MAPP &
LUCIA

E. F. Benson

MAPP & LUCIA

QUEEN LUCIA
MISS MAPP
MAPP AND LUCIA

E. F. Benson

With an introduction by
Steve Pemberton

BOOKS

1 3 5 7 9 10 8 6 4 2

BBC Books, an imprint of Ebury Publishing
20 Vauxhall Bridge Road,
London, SW1V 2SA

BBC Books is part of the Penguin Random House group of companies whose
addresses can be found at: global.penguinrandomhouse.com

This book is published to accompany the television series entitled
Mapp and Lucia first broadcast on BBC One in 2014.
Mapp and Lucia is a BBC Drama Production.

Executive producer: Lisa Osborne

First published by BBC Books in 2014.

www.eburypublishing.co.uk

A CIP catalogue record for this book is available from the British Library

ISBN 9781849908474

Commissioning Editor: Lorna Russell
Project Editor: Lizzy Gaisford
Production: Serena Nazareth

Printed and bound by CPI Group (UK) Ltd, Croydon, CR0 4YY

CONTENTS

INTRODUCTION

On the boil! That's what we all ought to be, with a thousand things to do that seem immensely important and which are important because they seem so.

Lucia in London

When my friend Mark [Gatiss] first told me that the BBC were interested in making a new series based on E.F. Benson's wonderful 'Mapp and Lucia' novels I was completely thrilled. 'No!' I exhaled down the telephone in the true Riseholme way. Yet the excitement was tinged with apprehension, for the previous adaptation made for Channel 4 in the mid-80s had been one of my favourite TV shows as a teenager. The performances were pin-sharp and the characters so well defined that when I went out and bought the books I was instantly able to see Geraldine McEwan, Prunella Scales, Nigel Hawthorne *et al* tripping through the streets of Tilling with gay abandon. So it was a difficult decision when I was asked if I wanted to pen the new series, one that I wrestled with for all of five seconds before blurting out 'Alright, as long as I can play Georgie!'

Edward Frederic Benson was a prolific author, biographer, archaeologist and some-time figure skater. He wrote *Queen Lucia* in 1920 and *Miss Mapp* in 1922, but it wasn't until a decade later that he had the delicious idea of pitting these two formidable ladies against each other. Lucia was a glorious snob, a ruthlessly ambitious social climber who ruled the cultural life of Riseholme with an iron fist. She spent an upwardly-mobile season in the capital (*Lucia in London*, 1927) and was seemingly unassailable. Miss Mapp was a scheming spinster who made it her business to rule the roost in her hometown of Tilling. She spied on her neighbours from her grand Queen Anne house and in spite of having troublesome quarrels and spats, always managed to come out on top. Perhaps Benson thought that they both had it too easy, so he decided to write *Mapp and Lucia* in 1931.

Benson lived in the picturesque town of Rye in East Sussex, and what he saw from the window of his beloved garden room at Lamb House began to shape his writing. The sight of ladies gossiping on the High Street with shopping baskets on their arms and outraged looks on their faces gave him the idea to turn Rye into Tilling. For the filming of the new series we were lucky enough to be given access to Lamb House, as well as many other local properties, and therefore were presenting Tilling pretty much as Benson intended it. From the crooked chimney on West Street sketched by Georgie to the church tower overlooking Mallards garden where Mapp spies Lucia skipping, the *mise en scene* of *Mapp and Lucia* was all available to us and it was a total joy to know that we were literally walking in Benson's footsteps (albeit slightly unsteadily, given the cobbled streets. Much easier to take the Royce).

One of the first things I wrote down in my notebook was 'She's stolen *au reservoir*! She heard it in Riseholme and smuggled it into Tilling!' The idea that Mapp's appropriation of one of Lucia's witty remarks carries the weight of Hitler invading Poland was the key to unlocking Benson's central comic conceit. As Henry Kissinger was fond of quoting, 'Academic politics are so vicious precisely because the stakes are so small.' That goes to heart of every dispute in Tilling: whether someone stole a dress colour, overbid their hand at bridge or failed to reciprocate a dinner invitation, the most trivial slight is elevated to the level of the highest scandal. Mapp and Lucia's battle for social domination isn't a cosy comedy of manners, it is a war story; may the worst-behaved woman win.

Benson uses war metaphors throughout his books, from Georgie's 'I feel like the fourth of August, 1914' (on the occasion of a broken door chain) to Mapp's 'Night marches. Maneuvers' (over the ownership of garden produce). Every use of 'dear' and 'darling' is a weapon, every wide teeth-baring smile a shield. This is war as theatre, where the residents of Tilling have a ringside seat as two heavyweights go head to head over several rounds. Of the two combatants, Lucia would appear at first to have our sympathy as she is more sinned against than sinning, but as I worked on the adaptation I found myself rooting for Miss Mapp, as 'this alien from Riseholme had appeared and had not so much challenged her as just taken her sceptre and her crown and worn them now for a couple of months.' Mapp suffers 'manifold reverses' whereas Lucia is seemingly Teflon-coated; nothing sticks.

The next decision I took was not to limit myself to the events of the *Mapp and Lucia* novel, but to incorporate elements of the earlier stories too. The Guru and Georgie's sisters (Hermy and Ursy) visit Riseholme in *Queen Lucia*, and the dress-wars and the Prince of Wales' visit are from *Miss Mapp* with no Lucia or Georgie in sight. I felt it would be a treat to weave these stories into a loose narrative of Lucia's first summer in Tilling, not only because they are some of my favourites, but also because they haven't been seen on screen before (the Channel 4 version was very much based on the events of *Mapp and Lucia* for its first series.)

I therefore sketched out a through-line which would see Lucia conquer Tilling in episode one, an uneasy truce break out in episode two and Mapp snatch defeat from the jaws of victory in episode three. The first episode was in some ways the easiest as we view Tilling through the eyes of the incomers, Lucia and Georgie. Much as I wanted to begin in Riseholme and revel in the Elizabethan fete (especially Lucia's reaction to being offered the role of Drake's wife by Daisy Quantock), ultimately I felt it best to begin with the journey into Tilling, intercut with establishing Mapp's social dominance. The opening scenes pose the age-old question: what happens when an unstoppable force meets an immoveable object.

The Guru storyline was useful because it shows Lucia on the back foot. Mapp is the one who introduces Tilling to yoga and meditation, and as such Lucia cannot enjoy the game as she didn't bring it to the party. She can't bear not to be involved, but doesn't want to be seen to be making an effort. The other Tillingites, though wonderfully characterised as individuals, move like sheep from Lucia's house to Mapp's. They congratulate themselves for not being faddish, whilst being open to every new fad and novelty the world has to offer them. The transposition of this storyline from Riseholme to Tilling did mean a fair amount of manipulation and invention on my part, but I felt comfortable dishing out some of Daisy Quantock's traits to dear Diva Plaistow, and some to Miss Mapp. I hope I may be forgiven for these contrivances, but it seemed perfectly right that Mapp should somehow annexe Diva's Guru, and Georgie have to visit Major Benjy to discuss golf for his sisters.

Once these battle lines had been drawn and an end point reached (Lucia decides to buy a house in Tilling, much to Mapp's obvious chagrin), the cherry on top was working with the wonderful ensemble of Tilling characters. The strangely proper and unctuous Wyses, thrifty and fretful widow Diva Plaistow, provocative artist and 'disgrace of Tilling' Irene Coles, the Scots-spouting Padre and mousy wife Evie, and the bellicose boozer Major Benjy all have their parts to play, as does Lucia's dapper confidante, the 'not obtrusively masculine' Georgie Pillson. With this cast of colourful characters, waspishly funny set pieces, stunning location and exquisite period detail, I said to Mark as we embarked on filming 'This could be the most *parfect* summer job ever!' – and so it proved. Whether the TV series has brought you to these pages, or indeed vice versa, I hope you enjoy reveling in Benson's wonderful comic creations, and that they bring you as much pleasure over the years as they have brought to me. *Au reservoir!*

Steve Pemberton
Writer of the BBC TV series, 2014

QUEEN
LUCIA

CHAPTER ONE

Though the sun was hot on this July morning, Mrs Lucas preferred to cover the half-mile that lay between the station and her house on her own brisk feet, and sent on her maid and her luggage in the fly that her husband had ordered to meet her. After those four hours in the train a short walk would be pleasant, but, though she veiled it from her conscious mind, another motive, subconsciously engineered, prompted her action. It would, of course, be universally known to all her friends in Riseholme that she was arriving today by the twelve twenty-six, and at that hour the village street would be sure to be full of them. They would see the fly with luggage draw up at the door of The Hurst, and nobody except her maid would get out.

That would be an interesting thing for them: it would cause one of those little thrills of pleasant excitement and conjectural exercise which supplied Riseholme with its emotional daily bread. They would all wonder what had happened to her, whether she had been taken ill at the very last moment before leaving town, and with her well-known fortitude and consideration for the feelings of others, had sent her maid on to assure her husband that he need not be anxious. That would clearly be Mrs Quantock's suggestion, for Mrs Quantock's mind, devoted as it was now to the study of Christian Science, and the determination to deny the existence of pain, disease and death as regards herself, was always full of the gloomiest views as regards her friends, and on the slightest excuse, pictured that they, poor blind things, were suffering from false claims. Indeed, given that the fly had already arrived at The Hurst, and that its arrival had at this moment been seen by or reported to Daisy Quantock, the chances were vastly in favour of that lady's having already started in to give Mrs Lucas absent treatment. Very likely Georgie Pillson had also seen the anticlimax of the fly's arrival, but he would hazard a much more probable though erroneous solution of her absence. He would certainly guess that she had sent on her maid with her luggage to the station in order to take a seat for her, while she herself, oblivious of the passage of time, was spending her last half-hour in contemplation of the Italian masterpieces at the National Gallery, or the Greek bronzes at the British Museum. Certainly she would not be at the Royal Academy, for the culture of Riseholme, led by herself, rejected as valueless all artistic efforts later than the death of Sir Joshua Reynolds, and a great deal of what went before. Her husband with his firm grasp of the obvious, on the other hand, would be disappointingly capable, even before her maid confirmed his conjecture, of concluding that she had merely walked from the station.

The motive, then, that made her send her cab on, though subconsciously generated, soon penetrated into her consciousness, and these guesses at what other people would think when they saw it arrive without her, sprang from the dramatic element that formed so large a part of her mentality, and made her always take, as by right divine, the leading part in the histrionic entertainments with which the cultured of Riseholme beguiled or rather strenuously occupied such moments as could be spared from their studies of art and literature, and their social engagements. Indeed she did not usually stop at taking the leading part, but, if possible, doubled another character with it, as well as being stage manager and adapter, if not designer of scenery. Whatever she did – and really she did an incredible deal – she did it with all the might of her dramatic perception, did it in fact with such earnestness that she had no time to have an eye to the gallery at all, she simply contemplated herself and her own vigorous accomplishment. When she played the piano as she frequently did (reserving an hour for practice every day), she cared not in the smallest degree for what anybody who passed down the road outside her house might be thinking of the roulades that poured from her open window: she was simply Emmeline Lucas, absorbed in glorious Bach or dainty Scarlatti, or noble Beethoven. The latter perhaps was her favourite composer, and many were the evenings when with lights quenched and only the soft effulgence of the moon pouring in through the uncurtained windows, she sat with her profile, cameo-like (or liker perhaps to the head on a postage stamp) against the dark oak walls of her music room, and entranced herself and her listeners, if there were people to dinner, with the exquisite pathos of the first movement of the 'Moonlight Sonata'. Devotedly as she worshipped the Master, whose picture hung above her Steinway Grand, she could never bring herself to believe that the two succeeding movements were on the same sublime level as the first, and besides they 'went' very much faster. But she had seriously thought, as she came down in the train today and planned her fresh activities at home, of trying to master them, so that she could get through their intricacies with tolerable accuracy. Until then, she would assuredly stop at the end of the first movement in these moonlit séances, and say that the other two were more like morning and afternoon. Then with a sigh she would softly shut the piano lid, and perhaps wiping a little genuine moisture from her eyes, would turn on the electric light and taking up a book from the table, in which a paperknife marked the extent of her penetration, say: 'Georgie, you must really promise me to read this life of Antonio Caporelli the moment I have finished it. I never understood the rise of the Venetian School before. As I read I can smell the salt tide creeping up over the lagoon, and see the campanile of dear Torcello.'

And Georgie would put down the tambour on which he was working his copy of an Italian cope and sigh too.

'You are too wonderful!' he would say. 'How do you find time for everything?'

She rejoined with the apophthegm that made the rounds of Riseholme next day.

'My dear, it is just busy people that have time for everything.'

*   *   *

It might be thought that even such activities as have here been indicated would be enough to occupy anyone so busily that he would positively not have time for more, but such was far from being the case with Mrs Lucas. Just as the painter Rubens amused himself with being the ambassador to the court of St James's – a sufficient career in itself for most busy men – so Mrs Lucas amused herself, in the intervals of her pursuit of art for art's sake, with being not only an ambassador but a monarch. Riseholme might perhaps, according to the crude materialism of maps, be included in the kingdom of Great Britain, but in a more real and inward sense it formed a complete kingdom of its own, and its queen was undoubtedly Mrs Lucas, who ruled it with a secure autocracy pleasant to contemplate at a time when thrones were toppling, and imperial crowns whirling like dead leaves down the autumn winds. The ruler of Riseholme, happier than he of Russia, had no need to fear the finger of Bolshevism writing on the wall, for there was not in the whole of that vat, which seethed so pleasantly with culture, one bubble of revolutionary ferment. Here there was neither poverty nor discontent nor muttered menace of any upheaval: Mrs Lucas, busy and serene, worked harder than any of her subjects, and exercised an autocratic control over a nominal democracy.

Something of the consciousness of her sovereignty was in her mind, as she turned the last hot corner of the road and came in sight of the village street that constituted her kingdom. Indeed it belonged to her, as treasure trove belongs to the Crown, for it was she who had been the first to begin the transformation of this remote Elizabethan village into the palace of culture that was now reared on the spot where ten years ago an agricultural population had led bovine and unilluminated lives in their cottages of grey stone or brick and timber. Before that, while her husband was amassing a fortune, comfortable in amount and respectable in origin, at the Bar, she had merely held up a small dim lamp of culture in Onslow Gardens. But both her ambition and his had been to bask and be busy in artistic realms of their own when the materialistic needs were provided for by sound investments, and so when there were the requisite thousands of pounds in secure securities she had easily persuaded him to buy three of these cottages that stood together in a low two-storeyed block. Then, by judicious removal of partition walls, she had, with the aid of a sympathetic architect, transmuted them into a most comfortable dwelling, subsequently building on to them a new wing, that ran at right angles at the back, which was, if anything, a shade more inexorably Elizabethan than the stem on to which it was grafted, for here was situated the famous smoking parlour, with rushes on the floor, and a dresser ranged with pewter tankards, and leaded lattice windows of glass so antique that it was practically impossible to see out of them. It had a huge open fireplace framed in oak beams with a seat on each side of the iron-backed hearth within the chimney, and a genuine spit hung over the middle of the fire. Here, though in the rest of the house she had for the sake of convenience allowed the installation of electric light, there was no such concession made, and sconces on the walls held dim iron lamps, so that only those of the most acute vision were able to read. Even then reading was difficult, for the bookstand on the table contained nothing but a few crabbed black-letter volumes dating from not later than the early seventeenth century, and you had to be in a frantically Elizabethan frame of mind to be at ease there. But Mrs Lucas often spent some of her rare leisure moments in the smoking parlour, playing on the virginal that stood in the window, or kippering herself in the fumes of the wood fire as with streaming eyes she deciphered an Elzevir Horace rather late for inclusion under the rule, but an undoubted bargain.

The house stood at the end of the village that was nearest the station, and thus, when the panorama of her kingdom opened before her, she had but a few steps further to go. A yew hedge, bought entire from a neighbouring farm, and transplanted with solid lumps of earth and indignant snails around its roots, separated the small oblong of garden from the road, and cast monstrous shadows of the shapes into which it was cut, across the little lawns inside. Here, as was only right and proper, there was not a flower to be found save such as were mentioned in the plays of Shakespeare; indeed it was called Shakespeare's garden, and the bed that ran below the windows of the dining room was Ophelia's border, for it consisted solely of those flowers which that distraught maiden distributed to her friends when she should have been in a lunatic asylum. Mrs Lucas often reflected how lucky it was that such institutions were unknown in Elizabeth's day, or that, if known, Shakespeare artistically ignored their existence. Pansies, naturally, formed the chief decoration – though there were some very flourishing plants of rue. Mrs Lucas always wore a little bunch of them when in flower, to inspire her thoughts, and found them wonderfully efficacious. Round the sundial, which was set in the middle of one of the squares of grass between which a path of broken paving stones led to the front door, was a circular border, now, in July, sadly vacant, for it harboured only the spring flowers enumerated by Perdita. But the first day every year when Perdita's border put forth its earliest blossom was a delicious anniversary, and the news of it spread like wildfire through Mrs Lucas's kingdom, and her subjects were very joyful, and came to salute the violet or daffodil, or whatever it was.

The three cottages dexterously transformed into The Hurst presented a charmingly irregular and picturesque front. Two were of the grey stone of the district and the middle one, to the door of which led the paved path, of brick and timber; latticed windows with stone mullions gave little light to the room within, and certain new windows had been added; these could be detected by the observant eye, for they had a markedly older appearance than the rest. The front door, similarly, seemed as if it must have been made years before the house, the fact being that the one which Mrs Lucas had found there was too dilapidated to be of the slightest service in keeping out wind or wet or undesired callers. She had therefore caused to be constructed an even older one made from the oak planks of a dismantled barn, and had it studded with large iron nails of antique pattern made by the village blacksmith. He had arranged some of them to look as if they spelt AD 1603. Over the door hung an inn sign, and into the space where once the sign had swung was now inserted a lantern, in which was ensconced, well hidden from view by its patinated glass sides, an electric light. This was one of the necessary concessions to modern convenience, for no lamp nurtured on oil would pierce those genuinely opaque panes, and illuminate the path to the gate. Better to have an electric light than cause your guests to plunge into Perdita's border. By the side of this fortress door hung a heavy iron bell pull, ending in a mermaid. When first Mrs Lucas had that installed, it was a bell pull in the sense that an extremely athletic man could, if he used both hands and planted his feet firmly, cause it to move, so that a huge bronze bell swung in the servants' passage and eventually gave tongue (if the athlete continued pulling) with vibrations so sonorous that the whitewash from the ceiling fell down in flakes. She had therefore made another concession to the frailty of the present generation and the inconveniences of having whitewash falling into salads and puddings on their way to the dining room, and now at the back of the mermaid's tail was a potent little bone button, coloured black and practically invisible, and thus the bell pull had been converted into an electric bell push. In this way visitors could make their advent known without violent exertion, the mermaid lost no visible whit of her Elizabethan virginity, and the spirit of Shakespeare wandering in his garden would not notice any anachronism. He could not in fact, for there was none to notice.

Though Mrs Lucas's parents had bestowed the name of Emmeline on her, it was not to be wondered at that she was always known among the more intimate of her subjects as Lucia, pronounced, of course, in the Italian mode – La Lucia, the wife of Lucas; and it was as '*Lucia mia*' that her husband hailed her as he met her at the door of The Hurst.

He had been watching for her arrival from the panes of the parlour while he meditated upon one of the little prose poems which formed so delectable a contribution to the culture of Riseholme, for though, as has been hinted, he had in practical life a firm grasp of the obvious, there were windows in his soul which looked out on to vague and ethereal prospects which so far from being obvious were only dimly intelligible. In form these odes were cast in the loose rhythms of Walt Whitman, but their smooth suavity and their contents bore no resemblance whatever to the productions of that barbaric bard, whose works were quite unknown in Riseholme. Already a couple of volumes of these prose poems had been published, not of course in the hard businesslike establishment of London, but at Ye Sign of Ye Daffodil, on the village green, where type was set up by hand, and very little, but that of the best, was printed. The press had only been recently started at Mr Lucas's expense, but it had put forth a reprint of Shakespeare's sonnets already, as well as his own poems. They were printed in blunt type on thick yellowish paper, the edges of which seemed as if they had been cut by the forefinger of an impatient reader, so ragged and irregular were they, and they were bound in vellum. The titles of these two slim flowers of poetry, *Flotsam* and *Jetsam*, were printed in black letter type and the covers were further adorned with a sort of embossed seal and with antique-looking tapes so that when you had finished with Mr Lucas's *Flotsam* you could tie it up with two bows before you turned to untie *Jetsam*.

Today the prose poem of 'Loneliness' had not been getting on very well, and Philip Lucas was glad to hear the click of the garden gate, which showed that his loneliness was over for the present, and looking up he saw his wife's figure waveringly presented to his eyes through the twisted and knotty glass of the parlour window, which had taken so long to collect, but which now completely replaced the plain, commonplace unrefracting stuff which was there before. He jumped up with an alacrity remarkable in so solid and well-furnished a person, and had thrown open the nail-studded front door before Lucia had traversed the path of broken paving-stones, for she had lingered for a sad moment at Perdita's empty border.

'*Lucia mia!*' he exclaimed. '*Ben arrivata!* So you walked from the station?'

'*Si, Peppino, mio caro,*' she said. '*Sta bene?*'

He kissed her and relapsed into Shakespeare's tongue, for their Italian, though firm and perfect as far as it went, could not be considered as going far, and was useless for conversational purposes, unless they merely wanted to greet each other, or to know the time. But it was interesting to talk Italian, however little way it went.

'*Molto bene,*' said he, 'and it's delightful to have you home again. And how was London?' he asked in the sort of tone in which he might have enquired after the health of a poor relation, who was not likely to recover. She smiled rather sadly.

'Terrifically busy about nothing,' she said. 'All this fortnight I have scarcely had a moment to myself. Lunches, dinners, parties of all kinds; I could not go to half the gatherings I was bidden to. Dear good South Kensington! Chelsea too!'

'*Carissima,* when London does manage to catch you, it is no wonder it makes the most of you,' he said. 'You mustn't blame London for that.'

'No, dear, I don't. Everyone was tremendously kind and hospitable; they all did their best. If I blame anyone, I blame myself. But I think this Riseholme life with its finish and its exquisiteness spoils one for other places. London is like a railway junction: it has no true life of its own. There is no delicacy, no appreciation of fine shades. Individualism has no existence there; everyone gabbles together, gabbles and gobbles: am not I naughty? If there is a concert in a private house – you know my views about music and the impossibility of hearing music at all if you are stuck in the middle of a row of people – even then, the moment it is over you are whisked away to supper, or somebody wants to have a few words. There is always a crowd, there is always food, you cannot be alone, and it is only in loneliness, as Goethe says, that your perceptions put forth their flowers. No one in London has time to listen: they are all thinking about who is there and who isn't there, and what is the next thing. The exquisite present, as you put it in one of your poems, has no existence there: it is always the feverish future.'

'Delicious phrase! I should have stolen that gem for my poor poems, if you had discovered it before.'

She was too much used to this incense to do more than sniff it in unconsciously, and she went on with her tremendous indictment.

'It isn't that I find fault with London for being so busy,' she said with strict impartiality, 'for if being busy was a crime, I am sure there are few of us here who would escape hanging. But take my life here, or yours for that matter. Well, mine if you like. Often and often I am alone from breakfast till lunchtime, but in those hours I get through more that is worth doing than London gets through in a day and a night. I have an hour at my music, not looking about and wondering who my neighbours are, but learning, studying, drinking in divine melody. Then I have my letters to write, and you know what that means, and I still have time for an hour's reading so that when you come to tell me lunch is ready, you will find that I have been wandering through Venetian churches or sitting in that little dark room at Weimar, or was it Leipzig? How would those same hours have passed in London?

'Sitting perhaps for half an hour in the park, with dearest Aggie pointing out to me, with thrills of breathless excitement, a woman who was in the divorce court, or a coroneted bankrupt. Then she would drag me off to some terrible private view full of the same people all staring at and gabbling to each other, or looking at pictures that made poor me gasp and shudder. No, I am thankful to be back at my own sweet Riseholme again. I can work and think here.'

She looked round the panelled entrance hall with a glow of warm content at being at home again that quite eclipsed the mere physical heat produced by her walk from the station. Wherever her eyes fell, those sharp dark eyes that resembled buttons covered with shiny American cloth, they saw nothing that jarred, as so much in London jarred. There were bright brass jugs on the window sill, a bowl of potpourri on the black table in the centre, an oak settee by the open fireplace, a couple of Persian rugs on the polished floor. The room had its quaintness, too, such as she had alluded to in her memorable essay read before the Riseholme Literary Society, called 'Humour in Furniture', and a brass milk can served as a receptacle for sticks and umbrellas. Equally quaint was the dish of highly realistic stone fruit that stood beside the potpourri and the furry Japanese spider that sprawled in a silk web over the window.

Such was the fearful verisimilitude of this that Lucia's new housemaid had once fled from her duties in the early morning, to seek the assistance of the gardener in killing it. The dish of stone fruit had scored a similar success, for once she had said to Georgie Pillson, 'Ah, my gardener has sent in some early apples and pears, won't you take one home with you?' It was not till the weight of the pear (he swiftly selected the largest) betrayed the joke that he had any notion that they were not real ones. But then Georgie had had his revenge, for waiting his opportunity he had inserted a real pear among those stony specimens and again passing through with Lucia, he picked it out, and with lips drawn back had snapped at it with all the force of his jaws. For the moment she had felt quite faint at the thought of his teeth crashing into fragments . . . These humorous touches were altered from time to time; the spider for instance might be taken down and replaced by a china canary in a Chippendale cage, and the selection of the entrance hall for those whimsicalities was intentional, for guests found something to smile at, as they took off their cloaks and entered the drawing room with a topic on their lips, something light, something amusing about what they had seen. For the gong similarly was sometimes substituted a set of bells that had once decked the collar of the leading horse in a waggoner's team somewhere in Flanders; in fact when Lucia was at home there was often a new little quaintness for quite a sequence of days, and she had held out hopes to the Literary Society that perhaps some day, when she was not so rushed, she would jot down material for a sequel to her essay, or write another covering a rather larger field on 'The Gambits of Conversation Derived from Furniture'.

On the table there was a pile of letters waiting for Mrs Lucas, for yesterday's post had not been forwarded her, for fear of its missing her – London postmen were probably very careless and untrustworthy – and she gave a little cry of dismay as she saw the volume of her correspondence.

'But I shall be very naughty,' she said, 'and not look at one of them till after lunch. Take them away, *caro*, and promise me to lock them up till then, and not give them me however much I beg. Then I will get into the saddle again, such a dear saddle, too, and tackle them. I shall have a stroll in the garden till the bell rings. What is it that Nietzsche says about the necessity to *Mediterraniser* yourself every now and then? I must *Riseholmer* myself.'

Peppino remembered the quotation, which had occurred in a review of some work of that celebrated author, where Lucia had also seen it, and went back, with the force of contrast to aid him, to his prose poem of 'Loneliness', while his wife went through the smoking parlour into the garden, in order to soak herself once more in the cultured atmosphere.

In this garden behind the house there was no attempt to construct a Shakespearian plot, for, as she so rightly observed, Shakespeare, who loved flowers so well, would wish her to enjoy every conceivable horticultural treasure. But furniture played a prominent part in the place, and there were statues and sundials and stone-seats scattered about with almost too profuse a hand. Mottos also were in great evidence, and while a sundial reminded you that '*Tempos fugit*', an enticing resting place somewhat bewilderingly bade you to 'Bide a wee'. But then again the rustic seat in the pleached alley of laburnums had carved on its back, 'Much have I travelled in the realms of gold', so that, meditating on Keats, you could bide a wee with a clear conscience. Indeed so copious was the wealth of familiar and stimulating quotations that one of her subjects had once said that to stroll in Lucia's garden was not only to enjoy her lovely flowers, but to spend a simultaneous half-hour with the best authors. There was a dovecote of course, but since the cats always killed the doves, Mrs Lucas had put up round the desecrated home several pigeons of Copenhagen china, which were both imperishable as regards cats, and also carried on the suggestion of humour in furniture. The humour had attained the highest point of felicity when Peppino concealed a mechanical nightingale in a bush, which sang 'Jug-jug' in the most realistic manner when you pulled a string. Georgie had not yet seen the Copenhagen pigeons, or being rather short-sighted thought they were real. Then, oh then, Peppino pulled the string, and for quite a long time Georgie listened entranced to their melodious cooings. That served him out for his 'trap' about the real pear introduced among the stone specimens. For in spite of the rarefied atmosphere of culture at Riseholme, Riseholme knew how to '*desipere in loco*', and its strenuous culture was often refreshed by these light refined touches.

Mrs Lucas walked quickly and decisively up and down the paths as she waited for the summons to lunch, for the activity of her mind reacted on her body, making her brisk in movement. On each side of her forehead were hard neat undulations of black hair that concealed the tips of her ears. She had laid aside her London hat, and carried a red cotton Contadina's umbrella, which threw a rosy glow on to the oval of her thin face and its colourless complexion. She bore the weight of her forty years extremely lightly, and but for the droop of skin at the corners of her mouth, she might have passed as a much younger woman. Her face was otherwise unlined and bore no trace of the ravages of emotional living, which both ages and softens. Certainly there was nothing soft about her, and very little of the signs of age, and it would have been reasonable to conjecture that twenty years later she would look but little older than she did today. For such emotions as she was victim of were the sterile and ageless ecstasies of art; such desires as beset her were not connected with her affections, but her ambitions. Dynasty she had none, for she was childless, and thus her ambitions were limited to the permanence and security of her own throne as queen of Riseholme. She really asked nothing more of life than the continuance of such harvests as she had so plenteously reaped for these last ten years. As long as she directed the life of Riseholme, took the lead in its culture and entertainment, and was the undisputed fountainhead of all its inspirations, and from time to time refreshed her memory as to the utter inferiority of London, she wanted nothing more.

But to secure that she dedicated all that she had of ease, leisure and income. Being practically indefatigable the loss of ease and leisure troubled her but little, and being in extremely comfortable circumstances, she had no need to economize in her hospitalities. She might easily look forward to enjoying an unchanging middle-aged activity, while generations of youth withered round her, and no star, remotely rising, had as yet threatened to dim her unrivalled effulgence. Though essentially autocratic, her subjects were allowed and even encouraged to develop their own minds on their own lines, provided always that those lines met at the junction where she was station master. With regard to religion finally, it may be briefly said that she believed in God in much the same way as she believed in Australia, for she had no doubt whatever as to the existence of either, and she went to church on Sunday in much the same spirit as she would look at a kangaroo in the Zoological Gardens, for kangaroos come from Australia.

A low wall separated the far end of her garden from the meadow outside; beyond that lay the stream which flowed into the Avon, and it often seemed wonderful to her that the water which wimpled by would (unless a cow happened to drink it) soon be stealing along past the church at Stratford where Shakespeare lay. Peppino had written a very moving little prose poem about it, for she had royally presented him with the idea, and had suggested a beautiful analogy between the earthly dew that refreshed the grasses, and was drawn up into the fire of the sun, and Thought, the spiritual dew that refreshed the mind and thereafter, rather vaguely, was drawn up into the Full-Orbed Soul of the World.

At that moment Lucia's eye was attracted by an apparition on the road which lay adjacent to the further side of the happy stream which flowed into the Avon. There was no mistaking the identity of the stout figure of Mrs Quantock with its short steps and its gesticulations, but why in the name of wonder should that Christian Scientist be walking with the draped and turbaned figure of a man with a tropical complexion and a black beard? His robe of saffron yellow with a violently green girdle was hitched up for ease in walking, and unless he had chocolate-coloured stockings on, Mrs Lucas saw human legs of the same shade. Next moment that debatable point was set at rest for she caught sight of short pink socks in red slippers. Even as she looked Mrs Quantock saw her (for owing to Christian Science she had recaptured the quick vision of youth) and waggled her hand and kissed it, and evidently called her companion's attention, for the next moment he was salaaming to her in some stately Oriental manner. There was nothing to be done for the moment except return these salutations, as she could not yell an aside to Mrs Quantock, screaming out 'Who is that Indian?' for if Mrs Quantock heard the Indian would hear too, but as soon as she could, she turned back towards the house again, and when once the lilac bushes were between her and the road she walked with more than her usual speed, in order to learn with the shortest possible delay from Peppino who this fresh subject of hers could be. She knew there were some Indian princes in London; perhaps it was one of them, in which case it would be necessary to read up Benares or Delhi in the encyclopaedia without loss of time.

CHAPTER TWO

As she traversed the smoking parlour the cheerful sounds that had once tinkled from the collar of a Flemish horse chimed through the house, and simultaneously she became aware that there would be macaroni au gratin for lunch, which was very dear and remembering of Peppino. But before setting fork to her piled-up plate, she had to question him, for her mental craving for information was far keener than her appetite for food.

'*Caro*, who is an Indian,' she said, 'whom I saw just now with Daisy Quantock? They were the other side of *il piccolo* Avon.'

Peppino had already begun his macaroni and must pause to shovel the outlying strings of it into his mouth. But the haste with which he did so was sufficient guarantee for his eagerness to reply as soon as it was humanly possible to do so.

'Indian, my dear?' he asked with the greatest interest.

'Yes; turban and burnous and calves and slippers,' she said rather impatiently, for what was the good of Peppino having remained in Riseholme if he could not give her precise and certain information on local news when she returned. His prose poems were all very well, but as prince consort he had other duties of state which must not be neglected for the calls of Art.

This slight asperity on her part seemed to sharpen his wits.

'Really, I don't know for certain, Lucia,' he said, 'for I have not set my eyes on him. But putting two and two together, I might make a guess.'

'Two and two make four,' she said with that irony for which she was feared and famous. 'Now for your guess. I hope it is equally accurate.'

'Well, as I told you in one of my letters,' said he, 'Mrs Quantock showed signs of being a little off with Christian Science. She had a cold, and though she recited the True Statement of Being just as frequently as before, her cold got no better. But when I saw her on Tuesday last, unless it was Wednesday – no, it couldn't have been Wednesday, so it must have been Tuesday – '

'Whenever it was then,' interrupted his wife, brilliantly summing up his indecision.

'Yes; whenever it was, as you say, on that occasion Mrs Quantock was very full of some Indian philosophy which made you quite well at once. What did she call it now? Yoga! Yes, that was it!'

'And then?' asked Lucia.

'Well, it appears you must have a teacher in Yoga or else you may injure yourself. You have to breathe deeply and say "Om" – '

'Say what?'

'Om. I understand the ejaculation to be Om. And there are very curious physical exercises; you have to hold your ear with one hand and your toes with the other, and you may strain yourself unless you do it properly. That was the general gist of it.'

'And shall we come to the Indian soon?' said Lucia.

'*Carissima*, you have come to him already. I suggest that Mrs Quantock has applied for a teacher and got him. *Ecco!*'

Mrs Lucas wore a heavily corrugated forehead at this news. Peppino had a wonderful *flair* in explaining unusual circumstances in the life of Riseholme and his conjectures were generally correct. But if he was right in this instance, it struck Lucia as being a very irregular thing that anyone should have imported a mystical Indian into Riseholme without consulting her. It is true that she had been away, but still there was the medium of the post.

'*Ecco* indeed!' she said. 'It puts me in rather a difficult position, for I must send out my invitations to my garden party today, and I really don't know whether I ought to be officially aware of this man's existence or not. I can't write to Daisy Quantock and say "Pray bring your black friend Om", or whatever his name proves to be, and on the other hand, if he is the sort of person whom one would be sorry to miss, I should not like to have passed over him.'

'After all, my dear, you have only been back in Riseholme half an hour,' said her husband. 'It would have been difficult for Mrs Quantock to have told you yet.'

Her face cleared.

'Perhaps Daisy has written to me about him,' she said. 'I may find a full account of it all when I open my letters.'

'Depend upon it you will. She would hardly have been so wanting in proper feeling as not to have told you. I think, too, that her visitor must only have just arrived, or I should have been sure to see him about somewhere.'

She rose.

'Well, we will see,' she said. 'Now I shall be very busy all afternoon, but by teatime I shall be ready to see anyone who calls. Give me my letters, *caro*, and I will find out if Daisy has written to me.'

She turned them over as she went to her room, and there among them was a bulky envelope addressed in Mrs Quantock's great sprawling hand, which looked at first sight so large and legible, but on closer examination turned out to be so baffling. You had to hold it at some distance off to make anything out of it, and look at it in an abstracted general manner much as you would look at a view. Treated thus, scattered words began to leap into being, and when you had got a sufficiency of these, like glimpses of the country seen by flashes of lightning, you could hope to get a collective idea of it all. The procedure led to the most promising results as Mrs Lucas sat with the sheets at arm's length, occasionally altering the range to try the effect of a different focus. 'Benares' blinked at her, also 'Brahmin'; also 'highest caste'; 'extraordinary sanctity', and 'guru'. And when the meaning of this latter was ascertained from the article on 'Yoga' in her encyclopaedia, she progressed very swiftly towards a complete comprehension of the letter.

When fully pieced together it was certainly enough to rivet her whole attention, and make her leave unopened the rest of the correspondence, for such a prelude to adventure had seldom sounded in Riseholme. It appeared, even as her husband had told her at lunch, that Mrs Quantock found her cold too obstinate for all the precepts of Mrs Eddy; the True Statement of Being, however often repeated, only seemed to inflame it further, and one day, when confined to the house, she had taken a book 'quite at random' from the shelves in her library, under, she supposed, the influence of some interior compulsion. This then was clearly a 'leading'.

Mrs Lucas paused a moment as she pieced together these first sentences. She seemed to remember that Mrs Quantock had experienced a similar leading when first she took up Christian Science. It was a leading from the sight of a new church off Sloane Street that day; Mrs Quantock had entered (she scarcely knew why) and had found herself in a testimony meeting, where witness after witness declared the miraculous healings they had experienced. One had had a cough, another cancer, another a fractured bone, but all had been cured by the blessed truths conveyed in the gospel according to Mrs Eddy. However, her memories on this subject were not to the point now; she burned to arrive at the story of the new leading.

Well, the book that Mrs Quantock had taken down in obedience to the last leading proved to be a little handbook of Oriental Philosophies, and it opened, all of its own accord, at a chapter called Yoga. Instantly she perceived, as by the unclosing of an inward eye that Yoga was what she wanted and she instantly wrote to the address from which this book was issued asking for any guidance on the subject. She had read in *Oriental Philosophies* that for the successful practice of Yoga, it was necessary to have a teacher, and did they know of any teacher who could give her instruction? A wonderful answer came to that, for two days afterwards her maid came to her and said that an Indian gentleman would like, to see her. He was ushered in, and with a profound obeisance said: 'Beloved lady, I am the teacher you asked for; I am your guru. Peace be to this house! Om!'

Mrs Lucas had by this time got her view of Mrs Quantock's letter into perfect focus, and she read on without missing a word.

Is it not wonderful, dearest Lucia [it ran] that my desire for light should have been so instantly answered? And yet my guru tells me that it always happens so. I was sent to him, and he was sent to me, just like that! He had been expecting some call when my letter asking for guidance came, and he started at once because he knew he was sent. Fancy! I don't even know his name, and his religion forbids him to tell it me. He is just my guru, my guide, and he is going to be with me as long as he knows I need him to show me the True Path. He has the spare bedroom and the little room adjoining where he meditates and does Postures and Pranayama, which is breathing. If you persevere in them under instruction, you have perfect health and youth, and my cold is gone already. He is a Brahmin of the very highest caste, indeed caste means nothing to him any longer, just as a Baronet and an Honourable must seem about the same thing to the King. He comes from Benares where he used to meditate all day by the Ganges and I can see for myself that he is a person of the most extraordinary sanctity. But he can meditate just as well in my little room, for he says he was never in any house that had such a wonderful atmosphere. He has no money at all which is so beautiful of him, and looked so pained and disappointed when I asked him if I might not give him some. He doesn't even know how he got here from London; he doesn't think he came by train, so perhaps he was wafted here in some astral manner. He looked so bewildered too when I said the word 'money', and evidently he had to think what it was, because it is so long since it has meant anything to him. So if he wants anything, I have told him to go into any shop and ask that it shall be put down to me. He has often been without food or sleep for days together when he is meditating. Just think!

Shall I bring him to see you, or will you come here? He wants to meet you, because he feels you have a beautiful soul and may help him in that way, as well as his helping you. I am helping him too he says, which seems more wonderful than I can believe. Send me a line as soon as you get back. *Tante salute!*

Your own,

Daisy

The voluminous sheets had taken long in reading and Mrs Lucas folded them up slowly and thoughtfully. She felt that she had to make a swift decision that called into play all her mental powers. On the one hand it was 'up to her' to return a frigid reply, conveying, without making any bones about the matter, that she had no interest in nameless gurus who might or might not be Brahmins from Benares and presented themselves at Daisy's door in a penniless condition without clear knowledge whether they had come by train or not. In favour of such prudent measures was the truly Athenian character of Daisy's mind, for she was always enquiring into 'some new thing', which was the secret of life when first discovered, and got speedily relegated to the dust-heap. But against such a course was the undoubted fact that Daisy did occasionally get hold of somebody who subsequently proved to be of interest, and Lucia would never forget to her dying day the advent in Riseholme of a little Welsh attorney, in whom Daisy had discovered a wonderful mentality. Lucia had refused to extend her queenly hospitality to him, or to recognize his existence in any way during the fortnight when he stayed with Daisy, and she was naturally very much annoyed to find him in a prominent position in the Government not many years later. Indeed she had snubbed him so markedly on his first appearance at Riseholme that he had refused on subsequent visits to come to her house at all, though he several times visited Mrs Quantock again, and told her all sorts of political secrets (so she said) which she would not divulge for anything in the world. There must never be a repetition of so fatal an error.

Another thing inclined the wavering balance. She distinctly wanted some fresh element at her court, that should make Riseholme know that she was in residence again. August would soon be here with its languors and absence of stimulus, when it was really rather difficult in the drowsy windless weather to keep the flag of culture flying strongly from her own palace. The guru had already said that he felt sure she had a beautiful soul, and – The outline of the scheme flashed upon her. She would have Yoga evenings in the hot August weather, at which, as the heat of the day abated, graceful groups should assemble among the mottos in the garden and listen to high talk on spiritual subjects. They would adjourn to delicious moonlit suppers in the pergola, or if the moon was indisposed – she could not be expected to regulate the affairs of the moon as well as of Riseholme – there would be dim séances and sandwiches in the smoking parlour. The humorous furniture should be put in cupboards, and as they drifted towards the front hall again, when the clocks struck an unexpectedly late hour, little whispered colloquies of 'How wonderful he was tonight' would be heard, and there would be faraway looks and sighs, and the notings down of the titles of books that conducted the pilgrim on the Way. Perhaps as they softly assembled for departure, a little music would be suggested to round off the evening, and she saw herself putting down the soft pedal as people rustled into their places, for the first movement of the 'Moonlight Sonata'. Then at the end there would be silence, and she would get up with a sigh, and someone would say, '*Lucia mia!*' and somebody else, 'Heavenly music,' and perhaps the guru would say, 'Beloved lady,' as he had *apparently* said to poor Daisy Quantock. Flowers, music, addresses from the guru, soft partings, sense of refreshment. . . With the memory of the Welsh attorney in her mind, it seemed clearly wiser to annex rather than to repudiate the guru. She seized a pen and drew a pile of postcards towards her, on the top of which was printed her name and address.

> Too wonderful [she wrote]. Pray bring him yourself to my little garden-party on Friday. There will be only a few. Let me know if he wants a quiet room ready for him.

All this had taken time, and she had but scribbled a dozen postcards to friends bidding them come to her garden party on Friday, when tea was announced. These invitations had the mystic word 'Hightum' written at the bottom left-hand corner, which conveyed to the enlightened recipient what sort of party it was to be, and denoted the standard of dress. For one of Lucia's quaint ideas was to divide dresses into three classes, 'Hightum', 'Tightum' and 'Scrub'. 'Hightum' was your very best dress, the smartest and newest of all, and when 'Hightum' was written on a card of invitation, it implied that the party was a very resplendent one. 'Tightum' similarly indicated a moderately smart party, 'Scrub' carried its own significance on the surface. These terms applied to men's dress as well and as regards evening parties: a dinner party 'Hightum' would indicate a white tie and a tail coat; a dinner party 'Tightum' a black tie and a short coat, and a dinner 'Scrub' would mean morning clothes.

With tea was announced also the advent of Georgie Pillson, who was her gentleman-in-waiting when she was at home, and her watchdog when she was not. In order to save subsequent disappointment, it may be at once stated that there never had been, was, or ever would be the smallest approach to a flirtation between them. Neither of them, she with her forty respectable years and he with his blameless forty-five years, had ever flirted, with anybody at all. But it was one of the polite and pleasant fictions of Riseholme that Georgie was passionately attached to her and that it was for her sake that he had settled in Riseholme now some seven years ago, and that for her sake he remained still unmarried. She never, to do her justice, had affirmed anything of the sort, but it is a fact that sometimes when Georgie's name came up in conversation, her eyes wore that 'faraway' look that only the masterpieces of art could otherwise call up, and she would sigh and murmur, 'Dear Georgie!' and change the subject, with the tact that characterized her. In fact their mutual relations were among the most Beautiful Things of Riseholme, and hardly less beautiful was Peppino's attitude towards it all. That large-hearted man trusted them both, and his trust was perfectly justified. Georgie was in and out of the house all day, chiefly in; and not only did scandal never rear its hissing head, but it positively had not a head to hiss with, or a foot to stand on. On his side again Georgie had never said that he was in love with her (nor would it have been true if he had), but by his complete silence on the subject coupled with his constancy he seemed to admit the truth of this bloodless idyll. They talked and walked and read the masterpieces of literature and played duets on the piano together. Sometimes (for he was the more brilliant performer, though as he said 'terribly lazy about practising', for which she scolded him) he would gently slap the back of her hand, if she played a wrong note, and say 'Naughty!' And she would reply in baby language 'Me vewy sowwy! Oo naughty too to hurt Lucia!' That was the utmost extent of their carnal familiarities, and with bright eyes fixed on the music they would break into peals of girlish laughter, until the beauty of the music sobered them again.

Georgie (he was Georgie or Mr Georgie, never Pillson to the whole of Riseholme) was not an obtrusively masculine sort of person. Such masculinity as he was possessed of was boyish rather than adult, and the most important ingredients in his nature were womanish. He had, in common with the rest of Riseholme, strong artistic tastes, and in addition to playing the piano, made charming little watercolour sketches, many of which he framed at his own expense and gave to friends, with slightly sentimental titles, neatly printed in gilt letters on the mount. *Golden Autumn Woodland*, *Bleak December*, *Yellow Daffodils* and *Roses of Summer* were perhaps his most notable series, and these he had given to Lucia, on the occasion of four successive birthdays. He did portraits as well in pastel; these were of two types, elderly ladies in lace caps with a row of pearls, and boys in cricket shirts with their sleeves rolled up. He was not very good at eyes, so his sitters always were looking down, but he was excellent at smiles, and the old ladies smiled patiently and sweetly, and the boys gaily. But his finest accomplishment was needlework and his house was full of the creations of his needle: wool-work curtains, petit-point chair seats, and silk embroideries framed and glazed. Next to Lucia he was the hardest-worked inhabitant of Riseholme, but not being so strong as the Queen, he had often to go away for little rests by the seaside. Travelling by train fussed him a good deal, for he might not be able to get a corner seat, or somebody with a pipe or a baby might get into his carriage, or the porter might be rough with his luggage, so he always went in his car to some neighbouring watering place where they knew him. Dicky, his handsome young chauffeur, drove him, and by Dicky's side sat Foljambe, his very pretty parlour maid who valeted him. If Dicky took the wrong turn his master called 'Naughty boy' through the tube, and Foljambe smiled respectfully. For the month of August, his two plain strapping sisters (Hermione and Ursula, alas!) always came to stay with him. They liked pigs and dogs and otter-hunting and mutton-chops, and were rather a discordant element in Riseholme. But Georgie had a kind heart, and never even debated whether he should ask Hermy and Ursy or not, though he had to do a great deal of tidying up after they had gone.

There was always a playful touch between the meetings of these two when either of them had been away from Riseholme that very prettily concealed the depth of Georgie's supposed devotion, and when she came out into the garden where her Cavalier and her husband were waiting for their tea under the pergola, Georgie jumped up very nimbly and took a few chassée-ing steps towards her with both hands outstretched in welcome. She caught at his humour, made him a curtsey, and next moment they were treading a little improvised minuet together with hands held high, and pointed toes. Georgie had very small feet, and it was a really elegant toe that he pointed, encased in cloth-topped boots. He had on a suit of fresh white flannels and over his shoulders, for fear of the evening air being chilly after this hot day, he had a little cape of a military cut, like those in which young ladies at music halls enact the part of colonels. He had a straw hat on, with a blue riband, a pink shirt and a red tie, rather loose and billowy. His face was pink and round, with blue eyes, a short nose and very red lips. An almost complete absence of eyebrow was made up for by a firm little brown moustache clipped very short, and brushed upwards at its extremities. Contrary to expectation he was quite tall and fitted very neatly into his clothes.

The dance came to an end with a low curtsey on Lucia's part, an obeisance hat in hand from Georgie (this exposure showing a crop of hair grown on one side of his head and brushed smoothly over the top until it joined the hair on the other side) and a clapping of the hands from Peppino.

'Bravo, bravo,' he cried from the tea table. 'Capital!'

Mrs Lucas blew him a kiss in acknowledgement of this compliment and smiled on her partner. '*Amico!*' she said. 'It is nice to see you again. How goes it?'

'*Va bene,*' said Georgie to show he could talk Italian too. '*Va* very *bene* now that you've come back.'

'*Grazie!* Now tell us all the news. We'll have a good gossip.'

Georgie's face beamed with a 'solemn gladness' at the word, like a drunkard's when brandy is mentioned.

'Where shall we begin?' he said. 'Such a lot to tell you. I think we must begin with a great bit of news. Something really mysterious.'

Lucia smiled inwardly. She felt that she knew for dead certain what the mysterious news was, and also that she knew far more about it than Georgie. This superiority she completely concealed. Nobody could have guessed it.

'*Presto, presto!*' she said. 'You excite me.'

'Yesterday morning I was in Rush's,' said Georgie, 'seeing about some *crème de menthe*, which ought to have been sent the day before. Rush is very negligent sometimes – and I was just saying a sharp word about it, when suddenly I saw that Rush was not attending at all, but was looking at something behind my back, and so I looked round. Guess!'

'Don't be tantalizing, *amico*,' said she. 'How can I guess? A pink elephant with blue spots!'

'No, guess again!'

'A red Indian in full war paint.'

'Certainly not! Guess again,' said Georgie, with a little sigh of relief. (It would have been awful if she had guessed.) At this moment Peppino suddenly became aware that Lucia had guessed and was up to some game.

'Give me your hand, Georgie,' she said, 'and look at me. I'm going to read your thoughts. Think of what you saw when you turned round.'

She took his hand and pressed it to her forehead, closing her eyes.

'But I do seem to see an Indian,' she said. 'Ah, not red Indian, other Indian. And – and he has slippers on and brown stockings – no, not brown stockings; it's legs. And there's a beard, and a turban.'

She gave a sigh.

'That's all I can see,' she said.

'My dear, you're marvellous,' said he. 'You're quite right.'

A slight bubbling sound came from Peppino, and Georgie began to suspect.

'I believe you've seen him!' he said. 'How tarsome you are . . .'

When they had all laughed a great deal, and Georgie had been assured that Lucia really, word of honour, had no idea what happened next, the narrative was resumed.

'So there stood the Indian, bowing and salaaming most politely and when Rush had promised me he would send my *crème de menthe* that very morning, I just looked through a wine list for a moment, and the Indian with quantities more bows came up to the counter and said, "If you will have the great goodness to give me a little brandy bottle." So Rush gave it him, and instead of paying for it, what do you think he said? Guess.'

Mrs Lucas rose with the air of Lady Macbeth and pointed her finger at Georgie.

'He said "Put it down to Mrs Quantock's account,"' she hissed.

Of course the explanation came now, and Lucia told the two men the contents of Mrs Quantock's letter. With that her cards were on the table, and though the fact of the Brahmin from Benares was news to Georgie, he had got many interesting things to tell her, for his house adjoined Mrs Quantock's and there were plenty of things which Mrs Quantock had not mentioned in her letter, so that Georgie was soon in the position of informant again. His windows overlooked Mrs Quantock's garden, and since he could not keep his eyes shut all day, it followed that the happenings there were quite common property. Indeed that was a general rule in Riseholme: anyone in an adjoining property could say, 'What an exciting game of lawn tennis you had this afternoon!' having followed it from his bedroom. That was part of the charm of Riseholme; it was as if it contained just one happy family with common interests and pursuits. What happened in the house was a more private matter, and Mrs Quantock, for instance, would never look from the rising ground at the end of her garden into Georgie's dining room or, if she did she would never tell anyone how many places were laid at table on that particular day when she had asked if he could give her lunch, and he had replied that to his great regret his table was full. But nobody could help seeing into gardens from back windows: the 'view' belonged to everybody.

Georgie had had wonderful views.

'That very day,' he said, 'soon after lunch, I was looking for a letter I thought I had left in my bedroom, and happening to glance out, I saw the Indian sitting under Mrs Quantock's pear tree. He was swaying a little backwards and forwards.'

'The brandy!' said Lucia excitedly. 'He has his meals in his own room.'

'No, *amica*, it was not the brandy. In fact I don't suppose the brandy had gone to Mrs Quantock's then, for he did not take it from Rush's, but asked that it should be sent . . .' He paused a moment – 'Or did he take it away? I declare I can't remember. But anyhow when he swayed backwards and forwards, he wasn't drunk, for presently he stood on one leg, and crooked the other behind it, and remained there with his hands up, as if he was praying, for quite a long time without swaying at all. So he couldn't have been tipsy.

And then he sat down again, and took off his slippers, and held his toes with one hand, while his legs were quite straight out, and put his other hand round behind his head, and grasped his other ear with it. I tried to do it on my bedroom floor, but I couldn't get near it. Then he sat up again and called "*Chela! Chela!*" and Mrs Quantock came running out.'

'Why did he say "*Chela*"?' asked Lucia.

'I wondered too. But I knew I had some clue to it, so I looked through some books by Rudyard Kipling, and found that *chela* meant "disciple". What you have told me just now about "guru" being "teacher", seems to piece the whole thing together.'

'And what did Daisy do?' asked Mrs Lucas breathlessly.

'She sat down too, and put her legs out straight in front of her like the guru, and tried to hold the toe of her shoe in her fingers, and naturally she couldn't get within yards of it. I got nearer than she did. And he said, "Beloved lady, not too far at first."'

'So you could hear too,' said Lucia.

'Naturally, for my window was open, and as you know Mrs Quantock's pear tree is quite close to the house. And then he told her to stop up one nostril with her finger and inhale through the other, and then hold her breath, while he counted six. Then she breathed it all out again, and started with the other side. She repeated that several times and he was very much pleased with her. Then she said, "It is quite wonderful; I feel so light and vigorous."'

'It would be very wonderful indeed if dear Daisy felt light,' remarked Lucia. 'What next?'

'Then they sat and swayed backwards and forwards again and muttered something that sounded like Pom!'

'That would be "Om"; and then?'

'I couldn't wait any longer for I had some letters to write.'

She smiled at him.

'I shall give you another cup of tea to reward you for your report,' she said. 'It has all been most interesting. Tell me again about the breathing in and holding your breath.'

Georgie did so, and illustrated in his own person what had happened. Next moment Lucia was imitating him, and Peppino came round in order to get a better view of what Georgie was doing. Then they all sat, inhaling through one nostril, holding their breath, and then expelling it again.

'Very interesting,' said Lucia at the end. 'Upon my word, it does give one a sort of feeling of vigour and lightness. I wonder if there is something in it.'

CHAPTER THREE

Though The Hurst was, as befitted its *châtelaine*, the most Elizabethanly complete abode in Riseholme, the rest of the village, in its due degrees, fell very little short of perfection. It had but its one street some half-mile in length but that street was a gem of medieval domestic architecture. For the most part the houses that lined it were blocks of contiguous cottages, which had been converted either singly or by twos and threes into dwellings containing the comforts demanded by the twentieth century, but externally they preserved the antiquity which, though it might be restored or supplemented by bathrooms or other conveniences, presented a truly Elizabethan appearance. There were, of course, accretions such as old inn signs above front doors and old bell pulls at their sides, but the doors were uniformly of inconveniently low stature, roofs were of stone slabs or old brick, in which a suspiciously abundant crop of antirrhinums and stone crops had anchored themselves, and there was hardly a garden that did not contain a path of old paving stones, a mulberry tree and some yews cut into shape.

Nothing in the place was more blatantly medieval than the village green, across which Georgie took his tripping steps after leaving the presence of his queen. Round it stood a row of great elms, and in its centre was the ducking pond, according to Riseholme tradition, though perhaps in less classical villages it might have passed merely for a duck pond. But in Riseholme it would have been rank heresy to dream, even in the most pessimistic moments, of its being anything but a ducking pond. Close by it stood a pair of stocks, about which there was no doubt whatever, for Mr Lucas had purchased them from a neighbouring iconoclastic village, where they were going to be broken up, and, after having them repaired, had presented them to the village green, and chosen their site close to the ducking pond. Round the green were grouped the shops of the village, slightly apart from the residential street, and at the far end of it was that undoubtedly Elizabethan hostelry, the Ambermere Arms, full to overflowing of ancient tables and bible boxes, and firedogs and fire backs, and bottles and chests and settles. These were purchased in large quantities by the American tourists who swarmed there during the summer months, at a high profit to the nimble proprietor, who thereupon purchased fresh antiquities to take their places. The Ambermere Arms in fact was the antique furniture shop of the place, and did a thriving trade, for it was much more interesting to buy objects out of a real old Elizabethan inn, than out of a shop.

Georgie had put his smart military cape over his arm for his walk, and at intervals applied his slim forefinger to one nostril, while he breathed in through the other, continuing the practice which he had observed going on in Mrs Quantock's garden. Though it made him a little dizzy, it certainly produced a sort of lightness, but soon he remembered the letter from Mrs Quantock which Lucia had read out, warning her that these exercises ought to be taken under instruction, and so desisted. He was going to deliver Lucia's answer at Mrs Quantock's house, and with a view to possibly meeting the guru, and being introduced to him, he said over to himself 'guru, guru, guru' instead of doing deep breathing, in order to accustom himself to the unusual syllables.

It would, of course, have been very strange and un-Riseholme-like to have gone to a friend's door, even though the errand was so impersonal a one as bearing somebody else's note, without enquiring whether the friend was in, and being instantly admitted if she was, and as a matter of fact, Georgie caught a glimpse, when the knocker was answered (Mrs Quantock did not have a bell at all), through the open door of the hall, of Mrs Quantock standing in the middle of the lawn on one leg. Naturally, therefore, he ran out into the garden without any further formality. She looked like a little round fat stork, whose legs had not grown, but who preserved the habits of her kind.

'Dear lady, I've brought a note for you,' he said. 'It's from Lucia.'

The other leg went down, and she turned on him the wide

firm smile that she had learned in the vanished days of Christian Science.

'Om,' said Mrs Quantock, expelling the remainder of her breath. 'Thank you, my dear Georgie. It's extraordinary what Yoga has done for me already. Cold quite gone. If ever you feel out of sorts, or depressed or cross, you can cure yourself at once. I've got a visitor staying with me.'

'Have you indeed?' asked Georgie, without alluding to the thrilling excitements which had trodden so close on each other's heels since yesterday morning when he had seen the guru in Rush's shop.

'Yes; and as you've just come from dear Lucia's perhaps she may have said something to you about him, for I wrote to her about him. He's a guru of extraordinary sanctity from Benares, and he's teaching me the Way. You shall see him too, unless he's meditating. I will call to him; if he's meditating he won't hear me, so we shan't be interrupting him. He wouldn't hear a railway accident if he was meditating.'

She turned round towards the house.

'Guru, dear!' she called.

There was a moment's pause, and the Indian's face appeared at a window.

'Beloved lady!' he said.

'Guru dear, I want to introduce a friend of mine to you,' she said. 'This is Mr Pillson, and when you know him a little better you will call him Georgie.'

'Beloved lady, I know him very well indeed. I see into his clear white soul. Peace be unto you, my friend.'

'Isn't he marvellous? Fancy!' said Mrs Quantock, in an aside.

Georgie raised his hat very politely.

'How do you do?' he said. (After his quiet practice he would have said 'How do you do, Guru?' but it rhymed in a ridiculous manner and his red lips could not frame the word.)

'I am always well,' said the guru, 'I am always young and well because I follow the Way.'

'Sixty at least he tells me,' said Mrs Quantock in a hissing aside, probably audible across the channel, 'and he thinks more, but the years make no difference to him. He is like a boy. Call him "Guru".'

'Guru – ' began Georgie.

'Yes, my friend.'

'I am very glad you are well,' said Georgie wildly. He was greatly impressed, but much embarrassed. Also it was so hard to talk at a second-storey window with any sense of ease, especially when you had to address a total stranger of extraordinary sanctity from Benares.

Luckily Mrs Quantock came to the assistance of his embarrassment.

'Guru dear, are you coming down to see us?' she asked.

'Beloved lady, no!' said the level voice. 'It is laid on me to wait here. It is the time of calm and prayer when it is good to be alone. I will come down when the guides bid me. But teach our dear friend what I have taught you. Surely before long I will grasp his earthly hand, but not now. Peace! Peace! and Light!'

'Have you got some guides as well?' asked Georgie when the guru disappeared from the window. 'And are they Indians too?'

'Oh, those are his spiritual guides,' said Mrs Quantock. 'He sees them and talks to them, but they are not in the body.'

She gave a happy sigh.

'I never have felt anything like it,' she said. 'He has brought such an atmosphere into the house that even Robert feels it, and doesn't mind being turned out of his dressing room. There, he has shut the window. Isn't it all marvellous?'

Georgie had not seen anything particularly marvellous yet, except the phenomenon of Mrs Quantock standing on one leg in the middle of the lawn, but presumably her emotion communicated itself to him by the subtle infection of the spirit.

'And what does he do?' he asked.

'My dear, it is not what he does, but what he is,' said she. 'Why, even my little bald account of him to Lucia has made her ask him to her garden party. Of course I can't tell whether he will go or not. He seems so very much – how shall I say it? – so very much sent to me. But I shall of course ask him whether he will consent. Trances and meditation all day! And in the intervals such serenity and sweetness. You know, for instance, how tiresome Robert is about his food. Well, last night the mutton, I am bound to say, was a little underdone, and Robert was beginning to throw it about his plate in the way he has. Well, my guru got up and just said, "Show me the way to kitchen" – he leaves out little words sometimes, because they don't matter – and I took him down, and he said "Peace!" He told me to leave him there, and in ten minutes he was up again with a little plate of curry and rice and what had been underdone mutton, and you never ate anything so good. Robert had most of it and I had the rest, and my guru was so pleased at seeing Robert pleased. He said Robert had a pure white soul, just like you, only I wasn't to tell him, because for him the Way ordained that he must find it out for himself. And today before lunch again, the guru went down in the kitchen, and my cook told me he only took a pinch of pepper and a tomato and a little bit of mutton fat and a sardine and a bit of cheese, and he brought up a dish that you never saw equalled. Delicious! I shouldn't a bit wonder if Robert began breathing exercises soon. There is one that makes you lean and young and exercises the liver.'

This sounded very entrancing.

'Can't you teach me that?' asked Georgie eagerly. He had been rather distressed about his increasing plumpness for a year past, and about his increasing age for longer than that. As for his liver he always had to be careful.

She shook her head.

'You cannot practise it except under tuition from an expert,' she said.

Georgie rapidly considered what Hermy's and Ursy's comments would be if, when they arrived tomorrow, he was found doing exercises under the tuition of a guru. Hermy, when she was not otter-hunting, could be very sarcastic, and he had a clear month of Hermy in front of him, without any otter-hunting, which, so she had informed him, was not possible in August. This was mysterious to Georgie, because it did not seem likely that all otters died in August, and a fresh brood came in like caterpillars. If Hermy was here in October, she would otter-hunt all morning and snore all afternoon, and be in the best of tempers, but the August visit required more careful steering. Yet the prospect of being lean and young and internally untroubled was wonderfully tempting.

'But couldn't he be my guru as well?' he asked.

Quite suddenly and by some demoniac possession, a desire

that had been only intermittently present in Mrs Quantock's consciousness took full possession of her, a red revolutionary insurgence hoisted its banner. Why with this stupendous novelty in the shape of a guru shouldn't she lead and direct Riseholme instead of Lucia? She had long wondered why darling Lucia should be Queen of Riseholme, and had, by momentary illumination, seen herself thus equipped as far more capable of exercising supremacy. After all, everybody in Riseholme knew Lucia's old tune by now, and was in his secret consciousness quite aware that she did not play the second and third movements of the 'Moonlight Sonata', simply because they 'went faster', however much she might cloak the omission by saying that they resembled eleven o'clock in the morning and 3 p.m. And Mrs Quantock had often suspected that she did not read one quarter of the books she talked about, and that she got up subjects in the encyclopaedia, in order to make a brave show that covered essential ignorance. Certainly she spent a good deal of money over entertaining, but Robert had lately made twenty times daily what Lucia spent annually, over Roumanian oils. As for her acting, had she not completely forgotten her words as Lady Macbeth in the middle of the sleep-walking scene?

But here was Lucia, as proved by her note, and her ADC Georgie, wildly interested in the guru. Mrs Quantock conjectured that Lucia's plan was to launch the guru at her August parties, as her own discovery. He would be a novelty, and it would be Lucia who gave Omparties and breathing parties and standing-on-one-leg parties, while she herself, Daisy Quantock, would be bidden to these as a humble guest, and Lucia would get all the credit, and, as likely as not, invite the discoverer, the inventress, just now and then. Mrs Quantock's guru would become Lucia's guru and all Riseholme would flock hungrily for light and leading to The Hurst. She had written to Lucia in all sincerity, hoping that she would extend the hospitality of her garden parties to the guru, but now the very warmth of Lucia's reply caused her to suspect this ulterior motive. She had been too precipitate, too rash, too ill-advised, too sudden, as Lucia would say. She ought to have known that Lucia, with her August parties coming on, would have jumped at a guru, and withheld him for her own parties, taking the wind out of

Lucia's August sails. Lucia had already suborned Georgie to leave this note, and begin to filch the guru away. Mrs Quantock saw it all now, and clearly this was not to be borne. Before she answered, she steeled herself with the triumph she had once scored in the matter of the Welsh attorney.

'Dear Georgie,' she said, 'no one would be more delighted than I if my guru consented to take you as a pupil. But you can't tell what he will do, as he said to me today, apropos of myself, "I cannot come unless I'm sent." Was not that wonderful? He knew at once he had been sent to me.'

By this time Georgie was quite determined to have the guru. The measure of his determination may be gauged from the fact that he forgot all about Lucia's garden party.

'But he called me his friend,' he said. 'He told me I had a clean white soul.'

'Yes; but that is his attitude towards everybody,' said Mrs Quantock. 'His religion makes it impossible for him to think ill of anybody.'

'But he didn't say that to Rush,' cried Georgie, 'when he asked for some brandy, to be put down to you.'

Mrs Quantock's expression changed for a moment, but that moment was too short for Georgie to notice it. Her face instantly cleared again.

'Naturally he cannot go about saying that sort of thing,' she observed. 'Common people – he is of the highest caste – would not understand him.'

Georgie made the direct appeal.

'Please ask him to teach me,' he said.

For a moment Mrs Quantock did not answer, but cocked her head sideways in the direction of the pear tree where a thrush was singing. It fluted a couple of repeated phrases and then was silent again.

Mrs Quantock gave a great smile to the pear tree.

'Thank you, little brother,' she said.

She turned to Georgie again.

'That comes out of St Francis,' she said, 'but Yoga embraces all that is true in every religion. Well, I will ask my guru whether he will take you as a pupil, but I can't answer for what he will say.'

'What does he – what does he charge for his lesson?' asked Georgie.

The Christian Science smile illuminated her face again.

'The word "money" never passes his lips,' she said. 'I don't think he really knows what it means. He proposed to sit on the green with a beggar's bowl but of course I would not permit that, and for the present I just give him all he wants. No doubt when he goes away, which I hope will not be for many weeks yet, though no one can tell when he will have another call, I shall slip something suitably generous into his hand, but I don't think about that. Must you be going? Good night, dear Georgie. Peace! Om!'

His last backward glance as he went out of the front door revealed her standing on one leg again, just as he had seen her first. He remembered a print of a fakir at Benares, standing in that attitude; and if the stream that flowed into the Avon could be combined with the Ganges, and the garden into the burning ghaut, and the swooping swallows into the kites, and the neat parlour-maid who showed him out, into a Brahmin, and the Chinese gong that was so prominent an object in the hall into a piece of Benares brassware, he could almost have fancied himself as standing on the brink of the sacred river. The marigolds in the garden required no transmutation . . .

Georgie had quite 'to pull himself together', as he stepped round Mrs Quantock's mulberry tree, and ten paces later round his own, before he could recapture his normal evening mood, on those occasions when he was going to dine alone. Usually these evenings were very pleasant and much occupied, for they did not occur very often in this whirl of Riseholme life, and it was not more than once a week that he spent a solitary evening, and then, if he got tired of his own company, there were half a dozen houses, easy of access, where he could betake himself in his military cloak, and spend a postprandial hour. But oftener than not when these occasions occurred, he would be quite busy at home, dusting a little china, and rearranging ornaments on his shelves, and, after putting his rings and handkerchief in the candle bracket of the piano, spending a serious hour (with the soft pedal down, for fear of irritating Robert) in reading his share of such duets as he would be likely to be called upon to play with Lucia during the next day or two. Though he read music much better than she did, he used to 'go over' the part alone first, and let it be understood that he had not seen it before. But then he was sure that she had done precisely the same, so they started fair. Such things whiled away very pleasantly the hours till eleven, when he went to bed, and it was seldom that he had to set out Patience cards to tide him over the slow minutes.

But every now and then – and tonight was one of those occasions – there occurred evenings when he never went out to dinner even if he was asked, because he 'was busy indoors'. They occurred about once a month (these evenings that he was 'busy indoors') – and even an invitation from Lucia would not succeed in disturbing them. Ages ago Riseholme had decided what made Georgie 'busy indoors' once a month, and so none of his friends chatted about the nature of his engagements to anyone else, simply because everybody else knew. His business indoors, in fact, was a perfect secret, from having been public property for so long.

June had been a very busy time, not 'indoors', but with other engagements, and as Georgie went up to his bedroom, having been told by Foljambe that the hairdresser was waiting for him, and had been waiting 'this last ten minutes', he glanced at his hair in the Cromwellian mirror that hung on the stairs, and was quite aware that it was time he submitted himself to Mr Holroyd's ministrations. There was certainly an undergrowth of grey hair visible beneath his chestnut crop, that should have been attended to at least a fortnight ago. Also there was a growing thinness in the locks that crossed his head; Mr Holroyd had attended to that before, and had suggested a certain remedy, not in the least inconvenient, unless Georgie proposed to be athletic without a cap, in a high wind, and even then not necessarily so. But as he had no intention of being athletic anywhere, with or without a cap, he determined as he went up the stairs that he would follow Mr Holroyd's advice. Mr Holroyd's procedure, without this added formula, entailed sitting 'till it dried', and after that he would have dinner, and then Mr Holroyd would begin again. He was a very clever person with regard to the face and the hands and the feet. Georgie had been conscious of walking a little lamely lately; he had been even more conscious of the need of hot towels on his face and the 'tap-tap' of Mr Holroyd's fingers, and the stretchings of Mr Holroyd's thumb across rather slack surfaces of cheek and chin. In the interval between the hair and the face, Mr Holroyd should have a good supper downstairs with Foljambe and the cook. And tomorrow morning, when he met Hermy and Ursy, Georgie would be just as spick and span and young as ever, if not more so.

Georgie (happy innocent!) was completely unaware that the whole of Riseholme knew that the smooth chestnut locks which covered the top of his head were trained like the tendrils of a grapevine from the roots, and flowed like a river over a bare head, and consequently when Mr Holroyd explained the proposed innovation, a little central wig, the edges of which would mingle in the most natural manner with his own hair, it seemed to Georgie that nobody would know the difference. In addition he would be spared those risky moments when he had to take off his hat to a friend in a high wind, for there was always the danger of his hair blowing away from the top of his head, and hanging down, like the tresses of a Rhine-maiden over one shoulder. So Mr Holroyd was commissioned to put that little affair in hand at once, and when the greyness had been attended to, and Georgie had had his dinner, there came hot towels and tappings on his face, and other ministrations. All was done about half-past ten, and when he came downstairs again for a short practice at the bass part of Beethoven's fifth symphony, ingeniously arranged for two performers on the piano, he looked with sincere satisfaction at his rosy face in the Cromwellian mirror, and his shoes felt quite comfortable again, and his nails shone like pink stars, as his hands dashed wildly about the piano in the quicker passages. But all the time the thought of the guru next door, under whose tuition he might be able to regain his youth without recourse to those expensive subterfuges (for the price of the undetectable *toupée* astonished him) rang in his head with a melody more haunting than Beethoven's. What he would have liked best of all would have been to have the guru all to himself, so that he should remain perpetually young, while all the rest of Riseholme, including Hermy and Ursy, grew old. Then, indeed, he would be king of the place, instead of serving the interests of its queen.

He rose with a little sigh, and after adjusting the strip of flannel over the keys, shut his piano and busied himself for a little with a soft duster over his cabinet of bibelots which not even Foljambe was allowed to touch. It was generally understood that he had inherited them, though the inheritance had chiefly passed to him through the medium of curiosity shops, and there were several pieces of considerable value among them. There were a gold Louis XVI snuff box, a miniature by Karl Huth, a silver toy porringer of the time of Queen Anne, a piece of Bow china, an enamelled cigarette case by Fabergé. But tonight his handling of them was not so dainty and delicate as usual, and he actually dropped the porringer on the floor as he was dusting it, for his mind still occupied itself with the guru and the practices that led to permanent youth. How quick Lucia had been to snap him up for her garden party. Yet perhaps she would not get him, for he might say he was not sent. But surely he would be sent to Georgie, whom he knew, the moment he set eyes on him, to have a clean white soul . . .

The clock struck eleven, and, as usual on warm nights, Georgie opened the glass door into his garden and drew in a breath of the night air. There was a slip of moon in the sky which he most punctiliously saluted, wondering (though he did not seriously believe in its superstition) how Lucia could be so foolhardy as to cut the new moon. She had seen it yesterday, she told him, in London, and had taken no notice whatever of it . . . The heavens were quickly peppered with pretty stars, which Georgie after his busy interesting day enjoyed looking at, though if he had had the arrangement of them, he would certainly have put them into more definite patterns. Among them was a very red planet, and Georgie, with recollections of his classical education, easily remembered that Mars, the God of War, was symbolized in the heavens by a red star. Could that mean anything to peaceful Riseholme? Was internal warfare, were revolutionary movements possible in so serene a realm?

CHAPTER FOUR

Pink irascible Robert, prone to throw his food about his plate, if it did not commend itself to him, felt in an extremely good-natured mood that same night after dinner, for the guru had again made a visit to the kitchen with the result that instead of a slab of pale dead codfish being put before him after he had eaten some tepid soup, there appeared a delicious little fish curry. The guru had behaved with great tact; he had seen the storm gathering on poor Robert's face, as he sipped the cool effete concoction and put down his spoon again with a splash in his soup plate, and thereupon had bowed and smiled and scurried away to the kitchen to intercept the next abomination. Then returning with the little curry he explained that it was entirely for Robert, since those who sought the Way did not indulge in hot sharp foods, and so he had gobbled it up to the very last morsel.

In consequence when the guru salaamed very humbly, and said that with gracious permission of beloved lady and kind master he would go and meditate in his room, and had shambled away in his red slippers, the discussion which Robert had felt himself obliged to open with his wife, on the subject of having an unknown Indian staying with them for an indefinite period, was opened in a much more amicable key than it would have been on a slice of codfish.

'Well, now, about this Golliwog – ha-ha – I should say guru, my dear,' he began, 'what's going to happen?'

Daisy Quantock drew in her breath sharply and winced at this irreverence, but quickly remembered that she must always be sending out messages of love, north, east, south, and west. So she sent a rather spiky one in the direction of her husband who was sitting due east, so that it probably got to him at once, and smiled the particular hard firm smile which was an heirloom inherited from her last rule of life.

'No one knows,' she said brightly. 'Even the Guides can't tell where and when a guru may be called.'

'Then do you propose he should stop here till he's called somewhere else?'

She continued smiling.

'I don't propose anything,' she said. 'It's not in my hands.'

Under the calming influence of the fish curry, Robert remained still placid.

'He's a first-rate cook anyhow,' he said. 'Can't you engage him as that? Call to the kitchen, you know.'

'Darling!' said Mrs Quantock, sending out more love. But she had a quick temper, and indeed the two were outpoured together, like hot and cold taps turned on in a bath. The pellucid stream of love served to keep her temper moderately cool.

'Well, ask him,' suggested Mr Quantock, 'as you say, you never can tell where a guru may be called. Give him forty pounds a year and beer money.'

'Beer!' began Mrs Quantock, when she suddenly remembered Georgie's story about Rush and the guru and the brandy bottle, and stopped.

'Yes, dear, I said "beer",' remarked Robert a little irritably, 'and in any case I insist that you dismiss your present cook. You only took her because she was a Christian Scientist, and you've left that little sheepfold now. You used to talk about false claims I remember. Well her claim to be a cook is the falsest I ever heard of. I'd sooner take my chance with an itinerant organ grinder. But that fish curry tonight and that other thing last night, that's what I mean by good eating.'

The thought even of good food always calmed Robert's savage breast; it blew upon him as the wind on an Aeolian harp hung in the trees, evoking faint sweet sounds.

'I'm sure, my dear,' he said, 'that I shall be willing to fall in with any pleasant arrangement about your guru, but it really isn't unreasonable in me to ask what sort of arrangement you propose. I haven't a word to say against him, especially when he goes to the kitchen; I only want to know if he is going to stop here a night or two or a year or two. Talk to him about it tomorrow with my love. I wonder if he can make bisque soup.'

Daisy Quantock carried quite a quantity of material for reflection upstairs with her, then she went to bed, pausing a moment opposite the guru's door, from inside of which came sounds of breathing so deep that it sounded almost like snoring. But she seemed to detect a timbre of spirituality about it which convinced her that he was holding high communion with the Guides. It was round him that her thoughts centred; he was the tree through the branches of which they scampered chattering.

Her first and main interest in him was sheer guruism, for she was one of those intensely happy people who pass through life in ecstatic pursuit of some idea which those who do not share it call a fad. Well might poor Robert remember the devastation of his home when Daisy, after the perusal of a little pamphlet which she picked up on a bookstall called 'The Uric Acid Monthly', came to the shattering conclusion that her buxom frame consisted almost entirely of waste products which must be eliminated. For a greedy man the situation was frankly intolerable, for when he continued his ordinary diet (this was before the cursed advent of the Christian Science cook) she kept pointing to his well-furnished plate, and told him that every atom of that beef or mutton and potatoes turned from the moment he swallowed it into chromogens and toxins, and that his apparent appetite was merely the result of fermentation. For herself her platter was an abominable mess of cheese and protein powder and apples and salad oil, while round her, like saucers of specimen seeds, were ranged little piles of nuts and pine branches, which supplied body-building material, and which she weighed out with scrupulous accuracy, in accordance with the directions of the 'Uric Acid Monthly'. Tea and coffee were taboo, since they flooded the blood with poisons, and the kitchen boiler rumbled day and night to supply the rivers of boiling water with which (taken in sips) she inundated her system. Strange gaunt females used to come down from London, with small parcels full of tough food that tasted of travelling bags and contained so much nutrition that a portmanteau full of it would furnish the daily rations of an army. Luckily even her iron constitution could not stand the strain of such ideal living for long, and her growing anaemia threatened to undermine a constitution seriously impaired by the precepts of perfect health. A course of beef steaks and other substantial viands loaded with uric acid restored her to her former vigour.

Thus reinforced, she plunged with the same energy as she had devoted to repelling uric acid into the embrace of Christian Science. The inhumanity of that sect towards both herself and others took complete possession of her, and when her husband complained on a bitter January morning that his smoking room was like an icehouse, because the housemaid had forgotten to light the fire, she had no touch of pity for him, since she knew that there was no such thing as cold or heat or pain, and therefore you could not feel cold. But now, since, according to the new creed, such things as uric acid, chromogens and poisons had no existence, she could safely indulge in decent viands again. But her unhappy husband was not a real gainer in this respect, for while he ate, she tirelessly discoursed to him on the new creed, and asked him to recite with her the True Statement of Being. And on the top of that she dismissed the admirable cook, and engaged the miscreant from whom he suffered still, though Christian Science, which had allowed her cold to make so long a false claim on her, had followed the uric-acid fad into the limbo of her discarded beliefs.

But now once more she had temporarily discovered the secret of life in the teachings of the guru, and it was, as has been mentioned, sheer guruism that constituted the main attraction of the new creed. That then being taken for granted, she turned her mind to certain side issues, which to a true Riseholmite were of entrancing interest. She felt a strong suspicion that Lucia contemplated annexing her guru altogether, for otherwise she would not have returned so enthusiastic a response to her note, nor have sent Georgie to deliver it, nor have professed so violent an interest in the guru. What then was the correctly diabolical policy to pursue? Should Daisy Quantock refuse to take him to Mrs Lucas altogether, with a message of regret that he did not feel himself sent? Even if she did this, did she feel herself strong enough to throw down the gauntlet (in the shape of the guru) and, using him as the attraction, challenge darling Lucia to mutual combat, in order to decide who should be the leader of all that was advanced and cultured in Riseholme society? Still following that ramification of this policy, should she bribe Georgie over to her own revolutionary camp, by promising him instruction from the guru? Or following a less dashing line, should she take darling Lucia and Georgie into the charmed circle, and while retaining her own right of treasure trove, yet share it with them in some inner ring, dispensing the guru to them, if they were good, in small doses?

Mrs Quantock's mind resembled in its workings the manoeuvres of a moth distracted by the glory of several bright lights. It dashed at one, got slightly singed, and forgetting all about that turned its attention to the second, and the third, taking headers into each in turn, without deciding which, on the whole, was the most enchanting of those luminaries. So, in order to curb the exuberance of these frenzied excursions she got a half-sheet of paper, and noted down the alternatives that she must choose from.

(i)   Shall I keep him entirely to myself?
(ii) Shall I run him for all he is worth, and leave out L?
(iii) Shall I get G on my side?
(iv) Shall I give L and G bits?

She paused a moment: then remembering that he had voluntarily helped her very pretty housemaid to make the beds that morning, saying that his business (like the Prince of Wales's) was to serve, she added:

(v)   Shall I ask him to be my cook?

For a few seconds the brightness of her eager interest was dimmed as the unworthy suspicion occurred to her that perhaps the prettiness of her housemaid had something to do with his usefulness in the bedrooms, but she instantly dismissed it. There was the bottle of brandy, too, which he had ordered from Rush's. When she had begged him to order anything he wanted and cause it to be put down to her account, she had not actually contemplated brandy. Then remembering that one of the most necessary conditions for progress in Yoga, was that the disciple should have complete confidence in the guru, she chased that also out of her mind. But still, even when the lines of all possible policies were written down, she could come to no decision, and putting her paper by her bed, decided to sleep over it. The rhythmical sounds of hallowed breathing came steadily from next door, and she murmured 'Om, Om,' in time with them.

*   *   *

The hours of the morning between breakfast and lunch were the time which the inhabitants of Riseholme chiefly devoted to spying on each other. They went about from shop to shop on household businesses, occasionally making purchases which they carried away with them in little paper parcels with convenient loops of string, but the real object of these excursions was to see what everybody else was doing, and learn what fresh interests had sprung up like mushrooms during the night. Georgie would be matching silks at the draper's, and very naturally he would carry them from the obscurity of the interior to the door in order to be certain about the shades, and keep his eye on the comings and goings in the street, and very naturally Mr Lucas on his way to the market gardener's to enquire whether he had yet received the bulbs from Holland, would tell him that Lucia had received the piano arrangement of the Mozart trio. Georgie for his part would mention that Hermy and Ursy were expected that evening, and Peppino enriched by this item would 'toddle on', as his phrase went, to meet and exchange confidences with the next spy. He had noticed incidentally that Georgie carried a small oblong box with hard corners, which, perfectly correctly, he conjectured to be cigarettes for Hermy and Ursy, since Georgie never smoked.

'Well, I must be toddling on,' he said, after identifying Georgie's box of cigarettes, and being rather puzzled by a bulge in Georgie's pocket. 'You'll be looking in some time this morning, perhaps.'

Georgie had not been quite sure that he would (for he was very busy owing to the arrival of his sisters, and the necessity of going to Mr Holroyd's, in order that that artist might accurately match the shade of his hair with a view to the expensive *toupée*), but the mention of the arrival of the Mozart now decided him. He intended anyhow before he went home for lunch to stroll past The Hurst, and see if he did not hear – to adopt a mixed metaphor – the sound of the diligent practice of that classical morsel going on inside. Probably the soft pedal would be down, but he had marvellously acute hearing, and he would be very much surprised if he did not hear the recognizable chords, and even more surprised if, when they came to practise the piece together, Lucia did not give him to understand that she was reading it for the first time. He had already got a copy, and had practised his part last night, but then he was in the superior position of not having a husband who would inadvertently tell on him! Meantime it was of the first importance to get that particular shade of purple silk that had none of that 'tarsome' magenta tint in it. Meantime also, it was of even greater importance to observe the movements of Riseholme.

Just opposite was the village green, and as nobody was quite close to him Georgie put on his spectacles, which he could whisk off in a moment. It was these which formed that bulge in his pocket which Peppino had noticed, but the fact of his using spectacles at all was a secret that would have to be profoundly kept for several years yet. But as there was no one at all near him, he stealthily adjusted them on his small straight nose. The morning train from town had evidently come in, for there was a bustle of cabs about the door of the Ambermere Arms, and a thing that thrilled him to the marrow was the fact that Lady Ambermere's motor was undoubtedly among them. That must surely mean that Lady Ambermere herself was here, for when poor thin Miss Lyall, her companion, came in to Riseholme to do shopping, or transact such business as the majestic life at The Hall required, she always came on foot, or in very inclement weather in a small two-wheeled cart like a hip bath. At this moment, steeped in conjecture, who should appear, walking stiffly, with her nose in the air, as if suspecting, and not choosing to verify, some faint unpleasant odour, but Lady Ambermere herself, coming from the direction of The Hurst . . . Clearly she must have got there after Peppino had left, or he would surely have mentioned the fact that Lady Ambermere had been at The Hurst, if she *had* been at The Hurst. It is true that she was only coming from the direction of The Hurst, but Georgie put into practice, in his mental processes, Darwin's principle, that in order to observe usefully, you must have a theory. Georgie's theory was that Lady Ambermere had been at The Hurst just for a minute or two, and hastily put his spectacles in his pocket. With the precision of a trained mind he also formed the theory that some business had brought Lady Ambermere into Riseholme, and that taking advantage of her presence there, she had probably returned a verbal answer to Lucia's invitation to her garden party, which she would have received by the first post this morning. He was quite ready to put his theory to the test when Lady Ambermere had arrived at the suitable distance for his conveniently observing her, and for taking off his hat. She always treated him like a boy, which he liked. The usual salutation passed.

'I don't know where my people are,' said Lady Ambermere majestically. 'Have you seen my motor?'

'Yes, dear lady, it's in at your own arms,' said Georgie brightly. 'Happy motor!'

If Lady Ambermere unbent to anybody, she unbent to Georgie. He was of quite good family, because his mother had been a Bartlett and a second cousin of her deceased husband. Sometimes when she talked to Georgie she said 'we', implying thereby his connection with the aristocracy, and this gratified Georgie nearly as much as did her treatment of him as being quite a boy still. It was to him, as a boy still, that she answered.

'Well, the happy motor, you little rascal, must come to my arms instead of being at them,' she said with the quick wit for which Riseholme pronounced her famous. 'Fancy being able to see my motor at that distance. Young eyes!'

It was really young spectacles, but Georgie did not mind that. In fact, he would not have corrected the mistake for the world.

'Shall I run across and fetch it for you?' he asked.

'In a minute. Or whistle on your fingers like a vulgar street boy,' said Lady Ambermere. 'I'm sure you know how to.'

Georgie had not the slightest idea, but with the courage of youth, presuming, with the prudence of middle age, that he would not really be called upon to perform so unimaginable a feat, he put two fingers up to his mouth.

'Here goes then!' he said, greatly daring. (He knew perfectly well that the dignity of Lady Ambermere would not permit rude vulgar whistling, of which he was hopelessly incapable, to summon her motor. She made a feint of stopping her ears with her hands.)

'Don't do anything of the kind,' she said. 'In a minute you shall walk with me across to the Arms, but tell me this first. I have just been to say to our good Mrs Lucas that very likely I will look in at her garden party on Friday, if I have nothing else to do. But who is this wonderful creature she is expecting? Is it an Indian conjurer? If so, I should like to see him, because when Ambermere was in Madras I remember one coming to the Residency who had cobras and that sort of thing. I told her I didn't like snakes, and she said there shouldn't be any. In fact, it was all rather mysterious, and she didn't at present know if he was coming or not. I only said, "No snakes: I insist on no snakes."'

Georgie relieved her mind about the chance of there being snakes, and gave a short *précis* of the ascertained habits of the guru, laying special stress on his high caste.

'Yes, some of these Brahmins are of very decent family,' admitted Lady Ambermere. 'I was always against lumping all dark-skinned people together. When we were at Madras I was famed for my discrimination.'

They were walking across the green as Lady Ambermere gave vent to these liberal sentiments, and Georgie even without the need of his spectacles could see Peppino, who had spied Lady Ambermere from the door of the market gardener's, hurrying down the street, in order to get a word with her before 'her people' drove her back to The Hall.

'I came into Riseholme today to get rooms at the Arms for Olga Bracely,' she observed.

'The prima donna?' asked Georgie, breathless with excitement.

'Yes; she is coming to stay at the Arms for two nights with Mr Shuttleworth.'

'Surely – ' began Georgie.

'No, it is all right, he is her husband, they were married last week,' said Lady Ambermere. 'I should have thought that Shuttleworth was a good enough name, as the Shuttleworths are cousins of the late lord, but she prefers to call herself Miss Bracely. I don't dispute her right to call herself what she pleases: far from it, though who the Bracelys were, I have never been able to discover. But when George Shuttleworth wrote to me saying that he and his wife were intending to stay here for a couple of days, and proposing to come over to The Hall to see me, I thought I would just look in at the Arms myself, and see that they were promised proper accommodation. They will dine with me tomorrow. I have a few people staying, and no doubt Miss Bracely will sing afterwards. My Broadwood was always considered a remarkably fine instrument. It was very proper of George Shuttleworth to say that he would be in the neighbourhood, and I dare say she is a very decent sort of woman.'

They had come to the motor by this time – the rich, the noble motor, as Mr Pepys would have described it – and there was poor Miss Lyall hung with parcels, and wearing a faint sycophantic smile. This miserable spinster, of age so obvious as to be called not the least uncertain, was Lady Ambermere's companion, and shared with her the glories of The Hall, which had been left to Lady Ambermere for life. She was provided with food and lodging and the use of the cart like a hip bath when Lady Ambermere had errands for her to do in Riseholme, so what could a woman want more? In return for these bounties, her only duty was to devote herself body and mind to her patroness, to read the paper aloud, to set Lady Ambermere's patterns for needlework, to carry the little Chinese dog under her arm, and wash him once a week, to accompany Lady Ambermere to church, and never to have a fire in her bedroom. She had a melancholy wistful little face: her head was inclined with a backward slope on her neck, and her mouth was invariably a little open showing long front teeth, so that she looked rather like a roast hare sent up to table with its head on. Georgie always had a joke ready for Miss Lyall, of the sort that made her say, 'Oh, Mr Pillson!' and caused her to blush. She thought him remarkably pleasant.

Georgie had his joke ready on this occasion.

'Why, here's Miss Lyall!' he said. 'And what has Miss Lyall been doing while her ladyship and I have been talking? Better not ask, perhaps.'

'Oh, Mr Pillson!' said Miss Lyall, as punctually as a cuckoo clock when the hands point to the hour.

Lady Ambermere put half her weight on to the step of the motor, causing it to creak and sway.

'Call on the Shuttleworths, Georgie,' she said. 'Say I told you to. Home!'

Miss Lyall effaced herself on the front seat of the motor, like a mouse hiding in a corner, after Lady Ambermere had got in, and the footman mounted on to the box. At that moment Peppino with his bag of bulbs, a little out of breath, squeezed his way between two cabs by the side of the motor. He was just too late, and the motor moved off. It was very improbable that Lady Ambermere saw him at all.

Georgie felt very much like a dog with a bone in his mouth, who only wants to get away from all the other dogs and discuss it quietly. It is safe to say that never in twenty-four hours had so many exciting things happened to him. He had ordered a *toupée*, he had been looked on with favour by a guru, all Riseholme knew that he had had quite a long conversation with Lady Ambermere and nobody in Riseholme, except himself, knew that Olga Bracely was going to spend two nights here. Well he remembered her marvellous appearance last year at Covent Garden in the part of Brünnhilde. He had gone to town for a rejuvenating visit to his dentist, and the tarsomeness of being betwixt and between had been quite forgotten by him when he saw her awake to Siegfried's line on the mountain top. '*Das ist keine mann,*' Siegfried had said, and, to be sure, that was very clever of him, for she looked like some slim beardless boy, and not in the least like those great fat Fraus at Baireuth, whom nobody could have mistaken for a man as they bulged and heaved even before the strings of the breastplate were uncut by his sword. And then she sat up and hailed the sun, and Georgie felt for a moment that he had quite taken the wrong turn in life, when he settled to spend his years in this boyish, maidenly manner with his embroidery and his china-dusting at Riseholme. He ought to have been Siegfried . . . He had brought a photograph of her in her cuirass and helmet, and often looked at it when he was not too busy with something else. He had even championed his goddess against Lucia, when she pronounced that Wagner was totally lacking in knowledge of dramatic effects. To be sure she had never seen any Wagner opera, but she had heard the overture to *Tristan* performed at the Queen's Hall, and if that was Wagner, well –

* * *

Already, though Lady Ambermere's motor had not yet completely vanished up the street, Riseholme was gently closing in round him, in order to discover by discreet questions (as in the game of Clumps) what he and she had been talking about. There was Colonel Boucher with his two snorting bulldogs closing in from one side, and Mrs Weston in her bath chair being wheeled relentlessly towards him from another, and the two Miss Antrobuses sitting playfully in the stocks, on the third, and Peppino at close range on the fourth. Everyone knew, too, that he did not lunch till half-past one, and there was really no reason why he should not stop and chat as usual. But with the eye of the true general, he saw that he could most easily break the surrounding cordon by going off in the direction of Colonel Boucher, because Colonel Boucher always said 'Haw, hum, by Jove,' before he descended into coherent speech, and thus Georgie could forestall him with 'Good morning, Colonel,' and pass on before he got to business. He did not like passing close to those slobbering bulldogs, but something had to be done . . . Next moment he was clear and saw that the other spies by their original impetus were still converging on each other and walked briskly down towards Lucia's house, to listen for any familiar noises out of the Mozart trio. The noises were there, and the soft pedal was down just as he expected, so, that business being off his mind, he continued his walk for a few hundred yards more, meaning to make a short circuit through fields, cross the bridge, over the happy stream that flowed into the Avon, and regain his house by the door at the bottom of the garden. Then he would sit and think . . . the guru, Olga Bracely . . . What if he asked Olga Bracely and her husband to dine, and persuaded Mrs Quantock to let the guru come? That would be three men and one woman, and Hermy and Ursy would make all square. Six for dinner was the utmost that Foljambe permitted.

He had come to the stile that led into the fields, and sat there for a moment. Lucia's tentative melodies were still faintly audible, but soon they stopped, and he guessed that she was looking out of the window. She was too great to take part in the morning spying that went on round about the green, but she often saw a good deal from her window. He wondered what Mrs Quantock was meaning to do. Apparently she had not promised the guru for the garden party, or else Lady Ambermere would not have said that Lucia did not know whether he was coming or not. Perhaps Mrs Quantock was going to run him herself, and grant him neither to Lucia nor Georgie. In that case he would certainly ask Olga Bracely and her husband to dine, and should he or should he not ask Lucia?

The red star had risen in Riseholme: Bolshevism was treading in its peaceful air, and if Mrs Quantock was going to secrete her guru, and set up her own standard on the strength of him, Georgie felt much inclined to ask Olga Bracely to dinner, without saying anything whatever to Lucia about it, and just see what would happen next. Georgie was a Bartlett on his mother's side, and he played the piano better than Lucia, and he had twenty-four hours' leisure every day, which he could devote to being king of Riseholme . . . His nature flared up, burning with a red revolutionary flame, that was fed by his secret knowledge about Olga Bracely. Why should Lucia rule everyone with her rod of iron? Why, and again why?

Suddenly he heard his name called in the familiar alto, and there was Lucia in her Shakespeare's garden.

'*Georgino! Georgino. Mio!*' she cried. '*Gino!*'

Out of mere habit Georgie got down from his stile, and tripped up the road towards her. The manly seething of his soul's insurrection rebuked him, but unfortunately his legs and his voice surrendered. Habit was strong . . .

'*Amica!*' he answered. '*Buon giorno.*' ('And why do I say it in Italian?' he vainly asked himself.)

'Geordie, come and have ickle talk,' she said. 'Me want 'oo wise man to advise ickle Lucia.'

'What 'oo want?' asked Georgie, now quite quelled for the moment.

'Lots things. Here's pwetty flower for button-holie. Now tell me about black man. Him no snakes have? Why Mrs Quantock say she thinks he no come to poo' Lucia's party garden?'

'Oh, did she?' asked Georgie, relapsing into the vernacular.

'Yes, oh, and by the way there's a parcel come which I think must be the Mozart trio. Will you come over tomorrow morning and read it with me? Yes? About half-past eleven, then. But never mind that.'

She fixed him with her ready, birdy eye.

'Daisy asked me to ask him,' she said, 'and so to oblige poor Daisy I did. And now she says she doesn't know if he'll come. What does that mean? Is it possible that she wants to keep him to herself? She has done that sort of thing before, you know.'

This probably represented Lucia's statement of the said case about the Welsh attorney, and Georgie taking it as such felt rather embarrassed. Also that birdlike eye seemed to gimlet its way into his very soul, and divine the secret disloyalty that he had been contemplating. If she had continued to look into him, he might not only have confessed to the gloomiest suspicions about Mrs Quantock, but have let go of his secret about Olga Bracely also, and suggested the possibility of her and her husband being brought to the garden party. But the eye at this moment unscrewed itself from him again and travelled up the road.

'There's the guru,' she said. 'Now we will see!'

Georgie, faint with emotion, peered out between the form of the peacock and the pineapple on the yew hedge, and saw what followed. Lucia went straight up to the guru, bowed and smiled and clearly introduced herself. In another moment he was showing his white teeth and salaaming, and together they walked back to The Hurst, where Georgie palpitated behind the yew hedge. Together they entered and Lucia's eye wore its most benignant aspect.

'I want to introduce to you, Guru,' she said without a stumble, 'a great friend of mine. This is Mr Pillson, Guru; Guru, Mr Pillson. The guru is coming to tiffin with me, Georgie. Cannot I persuade you to stop?'

'Delighted!' said Georgie. 'We met before in a sort of way, didn't we?'

'Yes, indeed. So pleased,' said the guru.

'Let us go in,' said Lucia. 'It is close on lunchtime.'

Georgie followed, after a great many bowings and politenesses from the guru. He was not sure if he had the makings of a Bolshevist. Lucia was so marvellously efficient.

CHAPTER FIVE

One of Lucia's greatnesses lay in the fact that when she found anybody out in some act of atrocious meanness, she never indulged in any idle threats of revenge: it was sufficient that she knew, and would take suitable steps on the earliest occasion. Consequently when it appeared, from the artless conversation of the guru at lunch, that the perfidious Mrs Quantock had not even asked him whether he would like to go to Lucia's garden party or not (pending her own decision as to what she was meaning to do with him) Lucia received the information with the utmost good humour, merely saying, 'No doubt dear Mrs Quantock forgot to tell you,' and did not announce acts of reprisal, such as striking Daisy off the list of her habitual guests for a week or two, just to give her a lesson. She even, before they sat down to lunch, telephoned over to that thwarted woman to say that she had met the guru in the street, and they had both felt that there was some wonderful bond of sympathy between them, so he had come back with her, and they were just sitting down to tiffin. She was pleased with the word 'tiffin', and also liked explaining to Daisy what it meant.

Tiffin was a great success, and there was no need for the guru to visit the kitchen in order to make something that could be eaten without struggle. He talked quite freely about his mission here, and Lucia and Georgie and Peppino, who had come in rather late, for he had been obliged to go back to the market gardener's about the bulbs, listened entranced.

'Yes, it was when I went to my friend who keeps the bookshop,' he said, 'that I knew there was English lady who wanted guru, and I knew I was called to her. No luggage, no anything at all: as I am. Such a kind lady, too, and she will get on well, but she will find some of the postures difficult, for she is what you call globe, round.'

'Was that postures when I saw her standing on one leg in the garden?' asked Georgie, 'and when she sat down and tried to hold her toes?'

'Yes, indeed, quite so, and difficult for globe. But she has white soul.'

He looked round with a smile.

'I see many white souls here,' he said. 'It is happy place, when there are white souls, for to them I am sent.'

This was sufficient: in another minute Lucia, Georgie and Peppino were all accepted as pupils, and presently they went out into the garden, where the guru sat on the ground in a most complicated attitude which was obviously quite out of reach of Mrs Quantock.

'One foot on one thigh, other foot on other thigh,' he explained. 'And the head and back straight: it is good to meditate so.'

Lucia tried to imagine meditating so, but felt that any meditation so would certainly be on the subject of broken bones.

'Shall I be able to do that?' she asked. 'And what will be the effect?'

'You will be light and active, dear lady, and ah – here is other dear lady come to join us.'

Mrs Quantock had certainly made one of her diplomatic errors on this occasion. She had acquiesced on the telephone in her guru going to tiffin with Lucia, but about the middle of her lunch, she had been unable to resist the desire to know what was happening at The Hurst. She could not bear the thought that Lucia and her guru were together now, and her own note, saying that it was uncertain whether the guru would come to the garden party or not, filled her with the most uneasy apprehensions. She would sooner have acquiesced in her guru going to fifty garden parties, where all was public, and she could keep an eye and a control on him, rather than that Lucia should have 'enticed him in' – that was her phrase – like this to tiffin. The only consolation was that her own lunch had been practically inedible, and Robert had languished lamentably for the guru to return, and save his stomach. She had left him glowering over a little mud and water called coffee. Robert, at any rate, would welcome the return of the guru.

She waddled across the lawn to where this harmonious party was sitting, and at that moment Lucia began to feel vindictive. The calm of victory which had permeated her when she brought the guru in to lunch, without any bother at all, was troubled and broken up, and darling Daisy's note, containing the outrageous falsity that the guru would not certainly accept an invitation which had never been permitted to reach him at all, assumed a more sinister aspect. Clearly now Daisy had intended to keep him to herself, a fact that she already suspected, and had made a hostile invasion.

'Guru, dear, you naughty thing,' said Mrs Quantock playfully, after the usual salutations had passed, 'why did you not tell your Chela you would not be home for tiffin?'

The guru had unwound his legs, and stood up.

'But see, beloved lady,' he said, 'how pleasant we all are! Take not too much thought, when it is only white souls who are together.'

Mrs Quantock patted his shoulder.

'It is all good and kind Om,' she said. 'I send out my message of love. There!'

It was necessary to descend from these high altitudes, and Lucia proceeded to do so, as in a parachute that dropped swiftly at first, and then floated in still air.

'And we're making such a lovely plan, dear Daisy,' she said. 'The guru is going to teach us all. Classes! Aren't you?'

He held his hands up to his head, palms outwards, and closed his eyes.

'I seem to feel call,' he said. 'I am sent. Surely the Guides tell me there is a sending of me. What you call classes? Yes? I teach: you learn. We all learn . . . I leave all to you. I will walk a little way off to arbour, and meditate, and then when you have arranged, you will tell guru, who is your servant. Salaam! Om!'

With the guru in her own house, and with every intention to annex him, it was no wonder that Lucia took the part of chairman in this meeting that was to settle the details of the esoteric brotherhood that was to be formed in Riseholme. Had not Mrs Quantock been actually present, Lucia in revenge for her outrageous conduct about the garden party invitation would probably have left her out of the classes altogether, but with her sitting firm and square in a basket chair, that creaked querulously as she moved, she could not be completely ignored. But Lucia took the lead throughout, and suggested straight away that the smoking parlour would be the most convenient place to hold the classes in.

'I should not think of invading your house, dear Daisy,' she said, 'and here is the smoking parlour which no one ever sits in, so quiet and peaceful. Yes. Shall we consider that settled, then?'

She turned briskly to Mrs Quantock.

'And now where shall the guru stay?' she said. 'It would be too bad, dear Daisy, if we are all to profit by his classes, that you should have all the trouble and expense of entertaining him, for in your sweet little house he must be a great inconvenience, and I think you said that your husband had given up his dressing room to him.'

Mrs Quantock made a desperate effort to retain her property.

'No inconvenience at all,' she said, 'quite the contrary in fact, dear. It is delightful having him, and Robert regards him as a most desirable inmate.'

Lucia pressed her hand feelingly.

'You and your husband are too unselfish,' she said. 'Often have I said, "Daisy and Mr Robert are the most unselfish people I know." Haven't I, Georgie? But we can't permit you to be so crowded. Your only spare room, you know, *and* your husband's dressing room! Georgie, I know you agree with me; we must not permit dear Daisy to be so unselfish.'

The birdlike eye produced its compelling effect on Georgie. So short a time ago he had indulged in revolutionary ideas, and had contemplated having the guru and Olga Bracely to dinner, without even asking Lucia: now the faint stirrings of revolt faded like snow in summer. He knew quite well what Lucia's next proposition would be: he knew, too, that he would agree to it.

'No, that would never do,' he said. 'It is simply trespassing on Mrs Quantock's good nature, if she is to board and lodge him, while he teaches all of us. I wish I could take him in, but with Hermy and Ursy coming tonight, I have as little room as Mrs Quantock.'

'He shall come here,' said Lucia brightly, as if she had just that moment thought of it. 'There are Hamlet and Othello vacant' – all her rooms were named after Shakespearian plays – 'and it will not be the least inconvenient. Will it, Peppino? I shall really like having him here. Shall we consider that settled, then?'

Daisy made a perfectly futile effort to send forth a message of love to all quarters of the compass. Bitterly she repented of having ever mentioned her guru to Lucia: it had never occurred to her that she would annex him like this. While she was cudgelling her brains as to how she could arrest this powerful offensive, Lucia went sublimely on.

'Then there's the question of what we shall pay him,' she said. 'Dear Daisy tells us that he scarcely knows what money is, but I for one could never dream of profiting by his wisdom, if I was to pay nothing for it. The labourer is worthy of his hire, and so I suppose the teacher is. What if we pay him five shillings each a lesson: that will make a pound a lesson. Dear me! I shall be busy this August. Now how many classes shall we ask him to give us? I should say six to begin with, if everybody agrees. One every day for the next week except Sunday. That is what you all wish? Yes? Then shall we consider that settled?'

Mrs Quantock, still impotently rebelling, resorted to the most dire weapon in her armoury, namely, sarcasm.

'Perhaps, darling Lucia,' she said, 'it would be well to ask my guru if he has anything to say to your settlings. England is a free country still, even if you happen to have come from India.'

Lucia had a deadlier weapon than sarcasm, which was the apparent unconsciousness of there having been any. For it is no use plunging a dagger into your enemy's heart, if it produces no effect whatever on him. She clapped her hands together, and gave her peal of silvery laughter.

'What a good idea!' she said. 'Then you would like me to go and tell him what we propose? Just as you like. I will trot away, shall I, and see if he agrees. Don't think of stirring, dear Daisy, I know how you feel the heat. Sit quiet in the shade. As you know, I am a real salamander, the sun is never *troppo caldo* for me.'

She tripped off to where the guru was sitting in that wonderful position. She had read the article in the encyclopaedia about Yoga right through again this morning, and had quite made up her mind, as indeed her proceedings had just shown, that Yoga was, to put it irreverently, to be her August stunt. He was still so deep in meditation that he could only look dreamily in her direction as she approached, but then with a long sigh he got up.

'This is beautiful place,' he said. 'It is full of sweet influences and I have had high talk with Guides.'

Lucia felt thrilled.

'Ah, do tell me what they said to you,' she exclaimed.

'They told me to follow where I was led: they said they would settle everything for me in wisdom and love.'

This was most encouraging, for decidedly Lucia had been settling for him, and the opinion of the Guides was thus a direct personal testimonial. Any faint twitchings of conscience (they were of the very faintest) that she had grabbed dear Daisy's property were once and for ever quieted, and she proceeded confidently to unfold the settlements of wisdom and love, which met with the guru's entire approval. He shut his eyes a moment and breathed deeply.

'They give peace and blessing,' he said. 'It is they who ordered that it should be so. Om!'

He seemed to sink into profound depths of meditation, and Lucia hurried back to the group she had left.

'It is all too wonderful,' she said. 'The Guides have told him that they were settling everything for him in wisdom and love, so we may be sure we were right in our plans. How lovely to think that we have been guided by them! Dear Daisy, how wonderful he is! I will send across for his things, shall I, and I will have Hamlet and Othello made ready for him!'

Bitter though it was to part with her guru, it was impious to rebel against the ordinances of the Guides, but there was a trace of human resentment in Daisy's answer.

'Things!' she exclaimed. 'He hasn't got a thing in the world. Every material possession chains us down to earth. You will soon come to that, darling Lucia.'

It occurred to Georgie that the guru had certainly got a bottle of brandy, but there was no use in introducing a topic that might lead to discord, and indeed, even as Lucia went indoors to see about Hamlet and Othello, the guru himself, having emerged from meditation, joined them and sat down by Mrs Quantock.

'Beloved lady,' he said, 'all is peace and happiness. The Guides have spoken to me so lovingly of you, and they say it is best your guru should come here. Perhaps I shall return later to your kind house. They smiled when I asked that. But just now they send me here: there is more need of me here, for already you have so much light.'

Certainly the Guides were very tactful people, for nothing could have soothed Mrs Quantock so effectually as a message of that kind, which she would certainly report to Lucia when she returned from seeing about Hamlet and Othello.

'Oh, do they say I have much light already, Guru, dear?' she asked. 'That is nice of them.'

'Surely they said it, and now I shall go back to your house, and leave sweet thoughts there for you. And shall I send sweet thoughts to the home of the kind gentleman next door?'

Georgie eagerly welcomed this proposition, for with Hermy and Ursy coming that evening, he felt that he would have plenty of use for sweet thoughts. He even forbore to complete in his own mind the conjecture that was forming itself there, namely, that though the guru would be leaving sweet thoughts for Mrs Quantock, he would probably be taking away the brandy bottle for himself. But Georgie knew he was only too apt to indulge in secret cynicisms and perhaps there was no brandy to take away by this time . . . and lo and behold, he was being cynical again.

The sun was still hot when, half an hour afterwards, he got into the open cab which he had ordered to take him to the station to meet Hermy and Ursy, and he put up his umbrella with its white linen cover, to shield him from it. He did not take the motor, because either Hermy or Ursy would have insisted on driving it, and he did not choose to put himself in their charge. In all the years that he had lived at Riseholme, he never remembered a time when social events – 'work', he called it – had been so exciting and varied. There were Hermy and Ursy coming this evening, and Olga Bracely and her husband (Olga Bracely and Mr Shuttleworth sounded vaguely improper: Georgie rather liked that) were coming tomorrow, and there was Lucia's garden party the day after, and every day there was to be a lesson from the guru, so that God alone knew when Georgie would have a moment to himself for his embroidery or to practise the Mozart trio. But with his hair chestnut-coloured to the very roots, and his shining nails, and his comfortable boots, he felt extremely young and fit for anything. Soon, under the influence of the new creed with its postures and breathings, he would feel younger and more vigorous yet.

But he wished that it had been he who had found this pamphlet on Eastern philosophies, which had led Mrs Quantock to make the enquiries that had resulted in the epiphany of the guru. Of course when once Lucia had heard about it, she was certain to constitute herself head and leader of the movement, and it was really remarkable how completely she had done that. In that meeting in the garden just now she had just sailed through Mrs Quantock as calmly as a steamer cuts through the waters of the sea, throwing her off from her penetrating bows like a spent wave. But baffled though she was for the moment, Georgie had been aware that Mrs Quantock seethed with revolutionary ideas: she deeply resented this confiscation of what was certainly her property, though she was impotent to stop it, and Georgie knew just what she felt. It was all very well to say that Lucia's schemes were entirely in accord with the purposes of the Guides. That might be so, but Mrs Quantock would not cease to think that she had been robbed . . .

Yet nothing mattered if all the class found themselves getting young and active and loving and excellent under this tuition. It was that notion which had taken such entire command of them all, and for his part Georgie did not really care who owned the guru, so to speak, if only he got the benefit of his teachings. For social purposes Lucia had annexed him, and doubtless with him in the house she could get little instructions and hints that would not count as a lesson, but after all, Georgie had still got Olga Bracely to himself, for he had not breathed a word of her advent to Lucia. He felt rather like one who, when revolutionary ideas are in the air, had concealed a revolver in his pocket. He did not formulate to himself precisely what he was going to do with it, but it gave him a sense of power to know it was there.

The train came in, but he looked in vain for his sisters. They had distinctly said they were arriving by it, but in a couple of minutes it was perfectly clear that they had done nothing of the kind, for the only person who got out was Mrs Weston's cook, who as all the world knew went into Brinton every Wednesday to buy fish. At the rear of the train, however, was an immense quantity of luggage being taken out, which could not all be Mrs Weston's fish, and indeed, even at that distance there was something familiar to Georgie about a very large green holdall which was dumped there. Perhaps Hermy and Ursy had travelled in the van, because 'it was such a lark', or for some other tomboy reason, and he went down the platform to investigate. There were bags of golf clubs, and a dog, and portmanteaux, and even as the conviction dawned on him that he had seen some of these objects before, the guard, to whom Georgie always gave half a crown when he travelled by this train, presented him with a note scrawled in pencil. It ran:

Dearest Georgie – It was such a lovely day that when we got to Paddington Ursy and I decided to bicycle down instead, so for a lark we sent our things on, and we may arrive tonight, but probably tomorrow. Take care of Tiptree: and give him plenty of jam. He loves it.
Yours,

Hermy

PS – Tipsipoozie doesn't really bite: it's only his fun.

Georgie crumpled up this odious epistle, and became aware that Tipsipoozie, a lean Irish terrier, was regarding him with peculiar disfavour, and showing all his teeth, probably in fun. In pursuance of this humorous idea, he then darted towards Georgie, and would have been extremely funny, if he had not been handicapped by the bag of golf clubs to which he was tethered. As it was, he pursued him down the platform, towing the clubs after him, till he got entangled in them and fell down.

Georgie hated dogs at any time, though he had never hated one so much as Tipsipoozie, and the problems of life became more complicated than ever. Certainly he was not going to drive back with Tipsipoozie in his cab, and it became necessary to hire another for that abominable hound and the rest of the luggage. And what on earth was to happen when he arrived home, if Tipsipoozie did not drop his fun and become serious? Foljambe, it is true, liked dogs, so perhaps dogs liked her . . . 'But it is most tarsome of Hermy!'

thought Georgie bitterly. 'I wonder what the guru would do.' There ensued a very trying ten minutes, in which the station master, the porters, Georgie and Mrs Weston's maid all called Tipsipoozie a good dog as he lay on the ground snapping promiscuously at those who praised him. Eventually a valiant porter picked up the bag of clubs, and by holding them out in front of him at the extreme length of his arms, in the manner of a fishing rod, with Tipsipoozie on a short chain at the other end of the bag, like a savage fish, cursing and swearing, managed to propel him into the cab, and there was another half-crown gone. Georgie thereupon got into his cab and sped homewards in order to arrive there first, and consult with Foljambe. Foljambe usually thought of something.

Foljambe came out at the noise of the arriving wheels and Georgie explained the absence of his sisters and the advent of an atrocious dog.

'He's very fierce,' he said, 'but he likes jam.'

Foljambe gave that supreme smile which sometimes Georgie resented. Now he hailed it, as if it was 'an angel-face's smile'.

'I'll see to him, sir,' she said. 'I've brought up your tea.'

'But you'll take care, Foljambe, won't you?' he asked.

'I expect he'd better take care,' returned the intrepid woman.

Georgie, as he often said, trusted Foljambe completely, which must explain why he went into his drawing room, shut the door, and looked out of the window when the second cab arrived. She opened the door, put her arms inside, and next moment emerged again with Tipsipoozie on the end of the chain, making extravagant exhibitions of delight. Then to Georgie's horror, the drawing-room door opened, and in came Tipsipoozie without any chain at all. Rapidly sending a message of love in all directions like an SOS call, Georgie put a small chair in front of him, to shield his legs. Tipsipoozie evidently thought it was a game, and hid behind the sofa to rush out again from ambush.

'Just got snappy being tied to those golf clubs,' remarked Foljambe.

But Georgie, as he put some jam into his saucer, could not help wondering whether the message of love had not done it.

He dined alone, for Hermy and Ursy did not appear, and had a great polishing of his knick-knacks afterwards, while waiting for them. No one ever felt anxious at the non-arrival of those sisters, for they always turned up from their otter-hunting or their golf sooner or later, chiefly later, in the highest spirits at the larks they had had, with amazingly dirty hands and prodigious appetites. But when twelve o'clock struck, he decided to give up all idea of their appearance that night, and having given Tipsipoozie some more jam and a comfortable bed in the woodshed, he went upstairs to his room. Though he knew it was still possible that he might be roused by wild 'Cooees!' and showers of gravel at his window, and have to come down and minister to their gross appetites, the prospect seemed improbable and he soon went to sleep.

Georgie awoke with a start some hours later, wondering what had disturbed him. There was no gravel rattling on his window, no violent ringing of bicycle bells, nor loud genial shouts outraging the decorous calm of Riseholme, but certainly he had heard something. Next moment, the repeated noise sent his heart leaping into his throat, for quite distinctly he heard a muffled sound in the room below, which he instantly diagnosed with fatal certainty as burglars. The first emotion that mingled itself with the sheer terror was a passionate regret that Hermy and Ursy had not come. They would have thought it tremendous larks, and would have invented some wonderful offensive with fire irons and golf clubs and dumbbells. Even Tipsipoozie, the lately abhorred, would have been a succour in this crisis, and why, oh why, had not Georgie had him to sleep in his bedroom instead of making him cosy in the woodshed? He would have let Tipsipoozie sleep on his lovely blue quilt for the remainder of his days, if only Tipsipoozie could have been with him now, ready to have fun with the burglar below. As it was, the servants were in the attics at the top of the house, Dicky slept out, and Georgie was all alone, with the prospect of having to defend his property at risk of his life. Even at this moment, as he sat up in bed, blanched with terror, these miscreants might be putting his treasure into their pockets. The thought of the Faberge cigarette case, and the Louis XVI snuff box, and the Queen Anne toy porringer which he had inherited all these years, made even life seem cheap, for life would be intolerable without them, and he sprang out of bed, groped for his slippers, since until he had made a plan it was wiser not to show a light, and shuffled noiselessly towards the door.

CHAPTER SIX

The door handle felt icy to fingers already frozen with fright, but he stood firmly grasping it, ready to turn it noiselessly when he had quite made up his mind what to do. The first expedient that suggested itself, with an overpowering sweetness of relief, was that of locking his door, going back to bed again, and pretending that he had heard nothing. But apart from the sheer cowardice of that, which he did not mind so much, as nobody else would ever know his guilt, the thought of the burglar going off quite unmolested with his property was intolerable. Even if he could not summon up enough courage to get downstairs with his life and a poker in his hand, he must at least give them a good fright. They had frightened him, and so he would frighten them. They should not have it all their own way, and if he decided not to attack them (or him) single-handed, he could at least thump on the floor, and call out 'Burglars!' at the top of his voice, or shout 'Charles! Henry! Thomas!' as if summoning a bevy of stalwart footmen. The objection to this course, however, would be that Foljambe or somebody else might hear him, and in this case, if he did not then go downstairs to mortal combat, the knowledge of his cowardice would be the property of others beside himself . . . And all the time he hesitated, they were probably filling their pockets with his dearest possessions.

He tried to send out a message of love, but he was totally unable to do so.

Then the little clock on his mantelpiece struck two, which was a miserable hour, sundered so far from dawn.

Though he had lived through years of agony since he got out of bed, the actual passage of time, as he stood frozen to the door handle, was but the duration of a few brief seconds, and then making a tremendous call on his courage he felt his way to his fireplace, and picked up the poker. The tongs and shovel rattled treacherously, and he hoped that had not been heard, for the essence of his plan (though he had yet no idea what that plan was) must be silence till some awful surprise broke upon them. If only he could summon the police, he could come rushing downstairs with his poker, as the professional supporters of the law gained an entrance to his house, but unfortunately the telephone was downstairs, and he could not reasonably hope to carry on a conversation with the police station without being overheard by the burglars.

He opened his door with so masterly a movement that there was no sound either from the hinges nor from the handle as he turned it, and peered out. The hall below was dark, but a long pencil of light came from the drawing room, which showed where the reckless brutes must be, and there, too, alas! was his case of treasures. Then suddenly he heard the sound of a voice, speaking very low, and another voice answered it. At that Georgie's heart sank, for this proved that there must be at least two burglars, and the odds against him were desperate. After that came a low, cruel laugh, the unmistakable sound of the rattle of knives and forks, and the explosive uncorking of a bottle. At that his heart sank even lower yet, for he had read that cool habitual burglars always had supper before they got to work, and therefore he was about to deal with a gang of professionals. Also that explosive uncorking clearly indicated champagne, and he knew that they were feasting on his best. And how wicked of them to take their unhallowed meal in his drawing room, for there was no proper table there, and they would be making a dreadful mess over everything.

A current of cool night air swept up the stairs, and Georgie saw the panel of light from the open drawing-room door diminish in width, and presently the door shut with a soft thud, leaving him in the dark. At that his desperation seemed pressed and concentrated into a moment of fictitious courage, for he unerringly reasoned that they had left the drawing-room window open, and that perhaps in a few moments now they would have finished their meal and with bulging pockets would step forth unchallenged into the night. Why had he never had bolts put on his shutters, like Mrs Weston, who lived in nightly terror of burglars? But it was too late to think of that now, for it was impossible to ask them to step out till he had put bolts up, and then when he was ready begin again.

He could not let them go gorged with his champagne and laden with his treasures without reprisals of some sort, and keeping his thoughts steadily away from revolvers and clubs and sandbags, walked straight downstairs, threw open the drawing-room door, and with his poker grasped in his shaking hand, cried out in a faint, thin voice:

'If you move I shall fire.'

There was a moment of dead silence, and a little dazzled with the light he saw what faced him.

At opposite ends of his Chippendale sofa sat Hermy and Ursy. Hermy had her mouth open and held a bun in her dirty hands. Ursy had her mouth shut and her cheeks were bulging. Between them was a ham and a loaf of bread, and a pot of marmalade and a Stilton cheese, and on the floor was the bottle of champagne with two brimming bubbling tea cups full of wine. The cork and the wire and the tinfoil they had, with some show of decency, thrown into the fireplace.

Hermy put down her bun, and gave a great shout of laughter; Ursy's mouth was disgustingly full and she exploded. Then they lay back against the arms of the sofa and howled.

Georgie was very much vexed.

'Upon my word, Hermy!' he said, and then found it was not nearly a strong enough expression. And in a moment of ungovernable irritation he said: 'Damn it all!'

Hermy showed signs of recovery first, and as Georgie came back after shutting the window, could find her voice, while Ursy collected small fragments of ham and bread which she had partially chewed.

'Lord! What a lark!' she said. 'Georgie, it's *the* most ripping lark.'

Ursy pointed to the poker.

'He'll fire if we move,' she cried. 'Or poke the fire, was it?'

'Ask another!' screamed Hermy. 'Oh, dear, he thought we were burglars, and came down with a poker, brave boy! It's positively the limit. Have a drink, Georgie.'

Suddenly her eyes grew round and awestruck, and pointing

with her finger to Georgie's shoulder, she went off into another yell of laughter.

'Ursy! His hair!' she said, and buried her face in a soft cushion.

Naturally Georgie had not put his hair in order when he came downstairs, for nobody thinks about things like that when he is going to encounter burglars single-handed, and there was his bald pate and his long tresses hanging down one side.

It was most annoying, but when an irremediable annoyance has absolutely occurred, the only possible thing for a decent person to do is to take it as lightly as possible. Georgie rose gallantly to the occasion, gave a little squeal and ran from the room.

'Down again presently,' he called out, and had a heavy fall on the stairs, as he went up to his bedroom. There he had a short argument with himself. It was possible to slam his door, go to bed, and be very polite in the morning. But that would never do: Hermy and Ursy would have a joke against him for ever. It was really much better to share in the joke, identifying himself with it. So he brushed his hair in the orthodox fashion, put on a very smart dressing gown, and came tripping downstairs again.

'My dears, what fun!' he said. 'Let's all have supper. But let's move into the dining room, where there's a table, and I'll get another bottle of wine, and some glasses, and we'll bring Tipsipoozie in. You naughty girls, fancy arriving at a time like this. I suppose your plan was to go very quietly to bed, and come down to breakfast in the morning, and give me a fine surprise. Tell me about it now.'

So presently Tipsipoozie was having his marmalade, which did just as well as jam, and they were all eating slices off the ham, and stuffing them into split buns.

'Yes, we thought we might as well do it all in one go,' said Hermy, 'and it's a hundred and twenty miles, if it's a yard. And then it was so late when we got here, we thought we wouldn't disturb you, specially as the drawing-room window wasn't bolted.'

'Bicycles outside,' said Ursy, 'they'll just have to be out at grass till morning. Oh, Tipsi-ipsi-poozie-woozy, how is you? Hope he behaved like the good little Tiptree that he is, Georgie?'

'Oh yes, we made great friends,' said Georgie sketchily. 'He was a wee bit upset at the station, but then he had a good tea with his Uncle Georgie and played hide and seek.'

Rather rashly, Georgie made a face at Tiptree, the sort of face which amuses children. But it didn't amuse Tiptree, who made another face, in which teeth played a prominent part.

'Fool dog,' said Hermy, carelessly smacking him across the nose. 'Always hit him if he shows his teeth, Georgie. Pass the fizz.'

'Well, so we got through the drawing-room window,' continued Ursy, 'and golly, we were hungry. So we foraged, and there we were! Jolly plucky of you, Georgie, to come down and beard us.'

'Real sport,' said Hermy. 'And how's old Fol-de-rol-de-ray? Why didn't she come down and fight us, too?'

Georgie guessed that Hermy was making a humorous allusion to Foljambe, who was the one person in Riseholme whom his two sisters seemed to hold in respect. Ursy had once set a booby trap for Georgie, but the mixed biscuits and Brazil nuts had descended on Foljambe instead. On that occasion Foljambe, girt about in impenetrable calm, had behaved as if nothing had happened and trod on biscuits and Brazil nuts without a smile, unaware to all appearance that there was anything whatever crunching and exploding beneath her feet. That had somehow quelled the two, who, as soon as she left the room again, swept up the mess, and put the uninjured Brazil nuts back into the dessert dish . . . It would never do if Foljambe lost her prestige and was alluded to by some outrageously slangy name.

'If you mean Foljambe,' said Georgie icily, 'it was because I didn't think it worth while to disturb her.'

* * *

In spite of their ride, the indefatigable sisters were up early next morning, and the first thing Georgie saw out of his bathroom window was the pair of them practising lifting shots over the ducking pond on the green till breakfast was ready. He had given a short account of last night's adventure to Foljambe when she called him, omitting the episode about his hair, and her disapproval was strongly indicated by her silence then, and the studied contempt of her manner to the sisters when they came in to breakfast.

'Hello, Foljambe,' said Hermy. 'We had a rare lark last night.'

'So I understand, miss,' said Foljambe.

'Got in through the drawing-room window,' said Hermy, hoping to make her smile.

'Indeed, miss,' said Foljambe. 'Have you any orders for the car, sir?'

'Oh, Georgie, may we run over to the links this morning?' asked Hermy. 'Mayn't Dickie-bird take us there?'

She glanced at Foljambe to see whether this brilliant wit afforded her any amusement. Apparently it didn't.

'Tell Dicky to be round at half-past ten,' said Georgie.

'Yes, sir.'

'Hurrah!' said Ursy. 'Come, too, Foljambe, and we'll have a three-ball match.'

'No, thank you, miss,' said Foljambe, and sailed from the room, looking down her nose.

'Golly, what an iceberg!' said Hermy when the door was quite shut.

*　　*　　*

Georgie was not sorry to have the morning to himself, for he wanted to have a little quiet practice at the Mozart trio, before he went over to Lucia's at half-past eleven, the hour when she had arranged to run through it for the first time. He would also have time to do a few posturing exercises before the first Yoga class, which was to take place in Lucia's smoking parlour at half-past twelve. That would make a pretty busy morning, and as for the afternoon, there would be sure to be some callers, since the arrival of his sisters had been expected, and after that he had to go to the Ambermere Arms for his visit to Olga Bracely . . . And what was he to do about her with regard to Lucia? Already he had been guilty of disloyalty, for Lady Ambermere had warned him of the prima donna's arrival yesterday, and he had not instantly communicated that really great piece of news to Lucia. Should he make such amends as were in his power for that omission, or, greatly daring, should he keep her to himself, as Mrs Quantock so fervently wished that she had done with regard to the guru? After the adventure of last night, he felt he ought to be able to look any situation in the face, but he found himself utterly unable to conceive himself manly and erect before the birdlike eyes of the Queen, if she found out that Olga Bracely had been at Riseholme for the day of her garden party, and that Georgie, knowing it and having gone to see her, had not informed the Court of that fact.

The spirit of Bolshevism, the desire to throw off all authority and act independently, which had assailed him yesterday returned now with redoubled force. If he had been perfectly certain that he would not be found out, there is no doubt he would have kept it from her, and yet, after all, what was the glory of going to see Olga Bracely (and perhaps even entertaining her here) if all Riseholme did not turn green with jealousy? Moreover there was every chance of being found out, for Lady Ambermere would be at the garden party tomorrow, and she would be sure to wonder why Lucia had not asked Olga. Then it would come out that Lucia didn't know of that eminent presence, and Lady Ambermere would be astonished that Georgie had not told her. Thus he would be in the situation which his imagination was unable to face, although he had thrown the drawing-room door open in the middle of the night, and announced that he would fire with his poker.

No; he would have to tell Lucia, when he went to read the Mozart trio with her for the first time, and very likely she would call on Olga Bracely herself, though nobody had asked her to, and take all the wind out of Georgie's sails. Sickening though that would be, he could not face the alternative, and he opened his copy of the Mozart trio with a sigh. Lucia *did* push and shove, and have everything her own way. Anyhow he would *not* tell her that Olga and her husband were dining at The Hall tonight; he would not even tell her that her husband's name was Shuttleworth, and Lucia might make a dreadful mistake, and ask Mr and Mrs Bracely. That would be jam for Georgie, and he could easily imagine himself saying to Lucia, 'My dear, I thought you must have known that she had married Mr Shuttleworth and kept her maiden name! How tarsome for you! They are so touchy about that sort of thing.'

* * *

Georgie heard the tinkle of the treble part of the Mozart trio (Lucia always took the treble, because it had more tune in it, though she

pretended that she had not Georgie's fine touch, which made the
bass effective) as he let himself in to Shakespeare's garden a few
minutes before the appointed time. Lucia must have seen him from
the window, for the subdued noise of the piano ceased even before
he had got as far as Perdita's garden round the sundial, and she
opened the door to him. The faraway look was in her eyes, and the
black undulations of hair had encroached a little on her forehead,
but, after all, others besides Lucia had trouble with their hair, and
Georgie only sympathized.

'*Georgino mio!*' she said. 'It is all being so wonderful. There
seems a new atmosphere about the house since my guru came.
Something holy and peaceful; do you not notice it?'

'Delicious!' said Georgie, inhaling the potpourri. 'What is he
doing now?'

'Meditating, and preparing for our class. I do hope dear Daisy
will not bring in discordant elements.'

'Oh, but that's not likely, is it?' said Georgie. 'I thought he said
she had so much light.'

'Yes, he did. But now he is a little troubled about her, I think.
She did not want him to go away from her house, and she sent
over here for some silk pyjamas belonging to her husband, which
he thought she had given him. But Robert didn't think so at all.
The guru brought them across yesterday after he had left good
thoughts for her in her house. But it was the Guides who wished
him to come here; they told him so distinctly. It would have been
very wrong of me not to do as they said.'

She gave a great sigh.

'Let us have an hour with Mozart,' she said, 'and repel all
thought of discord. My guru says that music and flowers are good
influences for those who are walkers on the Way. He says that my
love for both of them which I have had all my life will help me very
much.'

For one moment the mundane world obtruded itself into the
calm peace.

'Any news in particular?' she asked. 'I saw you drive back from
the station yesterday afternoon, for I happened to be looking out
of the window, in a little moment of leisure – the guru says I work
too hard, by the way – and your sisters were not with you. And

yet there were two cabs, and a quantity of luggage. Did they not come?'

Georgie gave a respectably accurate account of all that had happened, omitting the fact of his terror when first he awoke, for that was not really a happening, and had had no effect on his subsequent proceedings. He also omitted the adventure about his hair, for that was quite extraneous, and said what fun they had all had over their supper at half-past two this morning.

'I think you were marvellously brave, Georgie,' said she, 'and most good-natured. You must have been sending out love, and so were full of it yourself, and that casts out fear.'

She spread the music open.

'Anything else?' she asked.

Georgie took his seat and put his rings on the candle bracket.

'Oh yes,' he said, 'Olga Bracely, the prima donna, you know, and her husband are arriving at the Ambermere Arms this afternoon for a couple of days.'

The old fire kindled.

'No!' exclaimed Lucia. 'Then they'll be here for my party tomorrow. Fancy if she would come and sing for us! I shall certainly leave cards today, and write later in the evening, asking her.'

'I have been asked to go and see her,' said Georgie, not proudly.

The music rest fell down with a loud slap, but Lucia paid no attention.

'Let us go together then,' she said. 'Who asked you to call on her?'

'Lady Ambermere,' said he.

'When she was in here yesterday? She never mentioned it to me. But she would certainly think it very odd of me not to call on friends of hers, and be polite to them. What time shall we go?'

Georgie made up his mind that wild horses should not drag from him the fact that Olga's husband's name was Shuttleworth, for here was Lucia grabbing at his discovery, just as she had grabbed at Daisy's discovery who was now 'her guru'. She should call him Mr Bracely then.

'Somewhere about six, do you think?' said he, inwardly raging.

He looked up and distinctly saw that sharp foxy expression cross Lucia's face, which from long knowledge of her he knew to betoken that she had thought of some new plan. But she did not choose to reveal it and re-erected the music rest.

'That will do beautifully,' she said. 'And now for our heavenly Mozart. You must be patient with me, Georgie, for you know how badly I read. *Caro!* How difficult it looks. I am frightened! Lucia never saw such a dwefful thing to read!'

And it had been those very bars which Georgie had heard through the open window just now.

'Georgie's is much more dwefful!' he said, remembering the double sharp that came in the second bar. 'Georgie fwightened too at reading it. O-o-h,' and he gave a little scream. *'Cattivo* Mozart to wite anything so dwefful diffy!'

*   *   *

It was quite clear at the class this morning that though the pupils were quite interested in the abstract messages of love which they were to shoot out in all directions, and in the atmosphere of peace with which they were to surround themselves, the branch of the subject which thrilled them to the marrow was the breathing exercises and contortions which, if persevered in, would give them youth and activity, faultless digestions and indefatigable energy. They all sat on the floor, and stopped up alternate nostrils, and held their breath till Mrs Quantock got purple in the face, and Georgie and Lucia red, and expelled their breath again with sudden puffs that set the rushes on the floor quivering, or with long quiet exhalations. Then there were certain postures to be learned, in one of which, entailing the bending of the body backwards, two of Georgie's trouser buttons came off with a sharp snap and he felt the corresponding member of his braces, thus violently released, spring up to his shoulder. Various other embarrassing noises issued from Lucia and Daisy that sounded like the bursting of strings and tapes, but everybody pretended to hear nothing at all, or covered up the report of those explosions with coughings and clearings of the throat. But apart from these discordances, everything was fairly harmonious. Indeed, so far from Daisy introducing discords, she wore a fixed smile, which it would have been purely cynical to call superior, when Lucia asked some amazingly simple question with regard to Om. She sighed too, at intervals, but these sighs were expressive of nothing but patience and resignation, till Lucia's ignorance of the most elementary doctrines was enlightened, and though she rather pointedly looked in any direction but hers, and appeared completely unaware of her presence, she had not, after all, come here to look at Lucia, but to listen to her own (whatever Lucia might say) guru.

At the end Lucia, with her faraway look, emerged, you might say, in a dazed condition from hearing about the fastness of Thibet, where the guru had been in commune with the Guides, whose wisdom he interpreted to them.

'I feel such a difference already,' she said dreamily. 'I feel as if I could never be hasty or worried any more at all. Don't you experience that, dear Daisy?'

'Yes, dear,' said she. 'I went through all that at my first lesson. Didn't I, Guru dear?'

'I felt it too,' said Georgie, unwilling not to share in these benefits, and surreptitiously tightening his trouser strap to compensate for the loss of buttons. 'And am I to do that swaying exercise before every meal?'

'Yes, Georgie,' said Lucia, saving her guru from the trouble of answering. 'Five times to the right and five times to the left and then five times backwards and forwards. I felt so young and light just now when we did it that I thought I was rising into the air. Didn't you, Daisy?'

Daisy smiled kindly.

'No, dear, that is levitation,' she said, 'and comes a very long way on.'

She turned briskly towards her guru.

'Will you tell them about that time when you levitated at Paddington Station?' she said. 'Or will you keep that for when Mrs Lucas gets rather further on? You must be patient, dear Lucia; we all have to go through the early stages, before we get to that.'

Mrs Quantock spoke as if she was in the habit of levitating herself, and it was but reasonable, in spite of the love that was swirling about them all, that Lucia should protest against such an attitude. Humility, after all, was the first essential to progress on the Way.

'Yes, dear,' she said. 'We will tread these early stages together, and encourage each other.'

* * *

Georgie went home, feeling also unusually light and hungry, for he had paid special attention to the exercise that enabled him to have his liver and digestive organs in complete control, but that did not prevent him from devoting his mind to arriving at that which had made Lucia look so sharp and foxy during their conversation about Olga Bracely. He felt sure that she was meaning to steal a march on him, and she was planning to draw first blood with the prima donna, and, as likely as not, claim her for her own, with the same odious greed as she was already exhibiting with regard to the guru. All these years Georgie had been her faithful servant and coadjutor; now for the first time the spirit of independence had begun to seethe within him. The scales were falling from his eyes, and just as he turned into shelter of his mulberry tree, he put on his spectacles to see how Riseholme was getting on without him to assist at the morning parliament. His absence and Mrs Quantock's would be sure to evoke comment, and since the Yoga classes were always to take place at half-past twelve, the fact that they would never be there, would soon rise to the level of a first-class mystery. It would, of course, begin to leak out that they and Lucia were having a course of Eastern philosophy that made its pupils young and light and energetic, and there was a sensation!

Like all great discoveries, the solution of Lucia's foxy look broke on him with the suddenness of a lightning flash, and since it had been settled that she should call for him at six, he stationed himself in the window of his bathroom, which commanded a perfect view of the village green and the entrance to the Ambermere Arms at five. He had brought up with him a pair of opera glasses, with the intention of taking them to bits, so he had informed Foljambe, and washing their lenses, but he did not at once proceed about this, merely holding them ready to hand for use. Hermy and Ursy had gone back to their golf again after lunch, and so callers would be told that they were all out. Thus he could wash the lenses, when he chose to do so, uninterrupted.

* * *

The minutes passed on pleasantly enough, for there was plenty going on. The two Miss Antrobuses frisked about the green, jumping over the stocks in their playful way, and running round the duck pond in the eternal hope of attracting Colonel Boucher's attention to their pretty nimble movements. For many years past, they had tried to gain Georgie's serious attention, without any result, and lately they had turned to Colonel Boucher. There was Mrs Antrobus there, too, with her ham-like face and her ear trumpet, and Mrs Weston was being pushed round and round the asphalt path below the elms in her bath chair. She hated going slow, and her gardener and his boy took turns with her during her hour's carriage exercise, and propelled her, amid streams of perspiration, at a steady four miles an hour. As she passed Mrs Antrobus she shouted something at her, and Mrs Antrobus returned her reply, when next she came round.

Suddenly all these interesting objects vanished completely from Georgie's ken, for his dark suspicions were confirmed, and there was Lucia in her 'Hightum' hat and her 'Hightum' gown making her gracious way across the green. She had distinctly been wearing one of the 'Scrub' this morning at the class, so she must have changed after lunch, which was an unheard-of thing to do for a mere stroll on the green. Georgie knew well that this was no mere stroll; she was on her way to pay a call of the most formal and magnificent kind. She did not deviate a hair breadth from her straight course to the door of the Arms, she just waggled her hand to Mrs Antrobus, blew a kiss to her sprightly daughters, made a gracious bow to Colonel Boucher, who stood up and took his hat off, and went on with the inexorability of the march of destiny, or of fate knocking at the door in the immortal fifth symphony. And in her hand she carried a note. Through his glasses Georgie could see it quite plainly, and it was not a little folded-up sheet, such as she commonly used, but a square thick envelope. She disappeared in the Arms and Georgie began thinking feverishly. A great deal depended on how long she stopped there.

A few little happenings beguiled the period of waiting. Mrs Weston desisted from her wild career, and came to anchor on the path just opposite the door into the Arms, while the gardener's boy sank exhausted on to the grass. It was quite easy to guess that she proposed to have a chat with Lucia when she came out.

Similarly the Miss Antrobuses, who had paid no attention to her at all before, ceased from their pretty gambolings, and ran up to talk to her, so they wanted a word too. Colonel Boucher, a little less obviously, began throwing sticks into the ducking pond for his bulldog (for Lucia would be obliged to pass the ducking pond) and Mrs Antrobus examined the stocks very carefully, as if she had never seen them before.

And then, before a couple of minutes had elapsed Lucia came out. She had no longer the note in her hand, and Georgie began taking his opera glasses to bits, in order to wash the lenses. For the present they had served their purpose. 'She has left a note on Olga Bracely,' said Georgie quite aloud, so powerful was the current of his thoughts. Then as a corollary came the further proposition which might be considered as proved, 'But she has not seen her.'

The justice of this conclusion was soon proved, for Lucia had hardly disengaged herself from the group of her subjects, and traversed the green on her way back to her house, when a motor passed Georgie's bathroom window, closely followed by a second; both drew up at the entrance to the Ambermere Arms. With the speed of a practised optician Georgie put his opera glass together again, and after looking through the wrong end of it in his agitation was in time to see a man get out of the second car, and hold the carriage door open for the occupants of the first. A lady got out first, tall and slight in figure, who stood there unwinding her motor veil, then she turned round again, and with a thump of his heart that surprised Georgie with its violence, he beheld the well-remembered features of his Brünnhilde.

Swiftly he passed into his bedroom next door, and arrayed himself in his summer Hightums; a fresh (almost pearly) suit of white duck, a mauve tie with an amethyst pin in it, socks, tightly braced up, of precisely the same colour as the tie, so that an imaginative beholder might have conjectured that on this warm day the end of his tie had melted and run down his legs; buckskin shoes with tall slim heels and a straw hat completed this pretty Hightum. He had meant to wear it for the first time at Lucia's party tomorrow, but now, after her meanness, she deserved to be punished. All Riseholme should see it before she did.

The group round Mrs Weston's chair was still engaged in conversation when Georgie came up, and he casually let slip what a bore it was to pay calls on such a lovely day, but he had promised to visit Miss Olga Bracely, who had just arrived. So there was another nasty one for Lucia, since now all Riseholme would know of her actual arrival before Lucia did.

'And who, Mr Georgie,' asked Mrs Antrobus, presenting her trumpet to him in the manner in which an elephant presents its trunk to receive a bun, 'who was that with her?'

'Oh, her husband, Mr Shuttleworth,' said Georgie. 'They have just been married, and are on their honeymoon.' And if that was not another staggerer for Lucia, it is diffy, as Georgie would say, to know what a staggerer is. For Lucia would be last of all to know that this was not Mr Bracely.

'And will they be at Mrs Lucas's party tomorrow?' asked Mrs Weston.

'Oh, does she know them?' asked Georgie.

'Haw, haw, by Jove!' began Colonel Boucher. 'Very handsome woman. Envy you, my boy. Pity it's their honeymoon. Haw!'

Mrs Antrobus's trumpet was turned in his direction at this moment, and she heard these daring remarks.

'Naughty!' she said, and Georgie, the envied, passed on into the inn.

He sent in his card, on which he had thought it prudent to write 'From Lady Ambermere', and was presently led through into the garden behind the building. There she was, tall and lovely and welcoming, and held out a most cordial hand.

'How kind of you to come and see us,' she said. 'Georgie, this is Mr Pillson. My husband.'

'How do you do, Mr Shuttleworth,' said Georgie to show he knew, though his own Christian name had given him quite a start. For the moment he had almost thought she was speaking to him.

'And so Lady Ambermere asked you to come and see us?' Olga went on. 'I think that was much kinder of her than to ask us to dinner. I hate going out to dinner in the country almost as much as I hate not going out to dinner in town. Besides with that great hook nose of hers, I'm always afraid that in an absent moment I might scratch her on the head and say "Pretty Polly". Is she a great friend of yours, Mr Pillson? I hope so, because everyone likes his best friends being laughed at.'

Up till that moment Georgie was prepared to indicate that Lady Ambermere was the hand and he the glove. But evidently that would not impress Olga in the least. He laughed in a most irreverent manner instead.

'Don't let us go,' she went on. 'Georgie, can't you send a telegram saying that we have just discovered a subsequent engagement and then we'll ask Mr Pillson to show us round this utterly adorable place, and dine with us afterwards. That would be so much nicer. Fancy living here! Oh, and do tell me something, Mr Pillson. I found a note when I arrived half an hour ago, from Mrs Lucas asking me and Mr Shuttleworth to go to a garden party tomorrow. She said she didn't even hope that I should remember her, but would we come. Who is she? Really I don't think she can remember me very well, if she thinks I am Mrs Bracely. Georgie says I must have been married before, and that I have caused him to commit bigamy. That's pleasant conversation for a honeymoon, isn't it? Who is she?'

'Oh, she's quite an old friend of mine,' said Georgie, 'though I never knew she had met you before; I'm devoted to her.'

'Extremely proper. But now tell me this, and look straight in my face, so that I shall know if you're speaking the truth. Should I enjoy myself more wandering about this heavenly place than at her garden party?'

Gedrgie felt that poor Lucia was really punished enough by this time.

'You will give her a great deal of pleasure if you go,' he began.

'Ah, that's not fair; it is hitting below the belt to appeal to unselfish motives. I have come here simply to enjoy myself. Go on; eyes front.'

The candour and friendliness of that beautiful face gave Georgie an impulse of courage. Besides, though no doubt in fun, she had already suggested that it would be much nicer to wander about with him and dine together than spend the evening among the splendours of The Hall.

'I've got a suggestion,' he said. 'Will you come and lunch with me first, and we'll stroll about, and then we can go to the garden party, and if you don't like it I'll take you away again?'

'Done!' she said. 'Now don't you try to get out of it, because my husband is a witness. Georgie, give me a cigarette.'

In a moment Riseholme-Georgie had his cigarette case open.

'Do take one of mine,' he said, 'I'm Georgie too.'

'You don't say so! Let's send it to the Psychical Research, or whoever those people are who collect coincidences and say it's spooks. And a match please, one of you Georgies. Oh, how I should like never to see the inside of an opera house again. Why mayn't I grow on the walls of a garden like this, or better still, why shouldn't I have a house and garden of my own here, and sing on the village green, and ask for halfpennies? Tell me what happens here! I've always lived in town since the time a hook-nosed Hebrew, rather like Lady Ambermere, took me out of the gutter.'

'My dear!' said Mr Shuttleworth.

'Well, out of an orphan school at Brixton and I would much prefer the gutter. That's all about my early life just now, because I am keeping it for my memoirs which I shall write when my voice becomes a little more like a steam whistle. But don't tell Lady Ambermere, for she would have a fit, but say you happen to know that I belong to the Surrey Bracelys. So I do; Brixton is on the Surrey side. Oh, my dear, look at the sun. It's behaving like the best sort of Claude! *Heile Sonne!*'

'I heard you do that last May,' said Georgie.

'Then you heard a most second-rate performance,' said she. 'But really being unlaced by that Thing, that great fat profligate beery Prussian, was almost too much for me. And the duet! But it was very polite of you to come, and I will do better next time. Siegfried! Brünnhilde! Siegfried! Miaou! Miaou! Bring on the next lot of cats! Darling Georgie, wasn't it awful? And you had proposed to me only the day before.'

'I was absolutely enchanted,' said Riseholme-Georgie.

'Yes, but then you didn't have that Thing breathing beer into your innocent face.' Georgie rose; the first call on a stranger in Riseholme was never supposed to last more than half an hour, however much you were enjoying it, and never less, however bored you might be, and he felt sure he had already exceeded this.

'I must be off,' he said. 'Too delightful to think that you and Mr Shuttleworth will come to lunch with me tomorrow. Half-past one, shall we say?'

'Excellent; but where do you live?'

'Just across the green. Shall I call for you?' he asked.

'Certainly not. Why should you have that bother?' she said. 'Ah, let me come with you to the inn door, and perhaps you will show me from there.'

She passed through the hall with him, and they stood together in the sight of all Riseholme, which was strolling about the green at this as at most other hours. Instantly all faces turned round in their direction, like so many sunflowers following the sun, while Georgie pointed out his particular mulberry tree. When everybody had had a good look, he raised his hat.

'*A domani* then,' she said. 'So many thanks.'

And quite distinctly she kissed her hand to him as he turned away . . .

'So she talks Italian too,' thought Georgie, as he dropped little crumbs of information to his friends on his way to his house. '*Domani*, that means tomorrow. Oh yes; she was meaning lunch.'

It is hardly necessary to add that on the table in his hall there was one of Lucia's commoner kinds of note, merely a half-sheet folded together in her own manner. Georgie felt that it was scarcely more necessary to read it, for he felt quite sure that it contained some excuse for not coming to his house at six in order to call on Mr and Mrs Bracely. But he gave a glance at it before he rolled it up in a ball for Tipsipoozie to play with, and found its contents to be precisely what he expected, the excuse being that she had not done her practising. But the postscript was interesting, for it told him that she had asked Foljambe to give her his copy of *Siegfried* . . .

Georgie strolled down past The Hurst before dinner. Mozart was silent now, but there came out of the open windows the most amazing hash of sound, which he could just recognize as being the piano arrangement of the duet between Brünnhilde and Siegfried at the end. He would have been dull indeed if he had not instantly guessed what *that* signified.

CHAPTER SEVEN

A fresh thrill went through an atmosphere already super-saturated with excitement, when next morning all Lucia's friends who had been bidden to the garden party (Tightum) were rung up on the telephone and informed that the party was Hightum. That caused a good deal of extra work, because the Tightum robes had to be put away again, and the Hightums aired and brushed and valeted. But it was well worth it, for Riseholme had not the slightest difficulty in conjecturing that Olga Bracely was to be among the guests. For a cultured and artistic centre the presence of a star that blazed so regally in the very zenith of the firmament of art absolutely demanded the Hightum which the presence of poor Lady Ambermere (though she would not have liked that) had been powerless to bring out of their cupboards. And these delightful anticipations concentrated themselves into one rose-coloured point of joy, when no less than two independent observers, without collusion, saw the piano tuner either entering or leaving The Hurst, while a third, an ear witness, unmistakably heard the tuning of the piano actually going on. It was thus clear to all penetrating minds that Olga Bracely was going to sing. It was further known that something was going on between her and Georgie, for she had been heard by one Miss Antrobus to ask for Georgie's number at the telephone in the Ambermere Arms. Etiquette forbade her actually to listen to what passed, but she could not help hearing Olga laugh at something (presumably) that Georgie said. He himself took no part in the green parliament that morning, but had been seen to dash into the fruiterer's and out again, before he went in a great hurry to The Hurst, shortly after twelve-thirty. Classes on Eastern philosophy under the tuition of Mrs Quantock's Indian were already beginning to be hinted at, but today in the breathless excitement about the prima donna nobody cared about that; they might all have been taking lessons in cannibalism, and nobody would have been interested. Finally about one o'clock one of the motors in which the party had arrived yesterday drew up at the door of the Ambermere Arms, and presently Mr Bracely – no, dear, Mr Shuttleworth – got in and drove off alone. That was very odd conduct in a lately married bridegroom, and it was hoped that there had been no quarrel.

Olga had, of course, been given no directions as to Hightum or Tightum, and when she walked across to Georgie's house shortly after half-past one only Mrs Weston who was going back home to lunch at top speed was aware that she was dressed in a very simple dark blue morning frock, that would almost have passed for Scrub. It is true that it was exceedingly well cut, and had not the look of having been rolled up in a ball and hastily ironed out again that usually distinguished Scrub, and she also wore a string of particularly fine pearls round her neck, the sort of ornament that in Riseholme would only be seen in an evening Hightum, even if anybody in Riseholme had owned such things. Lucia, not long ago, had expressed the opinion that jewels were vulgar except at night, and for her part she wore none at all, preferring one Greek cameo of uncertain authenticity.

Georgie received Olga alone, for Hermy and Ursy were not yet back from their golf.

'It is good of you to let me come without my husband,' she said. 'His excuse is toothache and he has driven into Brinton – '

'I'm very sorry,' said Georgie.

'You needn't be, for now I'll tell you his real reason. He thought that if he lunched with you he would have to come on to the garden party, and that he was absolutely determined not to do. You were the thin edge of the wedge, in fact. My dear, what a delicious house. All panelled, with that lovely garden behind. And croquet – may we play croquet after lunch? I always try to cheat, and if I'm found out I lose my temper. Georgie won't play with me, so I play with my maid.'

'This Georgie will,' said he.

'How nice of him! And do you know what we did this morning, before the toothache didn't begin? We went all over that house three doors away, which is being done up. It belongs to the proprietor of the Ambermere Arms. And – oh, I wonder if you can keep a secret?'

'Yes,' said Georgie. He probably had never kept one yet, but there was no reason why he shouldn't begin now.

'Well, I'm absolutely determined to buy it, only I daren't tell my husband until I've done it. He has an odd nature. When a thing is done, settled, and there's no help for it, he finds it adorable, but he also finds fatal objections to doing it at all, if he is consulted about it before it is done. So not a word! I shall buy it, make the garden, furnish it, down to the minutest detail, and engage the servants, and then he'll give it me for a birthday present. I had to tell somebody or I should burst.'

Georgie nearly swooned with fervour and admiration.

'But what a perfect plan!' he said. 'You really like our little Riseholme?'

'It's not a question of liking; it's a mere detail of not being able to do without it. I don't like breathing, but I should die if I didn't. I want some delicious, hole-in-the-corner, lazy backwater sort of place, where nothing ever happens, and nobody ever does anything. I've been observing all the morning, and your habits are adorable. Nothing ever happens here, and that will precisely suit me, when I get away from my work.'

Georgie was nearer swooning than ever at this. He could hardly believe his ears when she talked of Riseholme being a lazy backwater, and almost thought she must have been speaking of London, where, as Lucia had acutely observed, people sat in the park all morning and talked of each other's affairs, and spent the afternoon at picture galleries, and danced all night. There was a flippant, lazy existence.

But she was far too much absorbed in her project to notice his stupefaction.

'But if you breathe a word,' she said, 'everything will be spoilt. It has to burst on Georgie. Oh, and there's another mulberry tree in your garden as well as the one in front. It's too much.'

Her eyes followed Foljambe out of the door.

'And I know your parlour maid is called Paravicini or Grosvenor,' she said.

'No, she is Foljambe,' said Georgie.

She laughed.

'I knew I was right,' she said. 'It's practically the same thing. Oh, and last night! I never had such an awful evening. Why didn't you warn me, and my husband should have had toothache then instead of this morning.'

'What happened?' asked he.

'But the woman's insane, that Ambermere parrot, I mean. Georgie and I were ten minutes late, and she had a jet tiara on, and why did she ask us to dine at a quarter to eight, if she meant a quarter to eight, instead of saying half-past seven? They were actually going into dinner when we came, a mournful procession of three moth-eaten men and three whiskered women. Upon which the procession broke up, as if we had been the riot act, and was arranged again, as a funeral procession, and Georgie with Lady Ambermere was the hearse. We dined in the family vault and talked about Lady Ambermere's pug. She talked about you, too, and said you were of county family, and that Mrs Lucas was a very decent sort of woman, and that she herself was going to look in on her garden party today. Then she looked at my pearls, and asked if they were genuine. So I looked at her teeth, and there was no need to ask about them.'

'Don't miss out a moment,' said Georgie greedily.

'Whenever Lady Ambermere spoke, everybody else was silent. I didn't grasp that at first, for no one had explained the rules. So she stopped in the middle of a sentence and waited till I had finished. Then she went on again, precisely where she had left off. Then when we came into the drawing room, the whiskered ladies and I, there was a little woman like a mouse sitting there, and nobody introduced her. So naturally I went to talk to her, before which the great parrot said, "Will you kindly fetch my wool-work, Miss Lyall?" and Miss Lyall took a sack out of the corner, and inside was the sacred carpet. And then I waited for some coffee and cigarettes, and I waited, and I waited, and I am waiting still. The Parrot said that coffee always kept her awake, and that was why. And then Georgie came in with the others, and I could see by his face that he hadn't had a cigarette either. It was then half-past nine. And then each man sat down between two women, and Pug sat in the middle and looked for fleas. Then Lady Ambermere got up, and came across the charmed circle to me. She said: "I hope you have brought your music, Mrs Shuttleworth. Kindly open the piano, Miss Lyall. It was always considered a remarkably fine instrument.'"

Olga waved the fork on which was impaled a piece of the pineapple which Georgie had purchased that morning at the fruiterer's.

'The stupendous cheek!' she said. 'I thought it must be a joke, and laughed with the greatest politeness. But it wasn't! You'll hardly believe it, but it wasn't! One of the whiskered ones said, "That will be a great treat," and another put on the face that everyone wears at concerts. And I was so stunned that I sang, and Lady Ambermere beat time, and Pug barked.'

She pointed a finger at Georgie.

'Never till the Day of Judgement,' she said, 'when Lady Ambermere gnashes her beautiful teeth for ever and ever, will I set foot in that house again. Nor she in my house. I will set fire to it sooner. There! My dear, what a good lunch you have given me. May we play croquet at once?'

Lucia's garden parties were scheduled from four to seven and half an hour before the earliest guest might be expected, she was casting an eagle eye over the preparations which today were on a very sumptuous scale. The bowls were laid out in the bowling alley, not because anybody in Hightums dresses was the least likely to risk the stooping down and the strong movements that the game entailed, but because bowls were Elizabethan. Between the alley and the lawn nearer to the house was a large marquee, where the commoner crowd – though no crowd could be really common in Riseholme – would refresh itself. But even where none are common there may still be degrees in rarity, and by the side of this general refreshment room was a smaller tent carpeted with Oriental rugs, and having inside it some half-dozen chairs, and two seats which can only be described as thrones, for Lady Ambermere or Olga Bracely, while Lucia's guru, though throneworthy, would very kindly sit in one of his most interesting attitudes on the floor. This tent was designed only for high converse, and common guests (if they were good) would be led into it and introduced to the great presences, while for the refreshment of the presences, in intervals of audience, a more elaborate meal, with peaches and four sorts of sandwiches, was laid in the smoking parlour. Thus those guests for whom audiences were not provided could have the felicity of seeing the great ones pass across the lawn on their excursions for food, and possibly trip over the croquet hoops, which had been left up to give an air of naturalness to the lawn. In the smoking parlour an Elzevir or two were left negligently open, as if Mr and Mrs Lucas had been reading the works of Persius and Juvenal when the first guests arrived. In the music room, finally, which was not usually open on these occasions, there were fresh flowers: the piano, too, was open, and if you had not seen the Elzevirs in the smoking parlour, it would have been reasonable for the early guests, if they penetrated here, to imagine that Mrs Lucas had been running over the last act of *Siegfried* a minute before.

In this visit of final inspection Lucia was accompanied by her guru, for he was part of the domestic *dramatis personae*, and she wanted him to be 'discovered' in the special tent. She pointed out the site of his proposed 'discovery' to him.

'Probably the first person I shall bring in here,' she said, 'will be Lady Ambermere, for she is noted for her punctuality. She is so anxious to see you, and would it not be exciting if you found you had met before? Her husband was Governor of Madras, and she spent many years in India.'

'Madras, gracious lady?' asked the guru. 'I, too, know Madras: there are many dark spirits in Madras. And she was at English Residency?'

'Yes. She says Mr Kipling knows nothing about India. You and she will have much to talk about. I wish I could sit on the floor, too, and listen to what you say to each other.'

'It will be great treat,' said the guru thoughtfully, 'I love all who love my wonderful country.'

Suddenly he stopped, and put his hands up to his head, palms outward.

'There are wonderful vibrations today,' he said. 'All day I feel that some word is on way from the Guides, some great message of light.'

'Oh, wouldn't it be wonderful if it came to you in the middle of my garden party?' said Lucia enthusiastically.

'Ah, gracious lady, the great word comes not so. It comes always in solitude and quiet. Gracious lady knows that as well as Guru.'

Pure guruism and social pre-eminence struggled together in Lucia. Guruism told her that she ought to be ecstatic at the idea of a great message coming and should instantly smile on his desire for solitude and quiet, while social pre-eminence whispered to her that she had already dangled the presence of a high-caste mystic from Benares before the eyes of Lady Ambermere, who only came from Madras. On the other hand Olga Bracely was to be an even more resplendent guest than either Lady Ambermere or the guru; surely Olga Bracely was enough to set this particular garden party on the giddiest of pinnacles. And an awful consequence lurked as a possibility if she attempted to force her guru not to immure himself in solitude and quiet, which was that conceivably he might choose to go back to the pit whence he was digged, namely the house of poor Daisy Quantock. The thought was intolerable, for with him in her house, she had seen herself as dispenser of Eastern Mysteries, and Mistress of Omism to Riseholme. In fact the guru was her August stunt; it would never do to lose him before the end of July, and rage to see all Riseholme making pilgrimages to Daisy. There was a thin-lipped firmness, too, about him at this moment: she felt that under provocation he might easily defy or desert her. She felt she had to yield, and so decided to do so in the most complete manner.

'Ah, yes,' she said. 'I know how true that is. Dear Guru, go up to Hamlet: no one will disturb you there. But if the message comes through before Lady Ambermere goes away, promise me you will come back.'

He went back to the house, where the front door was already open to admit Lady Ambermere, who was telling 'her people' when to come back for her, and fled with the heels of his slippers tapping on the oak stairs up to Hamlet. Softly he shut out the dark spirits from Madras, and made himself even more secure by turning the key in his door. It would never do to appear as a high-caste Brahmin from Benares before anyone who knew India with such fatal intimacy, for he might not entirely correspond with her preconceived notions of such a person.

Lady Ambermere's arrival was soon followed by that of other

guests, and instead of going into the special tent reserved for the lions, she took up a commanding position in the middle of the lawn, where she could examine everybody through her tortoiseshell-handled lorgnette. She kept Peppino by her, who darted forward to shake hands with his wife's guests, and then darted back again to her. Poor Miss Lyall stood behind her chair, and from time to time as ordered, gave her a cape, or put up her parasol, or adjusted her footstool for her, or took up Pug or put him down as her patroness required. Most of the time Lady Ambermere kept up a majestic monologue.

'You have a pretty little garden here, Mr Lucas,' she said, 'though perhaps inconveniently small. Your croquet lawn does not look to me the full size, and then there is no tennis court. But I think you have a little strip of grass somewhere, which you use for bowls, have you not? Presently I will walk around with you and see your domain. Put Pug down again, please, Miss Lyall, and let him run about. See, he wants to play with one of those croquet balls. Put it in motion for him, and he will run with it. Bless me, who is that coming up the path at such a tremendous speed in a bath chair? Oh, I see, it is Mrs Weston. She should not go as fast as that. If Pug was to stray on to the path he would be run over. Better pick up Pug again, Miss Lyall, till she has gone by. And here is Colonel Boucher. If he had brought his bulldogs, I should have asked him to take them away again. I should like a cup of tea, Miss Lyall, with plenty of milk in it, and not too strong. You know how I like my tea. And a biscuit or something for Pug, with a little cream in a saucer or anything that's handy.'

'Won't you come into the smoking parlour, and have tea there, Lady Ambermere?' asked Peppino.

'The smoking parlour?' asked she. 'How very strange to lay tea in a smoking room.'

Peppino explained that nobody had in all probability used the smoking parlour to smoke in for five or six years.

'Oh, if that is so, I will come,' said she. 'Better bring Pug along, too, Miss Lyall. There is a croquet hoop. I am glad I saw it or I should have stumbled over it perhaps. Oh, this is the smoking parlour, is it? Why do you have rushes on the floor? Put Pug in a chair, Miss Lyall, or he may prick his paws. Books, too, I see. That one lying open is an old one. It is Latin poetry. The library at The Hall is very famous for its classical literature. The first Viscount collected it, and it numbers many thousands of volumes.'

'Indeed, it is the most wonderful library,' said Peppino. 'I can never tear myself away from it, when I am at The Hall.'

'I do not wonder. I am a great student myself and often spend a morning there, do I not, Miss Lyall? You should have some new glass put in those windows, Mr Lucas. On a dark day it must be very difficult to see here. By the way, your good wife told me that there would probably be a very remarkable Indian at her party, a Brahmin from Benares, she said. I should like to have a talk with him while I am having my tea. Kindly prepare a peach for me, Miss Lyall.'

Peppino had heard about the retirement of the guru, in consequence of a message from the Guides being expected, and proceeded to explain this to Lady Ambermere, who did not take the slightest notice, as she was looking at the peaches through her lorgnette.

'That one nearest me looks eatable,' she said. 'And then I do not see Miss Olga Bracely, though I distinctly told her I should be here this afternoon, and she said Mrs Lucas had asked her. She sang to us yesterday evening at The Hall, and very creditably indeed. Her husband, Mr Shuttleworth, is a cousin of the late lord's.'

Lucia had come into the smoking parlour during this speech, and heard these fatal words. At the moment she would gladly have recalled her invitation to Olga Bracely altogether, sooner than have alluded therein to Mr Bracely. But that was one of the irremediable things of life, and since it was no use wasting regret on that, she was only the more eager for Olga to come, whatever her husband's name was. She braced herself up to the situation.

'Peppino, are you looking after Lady Ambermere?' she said. 'Dear Lady Ambermere, I hope they are all taking care of you.'

'A very decent peach,' said Lady Ambermere. 'The south wall of my garden is covered with them, and they are always of a peculiarly delicious flavour. The Hall is famed for its peaches. I understood that Miss Bracely was going to be here, Mrs Lucas. I cannot imagine what makes her so late. I was always famed for my punctuality myself. I have finished my tea.'

The lawn outside was now growing thick with people all in their Hightums, and Lady Ambermere as she emerged from the smoking parlour again viewed the scene with marked disfavour. The two Miss Antrobuses had just arrived, and skipped up to their hostess with pretty cries.

'We are dreadfully late,' said the eldest, 'but it was all Piggy's fault.'

'No, Goosie, it was yours,' said the other. 'How can you be so naughty as to say it was mine? Dear Mrs Lucas, what a lovely party it's being, and may we go and play bowls?'

Lady Ambermere regarded their retreating backs, as they raced off with arms intertwined to the bowling green.

'And who are those young ladies?' she asked. 'And why Piggy and Goosie? Miss Lyall, do not let Pug go to the bowls. They are very heavy.'

Elsewhere Mrs Antrobus was slowly advancing from group to group, with her trumpet violently engaged in receiving refreshment. But conversation was not quite so varied as usual, for there was an attitude of intense expectation about with regard to the appearance of Miss Bracely, that made talk rather jerky and unconsecutive. Then also it had gone about that the mysterious Indian, who had been seen now and then during the last week, was actually staying with Mrs Lucas, and why was he not here? More unconjecturable yet, though not so thrillingly interesting, was the absence of Mr Georgie. What could have happened to him, that he was not flitting about on his hostess's errands, and being the life and soul of the party? It was in vain that Mrs Antrobus plodded on her methodical course, seeking answers to all these riddles, and that Mrs Weston in her swifter progression dashed about in her bath chair from group to group, wherever people seemed to be talking in an animated manner. She could learn nothing, and Mrs Antrobus could learn nothing, in fact the only information to be had on the subject was what Mrs Weston herself supplied. She had a very high-coloured handsome face, and an extremely impressive manner, as if she was imparting information of the very highest importance. She naturally spoke in a loud, clear voice, so that she had not got to raise it much even when she addressed Mrs Antrobus. Her wealth of discursive detail was absolutely unrivalled, and she was quite the best observer in Riseholme.

'The last I saw of Miss Bracely,' she said, exactly as if she had been told to describe something on oath in the witness box, 'was a little after half-past one today. It must have been after half-past because when I got home it was close on a quarter to two, and I wasn't a hundred yards from my house when I saw her. As soon as I saw her I said to my gardener boy, Henry Luton, who was pushing me – he's the son of old Mrs Luton who kept the fish shop, and when she died last year, I began to get my fish from Brinton, for I didn't fancy the look of the new person who took on the business, and Henry went to live with his aunt. That was his father's sister, not his mother's, for Mrs Luton never had a sister, and no brothers either. Well, I said to Henry, "You can go a bit slower, Henry, as we're late, we're late, and a minute or two more doesn't make any difference." "No, ma'am," said Henry, touching his cap, so we went slower. Miss Bracely was just opposite the ducking pond then, and presently she came out between the elms. She had just an ordinary morning frock on; it was dark blue, about the same shade as your cape, Mrs Antrobus, or perhaps a little darker, for the sunshine brightened it up. Quite simple it was, nothing grand. And she looked at the watch on her wrist, and she seemed to me to walk a little quicker after that, as if she was a bit late, just as I was. But slower than I was going, I could not go, for I was crawling along, and before she got off the grass, I had come to the corner of Church Lane, and though I turned my head round sharp, like that, at the very last moment, so as to catch the last of her, she hadn't more than stepped off the grass on to the road before the laurestinus at the corner of Colonel Boucher's garden – no, of the Vicar's garden – hid her from me. And if you ask me – '

Mrs Weston stopped for a moment, nodding her head up and down, to emphasize the importance of what she had said, and to raise the expectations of Mrs Antrobus to the highest pitch, as to what was coming.

'And if you ask me where I think she was going and what she was going to do,' she said, 'I believe she was going out to lunch and that she was going to one of those houses there, just across the road, for she made a beeline across the green towards them.

Well, there are three houses there: there's Mrs Quantock's, and it couldn't have been that, or else Mrs Quantock would have had some news of her, or Colonel Boucher's, and it wouldn't have been that, for the Colonel would have had news of her, and we all know whose the third house just there is.'

Mrs Antrobus had not completely followed this powerful reasoning.

'But Colonel Boucher and Mrs Quantock are both here, eh?' said she.

Mrs Weston raised her voice a little.

'That's what I'm saying,' she announced, 'but who isn't here whom we should expect to see, and where's his house?'

It was generally felt that Mrs Weston had hit the nail on the head. What that nail precisely was no one knew, because she had not explained why both Olga Bracely and Georgie were absentees. But now came the climax, bang on the top of the nail, a shrewd straight stroke.

'So there she was having her lunch with Mr Georgie,' said Mrs Weston, now introducing this name for the first time, with the highest dramatic art, 'and they would be seeing round his house afterwards. And then when it was time to come here, Mr Georgie would have remembered that the party was Hightum not Tightum, and there was Miss Bracely not in Hightum at all, nor even Tightum, in my opinion, but Scrub. No doubt she said to him, "Is it a very grand sort of party, Mr Pillson?" and he couldn't do other than reply, for we all received notice that it was Hightum – mine came about twelve – he couldn't do other than reply, "Yes, Miss Bracely, it is." "Good gracious me," she would say, "and I've only got this old rag on. I must go back to the Ambermere Arms, and tell my maid – for she brought a maid in that second motor – and tell my maid to put me out something tidy." "But that will be a great bother for you," he would say, or something of that sort, for I don't pretend to know what he actually did say, and she would reply, "Oh Mr Pillson, but I must put on something tidy, and it would be so kind of you, if you would wait for me, while I do that, and let us go together." That's what *she* said.'

Mrs Weston made a sign to her gardener to proceed, wishing to leave the stage at the moment of climax.

'And that's why they're both late,' she said, and was whirled away in the direction of the bowling green.

The minutes went on, and still nobody appeared who could possibly have accounted for the three-lined whip of Hightams, but by degrees Lucia, who had utterly failed to decoy Lady Ambermere into the place of thrones, began to notice a certain thinning on her lawns. Her guests, it would seem, were not in process of dispersal, for it was a long way off seven o'clock yet, and also none would be so ill-mannered as to leave without shaking hands and saying what a delicious afternoon they had spent. But certainly the lawns grew emptier, and she was utterly unable to explain this extraordinary phenomenon, until she happened to go close to the windows of her music room. Then, looking in, she saw that not only was every chair there occupied, but people were standing about in expectant groups. For a moment, her heart beat high . . . Could Olga have arrived and by some mistake have gone straight in there? It was a dreamlike possibility, but it burst like a ray of sunshine on the party that was rapidly becoming a nightmare to her – for everyone, not Lady Ambermere alone, was audibly wondering when the guru was coming, and when Miss Bracely was going to sing.

At the moment as she paused, a window in the music room was opened, and Piggy's odious head looked out.

'Oh, Mrs Lucas,' she said. 'Goosie and I have got beautiful seats, and Mamma is quite close to the piano where she will hear excellently. Has she promised to sing *Siegfried*? Is Mr Georgie going to play for her? It's *the* most delicious surprise; how could you be so sly and clever as not to tell anybody?'

Lucia cloaked her rage under the most playful manner, as she ran into the music room through the hall.

'You naughty things!' she said. 'Do all come into the garden! It's a garden party, and I couldn't guess where you had all gone. What's all this about singing and playing? I know nothing of it.'

She herded the incredulous crowd out into the garden again, all in their Hightums, every one of them, only to meet Lady Ambermere with Pug and Miss Lyall coming in.

'Better be going, Miss Lyall,' she said. 'Kindly run out and find my people. Oh, here's Mrs Lucas. Been very pleasant indeed, thank you, goodbye. Your charming garden. Yes.'

'Oh, but it's very early,' said Lucia. 'It's hardly six yet.'

'Indeed!' said Lady Ambermere. 'Been so charming,' and she marched out after Miss Lyall into Shakespeare's garden.

It was soon terribly evident that other people were sharing Lady Ambermere's conclusion about the delights of the afternoon, and the necessity of getting home. Colonel Boucher had to take his bulldogs for a run and walk off the excitement of the party; Piggy and Goosie explained to their mother that nobody was going to sing, and by silvery laughter tried to drown her just indignation, and presently Lucia had the agony of seeing Mrs Quantock seated on one of the thrones, that had been designed for much worthier ends, and Peppino sitting in the other, while a few guests drifted about the lawn with all the purposelessness of autumn leaves. What with the guru, presumably meditating upstairs still, and with Olga Bracely most conspicuously absent, she had hardly nervous energy left to wonder what could have become of Georgie. Never in all the years of his ministry had he failed to be at her elbow through the entire duration of her garden parties, flying about on her errands like a tripping Hermes, herding her flocks if she wanted them in one part of the garden rather than another, like a sagacious sheepdog, and coming back to heel again ready for further tasks. But today Georgie was mysteriously away, for he had neither applied for leave nor given any explanation, however improbable, of his absence. He at least would have prevented Lady Ambermere, the only cornerstone of the party, from going away in what must be called a huff, and have continued to tell Lucia how marvellous she was, and what a beautiful party they were having. With the prospect of two other much more magnificent cornerstones, Lucia had not provided any further entertainment for her guests: there was not the conjurer from Brinton, nor the three young ladies who played banjo trios, nor even the mild performing doves which cooed so prettily, and walked up their mistress's outstretched fingers according to order, if they felt disposed. There was nothing to justify Hightums, there was scarcely even sufficient to warrant Tightums. Scrub was written all over 'the desert's dusty face'.

It was about half-past six when the miracles began, and without warning the guru walked out into the garden. Probably he had watched the departure of the great motor with its chauffeur and footman, and Miss Lyall and Lady Ambermere and Pug, and with his intuitive sagacity had conjectured that the danger from Madras was over. He wore his new red slippers, a wonderful turban and an ecstatic smile. Lucia and Daisy met him with cries of joy, and the remaining guests, those drifting autumn leaves, were swept up, as it were, by some compelling broom and clustered in a heap in front of him. There had been a Great Message, a Word of Might, full of Love and Peace. Never had there been such a Word . . .

And then, even before they had all felt the full thrill of that, once more the door from the house opened, and out came Olga Bracely and Georgie. It is true that she had still her blue morning frock, which Mrs Weston had designated as Scrub, but it was a perfectly new Scrub, and if it had been completely covered with Paris labels, they would not have made its *provenance* one whit clearer. 'Dear Mrs Lucas,' she said, 'Mr Georgie and I are terribly late, and it was quite my fault. There was a game of croquet that wouldn't come to an end, and my life has been guided by only one principle, and that is to finish a game of croquet whatever happens. I missed six trains once by finishing a game of croquet. And Mr Georgie was so unkind: he wouldn't give me a cup of tea, or let me change my frock, but dragged me off to see you. And I won!'

The autumn leaves turned green and vigorous again, while Georgie went to get refreshment for his conqueror, and they were all introduced. She allowed herself to be taken with the utmost docility – how unlike Somebody – into the tent with the thrones: she confessed to having stood on tiptoe and looked into Mrs Quantock's garden and wanted to see it so much from the other side of the wall. And this garden, too – might she go and wander all over this garden when she had finished the most delicious peach that the world held? She was so glad she had not had tea with Mr Georgie: he would never have given her such a good peach . . .

Now the departing guests in their Hightums, lingering on the village green a little, and being rather sarcastic about the utter failure of Lucia's party, could hardly help seeing Georgie and Olga emerge from his house and proceed swiftly in the direction of The Hurst, and Mrs Antrobus, who retained marvellous eyesight as compensation for her defective hearing, saw them go in, and simultaneously thought that she had left her parasol at The Hurst.

Next moment she was walking thoughtfully away in that direction. Mrs Weston had been the next to realize what had happened, and though she had to go round by the road in her bath chair, she passed Mrs Antrobus a hundred yards from the house, her pretext for going back being that Lucia had promised to lend her the book by Antonio Caporelli (or was it Caporetto?).

So once more the door into the garden opened, and out shot Mrs Weston. Olga by this time had made her tour of the garden, and might she see the house? She might. There was a pretty music room. At this stage, just as Mrs Weston was poured out in the garden, as with the floodgates being opened, the crowd that followed her came surging into Shakespeare's garden, and never had the mermaid's tail, behind which was secreted the electric bell, experienced such feverish usage. Pressure after pressure invoked its aid, and the pretexts for readmission were soon not made at all, or simply disregarded by the parlour maid. Colonel Boucher might have left a bulldog, and Mrs Antrobus an ear trumpet, or Miss Antrobus (Piggy) a shoelace, and the other Miss Antrobus (Goosie) a shoehorn: but in brisk succession the guests who had been so sarcastic about the party on the village green jostled each other in order to revisit the scenes of their irony. Miss Olga Bracely had been known to enter the portals, and as many of them who entered after her, found a guru as well.

Olga was in the music room when the crowd had congested the hall. People were introduced to her, and sank down into the nearest chairs. Mrs Antrobus took up her old place by the keyboard of the piano. Everybody seemed to be expecting something, and by degrees the import of their longing was borne in upon Olga. They waited, and waited and waited, much as she had waited for a cigarette the evening before. She looked at the piano, and there was a comfortable murmur from her audience. She looked at Lucia, who gave a great gasp, and said nothing at all. She was the only person present who was standing now except her hostess, and Mrs Weston's gardener, who had wheeled his mistress's chair into an admirable position for hearing. She was not too well pleased, but after all . . .

'Would you like me to sing?' she asked Lucia. 'Yes? Ah, there's a copy of *Siegfried*. Do you play?'

Lucia could not smile any more than she was smiling already.

'Is it very diffy?' she asked. 'Could I read it, Georgie? Shall I try?'

She slid on to the music stool.

'Me to begin?' she asked, finding that Olga had opened the book at the salutation of Brünnhilde, which Lucia had practised so diligently all the morning.

She got no answer. Olga, standing by her, had assumed a perfectly different aspect. For her gaiety, her lightness, was substituted some air of intense concentrated seriousness which Lucia did not understand at all. She was looking straight in front of her, gathering herself in, and paying not the smallest attention to Lucia or anybody else.

'One, two,' said Lucia. 'Three. Now,' and she plunged wildly into a sea of demi-semi-quavers. Olga had just opened her mouth, but shut it again.

'No,' she said. 'Once more,' and she whistled the *motif*.

'Oh! it's so diffy!' said Lucia, beginning again. 'Georgie! Turn over!'

Georgie turned over, and Lucia, counting audibly to herself, made an incomparable mess all over the piano.

Olga turned to her accompanist.

'Shall I try?' she said.

She sat down at the piano, and made some sort of sketch of the accompaniment, simplifying, and yet retaining the essence. And then she sang.

CHAPTER EIGHT

Throughout August, guruism reigned supreme over the cultured life of Riseholme, and the priestess and dispenser of its mysteries was Lucia. Never before had she ruled from so elate a pinnacle, nor wielded so secure a supremacy. None had access to the guru but through her: all his classes were held in the smoking parlour and he meditated only in Hamlet or in the sequestered arbour at the end of the laburnum walk. Once he had meditated on the village green, but Lucia did not approve of that and had led him, still rapt, home by the hand.

The classes had swelled prodigiously, for practically all Riseholmites now were at some stage of instruction, with the exception of Hermy and Ursy, who pronounced the whole thing 'piffle', and, as gentle chaff for Georgie, sometimes stood on one leg in the middle of the lawn and held their breath. Then Hermy would say 'One, two, three!' and they shouted 'Om!' at the tops of their discordant voices. Now that the guru was practically interned in The Hurst, they had actually never set eyes on him, for they had not chosen to come to the Hightum garden party, preferring to have a second round of golf, and meeting Lucia next day had been distinctly irreverent on the subject of Eastern philosophy. Since then she had not been aware of their existence.

Lucia now received special instruction from the guru in a class all by herself, so prodigious was her advance in Yoga, for she could hold her breath much longer than anybody else, and had mastered six postures, while the next class which she attended also consisted of the other original members, namely Daisy Quantock, Georgie and Peppino. They had got on very well, too, but Lucia had quite shot away from them, and now if the guru had other urgent spiritual claims on him, she gave instruction to a less advanced class herself.

For this purpose she habited herself in a peculiarly becoming dress of white linen, which reached to her feet and had full flowing sleeves like a surplice. It was girdled with a silver cord with long tassels, and had mother-of-pearl buttons and a hood at the back lined with white satin which came over her head. Below its hem as she sat and taught in a really rather advanced posture showed the toes of her white morocco slippers, and she called it her 'Teacher's Robe'. The class which she taught consisted of Colonel Boucher, Piggy Antrobus and Mrs Weston: sometimes the Colonel brought his bulldogs with him, who lay and snorted precisely as if they were doing breathing exercises, too. A general air of joyful mystery and spiritual endeavour blew balmily round them all, and without any doubt the exercises and the deep breathing were extremely good for them.

One evening, towards the end of the month, Georgie was sitting in his garden, for the half-hour before dressing time, thinking how busy he was, and yet how extraordinarily young and fresh he felt. Usually this month when Hermy and Ursy were with him was very fatiguing, and in ordinary years he would have driven away with Foljambe and Dicky on the day after their departure, and had a quiet week by the seaside. But now, though his sisters were going away tomorrow morning, he had no intention of taking a well-earned rest, in spite of the fact that not only had he been their host all this time, but had done an amazing quantity of other things as well. There had been the daily classes to begin with, which entailed much work in the way of meditation and exercises, as well as the actual learning, and also he had had another job which might easily have taxed his energies to the utmost any other year. For Olga Bracely had definitely bought that house without which she had felt that life was not worth living, and Georgie all this month had at her request been exercising a semi-independent supervision over its decoration and furnishing. She had ordered the general scheme herself and had sent down from London the greater part of the furniture, but Georgie was commissioned to report on any likely pieces of old stuff that he could find, and if expedition was necessary to act on his own responsibility and buy them. But above all secrecy was still necessary till the house was so complete that her Georgie might be told, and by the end of the month Riseholme generally was in a state of prostration following on the violent and feverish curiosity as to who had taken the house. Georgie had gone so far as to confess that he knew, but the most pathetic appeals as to the owner's identity had fallen on obdurate, if not deaf, ears. Not the smallest hint would he give on the subject, and though those incessant visits to the house, those searchings for furniture, the bestowal of it in suitable places, the superintendence of the making of the garden, the interviewings of paperhangers, plumbers, upholsterers, painters, carpenters and so forth occupied a great deal of time, the delicious mystery about it all, and the fact that he was doing it for so adorable a creature, rendered his exertions a positive refreshment. Another thing which, in conjunction with this and his youth-giving studies, made him feel younger than ever was the discreet arrival and perfect success of his *toupée*. No longer was there any need to fear the dislocation of his espaliered locks. He felt so secure and undetectable in that regard that he had taken to wearing no hat, and was soon about to say that his hair was growing more thickly than ever in consequence. But it was not quite time for that yet: it would be inartistic to suggest that just a couple of weeks of hatlessness had produced so desirable a result.

* * *

As he sat at ease after the labours of the day he wondered how the coming of Olga Bracely to Riseholme would affect the economy of the place. It was impossible to think of her with her beauty, her charm, her fame, her personality as taking any second place in its life. Unless she was really meaning to use Riseholme as a retreat, to take no part in its life at all, it was hard to see what part she would take except the first part. One who by her arrival at Lucia's ever-memorable party had converted it in a moment from the most dire of Scrubs (in a psychical sense) to the Hightumest gathering ever known could not lay aside her distinction and pre-eminence. Never had Lucia 'scored' so amazingly as over Olga's late appearance, which had the effect of bringing back all her departed guests with the compulsion of a magnet over iron filings, and sending up the whole party like a rocket into the zenith of social success. All Riseholme knew that Olga had come (after playing croquet with Georgie the entire afternoon) and had given them free, gratis and for nothing, such a treat as only the wealthiest could obtain with the most staggering fees. Lady Ambermere alone, driving back to The Hall with Pug and poor Miss Lyall, was the only person who had not shared in that, and she knew all about it next day, for Georgie had driven out on purpose to tell her, and met Lucia coming away. How, then, would the advent of Olga affect Riseholme's social working generally, and how would it affect Lucia in particular? And what would Lucia say when she knew on whose behalf Georgie was so busy with plumbers and painters, and with buying so many of the desirable treasures in the Ambermere Arms?

Frankly he could not answer these conundrums: they presupposed inconceivable situations, which yet, though inconceivable, were shortly coming to pass, for Olga's advent might be expected before October, that season of tea parties that ushered in the multifarious gaieties of the winter. Would Olga form part of the moonlit circle to whom Lucia played the first movement of the 'Moonlight Sonata', and give a long sigh at the end like the rest of them? And would Lucia when they had all recovered a little from the invariable emotion go to her and say, 'Olga *mia*, just a little bit out of the *Valkyrie*? It would be so pleasant.' Somehow Georgie, with all his imagination, could not picture such a scene. And would Olga take the part of second citizenness or something of the sort when Lucia played Portia? Would Olga join the elementary class of Yoga, and be instructed by Lucia in her Teacher's Robe? Would she sing treble in the Christmas carols, while Lucia beat time, and said in syllables dictated by the rhythm, 'Trebles a little flat! My poor ears!'? Georgie could not imagine any of these things, and yet, unless Olga took no part in the social life of Riseholme at all (and that was equally inconceivable) what was the alternative? True, she had said that she was coming here because it was so ideally lazy a backwater, but Georgie did not take that seriously. She would soon see what Riseholme was when its life poured down in spate, whirling her punt along with it.

And finally, what would happen to him, when Olga was set as a shining star in this firmament? Already he revolved about her, he was aware, like some eager delighted little moon, drawn away from the orbit where it had encircled so contentedly by the more potent planet. And the measure of his detachment from that old orbit might be judged precisely by the fact that the process of detachment which was already taking place was marked by no sense of the pull of opposing forces at all. The great new star sailing into the heavens had just picked him up by force of its superior power of attraction, even as by its momentary conjunction with Lucia at the garden party it had raised her to a magnitude she had never possessed before. That magnitude was still Lucia's, and no doubt would be until the great star appeared again. Then without effort its shining must surely eclipse every other illumination, just as without effort it must surely attract all the little moons to itself. Or would Lucia manage somehow or other, either by sheer force of will, by desperate and hostile endeavour, or, on the other hand, by some supreme tact and cleverness, to harness the great star to her own chariot? He thought the desperate and hostile endeavour was more in keeping with Lucia's methods, and this quiet evening hour represented itself to him as the lull before the storm.

The actual quiet of the moment was suddenly broken into. His front door banged, and the house was filled with running footsteps and screams of laughter. But it was not uncommon for Hermy and Ursy to make this sort of entrance, and at the moment Georgie had not the slightest idea of how much further reaching was the disturbance of the tranquillity. He but drew a couple of long breaths, said 'Om' once or twice, and was quite prepared to find his deeper calm unshattered.

Hermy and Ursy ran down the steps into the garden where he sat still yelling with laughter, and still Georgie's imagination went no further than to suppose that one of them had laid a stymie for the other at their golf, or driven a ball out of bounds or done some other of these things that appeared to make the game so diverting to them.

'Georgie, you'll never guess!' cried Hermy.

'The guru: the Om, of high caste and extraordinary sanctity,' cried Ursy.

'The Brahmin from Benares,' shrieked Hermy.

'The great Teacher! Who do you think he is?' said Ursy. 'We'd never seen him before – '

'But we recognized him at once – '

'He recognized us, too, and didn't he run? – '

'Into The Hurst and shut the door – '

Georgie's deeper calm suddenly quivered like a jelly.

'My dears, you needn't howl so, or talk quite so loud,' he said. 'All Riseholme will hear you. Tell me without shouting who it was you thought you recognized.'

'There's no think about it,' said Hermy. 'It was one of the cooks from the Calcutta Restaurant in Bedford Street – '

'Where we often have lunch,' said Ursy. 'He makes the most delicious curries.'

'Especially when he's a little tipsy,' said Hermy.

'And is about as much a Brahmin as I am.'

'And always said he came from Madras.'

'We always tip him to make the curry himself, so he isn't quite ignorant about money.'

'O Lord!' said Hermy, wiping her eyes. 'If it isn't the limit!'

'And to think of Mrs Lucas and Colonel Boucher and you and Mrs Quantock, and Piggy and all the rest of them sitting round a cook,' said Ursy, 'and drinking in his wisdom. Mr Quantock was on the right track after all when he wanted to engage him.'

Georgie with a fallen heart had first to satisfy himself that this was not one of his sisters' jokes, and then tried to raise his fallen heart by remembering that the guru had often spoken of the dignity of simple manual work, but somehow it was a blow, if Hermy and Ursy were right, to know that this was a tipsy contriver of curry. There was nothing in the simple manual office of curry-making that could possibly tarnish sanctity, but the amazing tissue of falsehoods with which the guru had modestly masked his innocent calling was not so markedly in the spirit of the Guides, as retailed by him. It was of the first importance, however, to be assured that his sisters had not at present communicated their upsetting discovery to anybody but himself, and after that to get their promise that they would not do so.

This was not quite so easy, for Hermy and Ursy had projected a round of visits after dinner to every member of the classes with the exception of Lucia, who should wake up next morning to find herself the only illusioned person in the place.

'She wouldn't like that, you know,' said Hermy with brisk

malice. 'We thought it would serve her out for never asking us to her house again after her foolish old garden party.'

'My dear, you never wanted to go,' said Georgie.

'I know we didn't, but we rather wanted to tell her we didn't want to go. She wasn't nice. Oh, I don't think we can give up telling everybody. It has made such sillies of you all. I think he's a real sport.'

'So do I,' said Ursy. 'We shall soon have him back at his curry oven again. What a laugh we shall have with him.'

They subsided for just as long as it took Foljambe to come out of the house, inform them that it was a quarter of an hour to dinner time, and return again. They all rose obediently.

'Well, we'll talk about it at dinner time,' said Georgie diplomatically. 'And I'll just go down to the cellar first to see if I can find something you like.'

'Good old Georgie,' said Hermy. 'But if you're going to bribe us, you must bribe us well.'

'We'll see,' said he.

Georgie was quite right to be careful over his Veuve Clicquot, especially since it was a bottle of that admirable beverage that Hermy and Ursy had looted from his cellar on the night of their burglarious entry. He remembered that well, though he had – chiefly from the desire to keep things pleasant about his hair – joined in 'the fan', and had even produced another half-bottle. But tonight, even more than then, there was need for the abolition of all petty economies, for the situation would be absolutely intolerable if Hermy and Ursy spread about Riseholme the fact that the introducers and innermost circle of Yoga philosophers had sat at the feet of no Gamaliel at all, but at those of a curry cook from some low restaurant. Indeed he brought up a second bottle tonight with a view, if Hermy and Ursy were not softened by the first, to administer that also. They would then hardly be in a condition to be taken seriously if they still insisted on making a house-to-house visit in Riseholme, and tearing the veil from off the features of the guru. Georgie was far too upright of purpose to dream of making his sisters drunk, but he was willing to make great sacrifices in order to render them kind. What the inner circle would do about this cook he had no idea; he must talk to Lucia about it, before the advanced class tomorrow morning. But anything was better than letting Hermy and Ursy loose in Riseholme with their rude laughs and discreditable exposures. This evening safely over, he could discuss with Lucia what was to be done, for Hermy and Ursy would have vanished at cockcrow, as they were going in for some golf competition at a safe distance. Lucia might recommend doing nothing at all, and wish to continue enlightening studies as if nothing had happened. But Georgie felt that the romance would have evaporated from the classes as regards himself. Or again they might have to get rid of the guru somehow. He only felt quite sure that Lucia would agree with him that Daisy Quantock must not be told. She with her thwarted ambitions of being the prime dispenser of guruism to Riseholme might easily 'turn nasty' and let it be widely known that she and Robert had seen through that fraud long ago, and had considered whether they should not offer the guru the situation of cook in their household, for which he was so much better qualified. She might even add that his leanings towards her pretty housemaid had alone dissuaded her.

The evening went off with a success more brilliant than Georgie had anticipated, and it was quite unnecessary to open the second bottle of champagne. Hermy and Ursy, perhaps under the influence of the first, perhaps from innate good nature, perhaps because they were starting so very early next morning, and wanted to be driven into Brinton, instead of taking a slower and earlier train at Riseholme, readily gave up their project of informing the whole of Riseholme of their discovery, and went to bed as soon as they had rooked their brother of eleven shillings at cutthroat bridge. They continued to say, 'I'll play the guru,' whenever they had to play a knave, but Georgie found it quite easy to laugh at that, so long as the humour of it did not spread. He even himself said, 'I'll guru you, then,' when he took a trick with the Knave of Trumps.

The agitation and uncertainty caused him not to sleep very well, and in addition there was a good deal of disturbance in the house, for his sisters had still all their packing in front of them when they went to bed and the doze that preceded sleep was often broken by the sound of the banging of luggage, the clash of golf clubs and steps on the stairs as they made ready for their departure.

But after a while these disturbances ceased, and it was out of a deep sleep that he awoke with the sense that some noise had awakened him. Apparently they had not finished yet, for there was surely some faint stir of movement somewhere. Anyhow they respected his legitimate desire for quiet, for the noise, whatever it was, was extremely stealthy and subdued. He thought of his absurd lark about burglars on the night of their arrival, and smiled at the notion. His *toupée* was in a drawer close to his bed, but he had no substantial impulse to put it on, and make sure that the noise was not anything other than his sisters' preparations for their early start. For himself, he would have had everything packed and corded long before dinner, if he was to start next day, except just a suitcase that would hold the apparatus of immediate necessities, but then dear Hermy and Ursy were so ramshackle in their ways. Some time he would have bells put on all the shutters as he had determined to do a month ago, and then no sort of noise would disturb him any more . . .

The Yoga class next morning was (unusually) to assemble at ten, since Peppino, who would not miss it for anything, was going to have a day's fishing in the happy stream that flowed into the Avon, and he wanted to be off by eleven. Peppino had made great progress lately and had certain curious dizzy symptoms when he meditated which were highly satisfactory.

Georgie breakfasted with his sisters at eight (they had enticed the motor out of him to convey them to Brinton) and when they were gone, Foljambe informed him that the housemaid had a sore throat, and had not 'done' the drawing room. Foljambe herself would 'do' it, when she had cleaned the 'young ladies'' rooms (there was a hint of scorn in this) upstairs, and so Georgie sat on the window seat of the dining room, and thought how pleasant peace and quietness were. But just when it was time to start for The Hurst in order to talk over the disclosures of the night before with Lucia before the class, and perhaps to frame some secretive policy which would obviate further exposure, he remembered that he had left his cigarette case (the pretty straw one with the turquoise in the corner) in the drawing room and went to find it. The window was open, and apparently Foljambe *had* just come in to let fresh air into the atmosphere which Hermy and Ursy had so uninterruptedly contaminated last night with their 'fags', as they called them, but his cigarette case was not on the table where he thought he had left it. He looked round, and then stood rooted to the spot.

His glass case of treasures was not only open but empty. Gone was the Louis XVI snuffbox, gone was the miniature of Karl Huth, gone the piece of Bow china, and gone the Fabergé cigarette case. Only the Queen Anne toy porringer was there, and in the absence of the others, it looked to him, as no doubt it had looked to the burglar, indescribably insignificant.

Georgie gave a little low wailing cry, but did not tear his hair for obvious reasons. Then he rang the bell three times in swift succession, which was the signal to Foljambe that even if she was in her bath, she must come at once. In she came with one of Hermy's horrid woollen jerseys that had been left behind, in her hand.

'Yes, sir, what is it?' she asked, in an agitated manner, for never could she remember Georgie having rung the bell three times except once when a fish bone had stuck in his throat, and once again when a note had announced to him that Piggy was going to call and hoped to find him alone. For answer Georgie pointed to the rifled treasure case. 'Gone! Burgled!' he said. 'Oh, my God!'

At that supreme moment the telephone bell sounded.

'See what it is,' he said to Foljambe, and put the Queen Anne toy porringer in his pocket.

She came hurrying back.

'Mrs Lucas wants you to come around at once,' she said.

'I can't,' said Georgie. 'I must stop here and send for the police. Nothing must be moved,' and he hastily replaced the toy porringer on the exact circle of pressed velvet where it had stood before.

'Yes, sir,' said Foljambe, but in another moment she returned.

'She would be very much obliged if you would come at once,' she said. 'There's been a robbery in the house.'

'Well, tell her there's been one in mine,' said Georgie irritably. Then good nature mixed with furious curiosity came to his aid.

'Wait here, then, Foljambe, on this very spot,' he said, 'and see that nobody touches anything. I shall probably ring up the police from The Hurst. Admit them.'

In his agitation he put on his hat, instead of going bareheaded, and was received by Lucia, who had clearly been looking out of the music-room window, at the door. She wore her Teacher's Robe.

'Georgie,' she said, quite forgetting to speak Italian in her greeting, 'someone broke into Philip's safe last night, and took a hundred pounds in bank notes. He had put them there only yesterday in order to pay in cash for that cob. And my Roman pearls.'

Georgie felt a certain pride of achievement.

'I've been burgled, too,' he said. 'My Louis XVI snuffbox is worth more than that, and there's the piece of Bow china, and the cigarette case, and the Karl Huth as well.'

'My dear! Come inside,' said she. 'It's a gang. And I was feeling so peaceful and exalted. It will make a terrible atmosphere in the house. My guru will be profoundly affected. An atmosphere where thieves have been will stifle him. He has often told me how he cannot stop in a house where there have been wicked emotions at play. I must keep it from him. I cannot lose him.'

Lucia had sunk down on a spacious Elizabethan settle in the hall. The humorous spider mocked them from the window, the humorous stone fruit from the plate beside the potpourri bowl. Even as she repeated, 'I cannot lose him,' again, a tremendous rap came on the front door, and Georgie, at a sign from his queen, admitted Mrs Quantock.

'Robert and I have been burgled,' she said. 'Four silver spoons – thank God, most of our things are plate – eight silver forks and a Georgian tankard. I could have spared all but the last.'

A faint sign of relief escaped Lucia. If the foul atmosphere of thieves permeated Daisy's house, too, there was no great danger that her guru would go back there. She instantly became sublime.

'Peace!' she said. 'Let us have our class first, for it is ten already, and not let any thought of revenge or evil spoil that for us. If I sent for the police now I could not concentrate. I will not tell my guru what has happened to any of us, but for poor Peppino's sake I will ask him to give us rather a short lesson. I feel completely calm. Om.'

Vague nightmare images began to take shape in Georgie's mind, unworthy suspicions based on his sisters' information the evening before. But with Foljambe keeping guard over the Queen Anne porringer, there was nothing more to fear, and he followed Lucia, her silver cord with tassels gently swinging as she moved, to the smoking parlour, where Peppino was already sitting on the floor, and breathing in a rather more agitated manner than was usual with the advanced class. There were fresh flowers on the table, and the scented morning breeze blew in from the garden. According to custom they all sat down and waited, getting calmer and more peaceful every moment. Soon there would be the tapping of slippered heels on the walk of broken paving stones outside, and for the time they would forget all these disturbances. But they were all rather glad that Lucia was to ask the guru to give them a shorter lesson than usual.

They waited. Presently the hands of the Cromwellian timepiece which was the nearest approach to an Elizabethan clock that Lucia had been able at present to obtain, pointed to a quarter past ten.

'My guru is a little late,' said she.

Two minutes afterwards, Peppino sneezed. Two minutes after that Daisy spoke, using irony.

'Would it not be well to see what has happened to your guru, dear?' she asked. 'Have you seen your guru this morning?'

'No, dear,' said Lucia, not opening her eyes, for she was 'concentrating', 'he always meditates before a class.'

'So do I,' said Daisy, 'but I have meditated long enough.'

'Hush!' said Lucia. 'He is coming.'

That proved to be a false alarm, for it was nothing but Lucia's Persian cat, who had a quarrel with some dead laurel leaves. Lucia rose.

'I don't like to interrupt him,' she said, 'but time is getting on.'

She left the smoking parlour with the slow supple walk that she adopted when she wore her Teacher's Robe. Before many seconds had passed, she came back more quickly and with no suppleness.

'His door is locked,' she said; 'and yet there's no key in it.'

'Did you look through the keyhole, Lucia *mia*?' asked Mrs Quantock, with irrepressible irony.

Naturally Lucia disregarded this.

'I knocked,' she said, 'and there was no reply. I said, "Master, we are waiting," and he didn't answer.'

Suddenly Georgie spoke, as with the report of a cork flying out of a bottle.

'My sisters told me last night that he was the curry cook at the Calcutta Restaurant,' he said. 'They recognized him, and they thought he recognized them. He comes from Madras, and is no more a Brahmin than Foljambe.'

Peppino bounded to his feet.

'What?' he said. 'Let's get a poker and break in the door! I believe he's gone and I believe he's the burglar. Ring for the police.'

'Curry cook, is he?' said Daisy. 'Robert and I were right after all. We knew what your guru was best fitted for, dear Lucia, but then of course you always know best, and you and he have been fooling us finely. But you didn't fool me. I knew when you took him away from me, what sort of a bargain you had made. Guru, indeed! He's the same class as Mrs Eddy, and I saw through her fast enough. And now what are we to do? For my part, I shall just get home, and ring up for the police, and say that the Indian who has been living with you all these weeks has stolen my spoons and forks and my Georgian tankard. Guru, indeed! Burglaroo, I call him! There!'

Her passion, like Hyperion's, had lifted her upon her feet, and she stood there defying the whole of the advanced class, short and stout and wholly ridiculous, but with some revolutionary menace about her. She was not exactly 'terrible as an army with banners', but she was terrible as an elderly lady with a long-standing grievance that had been accentuated by the loss of a Georgian tankard, and that was terrible enough to make Lucia adopt a conciliatory attitude. Bitterly she repented having stolen Daisy's guru at all, if the suspicions now thickening in the air proved to be true, but after all they were not proved yet. The guru might still walk in from the arbour on the laburnum alley which they had not yet searched, or he might be levitating with the door key in his pocket. It was not probable but it was possible, and at this crisis possibilities were things that must be clung to, for otherwise you would simply have to submerge, like those U-boats.

They searched all the garden, but found no trace of the curry cook: they made guarded enquiries of the servants as to whether he had been seen, but nothing whatever could be learned about him. So when Peppino took a ponderous hammer and a stout chisel from his tool chest and led the way upstairs, they all knew that the decisive moment had come. Perhaps he might be meditating (for indeed it was likely that he had a good deal to meditate about), but perhaps Peppino called to him in his most sonorous tones, and said that he would be obliged to break his lock if no answer came, and presently the house resounded with knockings as terrible as those in Macbeth, and much louder. Then suddenly the lock gave, and the door was open.

The room was empty, and as they had all conjectured by now, the bed was unslept in. They opened the drawers of the wardrobe and they were as empty as the room. Finally, Peppino unlocked the door of a large cupboard that stood in the corner, and with a clinking and crashing of glass there poured out a cataract of empty brandy bottles. Emptiness: that was the keynote of the whole scene, and blank consternation its effect.

'My brandy!' said Mrs Quantock in a strangled voice. 'There are fourteen or fifteen bottles. That accounts for the glazed look in his eyes which you, dear Lucia, thought was concentration. I call it distillation.'

'Did he take it from your cellar?' asked Lucia, too shattered to feel resentment, but still capable of intense curiosity.

'No: he had a standing order from me to order any little things he might want from my tradesmen. I wish I had my bills sent in every week.'

'Yes, dear,' said Lucia.

Georgie's eyes sought hers.

'I saw him buy the first bottle,' he said. 'I remember telling you about it. It was at Rush's.'

Peppino gathered up his hammer and chisel.

'Well, it's no use sitting here and thinking of old times,' he observed. 'I shall ring up the police station and put the whole matter into their hands, as far as I am concerned. They'll soon lay hands on him, and he can do his postures in prison for the next few years.'

'But we don't know that it was he who committed all these burglaries yet,' said Lucia.

No one felt it was worth answering this, for the others had all tried and convicted him already.

'I shall do the same,' said Georgie.

'My tankard,' said Mrs Quantock.

Lucia got up. '*Peppino mio*,' she said, 'and you, Georgie, and you, Daisy, I want you before you do anything at all to listen to me for five minutes. Just consider this. What sort of figure shall we all cut if we put the matter into the hands of the police? They will probably catch him, and it will all come out that we have been the dupes of a curry cook. Think what we have all been doing for this last month, think of our classes, our exercises, our – everything. We have been made fools of, but for my part, I simply couldn't bear that everybody should know I had been made a fool of. Anything but that. What's a hundred pounds compared to that, or a tankard – '

'My Louis XVI snuff box was worth at least that without the other things,' said Georgie, still with a secret satisfaction in being the greatest sufferer.

'And it was my hundred pounds, not yours, *carissima*,' said Peppino. But it was clear that Lucia's words were working within him like leaven.

'I'll go halves with you,' she said. 'I'll give you a cheque for fifty pounds.'

'And who would like to go halves in my tankard?' said Daisy with bitter irony. 'I want my tankard.'

Georgie said nothing, but his mind was extremely busy. There was Olga soon coming to Riseholme, and it would be awful if she found it ringing with the tale of the guru, and glancing across to Peppino, he saw a thoughtful and sympathetic look in his eyes, that seemed to indicate that his mind was working on parallel lines. Certainly Lucia had given them all something to meditate upon. He tried to imagine the whole story being shouted into Mrs Antrobus's ear trumpet on the village green, and could not endure the idea. He tried to imagine Mrs Weston ever ceasing to talk about it, and could not picture her silence. No doubt they had all been taken in, too, but here in this empty bedroom were the original dupes, who encouraged the rest.

After Mrs Quantock's enquiry a dead silence fell.

'What do you propose, then?' asked Peppino, showing signs of surrender.

Lucia exerted her utmost wiles.

'*Caro!*' she said. 'I want 'oo to propose. Daisy and me, we silly women, we want 'oo and Georgie to tell us what to do. But if Lucia must speak, I fink – '

She paused a moment, and observing strong disgust at her playfulness on Mrs Quantock's face, reverted to ordinary English again.

'I should do something of this sort,' she said. 'I should say that dear Daisy's guru had left us quite suddenly, and that he has had a call somewhere else. His work here was done; he had established our classes, and set all our feet upon the Way. He always said that something of the sort might happen to him – '

'I believe he had planned it all along,' said Georgie. 'He knew the thing couldn't last for ever, and when my sisters recognized him, he concluded it was time to bolt.'

'With all the available property he could lay hands on,' said Mrs Quantock.

Lucia fingered her tassel.

'Now about the burglaries,' she said. 'It won't do to let it be known that three burglaries were committed in one night, and that simultaneously Daisy's guru was called away – '

'My guru, indeed!' said Mrs Quantock, fizzing with indignation at the repetition of this insult.

'That might give rise to suspicion,' continued Lucia calmly, disregarding the interruption, 'and we must stop the news from spreading. Now with regard to our burglary . . . let me think a moment.'

She had got such complete control of them all now that no one spoke.

'I have it,' she said. 'Only Boaler knows, for Peppino told her not to say a word till the police had been sent for. You must tell her, *carissimo*, that you have found the hundred pounds. That settles that. Now you, Georgie.'

'Foljambe knows,' said Georgie.

'Then tell her not to say a word about it. Put some more things out in your lovely treasure case, no one will notice. And you, Daisy.'

'Robert is away,' said she, quite meekly, for she had been thinking things over. 'My maid knows.'

'And when he comes back, will he notice the loss of the tankard? Did you often use it?'

'About once in ten years.'

'Chance it, then,' said Lucia. 'Just tell your maid to say nothing about it.'

She became deliciously modest again.

'There!' she said. 'That's just a little rough idea of mine and now Peppino and Georgie will put their wise heads together, and tell us what to do.'

That was easily done: they repeated what she had said, and she corrected them if they went wrong. Then once again she stood fingering the tassels of her Teacher's Robe.

'About our studies,' she said. 'I for one should be very sorry to drop them altogether, because they made such a wonderful difference to me, and I think you all felt the same. Look at Georgie now: he looks ten years younger than he did a month ago, and as for Daisy, I wish I could trip about as she does. And it wouldn't do, would it, to drop everything just because Daisy's guru – I mean our guru – had been called away. It would look as if we weren't really interested in what he taught us, as if it was only the novelty of having a – a Brahmin among us that had attracted us.'

Lucia smiled benignly at them all.

'Perhaps we shall find, by and by, that we can't progress much all by ourselves,' she said, 'and it will all drop quietly. But don't let us drop it with a bang. I shall certainly take my elementary class as usual this afternoon.'

She paused.

'In my Robe, just as usual,' she said.

CHAPTER NINE

The fish for which Mrs Weston sent to Brinton every week since she did not like the look of the successor to Tommy Luton's mother lay disregarded on the dish, while with fork and fish slice in her hand, as aids to gesticulation, she was recounting to Colonel Boucher the complete steps that had led up to her remarkable discovery.

'It was the day of Mrs Lucas's garden party,' she said, 'when first I began to have my ideas, and you may be sure I kept them to myself, for I'm not one to speak before I'm pretty sure, but now if the King and Queen came to me on their bended knee and said it wasn't so, I shouldn't believe them. Well – as you may remember, we all went back to Mrs Lucas's party again about half-past six, and it was an umbrella that one had left behind, and a stick that another had forgotten, and what not, for me it was a book all about Venice, that I wanted to borrow, most interesting I am sure, but I haven't had time to glance at it yet, and there was Miss Bracely just come!'

Mrs Weston had to pause a moment for her maid, Elizabeth Luton (cousin of Tommy), jogged her elbow with the dish cover in a manner that could not fail to remind her that Colonel Boucher was still waiting for his piece of brill. As she carved it for him, he rapidly ran over in his mind what seemed to be the main points so far, for as yet there was no certain clue as to the purpose of this preliminary matter. He guessed either Guru or Miss Bracely. Then he received his piece of brill, and Mrs Weston laid down her carving implements again.

'You'd better help yourself, ma'am,' said Elizabeth discreetly.

'So I had, and I'll give you a piece of advice too, Elizabeth, and that is to give the Colonel a glass of wine. Burgundy! I was only wondering this afternoon when it began to turn chilly, if there was a bottle or two of the old Burgundy left, which Mr Weston used to be so fond of, and there was. He bought it on the very spot where it was made, and he said there wasn't a headache in it, not if you drank it all night. He never did, for a couple of glasses and one more was all he ever took, so I don't know how he knew about drinking it all night, but he was a very fine judge of wine. So I said to Elizabeth, "A bottle of the old Burgundy, Elizabeth." Well, on that evening I stopped behind a bit, to have another look at the guru, and get my book, and when I came up the street again, what should I see but Miss Bracely walking in to the little front garden at "Old Place". It was getting dark, I know, and my eyes aren't like Mrs Antrobus's, which I call gimlets, but I saw her plain enough. And if it wasn't the next day, it was the day after that, that they began mending the roof, and since then, there have been plumbers and painters and upholsterers and furniture vans at the door day and night.'

'Haw, hum,' said the Colonel, 'then do you mean that it's Miss Bracely who has taken it?'

Mrs Weston nodded her head up and down.

'I shall ask you what you think when I've told you all,' she said. 'Well! There came a day, and if today's Friday it would be last Tuesday fortnight, and if today's Thursday, for I get mixed about it this morning, and then I never get it straight till next Sunday, but if today's Thursday, then it would be last Monday fortnight, when the guru went away very suddenly, and I'm sure I wasn't very sorry, because those breathings made me feel very giddy and yet I didn't like to be out of it all. Mr Georgie's sisters went away the same day, and I've often wondered whether there was any connection between the two events, for it was odd their happening together like that, and I'm not sure we've heard the last of it yet.'

Colonel Boucher began to wonder whether this was going to be about the guru after all and helped himself to half a partridge. This had the effect of diverting Mrs Weston's attention.

'No,' she said. 'I insist on your taking the whole bird. They are quite small, and I was disappointed when I saw them plucked, and a bit of cold ham and a savoury is all the rest of your dinner. Mary asked me if I wouldn't have an apple tart as well, but I said, "No; the Colonel never touches sweets, but he'll have a partridge, a whole partridge," I said, "and he won't complain of his dinner."

Well! On the day that they all went away, whatever the explanation of that was, I was sitting in my chair opposite the Arms, when out came the landlord followed by two men carrying the settle that stood on the right of the fireplace in the hall. So I said, "Well, landlord, who has ordered that handsome piece?" For handsome it was with its carved arms. And he said, "Good morning, ma'am" – no, "Good afternoon, ma'am," it would be – "It's for Miss" – and then he stopped dead and corrected himself, "It's for Mr Pillson."'

Mrs Weston rapidly took a great quantity of mouthfuls of partridge. As soon as possible she went on.

'So perhaps you can tell me where it is now, if it was for Mr Georgie,' she said. 'I was there only two days ago, and it wasn't in his hall, or in his dining room, or in his drawing room, for though there are changes there, that settle isn't one of them. It's his treasure case that's so altered. The snuff box is gone, and the cigarette case and the piece of Bow china, and instead there's a rat-tail spoon which he used to have on his dinner table, and made a great fuss with, and a bit of Worcester china that used to stand on the mantelpiece, and a different cigarette case, and a bead bag. I don't know where that came from, but if he inherited it, he didn't inherit much that time, I priced it at five shillings. But there's no settle in the treasure case or out of it, and if you want to know where that settle is, it's in Old Place, because I saw it there myself, when the door was open, as I passed. He bought it – Mr Georgie – on behalf of Miss Bracely, unless you suppose that Mr Georgie is going to live in Old Place one day and his own house the next. No; it's Miss Bracely who is going to live at Old Place and that explains the landlord saying "Miss" and then stopping. For some reason, and I dare say that won't puzzle me long, now I can give my mind to it, she's making a secret about it, and only Mr Georgie and the landlord of the Arms know. Of course he had to, for Old Place is his, and I wish I had bought it myself now, for he got it for an old song.'

'Well, by Jove, you have pieced it together finely,' said Colonel Boucher.

'Wait a bit,' said Mrs Weston, rising to her climax. 'This very day, when Mary, that's my cook as you know, was coming back from Brinton with that bit of brill we've been eating, for they hadn't got an ounce of turbot, which I wanted, a luggage train was standing at Riseholme station, and they had just taken out of it a case that could have held nothing but a grand piano. And if that's not enough for you, Colonel, there were two big dress baskets as well, which I think must have contained linen, for they were corded, and it took two men to move each of them, so Mary said, and there's nothing so heavy as linen properly packed, unless it's plate, and there printed on them in black – no, it would be white, because the dress baskets are black, were two initials, O. B. And if you can point to another O. B. in Riseholme I shall think I've lost my memory.'

At this moment of supreme climax, the telephone bell rang in the hall, shrill through the noise of cracking walnuts, and in came Elizabeth with the news that Mr Georgie wanted to know if he might come in for half an hour and chat. If it had been Olga Bracely herself, she could hardly have been more welcome; virtue (the virtue of observation and inference) was receiving its immediate reward.

'Delighted; say I'm delighted, Elizabeth,' said Mrs Weston, 'and now, Colonel, why should you sit all alone here, and I all alone in the drawing room? Bring your decanter and your glass with you, and you shall spare me half a glass for myself, and if you can't guess what one of the questions that I shall ask Mr Georgie is: well – '

Georgie made haste to avail himself of this hospitality for he was bursting with the most important news that had been his since the night of the burglaries. Today he had received permission to let it be known that Olga was coming to Old Place, for Mr Shuttleworth had been informed of the purchase and furnishing of the house, and had, as expected, presented his wife with it, a really magnificent gift. So now Riseholme might know, too, and Georgie, as eager as Hermes, if not quite so swift, tripped across to Mrs Weston's, on his delightful errand. It was, too, of the nature of just such a punitive expedition as Georgie thoroughly enjoyed, for Lucia all this week had been rather haughty and cold with him for his firm refusal to tell her who the purchaser of Old Place was. He had admitted that he knew, but had said that he was under promise not to reveal that, until permitted, and Lucia had been haughty in consequence. She had, in fact, been so haughty that when Georgie rang her up just now, before ringing Mrs Weston up, to ask if he might spend an hour after dinner there, fully intending to tell her the great news, she had replied through her parlour maid that she was very busy at the piano. Very well, if she preferred the second and third movements of the 'Moonlight Sonata', which she had seriously taken in hand, to Georgie's company, why, he would offer himself and his great news elsewhere. But he determined not to bring it out at once; that sort of thing must be kept till he said it was time to go away. Then he would bring it out, and depart in the blaze of success.

He had brought a pretty piece of embroidery with him to occupy himself with, for his work had fallen into sad arrears during August, and he settled himself comfortably down close to the light, so that at the cost of very little eyestrain, he need not put on his spectacles.

'Any news?' he asked, according to the invariable formula. Mrs Weston caught the Colonel's eye. She was not proposing to bring out her tremendous interrogation just yet.

'Poor Mrs Antrobus. Toothache!' she said. 'I was in the chemist's this morning and who should come in but Miss Piggy, and she wanted a drop of laudanum and had to say what it was for, and even then she had to sign a paper. Very unpleasant, I call it, to be obliged to let a chemist know that your mother has a toothache. But there it was, tell him she had to, or go away without any laudanum. I don't know whether Mr Doubleday wasn't asking more than he should, just out of inquisitiveness, for I don't see what business it is of his. I know what I should have said: "Oh, Mr Doubleday, I want it to make laudanum tartlets, we are all so fond of laudanum tartlets." Something sharp and sarcastic like that, to show him his place. But I expect it did Mrs Antrobus good, for there she was on the green in the afternoon, and her face wasn't swollen for I had a good look at her. Oh, and there was something I wanted to ask you, Mr Georgie, and I had it on the tip of my tongue a moment ago. We talked about it at dinner, the Colonel and I, while we were eating our bit of partridge, and I thought "Mr Georgie will be sure to be able to tell us," and if you didn't ring up on the telephone immediately afterwards! That seemed just

Providential, but what's the use of that, if I can't remember what it was that I wanted to ask you.'

This seemed a good opening for his startling news, but Georgie rejected it, as it was too early yet. 'I wonder what it could have been,' he said.

'Well, it will come back to me presently, and here's our coffee, and I see Elizabeth hasn't forgotten to bring a drop of something good for you two gentlemen. And I don't say that I won't join you, if Elizabeth will bring another glass. What with a glass of Burgundy at my dinner, and a drop of brandy now, I shall be quite tipsy unless I take care. The guru now, Mr Georgie, no, that's not what I wanted to ask you about – but has there been any news of the guru?'

For a moment in this juxtaposition of the topics of brandy and guru, Georgie was afraid that something might have leaked out about the contents of the cupboard in Othello. But it was evidently a chance combination, for Mrs Weston went straight on without waiting for an answer.

'What a day that was,' she said, 'when he and Miss Olga Bracely were both at Mrs Lucas's garden party. Ah, now I've got it; now I know what I wanted to ask. When will Miss Olga Bracely come to live at Old Place? Quite soon now, I suppose.'

If Georgie had not put down his embroidery with great expedition, he would undoubtedly have pricked his finger.

'But how on earth did you know she was coming at all?' he said. 'I was just going to tell you that she was coming, as a great bit of news. How tarsome! It's spoiled all my pleasure.'

'Haw, hum, not a very gallant speech, when you're talking to Mrs Weston,' said the Colonel, who hated Georgie's embroidery.

Luckily the pleasure in the punitive part of the expedition remained and Georgie recovered himself. He had some news too; he could answer Mrs Weston's question.

'But it was to have been such a secret until the whole thing was ready,' he said. 'I knew all along; I have known since the day of the garden party. No one but me, not even her husband.'

He was well rewarded for the recovery of his temper. Mrs Weston put down her glass of something good untasted.

'What?' she said. 'Is she going to live here alone in hiding from him? Have they quarrelled so soon?'

Georgie had to disappoint her about this, and gave the authentic version.

'And she's coming next week, Monday probably,' he said.

They were all now extremely happy, for Mrs Weston felt convinced that nobody else had put two and two together with the same brilliant result as herself, and Georgie was in the even superior position of having known the result without having to do any addition at all, and Colonel Boucher enjoyed the first fruits of it all. When they parted, having thoroughly discussed it, the chief preoccupation in the minds of all was the number of Riseholmites that each of them would be the first to pass on the news to. Mrs Weston could tell Elizabeth that night, and Colonel Boucher his bulldogs, but the first blood was really drawn by Georgie, who seeing a light in Mrs Quantock's drawing room when he returned, dropped in for a moment and scored a right and left by telling Robert who let him in, before going upstairs, and Mrs Quantock when he got there. It was impossible to do any more that night.

* * *

Lucia was always very busy of a morning in polishing the sword and shield of Art, in order to present herself daily to her subjects in shining armour, and keep a little ahead of them all in culture, and thus did not as a rule take part in the parliament on the green. Moreover Georgie usually dropped in before lunch, and her casual interrogation 'Any news?' as they sat down to the piano, elicited from him, as in a neat little jug, the cream of the morning's milkings. Today she was attired in her Teacher's Robe, for the elementary class, though not always now in full conclave, gathered at her house on Tuesdays and Fridays. There had been signs of late that the interest of her pupils was on the wane, for Colonel Boucher had not appeared for two meetings, nor had Mrs Weston come to the last, but it was part of Lucia's policy to let guruism die a natural death without herself facilitating its happy release, and she meant to be ready for her class at the appointed times as long as anybody turned up. Besides the Teacher's Robe was singularly becoming and she often wore it when there was no question of teaching at all.

But today, though she would not have been surprised at the

complete absence of pupils, she was still in consultation with her cook over the commissariat of the day, when a succession of tinklings from the mermaid's tail announced that a full meeting was assembling. Her maid in fact had announced to her without pause except to go to the door and back, though it still wanted a few minutes to eleven, that Colonel Boucher, Mrs Weston, Mrs Antrobus and Piggy were all assembled in the smoking parlour. Even as she passed through the hall on her way there, Georgie came hurrying across Shakespeare's garden, his figure distorted through the wavy glass of the windows, and she opened the door to him herself.

'*Georgino mio*,' she said, ''oo not angry with Lucia for saying she was busy last night? And now I'm just going to take my Yoga class. They all came rather early and I haven't seen any of them yet. Any news?'

Georgie heaved a sigh; all Riseholme knew by this time, and he was going to score one more by telling Lucia.

'My dear, haven't you heard yet?' he asked. 'I was going to tell you last night.'

'The tenant of Old Place?' asked Lucia unerringly.

'Yes. Guess!' said Georgie tantalizingly. This was his last revelation and he wanted to spin it out.

Lucia decided on a great stroke, involving risks but magnificent if it came off. In a flash she guessed why all the Yoga class had come so super-punctually; each of them she felt convinced wanted to have the joy of telling her, after everybody else knew, who the new tenant was. On the top of this bitterness was the added acrimony of Georgie, whose clear duty it was to have informed her the moment he knew, wanting to make the same revelation to her, last of all Riseholme. She had already had her suspicions, for she had not forgotten the fact that Olga Bracely and Georgie had played croquet all afternoon when they should have been at her garden party, and she determined to risk all for the sake of spoiling Georgie's pleasure in telling her. She gave her silvery laugh, that started, so she had ascertained, on A flat above the treble clef.

'*Georgino*, did all my questions as to who it was really take you in?' she asked. 'Just as if I hadn't known all along! Why, Miss Olga Bracely, of course!'

Georgie's fallen face showed her how completely she had spoiled his pleasure.

'Who told you?' he asked.

She rattled her tassels.

'Little bird!' she said. 'I must run away to my class, or they will scold me.'

Once again before they settled down to high philosophies, Lucia had the pleasure of disappointing the ambitions of her class to surprise, inform and astonish her.

'Good morning to you all,' she said, 'and before we settle down I'll give you a little bit of news now that at last I'm allowed to. Dear Miss Olga Bracely, whom I think you all met here, is coming to live at Old Place. Will she not be a great addition to our musical parties? Now, please.'

But this splendid bravado was but a scintillation, on a hard and highly polished surface, and had Georgie been able to penetrate into Lucia's heart he would have found complete healing for his recent severe mortification. He did not really believe that Lucia had known all along, like himself, who the new tenant was, for her enquiries had seemed to be pointed with the most piercing curiosity, but, after all, Lucia (when she did not forget her part) was a fine actress, and perhaps all the time he thought he had been punishing her, she had been fooling him. And, in any case, he certainly had not had the joy of telling her; whether she had guessed or really knew, it was she who had told him, and there was no getting over it. He went back straight home and drew a caricature of her.

But if Georgie was sitting with a clouded brow, Lucia was troubled by nothing less than a raging tornado of agitated thought. Though Olga would undoubtedly be a great addition to the musical talent of Riseholme, would she fall into line, and, for instance, 'bring her music' and sing after dinner when Lucia asked her? As regards music, it was possible that she might be almost too great an addition, and cause the rest of the gifted amateurs to sink into comparative insignificance. At present Lucia was high priestess at every altar of Art, and she could not think with equanimity of seeing anybody in charge of the ritual at any. Again to so eminent an opera singer there must be conceded a certain dramatic knowledge, and indeed Georgie had often spoken to Lucia of that superb moment when Brünnhilde woke and hailed the sun. Must Lucia give up the direction of dramatic art as well as of music?

Point by point pricked themselves out of the general gloom, and hoisted danger signals; then suddenly the whole was in blaze together. What if Olga took the lead, not in this particular or in that, but attempted to constitute herself supreme in the affairs of Riseholme? It was all very well for her to be a brilliant bird of passage just for a couple of days, and drop, so to speak, 'a moulted feather, an eagle's feather' on Lucia's party, thereby causing it to shine out from all previous festivities, making it the Hightumest affair that had ever happened, but it was a totally different matter to contemplate her permanent residence here. It seemed possible that then she might keep her feathers to line her own eyrie. She thought of Belshazzar's feast, and the writing of doom on the wall which she was Daniel enough to interpret herself. 'Thy kingdom is divided,' it said, 'and given to the Bracelys or the Shuttleworths.'

She rallied her forces. If Olga meant to show herself that sort of woman, she should soon know with whom she had to deal. Not but what Lucia would give her the chance first of behaving with suitable loyalty and obedience; she would even condescend to cooperate with her so long as it was perfectly clear that she aimed at no supremacy. But there was only one lawgiver in Riseholme, one court of appeal, one dispenser of destiny.

Her own firmness of soul calmed and invigorated her, and changing her Teacher's Robe for a walking dress, she went out up the road that led by Old Place, to see what could be observed of the interior from outside.

CHAPTER TEN

One morning about the middle of October, Lucia was seated at breakfast and frowning over a note she had just received. It began without any formality and was written in pencil.

> Do look in about half-past nine on Saturday and be silly for an hour or two. We'll play games and dance, shall we? Bring your husband of course, and don't bother to reply.
>
> O. B.

'An invitation,' she said icily, as she passed it to her husband. 'Rather short notice.'

'We're not doing anything, are we?' he asked.

Peppino was a little imperceptive sometimes.

'No, it wasn't that I meant,' she said. 'But there's a little more informality about it than one would expect.'

'Probably it's an informal party,' said he.

'It certainly seems most informal. I am not accustomed to be asked quite like that.'

Peppino began to be aware of the true nature of the situation.

'I see what you mean, *cara*,' he said. 'So don't let us go. Then she will take the hint perhaps.'

Lucia thought this over for a moment and found that she rather wanted to go. But a certain resentment that had been slowly accumulating in her mind for some days past began to leak out first, before she consented to overlook Olga's informality.

'It is a fortnight since I called on her,' she said, 'and she has not even returned the call. I dare say they behave like that in London in certain circles, but I don't know that London is any better for it.'

'She has been away twice since she came,' said Peppino. 'She has hardly been here for a couple of days together yet.'

'I may be wrong,' said Lucia. 'No doubt I am wrong. But I should have thought that she might have spared half an hour out of these days in returning my call. However, she thought not.'

Peppino suddenly recollected a thrilling piece of news which most unaccountably he had forgotten to tell Lucia.

'Dear me, something slipped my memory,' he said. 'I met Mrs Weston yesterday afternoon, who told me that half an hour ago Miss Bracely had seen her in her bath chair and had taken the handles from Tommy Luton, and pushed her twice round the green, positively running.'

'That does not seem to me of very prime importance,' said Lucia, though she was thrilled to the marrow. 'I do not wonder it slipped your memory, *caro*.'

'*Carissima*, wait a minute. That is not all. She told Mrs Weston that she would have returned her call, but that she hadn't got any calling cards.'

'Impossible!' cried Lucia. 'They could have printed them at Ye Olde Booke Shop in an afternoon.'

'That may be so, indeed, if you say so, it is,' said Peppino. 'Anyhow she said she hadn't got any calling cards, and I don't see why she should lie about it.'

'No, it is not the confession one would be likely to make,' said she, 'unless it was true. Or even if it was,' she added.

'Anyhow it explains why she has not been here,' said Peppino. 'She would naturally like to do everything in order, when she called on you, *carissima*. It would have been embarrassing if you were out, and she could not hand in her card.'

'And about Mr Shuttleworth?' asked she in an absent voice, as if she had no real interest in her question.

'He has not been seen yet at all, as far as I can gather.'

'Then shall we have no host, if we drop in tomorrow night?'

'Let us go and see, *cara*,' said he gaily.

Apart from this matter of her call not being returned, Lucia had not as yet had any reason to suspect Olga of revolutionary designs on the throne. She had done odd things – pushing Mrs Weston's chair round the green was one of them, smoking a cigarette as she came back from church on Sunday was another – but these she set down to the Bohemianism and want of polish which might be expected from her upbringing, if you could call an orphan school at Brixton an upbringing at all. This terrific fact Georgie had let slip in his stern determination to know twice as much about Olga as anybody else, and Lucia had treasured it. She had in the last fortnight labelled Olga as 'rather common', retaining, however, a certain respect for her professional career, given that that professional career was to be thrown down as a carpet for her own feet. But, after all, if Olga was a bit Bohemian in her way of life, as exhibited by the absence of calling cards, Lucia was perfectly ready to overlook that (confident in the refining influence of Riseholme), and to go to the informal party next day, if she felt so disposed, for no direct answer was asked for.

There was a considerable illumination in the windows of Old Place when she and Peppino set out after dinner next night to go to the 'silly' party, kindly overlooking the informality and the absence of a return visit to her call. It had been a sloppy day of rain, and, as was natural, Lucia carried some very smart indoor shoes in a paper parcel and Peppino had his Russian goloshes on. These were immense snow boots, in which his evening shoes were completely encased, but Lucia preferred not to disfigure her feet to that extent, and was clad in neat walking boots which she could exchange for her smart satin footwear in the cloakroom. The resumption of walking boots when the evening was over was rather a feature among the ladies and was called 'the cobbler's at-home'. The two started rather late, for it was fitting that Lucia should be the last to arrive.

They had come to the door of Old Place, and Peppino was fumbling in the dark for the bell, when Lucia gave a little cry of agony and put her hands over her ears, just as if she had been seized with a double-earache of peculiar intensity.

'Gramophone,' she said faintly.

There could be no doubt about that. From the window close at hand came out the excruciating strains of a very lusty instrument, and the record was that of a vulgar 'catchy' waltz tune, taken down from a brass band. All Riseholme knew what her opinion about gramophones was; to the lover of Beethoven they were like indecent and profane language loudly used in a public place. Only one, so far as was known, had ever come to Riseholme, and that was introduced by the misguided Robert Quantock. Once he had turned it on in her presence; but the look of agony which crossed her face was such that he had to stop it immediately. Then the door was opened, and the abominable noise poured out in increased volume.

Lucia paused for a moment in indecision. Would it be the great, the magnificent thing to go home without coming in, trusting to Peppino to let it be widely known what had turned her back from the door? There was a good deal to be said for that, for it would be living up to her own high and immutable standards. On the other hand she particularly wanted to see what standard of entertaining Olga was initiating. The 'silly evening' was quite a new type of party, for since she had directed and controlled the social side of things there had been no 'silly evenings' of any kind in Riseholme, and it might be a good thing to ensure the failure of this (in case she did not like it) by setting the example of a bored and frosty face. But if she went in, the gramophone must be stopped. She would sit and wince, and Peppino must explain her feeling about gramophones. That would be a suitable exhibition of authority. Or she might tell Olga.

Lucia put on her satin shoes, leaving her boots till the hour of the cobbler's at-home came, and composing her face to a suitable wince was led by a footman on tiptoe to the door of the big music room which Georgie had spoken of.

'If you'll please to step in very quietly, ma'am,' he said.

The room was full of people; all Riseholme was there, and since there were not nearly enough chairs (Lucia saw *that* at once) a large number were sitting on the floor on cushions. At the far end of the room was a slightly raised dais, to the corner of which the grand piano had been pushed, on the top of which, with its braying trumpet pointing straight at Lucia, was an immense gramophone. On the dais was Olga dancing. She was dressed in some white soft fabric shimmering with silver, which left her beautiful arms bare to the shoulder. It was cut squarely and simply about the neck, and hung in straight folds down to just above her ankles. She held in her hands some long shimmering scarf of brilliant red, that floated and undulated as she moved, as if inspired by some life of its own that it drew out of her slim superb vitality. From the cloud of shifting crimson, with the slow billows of silver moving rhythmically round her body, that beautiful face looked out deliciously smiling and brimming with life . . .

Lucia had hardly entered when with a final bray the gramophone came to the end of its record, and Olga swept a great curtsey, threw down her scarf, and stepped off the dais. Georgie was sitting on the floor close to it, and jumped up, leading the applause. For a moment, though several heads had been turned at Lucia's entrance, nobody took the slightest notice of her, indeed, the first apparently to recognize her presence was her hostess, who just kissed her hand to her, and then continued talking to Georgie. Then Olga threaded her way through the besprinkled floor, and came up to her.

'How wise you were to miss that very poor performance,' she said. 'But Mr Georgie insisted that I should make a fool of myself.'

'Indeed, I am sorry not to have been here for it,' said Lucia in her most stately manner. 'It seemed to me very far from being a poor performance, very far indeed. *Caro mio*, you remember Miss Bracely.'

'*Si, si molto bene*,' said Peppino, shaking hands.

'Ah, and you talk Italian,' said Olga. '*Che bella lingua!* I wish I knew it.'

'You have a very good pronunciation,' said Lucia.

'*Tante grazie.* You know everyone here of course. Now, what shall we do next? Clumps or charades or what? Ah, there are some cigarettes. Won't you have one?'

Lucia gave a little scream of dismay.

'A cigarette for me? That would be a very odd thing,' she said. Then relenting, as she remembered that Olga must be excused for her ignorance, she added: 'You see I never smoke. Never.'

'Oh, you should learn,' said Olga. 'Now let's play clumps. Does everyone know clumps? If they don't they will find out. Or shall we dance? There's the gramophone to dance to.'

Lucia put up her hands in playful petition.

'Oh please, no gramophone!' she said.

'Oh, don't you like it?' said Olga. 'It's so horrible that I adore it, as I adore dreadful creatures in an aquarium. But I think we won't dance till after supper. We'll have supper extremely soon, partly because I am dying of famine, and partly because people are sillier afterwards. But just one game of clumps first. Let's see; there are but enough for four clumps. Please make four clumps, everybody, and – and will you and two more go out with Mr Georgie, Mrs Lucas? We will be as quick as we can, and we won't think of anything that will make Mr Georgie blush. Oh, there he is! He heard!'

Olga's intense enjoyment of her own party was rapidly galvanizing everybody into a much keener gaiety than was at all usual in Riseholme, where as a rule, the hostess was somewhat anxious and watchful, fearing that her guests were not amusing themselves, and that the sandwiches would give out. There was a sit-down supper when the clumps were over (Mrs Quantock had been the first to guess Beethoven's little toe on his right foot, which made Lucia wince) and there were not enough men and maids to wait, and so people foraged for themselves, and Olga paraded up and down the room with a bottle of champagne in one hand, and a dish of lobster salad in the other. She sat for a minute or two first at one table and then at another, and asked silly riddles, and sent to the kitchen for a ham, and put out all the electric light by mistake, when she meant to turn on some more. Then when supper was over they all took their seats back into the music room and played musical chairs, at the end of which Mrs Quantock was left in with Olga, and it was believed that she said 'Damn', when Mrs Quantock won. Georgie was in charge of the gramophone which supplied deadly music, quite forgetting that this was agony to Lucia, and not even being aware when she made a sign to Peppino, and went away having a cobbler's at-home all to herself. Nobody noticed when Saturday ended and Sunday began, for Georgie and Colonel Boucher were cockfighting on the floor, Georgie screaming out 'How tarsome' when he was upset, and Colonel Boucher very red in the face saying 'Haw, hum. Never thought I should romp again like this. By Jove, most amusing!' Georgie was the last to leave and did not notice till he was halfway home that he had a ham frill adorning his shirt front. He hoped that it had been Olga who put it there, when he had to walk blindfold across the floor and try to keep in a straight line.

Riseholme got up rather late next morning, and had to hurry over its breakfast in order to be in time for church. There was a slight feeling of reaction abroad, and a sense of having been young and amused, and of waking now to the fact of church bells and middle age. Colonel Boucher, singing the bass of 'A few more years shall roll', felt his mind instinctively wandering to the cockfight the evening before, and depressedly recollecting that a considerable number of years had rolled already. Mrs Weston, with her bath chair in the aisle and Tommy Luton to hand her hymn book and prayer book as she required, looked sideways at Mrs Quantock, and thought how strange it was that Daisy, so few hours ago, had been racing round a solitary chair with Georgie's finger on the gramophone, while Georgie, singing tenor by Colonel Boucher's ample side, saw with keen annoyance that there was a stain of tarnished silver on his forefinger, accounted for by the fact that after breakfast he had been cleaning the frame which held the photograph of Olga Bracely and had been astonished to hear the church bells beginning. Another conducement to depression on his part was the fact that he was lunching with Lucia, and he could not imagine what Lucia's attitude would be towards the party last night. She had come to church rather late, having no use for the General Confession, and sang with stony fervour. She wore her usual church face, from which nothing whatever could be gathered. A great many stealthy glances right and left from everybody failed to reveal the presence of their hostess of last night. Georgie, in particular, was sorry for this; he would have liked her to show that capacity for respectable seriousness which her presence at church that morning would have implied; while Lucia, in particular, was glad of this, for it confirmed her view that Miss Bracely was not, nor could ever be, a true Riseholmite. She had thought as much last night, and had said so to Peppino. She proposed to say the same to Georgie today.

Then came a stupefying surprise as Mr Rumbold walked from his stall to the pulpit for the sermon. Generally he gave out the number of the short anthem which accompanied this manoeuvre, but today he made no such announcement. A discreet curtain hid the organist from the congregation, and veiled his gymnastics with the stops and his antic dancing on the pedals, and now when

Mr Rumbold moved from his stall, there came from the organ the short introduction to Bach's 'Mein gläubiges Herze', which even Lucia had allowed to be nearly 'equal' to Beethoven. And then came the voice . . .

The reaction after the romp last night went out like a snuffed candle at this divine singing, which was charged with the joyfulness of some heavenly child. It grew low and soft, it rang out again, it lingered and tarried, it quickened into the ultimate triumph. No singing could have been simpler, but that simplicity could only have sprung from the highest art. But now the art was wholly unconscious; it was part of the singer who but praised God as the thrushes do. She who had made gaiety last night, made worship this morning.

As they sat down for the discourse, Colonel Boucher discreetly whispered to Georgie 'By Jove.' And Georgie rather more audibly answered 'Adorable.' Mrs Weston drew a half a crown from her purse instead of her usual shilling, to be ready for the offertory, and Mrs Quantock wondered if she was too old to learn to sing.

*　*　*

Georgie found Lucia very full of talk that day at luncheon, and markedly more Italian than usual. Indeed she put down an Italian grammar when he entered the drawing room, and covered it up with the essays of Antonio Caporelli. This possibly had some connection with the fact that she had encouraged Olga last night with regard to her pronunciation.

'*Ben arrivato, Georgio*,' she said. '*Ho finito il libro di Antonio Caporelli quanta memento. E magnifico!*'

Georgie thought she had finished it long ago, but perhaps he was mistaken. The sentence flew off Lucia's tongue as if it was perched there all quite ready.

'*Sono un poco fatigata dopo il* – dear me how rusty I am getting in Italian for I can't remember the word,' she went on. 'Anyhow I am a little tired after last night. A delightful little party, was it not? It was clever of Miss Bracely to get so many people together at so short a notice. Once in a while that sort of romp is very well.'

'I enjoyed it quite enormously,' said Georgie.

'I saw you did, *cattivo ragazzo*,' said she. 'You quite forgot about your poor Lucia and her horror of that dreadful gramophone. I had to exert all the calmness that Yoga has given me not to scream. But you were naughty with the gramophone over those musical chairs – unmusical chairs, as I said to Peppino, didn't I, *caro*? – taking it off and putting it on again so suddenly. Each time I thought it was the end. *E pronta la colazione. Andiamo.*'

Presently they were seated; the menu, an unusual thing in itself at luncheon, was written in Italian, the scribe being clearly Lucia.

'I shall want a lot of Georgino's *tempo* this week,' she said, 'for Peppino and I have quite settled we must give a little after-dinner party next Saturday, and I want you to help me to arrange some impromptu tableaux. Everything impromptu must just be sketched out first, and I dare say Miss Bracely worked a great deal at her dance last night and I wish I had seen more of it. She was a little awkward in the management of her draperies I thought, but I dare say she does not know much about dancing. Still it was very graceful and effective for an amateur, and she carried it off very well.'

'Oh, but she is not quite an amateur,' said Georgie. 'She has played in *Salome.*'

Lucia pursed her lips.

'Indeed, I am sorry she played in that,' she said. 'With her undoubtedly great gifts I should have thought she might have found a worthier object. Naturally I have not heard it. I should be very much ashamed to be seen there. But about our tableaux now. Peppino thought we might open with the execution of Mary Queen of Scots. It is a dreadful thing that I have lost my pearls. He would be the executioner and you the priest. Then I should like to have the awakening of Brünnhilde.'

'That would be lovely,' said Georgie. 'Have you asked Miss Olga if she will?'

'*Georgino mio*, you don't quite understand,' said Lucia. 'This party is to be for Miss Bracely. I was her guest last night in spite of the gramophone, and indeed I hope she will find nothing in my house that jars on her as much as her gramophone jarred on me. I had a dreadful nightmare last night – didn't I, Peppino? – in consequence. About the Brünnhilde tableau, I thought Peppino would be Siegfried – and perhaps you could learn just fifteen or twenty bars of the music and play it while the curtain was up. You can play the same over again if it is encored. Then how about King Cophetua and the beggar maid? I should be with my back to the audience, and should not turn round at all; it would be quite your tableau. We will just sketch them out, as I said, and have a grouping or two to make sure we don't get in each other's way, and I will see that there are some dresses of some kind which we can just throw on. The tableaux with a little music, serious music, would be quite sufficient to keep everybody interested.'

By this time Georgie had got a tolerable inkling of the import of all this. It was not at present to be war; it was to be magnificent rivalry, a throwing down perhaps of a gauntlet, which none would venture to pick up. To confirm this view, Lucia went on with gathering animation.

'I do not propose to have games, romps shall I call them?' she said, 'for as far as I know Riseholme, and perhaps I know it a little better than dear Miss Bracely, Riseholme does not care for that sort of thing. It is not quite in our line; we may be right or wrong, I am sure I do not know, but as a matter of fact, we *don't* care for that sort of thing. Dear Miss Bracely did her very best last night; I am sure she was prompted only by the most hospitable motives, but how should she know? The supper too. Peppino counted nineteen empty champagne bottles.'

'Eighteen, *carissima*,' said Peppino.

'I think you told me nineteen, *caro*, but it makes very little difference. Eighteen empty champagne bottles standing on the sideboard, and no end to the caviare sandwiches which were left over. It was all too much, though there were not nearly enough chairs, and indeed I never got one at all except just at supper.'

Lucia leaned forward over the table, with her hands clasped.

'There was display about it, *Georgino*, and you know how I hate display,' she said. 'Shakespeare was content with the most modest scenery for his masterpieces, and it would be a great mistake if we allowed ourselves to be carried away by mere wasteful opulence. In all the years I have lived here, and contributed in my humble way to the life of the place, I have heard no complaints about my suppers or teas, nor about the quality of entertainment which I offer my guests when they are so good as to say "*Si*," to *le mie invitazione*. Art is not advanced by romping, and we are able to enjoy ourselves without two hundred caviare sandwiches being left over. And such wasteful cutting of the ham; I had to slice the chunk she gave me over and over again before I could eat it.'

Georgie felt he could not quite let this pass.

'Well, I had an excellent supper,' he said, 'and I enjoyed it very much. Besides, I saw Peppino tucking in like anything. Ask him what he thought of it.'

Lucia gave her silvery laugh.

'*Georgino*, you are a boy,' she said artfully, 'and "tuck in" as you so vulgarly call it without thinking. I'm saying nothing against the supper, but I'm sure that Peppino and Colonel Boucher would have felt better this morning if they had been wiser last night. But that's not the real point. I want to show Miss Bracely, and I'm sure she will be grateful for it, the sort of entertainment that has contented us at Riseholme for so long. I will frame it on her lines; I will ask all and sundry to drop in with just a few hours' notice, as she did. Everything shall be good, and there shall be about it all something that I seemed to miss last night. There was a little bit – how shall I say it? – a little bit of the footlights about it all. And the footlights didn't seem to me to have been extinguished at church time this morning. The singing of that very fine aria was theatrical, I can't call it less than theatrical.'

She fixed Georgie with her black beady eye, and smoothed her undulated hair.

'Theatrical,' she said again. 'Now let us have our coffee in the music room. Shall Lucia play a little bit of Beethoven to take out any nasty taste of gramophone? Me no likey gramophone at all. Nebber!'

*   *   *

Georgie now began to feel himself able to sympathize with that surfeited swain who thought how happy he could be with either, were t'other dear charmer away. Certainly he had been very happy with Lucia all these years, before t'other dear charmer alighted in Riseholme, and now he felt that should Lucia decide, as she had often so nearly decided, to spend the winter on the Riviera, Riseholme would still be a very pleasant place of residence. He never was quite sure how seriously she had contemplated a winter on the Riviera, for the mere mention of it had always been enough to make him protest that Riseholme could not possibly exist without her, but today, as he sat and heard (rather than listened to) a series of slow movements, with a brief and hazardous attempt at the scherzo of the 'Moonlight', he felt that if any talk of the Riviera came up, he would not be quite so insistent as to the impossibility of Riseholme continuing to exist without her. He could, for instance, have existed perfectly well this Sunday afternoon if Lucia had been even at Timbuctoo or the Antipodes, for as he went away last night, Olga had thrown a casual intimation to him that she would be at home, if he had nothing better to do, and cared to drop in. Certainly he had nothing better to do but he had something worse to do . . .

Peppino was sitting in the window seat, with eyes closed, because he listened to music better so, and with head that nodded occasionally, presumably for the same reason. But the cessation of the slow movement naturally made him cease to listen, and he stirred and gave the sigh with which Riseholme always acknowledged the end of a slow movement. Georgie sighed too, and Lucia sighed; they all sighed, and then Lucia began again. So Peppino closed his eyes again, and Georgie continued his mental analysis of the situation.

At present, so he concluded, Lucia did not mean war. She meant, as by some great armed demonstration, to exhibit the Riseholme spirit in its full panoply, and then crush into dazzled submission any potential rivalry. She meant also to exert an educational influence, for she allowed that Olga had great gifts, and she meant to train and refine those gifts so that they might, when exercised under benign but autocratic supervision, conduce to the strength and splendour of Riseholme. Naturally she must be loyally and ably assisted, and Georgie realized that the tableau of King Cophetua (his tableau as she had said) partook of the nature of a bribe, and, if that word was invidious, of a raising of his pay. It was equally certain that this prolonged recital of slow movements was intended to produce in his mind a vivid consciousness of the contrast between the romp last night and the present tranquil hour, and it did not fail in this respect.

Lucia shut the piano lid, and almost before they had given their sighs, spoke.

'I think I will have a little dinner party first,' she said. 'I will ask Lady Ambermere. That will make us four, with you Georgie, and Miss Bracely and Mr Shuttleworth will make six. The rest I shall ask to come in at nine, for I know Lady Ambermere does not like late hours. And now shall we talk over our tableaux?'

So even Lucia's mind had not been wholly absorbed in Beethoven, though Georgie, as usual, told her she had never played so divinely.

CHAPTER ELEVEN

The manoeuvres of the next week became so bewilderingly complicated that by Wednesday Georgie was almost thinking of going away to the seaside with Foljambe and Dicky in sheer despair, and in after years he could not without great mental effort succeed in straightening it all out, and the effort caused quite a buzzing in his head . . . That Sunday evening Lucia sent an invitation to Lady Ambermere for 'dinner and tableaux', to which Lady Ambermere's 'people' replied by telephone on Monday afternoon that her ladyship was sorry to be unable. Lucia therefore gave up the idea of a dinner party, and reverted to her original scheme of an evening party like Olga's got up on the spur of the moment, with great care and most anxious preparation. The rehearsals for the impromptu tableaux meantime went steadily forward behind closed doors, and Georgie wrestled with twenty bars of the music of the 'Awakening of Brünnhilde'. Lucia intended to ask nobody until Friday evening, and Olga should see what sort of party Riseholme could raise at a moment's notice.

Early on Tuesday morning the devil entered into Daisy Quantock, probably by means of subconscious telepathy, and she proceeded to go round the green at the morning parliament, and ask everybody to come in for a good romp on Saturday evening, and they all accepted. Georgie, Lucia and Olga were absentees, and so, making a house-to-house visitation she went first to Georgie. He with secret knowledge of the tableaux (indeed he was stitching himself a robe to be worn by King Cophetua at the time and hastily bundled it under the table) regretted that he was already engaged. This was rather mysterious, but he might have planned, for all Mrs Quantock knew, an evening when he would be 'busy indoors', and since those evenings were never to be pried upon, she asked no questions, but went off to Lucia's to give her invitation there. There again she was met with a similarly mysterious refusal. Lucia much regretted that she and Peppino were unable to come, and she hoped Daisy would have a lovely party. Even as she spoke, she heard her telephone bell ringing, and hurried off to find that Georgie, faithful lieutenant, was acquainting her with the fact that Mrs Quantock was planning a party for Saturday; he did not know how far she had got. At that moment she had got just halfway to Old Place, walking at unusual speed. Lucia grasped the situation with amazing quickness, and cutting off Georgie with a snap, she abandoned all idea of her party being impromptu, and rang up Olga. She would secure her anyhow . . .

The telephone was in the hall, and Olga, with her hat on, was just preparing to go out, when the bell sounded. The words of grateful acceptance were on her very lips when her front-door bell rang too, very long and insistently, and had hardly left off when it began again. Olga opened the door herself and there was Mrs Quantock on the doorstep with her invitation for Saturday night. She was obliged to refuse, but promised to look in, if she was not very late in getting away from Mrs Lucas's (and pop went the cat out of the bag). Another romp would be lovely.

Already the evils of decentralization and overlapping were becoming manifest. Lucia rang up house after house, only to find that its inhabitants were already engaged. She had got Olga and Georgie, and could begin the good work of education and the crushing of rivalry, not by force but by pure and refined example, but Mrs Quantock had got everybody else. In the old days this could never have happened, for everything revolved round one central body. Now with the appearance of this other great star, all the known laws of gravity and attraction were upset.

Georgie, again summoned to the telephone, recommended an appeal to Mrs Quantock's better nature, which Lucia rejected, doubting whether she had one.

'But what about the tableaux?' asked Georgie. 'We three can't very well do tableaux for Miss Olga to look at.'

Then Lucia showed herself truly great.

'The merit of the tableaux does not consist in the number of the audience,' she said.

She paused a moment.

'Have you got the Cophetua robe to set properly?' she asked.

'Oh, it'll do,' said Georgie dejectedly.

* * *

On Tuesday afternoon Olga rang up Lucia again to say that her husband was arriving that day, so might she bring him on Saturday? To this Lucia cordially assented, but she felt that a husband and wife sitting together and looking at another husband and wife doing tableaux would be an unusual entertainment, and not characteristic of Riseholme's best. She began to waver about the tableaux and to consider dinner instead. She also wondered whether she had been wronging dear Daisy, and whether she had a better nature after all. Perhaps Georgie might ascertain.

Georgie was roused from a little fatigued nap by the telephone, for he had fallen asleep over King Cophetua's robe. Lucia explained the situation and delicately suggested that it would be so easy for him to 'pop in' to dear Daisy's, and be very diplomatic. There was nobody like Georgie for tact. So with a heavy yawn he popped in.

'You've come about this business on Saturday,' said Daisy unerringly. 'Haven't you?'

Georgie remembered his character for tact.

'How wonderful of you to guess that!' he said. 'I thought we might see if we couldn't arrange something, if we put our heads together. It's such a pity to split up. We – I mean Lucia has got Miss Olga and her husband coming, and – '

'And I've got everybody else,' said Daisy brightly. 'And Miss Bracely is coming over here, if she gets away early. Probably with such a small party she will.'

'Oh, I shouldn't count on that,' said he. 'We are having some tableaux, and they always take longer than you think. Dear me, I shouldn't have said that, as they were to be impromptu, but I really believe my head is going. You know how thorough Lucia is; she is taking a great deal of trouble about them.'

'I hadn't heard about that,' said Mrs Quantock.

She thought a moment.

'Well; I don't want to spoil Lucia's evening,' she said, 'for I'm sure nothing could be so ridiculous as three people doing tableaux for two others. And on the other hand, I don't want her to spoil mine, for what's to prevent her going on with the tableaux till church time next morning if she wishes to keep Miss Bracely away from my house? I'm sure after the way she behaved about my guru – Well, never mind that. How would it be if we had the tableaux first at Lucia's, and then came on here? If Lucia cares to suggest that to me, and my guests consent, I don't mind doing that.'

By six o'clock on Tuesday evening therefore all the telephone bells of Riseholme were merrily ringing again. Mrs Quantock stipulated that Lucia's party should end at 10.45 precisely, if it didn't end before, and that everyone should then be free to flock across to her house. She proposed a romp that should even outshine Olga's, and was deep in the study of a manual of 'Round Games', which included 'Hunt the Slipper' . . .

*　　*　　*

Georgie and Peppino took turns at the telephone, ringing up all Mrs Quantock's guests, and informing them of the double pleasure which awaited them on Saturday. Since Georgie had let out the secret of the impromptu tableaux to Mrs Quantock there was no reason why the rest of Riseholme should not learn of this first-hand from The Hurst, instead of second-hand (with promises not to repeat it) from Mrs Quantock. It appeared that she had a better nature than Lucia credited her with, but to expect her not to tell everybody about the tableaux would be putting virtue to an unfair test.

'So that's all settled,' said Georgie, as he returned with the last acceptance, 'and how fortunately it has happened after all. But what a day it has been. Nothing but telephoning from morning till night. If we go on like this the company will pay a dividend this year, and return us some of our own pennies.'

Lucia had got a quantity of pearl beads and was stringing them for the tableau of Mary Queen of Scots.

'Now that everyone knows,' she said, 'we might allow ourselves a little more elaboration in our preparations. There is an Elizabethan axe at the Ambermere Arms which I might borrow for Peppino. Then about the Brannhilde tableau. It is dawn, is it not? We might have the stage quite dark when the curtain goes up, and turn up a lamp very slowly behind the scene, so that it shines on my face. A lamp being turned up very slowly is wonderfully effective. It produces a perfect illusion. Could you manage that with one hand and play the music of the awakening with the other, Georgino?'

'I'm quite sure I couldn't,' said he.

'Well then Peppino must do it before he comes on. We will have movement in this tableau; I think that will be quite a new idea. Peppino shall come in – just two steps – when he has turned the lamp up, and he will take off my shield and armour – '

'But the music will never last out,' cried Georgie. 'I shall have to start earlier.'

'Yes, perhaps that would be better,' said Lucia calmly. 'That real piece of chain armour too, I am glad I remembered Peppino had that. Marshall is cleaning it now, and it will give a far finer effect than the tawdry stuff they use in opera. Then I sit up very slowly, and wave first my right arm and then my left, and then both. I should like to practise that now on the sofa!'

Lucia had just lain down, when the telephone sounded again and Georgie got up.

'That's to announce a dividend,' he said, and tripped into the hall.

'Is that Mrs Lucas's?' said a voice he knew.

'Yes, Miss Olga,' he said, 'and this is me.'

'Oh, Mr Georgie, how fortunate,' she said. 'You can give my message now to Mrs Lucas, can't you? I'm a perfect fool, you know, and horribly forgetful.'

'What's the matter?' asked Georgie faintly.

'It's about Saturday. I've just remembered that Georgie and I – not you, you know – are going away for the weekend. Will you tell Mrs Lucas how sorry I am?'

Georgie went back to the music room, where Lucia had just got both her arms waving. But at the sight of his face she dropped them and took a firm hold of herself.

'Well, what is it?' she said.

Georgie gave the message, and she got off the sofa, rising to her feet, while her mind rose to the occasion.

'I am sorry that Miss Bracely will not see our tableaux,' she said.

'But as she was not acting in them I do not know that it makes much difference.'

A deadly flatness, although Olga's absence made no difference, descended on the three. Lucia did not resume her arm work, for after all these years her acting might be supposed to be good enough for Riseholme without farther practice, and nothing more was heard of the borrowing of the axe from the Ambermere Arms. But having begun to thread her pearl beads, she finished them; Georgie, however, cared no longer whether the gold border of King Cophetua's mantle went quite round the back or not, and having tacked on the piece he was working at, rolled it up. It was just going to be an ordinary party, after all. His cup was empty.

But Lucia's was not yet quite full, for at this moment Miss Lyall's pony hip bath stopped at the gate, and a small stableboy presented a note, which required an answer. In spite of all Lucia's self-control, the immediate answer it got was a flush of heightened colour.

'Mere impertinence,' she said. 'I will read it aloud.'

'Dear Mrs Lucas – I was in Riseholme this morning, and learn from Mrs Weston that Miss Bracely will be at your house on Saturday night. So I shall be enchanted to come to dinner after all. You must know that I make a rule of not going out in the evening, except for some special reason, but it would be a great pleasure to hear her sing again. I wonder if you would have dinner at 7.30 instead of 8, as I do not like being out very late.'

There was a short pause.

'*Caro,*' said Lucia, trembling violently, 'perhaps you would kindly tell Miss Lyall that I do not expect Miss Bracely on Saturday, and that I do not expect Lady Ambermere either.'

'My dear – ' he began.

'I will do it myself then,' she said.

*   *   *

It was as Georgie walked home after the delivery of this message that he wanted to fly away and be at rest with Foljambe and Dicky.

He had been frantically excited ever since Sunday at the idea of doing tableaux before Olga, and today in especial had been a mere feverish hash of telephoning and sewing which all ended in nothing at all, for neither tableaux nor romps seemed to hold the least attraction for him now that Olga was not going to be there. And then all at once it dawned on him that he must be in love with Olga, for why else should her presence or absence make such an astounding difference to him? He stopped dead opposite Mrs Quantock's mulberry tree.

'More misery! More unhappiness!' he said to himself. Really if life at Riseholme was to become a series of agitated days ending in devastating discoveries, the sooner he went away with Foljambe and Dicky the better. He did not quite know what it was like to be in love, for the nearest he had previously ever got to it was when he saw Olga awake on the mountain top and felt that he had missed his vocation in not being Siegfried, but from that he guessed. This time, too, it was about Olga, not about her as framed in the romance of legend and song, but of her as she appeared at Riseholme, taking as she did now, an ecstatic interest in the affairs of the place. So short a time ago, when she contemplated coming here first, she had spoken of it as a lazy backwater. Now she knew better than that, for she could listen to Mrs Weston far longer than anybody else, and ask for more histories when even she had run dry. And yet Lucia seemed hardly to interest her at all. Georgie wondered why that was.

He raised his eyes as he muttered these desolated syllables and there was Olga just letting herself out of the front garden of Old Place. Georgie's first impulse was to affect not to see her, and turn into his bachelor house, but she had certainly seen him, and made so shrill and piercing a whistle on her fingers that, pretend as he would not to have seen her, it was ludicrous to appear not to have heard her. She beckoned to him.

'Georgie, the most awful thing has happened,' she said, as they came within speaking distance. 'Oh, I called you Georgie by mistake then. When one once does that, one must go on doing it on purpose. Guess!' she said in the best Riseholme manner.

'You can come to Lucia's party after all,' said he.

'No, I can't. Well, you'll never guess because you move in such high circles, so I'll tell you. Mrs Weston's Elizabeth is going to be married to Colonel Boucher's Atkinson. I don't know his Christian name, nor her surname, but they're the ones!'

'You don't say so!' said Georgie, stung for a moment out of his own troubles. 'But will they both leave? What will either of the others do? Mrs Weston can't have a manservant, and how on earth is she to get on without Elizabeth? Besides – '

A faint flush mounted to his cheek.

'I know. You meant babies,' said Olga ruthlessly. 'Didn't you?'

'Yes,' said Georgie.

'Then why not say so? You and I were babies once, though no one is old enough to remember that, and we shouldn't have liked our parents and friends to have blushed when they mentioned us. Georgie, you are a prude.'

'No, I'm not,' said Georgie, remembering he was probably in love with a married woman.

'It doesn't matter whether you are or not. Now there's only one thing that can happen to Mrs Weston and the Colonel. They must marry each other too. Then Atkinson can continue to be Colonel Boucher's man and Elizabeth the parlour maid, unless she is busy with what made you blush. Then they can get help in; you will lend them Foljambe, for instance. It's time you began to be of some good in your wicked selfish life. So that's settled. It only remains for us to make them marry each other.'

'Aren't you getting on rather fast?' asked Georgie.

'I'm not getting on at all at present, I'm only talking. Come into my house instantly, and we'll drink vermouth. Vermouth always makes me brilliant unless it makes me idiotic, but we'll hope for the best.'

Presently they were seated in Olga's music room, with a bottle of vermouth between them.

'Now drink fair, Georgie,' she said, 'and as you drink tell me all about the young people's emotional history.'

'Atkinson and Elizabeth?' asked Georgie.

'No, my dear; Colonel Boucher and Mrs Weston. They have an emotional history. I am sure you all thought they were going to marry each other once. And they constantly dine together tête-à-tête. Now that's a very good start. Are you quite sure he hasn't got a wife and family in Egypt, or she a husband and family somewhere else? I don't want to rake up family skeletons.'

'I've never heard of them,' said Georgie.

'Then we'll take them as non-existent. You certainly would have heard of them if there were any, and very likely if there weren't. And they both like eating, drinking and the latest intelligence. Don't they?'

'Yes. But – '

'But what? What more do you or they want? Isn't that a better start for married life than many people get?'

'But aren't they rather old?' asked Georgie.

'Not much older than you and me, and if it wasn't that I've got my own Georgie, I would soon have somebody else's. Do you know who I mean?'

'No!' said Georgie firmly. Though all this came at the end of a most harrowing day, it or the vermouth exhilarated him.

'Then I'll tell you just what Mrs Weston told me. "He's always been devoted to Lucia," said Mrs Weston, "and he has never looked at anybody else. There was Piggy Antrobus – " Now do you know who I mean?'

Georgie suddenly giggled.

'Yes,' he said.

'Then don't talk about yourself so much, my dear, and let us get to the point. Now this afternoon I dropped in to see Mrs Weston and as she was telling me about the tragedy, she said by accident (just as I called you Georgie just now by accident) "And I don't know what Jacob will do without Atkinson." Now is or is not Colonel Boucher's name Jacob? There you are then! That's one side of the question. She called him Jacob by accident and so she'll call him Jacob on purpose before very long.'

Olga nodded her head up and down in precise reproduction of Mrs Weston.

'I'd hardly got out of the house,' she said in exact imitation of Mrs Weston's voice, 'before I met Colonel Boucher. It would have been about three o'clock – no it couldn't have been three, because I had got back home and was standing in the hall when it struck three, and my clock's a shade fast if anything. Well; Colonel Boucher said to me, "Haw, hum, quite a domestic crisis, by Jove."

And so I pretended I didn't know, and he told me all about it. So I said, "Well, it is a domestic crisis, and you'll lose Atkinson." "Haw, hum," said he, "and poor Jane, I should say, Mrs Weston, will lose Elizabeth." There!'

She got up and lit a cigarette.

'Oh, Georgie, do you grasp the inwardness of that?' she said. 'Their dear old hearts were laid bare by the trouble that had come upon them, and each of them spoke of the other, as each felt for the other. Probably neither of them had said Jacob or Jane in the whole course of their lives. But the Angel of the Lord descended and troubled the waters. If you think that's profane, have some more vermouth. It's making me brilliant, though you wouldn't have thought it. Now listen!'

She sat down again close to him, her face brimming with a humorous enthusiasm. Humour in Riseholme was apt to be a little unkind; if you mentioned the absurdities of your friends, there was just a speck of malice in your wit. But with her there was none of that; she gave an imitation of Mrs Weston with the most ruthless fidelity, and yet it was kindly to the bottom. She liked her for talking in that emphatic voice and being so particular as to what time it was. 'Now first of all you are coming to dine with me tonight,' said Olga.

'Oh, I'm afraid that tonight – ' began Georgie, shrinking from any further complications. He really must have a quiet evening, and go to bed very early.

'What are you afraid of tonight?' she asked. 'You're only going to wash your hair. You can do that tomorrow. So you and I, that's two, and Mrs Weston and Colonel Jacob, that's four, which is enough, and I don't believe there's anything to eat in the house. But there's something to drink, which is my point. Not for you and me, mind; we've got to keep our heads and be clever. Don't have any more vermouth. But Jane and Jacob are going to have quantities of champagne. Not tipsy, you, understand, but at their best, and unguardedly appreciative of each other and us. And when they go away, they will exchange a chaste kiss at Mrs Weston's door, and she will ask him in. No! I think she'll ask him in first. And when they wake up tomorrow morning, they will both wonder how they could possibly, and jointly ask themselves what everybody else will say. And then they'll thank God and Olga and Georgie that they did, and live happily for an extraordinary number of years. My dear, how infinitely happier they will be together than they are being now. Funny old dears! Each at its own fireside, saying that it's too old, bless them! And you and I will sing "Voice that breathed o'er Eden" and in the middle our angel voices will crack, and we will sob into our handkerchief, and Eden will be left breathing deeply all by itself like the guru. Why did you never tell me about the guru? Mrs Weston's a better friend to me than you are, and I must ring for my cook – no I'll telephone first to Jacob and Jane – and see what there is to eat afterwards. You will sit here quietly, and when I have finished I will tell you what your part is.'

During dinner, according to Olga's plan of campaign, the conversation was to be general, because she hated to have two conversations going on when only four people were present, since she found that she always wanted to join in the other one. This was the main principle she inculcated on Georgie, stamping it on his memory by a simile of peculiar vividness. 'Imagine there is an Elizabethan spittoon in the middle of the table,' she said, 'and keep on firmly spitting into it. I want you when there's any pause to spit about two things, one, how dreadfully unhappy both Jacob and Jane will be without their paragons, the other, how pleasant is conversation and companionship. I shall be chaffing you, mind, all the time and saying *you* must get married. After dinner I shall probably stroll in the garden with Jacob. Don't come! Keep him after dinner for some little time, for then's my opportunity of talking to Jane, and give him at least three glasses of port. Gracious, it's time to dress, and the Lord prosper us.'

Georgie found himself the last to arrive, when he got back to Olga's, and all three of them shook hands rather as people shake hands before a funeral. They went into dinner at once and Olga instantly began. 'How many years did you say your admirable Atkinson had been with you?' she asked Colonel Boucher.

'Twenty; getting on for twenty-one,' said he. 'Great nuisance; 'pon my word it's worse than a nuisance.'

Georgie had a bright idea.

'But what's a nuisance, Colonel?' he asked.

'Eh, haven't you heard? I thought it would have been all over the place by now. Atkinson's going to be married.'

'No!' said Georgie. 'Whom to?'

Mrs Weston could not bear not to announce this herself. 'To my Elizabeth,' she said. 'Elizabeth came to me this morning. "May I speak to you a minute, ma'am?" she asked, and I thought nothing more than that perhaps she had broken a teacup. "Yes," said I quite cheerfully, "and what have you come to tell me?"'

It was getting almost too tragic and Olga broke in.

'Let's try to forget all about it, for an hour or two,' she said. 'It was nice of you all to take pity on me and come and have dinner, otherwise I should have been quite alone. If there's one thing I cannot bear it's being alone in the evening. And to think that anybody chooses to be alone when he needn't! Look at that wretch there,' and she pointed to Georgie, 'who lives all by himself instead of marrying. Liking to be alone is the worst habit I know; much worse than drink.'

'Now do leave me alone,' said Georgie.

'I won't, my dear, and when dinner is over Mrs Weston and I are going to put our heads together, and when you come out we shall announce to you the name of your bride. I should put a tax of twenty shillings on the pound on all bachelors; they should all marry or starve.'

Suddenly she turned to Colonel Boucher.

'Oh, Colonel,' she said. 'What have I been saying? How dreadfully stupid of me not to remember that you were a bachelor too. But I wouldn't have you starve for anything. Have some more fish instantly to show you forgive me. Georgie, change the subject – you're always talking about yourself.'

Georgie turned with admirable docility to Mrs Weston.

'It's too miserable for you,' he said. 'How will you get on without Elizabeth? How long has she been with you?'

Mrs Weston went straight back to where she had left off.

'So I said, "What have you come to tell me?" quite cheerfully, thinking it was a teacup. And she said, "I'm going to be married, ma'am," and she blushed so prettily that you'd have thought she was a girl of twenty, though she was seventeen when she came to me – no, she was just eighteen, and that's fifteen years ago, and that makes her thirty-three. "Well, Elizabeth," I said, "you haven't told me yet who it is, but whether it's the Archbishop of Canterbury or the Prince of Wales – for I felt I had to make a little joke like that – I hope you'll make him as happy as you've made me all these years."'

'You old darling,' said Olga. 'I should have gone into hysterics, and forbade the banns.'

'No, Miss Bracely, you wouldn't,' said Mrs Weston, 'you'd have been just as thankful as me, that she'd got a good husband to take care of and to be taken care of by, because then she said, "Lor ma'am, it's none of they – not them great folks. It's the Colonel's Atkinson." You ask the Colonel for Atkinson's character, Miss Bracely, and then you'd be just as thankful as I was.'

'The Colonel's Atkinson is a slow coach, just like Georgie,' said Olga. 'He and Elizabeth have been living side by side all these years, and why couldn't the man make up his mind before? The only redeeming circumstance is that he has done it now. Our poor Georgie now – '

'Now you're going to be rude to Colonel Boucher again,' said Georgie. 'Colonel, we've been asked here to be insulted.'

Colonel Boucher had nothing stronger than a mild tolerance for Georgie and rather enjoyed snubbing him.

'Well, if you call a glass of wine and a dinner like this an insult,' he said, ''pon my word I don't know what you'd call a compliment.'

'I know what I call a compliment,' said Olga, 'and that's your all coming to dine with me at such short notice. About Georgie's approaching nuptials now – '

'You're too tarsome,' said he. 'If you go on like that, I shan't ask you to the wedding. Let's talk about Elizabeth's. When are they going to get married, Mrs Weston?'

'That's what I said to Elizabeth. "Get an almanack, Elizabeth," said I, "so that you won't choose a Sunday. Don't say the twentieth of next month without looking it out. But if the twentieth isn't a Sunday or a Friday mind, for though I don't believe in such things, still you never know – " There was Mrs Antrobus now,' said Mrs Weston suddenly, putting in a footnote to her speech to Elizabeth, 'it was on a Friday she married, and within a year she got as deaf as you see her now. Then Mr Weston's uncle, his uncle by marriage I should say, he was another Friday marriage and they missed their train when going off on their honeymoon, and had to stay all night where they were without a sponge or a toothbrush between them, for all their luggage was in the train being whirled away to Torquay. "So make it the twentieth, Elizabeth," I said, "if it isn't a Friday or a Sunday, and I shall have time to look round me, and so will the Colonel, though I don't expect that either of us will find your equals! And don't cry, Elizabeth," I said, for she was getting quite watery, "for if you cry about a marriage, what'll be left for a funeral?"'

'Ha! Upon my word, I call that splendid of you,' said the Colonel. 'I told Atkinson I wished I had never set eyes on him, before I wished him joy.'

Olga got up.

'Look after Colonel Boucher, Georgie,' she said, 'and ring for anything you want. Look at the moon! Isn't it heavenly. How Atkinson and Elizabeth must be enjoying it.'

The two men spent a half-hour of only moderately enjoyable conversation, for Georgie kept the grindstone of the misery of his lot without Atkinson, and the pleasure of companionship, firmly to the Colonel's nose. It was no use for him to attempt to change the subject to the approaching tableaux, to a vague rumour that Piggy had fallen face downwards in the ducking pond, that Mrs Quantock and her husband had turned a table this afternoon with remarkable results, for it had tapped out that his name was Robert and hers Daisy. Whichever way he turned, Georgie herded him back on to the stony path that he had been bidden to take, with the result that when Georgie finally permitted him to go into the music room, he was a-thirst for the more genial companionship of the ladies. Olga got up as they entered.

'Georgie's so lazy,' she said, 'that it's no use asking him. But do let you and me have a turn up and down my garden, Colonel. There's a divine moon and it's quite warm.'

They stepped out into the windless night.

'Fancy its being October,' she said. 'I don't believe there is any winter in Riseholme, nor autumn either, for that matter. You are all so young, so deliciously young. Look at Georgie in there: he's like a boy still, and as for Mrs Weston, she's twenty-five: not a day older.'

'Yes, wonderful woman,' said he. 'Always agreeable and lively.

Handsome, too: I consider Mrs Weston a very handsome woman. Hasn't altered an atom since I knew her.'

'That's the wonderful thing about you all!' said she. 'You are all just as brisk and young as you were ten years ago. It's ridiculous. As for you, I'm not sure that you're not the most ridiculous of the lot. I feel as if I had been having dinner with three delightful cousins a little younger – not much, but just a little – than myself. Gracious! How you all made me romp the other night here. What a pace you go, Colonel! What's your walking like if you call this a stroll?'

Colonel Boucher moderated his pace. He thought Olga had been walking so quickly.

'I'm very sorry,' he said. 'Certainly Riseholme is a healthy bracing place. Perhaps we do keep our youth pretty well. God bless me, but the days go by without one's noticing them. To think that I came here with Atkinson close on ten years ago.'

This did very well for Olga: she swiftly switched off on to it.

'It's quite horrid for you losing your servant,' she said. 'Servants do become friends, don't they, especially to anyone living alone. Georgie and Foljambe, now! But I shouldn't be a bit surprised if Foljambe had a mistress before very long.'

'No, really? I thought you were just chaffing him at dinner. Georgie marrying, is he? His wife'll take some of his needlework off his hands. May I – ah – may I enquire the lady's name?'

Olga decided to play a great card. She had just found it, so to speak, in her hand, and it was most tempting. She stopped.

'But can't you guess?' she said. 'Surely I'm not absolutely on the wrong track?'

'Ah, Miss Antrobus,' said he. 'The one I think they call Piggy. No, I should say there was nothing in that.'

'Oh, that had never occurred to me,' said she. 'I dare say I'm quite wrong. I only judged from what I thought I noticed in poor Georgie. I dare say it's only what he should have done ten years ago, but I fancy there's a spark alive still. Let us talk about something else, though we won't go in quite yet, shall we?' She felt quite safe in her apparent reluctance to tell him; the Riseholme gluttony for news made it imperative for him to ask more.

'Really, I must be very dull,' he said. 'I dare say an eye new to the place sees more. Who is it, Miss Bracely?'

She laughed.

'Ah, how bad a man is at observing a man!' she said. 'Didn't you see Georgie at dinner? He hardly took his eyes off her.'

She had a great and glorious reward. Colonel Boucher's face grew absolutely blank in the moonlight with sheer astonishment.

'Well, you surprise me,' he said. 'Surely a fine woman, though lame, wouldn't look at a needlewoman – well, leave it at that.'

He stamped his feet and put his hands in his pockets.

'It's growing a bit chilly,' he said. 'You'll be catching cold, Miss Bracely, and what will your husband say if he finds out I've been strolling about with you out of doors after dinner?'

'Yes, we'll go in,' she said. 'It is chilly. How thoughtful you are for me.'

Georgie, little knowing the cat's paw that had been made of him, found himself being detached from Mrs Weston by the Colonel, and this suited him very well, for presently Olga said she would sing, unless anybody minded, and called on him to accompany her. She stood just behind him, leaning over him sometimes with a hand on his shoulder, and sang three ruthless simple English songs, appropriate to the matter in hand. She sang, 'I Attempt from Love's Sickness to Fly', and 'Sally in Our Alley', and 'Come Live with Me', and sometimes beneath the rustle of leaves turned over she whispered to him. 'Georgie, I'm cleverer than anybody ever was, and I shall die in the night,' she said once. Again more enigmatically she said, 'I've been a cad, but I'll tell you about it when they've gone. Stop behind.' And then some whisky came in, and she insisted on the 'young people' having some of that; finally she saw them off at the door, and came running back to Georgie. 'I've been a cad,' she said, 'because I hinted that you were in love with Mrs Weston. My dear, it was simply perfect! I believe it to have been the last straw, and if you don't forgive me you needn't. Wasn't it clever? He simply couldn't stand that, for it came on the top of your being so young.'

'Well, really – ' said Georgie.

'I know. And I must be a cad again. I'm going up to my bedroom; you may come, too, if you like, because it commands a view of Church Road. I shouldn't sleep a wink unless I knew that he had gone in with her. It'll be precisely like Faust and Marguerite going into the house, and you and I are Mephistopheles and Martha. Come quick!'

From the dark of the window they watched Mrs Weston's bath chair being pushed up the lit road.

'It's the Colonel pushing it,' whispered Olga, squeezing him into a corner of the window. 'Look! There's Tommy Luton on the path. Now they've stopped at her gate . . . I can't bear the suspense . . . Oh, Georgie, they've gone in! And Atkinson will stop, and so will Elizabeth, and you've promised to lend them Foljambe. Which house will they live at, do you think? Aren't you happy?'

CHAPTER TWELVE

The miserable Lucia started a run of extreme bad luck about this time, of which the adventure or misadventure of the guru seemed to be the prelude, or perhaps the news of her want of recognition of the August moon, which Georgie had so carefully saluted, may have arrived at that satellite by October. For she had simply 'cut' the August moon . . .

There was the fiasco about Olga coming to the tableaux, which was the cause of her sending that very tart reply, via Miss Lyall, to Lady Ambermere's impertinence, and the very next morning, Lady Ambermere, coming again into Riseholme, perhaps for that very purpose, had behaved to Lucia as Lucia had behaved to the moon, and cut her. That was irritating, but the counter-irritant to it had been that Lady Ambermere had then gone to Olga's, and been told that she was not at home, though she was very audibly practising in her music room at the time. Upon which Lady Ambermere had said 'Home' to her people, and got in with such unconcern of the material world that she sat down on Pug.

Mrs Quantock had heard both 'Home' and Pug, and told the cut Lucia, who was a hundred yards away, about it. She also told her about the engagement of Atkinson and Elizabeth, which was all she knew about events in those houses. On which Lucia with a kind smile had said, 'Dear Daisy, what slaves some people are to their servants. I am sure Mrs Weston and Colonel Boucher will be quite miserable, poor things. Now I must run home. How I wish I could stop and chat on the green!' And she gave her silvery laugh, for she felt much better now that she knew Olga had said she was out to Lady Ambermere, when she was so audibly in.

Then came a second piece of bad luck. Lucia had not gone more than a hundred yards past Georgie's house, when he came out in a tremendous hurry. He rapidly measured the distance between himself and Lucia, and himself and Mrs Quantock, and made a beeline for Mrs Quantock, since she was the nearest. Olga had just telephoned to him . . .

'Good morning,' he said breathlessly, determined to cap anything she said. 'Any news?'

'Yes, indeed,' she said. 'Haven't you heard?'

Georgie had one moment of heart-sink.

'What?' he said.

'Atkinson and Eliz – ' she began.

'Oh, that,' said he scornfully. 'And talking of them, of course you've heard the rest. *Haven't* you? Why, Mrs Weston and Colonel Boucher are going to follow their example, unless they set it themselves, and get married first.'

'No!' said Mrs Quantock in the loudest possible Riseholme voice of surprise.

'Oh, yes. I really knew it last night. I was dining at Old Place and they were there. Olga and I both settled there would be something to talk in the morning. Shall we stroll on the green a few minutes?'

Georgie had a lovely time. He hurried from person to person, leaving Mrs Quantock to pick up a few further gleanings. Everyone was there except Lucia, and she, but for the accident of her being further off than Mrs Quantock, would have been the first to know.

When this tour was finished Georgie sat to enjoy the warm comforting glow of envy that surrounded him. Nowadays the meeting place at the green had insensibly transferred itself to just opposite Old Place, and it was extremely interesting to hear Olga practising as she always did in the morning. Interesting though it was, Riseholme had at first been a little disappointed about it, for everyone had thought that she would sing Brünnhilde's part or Salome's part through every day, or some trifle of that kind. Instead she would perform an upwards scale in gradual *crescendo*, and on the highest most magnificent note would enunciate at the top of her voice, 'Yawning York!' Then starting soft again she would descend in *crescendo* to a superb low note and enunciate 'Love's Lilies Lonely'. Then after a dozen repetitions of this, she would start off with full voice, and get softer and softer until she just whispered that York was yawning, and do the same with Love's

Lilies. But you never could tell what she might not sing, and some mornings there would be long trills and leapings on to high notes, long notes and leaping on to trills, and occasionally she sang a real song. That was worth waiting for, and Georgie did not hesitate to let drop that she had sung four last night to his accompaniment. And hardly had he repeated that the third time, when she appeared at her window, and before all Riseholme called out 'Georgie!' with a trill at the end, like a bird shaking its wings. Before all Riseholme!

So in he went. Had Lucia known that, it would quite have wiped the gilt off Lady Ambermere's being refused admittance. In point of fact it did wipe the gilt off when, about an hour afterwards, Georgie went to lunch, because he told her. And if there had been any gilt left about anywhere, that would have vanished, too, when in answer to some rather damaging remark she made about poor Daisy's interests in the love affairs of other people's servants, she learned that it was of the love affairs of their superiors that all Riseholme had been talking for at least an hour by now.

Again there was ill-luck about the tableaux on Saturday, for in the Brünnhilde scene, Peppino in his agitation turned the lamp that was to be a sunrise completely out, and Brünnhilde had to hail the midnight, or at any rate a very obscure twilight. Georgie, it is true, with wonderful presence of mind, turned on an electric light when he had finished playing, but it was more like a flash of lightning than a slow, wonderful dawn. The tableaux were over well before 10.45, and though Lucia, in answer to the usual pressings, said she would 'see about' doing them again, she felt that Mrs Weston and Colonel Boucher, who made their first public appearance as the happy pair, attracted more than their proper share of attention. The only consolation was that the romps that followed at poor Daisy's were a complete fiasco. It was in vain, too, at supper, that she went from table to table, and helped people to lobster salad and champagne, and had not enough chairs, and generally imitated all that had apparently made Olga's party so supreme a success. But on this occasion the recipe for the dish and not the dish itself was served up, and the hunting of the slipper produced no exhilaration in the chase . . .

But far more untoward events followed. Olga came back on the next Monday, and immediately after Lucia received a card for an evening 'At Home', with 'Music' in the bottom left-hand corner. It happened to be wet that afternoon, and seeing Olga's shut motor coming from the station with four men inside, she leaped to the conclusion that these were four musicians for the music. A second motor followed with luggage, and she quite distinctly saw the unmistakable shape of a cello against the window. After that no more guessing was necessary, for it was clear that poor Olga had hired the awful string quartet from Brinton, that played in the lounge at the Royal Hotel after dinner. The Brinton string quartet! She had heard them once at a distance and that was quite enough. Lucia shuddered as she thought of those doleful fiddlers. It was indeed strange that Olga, with all the opportunities she had had for hearing good music, should hire the Brinton string quartet, but, after all, that was entirely of a piece with her views about the gramophone. Perhaps the gramophone would have its share in this musical evening. But she had said she would go: it would be very unkind to Olga to stop away now, for Olga must know by this time her passion for music, so she went. She sincerely hoped that she would not be conducted to the seat of honour, and be obliged to say a few encouraging words to the string quartet afterwards.

Once again she came rather late, for the music had begun. It had only just begun, for she recognized – who should recognize if not she? – the early bars of a Beethoven quartet. She laid her hand on Peppino's arm.

'Brinton: Beethoven,' she said limply.

She slipped into a chair next to Daisy Quantock, and sat in her well-known position when listening to music, with her head forward, her chin resting on her hand, and the faraway look in her eyes. Nothing of course could wholly take away the splendour of that glorious composition, and she was pleased that there was no applause between the movements, for she had rather expected that Olga would clap, and interrupt the unity of it all. Occasionally, too, she was agreeably surprised by the Brinton string quartet: they seemed to have some inklings, though not many. Once she winced very much when a string broke.

Olga (she was rather a restless hostess) came up to her when it was over.

'So glad you could come,' she said. 'Aren't they divine?'

Lucia gave her most indulgent smile.

'Perfect music! Glorious!' she said. 'And they really played it very creditably. But I am a little spoiled, you know, for the last time I heard that it was performed by the Spanish Quartet. I know one ought never to compare, but have you ever heard the Spanish Quartet, Miss Bracely?'

Olga looked at her in surprise.

'But they are the Spanish Quartet!' she said, pointing to the players.

Lucia had raised her voice rather as she spoke, for when she spoke on music she spoke for everybody to hear. And a great many people undoubtedly did hear, among whom, of course, was Daisy Quantock. She gave one shrill squeal of laughter, like a slate pencil, and from that moment granted plenary absolution to *poor dear* Lucia for all her greed and grabbing with regard to the guru.

But instantly all Olga's good nature awoke: unwittingly (for her remark that this *was* the Spanish Quartet had been a mere surprised exclamation), she had made a guest of hers uncomfortable, and must at once do all she could to remedy that.

'It's a shocking room for echoes, this,' she said. 'Do all of you come up a little nearer, and you will be able to hear the playing so much better. You lose all shade, all fineness here. I came here on purpose to ask you to move up, Mrs Lucas: there are half a dozen chairs unoccupied near the platform.'

It was a kindly intention that prompted the speech, but for all real Riseholme practical purposes, quite barren, for many people had heard Lucia's remarks, and Peppino also had already been wincing at the Brinton quartet. In that fell moment the Bolshevists laid bony fingers on the sceptre of her musical autocracy . . . But who would have guessed that Olga would get the Spanish Quartet from London to come down to Riseholme?

Staggering from these blows, she had to undergo an even shrewder stroke yet. Already, in the intelligence department, she had been sadly behindhand in news, her tableaux party had been anything but a success, this one little remark of Olga's had shaken her musically, but at any rate up till this moment she had shown herself mistress of the Italian tongue, while to strengthen that she was being very diligent with her dictionary, grammar and Dante's *Paradiso*. Then as by a bolt out of a clear sky that temple, too, was completely demolished, in the most tragic fashion.

* * *

A few days after the disaster of the Spanish-Brinton Quartet, Olga received a letter from Signor Cortese, the eminent Italian composer, to herald the completion of his opera, *Lucretia*. Might he come down to Riseholme for a couple of nights, and, figuratively, lay it at her feet, in the hope that she would raise it up, and usher it into the world? All the time he had been writing it, as she knew, he had thought of her in the name part and he would come down today, tomorrow, at a moment's notice by day or night to submit it to her. Olga was delighted and sent an effusive telegram of many sheets, full of congratulation and welcome, for she wanted above all things to 'create' the part. So would Signor Cortese come down that very day?

She ran upstairs with the news to her husband.

'My dear, *Lucretia* is finished,' she said, 'and that angel practically offers it me. Now what are we to do about dinner tonight? Jacob and Jane are coming, and neither you nor they, I suppose, speak one word of Italian, and you know what mine is, firm and intelligible and operatic but not conversational. What are we to do? He hates talking English . . . Oh, I know, if I can only get Mrs Lucas. They always talk Italian, I believe, at home. I wonder if she can come. She's musical, too, and I shall ask her husband, I think: that'll be a man over, but it will be another *Italiano* – '

Olga wrote at once to Lucia, mentioning that Cortese was staying with them, but, quite naturally, saying nothing about the usefulness of Peppino and her being able to engage the musician in his own tongue, for that she took for granted. An eager affirmative (such a great pleasure) came back to her, and for the rest of the day, Lucia and Peppino made up neat little sentences to let off to the dazzled Cortese, at the moment when they said 'good night', to show that they could have talked Italian all the time, had there been any occasion for doing so.

Mrs Weston and Colonel Boucher had already arrived when Lucia and her husband entered, and Lucia had quite a shock to see on what intimate terms they were with their hostess. They actually called each other Olga and Jacob and Jane, which was most surprising and almost painful. Lucia (perhaps because she had not known about it soon enough) had been a little satirical about the engagement, rather as if it was a slight on her that Jacob had not been content with celibacy and Jane with her friendship, but she was sure she wished them both 'nothing but well'. Indeed the moment she got over the shock of seeing them so intimate with Olga, she could not have been surpassed in cordiality.

'We see but little of our old friends now,' she said to Olga and Jane jointly, 'but we must excuse their desire for solitude in their first glow of their happiness. Peppino and I remember that sweet time, oh, ever so long ago.'

This might have been tact, or it might have been cat. That Peppino and she sympathized as they remembered their beautiful time was tact, that it was so long ago was cat. Altogether it might be described as a cat chewing tact. But there was a slight air of patronage about it, and if there was one thing Mrs Weston would not, and could not and did not even intend to stand, it was that. Besides it had reached her ears that Mrs Lucas had said something about there being no difficulty in finding bridesmaids younger than the bride.

'Fancy! How clever of you to remember so long ago,' she said. 'But, then, you have the most marvellous memory, dear, and keep it wonderfully!'

Olga intervened.

'How kind of you and Mr Lucas to come at such short notice,' she said. 'Cortese hates talking English, so I shall put him between you and me, and you'll talk to him all the time, won't you? And you won't laugh at me, will you, when I join in with my atrocious attempts? And I shall buttress myself on the other side with your husband, who will firmly talk across me to him.'

Lucia had to say something. A further exposure was at hand, quite inevitably. It was no use for her and Peppino to recollect a previous engagement.

'Oh, my Italian is terribly rusty,' she said, knowing that Mrs Weston's eye was on her . . . Why had she not sent Mrs Weston a handsome wedding present that morning?

'Rusty? We will ask Cortese about that when you've had a good talk to him. Ah, here he is!'

Cortese came into the room, florid and loquacious, pouring out a stream of apology for his lateness to Olga, none of which was the least intelligible to Lucia. She guessed what he was saying, and next moment Olga, who apparently understood him perfectly, and told him with an enviable fluency that he was not late at all, was introducing him to her, and explaining that '*la Signora*' (Lucia understood this) and her husband talked Italian. She did not need to reply to some torrent of amiable words from him, addressed to her, for he was taken on and introduced to Mrs Weston, and the Colonel. But he instantly whirled round to her again, and asked her something. Not knowing the least what he meant, she replied:

'*Si; tante grazie.*'

He looked puzzled for a moment and then repeated his question in English.

'In what deestrict of Italy 'ave you voyaged most?'

Lucia understood that: so did Mrs Weston, and Lucia pulled herself together.

'*In Roma,*' she said. '*Che bella città! Adoro Roma, ed il mio marito. Non e vero, Peppino?*'

Peppino cordially assented: the familiar ring of this fine intelligible Italian restored his confidence, and he asked Cortese whether he was not very fond of music . . .

Dinner seemed interminable to Lucia. She kept a watchful eye on Cortese, and if she saw he was about to speak to her, she turned hastily to Colonel Boucher, who sat on her other side, and asked him something about his *can cani*, which she translated to him. While he answered she made up another sentence in Italian about the blue sky or Venice, or very meanly said her husband had been there, hoping to direct the torrent of Italian eloquence to him. But she knew that, as an Italian conversationalist, neither she nor Peppino had a rag of reputation left them, and she dismally regretted that they had not chosen French, of which they both knew about as much, instead of Italian, for the vehicle of their linguistic distinction.

Olga meantime continued to understand all that Cortese said, and to reply to it with odious fluency, and at the last, Cortese having said something to her which made her laugh, he turned to Lucia.

'I've said to Meesis Shottlewort' . . . and he proceeded to explain his joke in English.

'*Molto bene,*' said Lucia with a dying flicker. '*Molto divertente. Non e vero, Peppino?*'

'*Si, si,*' said Peppino miserably.

And then the final disgrace came, and it was something of a relief to have it over. Cortese, in excellent spirits with his dinner and his wine and the prospect of Olga taking the part of Lucretia, turned beamingly to Lucia again.

'Now we will all spick English,' he said. 'This is one very pleasant evening. I enjoy me very much. *Ecco!*'

Just once more Lucia shot up into flame.

'*Parlate Inglese molto bene,*' she said, and except when Cortese spoke to Olga, there was no more Italian that night.

Even the unique excitement of hearing Olga 'try over' the great scene in the last act could not quite absorb Lucia's attention after this awful fiasco, and though she sat leaning forward with her chin in her hand, and the faraway look in her eyes, her mind was furiously busy as to how to make anything whatever out of so bad a job. Everyone present knew that her Italian, as a medium for conversation, had suffered a complete breakdown, and it was no longer any real use, when Olga did not quite catch the rhythm of a passage, to murmur '*Uno, due, tre*' unconsciously to herself; she might just as well have said 'one, two, three' for any effect it had on Mrs Weston. The story would be all over Riseholme next day, and she felt sure that Mrs Weston, that excellent observer and superb reporter, had not failed to take it all in, and would not fail to do justice to it. Blow after blow had been rained upon her palace door; it was little wonder that the whole building was a-quiver. She had thought of starting a Dante class this winter, for printed Italian, if you had a dictionary and a translation in order to prepare for the class, could be easily interpreted: it was the spoken word which you had to understand without any preparation at all, and not in the least knowing what was coming, that had presented such insurmountable difficulties. And yet who, when the story of this evening was known, would seek instruction from a teacher of that sort? Would Mrs Weston come to her Dante class? Would she? Would she? No, she would not.

*   *   *

Lucia lay long awake that night, tossing and turning in her bed in that delightful apartment in 'Midsummer Night's Dream', and reviewing the fell array of these unlucky affairs. As she eyed them, black shapes against the glow of her firelight, it struck her that the same malevolent influence inspired them all. For what had caused the failure and flatness of her tableaux (omitting the unfortunate incident about the lamp) but the absence of Olga? Who was it who had occasioned her unfortunate remark about the Spanish Quartet but Olga, whose clear duty it had been, when she sent the invitation for the musical party, to state (so that there could be no mistake about it) that those eminent performers were to entrance them? Who could have guessed that she would have gone to the staggering expense of having them down from London? The Brinton Quartet was the utmost that any sane imagination could have pictured, and Lucia's extremely sane imagination had pictured just that, with such extreme vividness that it had never occurred to her that it could be anybody else. Certainly Olga should have put 'Spanish Quartet' in the bottom left-hand corner instead of 'Music' and then Lucia would have known all about it, and have been speechless with emotion when they had finished the Beethoven, and wiped her eyes, and pulled herself together again. It really looked as if Olga had laid a trap for her . . .

Even more like a trap were the horrid events of this evening. Trap was not at all too strong a word for them. To ask her to the house, and then suddenly spring upon her the fact that she was expected to talk Italian . . . Was that an open, an honourable proceeding? What if Lucia had actually told Olga (and she seemed to recollect it) that she and Peppino often talked Italian at home? That was no reason why she should be expected, offhand like that, to talk Italian anywhere else. She should have been told what was expected of her, so as to give her the chance of having a previous engagement. Lucia hated underhand ways, and they were particularly odious in one whom she had been willing to educate and refine up to the highest standards of Riseholme. Indeed it looked as if Olga's nature was actually incapable of receiving cultivation. She went on her own rough independent lines, giving a romp one night, and not coming to the tableaux on another, and getting the Spanish Quartet without consultation on a third, and springing this dreadful Pentecostal party on them on a fourth. Olga clearly meant mischief: she wanted to set herself up as leader of Art and Culture in Riseholme. Her conduct admitted of no other explanation.

Lucia's benevolent scheme of educating and refining vanished like morning mists, and through her drooping eyelids, the firelight seemed strangely red . . . She had been too kind, too encouraging: now she must collect her forces round her and be stern. As she dozed off to sleep, she reminded herself to ask Georgie to lunch next day. He and Peppino and she must have a serious talk. She had seen Georgie comparatively little just lately, and she drowsily and uneasily wondered how that was.

* * *

Georgie by this time had quite got over the desolation of the moment when standing in the road opposite Mrs Quantock's mulberry tree he had given vent to that bitter cry of 'More misery! more unhappiness!' His nerves on that occasion had been worn to fiddlestrings with all the fuss and fiasco of planning the tableaux, and thus fancying himself in love had been just the last straw. But the fact that he had been Olga's chosen confidant in her wonderful scheme of causing Mrs Weston and the Colonel to get engaged, and the distinction of being singled out by Olga to this friendly intimacy, had proved a great tonic. It was quite clear that the existence of Mr Shuttleworth constituted a hopeless bar to the fruition of his passion, and, if he was completely honest with himself, he was aware that he did not really hate Mr Shuttleworth for standing in his path. Georgie was gentle in all his ways, and his manner of falling in love was very gentle, too. He admired Olga immensely, he found her stimulating and amusing, and since it was out of the question really to be her lover, he would have enjoyed, next best to that, being her brother, and such little pangs of jealousy as he might experience from time to time, were rather in the nature of small electric shocks voluntarily received. He was devoted to her with a warmth that his supposed devotion to Lucia had never kindled in him; he even went so far as to dream about her in an agitated though respectful manner. Without being conscious of any unreality about his sentiments, he really wanted to dress up as a lover rather than to be one, for he could form no notion at present of what it felt to be absorbed in anyone else. Life was so full as it was: there really was no room for anything else, especially if that something else must be of the quality which rendered everything else colourless.

This state of mind, this quality of emotion was wholly pleasurable and quite exciting, and instead of crying out 'More misery! more unhappiness!' he could now, as he passed the mulberry, say to himself 'More pleasures! more happiness!'

Yet as he ran down the road to lunch with Lucia he was conscious that she was likely to stand, an angel perhaps, but certainly one with a flaming sword, between him and all the interests of the new life which was undoubtedly beginning to bubble in Riseholme, and to which Georgie found it so pleasant to take his little mug, and have it filled with exhilarating liquid. And if Lucia proved to be standing in his path, forbidding his approach, he, too, was armed for combat, with a revolutionary weapon, consisting of a rolled-up copy of some of Debussy's music for the piano – Olga had lent it him a few days ago – and he had been very busy over 'Poissons d'or'. He was further armed by the complete knowledge of the Italian débâcle of last night, which, from his knowledge of Lucia, he judged must constitute a crisis. Something would have to happen . . . Several times lately Olga had, so to speak, run full tilt into Lucia, and had passed on leaving a staggering form behind her. And in each case, so Georgie clearly perceived, Olga had not intended to butt into or stagger anybody. Each time, she had knocked Lucia down purely by accident, but if these accidents occurred with such awful frequency, it was to be expected that Lucia would find another name for them: they would have to be re-christened. With all his Riseholme appetite for complications and events Georgie guessed that he was not likely to go empty away from this lunch. In addition there were other topics of extraordinary interest, for really there had been very odd experiences at Mrs Quantock's last night, when the Italian débâcle was going on, a little way up the road. But he was not going to bring that out at once.

Lucia hailed him with her most cordial manner, and with a superb effrontery began to talk Italian just as usual, though she must have guessed that Georgie knew all about last night.

'*Bon arrivato, amico mio*,' she said. 'Why, it must be three days since we met. *Che ha fatto il signorino?* And what have you got there?'

Georgie, having escaped being caught over Italian, had made up his mind not to talk any more ever.

'Oh, they are some little things by Debussy,' he said. 'I want to play one of them to you afterwards. I've just been glancing through it.'

'*Bene, molto bene!*' said she. 'Come in to lunch. But I can't promise to like it, Georgino. Isn't Debussy the man who always makes me want to howl like a dog at the sound of the gong? Where did you get these from?'

'Olga lent me them,' said Georgie negligently. He really did call her Olga to her face now, by request.

Lucia's bugles began to sound.

'Yes, I should think Miss Bracely would admire that sort of music,' she said. 'I suppose I am too old-fashioned, though I will not condemn your little pieces of Debussy before I have heard them. Old-fashioned! Yes! I was certainly too old-fashioned for the music she gave us last night. *Dio mio!*'

'Oh, didn't you enjoy it?' asked he.

Lucia sat down, without waiting for Peppino.

'Poor Miss Bracely!' she said. 'It was very kind of her in intention to ask me, but she would have been kinder to have asked Mrs Antrobus instead, and have told her not to bring her ear trumpet. To hear that lovely voice, for I do her justice, and there are lovely notes in her voice, *lovely*, to hear that voice shrieking and screaming away, in what she called the great scene, was simply pitiful. There was no melody, and above all there was no form. A musical composition is like an architectural building; it must be built up and constructed. How often have I said that! You must have colour, and you must have line, otherwise I cannot concede you the right to say you have music.'

Lucia finished her egg in a hurry, and put her elbows on the table.

'I hope I am not hidebound and limited,' she said, 'and I think you will acknowledge, Georgie, that I am not. Even in the divinest music of all, I am not blind to defects, if there are defects. The "Moonlight Sonata", for instance. You have often heard me say that the two last movements do not approach the first in perfection of form. And if I am permitted to criticize Beethoven, I hope I may be allowed to suggest that Mr Cortese has not produced an opera which will render *Fidelio* ridiculous. But really I am chiefly sorry for Miss Bracely. I should have thought it worth her while to render herself not unworthy to interpret *Fidelio*, whatever time and trouble that cost her, rather than to seek notoriety by helping to foist on to the world a fresh combination of engine whistles and grunts. *Non e vero*, Peppino? How late you are.'

Lucia had not determined on this declaration of war without anxious consideration. But it was quite obvious to her that the enemy was daily gaining strength, and therefore the sooner she came to open hostilities the better, for it was equally obvious to her mind that Olga was a pretender to the throne she had occupied for so long. It was time to mobilize, and she had first to state her views and her plan of campaign to the chief of her staff.

'No, we did not quite like our evening, Peppino and I, did we, *caro*?' she went on. 'And Mr Cortese! His appearance! He is like a huge hairdresser. His touch on the piano: if you can imagine a wild bull butting at the keys, you will have some idea of it. And above all, his Italian! I gathered that he was a Neapolitan, and we all know what Neapolitan dialect is like. Tuscans and Romans, who between them, I believe – *lingua Toscano in bocca Romana*, you remember – know how to speak their own tongue, find Neapolitans totally unintelligible. For myself, and I speak for *mio sposo* as well, I do not want to understand what Romans do not understand. *La bella lingua* is sufficient for me.'

'I hear that Olga could understand him quite well,' said Georgie, betraying his complete knowledge of all that had happened.

'That may be so,' said Lucia. 'I hope she understood his English too, and his music. He had not an "h" when he spoke English, and I have not the slightest doubt in my own mind that his Italian was equally illiterate. It does not matter; I do not see that Mr Cortese's linguistic accomplishments concern us. But his music does, if poor

Miss Bracely, with her lovely notes, is going to study it, and appear as Lucretia. I am sorry if that is so. Any news?'

Really it was rather magnificent, and it was war as well; of that there could not be the slightest doubt. All Riseholme, by this time, knew that Lucia and Peppino had not been able to understand a word of what Cortese had said, and here was the answer to the backbiting suggestion, vividly put forward by Mrs Weston on the green that morning, that the explanation was that Lucia and Peppino did not know Italian. They could not reasonably be expected to know Neapolitan dialect; the language of Dante satisfied their humble needs. They found it difficult to understand Cortese when he spoke English, but that did not imply that they did not know English. Dante's tongue and Shakespeare's tongue sufficed them . . .

'And what were the words of the libretto like?' asked Georgie.

Lucia fixed him with her beady eyes, ready and eager to show how delighted she was to bestow approbation wherever it was deserved.

'Wonderful!' she said. 'I felt, and so did Peppino, that the words were as utterly wasted on that formless music as was poor Miss Bracely's voice. How did it go, Peppino? Let me think!'

Lucia raised her head again with the faraway look.

'*Amore misterio!*' she said. '*Amore profondo! Amore profondo delvasto mar.* Ah, there was our poor *bella lingua* again. I wonder who wrote the libretto.'

'Mr Cortese wrote the libretto,' said Georgie.

Lucia did not hesitate for a moment, but gave her silvery laugh.

'Oh, dear me, no,' she said. 'If you had heard him talk you would know he could not have. Well, have we not had enough of Mr Cortese and his works? Any news? What did you do last night, when Peppino and I were in our *purgatorio?*'

Georgie was almost equally glad to get off the subject of Italian. The less said in or of Italian the better.

'I was dining with Mrs Quantock,' he said. 'She had a very interesting Russian woman staying with her, Princess Popoffski.'

Lucia laughed again.

'Dear Daisy!' she said. 'Tell me about the Russian princess. Was she a guru? Dear me, how easily some people are taken in! The guru! Well, we were all in the same boat there. We took the guru on poor Daisy's valuation, and I still believe he had very remarkable gifts, curry cook or not. But Princess Popoffski now – '

'We had a séance,' said Georgie.

'Indeed! And Princess Popoffski was the medium?'

Georgie grew a little dignified.

'It is no use adopting that tone, *cara*,' he said, relapsing into Italian. 'You were not there; you were having your purgatory at Olga's. It was very remarkable. We touched hands all round the table; there was no possibility of fraud.'

Lucia's views on psychic phenomena were clearly known to Riseholme; those who produced them were fraudulent, those who were taken in by them were dupes. Consequently there was irony in the baby talk of her reply.

'Me dood!' she said. 'Me very dood, and listen carefully. Tell Lucia!'

Georgie recounted the experiences. The table had rocked and tapped out names. The table had whirled round, though it was a very heavy table. Georgie had been told that he had two sisters, one of whom in Latin was a bear.

'How did the table know that?' he asked. 'Ursa, a bear, you know. And then, while we were sitting there, the Princess went off into a trance. She said there was a beautiful spirit present, who blessed us all. She called Mrs Quantock Margarita, which, as you may know, is the Italian for Daisy.'

Lucia smiled.

'Thank you for explaining, Georgino,' she said.

There was no mistaking the irony of that, and Georgie thought he would be ironical too.

'I didn't know if you knew,' he said. 'I thought it might be Neapolitan dialect.'

'Pray, go on!' said Lucia, breathing through her nose.

'And she said I was Georgie,' said Georgie, 'but that there was another Georgie not far off. That was odd, because Olga's house, with Mr Shuttleworth, was so close. And then the Princess went into very deep trance, and the spirit that was there took possession of her.'

'And who was that?' asked Lucia.

'His name was Amadeo. She spoke in Amadeo's voice; indeed

it was Amadeo who was speaking. He was a Florentine and knew Dante quite well. He materialized; I saw him.'

A bright glorious vision flashed upon Lucia. The Dante class might not, even though it was clearly understood that Cortese spoke unintelligible Neapolitan, be a complete success, if the only attraction was that she herself taught Dante, but it would be quite a different proposition if Princess Popoffski, controlled by Amadeo, Dante's friend, was present. They might read a Canto first, and then hold a séance of which Amadeo – via Princess Popoffski – would take charge. While this was simmering in her mind, it was important to drop all irony and be extremely sympathetic.

'Georgino! How wonderful!' she said. 'As you know, I am sceptical by nature, and want all evidence carefully sifted. I dare say I am too critical, and that is a fault. But fancy getting in touch with a friend of Dante's! What would one not give? Tell me: what is this Princess like? Is she the sort of person one could ask to dinner?'

Georgie was still sore over the irony to which he had been treated. He had, moreover, the solid fact behind him that Daisy Quantock (Margarita) had declared that in no circumstances would she permit Lucia to annex her Princess. She had forgiven Lucia for annexing the guru (and considering that she had only annexed a curry cook, it was not so difficult) but she was quite determined to run her Princess herself.

'Yes, you might ask her,' he said. If irony was going about, there was no reason why he should not have a share.

Lucia bounced from her seat, as if it had been a spring cushion.

'We will have a little party,' she said. 'We three, and dear Daisy and her husband and the Princess. I think that will be enough; psychics hate a crowd, because it disturbs the influences. Mind! I do not say I believe in her power yet, but I am quite open-minded; I should like to be convinced. Let me see! We are doing nothing tomorrow. Let us have our little dinner tomorrow. I will send a line to dear Daisy at once, and say how enormously your account of the séance has interested me. I should like dear Daisy to have something to console her for that terrible fiasco about her guru. And then, Georgino *mio*, I will listen to your Debussy. Do not expect anything; if it seems to me formless, I shall say so. But if it seems to me promising, I shall be equally frank. Perhaps it is great;

I cannot tell you about that till I have heard it. Let me write my note first.'

That was soon done, and Lucia, having sent it by hand, came into the music room, and drew down the blinds over the window through which the autumn sun was streaming. Very little art, as she had once said, would 'stand' daylight; only Shakespeare or Dante or Beethoven and perhaps Bach, could compete with the sun.

Georgie, for his part, would have liked rather more light, but after all Debussy wrote such very odd chords and sequences that it was not necessary to wear his spectacles.

Lucia sat in a high chair near the piano, with her chin in her hand, tremendously erect.

Georgie took off his rings and laid them on the candle bracket, and ran his hands nimbly over the piano.

'*Poissons d'or*,' he said. 'Goldfish!'

'Yes; *pesci d'oro*,' said Lucia, explaining it to Peppino.

Lucia's face changed as the elusive music proceeded. The faraway look died away, and became puzzled; her chin came out of her hand, and the hand it came out of covered her eyes.

Before Georgie had got to the end the answer to her note came, and she sat with it in her hand, which, released from covering her eyes, tried to beat time. On the last note she got up with a regretful sigh.

'Is it finished?' she asked. 'And yet I feel inclined to say "When is it going to begin?" I haven't been fed; I haven't drunk in anything. Yes, I warned you I should be quite candid. And there's my verdict. I am sorry. Me vewy sowwy! But you played it, I am sure, beautifully, Georgino; you were a *buono avvocato*: you said all that could be said for your client. Shall I open this note before we discuss it more fully? Give Georgino a cigarette, Peppino! I am sure he deserves one, after all those accidentals.'

She pulled up the blind again in order to read her note and as she read her face clouded.

'Ah! I am sorry for that,' she said. 'Peppino, the Princess does not go out in the evening; they always have a séance there. I dare say Daisy means to ask us some evening soon. We will keep an evening or two open. It is a long time since I have seen dear Daisy; I will pop round this afternoon.'

CHAPTER THIRTEEN

Spiritualism, and all things pertaining to it, swept over Riseholme like the amazing growth of some tropical forest, germinating and shooting out its surprising vegetation, and rearing into huge fantastic shapes. In the centre of this wonderful jungle was a temple, so to speak, and that temple was the house of Mrs Quantock . . .

A strange Providence was the origin of it all. Mrs Quantock, a week before, had the toothache, and being no longer in the fold of Christian Science, found that it was no good at all to tell herself that it was a false claim. False claim it might be, but it was so plausible at once that it quite deceived her, and she went up to London to have its falsity demonstrated by a dentist. Since the collapse of Yoga and the flight of the curry cook, she had embarked on no mystical adventure, and she starved for some new fad. Then when her first visit to the dentist was over (the tooth required three treatments) and she went to a vegetarian restaurant to see if there was anything enlightening to be got out of that, she was delighted to find herself sitting at a very small table with a very communicative lady who ate cabbages in perfectly incredible quantities. She had a round pale face like the moon behind the clouds, enormous eyebrows that almost met over her nose, and a strange low voice, of husky tone, and a pronunciation quite as foreign as Signor Cortese's. She wore some very curious rings with large engraved amethysts and turquoises in them, and since in the first moments of their conversation she had volunteered the information that vegetarianism was the only possible diet for any who were cultivating their psychical powers, Mrs Quantock asked her if these weird finger ornaments had any mystical signification. They had; one was Gnostic, one was Rosicrucian, and the other was Cabalistic . . . It is easy to picture Mrs Quantock's delight;

adventure had met her with smiling mouth and mysterious eyes. In the course of an animated conversation of half an hour, the lady explained that if Mrs Quantock was, like her, a searcher after psychical truths, and cared to come to her flat at half-past four that afternoon, she would try to help her. She added with some little diffidence that the fee for a séance was a guinea, and, as she left, took a card out of a case, encrusted with glowing rubies, and gave it her. That was the Princess Popoffski.

Now here was a curious thing. For the last few evenings at Riseholme, Mrs Quantock had been experimenting with a table, and found that it creaked and tilted and tapped in the most encouraging way when she and Robert laid their hands on it. Then something – whatever it was that moved the table – had indicated by raps that her name was Daisy and his Robert, as well as giving them other information, which could not so easily be verified. Robert had grown quite excited about it, and was vexed that the séances were interrupted by his wife's expedition to London. But now how providential that was. She had walked straight from the dentist into the arms of Princess Popoffski.

It was barely half-past four when Mrs Quantock arrived at the Princess's flat, in a pleasant quiet side street off Charing Cross Road. A small dapper little gentleman received her, who explained that he was the Princess's secretary, and conducted her through several small rooms into the presence of the Sybil. These rooms, so Mrs Quantock thrillingly noticed, were dimly lit by oil lamps that stood in front of shrines containing images of the great spiritual guides from Moses down to Madame Blavatski, a smell of incense hung about, there were vases of flowers on the tables, and strange caskets set with winking stones. In the last of these rooms the Princess was seated, and for the moment Mrs Quantock hardly recognized her, for she wore a blue robe, which left her massive arms bare, and up them writhed serpent-shaped bracelets of many coils. She fixed her eyes on Mrs Quantock, as if she had never seen her before, and made no sign of recognition.

'The Princess has been meditating,' said the secretary in a whisper. 'She'll come to herself presently.'

For a moment meditation unpleasantly reminded Mrs Quantock of the guru, but nothing could have been less like that ill-starred curry cook than this majestic creature. Eventually she gave a great sigh and came out of her meditation.

'Ah, it is my friend,' she said. 'Do you know that you have a purple halo?'

This was very gratifying, especially when it was explained that only the most elect had purple halos, and soon other elect souls assembled for the séance. In the centre of the table was placed a musical box and a violin, and hardly had the circle been made, and the lights turned down, when the most extraordinary things began to happen. A perfect storm of rappings issued from the table, which began to rock violently, and presently there came peals of laughter in a high voice, and those who had been here before said that it was Pocky. He was a dear naughty boy, so Mrs Quantock's neighbour explained to her, so full of fun, and when on earth had been a Hungarian violinist. Still invisible, Pocky wished them all much laughter and joy, and then suddenly said "Ullo, 'ullo, 'ere's a new friend. I like her,' and Mrs Quantock's neighbour, with a touch of envy in her voice, told her that Pocky clearly meant her. Then Pocky said that they had been having heavenly music on the other side that day, and that if the new friend would say 'Please' he would play them some of it.

So Mrs Quantock, trembling with emotion, said, 'Please, Pocky,' and instantly he began to play on the violin the spirit tune which he had just been playing on the other side. After that, the violin clattered back on to the middle of the table again, and Pocky, blowing showers of kisses to them all, went away amid peals of happy laughter.

Silence fell, and then a deep bass voice said, 'I am coming, Amadeo!' and out of the middle of the table appeared a faint luminousness. It grew upwards and began to take form. Swathes of white muslin shaped themselves in the darkness, and there appeared a white face, in among the topmost folds of the muslin, with a Roman nose and a melancholy expression. He was not gay like Pocky, but he was intensely impressive, and spoke some lines in Italian, when asked to repeat a piece of Dante. Mrs Quantock knew they were Italian, because she recognised '*notte*' and '*uno*' and '*caro*', familiar words on Lucia's lips.

The séance came to an end, and Mrs Quantock having placed

a guinea with the utmost alacrity in a sort of offertory plate which the Princess's secretary negligently but prominently put down on a table in one of the other rooms, waited to arrange for another séance. But most unfortunately the Princess was leaving town next day on a much-needed holiday, for she had been giving three séances a day for the last two months and required rest.

'Yes, we're off tomorrow, the Princess and I,' said he, 'for a week at the Royal Hotel at Brinton. Pleasant bracing air, always sets her up. But after that she'll be back in town. Do you know that part of the country?'

Daisy could hardly believe her ears.

'Brinton?' she said. 'I live close to Brinton.'

Her whole scheme flashed completely upon her, even as Athene sprang full grown from the brain of Zeus.

'Do you think that she might be induced to spend a few days with me at Riseholme?' she said. 'My husband and I are so much interested in psychical things. You would be our guest, too, I hope. If she rested for a few days at Brinton first? If she came on to me afterwards? And then if she was thoroughly rested, perhaps she would give us a séance or two. I don't know – '

Mrs Quantock felt a great diffidence in speaking of guineas in the same sentence with Princesses, and had to make another start.

'If she were thoroughly rested,' she said, 'and if a little circle perhaps of four, at the usual price, would be worth her while. Just after dinner, you know, and nothing else to do all day but rest. There are pretty drives and beautiful air. All very quiet, and I think I may say more comfortable than the hotel. It would be such a pleasure.'

Mrs Quantock heard the clinking of bracelets from the room where the Princess was still reposing, and there she stood in the door, looking unspeakably majestic, but very gracious. So Mrs Quantock put her proposition before her, the secretary coming to the rescue on the subject of the usual fees, and when two days afterwards Mrs Quantock returned to Riseholme, it was to get ready the spare room and Robert's room next to it for these thrilling visitors, whose first séance Georgie and Piggy had attended, on the evening of the Italian débâcle . . .

*   *   *

The Quantocks had taken a high and magnificent line about the 'usual fees' for the séances, an expensive line, but then Roumanian oils had been extremely prosperous lately. No mention whatever of these fees was made to their guests, no offertory plate was put in a prominent position in the hall, there was no fumbling for change or the discreet pressure of coins into the secretary's hand; the entire cost was borne by Roumanian oils. The Princess and Mrs Quantock, apparently, were old friends; they spoke to each other at dinner as 'dear friend', and the Princess declared in the most gratifying way that they had been most intimate in a previous incarnation, without any allusion to the fact that in this incarnation they had met for the first time last week at a vegetarian restaurant. She was kind enough, it was left to be understood, to give a little séance after dinner at the house of her 'dear friend', and so, publicly, the question of money never came up.

Now the Princess was to stay three nights, and therefore, as soon as Mrs Quantock had made sure of that, she proceeded to fill up each of the séances without asking Lucia to any of them. It was not that she had not fully forgiven her for her odious grabbing of the guru, for she had done that on the night of the Spanish Quartet; it was rather that she meant to make sure that there would by no possibility be anything to forgive concerning her conduct with regard to the Princess. Lucia could not grab her and so call Daisy's powers of forgiveness into play again, if she never came near her, and Daisy meant to take proper precautions that she should not come near her. Accordingly Georgie and Piggy were asked to the first séance (if it did not go very well, it would not particularly matter with them), Olga and Mr Shuttleworth were bidden to the second, and Lady Ambermere with Georgie again to the third. This – quite apart from the immense interest of psychic phenomena – was deadly work, for it would be bitter indeed to Lucia to know, as she most undoubtedly would, that Lady Ambermere, who had cut her so firmly, was dining twice and coming to a séance. Daisy, it must again be repeated, had quite forgiven Lucia about the guru, but Lucia must take the consequences of what she had done.

It was after the first séance that the frenzy for spiritualism seized Riseholme. The Princess, with great good nature, gave some further exhibitions of her psychical power in addition to the séances, and even as Georgie the next afternoon was receiving Lucia's cruel verdict about Debussy, the Sybil was looking at the hands of Colonel Boucher and Mrs Weston, and unerringly probing into their past, and lifting the corner of the veil, giving them both glimpses into the future. She knew that the two were engaged, for that she had learned from Mrs Quantock in her morning's drive, and did not attempt to conceal the fact, but how could it be accounted for that, looking impressively from the one to the other, she said that a woman no longer young but tall, and with fair hair, had crossed their lives and had been connected with one of them for years past? It was impossible to describe Elizabeth more accurately than that, and Mrs Weston in high excitement confessed that her maid who had been with her for fifteen years entirely corresponded with what the Princess had seen in her hand. After that it took only a moment's further scrutiny for the Princess to discover that Elizabeth was going to be happy too. Then she found that there was a man connected with Elizabeth, and Colonel Boucher's hand, to which she transferred her gaze, trembled with delightful anticipation. She seemed to see a man there; she was not quite sure, but was there a man who perhaps had been known to him for a long time? There was. And then by degrees the affairs of Elizabeth and Atkinson were unerringly unravelled. It was little wonder that the Colonel pushed Mrs Weston's bath chair with record speed to Ye Signe of Ye Daffodil, and by the greatest good luck obtained a copy of *The Palmist's Manual*.

At another of these informal séances attended by Goosie and Mrs Antrobus, even stranger things had happened, for the Princess's hands, as they held a little preliminary conversation, began to tremble and twitch even more strongly than Colonel Boucher's, and Mrs Quantock hastily supplied her with a pencil and a quantity of sheets of foolscap paper, for this trembling and twitching implied that Reschia, an ancient Egyptian priestess, was longing to use the Princess's hand for automatic writing. After a few wild scrawls and plunges with the pencil, the Princess, though she still continued to talk to them, covered sheet after sheet in large flowing handwriting. This, when it was finished and the Princess sunk back in her chair, proved to be the most wonderful spiritual discourse, describing the happiness and harmony which pervaded the whole universe, and was only temporarily obscured by the mists of materiality. These mists were wholly withdrawn from the vision of those who had passed over. They lived in the midst of song and flowers and light and love . . . Towards the end there was a less intelligible passage about fire from the clouds. It was rendered completely intelligible the very next day when there was a thunderstorm, surely an unusual occurrence in November. If that had not happened Mrs Quantock's interpretation of it, as referring to Zeppelins, would have been found equally satisfactory. It was no wonder after that, that Mrs Antrobus, Piggy and Goosie spent long evenings with pencils and paper, for the Princess said that everybody had the gift of automatic writing, if they would only take pains and patience to develop it. Everybody had his own particular guide, and it was the very next day that Piggy obtained a script clearly signed Annabel Nicostratus and Jamifleg followed very soon after for her mother and sister, and so there was no jealousy.

But the crown and apex of these manifestations was undoubtedly the three regular séances which took place to the three select circles after dinner. Musical boxes resounded, violins gave forth ravishing airs, the sitters were touched by unseen fingers when everybody's hands were touching all around the table, and from the middle of it materializations swathed in muslin were built up. Pocky came, visible to the eye, and played spirit music. Amadeo, melancholy and impressive, recited Dante, and Cardinal Newman, not visible to the eye but audible to the ear, joined in singing 'Lead, Kindly Light', which the secretary requested them to encourage him with, and blessed them profusely at the conclusion. Lady Ambermere was so much impressed, and so nervous of driving home alone, that she insisted on Georgie's going back to The Hall with her, and consigning her person to Pug and Miss Lyall, and for the three days of the Princess's visit, there was practically no subject discussed at the parliaments on the green, except the latest manifestations. Olga went to town for a crystal, and Georgie for a planchette, and Riseholme temporarily became a spiritualistic republic, with the Princess as priestess and Mrs Quantock as President.

Lucia, all this time, was almost insane with pique and jealousy, for she sat in vain waiting for an invitation to come to a séance, and would, long before the three days were over, have welcomed with enthusiasm a place at one of the inferior and informal exhibitions. Since she could not procure the Princess for dinner, she asked Daisy to bring her to lunch or tea or at any hour day or night which was convenient. She made Peppino hang about opposite Daisy's house, with orders to drop his stick, or let his hat blow off, if he saw even the secretary coming out of the gate, so as possibly to enter into conversation with him, while she positively forced herself one morning into Daisy's hall, and cried 'Margarita' in silvery tones. On this occasion Margarita came out of the drawing room with a most determined expression on her face, and shut the door carefully behind her.

'Dearest Lucia,' she said, 'how nice to see you! What is it?'

'I just popped in for a chat,' said she. 'I haven't set eyes on you since the evening of the Spanish Quartet.'

'No! So long ago as that, is it? Well, you must come in again sometime very soon, won't you? The day after tomorrow I shall be much less busy. Promise to look in then.'

'You have a visitor with you, have you not?' asked Lucia desperately.

'Yes! Two, indeed, dear friends of mine. But I am afraid you would not like them. I know your opinion about anything connected with spiritualism, and – isn't it silly of us? – we've been dabbling in that.'

'Oh, but how interesting,' said Lucia. 'I – I am always ready to learn, and alter my opinions if I am wrong.'

Mrs Quantock did not move from in front of the drawing-room door.

'Yes?' she said. 'Then we will have a great talk about it, when you come to see me the day after tomorrow. But I know I shall find you hard to convince.'

She kissed the tips of her fingers in a manner so hopelessly final that there was nothing to do but go away.

Then with poor generalship, Lucia altered her tactics, and went up to the village green where Piggy was telling Georgie about the script signed Annabel. This was repeated again for Lucia's benefit.

'Wasn't it too lovely?' said Piggy. 'So Annabel's my guide, and she writes a hand quite unlike mine.'

Lucia gave a little scream, and put her fingers to her ears.

'Gracious me!' she said. 'What has come over Riseholme? Wherever I go I hear nothing but talk of séances, and spirits, and automatic writing. Such a pack of nonsense, my dear Piggy. I wonder at a sensible girl like you.'

Mrs Weston, propelled by the Colonel, whirled up in her bath-chair.

'*The Palmist's Manual* is too wonderful,' she said, 'and Jacob and I sat up over it till I don't know what hour. There's a break in his line of life, just at the right place, when he was so ill in Egypt, which is most remarkable, and when Tommy Luton brought round my bath chair this morning – I had it at the garden door, because the gravel's just laid at my front door, and the wheels sink so far into it – "Tommy," I said, "let me look at your hand a moment," and there on his line of fate, was the little cross that means bereavement. It came just right didn't it, Jacob? when he was thirteen, for he's fourteen this year, and Mrs Luton died just a year ago. Of course I didn't tell Tommy that, for I only told him to wash his hands, but it was most curious. And has your planchette come yet, Mr Georgie? I shall be most anxious to know what it writes, so if you've got an evening free any night soon just come round for a bit of dinner, and we'll make an evening of it, with table turning and planchette and palmistry. Now tell me all about the séance the first night. I wish I could have been present at a real séance, but of course Mrs Quantock can't find room for everybody, and I'm sure it was most kind of her to let the Colonel and me come in yesterday afternoon. We were thrilled with it, and who knows but that the Princess didn't write *The Palmist's Manual*, for on the title page it says it's by P. and that might be Popoffski as easily as not, or perhaps Princess.'

This allusion to there not being room for everybody was agony to Lucia. She laughed in her most silvery manner.

'Or, perhaps Peppino,' she said. 'I must ask *mio caro* if he wrote it. Or does it stand for Pillson? Georgino, are you the author of *The Palmist's Manual*? *Ecco!* I believe it was you.'

This was not quite wise, for no one detested irony more than Mrs Weston, or was sharper to detect it. Lucia should never have been ironical just then, nor indeed have dropped into Italian.

'No,' she said. 'I'm sure it was neither *il Signor Peppino* nor *il Signor Pillson* who wrote it. I believe it was the *Principessa*. So, *ecco*!

And did we not have a delicious evening at Miss Bracely's the other night? Such lovely singing, and so interesting to learn that Signor Cortese made it all up. And those lovely words, for though I didn't understand much of them, they sounded so exquisite. And fancy Miss Bracely talking Italian so beautifully when we none of us knew she talked it at all.'

Mrs Weston's amiable face was crimson with suppressed emotion, of which these few words were only the most insignificant leakage, and a very awkward pause succeeded which was luckily broken by everybody beginning to talk again very fast and brightly. Then Mrs Weston's chair scudded away; Piggy skipped away to the stocks where Goosie was sitting with a large sheet of foolscap, in case her hand twitched for automatic script, and Lucia turned to Georgie, who alone was left.

'Poor Daisy!' she said. 'I dropped in just now, and really I found her very odd and strange. What with her crazes for Christian Science, and uric acid and gurus and mediums, one wonders if she is quite sane. So sad! I should be dreadfully sorry if she had some mental collapse; that sort of thing is always so painful. But I know of a first-rate place for rest cures; I think it would be wise if I just casually dropped the name of it to Mr Robert, in case. And this last craze seems so terribly infectious. Fancy Mrs Weston dabbling in palmistry! It is too comical, but I hope I did not hurt her feelings by suggesting that Peppino or you wrote the *Manual*. It is dangerous to make little jokes to poor Mrs Weston.'

Georgie quite agreed with that, but did not think it necessary to say in what sense he agreed with it. Every day now Lucia was pouring floods of light on a quite new side of her character, which had been undeveloped, like the print from some photographic plate lying in the dark so long as she was undisputed mistress of Riseholme. But, so it struck him now, since the advent of Olga, she had taken up a critical ironical standpoint, which previously she had reserved for Londoners. At every turn she had to criticize and condemn where once she would only have praised. So few months ago, there had been that marvellous Hightum garden party, when Olga had sung long after Lady Ambermere had gone away. That was her garden party; the splendour and success of it had been hers, and no one had been allowed to forget that until Olga came back again. But the moment that happened, and Olga began to sing on her own account (which after all, so Georgie thought, she had a perfect right to do), the whole aspect of affairs was changed. She romped, and Riseholme did not like romps; she sang in church, and that was theatrical; she gave a party with the Spanish Quartet, and Brinton was publicly credited with the performance. Then had come Mrs Quantock and her Princess, and, lo, it would be kind to remember the name of an establishment for rest cures, in the hope of saving poor Daisy's sanity. Again Colonel Boucher and Mrs Weston were intending to get married, and consulted a *Palmist's Manual*, so they too helped to develop as with acid the print that had lain so long in the dark.

'Poor thing!' said Lucia, 'it is dreadful to have no sense of humour, and I'm sure I hope that Colonel Boucher will thoroughly understand that she has none before he speaks the fatal words. But then he has none either, and I have often noticed that two people without any sense of humour find each other most witty and amusing. A sense of humour, I expect, is not a very common gift; Miss Bracely has none at all, for I do not call romping humour. As for poor Daisy, what can rival her solemnity in sitting night after night round a table with someone who may or may not be a Russian princess – Russia of course is a very large place, and one does not know how many princesses there may be there – and thrilling over a pot of luminous paint and a false nose and calling it Amadeo the friend of Dante.'

This was too much for Georgie.

'But you asked Mrs Quantock and the Princess to dine with you,' he said, 'and hoped there would be a séance afterwards. You wouldn't have done that, if you thought it was only a false nose and a pot of luminous paint.'

'I may have been impulsive,' said Lucia, speaking very rapidly. 'I dare say I'm impulsive, and if my impulses lie in the direction of extending such poor hospitality as I can offer to my friends, and their friends, I am not ashamed of them. Far otherwise. But when I see and observe the awful effect of this so-called spiritualism on people whom I should have thought sensible and well balanced – I do not include poor dear Daisy among them – then I am only thankful that my impulses did not happen to lead me into countenancing such piffle, as your sister so truly observed about poor Daisy's guru.'

They had come opposite Georgie's house, and suddenly his drawing-room window was thrown up. Olga's head looked out.

'Don't have a fit, Georgie, to find me here,' she said. 'Good morning, Mrs Lucas; you were behind the mulberry, and I didn't see you. But something's happened to my kitchen range, and I can't have lunch at home. Do give me some. I've brought my crystal, and we'll gaze and gaze. I can see nothing at present except my own nose and the window. Are you psychical, Mrs Lucas?'

This was the last straw; all Lucia's grievances had been flocking together like swallows for their flight, and to crown all came this open annexation of Georgie. There was Olga, sitting in his window, all unasked, and demanding lunch, with her silly ridiculous crystal in her hand, wondering if Lucia was psychical.

Her silvery laugh was a little shrill. It started a full tone above its normal pitch.

'No, dear Miss Bracely,' she said. 'I am afraid I am much too commonplace and matter-of-fact to care about such things. It is a great loss I know, and deprives me of the pleasant society of Russian princesses. But we are all made differently; that is very lucky. I must get home, Georgie.'

It certainly seemed very lucky that everyone was not precisely like Lucia at that moment, or there would have been quarrelling.

She walked quickly off, and Georgie entered his house. Lucia had really been remarkably rude, and, if allusion was made to it, he was ready to confess that she seemed a little worried. Friendship would allow that, and candour demanded it. But no allusion of any sort was made. There was a certain flush on Olga's face, and she explained that she had been sitting over the fire.

The Princess's visit came to an end next day, and all the world knew that she was going back to London by the 11.00 a.m. express. Lady Ambermere was quite aware of it, and drove in with Pug and Miss Lyall, meaning to give her a lift to the station, leaving Mrs Quantock, if she wanted to see her guest off, to follow with the Princess's luggage in the fly which, no doubt, had been ordered. But Daisy had no intention of permitting this sort of thing, and drove calmly away with her dear friend in Georgie's motor, leaving the baffled Lady Ambermere to follow or not as she liked. She did like, though not much, and found herself on the platform among a perfect crowd of Riseholmites who had strolled down to the station on this lovely morning to see if parcels had come. Lady Ambermere took very little notice of them, but managed that Pug should give his paw to the Princess as she took her seat, and waved her hand to Mrs Quantock's dear friend, as the train slid out of the station.

'The late lord had some Russian relations,' she said majestically. 'How did you get to know her?'

'I met her at Tsarskoe Selo,' was on the tip of Mrs Quantock's tongue, but she was afraid that Lady Ambermere might not understand, and ask her when she had been to Tsarskoe Selo. It was grievous work making jokes for Lady Ambermere.

* * *

The train sped on to London, and the Princess opened the envelope which her hostess had discreetly put in her hand, and found that *that* was all right. Her hostess had also provided her with an admirable lunch, which her secretary took out of a Gladstone bag. When that was finished, she wanted her cigarettes, and as she looked for these, and even after she had found them, she continued to search for something else. There was the musical box there, and some curious pieces of elastic, and the violin was in its case, and there was a white mask. But she still continued to search . . .

* * *

About the same time as she gave up the search, Mrs Quantock wandered upstairs to the Princess's room. A less highly vitalized nature than hers would have been in a stupor of content, but she was more in a frenzy of content than in a stupor. How fine that frenzy was may be judged from the fact that perhaps the smallest ingredient in it was her utter defeat of Lucia. She cared comparatively little for that glorious achievement, and she was not sure that when the Princess came back again, as she had arranged to do on her next holiday, she would not ask Lucia to come to a séance. Indeed she had little but pity for the vanquished, so great were the spoils. Never had Riseholme risen to such a pitch of enthusiasm, and with good cause had it done so now, for of all the wonderful and exciting things that had ever happened there, these séances were the most delirious. And better even than the excitement of Riseholme was the cause of its excitement, for spiritualism and the truth of inexplicable psychic phenomena had flashed upon them all. Tableaux, romps, Yoga, the 'Moonlight Sonata', Shakespeare, Christian Science, Olga herself, uric acid, Elizabethan furniture, the engagement of Colonel Boucher and Mrs Weston, all these tremendous topics had paled like fire in the sunlight before the revelation that had now dawned. By practice and patience, by zealous concentration on crystals and palms, by the waiting for automatic script to develop, you attained to the highest mysteries, and could evoke Cardinal Newman, or Pocky . . .

There was the bed in which the Sybil had slept; there was the fresh vase of flowers, difficult to procure in November, but still obtainable, which she loved to have standing near her. There was the chest of drawers in which she had put her clothes, and Mrs Quantock pulled them open one by one, finding fresh emanations and vibrations everywhere. The lowest one stuck a little, and she had to use force to it . . .

The smile was struck from her face, as it flew open. Inside it were billows and billows of the finest possible muslin. Fold after fold of it she drew out, and with it there came a pair of false eyebrows. She recognised them at once as being Amadeo's. The muslin belonged to Pocky as well.

She needed but a moment's concentrated thought, and in swift succession rejected two courses of action that suggested themselves. The first was to use the muslin herself; it would make summer garments for years. The chief reason against that was that she was a little old for muslin. The second course was to send the whole paraphernalia back to her dear friend, with or without a comment. But that would be tantamount to a direct accusation of fraud. Never any more, if she did that, could she dispense her dear friend to Riseholme like an expensive drug. She would not so utterly burn her boats. There remained only one other judicious course of action, and she got to work.

It had been a cold morning, clear and frosty, and she had caused a good fire to be lit in the Princess's bedroom, for her to dress by. It still prospered in the grate, and Mrs Quantock, having shut the door and locked it, put on to it the false eyebrows, which, as they turned to ash, flew up the chimney. Then she fed it with muslin; yards and yards of muslin she poured on to it; never had there been so much muslin nor that so exquisitely fine. It went to her heart to burn it, but there was no time for minor considerations; every atom of that evidence must be purged by fire. The Princess would certainly not write and say that she had left some eyebrows and a hundred yards of muslin behind her, for, knowing what she did, it would be to her interests as well as Mrs Quantock's that those properties should vanish, as if they never had been.

Up the chimney in sheets of flame went this delightful fabric; sometimes it roared there, as if it had set the chimney on fire, and she had to pause, shielding her scorched face, until the hollow rumbling had died down. But at last the holocaust was over, and she unlocked the door again. No one knew but she, and no one should ever know. The guru had turned out to be a curry cook, but no intruding Hermy had been here this time. As long as crystals fascinated and automatic writing flourished, the secret of the muslin and the eyebrows should repose in one bosom alone. Riseholme had been electrified by spiritualism, and, even now, the séances had been cheap at the price, and in spite of this discovery, she felt by no means sure that she would not ask the Princess to come again and minister to their spiritual needs.

She had hardly got downstairs when Robert came in from the green, where he had been recounting the experiences of the last séance.

'Looked as if there was a chimney on fire,' he said. 'I wish it was the kitchen chimney. Then perhaps the beef mightn't be so raw as it was yesterday.'

Thus is comedy intertwined with tragedy!

CHAPTER FOURTEEN

Georgie was very busily engaged during the first weeks of December on a watercolour sketch of Olga sitting at her piano and singing. The difficulty of it was such that at times he almost despaired of accomplishing it, for the problem of how to draw her face and her mouth wide open and yet retain the likeness seemed almost insoluble. Often he sat in front of his own looking glass with his mouth open, and diligently drew his own face, in order to arrive at the principles of the changes of line which took place. Certainly the shape of a person's face, when his mouth was wide open, altered so completely that you would have thought him quite unrecognizable, however skilfully the artist reproduced his elongated countenance, and yet Georgie could easily recognize that face in the glass as his. Forehead, eyes and cheekbones alone retained their wonted aspect; even the nose seemed to lengthen if you opened your mouth very wide . . . Then how again was he to indicate that she was singing and not yawning, or preparing for a sneeze? His most successful sketch at present looked precisely as if she was yawning, and made Georgie's jaws long to yawn too. Perhaps the shape of the mouth in the two positions was really the same, and it was only the sound that led you to suppose that an open-mouthed person was singing. But perhaps the piano would supply the necessary suggestion; Olga would not sit down at the piano merely to yawn or sneeze, for she could do that anywhere.

Then a brilliant idea struck him: he would introduce a shaded lamp standing on the piano, and then her face would be in red shadow. Naturally this entailed fresh problems with regard to light, but light seemed to present less difficulty than likeness. Besides he could make her dress, and the keys of the piano very like indeed. But when he came to painting again he despaired. There must be red shadow on her face and yellow light on her hands, and on her green dress, and presently the whole thing looked not so much like Olga singing by lamplight, as a lobster salad spread out in the sunlight. The more he painted, the more vividly did the lettuce leaves and the dressing and the lobster emerge from the paper. So he took away the lamp, and shut Olga's mouth, and there she would be at her piano just going to sing.

These artistic agonies had rewards which more than compensated for them, for regularly now he took his drawing board and his paintbox across to her house, and sat with her while she practised. There were none of love's lilies low or yawning York now, for she was very busy learning her part in *Lucretia*, spending a solid two hours at it every morning, and Georgie began to perceive what sort of work it implied to produce the spontaneous ease with which Brünnhilde hailed the sun. More astounding even was the fact that this mere learning of notes was but the preliminary to what she called 'real work'. And when she had got through the mere mechanical part of it, she would have to study. Then when her practice was over, she would indulgently sit with her head in profile against a dark background, and Georgie would suck one end of his brush and bite the other, and wonder whether he would ever produce anything which he could dare to offer her. By daily poring on her face, he grew not to admire only but to adore its youth and beauty, by daily contact with her he began to see how fresh and how lovely was the mind that illuminated it.

'Georgie, I'm going to scold you,' she said one day, as she took up her place against the black panel. 'You're a selfish little brute. You think of nothing but your own amusement. Did that ever strike you?'

Georgie gasped with surprise. Here was he spending the whole of every morning trying to do something which would be a worthy Christmas present for her (to say nothing of the hours he had spent with his mouth open in front of his glass, and the cost of the beautiful frame which he had ordered) and yet he was supposed to be only thinking about himself. Of course Olga did not know that the picture was to be hers . . .

'How tarsome you are!' he said. 'You're always finding fault with me. Explain.'

'Well, you're neglecting your old friends for your new one,' she said. 'My dear, you should never drop an old friend. For instance, when did you last play duets with Mrs Lucas?'

'Oh, not so very long ago,' said Georgie.

'Quite long enough, I am sure. But I don't actually mean sitting down and thumping the piano with her. When did you last think about her and make plans for her and talk baby language?'

'Who told you I ever did?' asked Georgie.

'Gracious! How can I possibly remember that sort of thing? I should say at a guess that everybody told me. Now poor Mrs Lucas is feeling out of it, and neglected and dethroned. It's all on my mind rather, and I'm talking to you about it, because it's largely your fault. Now we're talking quite frankly, so don't fence, and say it's mine. I know exactly what you mean, but you are perfectly wrong. Primarily, it's Mrs Lucas's fault, because she's quite the stupidest woman I ever saw, but it's partly your fault too.'

She turned round.

'Come, Georgie, let's have it out,' she said. 'I'm perfectly powerless to do anything, because she detests me, and you've got to help her and help me, and drop your selfishness. Before I came here, she used to run you all, and give you treats like going to her tableaux and listening to her stupid old "Moonlight Sonata", and talking seven words of Italian. And then I came along with no earthly intention except to enjoy my holidays, and she got it into her head that I was trying to run the place instead of her. Isn't that so? Just say "yes".'

'Yes,' said Georgie.

'Well, that puts me in an odious position and a helpless position. I did my best to be nice to her; I went to her house until she ceased to ask me, and asked her here for everything that I thought would amuse her, until she ceased to come. I took no notice of her rudeness, which was remarkable, or of her absurd patronizing airs, which didn't hurt me in the smallest degree. But, Georgie, she would continue to make such a dreadful ass of herself, and think it was my fault. Was it my fault that she didn't know the Spanish Quartet when she heard it, or that she didn't know a word of Italian, when she pretended she did, or that the other day (it was the last time I saw her, when you played your

Debussy to us at Aunt Jane's) she talked to me about inverted fifths?'

Olga suddenly burst out laughing, and Georgie assumed the Riseholme face of intense curiosity.

'You must tell me all about that,' he said, 'and I'll tell you the rest which you don't know.'

Olga succumbed too, and began to talk in Aunt Jane's voice, for she had adopted her as an aunt.

'Well, it was last Monday week,' she said, 'or was it Sunday? No it couldn't have been Sunday because I don't have anybody to tea that day, as Elizabeth goes over to Jacob's and spends the afternoon with Atkinson, or the other way about, which doesn't signify, as the point is that Elizabeth should be free. So it was Monday, and Aunt Jane – it's me talking again – had the tea party at which you played "Poisson d'Or". And when it was finished, Mrs Lucas gave a great sigh, and said, "Poor Georgino! Wasting his time over that rubbish," though she knew quite well that I had given it to you. And so I said, "Would you call it rubbish, do you think?" and she said, "Quite. Every rule of music is violated. Don't those inverted fifths make you wince, Miss Bracely?"'

Olga laughed again, and spoke in her own voice.

'Oh, Georgie, she is an ass,' she said. 'What she meant I suppose was consecutive fifths; you can't invert a fifth. So I said (I really meant it as a joke), "Of course there is that, but you must forgive Debussy that for the sake of that wonderful passage of submerged tenths!" And she took it quite gravely and shook her head, and said she was afraid she was a purist. What happened next? That's all I know.'

'Directly afterwards,' said Georgie, 'she brought the music to me, and asked me to show her where the passage of tenths came. I didn't know, but I found some tenths, and she brightened up and said, "Yes, it is true; those submerged tenths are very impressive." Then I suggested that the submerged tenth was not a musical expression, but referred to a section of the population. On which she said no more, but when she went away she asked me to send her some book on harmony. I dare say she is looking for the submerged tenth still.'

Olga lit a cigarette and became grave again.

'Well, it can't go on,' she said. 'We can't have the poor thing feeling angry and out of it. Then there was Mrs Quantock absolutely refusing to let her see the Princess.'

'That was her own fault,' said Georgie. 'It was because she was so greedy about the guru.'

'That makes it all the bitterer. And I can't do anything, because she blames me for it all. I would ask her and her Peppino here every night, and listen to her dreary tunes every evening, and let her have it all her own way, if it would do any good. But things have gone too far; she wouldn't come. It has all happened without my noticing it. I never added it all up as it went along, and I hate it.'

Georgie thought of the spiritualistic truths.

'If you're an incarnation,' he said in a sudden glow of admiration, 'you're the incarnation of an angel. How you can forgive her odious manners to you – '

'My dear, shut up,' said Olga. 'We've got to do something. Now how would it be if you gave a nice party on Christmas night, and asked her at once? Ask her to help you in getting it up; make it clear she's going to run it.'

'All right. You'll come, won't you?'

'Certainly I will not. Perhaps I will come in after dinner with Goosie or someone of that sort. Don't you see it would spoil it all if I were at dinner? You must rather pointedly leave me out. Give her a nice expensive refined Christmas present too. You might give her that picture you're doing of me. No, I suppose she wouldn't like that. But just comfort her and make her feel you can't get on without her. You've been her right hand all these years. Make her give her tableaux again. And then I think you must ask me in afterwards. I long to see her and Peppino as Brünnhilde and Siegfried. Just attend to her, Georgie, and buck her up. Promise me you will. And do it as if your heart was in it, otherwise it's no good.'

Georgie began packing up his paintbox. This was not the plan he had hoped for on Christmas Day, but if Olga wished this, it had got to be done.

'Well, I'll do my best,' he said.

'Thanks ever so much. You're a darling. And how is your

planchette getting on? I've been lazy about my crystal, but I get so tired of my own nose.'

'Planchette would write nothing but a few names,' said Georgie, omitting the fact that Olga's was the most frequent. 'I think I shall drop it.'

This was but reasonable, for since Riseholme had some new and absorbing excitement every few weeks, to say nothing of the current excitement of daily life, it followed that even the most thrilling pursuits could not hold the stage for very long. Still, the interest in spiritualism had died down with the rapidity of the seed on stony ground.

'Even Mrs Quantock seems to have cooled,' said Olga. 'She and her husband were here last night, and they looked rather bored when I suggested table-turning. I wonder if anything has happened to put her off it?'

'What do you think could have?' asked Georgie with Riseholme alacrity.

'Georgie, do you really believe in the Princess and Pocky?' she asked.

Georgie looked round to see that there was no one within hearing.

'I did at the time,' he said, 'at least I think I did. But it seems less likely now. Who was the Princess anyway? Why didn't we ever hear of her before? I believe Mrs Quantock met her in the train or something.'

'So do I,' said Olga. 'But not a word. It makes Aunt Jane and Uncle Jacob completely happy to believe in it all. Their lines of life are enormous, and they won't die till they're over a hundred. Now go and see Mrs Lucas, and if she doesn't ask you to lunch you can come back here.'

Georgie put down his picture and painting apparatus at his house, and went on to Lucia's, definitely conscious that though he did not want to have her to dinner on Christmas Day, or go back to his duets and his ADC duties, there was a spice and savour in so doing that came entirely from the fact that Olga wished him to, that by this service he was pleasing her. In itself it was distasteful, in itself it tended to cut him off from her, if he had to devote his time to Lucia, but he still delighted in doing it.

'I believe I am falling in love with her this time,' said Georgie to himself . . . 'She's wonderful; she's big; she's – '

At that moment his thoughts were violently diverted, for Robert Quantock came out of his house in a tremendous hurry, merely scowling at Georgie, and positively trotted across the green in the direction of the newsagents. Instantly Georgie recollected that he had seen him there already this morning before his visit to Olga, buying a new twopenny paper in a yellow cover called *Todd's News*. They had had a few words of genial conversation, and what could have happened in the last two hours that made Robert merely gnash his teeth at Georgie now, and make a second visit to the paper shop?

It was impossible not to linger a moment and see what Robert did when he got to the paper shop, and with the aid of his spectacles Georgie perceived that he presently loaded himself with a whole packet of papers in yellow covers, presumably *Todd's News*. Flesh and blood could not resist the cravings of curiosity, and making a detour, so as to avoid being gnashed at again by Robert, who was coming rapidly back in his direction, he strolled round to the paper shop and asked for a copy of *Todd's News*. Instantly the bright December morning grew dark with mystery, for the proprietor told him that Mr Quantock had bought every copy he possessed of it. No further information could be obtained, except that he had bought a copy of every other daily paper as well.

Georgie could make nothing of it whatever, and having observed Robert hurry into his house again, went on his errand to Lucia. Had he seen what Robert did when he got home, it is doubtful if he could have avoided breaking into the house and snatching a copy of *Todd's News* from him . . .

Robert went to his study, and locked the door. He drew out from under his blotting pad the first copy of *Todd's News* that he had bought earlier in the morning, and put it with the rest. Then with a furrowed brow he turned to the police reports in *The Times* and after looking at them laid the paper down. He did the same to the *Daily Telegraph*, the *Daily Mail*, the *Morning Post*, the *Daily Chronicle*. Finally (this was the last of the daily papers) he perused the *Daily Mirror*, tore it in shreds, and said, 'Damn.'

He sat for a while in thought, trying to recollect if anybody in Riseholme except Colonel Boucher took in the *Daily Mirror*. But he felt morally certain that no one did, and letting himself out of his study, and again locking the door after him, he went into the street, and saw at a glance that the Colonel was employed in whirling Mrs Weston round the green. Instead of joining them he hurried to the Colonel's house and, for there was no time for half-measures, fixed Atkinson with his eye, and said he would like to write a note to Colonel Boucher. He was shown into his sitting room, and saw the *Daily Mirror* lying open on the table. As soon as he was left alone, he stuffed it into his pocket, told Atkinson he would speak to the Colonel instead, and intercepted the path of the bath chair. He was nearly run over, but stood his ground, and in a perfectly firm voice asked the Colonel if there was any news in the morning papers. With the Colonel's decided negative ringing joyfully in his ears, he went home again, and locked himself for the second time into his study.

There is a luxury, when some fell danger has been averted by promptness and presence of mind, in living through the moments of that danger again, and Robert opened *Todd's News*, for that gave the fuller account, and read over the paragraph in the police news headed 'Bogus Russian Princess'. But now he gloated over the lines which had made him shudder before when he read how Marie Lowenstein, of 15 Gerald Street, Charing Cross Road, calling herself Princess Popoffski, had been brought up at the Bow Street Police Court for fraudulently professing to tell fortunes and produce materialized spirits at a séance in her flat. Sordid details followed: a detective who had been there seized an apparition by the throat, and turned on the electric light. It was the woman Popoffski's throat that he held, and her secretary, Hezekiah Schwarz, was discovered under the table detaching an electric hammer. A fine was inflicted . . .

A moment's mental debate was sufficient to determine Robert not to tell his wife. It was true that she had produced Popoffski, but then he had praised and applauded her for that; he, no less than she, had been convinced of Popoffski's integrity, high rank and marvellous psychic powers, and together they had soared to a pinnacle of unexampled greatness in the Riseholme world. Besides, poor Daisy would be simply flattened out if she knew that Popoffski was no better than the guru. He glanced at the pile of papers, and at the fireplace . . .

It had been a cold morning, clear and frosty, and a good blaze prospered in the grate. Out of each copy of *Todd's News* he tore the page on which were printed the police reports, and fed the fire with them. Page after page he put upon it; never had so much paper been devoted to one grate. Up the chimney they flew in sheets of flame; sometimes he was afraid he had set it on fire, and he had to pause, shielding his scorched face, until the hollow rumbling had died down. With the page from two copies of the *Daily Mirror* the holocaust was over, and he unlocked the door again. No one in Riseholme knew but he, and no one should ever know. Riseholme had been electrified by spiritualism, and even now the séances had been cheap at the price.

The debris of all these papers he caused to be removed by the housemaid, and this was hardly done when his wife came in from the green.

'I thought there was a chimney on fire, Robert,' she said. 'You would have liked it to be the kitchen chimney as you said the other day.'

'Stuff and nonsense, my dear,' said he. 'Lunchtime, isn't it?'

'Yes. Ah, there's the post. None for me, and two for you.'

She looked at him narrowly as he took his letters. Perhaps their subconscious minds (according to her dear friend's theory) held communication, but only the faintest unintelligible ripple of that appeared on the surface.

'I haven't heard from my Princess since she went away,' she remarked.

Robert gave a slight start; he was a little off his guard from the reaction after his anxiety.

'Indeed!' he said. 'Have you written to her?'

She appeared to try to remember.

'Well, I really don't believe I have,' she said. 'That is remiss of me. I must send her a long budget one of these days.'

This time he looked narrowly at her. Had she a secret, he wondered, as well as he? What could it be? . . .

*   *   *

Georgie found his mission none too easy, and it was only the thought that it was a labour of love, or something very like it, that enabled him to persevere. Even then for the first few minutes he thought it might prove love's labour's lost, so bright and unreal was Lucia.

He had half crossed Shakespeare's garden, and had clearly seen her standing at the window of the music room, when she stole away, and next moment the strains of some slow movement, played very loud, drowned the bell on the mermaid's tail so completely that he wondered whether it had rung at all. As a matter of fact, Lucia and Peppino were in the midst of a most serious conversation when Georgie came through the gate, which was concerned with deciding what was to be done. A party at The Hurst sometime during Christmas week was as regular as the festival itself, but this year everything was so unusual. Who were to be asked in the first place? Certainly not Mrs Weston, for she had talked Italian to Lucia in a manner impossible to misinterpret, and probably, so said Lucia with great acidity, she would be playing children's games with her *promesso*. It was equally impossible to ask Miss Bracely and her husband, for relations were already severed on account of the Spanish Quartet and Signor Cortese, and as for the Quantocks, did Peppino expect Lucia to ask Mrs Quantock again ever? Then there was Georgie, who had become so different and strange, and . . . Well here was Georgie. Hastily she sat down at the piano, and Peppino closed his eyes for the slow movement.

The opening of the door was lost on Lucia, and Peppino's eyes were closed. Consequently Georgie sat down on the nearest chair, and waited. At the end Peppino sighed, and he sighed too.

'Who is that?' said Lucia sharply. 'Why, is it you, Georgie? What a stranger. Aren't you? Any news?'

This was all delivered in the coldest of tones, and Lucia snatched a morsel of wax off E flat.

'I've heard none,' said Georgie in great discomfort. 'I just dropped in.'

Lucia fixed Peppino with a glance. If she had shouted at the top of her voice she could not have conveyed more unmistakably that she was going to manage this situation.

'Ah, that is very pleasant,' she said. 'Peppino and I have been so busy lately that we have seen nobody. We are quite country cousins, and so the town mouse must spare us a little cheese. How is dear Miss Bracely now?'

'Very well,' said Georgie. 'I saw her this morning.'

Lucia gave a sigh of relief. 'That is good,' she said. 'Peppino, do you hear? Miss Bracely is quite well. Not overtired with practising that new opera? *Lucy Greecia*, was it? Oh, how silly I am! *Lucretia*; that was it, by that extraordinary Neapolitan. Yes. And what next? Our good Mrs Weston, now! Still thinking about her nice young man? Making orange-flower wreaths, and choosing bridesmaids? How naughty I am! Yes. And then dear Daisy? How is she? Still entertaining princesses? I look in the Court Circular every morning to see if Princess Pop – Pop – Popoff isn't it? if Princess Popoff has popped off to see her cousin the Czar again. Dear me!'

The amount of malice, envy and all uncharitableness which Lucia managed to put into this quite unrehearsed speech was positively amazing. She had not thought it over beforehand for a moment; it came out with the august spontaneity of lightning leaping from a cloud. Not till that moment had Georgie guessed at a tithe of all that Olga had felt so certain about, and a double emotion took hold of him. He was immensely sorry for Lucia, never having conjectured how she must have suffered before she attained to so superb a sourness, and he adored the intuition that had guessed it and wanted to sweeten it.

The outburst was not quite over yet, though Lucia felt distinctly better.

'And you, Georgie,' she said, 'though I'm sure we are such strangers that I ought to call you Mr Pillson, what have you been doing? Playing Miss Bracely's accompaniments, and sewing wedding dresses all day, and raising spooks all night? Yes.'

Lucia had caught this 'Yes' from Lady Ambermere, having found it peculiarly obnoxious. You laid down a proposition, or asked a question, and then confirmed it yourself.

'And Mr Cortese,' she said, 'is he still roaring out his marvellous English and Italian? Yes. What a full life you lead, Georgie. I suppose you have no time for your painting now.'

This was not a bow drawn at a venture, for she had seen Georgie come out of Old Place with his paintbox and drawing board, but this direct attack on him did not lessen the power of the 'sweet charity' which had sent him here. He blew the bugle to rally all the good nature for which he was capable.

'No, I have been painting lately,' he said, 'at least I have been trying to. I'm doing a little sketch of Miss Bracely at her piano, which I want to give her on Christmas Day. But it's so difficult. I wish I had brought it round to ask your advice, but you would only have screamed with laughter at it. It's a dreadful failure: much worse than those I gave you for your birthdays. Fancy your keeping them still in your lovely music room. Send them to the pantry, and I'll do something better for you next.'

Lucia, try as she might, could not help being rather touched by that. There they all were: *Golden Autumn Woodland, Bleak December, Yellow Daffodils,* and *Roses of Summer*. . .

'Or have them blacked over by the boot boy,' she said. 'Take them down, Georgie, and let me send them to be blacked.'

This was much better: there was playfulness behind the sarcasm now, which peeped out from it. He made the most of that.

'We'll do that presently,' he said. 'Just now I want to engage you and Peppino to dine with me on Christmas Day. Now don't be tarsome and say you're engaged. But one can never tell with you.'

'A party?' asked Lucia suspiciously.

'Well, I thought we would have just one of our old evenings together again,' said Georgie, feeling himself remarkably clever. 'We'll have the Quantocks, shan't we, and Colonel and Mrs Colonel, and you and Peppino, and me, and Mrs Rumbold? That'll make eight, which is more than Foljambe likes, but she must lump it. Mr Rumbold is always singing carols all Christmas evening with the choir, and she will be alone.'

'Ah, those carols,' said Lucia, wincing.

'I know: I will provide you with little wads of cotton wool. Do come and we'll have just a party of eight. I've asked no one yet and perhaps nobody will come. I want you and Peppino, and the rest may come or stop away. Do say you approve.'

Lucia could not yield at once. She had to press her fingers to her forehead.

'So kind of you, Georgie,' she said, 'but I must think. Are

we doing anything on Christmas night, *carrissimo*? Where's your engagement book? Go and consult it.'

This was a grand manoeuvre, for hardly had Peppino left the room when she started up with a little scream and ran after him.

'Me so stupid,' she cried. 'Me put it in smoking room, and poor *caro* will look for it ever so long. Back in minute, Georgino.'

Naturally this was perfectly clear to Georgie. She wanted to have a short private consultation with Peppino, and he waited rather hopefully for their return, for Peppino, he felt sure, was bored with this Achilles attitude of sitting sulking in the tent. They came back wreathed in smiles, and instantly embarked on the question of what to do after dinner. No romps: certainly not, but why not the tableaux again? The question was still under debate when they went in to lunch. It was settled affirmatively during the macaroni, and Lucia said that they all wanted to work her to death, and so get rid of her. They had thought – she and Peppino – of having a little holiday on the Riviera, but anyhow they would put it off till after Christmas. Georgie's mouth was full of crashing toast at the moment, and he could only shake his head. But as soon as the toast could be swallowed, he made the usual reply with great fervour.

Georgie was hardly at all complacent when he walked home afterwards, and thought how extremely good-natured he had been, for he could not but feel that this marvellous forbearance was a sort of mistletoe growth on him, quite foreign really to his nature. Never before had Lucia showed so shrewish and venomous a temper; he had not thought her capable of it. For the gracious queen, there was substituted a snarling fishwife, but then as Georgie calmly pursued the pacific mission of comfort to which Olga had ordained him, how the fishwife's wrinkles had been smoothed out, and the asps withered from her tongue. Had his imagination ever pictured Lucia saying such things to him, it would have supplied him with no sequel but a complete severance of relations between them. Instead of that he had consulted her and truckled to her: truckled, yes, he had truckled, and he was astonished at himself. Why had he truckled? And the beautiful mouth and kindly eyes of Olga supplied the answer. Certainly he must drop in at once, and tell her the result of the mission. Perhaps she would reward him by calling him a darling again. Really he deserved that she should say something nice to him.

It was a day of surprises for Georgie. He found Olga at home, and recounted, without losing any of the substance, the sarcasms of Lucia, and his own amazing tact and forbearance. He did not comment, he just narrated the facts in the vivid Riseholme manner, and waited for his reward.

Olga looked at him a moment in silence: then she deliberately wiped her eyes.

'Oh, poor Mrs Lucas,' she said. 'She must have been miserable to have behaved like that! I am so sorry. Now what else can you do, Georgie, to make her feel better?'

'I think I've done everything that could have been required of *me*,' said Georgie. 'It was all I could do to keep my temper at all. I will give my party at Christmas, because I promised you I would.'

'Oh, but it's ten days to Christmas yet,' said Olga. 'Can't you paint her portrait, and give it her for a present? Oh, I think you could, playing the "Moonlight Sonata".'

Georgie felt terribly inclined to be offended and tell Olga that she was tired of him; or to be dignified and say he was unusually busy. Never had he shown such forbearance towards downright rudeness as he had shown to Lucia, and though he had shown that for Olga's sake, she seemed to be without a single spark of gratitude, but continued to urge her request.

'Do paint a little picture of her,' she repeated. 'She would love it, and make it young and interesting. Think over it, anyhow: perhaps you'll think of something better than that. And now won't you go and secure all your guests for Christmas at once?'

Georgie turned to leave the room, but just as he got to the door she spoke again:

'I think you're a brick,' she said.

Somehow this undemonstrative expression of approval began to glow in Georgie's heart as he walked home. Apparently she took it for granted that he was going to behave with all the perfect tact and good temper that he had shown. It did not surprise her in the least; she had almost forgotten to indicate that she had noticed it at all. And that, as he thought about it, seemed a far deeper compliment than if she had told him how wonderful he was. She took it for granted, no more nor less, that he would be kind and pleasant, whatever Lucia said. He had not fallen short of her standard . . .

CHAPTER FIFTEEN

Georgie's Christmas party had just taken its seats at his round rosewood table without a cloth, and he hoped that Foljambe would be quick with the champagne, because there had been rather a long wait before dinner, owing to Lucia and Peppino being late, and conversation had been a little jerky. Lucia, as usual, had sailed into the room, without a word of apology, for she was accustomed to come last when she went out to dinner, and on her arrival dinner was always announced immediately. The few seconds that intervened were employed by her in saying just one kind word to everybody. Tonight, however, these gratifying utterances had not been received with the gratified responses to which she was accustomed: there was a different atmosphere abroad, and it was as if she were no more than one-eighth of the entire party. But it would never do to hurry Foljambe, who was a little upset already by the fact of there being eight to dinner, which was two more than she approved of.

Lucia was on Georgie's right, Mrs Colonel, as she had decided to call herself, on his left. Next her was Peppino, then Mrs Quantock, then the Colonel, then Mrs Rumbold (who resembled a grey hungry mouse), and Mr Quantock completed the circle round to Lucia again. Everyone had a small bunch of violets in the napkin, but Lucia had the largest. She had also a footstool.

'Capital good soup,' remarked Mr Quantock. 'Can't get soup like this at home.'

There was dead silence. Why was there never a silence when Olga was there, wondered Georgie. It wasn't because she talked, she somehow caused other people to talk.

'Tommy Luton hasn't got measles,' said Mrs Weston. 'I always said he hadn't, though there are measles about. He came to walk as usual this morning, and is going to sing in the carols tonight.'

She suddenly stopped.

Georgie gave an imploring glance at Foljambe, and looked at the champagne glasses. She took no notice. Lucia turned to Georgie, with an elbow on the table between her and Mr Quantock.

'And what news, Georgie?' she said. 'Peppino and I have been so busy that we haven't seen a soul all day. What have you been doing? Any planchette?'

She looked brightly at Mrs Quantock.

'Yes, dear Daisy, I needn't ask you what you've been doing. Table-turning, I expect. I know how interested you are in psychical matters. I should be, too, if only I could be certain that I was not dealing with fraudulent people.'

Georgie felt inclined to give a hollow groan and sink under the table when this awful polemical rhetoric began. To his unbounded surprise Mrs Quantock answered most cordially.

'You are quite right, dear Lucia,' she said. 'Would it not be terrible to find that a medium, some dear friend perhaps, whom one implicitly trusted, was exposed as fraudulent? One sees such exposures in the paper sometimes. I should be miserable if I thought I had ever sat with a medium who was not honest. They fine the wretches well, though, if they are caught, and they deserve it.'

Georgie observed, and couldn't the least understand, a sudden blank expression cross Robert's face. For the moment he looked as if he were dead but had been beautifully stuffed. But Georgie gave but a cursory thought to that, for the amazing supposition dawned on him that Lucia had not been polemical at all, but was burying instead of chopping with the hatchet. It was instantly confirmed, for Lucia took her elbow off the table, and turned to Robert.

'You and dear Daisy have been very lucky in your spiritualistic experiences,' she said. 'I hear on all sides what a charming medium you had. Georgie quite lost his heart to her.'

''Pon my word; she was delightful,' said Robert. 'Of course she was a dear friend of Daisy's, but one has to be very careful when one hears of the dreadful exposures, as my wife said, that occur sometimes. Fancy finding that a medium whom you believed to be perfectly honest had yards and yards of muslin and a false nose or two concealed about her. It would sicken me of the whole business.'

A loud pop announced that Foljambe had allowed them all some champagne at last, but Georgie hardly heard it, for glancing up at Daisy Quantock, he observed that the same dead and stuffed look had come over her face which he had just now noticed on her husband's countenance. Then they both looked up at each other with a glance that to him bristled with significance. An agonized questioning, an imploring petition for silence seemed to inspire it; it was as if each had made unwittingly some hopeless *faux pas*. Then they instantly looked away from each other again; their necks seemed to crack with the rapidity with which they turned them right and left, and they burst into torrents of speech to the grey hungry mouse and the Colonel respectively.

Georgie was utterly mystified: his Riseholme instinct told him that there was something below all this, but his Riseholme instinct could not supply the faintest clue as to what it was. Both of the Quantocks, it seemed clear, knew something perilous about the Princess, but surely if Daisy had read in the paper that the Princess had been exposed and fined, she would not have touched on so dangerous a subject. Then the curious incident about *Todd's News* inevitably occurred to him, but that would not fit the case, since it was Robert and not Daisy who had bought that inexplicable number of the yellow print. And then Robert had hinted at the discovery of yards and yards of muslin and a false nose. Why had he done that unless he had discovered them, or unless . . . Georgie's eyes grew round with the excitement of the chase . . . unless Robert had some other reason to suspect the integrity of the dear friend, and had said this at haphazard. In that case what was Robert's reason for suspicion? Had *he*, not Daisy, read in the paper of some damaging disclosures, and had Daisy (also having reason to suspect the Princess) alluded to the damaging exposures in the paper by pure haphazard? Anyhow they had both looked dead and stuffed when the other alluded to mediumistic frauds, and both had said how lucky their own experiences had been. 'Oh!' – Georgie almost said it aloud – What if Robert had seen a damaging exposure in *Todd's News*, and therefore bought up every copy that was to be had? Then, indeed, he would look dead and stuffed, when Daisy alluded to damaging exposures in the paper. Had a stray copy escaped him, and did Daisy know? What did Robert know? Had they exquisite secrets from each other?

Lucia was being talked to across him by Mrs Weston, who had also pinned down the attention of Peppino on the other side of her. At that precise moment the flood of Mrs Quantock's spate of conversation to the Colonel dried up, and Robert could find nothing more to say to the hungry mouse. Georgie in this backwater of his own thoughts was whirled into the current again. But before he sank he caught Mrs Quantock's eye and put a question that arose from his exciting backwater.

'Have you heard from the Princess lately?' he asked.

Robert's head went round with the same alacrity as he had turned it away.

'Oh, yes,' said she. 'Two days ago was it, Robert?'

'I heard yesterday,' said Robert firmly.

Mrs Quantock looked at her husband with an eager encouraging earnestness.

'So you did!' she said. 'I'm getting jealous. Interesting, dear?'

'Yes, dear, haw, haw,' said Robert, and again their eyes met.

This time Georgie had no doubts at all. They were playing the same game now: they smiled and smirked at each other. They had not been playing the same game before. Now they recognized that there was a conspiracy between them . . . But he was host; his business for the moment was to make his guests comfortable, and not pry into their inmost bosoms. So before Mrs Weston realized that she had the whole table attending to her, he said:

'I shall get it out of Robert after dinner. And I'll tell you, Mrs Quantock.'

'Before Atkinson came to the Colonel,' said Mrs Weston, going on precisely where she had left off, 'and that was five years before Elizabeth came to me – let me see – was it five or was it four and a half? – four and a half we'll say, he had another servant whose name was Ahab Crowe.'

'No!' said Georgie.

'Yes!' said Mrs Weston, hastily finishing her champagne, for she saw Foljambe coming near – 'Yes, Ahab Crowe. He married, too, just like Atkinson is going to, and that's an odd coincidence in itself. I tell the Colonel that if Ahab Crowe hadn't married, he would be with him still, and who can say that he'd have fancied Elizabeth? And if he hadn't, I don't believe that the Colonel and I would ever have – well, I'll leave that alone, and spare my blushes. But that's not what I was saying. Whom do you think Ahab Crowe married? You can have ten guesses each, and you would never come right, for it can't be a common name. It was Miss Jackdaw. Crowe, Jackdaw. I never heard anything like that, and if you ask the Colonel about it, he'll confirm every word I've said. Boucher, Weston: why that's quite commonplace in comparison, and I'm sure that's an event enough for me.'

Lucia gave her silvery laugh.

'Dear Mrs Weston,' she said, 'you must really tell me at once when the happy day will be. Peppino and I are thinking of going to the Riviera – '

Georgie broke in.

'You shan't do anything of the kind,' he said. 'What's to happen to us? 'Oo very selfish, Lucia.'

The conversation broke up again into duets and trios, and Lucia could have a private conversation with her host. But half an hour ago, so Georgie reflected, they had all been walking round each other like dogs going on tiptoe with their tails very tightly curled, and growling gently to themselves, aware that a hasty snap, or the breach of the smallest observance of etiquette, might lead to a general quarrel. But now they all had the reward of their icy politenesses: there was no more ice, except on their plates, and the politeness was not a matter of etiquette. At present, they might be considered a republic, but no one knew what was going to happen after dinner. Not a word had been said about the tableaux.

Lucia dropped her voice as she spoke to him, and put in a good deal of Italian for fear she might be overheard.

'*Non cognosce* anybody?' she asked. '*I tablini*, I mean. And are we all to sit in the *aula*, while the *salone* is being got ready?'

'*Si*,' said Georgie. 'There's a fire. When you go out, keep them there. *I domestichi* are making *salone* ready.'

'*Molto bene*. Then Peppino and you and I just steal away. *La lampa* is acting beautifully. We tried it over several times.'

'Everybody's tummin',' said Georgie, varying the cipher.

'Me so *nervosa*!' said Lucia. 'Fancy me doing Brünnhilde before opera-Brünnhilde. Me can't bear it.'

Georgie knew that Lucia had been thrilled and delighted to know that Olga so much wanted to come in after dinner and see the tableaux, so he found it quite easy to induce Lucia to nerve herself up to an ordeal so passionately desired. Indeed he himself was hardly less excited at the thought of being King Cophetua.

At that moment, even as the crackers were being handed round, the sound of the carol singers was heard from outside, and Lucia had to wince, as 'Good King Wenceslas' looked out. When the Page and the King sang their speeches, the other voices grew *piano*, so that the effect was of a solo voice accompanied. When the Page sang, Lucia shuddered.

'That's the small red-haired boy who nearly deafens me in church,' she whispered to Georgie. 'Don't you hope his voice will crack soon?'

She said this very discreetly, so as not to hurt Mrs Rumbold's feelings, for she trained the choir. Everyone knew that the King was Mr Rumbold, and said 'Charming' to each other, after he had sung.

'I liked that boy's voice, too,' said Mrs Weston. 'Tommy Luton used to have a lovely voice, but this one's struck me as better-trained even than Tommy Luton's. Great credit to you, Mrs Rumbold.'

The grey hungry mouse suddenly gave a shrill cackle of a laugh, quite inexplicable. Then Georgie guessed.

He got up.

'Now nobody must move,' he said, 'because we haven't drunk "absent friends" yet. I'm just going out to see that they have a bit of supper in the kitchen before they go on.'

His trembling legs would scarcely carry him to the door, and he ran out. There were half a dozen little choirboys, four men and one tall cloaked woman . . .

'Divine!' he said to Olga. 'Aunt Jane thought your voice very well trained. Come in soon, won't you?'

'Yes: all flourishing?'

'Swimming,' said Georgie. 'Lucia hoped your voice would crack soon. But it's all being lovely.'

He explained about food in the kitchen and hurried back to his guests. There was the riddle of the Quantocks to solve: there were the *tableaux vivants* imminent: there was the little red-haired boy coming in sOon. What a Christmas night!

* * *

Soon after Georgie's hall began to fill up with guests, and yet not a word was said about tableaux. It grew so full that nobody could have said for certain whether Lucia and Peppino were there or not. Olga certainly was: there was no mistaking that fact. And then Foljambe opened the drawing-room door and sounded a gong.

The lamp behaved perfectly and an hour later one Brünnhilde was being extremely kind to the other, as they sat together. 'If you really want to know my view, dear Miss Bracely,' said Lucia, 'it's just that. You must be Brünnhilde for the time being. Singing, of course, as you say, helps it out: you can express so much by singing. You are so lucky there. I am bound to say I had qualms when Peppino – or was it Georgie – suggested we should do Brünnhilde and Siegfried. I said it would be so terribly difficult. Slow: it has to be slow, and to keep gestures slow when you cannot make them mere illustrations of what you are singing – well, I am sure, it is very kind of you to be so flattering about it – but it is difficult to do that.'

'And you thought them all out for yourself?' said Olga. 'Marvellous!'

'Ah, if I had ever seen you do it,' said Lucia, 'I am sure I should have picked up some hints! And King Cophetua! Won't you give me a little word for our dear King Cophetua? I was so glad after the strain of Brünnhilde to have my back to the audience. Even then there is the difficulty of keeping quite still, but I am sure you know that quite as well as I do, from having played Brünnhilde yourself. Georgie was very much impressed by your performance of it. And Mary Queen of Scots now! The shrinking of the flesh, and the resignation of the spirit! That is what I tried to express. You must come and help me next time I attempt this sort of thing again. That will not be quite soon, I am afraid, for Peppino and I are thinking of going to the Riviera for a little holiday.'

'Oh, but how selfish!' said Olga. 'You mustn't do that.'

Lucia gave the silvery laugh.

'You are all very tiresome about my going to the Riviera,' she said. 'But I don't promise that I shall give it up yet. We shall see! Gracious! How late it is. We must have sat very late over dinner. Why were you not asked to dinner, I wonder! I shall scold Georgie for not asking you. Ah, there is dear Mrs Weston going away. I must say good night to her. She would think it very strange if I did not. Colonel Boucher, too! Oh, they are coming this way to save us the trouble of moving.'

A general move was certainly taking place, not in the direction of the door, but to where Olga and Lucia were sitting.

'It's snowing,' said Piggy excitedly to Olga. 'Will you mark my footsteps well, my page?'

'Piggy, you – you Goosie,' said Olga hurriedly. 'Goosie, weren't the tableaux lovely?'

'And the carols,' said Goosie. 'I adored the carols. I guessed. Did you guess, Mrs Lucas?'

Olga resorted to the mean trick of treading on Goosie's foot and apologizing. That was cowardly because it was sure to come out sometime. And Goosie again trod on dangerous ground by saving that if the Page had trod like that, there was no need for any footsteps to be marked for him.

*   *   *

It was snowing fast, and Mrs Weston's wheels left a deep track, but in spite of that, Daisy and Robert had not gone fifty yards from the door when they came to a full stop.

'Now, what is it?' said Daisy. 'Out with it. Why did you talk about the discovery of muslin?'

'I only said that we were fortunate in a medium whom after all you picked up at a vegetarian restaurant,' said he. 'I suppose I may indulge in general conversation. If it comes to that, why did you talk about exposure in the papers?'

'General conversation,' said Mrs Quantock all in one word. 'So that's all, is it?'

'Yes,' said Robert, 'you may know something, and – '

'Now don't put it all on me,' said Daisy. 'If you want to know what I think, it is that you've got some secret.'

'And if you want to know what I think,' he retorted, 'it is that I know you have.'

Daisy hesitated a moment; the snow was white on her shoulder and she shook her cloak.

'I hate concealment,' she said. 'I found yards and yards of muslin and a pair of Amadeo's eyebrows in that woman's bedroom the very day she went away.'

'And she was fined last Thursday for holding a séance at which a detective was present,' said Robert. 'Fifteen, Gerard Street. He seized Amadeo or Cardinal Newman by the throat, and it was that woman.'

She looked hastily round.

'When you thought that the chimney was on fire, I was burning muslin,' she said.

'When you thought the chimney was on fire, I was burning every copy of *Todd's News*,' said he. 'Also a copy of the *Daily Mirror*, which contained the case. It belonged to the Colonel. I stole it.'

She put her hand through his arm.

'Let's get home,' she said. 'We must talk it over. No one knows one word except you and me?'

'Not one, my dear,' said Robert cordially. 'But there are suspicions. Georgie suspects, for instance. He saw me buy all the copies of *Todd's News*, at least he was hanging about. Tonight he was clearly on the track of something, though he gave us a very tolerable dinner.' They went into Robert's study: it was cold, but neither felt it, for they glowed with excitement and enterprise.

'That was a wonderful stroke of yours, Robert,' said she. 'It was masterly: it saved the situation. The *Daily Mirror*, too: how right you were to steal it. A horrid paper I always thought. Yes, Georgie suspects something, but luckily he doesn't know what he suspects.'

'That's why we both said we had just heard from that woman,' said Robert.

'Of course. You haven't got a copy of *Todd's News*, have you?'

'No: at least I burned every page of the police reports,' said he. 'It was safer.'

'Quite so. I cannot show you Amadeo's eyebrows for the same reason. Nor the muslin. Lovely muslin, my dear: yards of it. Now what we must do is this: we must continue to be interested in psychical things; we mustn't drop them, or seem to be put off them.

I wish now I had taken you into my confidence at the beginning and told you about Amadeo's eyebrows.'

'My dear, you acted for the best,' said he. 'So did I when I didn't tell you about *Todd's News*. Secrecy even from each other was more prudent, until it became impossible. And I think we should be wise to let it be understood that we hear from the Princess now and then. Perhaps in a few months she might even visit us again. It – it would be humorous to be behind the scenes, so to speak, and observe the credulity of the others.'

Daisy broke into a broad grin.

'I will certainly ask dear Lucia to a séance, if we do,' she said. 'Dear me! How late it is: there was such a long wait between the tableaux. But we must keep our eyes on Georgie, and be careful how we answer his impertinent questions. He is sure to ask some. About getting that woman down again, Robert. It might be foolhardy, for we've had an escape, and shouldn't put our heads into the same noose again. On the other hand, it would disarm suspicion for ever, if, after a few months, I asked her to spend a few days of holiday here. You said it was a fine only, not imprisonment?'

The week was a busy one: Georgie in particular never had a moment to himself. The Hurst, so lately a desert, suddenly began to rejoice with joy and singing and broke out into all manner of edifying gaieties. Lucia, capricious queen, quite forgot all the vitriolic things she had said to him, and gave him to understand that he was just as high in favour as ever before, and he was as busy with his duties as ever he had been. Whether he would have fallen into his old place so readily if he had been a free agent, was a question that did not arise, for though it was Lucia who employed him, it was Olga who drove him there. But he had his consolation, for Lucia's noble forgiveness of all the disloyalties against her, included Olga's as well, and out of all the dinners and music parties, and recitations from Peppino's new book of prose poems which was already in proof, and was read to select audiences from end to end, there was none to which Olga was not bidden, and none at which she failed to appear. Lucia even overlooked the fact that she had sung in the carols on Christmas night, though she had herself declared that it was the voice of the red-haired boy which was so peculiarly painful to her. Georgie's picture of her (she never knew that Olga had really commissioned it) hung at the side of the piano in the music room, where the print of Beethoven had hung before, and it gave her the acutest gratification. It represented her sitting, with eyes cast down at her piano, and was indeed much on the same scheme as the yet unfinished one of Olga, which had been postponed in its favour, but there was no time for Georgie to think out another position, and his hand was in with regard to the perspective of pianos. So there it hung with its title, *The Moonlight Sonata*, painted in gilt letters on its frame, and Lucia, though she continued to say that he had made her far, far too young, could not but consider that he had caught her expression exactly . . .

So Riseholme flocked back to The Hurst like sheep that have been astray, for it was certain to find Olga there, even as it had turned there, deeply breathing, to the classes of the guru. It had to sit through the prose poems of Peppino, it had to listen to the old, old tunes and sigh at the end, but Olga mingled her sighs with theirs, and often after a suitable pause Lucia would say winningly to Olga: 'One little song, Miss Bracely. Just a stanza? Or am I trespassing too much on your good nature? Where is your accompanist? I declare I am jealous of him: I shall pop into his place someday! Georgino, Miss Bracely is going to sing us something. Is not that a treat? Sh-sh, please, ladies and gentlemen.'

And she rustled to her place, and sat with the furthest-away expression ever seen on mortal face, while she trespassed on Miss Bracely's good nature.

* * *

Then Georgie had the other picture to finish, which he hoped to get ready in time to be a New Year's present, since Olga had insisted on Lucia's being done first. He had certainly secured an admirable likeness of her, and there was in it just all that his stippled, fussy representation of Lucia lacked. *Bleak December* and *Yellow Daffodils* and the rest of the series lacked it, too: for once he had done something in the doing of which he had forgotten himself. It was by no means a work of genius, for Georgie was not possessed of one grain of that, and the talent it displayed was by no means of a high order, but it had something of the naturalness of a flower that grew from the earth which nourished it.

On the last day of the year he was putting a few final touches to it, little high reflected lights on the black keys, little blacknesses of shadow in the moulding of the panel behind his hand. He had finished with her altogether, and now she sat in the window seat, looking out, and playing with the blind tassel. He had been so much absorbed in his work that he had scarcely noticed that she had been rather unusually silent.

'I've got a piece of news for you,' she said at length.

Georgie held his breath, as he drew a very thin line of body colour along the edge of A flat.

'No! What is it?' he said. 'Is it about the Princess?'

Olga seemed to hail this as a diversion.

'Ah, let's talk about that for a minute,' she said. 'What you ought to have done was to order another copy of *Todd's News* at once.'

'I know I ought, but I couldn't get one when I thought of it afterwards. That was tarsome. But I feel sure there was something about her in it.'

'And you can't get anything out of the Quantocks?'

'No, though I've laid plenty of traps for them. There's an understanding between them now. They both know something. When I lay a trap, it isn't any use: they look at the trap, and then they look at each other afterwards.'

'What sort of traps?'

'Oh, anything. I say suddenly, "What a bore it is that there are so many frauds among mediums, especially paid ones." You see, I don't believe for a moment that these séances were held for nothing, though we didn't pay for going to them. And then Robert says that he would never trust a paid medium, and she looks at him approvingly, and says "Dear Princess!" The other day – it was a very good trap – I said, "Is it true that the Princess is coming to stay with Lady Ambermere?" It wasn't a lie: I only asked.'

'And then?' said Olga.

'Robert gave an awful twitch, not a jump exactly, but a twitch. But she was on the spot and said, "Ah, that would be nice. I wonder if it's true. The Princess didn't mention it in her last letter." And then he looked at her approvingly. There is something there, no one shall convince me otherwise.'

Olga suddenly burst out laughing.

'What's the matter?' asked Georgie.

'Oh, it's all so delicious!' she said. 'I never knew before how terribly interesting little things were. It's all wildly exciting, and there are fifty things going on just as exciting. Is it all of you who take such a tremendous interest in them that makes them so absorbing, or is it that they are absorbing in themselves, and ordinary dull people, not Riseholmites, don't see how exciting they are? Tommy Luton's measles: the Quantocks' secret: Elizabeth's lover! And to think that I believed I was coming to a backwater.'

Georgie held up his picture and half closed his eyes. 'I believe it's finished,' he said. 'I shall have it framed, and put it in my drawing room.'

This was a trap, and Olga fell into it.

'Yes, it will look nice there,' she said. 'Really, Georgie, it is very clever of you.'

He began washing his brushes.

'And what was your news?' he said.

She got up from her seat.

'I forgot all about it, with talking of the Quantocks' secret,' she said. 'That just shows you: I completely forgot, Georgie. I've just accepted an offer to sing in America, a four months' engagement, at fifty thousand million pounds a night. A penny less, and I wouldn't have gone. But I really can't refuse. It's all been very sudden, but they want to produce *Lucretia* there before it appears in England. Then I come back, and sing in London all the summer. Oh, me!'

There was dead silence, while Georgie dried his brushes.

'When do you go?' he asked.

'In about a fortnight.'

'Oh,' said he.

She moved down the room to the piano and shut it without speaking, while he folded the paper round his finished picture.

'Why don't you come, too?' she said at length. 'It would do you no end of good, for you would get out of this darling twopenny place which will all go inside a nutshell. There are big things in the world, Georgie: seas, continents, people, movements, emotions. I told my Georgie I was going to ask you, and he thoroughly approves. We both like you, you know. It would be lovely if you would come. Come for a couple of months, anyhow: of course you'll be our guest, please.'

The world, at that moment, had grown absolutely black to him, and it was by that that he knew who, for him, was the light of it. He shook his head.

'Why can't you come?' she said.

He looked at her straight in the face.

'Because I adore you,' he said.

EPILOGUE OR PREFACE

The glad word went round Riseholme one March morning that the earliest flower in Perdita's garden was in bloom. The day was one of those glories of the English springtime, with large white clouds blown across wide spaces of blue sky by the south-west wind, and with swift shadows that bowled across the green below them. Parliament was in full conclave that day, and in the elms the rooks were busy.

An awful flatness had succeeded Olga's departure. Riseholme naturally took a good deal of credit for the tremendous success which had attended the production of *Lucretia*, since it so rightly considered that the real cradle of the opera was here, where she had tried it over for the first time. Lucia seemed to remember it better than anybody, for she remembered all sorts of things which no one else had the faintest recollection of; how she had discussed music with Signor Cortese, and he had asked her where she had her musical training. Such a treat to talk Italian with a Roman – *lingua Toscana in bocca Romana* – and what a wonderful evening it was. Poor Mrs Colonel recollected very little of this, but Lucia had long been aware that her memory was going sadly. After producing *Lucretia* in New York, Olga had appeared in some of her old roles, notably in the part of Brünnhilde, and Lucia was very reminiscent of that charming party of Christmas Day at dear Georgino's, when they had the tableaux. Dear Olga was so simple and unspoiled: she had come to Lucia afterwards, and asked her to tell her how she had worked out her scheme of gestures in the awakening, and Lucia had been very glad, very glad indeed to give her a few hints. In fact, Lucia was quite herself: it was only her subjects whom it had been a little hard to stir up. Georgie in particular had been very listless and dull, and Lucia, for all her ingenuity, was at a complete loss to find a reason for it.

But today the warm inflowing tide of spring seemed to renovate the muddy flats, setting the weeds, that had lain dank and dispirited, a-floating again on the return of the water. No one could quite resist the magic of the season, and Georgie, who had intended out of mere politeness to go to see the earliest of Perdita's stupid flowers (having been warned of its epiphany by telephone from The Hurst) found, when he set foot outside his house on that warm windy morning, that it would be interesting to stroll across the green first, and see if there was any news. All the news he had really cared about for the last two months was news from America, of which he had a small packet done up in a pink riband.

After getting rid of Piggy, he went to the newspaper shop, to get his *Times*, which most unaccountably had not arrived, and the sight of *Todd's News* in its yellow cover stirred his drowsy interest. Not one atom of light had ever been thrown on that extraordinary occurrence when Robert bought the whole issue, and though Olga never failed to enquire, he had not been able to give her the slightest additional information. Occasionally he set a languid trap for one of the Quantocks, but they never by any chance fell into it. The whole affair must be classed with problems like the origin of evil, among the insoluble mysteries of life.

It was possible to get letters by the second post an hour earlier than the house-to-house delivery by calling at the office, and as Georgie was waiting for his *Times*, Mrs Quantock came hurrying out of the post office with a small packet in her hands, which she was opening as she walked. She was so much absorbed by this that she did not see Georgie at all, though she passed quite close to him, and soon after shed a registered envelope. At that the 'old familiar glamour' began to steal over him again, and he found himself wondering with intensity what it contained.

She was now some hundred yards in front of him, walking in the direction of The Hurst, and there could be no doubt that she, too, was on her way to see Perdita's first flower. He followed her going more briskly than she and began to catch her up. Soon (this time by accident, not in the manner in which, through eagerness, she had untidily cast the registered envelope away) she dropped a small paper, and Georgie picked it up, meaning to give it her. It had printed matter on the front of it, and was clearly a small pamphlet. He could not possibly help seeing what that printed matter was, for it was in capital letters:

INCREASE YOUR HEIGHT

Georgie quickened his step, and the old familiar glamour brightened round him. As soon as he got within speaking distance, he called to her, and turning round, 'like a guilty thing surprised', a little box flew out of her hand. As it fell the lid came off, and there was scattered on the green grass a multitude of red lozenges. She gave a cry of dismay.

'Oh! Mr Georgie, how you startled me,' she said. 'Do help me to pick them up. Do you think the damp will have hurt them? Any news? I was so wrapped up in what I was doing that I've spoken to nobody.'

Georgie assisted in the recovery of the red lozenges.

'You dropped this as you walked,' he said. 'I picked it up in order to give it you.'

'Ah, that is kind, and did you see what it was?'

'I couldn't help seeing the outside,' said Georgie.

She looked at him a moment, wondering what was the most prudent course. If she said nothing more, he would probably tell everybody . . .

'Well, then, I shall let you into the whole secret,' she said. 'It's the most wonderful invention, and increases your height, whatever your age is, from two to six inches. Fancy! There are some exercises you have to do, rather like those Yoga ones, every morning, and you eat three lozenges a day. Quite harmless they are, and then you soon begin to shoot up. It sounds incredible, doesn't it? but there are so many testimonials that I can't doubt it is genuine. Here's one of a man who grew six inches. I saw it advertised in some paper, and sent for it. Only a guinea! What fun when Robert begins to see that I am taller than he is! But now not a word! Don't tell dear Lucia whatever you do. She is half a head taller than I, and it would be no fun if everybody grew from two to six inches. You may write for them, and I'll give you the address, but you must tell nobody.'

'Too wonderful,' said Georgie. 'I shall watch you. Here we are. Look, there's Perdita's flower. What a beauty!'

It was not necessary to press the mermaid's tail, for Lucia had seen them from the music room, and they heard her high heels clacking over the polished floor of the hall.

'Listen! No more need of high heels!' said Mrs Quantock. 'And I've got something else to tell you. Lucia may hear that. Ah, dear Lucia, what a wonderful Perdita blossom!'

'Is it not?' said Lucia, blowing kisses to Georgie, and giving them to Daisy. 'That shows spring is here. *Primavera!* And Peppino's *piccolo libro* comes out today. I should not be a bit surprised if you each of you found a copy of it arrived before evening. Glorious! It's glorious!'

Surely it was no wonder that Georgie's blood began to canter along his arteries again. There had been very pleasant exciting years before now, requiring for their fuel no more than was ready at this moment to keep up the fire. Mrs Quantock was on tiptoe, so to speak, to increase her height, Peppino was just delivered of a second of these vellum volumes with seals and tapes outside, Mrs Weston was going to become Mrs Colonel at the end of the week, and at the same hour and church Elizabeth was going to become Mrs Atkinson. Had these things no savour, because –

'How is oo?' said Georgie, with a sudden flush of the springtime through him. 'Me vewy well, sank 'oo and me so want to read Peppino's bookie-bookie.'

''Oo come in,' said Lucia. 'Evewybody come in. Now, who's got ickle bit news?'

Mrs Quantock had been walking on her toes all across the hall, in anticipation of the happy time when she would be from two to six inches taller. As the animated pamphlet said, the world assumed a totally different aspect when you were even two inches taller. She was quite sorry to sit down.

'Is next week very fall with you, dear Lucia?' she asked.

Lucia pressed her finger to her forehead.

'Monday, Tuesday, Wednesday,' she began. 'No, not Tuesday, I am doing nothing on Tuesday. You want to be the death of me between you. Why?'

'I hope that my dear friend, Princess Popoffski, will be staying with me,' said Mrs Quantock. 'Do get over your prejudice against spiritualism, and give it a chance. Come to a séance on Tuesday. You, too, of course, Georgie: I know better than to invite Lucia without you.'

Lucia put on the faraway look which she reserved for the masterpieces of music, and for Georgie's hopeless devotion.

'Lovely! That will be lovely!' she said. 'Most interesting! I shall come with a perfectly open mind.'

Georgie scarcely lamented the annihilation of a mystery. He must surely have imagined the mystery, for it all collapsed like a card house, if the Princess was coming back. The séances had been most remarkable, too; and he would have to get out his planchette again.

'And what's going to happen on Wednesday?' he asked Lucia. 'All I know is that I've not been asked. Me's offended.'

'Ickle surprise,' said Lucia. 'You're not engaged that evening, are you? Nor you, dear Daisy? That's lovely. Eight o'clock? No, I think a quarter to. That will give us more time. I shan't tell you what it is.'

Mrs Quantock, grasping her lozenges, wondered how much taller she would be by then. As Lucia played to them, she drew a lozenge out of the box and put it into her mouth, in order to begin growing at once. It tasted rather bitter, but not unpleasantly so.

MISS MAPP

PREFACE

I lingered at the window of the garden room from which Miss Mapp so often and so ominously looked forth. To the left was the front of her house, straight ahead the steep cobbled way, with a glimpse of the High Street at the end, to the right the crooked chimney and the church.

The street was populous with passengers, but search as I might, I could see none who ever so remotely resembled the objects of her vigilance.

E. F. Benson
Lamb House, Rye

CHAPTER ONE

Miss Elizabeth Mapp might have been forty, and she had taken advantage of this opportunity by being just a year or two older. Her face was of high vivid colour and was corrugated by chronic rage and curiosity; but these vivifying emotions had preserved to her an astonishing activity of mind and body, which fully accounted for the comparative adolescence with which she would have been credited anywhere except in the charming little town which she had inhabited so long. Anger and the gravest suspicions about everybody had kept her young and on the boil.

She sat, on this hot July morning, like a large bird of prey at the very convenient window of her garden room, the ample bow of which formed a strategical point of high value. This garden room, solid and spacious, was built at right angles to the front of her house, and looked straight down the very interesting street which debouched at its lower end into the High Street of Tilling. Exactly opposite her front door the road turned sharply, so that as she looked out from this projecting window, her own house was at right angles on her left, the street in question plunged steeply downwards in front of her, and to her right she commanded an uninterrupted view of its further course which terminated in the disused graveyard surrounding the big Norman church. Anything of interest about the church, however, could be gleaned from a guidebook, and Miss Mapp did not occupy herself much with such coldly venerable topics. Far more to her mind was the fact that between the church and her strategic window was the cottage in which her gardener lived, and she could thus see, when not otherwise engaged, whether he went home before twelve, or failed to get back to her garden again by one, for he had to cross the street in front of her very eyes. Similarly she could observe whether any of his abandoned family ever came out from her garden door weighted with suspicious baskets, which might contain smuggled vegetables. Only yesterday morning she had hurried forth with a dangerous smile to intercept a laden urchin, with enquiries as to what was in 'that nice basket'. On that occasion that nice basket had proved to contain a strawberry net which was being sent for repair to the gardener's wife; so there was nothing more to be done except verify its return. This she did from a side window of the garden room which commanded the strawberry beds; she could sit quite close to that, for it was screened by the large-leaved branches of a fig tree and she could spy unseen.

Otherwise this road to the right leading up to the church was of no great importance (except on Sunday morning, when she could get a practically complete list of those who attended Divine Service), for no one of real interest lived in the humble dwellings which lined it. To the left was the front of her own house at right angles to the strategic window, and with regard to that a good many useful observations might be, and were, made. She could, from behind a curtain negligently half-drawn across the side of the window nearest the house, have an eye on her housemaid at work, and notice if she leaned out of a window, or made remarks to a friend passing in the street, or waved salutations with a duster. Swift upon such discoveries, she would execute a flank march across the few steps of garden and steal into the house, noiselessly ascend the stairs, and catch the offender red-handed at this public dalliance. But all such domestic espionage to right and left was flavourless and insipid compared to the tremendous discoveries which daily and hourly awaited the trained observer of the street that lay directly in front of her window.

There was little that concerned the social movements of Tilling that could not be proved, or at least reasonably conjectured, from Miss Mapp's eyrie. Just below her house on the left stood Major Flint's residence, of Georgian red brick like her own, and opposite was that of Captain Puffin. They were both bachelors, though Major Flint was generally supposed to have been the hero of some amazingly amorous adventures in early life, and always turned the subject with great abruptness when anything connected with duelling was mentioned. It was not, therefore, unreasonable to infer that he had had experiences of a bloody sort, and colour was added to this romantic conjecture by the fact that in damp, rheumatic weather his left arm was very stiff, and he had been known to say that his wound troubled him. What wound that was no one exactly knew (it might have been anything from a vaccination mark to a sabre cut), for having said that his wound troubled him, he would invariably add: 'Pshaw! that's enough about an old campaigner'; and though he might subsequently talk of nothing else except the old campaigner, he drew a veil over his old campaigns. That he had seen service in India was, indeed, probable by his referring to lunch as tiffin, and calling to his parlourmaid with the ejaculation of 'Quai-hai'. As her name was Sarah, this was clearly a reminiscence of days in bungalows. When not in a rage, his manner to his own sex was bluff and hearty; but whether in a rage or not, his manner to the fairies, or lovely woman, was gallant and pompous in the extreme. He certainly had a lock of hair in a small gold specimen case on his watchchain, and had been seen to kiss it when, rather carelessly, he thought that he was unobserved.

Miss Mapp's eye, as she took her seat in her window on this sunny July morning, lingered for a moment on the Major's house, before she proceeded to give a disgusted glance at the pictures on the back page of her morning illustrated paper, which chiefly represented young women dancing in rings in the surf, or lying on the beach in attitudes which Miss Mapp would have scorned to adjust herself to. Neither the Major nor Captain Puffin were very early risers, but it was about time that the first signals of animation might be expected. Indeed, at this moment, she quite distinctly heard that muffled roar which to her experienced ear was easily interpreted to be 'Quai-hai!'

'So the Major has just come down to breakfast,' she mechanically inferred, 'and it's close on ten o'clock. Let me see: Tuesday, Thursday, Saturday – Porridge morning.'

Her penetrating glance shifted to the house exactly opposite to that in which it was porridge morning, and even as she looked a hand was thrust out of a small upper window and deposited a sponge on the sill. Then from the inside the lower sash was thrust firmly down, so as to prevent the sponge from blowing away and falling into the street. Captain Puffin, it was therefore clear, was a little later than the Major that morning. But he always shaved and brushed his teeth before his bath, so that there was but a few minutes between them.

General manoeuvres in Tilling, the gradual burstings of fluttering life from the chrysalis of the night, the emergence of the ladies of the town with their wicker baskets in their hands for housekeeping purchases, the exodus of men to catch the 11.20 a.m. steam tram out to the golf links, and other first steps in the duties and diversions of the day, did not get into full swing till half-past ten, and Miss Mapp had ample time to skim the headlines of her paper and indulge in chaste meditations about the occupants of these two houses, before she need really make herself alert to miss nothing. Of the two, Major Flint, without doubt, was the more attractive to the feminine sense; for years Miss Mapp had tried to cajole him into marrying her, and had not nearly finished yet. With his record of adventure, with the romantic reek of India (and camphor) in the tigerskin of the rugs that strewed his hall and surged like a rising tide up the wall, with his haughty and gallant manner, with his loud pshawings and sniffs at 'nonsense and balderdash', his thumpings on the table to emphasize an argument, with his wound and his prodigious swipes at golf, his intolerance of any who believed in ghosts, microbes or vegetarianism, there was something dashing and risky about him; you felt that you were in the presence of some hot coal straight from the furnace of creation. Captain Puffin, on the other hand, was of clay so different that he could hardly be considered to be made of clay at all. He was lame and short and meagre, with strings of peaceful beads and Papuan aprons in his hall instead of wild tigerskins, and had a jerky, inattentive manner and a high-pitched voice. Yet to Miss Mapp's mind there was something behind his unimpressiveness that had a mysterious quality – all the more so, because nothing of it appeared on the surface. Nobody could call Major Flint, with his bawlings and his sniffings, the least mysterious. He laid all his loud cards on the table, great hulking kings and aces. But Miss Mapp felt far from sure that Captain Puffin did not hold a joker which would some time come to light. The idea of being Mrs Puffin was not so attractive as the other, but she occasionally gave it her remote consideration.

Yet there was mystery about them both, in spite of the fact that most of their movements were so amply accounted for. As a rule, they played golf together in the morning, reposed in the afternoon, as could easily be verified by anyone standing on a still day in the road between their houses and listening to the loud and rhythmical breathings that fanned the tranquil air, certainly went out to tea parties afterwards and played bridge till dinner time; or if no such entertainment was proffered them, occupied armchairs at the county club, or laboriously amassed a hundred at billiards. Though tea-parties were profuse, dining out was very rare at Tilling; Patience or a jigsaw puzzle occupied the hour or two that intervened between domestic supper and bedtime; but again and again, Miss Mapp had seen lights burning in the sitting room of those two neighbours at an hour when such lights as were still in evidence at Tilling were strictly confined to bedrooms, and should, indeed, have been extinguished there. And only last week, being plucked from slumber by some unaccountable indigestion (for which she blamed a small green apple), she had seen at no less than twelve-thirty in the morning the lights in Captain Puffin's sitting room still shining through the blind. This had excited her so much that at risk of toppling into the street, she had craned her neck from her window, and observed a similar illumination in the house of Major Flint. They were not together then, for in that case any prudent householder (and God knew that they both of them scraped and saved enough, or, if He didn't know, Miss Mapp did) would have quenched his own lights, if he were talking to his friend in his friend's house. The next night, the pangs of indigestion having completely vanished, she set her alarm clock at the same timeless hour, and had observed exactly the same phenomenon. Such late hours, of course, amply accounted for these late breakfasts; but why, so Miss Mapp pithily asked herself, why these late hours? Of course they both kept summertime, whereas most of Tilling utterly refused (except when going by train) to alter their watches because Mr Lloyd George told them to; but even allowing for that . . . then she perceived that summertime made it later than ever for its adherents, so that was no excuse.

Miss Mapp had a mind that was incapable of believing the improbable, and the current explanation of these late hours was very improbable, indeed. Major Flint often told the world in general that he was revising his diaries, and that the only uninterrupted time which he could find in this pleasant whirl of life at Tilling was when he was alone in the evening. Captain Puffin, on his part, confessed to a student's curiosity about the ancient history of Tilling, with regard to which he was preparing a monograph. He could talk, when permitted, by the hour about the reclamation from the sea of the marsh land south of the town, and about the old Roman road which was built on a raised causeway, of which traces remained; but it argued, so thought Miss Mapp, an unprecedented egoism on the part of Major Flint, and an equally unprecedented love of antiquities on the part of Captain Puffin, that they should prosecute their studies (with gas at the present price) till such hours. No; Miss Mapp knew better than that, but she had not made up her mind exactly what it was that she knew. She mentally rejected the idea that egoism (even in these days of diaries and autobiographies) and antiquities accounted for so much study, with the same healthy intolerance with which a vigorous stomach rejects unwholesome food, and did not allow herself to be insidiously poisoned by its retention. But as she took up her light aluminium opera glasses to make sure whether it was Isabel Poppit or not who was now stepping with that high, prancing tread into the stationer's in the High Street, she exclaimed to herself, for the three hundred and sixty-fifth time after breakfast: 'It's very baffling'; for it was precisely a year today since she had first seen those mysterious midnight squares of illuminated blind. 'Baffling', in fact, was a word that constantly made short appearances in Miss Mapp's vocabulary, though its retention for a whole year over one subject was unprecedented. But never yet had 'baffled' sullied her wells of pure undefiled English.

Movement had begun; Mrs Plaistow, carrying her wicker basket, came round the corner by the church, in the direction of Miss Mapp's window, and as there was a temporary coolness between them (following violent heat) with regard to some worsted of brilliant rose-madder hue, which a forgetful draper had sold to Mrs Plaistow, having definitely promised it to Miss Mapp . . . but Miss Mapp's large-mindedness scorned to recall the sordid details of this paltry appropriation. The heat had quite subsided, and Miss Mapp was, for her part, quite prepared to let the coolness regain the normal temperature of cordiality the moment that Mrs Plaistow returned that worsted. Outwardly and publicly friendly relationships had been resumed, and as the coolness had lasted six weeks or so, it was probable that the worsted had already been incorporated into the ornamental border of Mrs Plaistow's jumper or winter scarf, and a proper expression of regret would have to do instead. So the nearer Mrs Plaistow approached, the more invisible she became to Miss Mapp's eye, and when she was within saluting distance had vanished altogether. Simultaneously Miss Poppit came out of the stationer's in the High Street.

Mrs Plaistow turned the corner below Miss Mapp's window, and went bobbing along down the steep hill. She walked with the motion of those mechanical dolls sold in the street, which have three legs set as spokes to a circle, so that their feet emerge from their dress with Dutch and rigid regularity, and her figure had a certain squat rotundity that suited her gait. She distinctly looked into Captain Puffin's dining-room window as she passed, and with the misplaced juvenility so characteristic of her waggled her plump little hand at it. At the corner beyond Major Flint's house she hesitated a moment, and turned off down the entry into the side street where Mr Wyse lived. The dentist lived there, too, and as Mr Wyse was away on the continent of Europe, Mrs Plaistow was almost certain to be visiting the other. Rapidly Miss Mapp remembered that at Mrs Bartlett's bridge party yesterday Mrs Plaistow had selected soft chocolates for consumption instead of those stuffed with nougat or almonds. That furnished additional evidence for the dentist, for generally you could not get a nougat chocolate at all if Godiva Plaistow had been in the room for more than a minute or two . . . As she crossed the narrow cobbled roadway, with the grass growing luxuriantly between the rounded pebbles, she stumbled and recovered herself with a swift little forward run, and the circular feet twinkled with the rapidity of those of a thrush scudding over the lawn.

By this time Isabel Poppit had advanced as far as the fish shop three doors below the turning down which Mrs Plaistow had vanished. Her prancing progress paused there for a moment, and she waited with one knee highly elevated, like a statue of a curveting horse, before she finally decided to pass on. But she passed no further than the fruit shop next door, and took the three steps that elevated it from the street in a single prance, with her Roman nose high in the air. Presently she emerged, but with no obvious rotundity like that of a melon projecting from her basket, so that Miss Mapp could see exactly what she had purchased, and went back to the fish shop again. Surely she would not put fish on the top of fruit, and even as Miss Mapp's lucid intelligence rejected this supposition, the true solution struck her. 'Ice,' she said to herself, and, sure enough, projecting from the top of Miss Poppit's basket when she came out was an angular peak, wrapped up in paper already wet.

Miss Poppit came up the street and Miss Mapp put up her illustrated paper again, with the revolting picture of the Brighton sea nymphs turned towards the window. Peeping out behind it, she observed that Miss Poppit's basket was apparently oozing with bright venous blood, and felt certain that she had bought redcurrants. That, coupled with the ice, made conjecture complete. She had bought redcurrants slightly damaged (or they would not have oozed so speedily), in order to make that iced redcurrant fool of which she had so freely partaken at Miss Mapp's last bridge party. That was a very scurvy trick, for iced redcurrant fool was an invention of Miss Mapp's, who, when it was praised, said that she inherited the recipe from her grandmother. But Miss Poppit had evidently entered the lists against Grandmamma Mapp, and she had as evidently guessed that quite inferior fruit – fruit that was distinctly 'off' – was undetectable when severely iced. Miss Mapp could only hope that the fruit in the basket now bobbing past her window was so much 'off' that it had begun to ferment. Fermented redcurrant fool was nasty to the taste, and, if persevered in, disastrous in its effects. General unpopularity might be needed to teach Miss Poppit not to trespass on Grandmamma Mapp's preserves.

Isabel Poppit lived with a flashy and condescending mother just round the corner beyond the gardener's cottage, and opposite the west end of the church. They were comparatively new inhabitants of Tilling, having settled here only two or three years ago, and Tilling had not yet quite ceased to regard them as rather suspicious characters. Suspicion smouldered, though it blazed no longer. They were certainly rich, and Miss Mapp suspected them of being profiteers. They kept a butler, of whom they were both in considerable awe, who used almost to shrug his shoulders when Mrs Poppit gave him an order: they kept a motor car to which Mrs Poppit was apt to allude more frequently than would have been natural if she had always been accustomed to one, and they went to Switzerland for a month every winter and to Scotland 'for the shooting season', as Mrs Poppit terribly remarked, every summer. This all looked very black, and though Isabel conformed to the manners of Tilling in doing household shopping every morning with her wicker basket, and buying damaged fruit for fool, and in dressing in the original home-made manner indicated by good breeding and narrow incomes, Miss Mapp was sadly afraid that these habits were not the outcome of chaste and instinctive simplicity, but of the ambition to be received by the old families of Tilling as one of them. But what did a true Tillingite want with a butler and a motor car? And if these were not sufficient to cast grave doubts on the sincerity of the inhabitants of Ye Smalle House, there was still very vivid in Miss Mapp's mind that dreadful moment, undimmed by the years that had passed over it, when Mrs Poppit broke the silence at an altogether too sumptuous lunch by asking Mrs Plaistow if she did not find the supertax a grievous burden on 'our little incomes'. . . Miss Mapp had drawn in her breath sharply, as if in pain, and after a few gasps turned the conversation . . . Worst of all, perhaps, because more recent, was the fact that Mrs Poppit had just received the dignity of the MBE, or Member of the Order of the British Empire, and put it on her cards too, as if to keep the scandal alive. Her services in connection with the Tilling hospital had been entirely confined to putting her motor car at its disposal when she did not want it herself, and not a single member of the Tilling Working Club, which had knitted its fingers to the bone and made enough seven-tailed bandages to reach to the moon, had been offered a similar decoration. If anyone had she would have known what to do: a stinging letter to the Prime Minister saying that she worked not with hope of distinction, but from pure patriotism, would have certainly been Miss Mapp's rejoinder. She actually drafted the letter, when Mrs Poppit's name appeared, and diligently waded through column after column of subsequent lists, to make sure that she, the originator of the Tilling Working Club, had not been the victim of a similar insult.

Mrs Poppit was a climber: that was what she was, and Miss Mapp was obliged to confess that very nimble she had been. The butler and the motor car (so frequently at the disposal of Mrs Poppit's friends) and the incessant lunches and teas had done their work; she had fed rather than starved Tilling into submission, and Miss Mapp felt that she alone upheld the dignity of the old families. She was positively the only old family (and a solitary spinster at that) who had not surrendered to the Poppits. Naturally she did not carry her staunchness to the extent, so to speak, of a hunger strike, for that would be singular conduct, only worthy of suffragettes, and she partook of the Poppits' hospitality to the fullest extent possible, but (here her principles came in) she never returned the hospitality of the Member of the British Empire, though she occasionally asked Isabel to her house, and abused her soundly on all possible occasions . . .

This spiteful retrospect passed swiftly and smoothly through Miss Mapp's mind, and did not in the least take off from the acuteness with which she observed the tide in the affairs of Tilling which, after the ebb of the night, was now flowing again, nor did it, a few minutes after Isabel's disappearance round the corner, prevent her from hearing the faint tinkle of the telephone in her own house. At that she started to her feet, but paused again at the door. She had shrewd suspicions about her servants with regard to the telephone: she was convinced (though at present she had not been able to get any evidence on the point) that both her cook and her parlour maid used it for their own base purposes at her expense, and that their friends habitually employed it for conversation with them. And perhaps – who knows? – her housemaid was the worst of the lot, for she affected an almost incredible stupidity with regard to the instrument, and pretended not to be able either to speak through it or to understand its cacklings. All that might very well be assumed in order to divert suspicion, so Miss Mapp paused by the door to let any of these delinquents get deep in conversation with her friend: a soft and stealthy advance towards the room called the morning room (a small apartment opening out of the hall, and used chiefly for the bestowal of hats and cloaks and umbrellas) would then enable her to catch one of them red-mouthed, or at any rate to overhear fragments of conversation which would supply equally direct evidence.

She had got no further than the garden door into her house when Withers, her parlour maid, came out. Miss Mapp thereupon began to smile and hum a tune. Then the smile widened and the tune stopped.

'Yes, Withers?' she said. 'Were you looking for me?'

'Yes, Miss,' said Withers. 'Miss Poppit has just rung you up – '

Miss Mapp looked much surprised.

'And to think that the telephone should have rung without my hearing it,' she said. 'I must be growing deaf, Withers, in my old age. What does Miss Poppit want?'

'She hopes you will be able to go to tea this afternoon and play bridge. She expects that a few friends may look in at a quarter to four.'

A flood of lurid light poured into Miss Mapp's mind. To expect that a few friends may look in was the orthodox way of announcing a regular party to which she had not been asked, and Miss Mapp knew as if by a special revelation that if she went, she would find that she made the eighth to complete two tables of bridge. When the butler opened the door, he would undoubtedly have in his hand a half-sheet of paper on which were written the names of the expected friends, and if the caller's name was not on that list, he would tell her with brazen impudence that neither Mrs Poppit nor Miss Poppit were at home, while, before the baffled visitor had turned her back, he would admit another caller who duly appeared on his reference paper . . . So then the Poppits were giving a bridge party to which she had only been bidden at the last moment, clearly to take the place of some expected friend who had developed influenza, lost an aunt or been obliged to go to London: here, too, was the explanation of why (as she had overheard yesterday) Major Flint and Captain Puffin were only intending to play one round of golf today, and to come back by the two-twenty train. And why seek any further for the explanation of the lump of ice and the redcurrants (probably damaged) which she had observed

Isabel purchase? And anyone could see (at least Miss Mapp could) why she had gone to the stationer's in the High Street just before. Packs of cards.

Who the expected friend was who had disappointed Mrs Poppit could be thought out later: at present, as Miss Mapp smiled at Withers and hummed her tune again, she had to settle whether she was going to be delighted to accept, or obliged to decline. The argument in favour of being obliged to decline was obvious: Mrs Poppit deserved to be 'served out' for not including her among the original guests, and if she declined it was quite probable that at this late hour her hostess might not be able to get anyone else, and so one of her tables would be completely spoiled. In favour of accepting was the fact that she would get a rubber of bridge and a good tea, and would be able to say something disagreeable about the redcurrant fool, which would serve Miss Poppit out for attempting to crib her ancestral dishes . . .

A bright, a joyous, a diabolical idea struck her, and she went herself to the telephone, and genteelly wiped the place where Withers had probably breathed on it.

'So kind of you, Isabel,' she said, 'but I am very busy today, and you didn't give me much notice, did you? So I'll try to look in if I can, shall I? I might be able to squeeze it in.'

There was a pause, and Miss Mapp knew that she had put Isabel in a hole. If she successfully tried to get somebody else, Miss Mapp might find she could squeeze it in, and there would be nine. If she failed to get someone else, and Miss Mapp couldn't squeeze it in, then there would be seven . . . Isabel wouldn't have a tranquil moment all day.

'Ah, do squeeze it in,' she said in those horrid wheedling tones which for some reason Major Flint found so attractive. That was one of the weak points about him, and there were many, many others. But that was among those which Miss Mapp found it difficult to condone.

'If I possibly can,' said Miss Mapp. 'But at this late hour – Goodbye, dear, or only *au reservoir*, we hope.'

She heard Isabel's polite laugh at this nearly new and delicious malaprop before she rang off. Isabel collected malaprops and wrote them out in a notebook. If you reversed the notebook and began at the other end, you would find the collection of Spoonerisms, which were very amusing, too.

Tea, followed by a bridge party, was, in summer, the chief manifestation of the spirit of hospitality in Tilling. Mrs Poppit, it is true, had attempted to do something in the way of dinner parties, but though she was at liberty to give as many dinner parties as she pleased, nobody else had followed her ostentatious example. Dinner parties entailed a higher scale of living; Miss Mapp, for one, had accurately counted the cost of having three hungry people to dinner, and found that one such dinner party was not nearly compensated for, in the way of expense, by being invited to three subsequent dinner parries by your guests. Voluptuous teas were the rule, after which you really wanted no more than little bits of things, a cup of soup, a slice of cold tart, or a dished-up piece of fish and some toasted cheese. Then, after the excitement of bridge (and bridge was very exciting in Tilling), a jigsaw puzzle or Patience cooled your brain and composed your nerves. In winter, however, with its scarcity of daylight, Tilling commonly gave evening bridge parties, and asked the requisite number of friends to drop in after dinner, though everybody knew that everybody else had only partaken of bits of things. Probably the ruinous price of coal had something to do with these evening bridge parties, for the fire that warmed your room when you were alone would warm all your guests as well, and then, when your hospitality was returned, you could let your sitting-room fire go out. But though Miss Mapp was already planning something in connection with winter bridge, winter was a long way off yet. . .

Before Miss Mapp got back to her window in the garden room Mrs Poppit's great offensive motor car, which she always alluded to as 'the Royce', had come round the corner and, stopping opposite Major Flint's house, was entirely extinguishing all survey of the street beyond. It was clear enough then that she had sent the Royce to take the two out to the golf links, so that they should have time to play their round and catch the two-twenty back to Tilling again, so as to be in good time for the bridge party. Even as she looked, Major Flint came out of his house on one side of the Royce and Captain Puffin on the other. The Royce obstructed their view of each other, and simultaneously each of them shouted across to the house of the other. Captain Puffin emitted a loud 'Coo-ee, Major' (an Australian ejaculation, learned on his voyages), while Major Flint bellowed, '*Quai-hai*, Captain,' which, all the world knew, was of Oriental origin. The noise each of them made prevented him from hearing the other, and presently one in a fuming hurry to start ran round in front of the car at the precise moment that the other ran round behind it, and they both banged loudly on each other's knockers. These knocks were not so precisely simultaneous as the shouts had been, and this led to mutual discovery, hailed with peals of falsetto laughter on the part of Captain Puffin and the more manly guffaws of the Major . . . After that the Royce lumbered down the grass-grown cobbles of the street, and after a great deal of reversing managed to turn the corner.

Miss Mapp set off with her basket to do her shopping. She carried in it the weekly books, which she would leave, with payment but not without argument, at the tradesmen's shops. There was an item for suet which she intended to resist to the last breath in her body, though her butcher would probably surrender long before that. There was an item for eggs at the dairy which she might have to pay, though it was a monstrous overcharge. She had made up her mind about the laundry, she intended to pay that bill with an icy countenance and say 'Good morning for ever,' or words to that effect, unless the proprietor instantly produced the – the article of clothing which had been lost in the wash (like King John's treasures), or refunded an ample sum for the replacing of it. All these quarrelsome errands were meat and drink to Miss Mapp: Tuesday morning, the day on which she paid and disputed her weekly bills, was as enjoyable as Sunday mornings when, sitting close under the pulpit, she noted the glaring inconsistencies and grammatical errors in the discourse. After the bills were paid and business was done, there was pleasure to follow, for there was a fitting-on at the dressmakers, the fitting-on of a tea gown, to be worn at winter-evening bridge parties, which, unless Miss Mapp was sadly mistaken, would astound and agonize by its magnificence all who set eyes on it. She had found the description of it, as worn by Mrs Titus W. Trout, in an American fashion paper; it was of what was described as kingfisher blue, and had lumps and wedges of lace round the edge of the skirt, and orange chiffon round the neck. As she set off with her basket full of tradesmen's books, she pictured to herself with watering mouth the fury, the jealousy, the madness of envy which it would raise in all properly constituted breasts.

In spite of her malignant curiosity and her cancerous suspicions about all her friends, in spite, too, of her restless activities, Miss Mapp was not, as might have been expected, a lady of lean and emaciated appearance. She was tall and portly, with plump hands, a broad, benignant face and dimpled, well-nourished cheeks. An acute observer might have detected a danger warning in the sidelong glances of her rather bulgy eyes, and in a certain tightness at the corners of her expansive mouth, which boded ill for any who came within snapping distance, but to a more superficial view she was a rollicking, good-natured figure of a woman. Her mode of address, too, bore out this misleading impression: nothing, for instance, could have been more genial just now than her telephone voice to Isabel Poppit, or her smile to Withers, even while she so strongly suspected her of using the telephone for her own base purposes, and as she passed along the High Street, she showered little smiles and bows on acquaintances and friends. She markedly drew back her lips in speaking, being in no way ashamed of her long white teeth, and wore a practically perpetual smile when there was the least chance of being under observation. Though at sermon time on Sunday, as has been already remarked, she greedily noted the weaknesses and errors of which those twenty minutes was so rewardingly full, she sat all the time with down-dropped eyes and a pretty sacred smile on her lips, and now, when she spied on the other side of the street the figure of the vicar, she tripped slantingly across the road to him, as if by the move of a knight at chess, looking everywhere else, and only perceiving him with glad surprise at the very last moment. He was a great frequenter of tea parties and except in Lent an assiduous player of bridge, for a clergyman's duties, so he very properly held, were not confined to visiting the poor and exhorting the sinner. He should be a man of the world, and enter into the pleasures of his prosperous parishioners, as well as into the trials of the troubled. Being an accomplished card player he entered not only into their pleasures but their pockets, and there was no lady of Tilling who was not pleased to have Mr Bartlett for a partner. His winnings, so he said, he gave annually to charitable objects, though whether the charities he selected began at home was a point on which Miss Mapp had quite made up her mind. 'Not a penny of that will the poor ever see,' was the gist of her reflections when on disastrous days she paid him seven-and-ninepence. She always called him 'padre', and had never actually caught him looking over his adversaries' hands.

'Good morning, Padre,' she said as soon as she perceived him. 'What a lovely day! The white butterflies were enjoying themselves so in the sunshine in my garden. And the swallows!'

Miss Mapp, as every reader will have perceived, wanted to know whether he was playing bridge this afternoon at the Poppits. Major Flint and Captain Puffin certainly were, and it might be taken for granted that Godiva Plaistow was. With the Poppits and herself that made six . . .

Mr Bartlett was humorously archaic in speech. He interlarded archaisms with Highland expressions, and his face was knobby, like a chest of drawers.

'Ha, good morrow, fair dame,' he said. 'And prithee, art not thou even as ye white butterflies?'

'Oh, Mr Bartlett,' said the fair dame with a provocative glance. 'Naughty! Comparing me to a delicious butterfly!'

'Nay, prithee, why naughty?' said he. 'Yea, indeed, it's a day to make ye little fowles rejoice! Ha! I perceive you are on the errands of the guid wife Martha.' And he pointed to the basket.

'Yes; Tuesday morning,' said Miss Mapp. 'I pay all my household books on Tuesday. Poor but honest, dear Padre. What a rush life is today! I hardly know which way to turn. Little duties in all directions! And you; you're always busy! Such a busy bee!'

'Busy B? Busy Bartlett, quo' she! Yes, I'm a busy B today, Mistress Mapp. Sermon all morning: choir practice at three, a baptism at six. No time for a walk today, let alone a bit turn at the gowf.'

Miss Mapp saw her opening, and made a busy beeline for it.

'Oh, but you should get regular exercise, Padre,' said she. 'You take no care of yourself. After the choir practice now, and before the baptism, you could have a brisk walk. To please me!'

'Yes. I had meant to get a breath of air then,' said he. 'But ye guid Dame Poppit has insisted that I take a wee hand at the cartes with them, the wifey and I. Prithee, shall we meet there?'

('That makes seven without me,' thought Miss Mapp in parenthesis.) Aloud she said:

'If I can squeeze it in, Padre. I have promised dear Isabel to do my best.'

'Well, and a lassie can do no mair,' said he. '*Au reservoir* then.'

Miss Mapp was partly pleased, partly annoyed by the agility with which the Padre brought out her own particular joke. It was she who had brought it down to Tilling, and she felt she had an option on it at the end of every interview, if she meant (as she had done on this occasion) to bring it out. On the other hand it was gratifying to see how popular it had become. She had heard it last month when on a visit to a friend at that sweet and refined village called Riseholme. It was rather looked down on there, as not being sufficiently intellectual. But within a week of Miss Mapp's return, Tilling rang with it, and she let it be understood that she was the original humorist.

Godiva Plaistow came whizzing along the pavement, a short, stout, breathless body who might, so thought Miss Mapp, have acted up to the full and fell associations of her Christian name without exciting the smallest curiosity on the part of the lewd. (Miss Mapp had much the same sort of figure, but her height, so she was perfectly satisfied to imagine, converted corpulence into majesty.) The swift alternation of those Dutch-looking feet gave the impression that Mrs Plaistow was going at a prodigious speed, but they could stop revolving without any warning, and then she stood still. Just when a collision with Miss Mapp seemed imminent, she came to a dead halt.

It was as well to be quite certain that she was going to the Poppits, and Miss Mapp forgave and forgot about the worsted until she had found out. She could never quite manage the indelicacy of saying 'Godiva', whatever Mrs Plaistow's figure and age might happen to be, but always addressed her as 'Diva', very affectionately, whenever they were on speaking terms.

'What a lovely morning, Diva, darling,' she said; and noticing that Mr Bartlett was well out of earshot, 'The white butterflies were enjoying themselves so in the sunshine in my garden. And the swallows.'

Godiva was telegraphic in speech.

'Lucky birds,' she said. 'No teeth. Beaks.'

Miss Mapp remembered her disappearance round the dentist's corner half an hour ago, and her own firm inference on the problem.

'Toothache, darling?' she said. 'So sorry.'

'Wisdom,' said Godiva. 'Out at one o'clock. Gas. Ready for bridge this afternoon. Playing? Poppits.'

'If I can squeeze it in, dear,' said Miss Mapp. 'Such a hustle today.'

Diva put her hand to her face as 'wisdom' gave her an awful twinge. Of course she did not believe in the 'hustle', but her pangs prevented her from caring much.

'Meet you then,' she said. 'Shall be all comfortable then. *Au* – '

This was more than could be borne, and Miss Mapp hastily interrupted.

'*Au reservoir*, Diva dear,' she said with extreme acerbity, and Diva's feet began swiftly revolving again.

The problem about the bridge party thus seemed to be solved. The two Poppits, the two Bartletts, the Major and the Captain with Diva darling and herself made eight, and Miss Mapp with a sudden recrudescence of indignation against Isabel with regard to the redcurrant fool and the belated invitation, made up her mind that she would not be able to squeeze it in, thus leaving the party one short. Even apart from the redcurrant fool it served the Poppits right for not asking her originally, but only when, as seemed now perfectly clear, somebody else had disappointed them. But just as she emerged from the butcher's shop, having gained a complete victory in the matter of that suet, without expending the last breath in her body or anything like it, the whole of the seemingly solid structure came toppling to the ground. For on emerging, flushed with triumph, leaving the baffled butcher to try his tricks on somebody else if he chose but not on Miss Mapp, she ran straight into the Disgrace of Tilling and her sex, the suffragette, post-impressionist artist (who painted from the nude, both male and female), the socialist and the Germanophil, all incarnate in one frame. In spite of these execrable antecedents, it was quite in vain that Miss Mapp had tried to poison the collective mind of Tilling against this creature. If she hated anybody, and she undoubtedly did, she hated Irene Coles. The bitterest part of it all was that if Miss Coles was amused at anybody, and she undoubtedly was, she was amused at Miss Mapp.

Miss Coles was strolling along in the attire to which Tilling generally had got accustomed, but Miss Mapp never. She had an old wide-awake hat jammed down on her head, a tall collar and stock, a large loose coat, knickerbockers and grey stockings. In her mouth was a cigarette, in her hand she swung the orthodox wicker basket. She had certainly been to the other fishmonger's at the end of the High Street, for a lobster, revived perhaps after a sojourn on the ice, by this warm sun, which the butterflies and the swallows had been rejoicing in, was climbing with claws and waving legs over the edge of it.

Irene removed her cigarette from her mouth and did something in the gutter which is usually associated with the floor of third-class smoking carriages. Then her handsome, boyish face, more boyish because her hair was closely clipped, broke into a broad grin.

'Hello, Mapp!' she said. 'Been giving the tradesmen what for on Tuesday morning?'

Miss Mapp found it extremely difficult to bear this obviously insolent form of address without a spasm of rage. Irene called her Mapp because she chose to, and Mapp (more bitterness) felt it wiser not to provoke Coles. She had a dreadful, humorous tongue, an indecent disregard of public or private opinion, and her gift of mimicry was as appalling as her opinion about the Germans. Sometimes Miss Mapp alluded to her as 'quaint Irene', but that was as far as she got in the way of reprisals.

'Oh, you sweet thing!' she said. 'Treasure!'

Irene, in some ghastly way, seemed to take note of this. Why men like Captain Puffin and Major Flint found Irene 'fetching' and 'killing' was more than Miss Mapp could understand, or wanted to understand.

Quaint Irene looked down at her basket. 'Why, there's my lunch going over the top like those beastly British Tommies,' she said. 'Get back, love.'

Miss Mapp could not quite determine whether 'love' was a sarcastic echo of 'Treasure'. It seemed probable.

'Oh, what a dear little lobster,' she said. 'Look at his sweet claws.'

'I shall do more than look at them soon,' said Irene, poking it into her basket again. 'Come and have tiffin, *quai-hai*, I've got to look after myself today.'

'What has happened to your devoted Lucy?' asked Miss Mapp. Irene lived in a very queer way with one gigantic maid, who, but for her sex, might have been in the Guards.

'Ill. I suspect scarlet fever,' said Irene. 'Very infectious, isn't it? I was up nursing her all last night.'

Miss Mapp recoiled. She did not share Major Flint's robust views about microbes.

'But I hope, dear, you've thoroughly disinfected – '

'Oh, yes. Soap and water,' said Irene. 'By the way, are you Poppiting this afternoon?'

'If I can squeeze it in,' said Miss Mapp.

'We'll meet again, then. Oh – '

'*Au reservoir*,' said Miss Mapp instantly.

'No; not that silly old chestnut!' said Irene. 'I wasn't going to say that. I was only going to say: "Oh, do come to tiffin." You and me and the lobster. Then you and me. But it's a bore about Lucy. I was painting her. Fine figure, gorgeous legs. You wouldn't like to sit for me till she's well again?'

Miss Mapp gave a little squeal and bolted into her dressmaker's. She always felt battered after a conversation with Irene, and needed kingfisher blue to restore her.

CHAPTER TWO

There is not in all England a town so blatantly picturesque as Tilling, nor one, for the lover of level marsh land, of tall reedy dykes, of enormous sunsets and rims of blue sea on the horizon, with so fortunate an environment. The hill on which it is built rises steeply from the level land, and, crowned by the great grave church so conveniently close to Miss Mapp's residence, positively consists of quaint corners, rough-cast and timber cottages, and mellow Georgian fronts. Corners and quaintnesses, gems, glimpses and bits are an obsession to the artist, and in consequence, during the summer months, not only did the majority of its inhabitants turn out into the cobbled ways with sketching blocks, canvases and paintboxes, but every morning brought into the town charabancs from neighbouring places loaded with passengers, many of whom joined the artistic residents, and you would have thought (until an inspection of their productions convinced you of the contrary) that some tremendous outburst of Art was rivalling the Italian Renaissance. For those who were capable of tackling straight lines and the intricacies of perspective there were the steep cobbled streets of charming and irregular architecture, while for those who rightly felt themselves colourists rather than architectural draughtsmen, there was the view from the top of the hill over the marshes. There, but for one straight line to mark the horizon (and that could easily be misty) there were no petty conventionalities in the way of perspective, and the eager practitioner could almost instantly plunge into vivid greens and celestial blues, or, at sunset, into pinks and chromes and rose-madder.

Tourists who had no pictorial gifts would pick their way among the sketchers, and search the shops for cracked china and bits of brass. Few if any of them left without purchasing one of the famous

Tilling money-boxes, made in the shape of a pottery pig, who bore on his back that remarkable legend of his authenticity which ran:

> I won't be druv,
> Though I am willing.
> Good-morning, my love,
> Said the Pig of Tilling.

Miss Mapp had a long shelf full of these in every colour to adorn her dining room. The one which completed her collection, of a pleasant magenta colour, had only just been acquired. She called them 'my sweet rainbow of piggies', and often when she came down to breakfast, especially if Withers was in the room, she said: 'Good morning, quaint little piggies.' When Withers had left the room she counted them.

The corner where the street took a turn towards the church, just below the window of her garden room, was easily the most popular stance for sketchers. You were bewildered and bowled over by 'bits'. For the most accomplished of all there was that rarely attempted feat, the view of the steep downward street, which, in spite of all the efforts of the artist, insisted, in the sketch, on going up hill instead. Then, next in difficulty, was the street after it had turned, running by the gardener's cottage up to the churchyard and the church. This, in spite of its difficulty, was a very favourite subject, for it included, on the right of the street, just beyond Miss Mapp's garden wall, the famous crooked chimney, which was continually copied from every point of view. The expert artist would draw it rather more crooked than it really was, in order that there might be no question that he had not drawn it crooked by accident. This sketch was usually negotiated from the three steps in front of Miss Mapp's front door. Opposite the church-and-chimney artists would sit others, drawing the front door itself (difficult), and moistening their pencils at their cherry lips, while a little further down the street was another battalion hard at work at the gabled front of the garden room and its picturesque bow. It was a favourite occupation of Miss Mapp's, when there was a decent gathering of artists outside, to pull a table right into the window of the garden room, in full view of them, and, quite unconscious of their presence, to arrange flowers there with a smiling and pensive countenance. She had other little playful public pastimes: she would get her kitten from the house, and induce it to sit on the table while she diverted it with the tassel of the blind, and she would kiss it on its sweet little sooty head, or she would write letters in the window, or play Patience there, and then suddenly become aware that there was no end of ladies and gentlemen looking at her. Sometimes she would come out of the house, if the steps were very full, with her own sketching paraphernalia in her hands and say, ever so coyly: 'May I scriggle through?' or ask the squatters on her own steps if they could find a little corner for her. That was so interesting for them: they would remember afterwards that just while they were engaged on their sketches, the lady of that beautiful house at the corner, who had been playing with her kitten in the window, came out to sketch too. She addressed gracious and yet humble remarks to them: 'I see you are painting my sweet little home. May I look? Oh, what a lovely little sketch!' Once, on a never-to-be-forgotten day, she observed one of them take a camera from his pocket and rapidly focus her as she stood on the top step. She turned full-faced and smiling to the camera just in time to catch the click of the shutter, but then it was too late to hide her face, and perhaps the picture might appear in the *Graphic* or the *Sketch*, or among the posturing nymphs of a neighbouring watering place . . .

This afternoon she was content to 'scriggle' through the sketchers, and humming a little tune, she passed up to the church-yard. ('Scriggle' was one of her own words, highly popular; it connoted squeezing and wriggling.) There she carefully concealed herself under the boughs of the weeping ash tree directly opposite the famous south porch of the church. She had already drawn in the lines of this south porch on her sketching block, transferring them there by means of a tracing from a photograph, so that formed a very promising beginning to her sketch. But she was nicely placed not only with regard to her sketch, for, by peeping through the pretty foliage of the tree, she could command the front door of Mrs Poppit's (MBE) house.

Miss Mapp's plans for the bridge party had, of course, been completely upset by the encounter with Irene in the High Street. Up till that moment she had imagined that, with the two ladies of the house and the Bartletts and the Major and the Captain and Godiva and herself, two complete tables of bridge would be formed, and she had, therefore, determined that she would not be able to squeeze the party into her numerous engagements, thereby spoiling the second table. But now everything was changed: there were eight without her, and unless, at a quarter to four, she saw reason to suppose, by noting the arrivals at the house, that three bridge tables were in contemplation, she had made up her mind to 'squeeze it in', so that there would be nine gamblers, and Isabel or her mother, if they had any sense of hospitality to their guests, would be compelled to sit out for ever and ever. Miss Mapp had been urgently invited: sweet Isabel had made a great point of her squeezing it in, and if sweet Isabel, in order to be certain of a company of eight, had asked quaint Irene as well, it would serve her right. An additional reason, besides this piece of good nature in managing to squeeze it in, for the sake of sweet Isabel, lay in the fact that she would be able to take some redcurrant fool, and after one spoonful exclaim 'Delicious,' and leave the rest uneaten.

The white butterflies and the swallows were still enjoying themselves in the sunshine, and so, too, were the gnats, about whose pleasure, especially when they settled on her face, Miss Mapp did not care so much. But soon she quite ceased to regard them, for, before the quaint little gilded boys on each side of the clock above the north porch had hammered out the three-quarters after three on their bells, visitors began to arrive at the Poppits' door, and Miss Mapp was very active looking through the boughs of the weeping ash and sitting down again to smile and ponder over her sketch with her head a little on one side, if anybody approached. One by one the expected guests presented themselves and were admitted: Major Flint and Captain Puffin, the Padre and his wife, darling Diva with her head muffled in a 'cloud', and finally Irene, still dressed as she had been in the morning, and probably reeking with scarlet fever. With the two Poppits these made eight players, so as soon as Irene had gone in, Miss Mapp hastily put her sketching things away, and holding her admirably accurate drawing with its wash of sky not quite dry, in her hand, hurried to the door, for it would never do to arrive after the two tables had started, since in that case it would be she who would have to sit out.

Boon opened the door to her three staccato little knocks, and sulkily consulted his list. She duly appeared on it and was admitted. Having banged the door behind her he crushed the list up in his hand and threw it into the fireplace: all those whose presence was desired had arrived, and Boon would turn his bovine eye on any subsequent caller, and say that his mistress was out.

'And may I put my sketching things down here, please, Boon,' said Miss Mapp ingratiatingly. 'And will no one touch my drawing? It's a little wet still. The church porch.'

Boon made a grunting noise like the Tilling pig, and slouched away in front of her down the passage leading to the garden, sniffing. There they were, with the two bridge tables set out in a shady corner of the lawn, and a buffet vulgarly heaped with all sorts of dainty confections which made Miss Mapp's mouth water, obliging her to swallow rapidly once or twice before she could manage a wide, dry smile: Isabel advanced.

'De-do, dear,' said Miss Mapp. 'Such a rush! But managed to squeeze it in, as you wouldn't let me off.'

'Oh, that was nice of you, Miss Mapp,' said Isabel.

A wild and awful surmise seized Miss Mapp.

'And your dear mother?' she said. 'Where is Mrs Poppit?'

'Mamma had to go to town this morning, She won't be back till close on dinner time.'

Miss Mapp's smile closed up like a furled umbrella. The trap had snapped behind her: it was impossible now to scriggle away. She had completed, instead of spoiling, the second table.

'So we're just eight,' said Isabel, poking at her, so to speak, through the wires. 'Shall we have a rubber first and then some tea? Or tea first. What says everybody?'

Restless and hungry murmurs, like those heard at the sea lions' enclosure in the Zoological Gardens when feeding time approaches, seemed to indicate tea first, and with gallant greetings from the Major, and archaistic welcomes from the Padre, Miss Mapp headed the general drifting movement towards the buffet. There may have been tea there, but there was certainly iced coffee and lager beer and large jugs with dew on the outside and vegetables floating in a bubbling liquid in the inside, and it was all so vulgar and opulent that with one accord everyone set to work in earnest, in order that the garden should present a less gross and greedy appearance. But there was no sign at present of the redcurrant fool, which was baffling . . .

'And have you had a good game of golf, Major?' asked Miss Mapp, making the best of these miserable circumstances. 'Such a lovely day! The white butterflies were enjoying – '

She became aware that Diva and the Padre, who had already heard about the white butterflies, were in her immediate neighbourhood, and broke off.

'Which of you beat? Or should I say "won"!' she asked.

Major Flint's long moustache was dripping with lager beer, and he made a dexterous, sucking movement.

'Well, the Army and the Navy had it out,' he said. 'And if for once Britain's Navy was not invincible, eh, Puffin?'

Captain Puffin limped away pretending not to hear, and took his heaped plate and brimming glass in the direction of Irene.

'But I'm sure Captain Puffin played quite beautifully too,' said Miss Mapp in the vain attempt to detain him. She liked to collect all the men round her, and then scold them for not talking to the other ladies.

'Well, a game's a game,' said the Major. 'It gets through the hours, Miss Mapp. Yes: we finished at the fourteenth hole, and hurried back to more congenial society. And what have you done today? Fairy errands, I'll be bound. Titania! Ha!'

Suet errands and errands about a missing article of underclothing were really the most important things that Miss Mapp had done today, now that her bridge party scheme had so miscarried, but naturally she would not allude to these.

'A little gardening,' she said. 'A little sketching. A little singing. Not time to change my frock and put on something less shabby. But I wouldn't have kept sweet Isabel's bridge party waiting for anything, and so I came straight from my painting here. Padre, I've been trying to draw the lovely south porch. But so difficult! I shall give up trying to draw, and just enjoy myself with looking. And there's your dear Evie! How de do, Evie love?'

Godiva Plaistow had taken off her cloud for purposes of mastication, but wound it tightly round her head again as soon as she had eaten as much as she could manage. This had to be done on one side of her mouth, or with the front teeth in the nibbling manner of a rabbit. Everybody, of course, by now knew that she had had a wisdom tooth out at one o'clock with gas, and she could allude to it without explanation.

'Dreamed I was playing bridge,' she said, 'and had a hand of aces. As I played the first it went off in my hand. All over. Blood. Hope it'll come true. Bar the blood.'

Miss Mapp found herself soon afterwards partnered with Major Flint and opposed by Irene and the Padre. They had hardly begun to consider their first hands when Boon staggered out into the garden under the weight of a large wooden bucket, packed with ice, that surrounded an interior cylinder.

'Redcurrant fool at last,' thought Miss Mapp, adding aloud: 'Oh poor little me, is it, to declare? Shall I say "no trumps"?'

'Mustn't consult your partner, Mapp,' said Irene, puffing the end of her cigarette out of its holder. Irene was painfully literal.

'I don't, darling,' said Miss Mapp, beginning to fizz a little. 'No trumps. Not a trump. Not any sort of trump. There! What are we playing for, by the way?'

'Bob a hundred,' said the Padre, forgetting to be either Scotch or archaic.

'Oh, gambler! You want the poor box to be the rich box, Padre,' said Miss Mapp, surveying her magnificent hand with the greatest satisfaction. If it had not contained so many court cards, she would have proposed playing for sixpence, not a shilling a hundred.

All semblance of manners was invariably thrown to the winds by the ladies of Tilling when once bridge began; primeval hatred took their place. The winners of any hand were exasperatingly condescending to the losers, and the losers correspondingly bitter and tremulous. Miss Mapp failed to get her contract, as her partner's contribution to success consisted of more twos and threes than were ever seen together before, and when quaint Irene at the end said, 'Bad luck, Mapp,' Miss Mapp's hands trembled so much with passion that she with difficulty marked the score. But she could command her voice sufficiently to say, 'Lovely of you to be sympathetic, dear.' Irene in answer gave a short, hoarse laugh and dealt.

By this time Boon had deposited at the left hand of each player a cup containing a red creamy fluid, on the surface of which bubbles intermittently appeared. Isabel, at this moment being dummy, had strolled across from the other table to see that everybody was comfortable and provided with sustenance in times of stress, and here was clearly the proper opportunity for Miss Mapp to take a spoonful of this attempt at redcurrant fool, and with a wry face, hastily (but not too hastily) smothered in smiles, to push the revolting compound away from her. But the one spoonful that she took was so delicious and exhilarating, that she was positively unable to be good for Isabel. Instead, she drank her cup to the dregs in an absent manner, while considering how many trumps were out. The redcurrant fool made a similarly agreeable impression on Major Flint.

''Pon my word,' he said. 'That's amazingly good. Cooling on a hot day like this. Full of champagne.'

Miss Mapp, seeing that it was so popular, had, of course, to claim it again as a family invention.

'No, dear Major,' she said. 'There's no champagne in it. It's my Grandmamma Mapp's famous redcurrant fool, with little additions perhaps by me. No champagne: yolk of egg and a little cream. Dear Isabel has got it very nearly right.'

The Padre had promised to take more tricks in diamonds than he had the slightest chance of doing. His mental worry communicated itself to his voice.

'And why should there be nary a wee drappie o' champagne in it?' he said, 'though your Grandmamma Mapp did invent it. Weel, let's see your hand, partner. Eh, that's a sair sight.'

'And there'll be a sair wee score agin us when ye're through with the playin' o' it,' said Irene, in tones that could not be acquitted of a mocking intent. 'Why the hell – hallelujah did you go on when I didn't support you?'

Even that one glass of redcurrant fool, though there was no champagne in it, had produced, together with the certainty that her opponent had overbidden his hand, a pleasant exhilaration in Miss Mapp; but yolk of egg, as everybody knew, was a strong stimulant. Suddenly the name redcurrant fool seemed very amusing to her.

'Redcurrant fool!' she said. 'What a quaint, old-fashioned name! I shall invent some others. I shall tell my cook to make some gooseberry idiot, or strawberry donkey . . . My play, I think. A ducky little ace of spades.'

'Haw! haw! gooseberry idiot!' said her partner. 'Capital! You won't beat that in a hurry! And a two of spades on the top of it.'

'You wouldn't expect to find a two of spades at the bottom of it,' said the Padre with singular acidity.

The Major was quick to resent this kind of comment from a man, cloth or no cloth.

'Well, by your leave, Bartlett, by your leave, I repeat,' he said, 'I shall expect to find twos of spades precisely where I please, and when I want your criticism – '

Miss Mapp hastily intervened.

'And after my wee ace, a little king piece,' she said. 'And if my partner doesn't play the queen to it! Delicious! And I play just one more . . . Yes . . . lovely, partner puts wee trumpy on it! I'm not surprised; it takes more than that to surprise me; and then Padre's got another spade, I ken fine!'

'Hoots!' said the Padre with temperate disgust.

The hand proceeded for a round or two in silence, during which, by winks and gestures to Boon, the Major got hold of another cupful of redcurrant fool. There was already a heavy penalty of tricks against Miss Mapp's opponents, and after a moment's refreshment, the Major led a club, of which, at this period, Miss Mapp seemed to have none. She felt happier than she had been ever since, trying to spoil Isabel's second table, she had only succeeded in completing it.

'Little trumpy again,' she said, putting it on with the lightness of one of the white butterflies and turning the trick. 'Useful little trumpy – '

She broke off suddenly from the chant of victory which ladies of Tilling were accustomed to indulge in during cross-roughs, for she discovered in her hand another more than useless little clubby . . . The silence that succeeded became tense in quality. Miss Mapp knew she had revoked and squeezed her brains to think how she could possibly dispose of the card, while there was a certain calmness about the Padre, which but too clearly indicated that he was quite content to wait for the inevitable disclosure. This came at the last trick, and though Miss Mapp made one forlorn attempt to thrust the horrible little clubby underneath the other cards and gather them up, the Padre pounced on it.

'What ho, fair lady!' he said, now completely restored. 'Methinks thou art forsworn! Let me have a keek at the last trick but three! Verily I wis that thou didst trump ye club aforetime. I said so; there it is. Eh, that's bonny for us, partner!'

Miss Mapp, of course, denied it all, and a ruthless reconstruction of the tricks took place. The Major, still busy with redcurrant fool, was the last to grasp the disaster, and then instantly deplored the unsportsmanlike greed of his adversaries.

'Well, I should have thought in a friendly game like this – ' he said. 'Of course, you're within your right, Bartlett: might is right, hey? but upon my word, a pound of flesh, you know . . . Can't think what made you do it, partner.'

'You never asked me if I had any more clubs,' said Miss Mapp shrilly, giving up for the moment the contention that she had not revoked. 'I always ask if my partner has no more of a suit, and I always maintain that a revoke is more the partner's fault than the player's. Of course, if our adversaries claim it – '

'Naturally we do, Mapp,' said Irene. 'You were down on me sharp enough the other day.'

Miss Mapp wrinkled her face up into the sweetest and extremest smile of which her mobile features were capable.

'Darling, you won't mind my telling you that just at this moment you are being dummy,' she said, 'and so you mustn't speak a single word. Otherwise there is no revoke, even if there was at all, which I consider far from proved yet.'

There was no further proof possible beyond the clear and final evidence of the cards, and since everybody, including Miss Mapp herself, was perfectly well aware that she had revoked, their opponents merely marked up the penalty and the game proceeded. Miss Mapp, of course, following the rule of correct behaviour after revoking, stiffened into a state of offended dignity, and was extremely polite and distant with partner and adversaries alike. This demeanour became even more majestic when in the next hand the Major led out of turn. The moment he had done it, Miss Mapp hurriedly threw a random card out of her hand on to the table, in the hope that Irene, by some strange aberration, would think she had led first.

'Wait a second,' said she. 'I call a lead. Give me a trump, please.'

Suddenly the awful expression as of some outraged empress faded from Miss Mapp's face, and she gave a little shriek of laughter which sounded like a squeaking slate pencil.

'Haven't got one, dear,' she said. 'Now may I have your permission to lead what I think best? Thank you.'

There now existed between the four players that state of violent animosity which was the usual atmosphere towards the end of a rubber. But it would have been a capital mistake to suppose that they were not all enjoying themselves immensely. Emotion is the salt of life, and here was no end of salt. Everyone was overbidding his hand, and the penalty tricks were a glorious cause of vituperation, scarcely veiled, between the partners who had failed to make good, and caused epidemics of condescending sympathy from the adversaries which produced a passion in the losers far keener than their fury at having lost. What made the concluding stages of this contest the more exciting was that an evening breeze suddenly arising just as a deal was ended, made the cards rise in the air like a covey of partridges. They were recaptured, and all the hands were found to be complete with the exception of Miss Mapp's, which had a card missing. This, an ace of hearts, was discovered by the Padre, face upwards, in a bed of mignonette, and he was vehement in claiming a fresh deal, on the grounds that the card was exposed. Miss Mapp could not speak at all in answer to this preposterous claim: she could only smile at him, and proceed to declare trumps as if nothing had happened . . . The Major alone failed to come up to the full measure of these enjoyments, for though all the rest of them were as angry with him as they were with each other, he remained in a most indecorous state of good humour, drinking thirstily of the redcurrant fool, and when he was dummy, quite failing to mind whether Miss Mapp got her contract or not. Captain Puffin, at the other table, seemed to be behaving with the same impropriety, for the sound of his shrill, falsetto laugh was as regular as his visits to the bucket of redcurrant fool. What if there was champagne in it after all, so Miss Mapp luridly conjectured! What if this unseemly good humour was due to incipient intoxication? She took a little more of that delicious decoction herself.

It was unanimously determined, when the two rubbers

came to an end almost simultaneously, that, as everything was so pleasant and agreeable, there should be no fresh sorting of the players. Besides, the second table was only playing stakes of sixpence a hundred, and it would be very awkward and unsettling that anyone should play these moderate points in one rubber and those high ones the next. But at this point Miss Mapp's table was obliged to endure a pause, for the Padre had to hurry away just before six to administer the rite of baptism in the church which was so conveniently close. The Major afforded a good deal of amusement, as soon as he was out of hearing, by hoping that he would not baptize the child the Knave of Hearts if it was a boy, or, if a girl, the Queen of Spades; but in order to spare the susceptibilities of Mrs Bartlett, this admirable joke was not communicated to the next table, but enjoyed privately. The author of it, however, made a note in his mind to tell it to Captain Puffin, in the hopes that it would cause him to forget his ruinous half-crown defeat at golf this morning. Quite as agreeable was the arrival of a fresh supply of redcurrant fool, and as this had been heralded a few minutes before by a loud pop from the butler's pantry, which looked on to the lawn, Miss Mapp began to waver in her belief that there was no champagne in it, particularly as it would not have suited the theory by which she accounted for the Major's unwonted good humour, and her suggestion that the pop they had all heard so clearly was the opening of a bottle of stone ginger beer was not delivered with conviction. To make sure, however, she took one more sip of the new supply, and, irradiated with smiles, made a great concession.

'I believe I was wrong,' she said. 'There is something in it beyond yolk of egg and cream. Oh, there's Boon; he will tell us.'

She made a seductive face at Boon, and beckoned to him.

'Boon, will you think it very inquisitive of me,' she asked archly, 'if I ask you whether you have put a teeny drop of champagne into this delicious redcurrant fool?'

'A bottle and a half, Miss,' said Boon morosely, 'and half a pint of old brandy. Will you have some more, Miss?'

Miss Mapp curbed her indignation at this vulgar squandering of precious liquids, so characteristic of Poppits. She gave a shrill little laugh.

'Oh, no, thank you, Boon!' she said. 'I mustn't have any more. Delicious, though.'

Major Flint let Boon fill up his cup while he was not looking.

'And we owe this to your grandmother, Miss Mapp?' he asked gallantly. 'That's a second debt.'

Miss Mapp acknowledged this polite subtlety with a reservation.

'But not the champagne in it, Major,' she said. 'Grandmamma Nap – '

The Major beat his thigh in ecstasy.

'Ha! That's a good Spoonerism for Miss Isabel's book,' he said. 'Miss Isabel, we've got a new – '

Miss Mapp was very much puzzled at this slight confusion in her speech, for her utterance was usually remarkably distinct. There might be some little joke made at her expense on the effect of Grandmamma Mapp's invention if this lovely Spoonerism was published. But if she who had only just tasted the redcurrant fool tripped in her speech, how amply were Major Flint's good nature and Captain Puffin's incessant laugh accounted for. She herself felt very good-natured, too. How pleasant it all was!

'Oh, naughty!' she said to the Major. 'Pray, hush! you're disturbing them at their rubber. And here's the Padre back again!'

The new rubber had only just begun (indeed, it was lucky that they cut their cards without any delay) when Mrs Poppit appeared on her return from her expedition to London. Miss Mapp begged her to take her hand, and instantly began playing.

'It would really be a kindness to me, Mrs Poppit,' she said; '(No diamonds at all, partner?) but of course, if you won't – You've been missing such a lovely party. So much enjoyment!'

Suddenly she saw that Mrs Poppit was wearing on her ample breast a small piece of riband with a little cross attached to it. Her entire stock of good-humour vanished, and she smiled her widest.

'We needn't ask what took you to London,' she said. 'Congratulations! How was the dear King?'

This rubber was soon over, and even as they were adding up the score, there arose a shrill outcry from the next table, where Mrs Plaistow, as usual, had made the tale of her winnings sixpence in excess of what anybody else considered was due to her. The sound of that was so familiar that nobody looked up or asked what was going on.

'Darling Diva and her bawbees, Padre,' said Miss Mapp in an aside. 'So modest in her demands. Oh, she's stopped! Somebody has given her sixpence. Not another rubber? Well, perhaps it is rather late, and I must say good night to my flowers before they close up for the night. All those shillings mine? Fancy!'

Miss Mapp was seething with excitement, curiosity and rage, as with Major Flint on one side of her and Captain Puffin on the other, she was escorted home. The excitement was due to her winnings, the rage to Mrs Poppit's Order, the curiosity to the clue she believed she had found to those inexplicable lights that burned so late in the houses of her companions. Certainly it seemed that Major Flint was trying not to step on the joints of the paving stones, and succeeding very imperfectly, while Captain Puffin, on her left, was walking very unevenly on the cobbles. Even making due allowance for the difficulty of walking evenly there at any time, Miss Mapp could not help thinking that a teetotaller would have made a better job of it than that. Both gentlemen talked at once, very agreeably but rather carefully, Major Flint promising himself a studious evening over some very interesting entries in his Indian Diary, while Captain Puffin anticipated the speedy solution of that problem about the Roman road which had puzzled him so long. As they said their '*Au reservoirs*' to her on her doorstep, they took off their hats more often than politeness really demanded.

Once in her house Miss Mapp postponed her good nights to her sweet flowers, and hurried with the utmost speed of which she was capable to her garden room, in order to see what her companions were doing. They were standing in the middle of the street, and Major Flint, with gesticulating forefinger, was being very impressive over something . . .

* * *

Interesting as was Miss Mapp's walk home, and painful as was the light which it had conceivably thrown on the problem that had baffled her for so long, she might have been even more acutely disgusted had she lingered on with the rest of the bridge party in Mrs Poppit's garden, so revolting was the sycophantic loyalty of the newly decorated Member of the British Empire . . . She described minutely her arrival at the Palace, her momentary nervousness as she entered the Throne room, the instantaneousness with which that all vanished when she came face to face with her Sovereign.

'I assure you, he gave the most gracious smile,' she said, 'just as if we had known each other all our lives, and I felt at home at once. And he said a few words to me – such a beautiful voice he has. Dear Isabel, I wish you had been there to hear it, and then – '

'Oh, Mamma, what did he say?' asked Isabel, to the great relief of Mrs Plaistow and the Bartletts, for while they were bursting with eagerness to know with the utmost detail all that had taken place, the correct attitude in Tilling was profound indifference to anybody of whatever degree who did not live at Tilling, and to anything that did not happen there. In particular, any manifestation of interest in kings or other distinguished people was held to be a very miserable failing . . . So they all pretended to look about them, and take no notice of what Mrs Poppit was saying, and you might have heard a pin drop. Diva silently and hastily unwound her cloud from over her ears, risking catching cold in the hole where her tooth had been, so terrified was she of missing a single syllable.

'Well, it was very gratifying,' said Mrs Poppit; 'he whispered to some gentleman standing near him, who I think was the Lord Chamberlain, and then told me how interested he had been in the good work of the Tilling hospital, and how especially glad he was to be able – and just then he began to pin my Order on – to be able to recognize it. Now I call that wonderful to know all about the Tilling hospital! And such neat, quick fingers he has: I am sure it would take me double the time to make a safety pin hold, and then he gave me another smile, and passed me on, so to speak, to the Queen, who stood next him, and who had been listening to all he had said.'

'And did she speak to you too?' asked Diva, quite unable to maintain the right indifference.

'Indeed she did: she said, "So pleased," and what she put into those two words I'm sure I can never convey to you. I could hear how sincere they were: it was no set form of words, as if she meant nothing by it. She *was* pleased: she was just as interested in what I had done for the Tilling hospital as the King was. And the crowds outside: they lined the Mall for at least fifty yards. I was bowing and smiling on this side and that till I felt quite dizzy.'

'And was the Prince of Wales there?' asked Diva, beginning to wind her head up again. She did not care about the crowds.

'No, he wasn't there,' said Mrs Poppit, determined to have no embroidery in her story, however much other people, especially Miss Mapp, decorated remarkable incidents till you hardly recognized them. 'He wasn't there. I dare say something had unexpectedly detained him, though I shouldn't wonder if before long we all saw him. For I noticed in the evening paper which I was reading on the way down here, after I had seen the King, that he was going to stay with Lord Ardingly for this very next weekend. And what's the station for Ardingly Park if it isn't Tilling? Though it's quite a private visit, I feel convinced that the right and proper thing for me to do is to be at the station, or, at any rate, just outside, with my Order on. I shall not claim acquaintance with him, or anything of that kind,' said Mrs Poppit, fingering her Order; 'but after my reception today at the Palace, nothing can be more likely than that His Majesty might mention – quite casually, of course – to the Prince that he had just given a decoration to Mrs Poppit of Tilling. And it would make me feel very awkward to think that that had happened, and I was not somewhere about to make my curtsey.'

'Oh, Mamma, may I stand by you, or behind you?' asked Isabel, completely dazzled by the splendour of this prospect and prancing about the lawn . . .

This was quite awful: it was as bad as, if not worse than, the historically disastrous remark about supertax, and a general rigidity, as of some partial cataleptic seizure, froze Mrs Poppit's guests, rendering them, like incomplete Marconi installations, capable of receiving, but not of transmitting. They received these impressions, they also continued (mechanically) to receive more chocolates and sandwiches, and such refreshments as remained on the buffet; but no one could intervene and stop Mrs Poppit from exposing herself further. One reason for this, of course, as already indicated, was that they all longed for her to expose herself as much as she possibly could, for if there was a quality – and, indeed, there were many – on which Tilling prided itself, it was on its immunity from snobbishness: there were, no doubt, in the great world with which

Tilling concerned itself so little kings and queens and dukes and Members of the Order of the British Empire; but every Tillingite knew that he or she (particularly she) was just as good as any of them, and indeed better, being more fortunate than they in living in Tilling . . . And if there was a process in the world which Tilling detested, it was being patronized, and there was this woman telling them all what she felt it right and proper for her, as Mrs Poppit of Tilling (MBE), to do, when the Heir Apparent should pass through the town on Saturday. The rest of them, Mrs Poppit implied, might do what they liked, for they did not matter; but she – she must put on her Order and make her curtsey. And Isabel, by her expressed desire to stand beside, or even behind, her mother for this degrading moment had showed of what stock she came.

Mrs Poppit had nothing more to say on this subject; indeed, as Diva reflected, there was really nothing more that could be said, unless she suggested that they should all bow and curtsey to her for the future, and their hostess proceeded, as they all took their leave, to hope that they had enjoyed the bridge party which she had been unavoidably prevented from attending.

'But my absence made it possible to include Miss Mapp,' she said. 'I should not have liked poor Miss Mapp to feel left out; I am always glad to give Miss Mapp pleasure. I hope she won her rubber; she does not like losing. Will no one have a little more redcurrant fool? Boon has made it very tolerably today. A Scotch recipe of my great-grandmother's.'

Diva gave a little cackle of laughter as she enfolded herself in her cloud again. She had heard Miss Mapp's ironical enquiry as to how the dear King was, and had thought at the time that it was probably a pity that Miss Mapp had said that.

* * *

Though abhorrence of snobbery and immunity from any taint of it was so fine a characteristic of public social life at Tilling, the expected passage of this distinguished visitor through the town on Saturday next became very speedily known, and before the wicker baskets of the ladies in their morning marketings next day were half full, there was no quarter which the news had failed to reach. Major Flint had it from Mrs Plaistow, as he went down to the eleven-twenty tram out to the golf links, and though he had not much time to spare (for his work last night on his old diaries had caused him to breakfast unusually late that morning to the accompaniment of a dismal headache from over-application), he had stopped to converse with Miss Mapp immediately afterwards, with one eye on the time, for naturally he could not fire off that sort of news point blank at her, as if it was a matter of any interest or importance.

'Good morning, dear lady,' he said. 'By Jove! what a picture of health and freshness you are!'

Miss Mapp cast one glance at her basket to see that the paper quite concealed that article of clothing which the perfidious laundry had found. (Probably the laundry knew where it was all the time, and – in a figurative sense, of course – was 'trying it on'.)

'Early to bed and early to rise, Major,' she said. 'I saw my sweet flowers open their eyes this morning! Such a beautiful dew!'

'Well, my diaries kept me up late last night,' he said. 'When all you fascinating ladies have withdrawn is the only time at which I can bring myself to sit down to them.'

'Let me recommend six to eight in the morning, Major,' said Miss Mapp earnestly. 'Such a freshness of brain then.'

That seemed to be a cul-de-sac in the way of leading up to the important subject, and the Major tried another turning.

'Good, well-fought game of bridge we had yesterday,' he said. 'Just met Mrs Plaistow; she stopped on for a chat after we had gone.'

'Dear Diva; she loves a good gossip,' said Miss Mapp effusively. 'Such an interest she has in other people's affairs. So human and sympathetic. I'm sure our dear hostess told her all about her adventures at the Palace.'

There was only seven minutes left before the tram started, and though this was not a perfect opening, it would have to do. Besides, the Major saw Mrs Plaistow coming energetically along the High Street with whirling feet.

'Yes, and we haven't finished with – ha – royalty yet,' he said, getting the odious word out with difficulty. 'The Prince of Wales will be passing through the town on Saturday, on his way to Ardingly Park, where he is spending the Sunday.'

Miss Mapp was not betrayed into the smallest expression of interest.

'That will be nice for him,' she said. 'He will catch a glimpse of our beautiful Tilling.'

'So he will! Well, I'm off for my game of golf. Perhaps the Navy will be a bit more efficient today.'

'I'm sure you will both play perfectly!' said Miss Mapp.

Diva had 'popped' into the grocer's. She always popped everywhere just now; she popped across to see a friend, and she popped home again; she popped into church on Sunday, and occasionally popped up to town, and Miss Mapp was beginning to feel that somebody ought to let her know, directly or by insinuation, that she popped too much. So, thinking that an opportunity might present itself now, Miss Mapp read the newsboard outside the stationer's till Diva popped out of the grocer's again. The headlines of news, even the largest of them, hardly reached her brain, because it was entirely absorbed in another subject. Of course, the first thing was to find out by what train . . .

Diva trundled swiftly across the street.

'Good morning, Elizabeth,' she said. 'You left the party too early yesterday. Missed a lot. How the King smiled! How the Queen said "So pleased "'

'Our dear hostess would like that,' said Miss Mapp pensively. 'She would be so pleased, too. She and the Queen would both be pleased. Quite a pair of them.'

'By the way, on Saturday next – ' began Diva.

'I know, dear,' said Miss Mapp. 'Major Flint told me. It seemed quite to interest him. Now I must pop into the stationer's – '

Diva was really very obtuse.

'I'm popping in there, too,' she said. 'Want a timetable of the trains.'

Wild horses would not have dragged from Miss Mapp that this was precisely what she wanted.

'I only wanted a little ruled paper,' she said. 'Why, here's dear Evie popping out just as we pop in! Good morning, sweet Evie. Lovely day again.'

Mrs Bartlett thrust something into her basket which very much resembled a railway timetable. She spoke in a low, quick voice, as if afraid of being overheard, and was otherwise rather like a mouse. When she was excited she squeaked.

'So good for the harvest,' she said. 'Such an important thing to have a good harvest. I hope next Saturday will be fine; it would be a pity if he had a wet day. We were wondering, Kenneth and I, what would be the proper thing to do, if he came over for service – oh, here is Kenneth!'

She stopped abruptly, as if afraid that she had betrayed too much interest in next Saturday and Sunday. Kenneth would manage it much better.

'Ha! lady fair,' he exclaimed. 'Having a bit crack with wee wifey? Any news this bright morning?'

'No, dear Padre,' said Miss Mapp, showing her gums. 'At least, I've heard nothing of any interest. I can only give you the news of my garden. Such lovely new roses in bloom today, bless them!'

Mrs Plaistow had popped into the stationer's, so this perjury was undetected.

The Padre was noted for his diplomacy. Just now he wanted to convey the impression that nothing which could happen next Saturday or Sunday could be of the smallest interest to him; whereas he had spent an almost sleepless night in wondering whether it would, in certain circumstances, be proper to make a bow at the beginning of his sermon and another at the end; whether he ought to meet the visitor at the west door; whether the mayor ought to be told, and whether there ought to be special psalms . . .

'Well, lady fair,' he said. 'Gossip will have it that ye Prince of Wales is staying at Ardingly for the Sunday; indeed, he will, I suppose, pass through Tilling on Saturday afternoon – '

Miss Mapp put her forefinger to her forehead, as if trying to recollect something.

'Yes, now somebody did tell me that,' she said. 'Major Flint, I believe. But when you asked for news I thought you meant something that really interested me. Yes, Padre?'

'Aweel, if he comes to service on Sunday – ?'

'Dear Padre, I'm sure he'll hear a very good sermon. Oh, I see what you mean! Whether you ought to have any special hymn? Don't ask poor little me! Mrs Poppit, I'm sure, would tell you. She knows all about courts and etiquette.'

Diva popped out of the stationer's at this moment.

'Sold out,' she announced. 'Everybody wanted timetables this morning. Evie got the last. Have to go to the station.'

'I'll walk with you, Diva, dear,' said Miss Mapp. 'There's a parcel that – Goodbye, dear Eyie, *au reservoir.*'

She kissed her hand to Mrs Bartlett, leaving a smile behind it, as it fluttered away from her face, for the Padre.

Miss Mapp was so impenetrably wrapped in thought as she worked among her sweet flowers that afternoon, that she merely stared at a 'love-in-a-mist', which she had absently rooted up instead of a piece of groundsel, without any bleeding of the heart for one of her sweet flowers. There were two trains by which He might arrive – one at quarter-past four, which would get him to Ardingly for tea, the other at quarter to seven. She was quite determined to see him, but more inflexible than that resolve was the Euclidean postulate that no one in Tilling should think that she had taken any deliberate step to do so. For the present she had disarmed suspicion by the blankness of her indifference as to what might happen on Saturday or Sunday; but she herself strongly suspected that everybody else, in spite of the public attitude of Tilling to such subjects, was determined to see him too. How to see and not be seen was the question which engrossed her, and though she might possibly happen to be at that sharp corner outside the station where every motor had to go slow, on the arrival of the 4.15, it would never do to risk being seen there again precisely at 6.45. Mrs Poppit, shameless in her snobbery, would no doubt be at the station with her Order on at both these hours, if the arrival did not take place by the first train, and Isabel would be prancing by or behind her, and, in fact, dreadful though it was to contemplate, all Tilling, she reluctantly believed, would be hanging about . . . Then an idea struck her, so glorious, that she put the uprooted love-in-a-mist in the weed basket, instead of planting it again, and went quickly indoors, up to the attics, and from there popped – really popped, so tight was the fit – through a trapdoor on to the roof. Yes: the station was plainly visible, and if the quarter-past four was the favoured train, there would certainly be a motor from Ardingly Park waiting there in good time for its arrival. From the house roof she could ascertain that, and she would then have time to trip down the hill and get to her coal merchant's at that sharp corner outside the station, and ask, rather peremptorily, when the coke for her central heating might be expected. It was due now, and though it would be unfortunate if it arrived before Saturday, it was quite easy to smile away her peremptory manner, and say that Withers had not told her. Miss Mapp hated prevarication, but a major force sometimes came along . . . But if no motors from Ardingly Park were in waiting for the quarter-past four (as spied from her house roof), she need not risk being seen in the neighbourhood of the station, but would again make observations some few minutes before the quarter to seven was due. There was positively no other train by which He could come . . .

The next day or two saw no traceable developments in the situation, but Miss Mapp's trained sense told her that there was underground work of some kind going on: she seemed to hear faint hollow taps and muffled knockings, and, so to speak, the silence of some unusual pregnancy. Up and down the High Street she observed short whispered conversations going on between her friends, which broke off on her approach. This only confirmed her view that these secret colloquies were connected with Saturday afternoon, for it was not to be expected that, after her freezing reception of the news, any projected snobbishness should be confided to her, and though she would have liked to know what Diva and Irene and darling Evie were meaning to do, the fact that they none of them told her, showed that they were aware that she, at any rate, was utterly indifferent to and above that sort of thing. She suspected, too, that Major Flint had fallen victim to this un-Tillinglike mania, for on Friday afternoon, when passing his door, which happened to be standing open, she quite distinctly saw him in front of his glass in the hall (standing on the head of one of the tigers to secure a better view of himself), trying on a silk top hat. Her own errand at this moment was to the draper's, where she bought a quantity of pretty pale blue braid, for a little domestic dressmaking which was in arrears, and some riband of the same tint. At this clever and unusual hour for shopping, the High Street was naturally empty, and after a little hesitation and many anxious glances to right and left, she plunged into the toyshop and bought a pleasant little Union Jack with a short stick attached to it. She told Mr Dabnet very distinctly that it was a present for her nephew, and concealed it inside her parasol, where it lay quite flat and made no perceptible bulge . . .

At four o'clock on Saturday afternoon, she remembered that the damp had come in through her bedroom ceiling in a storm last winter, and told Withers she was going to have a look to see if any tiles were loose. In order to ascertain this for certain, she took up through the trap door a pair of binocular glasses, through which it was also easy to identify anybody who might be in the open yard outside the station. Even as she looked, Mrs Poppit and Isabel crossed the yard into the waiting room and ticket office. It was a little surprising that there were not more friends in the station yard, but at the moment she heard a loud *Quai-hai* in the street below, and cautiously peering over the parapet, she got an admirable view of the Major in a frock coat and tall hat. A 'Coo-ee' answered him, and Captain Puffin, in a new suit (Miss Mapp was certain of it) and a panama hat, joined him. They went down the street and turned the corner . . . Across the opening to the High Street there shot the figure of darling Diva.

While waiting for them to appear again in the station yard, Miss Mapp looked to see what vehicles were standing there. It was already ten minutes past four, and the Ardingly motors must have been there by this time, if there was anything 'doing' by the 4.15. But positively the only vehicle there was an open trolley laden with a piano in a sack. Apart from knowing all about that piano, for Mrs Poppit had talked about little else than her new upright Blüthner before her visit to Buckingham Palace, a moment's reflection convinced Miss Mapp that this was a very unlikely mode of conveyance for any guest . . . She watched for a few moments more, but as no other friends appeared in the station yard, she concluded that they were hanging about the street somewhere, poor things, and decided not to make enquiries about her coke just yet.

She had tea while she arranged flowers, in the very front of the window in her garden room, and presently had the satisfaction of seeing many of the baffled loyalists trudging home. There was no need to do more than smile and tap the window and kiss her hand: they all knew that she had been busy with her flowers, and that she knew what they had been busy about . . . Out again they all came towards half-past six, and when she had watched the last of them down the hill, she hurried back to the roof again, to make a final inspection of the loose tiles through her binoculars. Brief but exciting was that inspection, for opposite the entrance to the station was drawn up a motor. So clear was the air and so serviceable her binoculars that she could distinguish the vulgar coronet on the panels, and as she looked Mrs Poppit and Isabel hurried across the station yard. It was then but the work of a moment to slip on the dust cloak trimmed with blue braid, adjust the hat with the blue riband, and take up the parasol with its furled Union Jack inside it. The stick of the flag was uppermost; she could whip it out in a moment.

*　　*　　*

Miss Mapp had calculated her appearance to a nicety. Just as she got to the sharp corner opposite the station, where all cars slowed down and her coal merchant's office was situated, the train drew up. By the gates into the yard were standing the Major in his top hat, the Captain in his panama, Irene in a civilised skirt; Diva in a brand-new walking dress, and the Padre and wee wifey. They were all looking in the direction of the station, and Miss Mapp stepped into the coal merchant's unobserved. Oddly enough the coke had been sent three days before, and there was no need for peremptoriness.

'So good of you, Mr Wootten!' she said; 'and why is everyone standing about this afternoon?'

Mr Wootten explained the reason of this, and Miss Mapp, grasping her parasol, went out again as the car left the station. There were too many dear friends about, she decided, to use the Union Jack, and having seen what she wanted to she determined to slip quietly away again. Already the Major's hat was in his hand, and he was bowing low, so too were Captain Puffin and the Padre, while Irene, Diva and Evie were making little ducking movements . . . Miss Mapp was determined, when it came to her turn, to show them, as she happened to be on the spot, what a proper curtsey was.

The car came opposite her, and she curtseyed so low that

recovery was impossible, and she sat down in the road. Her parasol flew out of her hand and out of her parasol flew the Union Jack. She saw a young man looking out of the window, dressed in khaki, grinning broadly, but not, so she thought, graciously, and it suddenly struck her that there was something, beside her own part in the affair, which was not as it should be. As he put his head in again there was loud laughter from the inside of the car.

Mr Wootten helped her up and the entire assembly of her friends crowded round her, hoping she was not hurt.

'No, dear Major, dear Padre, not at all, thanks,' she said. 'So stupid: my ankle turned. Oh, yes, the Union Jack I bought for my nephew, it's his birthday tomorrow. Thank you. I just came to see about my coke: of course I thought the Prince had arrived when you all went down to meet the quarter-past four. Fancy my running straight into it all! How well he looked.'

This was all rather lame, and Miss Mapp hailed Mrs Poppit's appearance from the station as a welcome diversion . . . Mrs Poppit was looking vexed.

'I hope you saw him well, Mrs Poppit,' said Miss Mapp, 'after meeting two trains, and taking all that trouble.'

'Saw who?' said Mrs Poppit with a deplorable lack both of manner and grammar. 'Why' – light seemed to break on her odious countenance. 'Why, you don't think that was the Prince, do you, Miss Mapp? He arrived here at one, so the station master has just told me, and has been playing golf all afternoon.'

The Major looked at the Captain, and the Captain at the Major. It was months and months since they had missed their Saturday afternoon's golf.

'It was the Prince of Wales who looked out of that car window,' said Miss Mapp firmly. 'Such a pleasant smile. I should know it anywhere.'

'The young man who got into the car at the station was no more the Prince of Wales than you are,' said Mrs Poppit shrilly. 'I was close to him as he came out: I curtseyed to him before I saw.'

Miss Mapp instantly changed her attack: she could hardly hold her smile on to her face for rage.

'How very awkward for you,' she said. 'What a laugh they will all have over it this evening! Delicious!'

Mrs Poppit's face suddenly took on an expression of the tenderest solicitude.

'I hope, Miss Mapp, you didn't jar yourself when you sat down in the road just now,' she said.

'Not at all, thank you so much,' said Miss Mapp, hearing her heart beat in her throat . . . If she had had a naval fifteen-inch gun handy, and had known how to fire it, she would, with a sense of duty accomplished, have discharged it point-blank at the Order of the Member of the British Empire, and at anybody else who might be within range . . .

* * *

Sunday, of course, with all the opportunities of that day, still remained, and the seats of the auxiliary choir, which were advantageously situated, had never been so full, but as it was all no use, the Major and Captain Puffin left during the sermon to catch the twelve-twenty tram out to the links. On this delightful day it was but natural that the pleasant walk there across the marsh was very popular, and golfers that afternoon had a very trying and nervous time, for the ladies of Tilling kept bobbing up from behind sand dunes and bunkers, as, regardless of the players, they executed swift flank marches in all directions. Miss Mapp returned exhausted about teatime to hear from Withers that the Prince had spent an hour or more rambling about the town, and had stopped quite five minutes at the corner by the garden room. He had actually sat down on Miss Mapp's steps and smoked a cigarette. She wondered if the end of the cigarette was there still: it was hateful to have cigarette ends defiling the steps to her front door, and often before now, when sketchers were numerous, she had sent her housemaid out to remove these untidy relics. She searched for it, but was obliged to come to the reluctant conclusion that there was nothing to remove . . .

CHAPTER THREE

Diva was sitting at the open drawing room window of her house in the High Street, cutting with a pair of sharp nail scissors into the old chintz curtains which her maid had told her no longer 'paid for the mending'. So, since they refused to pay for their mending any more, she was preparing to make them pay, pretty smartly too, in other ways. The pattern was of little bunches of pink roses peeping out through trellis work, and it was these which she had just begun to cut out. Though Tilling was noted for the ingenuity with which its more fashionable ladies devised novel and quaint effects in their dress in an economical manner, Diva felt sure, ransack her memory though she might, that nobody had thought of *this* before.

The hot weather had continued late into September and showed no signs of breaking yet, and it would be agreeable to her and acutely painful to others that just at the end of the summer she should appear in a perfectly new costume, before the days of jumpers and heavy skirts and large woollen scarves came in. She was preparing, therefore, to take the light white jacket which she wore over her blouse, and cover the broad collar and cuffs of it with these pretty roses. The belt of the skirt would be similarly decorated, and so would the edge of it, if there were enough clean ones. The jacket and skirt had already gone to the dyer's, and would be back in a day or two, white no longer, but of a rich purple hue, and by that time she would have hundreds of these little pink roses ready to be tacked on. Perhaps a piece of the chintz, trellis and all, could be sewn over the belt, but she was determined to have single little bunches of roses peppered all over the collar and cuffs of the jacket and, if possible, round the edge of the skirt. She had already tried the effect, and was of the opinion that nobody could possibly guess what the origin of these roses was. When carefully sewn on they looked as if they were a design in the stuff.

She let the circumcised roses fall on to the window seat, and from time to time, when they grew numerous, swept them into a cardboard box. Though she worked with zealous diligence, she had an eye to the movements in the street outside, for it was shopping hour, and there were many observations to be made. She had not anything like Miss Mapp's genius for conjecture, but her memory was appallingly good, and this was the third morning running on which Elizabeth had gone into the grocer's. It was odd to go to your grocer's every day like that; groceries twice a week was sufficient for most people. From here on the floor above the street she could easily look into Elizabeth's basket, and she certainly was carrying nothing away with her from the grocer's, for the only thing there was a small bottle done up in white paper with sealing wax, which, Diva had no need to be told, certainly came from the chemist's, and was no doubt connected with too many plums.

Miss Mapp crossed the street to the pavement below Diva's house, and precisely as she reached it, Diva's maid opened the door into the drawing room, bringing in the second post, or rather not bringing in the second post, but the announcement that there wasn't any second post. This opening of the door caused a draught, and the bunches of roses which littered the window seat rose brightly in the air. Diva managed to beat most of them down again, but two fluttered out of the window. Precisely then, and at no other time, Miss Mapp looked up, and one settled on her face, the other fell into her basket. Her trained faculties were all on the alert, and she thrust them both inside her glove for future consideration, without stopping to examine them just then. She only knew that they were little pink roses, and that they had fluttered out of Diva's window . . .

She paused on the pavement, and remembered that Diva had not yet expressed regret about the worsted, and that she still 'popped' as much as ever. Thus Diva deserved a punishment of some sort, and happily, at that very moment she thought of a subject on which she might be able to make her uncomfortable. The street was full, and it would be pretty to call up to her, instead of ringing her bell, in order to save trouble to poor overworked Janet. (Diva only kept two servants, though of course poverty was no crime.)

'Diva darling!' she cooed.

Diva's head looked out like a cuckoo in a clock preparing to chime the hour.

'Hello!' she said. 'Want me?'

'May I pop up for a moment, dear?' said Miss Mapp. 'That's to say if you're not very busy.'

'Pop away,' said Diva. She was quite aware that Miss Mapp said 'pop' in crude inverted commas, so to speak, for purposes of mockery, and so she said it herself more than ever. 'I'll tell my maid to pop down and open the door.'

While this was being done, Diva bundled her chintz curtains together and stored them and the roses she had cut out into her work cupboard, for secrecy was an essential to the construction of these decorations. But in order to appear naturally employed, she pulled out the woollen scarf she was knitting for the autumn and winter, forgetting for the moment that the rose-madder stripe at the end on which she was now engaged was made of that fatal worsted which Miss Mapp considered to have been feloniously appropriated. That was the sort of thing Miss Mapp never forgot. Even among her sweet flowers. Her eye fell on it the moment she entered the room, and she tucked the two chintz roses more securely into her glove.

'I thought I would just pop across from the grocer's,' she said. 'What a pretty scarf, dear! That's a lovely shade of rose-madder. Where can I have seen something like it before?'

This was clearly ironical, and had best be answered by irony. Diva was no coward.

'Couldn't say, I'm sure,' she said.

Miss Mapp appeared to recollect, and smiled as far back as her wisdom teeth. (Diva couldn't do that.)

'I have it,' she said. 'It was the wool I ordered at Heynes's, and then he sold it you, and I couldn't get any more.'

'So it was,' said Diva. 'Upset you a bit. There was the wool in the shop. I bought it.'

'Yes, dear; I see you did. But that wasn't what I popped in about. This coal strike, you know.'

'Got a cellar full,' said Diva.

'Diva, you've not been hoarding, have you?' asked Miss Mapp with great anxiety. 'They can take away every atom of coal you've got, if so, and fine you I don't know what for every hundredweight of it.'

'Pooh!' said Diva, rather forcing the indifference of this rude interjection.

'Yes, love, pooh by all means, if you like poohing!' said Miss Mapp. 'But I should have felt very unfriendly if one morning I found you were fined – found you were fined – quite a play upon words – and I hadn't warned you.'

Diva felt a little less poohish.

'But how much do they allow you to have?' she asked.

'Oh, quite a little: enough to go on with. But I dare say they won't discover you. I just took the trouble to come and warn you.'

Diva did remember something about hoarding; there had surely been dreadful exposures of prudent housekeepers in the papers which were very uncomfortable reading.

'But all these orders were only for the period of the war,' she said.

'No doubt you're right, dear,' said Miss Mapp brightly. 'I'm sure I hope you are. Only if the coal strike comes on, I think you'll find that the regulations against hoarding are quite as severe as they ever were. Food hoarding, too. Twemlow – such a civil man – tells me that he thinks we shall have plenty of food, or anyhow sufficient for everybody for quite a long time, provided that there's no hoarding. Not been hoarding food, too, dear Diva? You naughty thing: I believe that great cupboard is full of sardines and biscuits and Bovril.'

'Nothing of the kind,' said Diva indignantly. 'You shall see for yourself' – and then she suddenly remembered that the cupboard was full of chintz curtains and little bunches of pink roses, neatly cut out of them, and a pair of nail scissors.

There was a perfectly perceptible pause, during which Miss Mapp noticed that there were no curtains over the window. There certainly used to be, and they matched with the chintz cover of the window seat, which was decorated with little bunches of pink roses peeping through trellis. This was in the nature of a bonus: she had not up till then connected the chintz curtains with the little things that had fluttered down upon her and were now safe in her glove; her only real object in this call had been to instil a general uneasiness into Diva's mind about the coal strike and the danger of being well provided with fuel. That she humbly hoped that she had accomplished. She got up.

'Must be going,' she said. 'Such a lovely little chat! But what has happened to your pretty curtains?'

'Gone to the wash,' said Diva firmly.

'Liar,' thought Miss Mapp, as she tripped downstairs. 'Diva would have sent the cover of the window seat too, if that was the case. Liar,' she thought again as she kissed her hand to Diva, who was looking gloomily out of the window.

* * *

As soon as Miss Mapp had gained her garden room, she examined the mysterious treasures in her left-hand glove. Without the smallest doubt Diva had taken down her curtains (and high time too, for they were sadly shabby), and was cutting the roses out of them. But what on earth was she doing that for? For what garish purpose could she want to use bunches of roses cut out of chintz curtains?

Miss Mapp had put the two specimens of which she had providentially become possessed in her lap, and they looked very pretty against the navy blue of her skirt. Diva was very ingenious: she used up all sorts of odds and ends in a way that did credit to her undoubtedly parsimonious qualities. She could trim a hat with a toothbrush and a banana in such a way that it looked quite Parisian till you firmly analysed its component parts, and most of her ingenuity was devoted to dress: the more was the pity that she had such a roundabout figure that her waistband always reminded you of the equator . . .

'Eureka!' said Miss Mapp aloud, and, though the telephone bell was ringing, and the postulant might be one of the servants' friends ringing them up at an hour when their mistress was usually in the High Street, she glided swiftly to the large cupboard underneath the stairs which was full of the things which no right-minded person could bear to throw away: broken basket chairs, pieces of brown paper, cardboard boxes without lids, and cardboard lids without boxes, old bags with holes in them, keys without locks and locks without keys and worn chintz covers. There was one – it had once adorned the sofa in the garden room – covered with red poppies (very easy to cut out), and Miss Mapp dragged it dustily from its corner, setting in motion a perfect cascade of cardboard lids and some door handles.

Withers had answered the telephone, and came to announce that Twemlow the grocer regretted he had only two large tins of corned beef, but –

'Then say I will have the tongue as well, Withers,' said Miss Mapp. 'Just a tongue – and then I shall want you and Mary to do some cutting out for me.'

The three went to work with feverish energy, for Diva had got a start, and by four o'clock that afternoon there were enough poppies cut out to furnish, when in seed, a whole street of opium dens. The dress selected for decoration was, apart from a few mildew spots, the colour of ripe corn, which was superbly appropriate for September. 'Poppies in the corn,' said Miss Mapp over and over to herself, remembering some sweet verses she had once read by Bernard Shaw or Clement Shorter or somebody like that about a garden of sleep somewhere in Norfolk . . .

'No one can work as neatly as you, Withers,' she said gaily, 'and I shall ask you to do the most difficult part. I want you to sew my lovely poppies over the collar and facings of the jacket, just spacing them a little and making a dainty irregularity. And then Mary – won't you, Mary? – will do the same with the waistband while I put a border of them round the skirt, and my dear old dress will look quite new and lovely. I shall be at home to nobody, Withers, this afternoon, even if the Prince of Wales came and sat on my doorstep again. We'll all work together in the garden, shall we, and you and Mary must scold me if you think I'm not working hard enough. It will be delicious in the garden.'

Thanks to this pleasant plan, there was not much opportunity for Withers and Mary to be idle . . .

*　*　*

Just about the time that this harmonious party began their work, a far from harmonious couple were being just as industrious in the grand spacious bunker in front of the tee to the last hole on the golf links. It was a beautiful bunker, consisting of a great slope of loose, steep sand against the face of the hill, and solidly shored up with timber. The Navy had been in better form today, and after a decisive victory over the Army in the morning and an indemnity of half a crown, its match in the afternoon, with just the last hole to play, was all square. So Captain Puffin, having the honour, hit a low, nervous drive that tapped loudly at the timbered wall of the bunker, and cuddled down below it, well protected from any future assault.

'Phew! That about settles it,' said Major Flint boisterously. 'Bad place to top a ball! Give me the hole?'

This insolent question needed no answer, and Major Flint drove, skying the ball to a prodigious height. But it had to come to earth sometime, and it fell like Lucifer, son of the morning, in the middle of the same bunker . . . So the Army played three more, and, sweating profusely, got out. Then it was the Navy's turn, and the Navy had to lie on its keel above the boards of the bunker, in order to reach its ball at all, and missed it twice.

'Better give it up, old chap,' said Major Flint. 'Unplayable.'

'Then see me play it,' said Captain Puffin, with a chewing motion of his jaws.

'We shall miss the tram,' said the Major, and, with the intention of giving annoyance, he sat down in the bunker with his back to Captain Puffin, and lit a cigarette. At his third attempt nothing happened; at the fourth the ball flew against the boards, rebounded briskly again into the bunker, trickled down the steep, sandy slope and hit the Major's boot.

'Hit you, I think,' said Captain Puffin. 'Ha! So it's my hole, Major!'

Major Flint had a short fit of aphasia. He opened and shut his mouth and foamed. Then he took a half-crown from his pocket.

'Give that to the Captain,' he said to his caddie, and without looking round, walked away in the direction of the tram. He had not gone a hundred yards when the whistle sounded, and it puffed away homewards with ever-increasing velocity.

Weak and trembling from passion, Major Flint found that after a few tottering steps in the direction of Tilling he would be totally unable to get there unless fortified by some strong stimulant, and turned back to the clubhouse to obtain it. He always went dead lame when beaten at golf, while Captain Puffin was lame in any circumstances, and the two, no longer on speaking terms, hobbled into the clubhouse, one after the other, each unconscious of the other's presence. Summoning his last remaining strength Major Flint roared for whisky, and was told that, according to regulation, he could not be served until six. There was lemonade and stone ginger beer . . . You might as well have offered a man-eating tiger bread and milk. Even the threat that he would instantly resign his membership unless provided with drink produced no effect on a polite steward, and he sat down to recover as best he might with an old volume of *Punch*. This seemed to do him little good. His forced abstemiousness was rendered the more intolerable by the fact that Captain Puffin, hobbling in immediately afterwards, fetched from his locker a large flask full of the required elixir, and proceeded to mix himself a long, strong tumblerful. After the Major's rudeness in the matter of the half-crown, it was impossible for any sailor of spirit to take the first step towards reconciliation.

Thirst is a great leveller. By the time the refreshed Puffin had penetrated halfway down his glass, the Major found it impossible to be proud and proper any longer. He hated saying he was sorry (no man more) and wouldn't have been sorry if he had been able to get a drink. He twirled his moustache a great many times and cleared his throat – it wanted more than that to clear it – and capitulated.

'Upon my word, Puffin, I'm ashamed of myself for – ha! – for not taking my defeat better,' he said. 'A man's no business to let a game ruffle him.'

Puffin gave his alto cackling laugh.

'Oh, mat's all right, Major,' he said. 'I know it's awfully hard to lose like a gentleman.'

He let this sink in, then added:

'Have a drink, old chap?'

Major Flint flew to his feet.

'Well, thank ye, thank ye,' he said. 'Now where's that soda water you offered me just now?' he shouted to the steward.

The speed and completeness of the reconciliation was in no way remarkable, for when two men quarrel whenever they meet, it follows that they make it up again with corresponding frequency, else there could be no fresh quarrels at all. This one had been a shade more acute than most, and the drop into amity again was a shade more precipitous.

Major Flint in his eagerness had put most of his moustache into the life-giving tumbler, and dried it on his handkerchief.

'After all, it was a most amusing incident,' he said. 'There was I with my back turned, waiting for you to give it up, when your bl – wretched little ball hit my foot. I must remember that. I'll serve you with the same spoon someday, at least I would if I thought it sportsmanlike. Well, well, enough said. Astonishing good whisky, that of yours.'

Captain Puffin helped himself to rather more than half of what now remained in the flask.

'Help yourself, Major,' he said.

'Well, thank ye, I don't mind if I do,' he said, reversing the flask over the tumbler. 'There's a good tramp in front of us now that the last tram has gone. Tram and tramp! Upon my word, I've half a mind to telephone for a taxi.'

This, of course, was a direct hint. Puffin ought clearly to pay for a taxi, having won two half-crowns today. This casual drink did not constitute the usual drink stood by the winner, and paid for with cash over the counter. A drink (or two) from a flask was not the same thing . . . Puffin naturally saw it in another light. He had paid for the whisky which Major Flint had drunk (or owed for it) in his wine-merchant's bill. That was money just as much as a florin pushed across the counter. But he was so excessively pleased with himself over the adroitness with which he had claimed the last hole, that he quite overstepped the bounds of his habitual parsimony.

'Well, you trot along to the telephone and order a taxi,' he said, 'and I'll pay for it.'

'Done with you,' said the other.

Their comradeship was now on its most felicitous level again, and they sat on the bench outside the clubhouse till the arrival of their unusual conveyance.

'Lunching at the Poppits' tomorrow?' asked Major Flint.

'Yes. Meet you there? Good. Bridge afterwards, I suppose.'

'Sure to be. Wish there was a chance of more redcurrant fool.

That was a decent tipple, all but the redcurrants. If I had had all the old brandy that was served for my ration in one glass, and all the champagne in another, I should have been better content.'

Captain Puffin was a great cynic in his own misogynistic way.

'Camouflage for the fair sex,' he said. 'A woman will lick up half a bottle of brandy if it's called plum pudding, and ask for more, whereas if you offered her a small brandy and soda, she would think you were insulting her.'

'Bless them, the funny little fairies,' said the Major.

'Well, what I tell you is true, Major,' said Puffin. 'There's old Mapp. Teetotaller she calls herself, but she played a bo'sun's part in that redcurrant fool. Bit rosy, I thought her, as we escorted her home.'

'So she was,' said the Major. 'So she was. Said goodbye to us on her doorstep as if she thought she was a perfect Venus Ana – Ana something.'

'*Anno Domini*,' giggled Puffin.

'Well, well, we all get long in the tooth in time,' said Major Flint charitably. 'Fine figure of a woman, though.'

'Eh?' said Puffin archly.

'Now none of your sailor talk ashore, Captain,' said the Major, in high good humour. 'I'm not a marrying man any more than you are. Better if I had been perhaps, more years ago than I care to think about. Dear me, my wound's going to trouble me tonight.'

'What do you do for it, Major?' asked Puffin.

'Do for it? Think of old times a bit over my diaries.'

'Going to let the world have a look at them someday?' asked Puffin.

'No, sir, I am not,' said Major Flint. 'Perhaps a hundred years hence – the date I have named in my will for their publication – someone may think them not so uninteresting. But all this toasting and buttering and grilling and frying your friends, and serving them up hot for all the old cats at a tea table to mew over – Pah!'

Puffin was silent a moment in appreciation of these noble sentiments.

'But you put in a lot of work over them,' he said at length. 'Often when I'm going up to bed, I see the light still burning in your sitting-room window.'

'And if it comes to that,' rejoined the Major, 'I'm sure I've often dozed off when I'm in bed and woken again, and pulled up my blind, and what not, and there's your light still burning. Powerful long roads those old Romans must have made, Captain.'

The ice was not broken, but it was cracking in all directions under this unexampled thaw. The two had clearly indicated a mutual suspicion of each other's industrious habits after dinner . . . They had never got quite so far as this before: some quarrel had congealed the surface again. But now, with a desperate disagreement just behind them, and the unusual luxury of a taxi just in front, the vernal airs continued blowing in the most springlike manner.

'Yes, that's true enough,' said Puffin. 'Long roads they were, and dry roads at that, and if I stuck to them from after my supper every evening till midnight or more, I should be smothered in dust.'

'Unless you washed the dust down just once in a while,' said Major Flint.

'Just so. Brain work's an exhausting process; requires a little stimulant now and again,' said Puffin. 'I sit in my chair, you understand, and perhaps doze for a bit after my supper, and then I'll get my maps out, and have them handy beside me. And then, if there's something interesting in the evening paper, perhaps I'll have a look at it, and bless me, if by that time it isn't already half-past ten or eleven, and it seems useless to tackle archaeology then. And I just – just while away the time till I'm sleepy. But there seems to be a sort of legend among the ladies here, that I'm a great student of local topography and Roman roads, and all sorts of truck, and I find it better to leave it at that. Tiresome to go into long explanations. In fact,' added Puffin in a burst of confidence, 'the study I've done on Roman roads these last six months wouldn't cover a threepenny piece.'

Major Flint gave a loud, choking guffaw and beat his fat leg.

'Well, if that's not the best joke I've heard for many a long day,' he said. 'There I've been in the house opposite you these last two years, seeing your light burning late night after night, and thinking to myself, "There's my friend Puffin still at it! Fine thing to be an enthusiastic archaeologist like that. That makes short work of a lonely evening for him if he's so buried in his books or his maps –

Mapps, ha! ha! – that he doesn't seem to notice whether it's twelve o'clock or one or two, maybe!" And all the time you've been sitting snoozing and boozing in your chair, with your glass handy to wash the dust down.'

Puffin added his falsetto cackle to this merriment.

'And, often I've thought to myself,' he said, ' "There's my friend the Major in his study opposite, with all his diaries round him, making a note here, and copying an extract there, and conferring with the Viceroy one day, and reprimanding the Maharajah of Bom-be-boo another. He's spending the evening on India's coral strand, he is, having tiffin and shooting tigers and Gawd knows what – "'

The Major's laughter boomed out again.

'And I never kept a diary in my life!' he cried. 'Why there's enough cream in this situation to make a dishful of meringues. You and I, you know, the students of Tilling! The serious-minded students who do a hard day's work when all the pretty ladies have gone to bed. Often and often has old – I mean has that fine woman, Miss Mapp, told me that I work too hard at night! Recommended me to get earlier to bed, and do my work between six and eight in the morning! Six and eight in the morning! That's a queer time of day to recommend an old campaigner to be awake at! Often she's talked to you, too, I bet my hat, about sitting up late and exhausting the nervous faculties.'

Major Flint choked and laughed and inhaled tobacco smoke till he got purple in the face.

'And you sitting up one side of the street,' he gasped, 'pretending to be interested in Roman roads, and me on the other pulling a long face over my diaries, and neither of us with a Roman road or a diary to our names. Let's have an end to such unsociable arrangements, old friend; you bring your Roman roads and the bottle to lay the dust over to me one night, and I'll bring my diaries and my peg over to you the next. Never drink alone – one of my maxims in life – if you can find someone to drink with you. And there were you within a few yards of me all the time sitting by your old solitary self, and there was I sitting by my old solitary self, and we each thought the other a serious-minded old buffer, busy on his life work. I'm blessed if I heard of two such pompous old frauds as you and I, Captain! What a sight of hypocrisy there is in the world, to be sure! No offence – mind: I'm as bad as you, and you're as bad as me, and we're both as bad as each other. But no more solitary confinement of an evening for Benjamin Flint, as long as you're agreeable.'

The advent of the taxi was announced, and arm in arm they limped down the steep path together to the road. A little way off to the left was the great bunker which, primarily, was the cause of their present amity. As they drove by it, the Major waggled his red hand at it.

'*Au reservoir*,' he said. 'Back again soon!'

*   *   *

It was late that night when Miss Mapp felt that she was physically incapable of tacking on a single poppy more to the edge of her skirt, and went to the window of the garden room where she had been working, to close it. She glanced up at the top storey of her own house, and saw that the lights in the servants' rooms were out: she glanced to the right and concluded that her gardener had gone to bed: finally, she glanced down the street and saw with a pang of pleasure that the windows of the Major's house showed no sign of midnight labour. This was intensely gratifying: it indicated that her influence was at work in him, for in response to her wish, so often and so tactfully urged on him, that he would go to bed earlier and not work so hard at night, here was the darkened window, and she dismissed as unworthy the suspicion which had been aroused by the redcurrant fool. The window of his bedroom was dark too: he must have already put out his light, and Miss Mapp made haste over her little tidyings so that she might not be found a transgressor to her own precepts. But there was a light in Captain Puffin's house: he had a less impressionable nature than the Major and was in so many ways far inferior. And did he really find Roman roads so wonderfully exhilarating? Miss Mapp sincerely hoped that he did, and that it was nothing else of less pure and innocent allurement that kept him up . . . As she closed the window very gently, it did just seem to her that there had been something equally baffling in Major Flint's egoistical vigils over his diaries; that she had wondered whether there was not something else (she had hardly formulated what) which kept his lights burning so late. But she would now cross him – dear man – and his late habits, out of the list of riddles about Tilling which awaited solution. Whatever it had been (diaries or what not) that used to keep him up, he had broken the habit now, whereas Captain Puffin had not. She took her poppy-bordered skirt over her arm, and smiled her thankful way to bed. She could allow herself to wonder with a little more definiteness, now that the Major's lights were out and he was abed, what it could be which rendered Captain Puffin so oblivious to the passage of time, when he was investigating Roman roads. How glad she was that the Major was not with him . . . 'Benjamin Flint!' she said to herself as, having put her window open, she trod softly (so as not to disturb the slumberer next door) across her room on her fat white feet to her big white bed. 'Good night, Major Benjy,' she whispered, as she put her light out.

* * *

It was not to be supposed that Diva would act on Miss Mapp's alarming hints that morning as to the fate of coal hoarders, and give, say, a ton of fuel to the hospital at once, in lieu of her usual smaller Christmas contribution, without making further enquiries in the proper quarters as to the legal liabilities of having, so she ascertained, three tons in her cellar, and as soon as her visitor had left her this morning, she popped out to see Mr Wootten, her coal merchant. She returned in a state of fury, for there were no regulations whatever in existence with regard to the amount of coal that any householder might choose to amass, and Mr Wootten complimented her on her prudence in having got in a reasonable supply, for he thought it quite probable that, if the coal strike took place, there would be some difficulty in a month's time from now in replenishing cellars. 'But we've had a good supply all the summer,' added agreeable Mr Wootten, 'and all my customers have got their cellars well stocked.'

Diva rapidly recollected that the perfidious Elizabeth was among them.

'Oh but, Mr Wootten,' she said, 'Miss Mapp popped – dropped in to see me just now. Told me she had hardly got any.'

Mr Wootten turned up his ledger. It was not etiquette to disclose the affairs of one client to another, but if there was a cantankerous customer, one who was never satisfied with prices and quality, that client was Miss Mapp . . . He allowed a broad grin to overspread his agreeable face.

'Well, ma'am, if in a month's time I'm short of coal, there are friends of yours in Tilling who can let you have plenty,' he permitted himself to say . . .

It was idle to attempt to cut out bunches of roses while her hand was so feverish, and she trundled up and down the High Street to cool off. Had she not been so prudent as to make enquiries, as likely as not she would have sent a ton of coal that very day to the hospital, so strongly had Elizabeth's perfidious warning inflamed her imagination as to the fate of hoarders, and all the time Elizabeth's own cellars were glutted, though she had asserted that she was almost fuelless. Why, she must have in her possession more coal than Diva herself, since Mr Wootten had clearly implied that it was Elizabeth who could be borrowed from! And all because of a wretched piece of rose-madder worsted . . .

By degrees she calmed down, for it was no use attempting to plan revenge with a brain at fever heat. She must be calm and icily ingenious. As the cooling process went on she began to wonder whether it was worsted alone that had prompted her friend's diabolical suggestion. It seemed more likely that another motive (one strangely Elizabethan) was the cause of it. Elizabeth might be taken for certain as being a coal hoarder herself, and it was ever so like her to divert suspicion by pretending her cellar was next to empty. She had been equally severe on any who might happen to be hoarding food, in case transport was disarranged and supplies fell short, and with a sudden flare of authentic intuition, Diva's mind blazed with the conjecture that Elizabeth was hoarding food as well.

Luck ever attends the bold and constructive thinker: the apple, for instance, fell from the tree precisely when Newton's mind was groping after the law of gravity, and as Diva stepped into her grocer's to begin her morning's shopping (for she had been occupied with roses ever since breakfast) the attendant was at the telephone at the back of the shop. He spoke in a lucid telephone voice.

'We've only two of the big tins of corned beef,' he said; and there was a pause, during which, to a psychic, Diva's ears might have seemed to grow as pointed with attention as a satyr's. But she could only hear little hollow quacks from the other end.

'Tongue as well. Very good. I'll send them up at once,' he added, and came forward into the shop.

'Good morning,' said Diva. Her voice was tremulous with anxiety and investigation. 'Got any big tins of corned beef? The ones that contain six pounds.'

'Very sorry, ma'am. We've only got two, and they've just been ordered.'

'A small pot of ginger then, please,' said Diva recklessly. 'Will you send it round immediately?'

'Yes, ma'am. The boy's just going out.'

That was luck. Diva hurried into the street, and was absorbed by the headlines of the news outside the stationer's. This was a favourite place for observation, for you appeared to be quite taken up by the topics of the day, and kept an oblique eye on the true object of your scrutiny . . . She had not got to wait long, for almost immediately the grocer's boy came out of the shop with a heavy basket on his arm, delivered the small pot of ginger at her own door, and proceeded along the street. He was, unfortunately, a popular and a conversational youth, who had a great deal to say to his friends, and the period of waiting to see if he would turn up the steep street that led to Miss Mapp's house was very protracted. At the corner he deliberately put down the basket altogether and lit a cigarette, and never had Diva so acutely deplored the spread of the tobacco habit among the juvenile population.

Having refreshed himself he turned up the steep street.

He passed the fishmonger's and the fruiterer's; he did not take the turn down to the dentist's and Mr Wyse's. He had no errand to the Major's house or to the Captain's. Then, oh then, he rang the bell at Miss Mapp's back door. All the time Diva had been following him, keeping her head well down so as to avert the possibility of observation from the window of the garden room, and walking so slowly that the motion of her feet seemed not circular at all . . . Then the bell was answered, and he delivered into Withers's hands one, two tins of corned beef and a round ox tongue. He put the basket on his head and came down the street again, shrilly whistling. If

Diva had had any reasonably small change in her pocket, she would assuredly have given him some small share in it. Lacking this, she trundled home with all speed, and began cutting out roses with swift and certain strokes of the nail scissors.

Now she had already noticed that Elizabeth had paid visits to the grocer's on three consecutive days (three consecutive days: think of it!), and given that her purchases on other occasions had been on the same substantial scale as today, it became a matter of thrilling interest as to where she kept these stores. She could not keep them in the coal cellar, for that was already bursting with coal, and Diva, who had assisted her (the base one) in making a prodigious quantity of jam that year from her well-stocked garden, was aware that the kitchen cupboards were like to be as replete as the coal cellar, before those hoardings of dead oxen began. Then there was the big cupboard under the stairs, but that could scarcely be the site of this prodigious cache, for it was full of cardboard and curtains and carpets and all the rubbishy accumulations which Elizabeth could not bear to part with. Then she had large cupboards in her bedroom and spare rooms full to overflowing of mouldy clothes, but there was positively not another cupboard in the house that Diva knew of, and she crushed her temples in her hands in the attempt to locate the hiding place of the hoard.

Diva suddenly jumped up with a happy squeal of discovery, and in her excitement snapped her scissors with so random a stroke that she completely cut in half the bunch of roses that she was engaged on. There was another cupboard, the best and biggest of all and the most secret and the most discreet. It lay embedded in the wall of the garden room, cloaked and concealed behind the shelves of a false bookcase, which contained no more than the simulacra of books, just books with titles that had never yet appeared on any honest book. There were twelve volumes of 'The Beauties of Nature', a shelf full of 'Elegant Extracts', there were volumes simply called 'Poems', there were 'Commentaries', there were 'Travels' and 'Astronomy' and the lowest and tallest shelf was full of 'Music'. A card table habitually stood in front of this false repository of learning, and it was only last week that Diva, prying casually round the room while Elizabeth had gone to take off her gardening gloves, had noticed a modest catch let into the woodwork. Without doubt, then, the bookcase was the door of the cupboard, and with a stroke of intuition, too sure to be called a guess, Diva was aware that she had correctly inferred the storage of this nefarious hoard. It only remained to verify her conclusion, and, if possible, expose it with every circumstance of public ignominy. She was in no hurry: she could bide her time, aware that, in all probability, every day that passed would see an addition to its damning contents. Someday, when she was playing bridge and the card table had been moved out, in some rubber when she herself was dummy and Elizabeth greedily playing the hand, she would secretly and accidentally press the catch which her acute vision had so providentially revealed to her . . .

She attacked her chintz curtains again with her appetite for the pink roses agreeably whetted. Another hour's work would give her sufficient bunches for her purpose, and unless the dyer was as perfidious as Elizabeth, her now purple jacket and skirt would arrive that afternoon. Two days' hard work would be sufficient for so accomplished a needlewoman as herself to make these original decorations.

In the meantime, for Diva was never idle, and was chiefly occupied with dress, she got out a certain American fashion paper. There was in it the description of a tea gown worn by Mrs Titus W. Trout which she believed was within her dressmaking capacity. She would attempt it, anyhow, and if it proved to be beyond her, she could entrust the more difficult parts to that little dressmaker whom Elizabeth employed, and who was certainly very capable. But the costume was of so daring and splendid a nature that she feared to take anyone into her confidence about it, lest some hint or gossip – for Tilling was a gossipy place – might leak out. Kingfisher blue! It made her mouth water to dwell on the sumptuous syllables!

*   *   *

Miss Mapp was so feverishly occupied all next morning with the application of poppies to the corn-coloured skirt that she paid very little attention to the opening gambits of the day, either as regards the world in general, or, more particularly, Major Benjy. After his early retirement last night he was probably up with the lark this morning, and when between half-past ten and eleven his sonorous

'*Quai-hai!*' sounded through her open window, the shock she experienced interrupted for a moment her floral industry. It was certainly very odd that, having gone to bed at so respectable an hour last night, he should be calling for his porridge only now, but with an impulse of unusual optimism, she figured him as having been at work on his diaries before breakfast, and in that absorbing occupation having forgotten how late it was growing. That, no doubt, was the explanation, though it would be nice to know for certain, if the information positively forced itself on her notice . . . As she worked (framing her lips with elaborate motions to the syllables), she dumbly practised the phrase 'Major Benjy'. Sometimes in moments of gallantry he called her 'Miss Elizabeth', and she meant, when she had got accustomed to it by practice, to say 'Major Benjy' to him by accident, and he would, no doubt, beg her to make a habit of that friendly slip of the tongue . . . 'Tongue' led to a new train of thought, and presently she paused in her work, and pulling the card table away from the deceptive bookcase, she pressed the concealed catch of the door, and peeped in.

There was still room for further small precautions against starvation owing to the impending coal strike, and she took stock of her provisions. Even if the strike lasted quite a long time, there would now be no immediate lack of the necessaries of life, for the cupboard glistened with tinned meats, and the flour merchant had sent a very sensible sack. This with considerable exertion she transferred to a high shelf in the cupboard, instead of allowing it to remain standing on the floor, for Withers had informed her of an unpleasant rumour about a mouse, which Mary had observed, lost in thought in front of the cupboard. 'So mousie shall only find tins on the floor now,' thought Miss Mapp. 'Mousie shall try his teeth on tins.' . . . There was tea and coffee in abundance, jars of jam filled the kitchen shelves, and if this morning she laid in a moderate supply of dried fruits, there was no reason to face the future with anything but fortitude. She would see about that now, for, busy though she was, she could not miss the shopping parade. Would Diva, she wondered, be at her window, snipping roses out of chintz curtains? The careful, thrifty soul. Perhaps this time tomorrow, Diva, looking out of her window, would see that somebody else had been quicker about being thrifty than she. That would be fun!

The Major's dining-room window was open, and as Miss Mapp passed it, she could not help hearing loud, angry remarks about eggs coming from inside. That made it clear that he was still at breakfast, and that if he had been working at his diaries in the fresh morning hours and forgetting the time, early rising, in spite of his early retirement last night, could not be supposed to suit his Oriental temper. But a change of habits was invariably known to be upsetting, and Miss Mapp was hopeful that in a day or two he would feel quite a different man. Further down the street was quaint Irene lounging at the door of her new studio (a converted coach house), smoking a cigarette and dressed like a jockey.

'Hello, Mapp,' she said. 'Come and have a look round my new studio. You haven't seen it yet. I shall give a house warming next week. Bridge party!'

Miss Mapp tried to steel herself for the hundredth time to appear quite unconscious that she was being addressed when Irene said 'Mapp' in that odious manner. But she never could summon up sufficient nerve to be rude to so awful a mimic . . .

'Good morning, dear one,' she said sycophantically. 'Shall I peep in for a moment?'

The decoration of the studio was even more appalling than might have been expected. There was a German stove in the corner made of pink porcelain, the rafters and roof were painted scarlet, the walls were of magenta distemper and the floor was blue. In the corner was a very large orange-coloured screen. The walls were hung with specimens of Irene's art, there was a stout female with no clothes on at all, whom it was impossible not to recognize as being Lucy; there were studies of fat legs and ample bosoms, and on the easel was a picture, evidently in process of completion, which represented a man. From this Miss Mapp instantly averted her eyes.

'Eve,' said Irene, pointing to Lucy.

Miss Mapp naturally guessed that the gentleman who was almost in the same costume was Adam, and turned completely away from him.

'And what a lovely idea to have a blue floor, dear,' she said. 'How original you are. And that pretty scarlet ceiling. But don't you find when you're painting that all these bright colours disturb you?'

'Not a bit: they stimulate your sense of colour.'

Miss Mapp moved towards the screen.

'What a delicious big screen,' she said.

'Yes, but don't go behind it, Mapp,' said Irene, 'or you'll see my model undressing.'

Miss Mapp retreated from it precipitately, as from a wasps' nest, and examined some of the studies on the wall, for it was more than probable from the unfinished picture on the easel that Adam lurked behind the delicious screen. Terrible though it all was, she was conscious of an unbridled curiosity to know who Adam was. It was dreadful to think that there could be any man in Tilling so depraved as to stand to be looked at with so little on . . .

Irene strolled round the walls with her.

'Studies of Lucy,' she said.

'I see, dear,' said Miss Mapp. 'How clever! Legs and things! But when you have your bridge party, won't you perhaps cover some of them up, or turn them to the wall? We should all be looking at your pictures instead of attending to our cards. And if you were thinking of asking the Padre, you know . . .'

They were approaching the corner of the room where the screen stood, when a movement there as if Adam had hit it with his elbow made Miss Mapp turn round. The screen fell flat on the ground and within a yard of her stood Mr Hopkins, the proprietor of the fish shop just up the street. Often and often had Miss Mapp had pleasant little conversations with him, with a view to bringing down the price of flounders. He had little bathing drawers on . . .

'Hello, Hopkins, are you ready?' said Irene. 'You know Miss Mapp, don't you?'

Miss Mapp had not imagined that Time and Eternity combined could hold so embarrassing a moment. She did not know where to look, but wherever she looked, it should not be at Hopkins. But (wherever she looked) she could not be unaware that Hopkins raised his large bare arm and touched the place where his cap would have been, if he had had one.

'Good morning, Hopkins,' she said. 'Well, Irene darling, I must be trotting, and leave you to your – ' she hardly knew what to call it – 'to your work.'

She tripped from the room, which seemed to be entirely full

of unclothed limbs, and redder than one of Mr Hopkins's boiled lobsters hurried down the street. She felt that she could never face him again, but would be obliged to go to the establishment in the High Street where Irene dealt, when it was fish she wanted from a fish shop . . . Her head was in a whirl at the brazenness of mankind, especially womankind. How had Irene started the overtures that led to this? Had she just said to Hopkins one morning: 'Will you come to my studio and take off all your clothes?' If Irene had not been such a wonderful mimic, she would certainly have felt it her duty to go straight to the Padre, and, pulling down her veil, confide to him the whole sad story. But as that was out of the question, she went into Twemlow's and ordered four pounds of dried apricots.

CHAPTER FOUR

The dyer, as Diva had feared, proved perfidious, and it was not till the next morning that her maid brought her the parcel containing the coat and skirt of the projected costume. Diva had already done her marketing, so that she might have no other calls on her time to interfere with the tacking on of the bunches of pink roses, and she hoped to have the dress finished in time for Elizabeth's afternoon bridge party next day, an invitation to which had just reached her. She had also settled to have a cold lunch today, so that her cook as well as her parlourmaid could devote themselves to the job.

She herself had taken the jacket for decoration, and was just tacking the first rose on to the collar, when she looked out of the window, and what she saw caused her needle to fall from her nerveless hand. Tripping along the opposite pavement was Elizabeth. She had on a dress, the material of which, after a moment's gaze, Diva identified: it was that corn-coloured coat and skirt which she had worn so much last spring. But the collar, the cuffs, the waistband and the hem of the skirt were covered with staring red poppies. Next moment, she called to remembrance the chintz that had once covered Elizabeth's sofa in the garden room.

Diva wasted no time, but rang the bell. She had to make certain.

'Janet,' she said, 'go straight out into the High Street, and walk close behind Miss Mapp. Look very carefully at her dress; see if the poppies on it are of chintz.'

Janet's face fell.

'Why, ma'am, she's never gone and – ' she began.

'Quick!' said Diva in a strangled voice.

Diva watched from her window. Janet went out, looked this way and that, spied the quarry, and skimmed up the High Street on feet that twinkled as fast as her mistress's. She came back much out of breath with speed and indignation.

'Yes, ma'am,' she said. 'They're chintz sure enough. Tacked on, too, just as you were meaning to do. Oh, ma'am – '

Janet quite appreciated the magnitude of the calamity and her voice failed.

'What are we to do, ma'am?' she added.

Diva did not reply for a moment, but sat with eyes closed in profound and concentrated thought. It required no reflection to decide how impossible it was to appear herself tomorrow in a dress which seemed to ape the costume which all Tilling had seen Elizabeth wearing today, and at first it looked as if there was nothing to be done with all those laboriously acquired bunches of rosebuds; for it was clearly out of the question to use them as the decoration for any costume, and idle to think of sewing them back into the snipped and gashed curtains. She looked at the purple skirt and coat that hungered for their flowers, and then she looked at Janet. Janet was a short, roundabout person; it was ill-naturedly supposed that she had much the same figure as her mistress . . .

Then the light broke, dazzling and diabolical, and Diva bounced to her feet, blinded by its splendour.

'My coat and skirt are yours, Janet,' she said. 'Get with the work both of you. Bustle. Cover it with roses. Have it finished tonight. Wear it tomorrow. Wear it always.'

She gave a loud cackle of laughter and threaded her needle.

'Lor, ma'am!' said Janet, admiringly. 'That's a teaser! And thank you, ma'am!'

'It was roses, roses all the way.' Diva had quite miscalculated the number required, and there were sufficient not only to cover collar, cuffs and border of the skirt with them but to make another line of them six inches above the hem. Original and gorgeous as the dress would be, it was yet a sort of parody of Elizabeth's costume which was attracting so much interest and attention as she popped in and out of shops today. Tomorrow that would be worn by Janet, and Janet (or Diva was much mistaken) should encourage her friends to get permission to use up old bits of chintz. Very likely chintz decoration would become quite a vogue among the servant maids of Tilling . . . How Elizabeth had got hold of the idea mattered nothing, but anyhow she would be surfeited with the idea before Diva had finished with her. It was possible, of course (anything was possible), that it had occurred to her independently, but Diva was loath to give so innocent an ancestry to her adoption of it. It was far more sensible to take for granted that she had got wind of Diva's invention by some odious, underhand piece of spying. What that might be must be investigated (and probably determined) later, but at present the business of Janet's roses eclipsed every other interest.

Miss Mapp's shopping that morning was unusually prolonged, for it was important that every woman in Tilling should see the poppies on the corn-coloured ground, and know that she had worn that dress before Diva appeared in some mean adaptation of it. Though the total cost of her entire purchases hardly amounted to a shilling, she went in and out of an amazing number of shops, and made a prodigious series of enquiries into the price of commodities that ranged from motor cars to sealing wax, and often entered a shop twice because (wreathed in smiling apologies for her stupidity) she had forgotten what she was told the first time. By twelve o'clock she was satisfied that practically everybody, with one exception, had seen her, and that her costume had aroused a deep sense of jealousy and angry admiration. So cunning was the handiwork of herself, Withers and Mary that she felt fairly sure that no one had the slightest notion of how this decoration of poppies was accomplished, for Evie had run round her in small mouse-like circles, murmuring to herself: 'Very effective idea; is it woven into the cloth, Elizabeth? Dear me, I wonder where I could get some like it,' and Mrs Poppit had followed her all up the street, with eyes glued to the hem of her skirt, and a completely puzzled face: 'But then,' so thought Elizabeth sweetly, 'even members of the Order of the British Empire can't have everything their own way.' As for the Major, he had simply come to a dead stop when he bounced out of his house as she passed, and said something very gallant and appropriate. Even the absence of that one inhabitant of Tilling, dear Diva, did not strike a jarring note in this paean of triumph, for Miss Mapp was quite satisfied that Diva was busy indoors, working her fingers to the bone over the application of bunches of roses, and, as usual, she was perfectly correct in her conjecture. But dear Diva would have to see the new frock tomorrow afternoon, at the latest, when she came to the bridge party. Perhaps she would then, for the first time, be wearing the roses herself, and everybody would very pleasantly pity her. This was so rapturous a thought, that when Miss Mapp, after her prolonged shopping and with her almost empty basket, passed Mr Hopkins standing outside his shop on her return home again, she gave him her usual smile, though without meeting his eye, and tried to forget how much of him she had seen yesterday. Perhaps she might speak to him tomorrow and gradually resume ordinary relations, for the prices at the other fish shop were as high as the quality of the fish was low . . . She told herself that there was nothing actually immoral in the human skin, however embarrassing it was.

*　*　*

Miss Mapp had experienced a cruel disappointment last night, though the triumph of this morning had done something to soothe it, for Major Benjy's window had certainly been lit up to a very late hour, and so it was clear that he had not been able, twice in succession, to tear himself away from his diaries, or whatever else detained him, and go to bed at a proper time. Captain Puffin, however, had not sat up late; indeed he must have gone to bed quite unusually early, for his window was dark by half-past nine. Tonight, again the position was reversed, and it seemed that Major Benjy was 'good' and Captain Puffin was 'bad'. On the whole, then, there was cause for thankfulness, and as she added a tin of biscuits and two jars of Bovril to her prudent stores, she found herself a conscious sceptic about those Roman roads. Diaries (perhaps) were a little different, for egoism was a more potent force than archaeology, and for her part she now definitely believed that Roman roads spelt some form of drink. She was sorry to believe it, but it was her duty to believe something of the kind, and she really did not know what else to believe. She did not go so far as mentally to accuse him of drunkenness, but considering the way he absorbed redcurrant fool, it was clear that he was no foe to alcohol and probably watered the Roman roads with it. With her vivid imagination she pictured him –

Miss Mapp recalled herself from this melancholy reflection and put up her hand just in time to save a bottle of Bovril which she had put on the top shelf in front of the sack of flour from tumbling to the ground. With the latest additions she had made to her larder, it required considerable ingenuity to fit all the tins and packages in, and for a while she diverted her mind from Captain Puffin's drinking to her own eating. But by careful packing and balancing she managed to stow everything away with sufficient economy of space to allow her to shut the door, and then put the card table in place again. It was then late, and with a fond look at her sweet flowers sleeping in the moonlight, she went to bed. Captain Puffin's sitting room was still alight, and even as she deplored this, his shadow in profile crossed the blind. Shadows were queer things – she could make a beautiful shadow rabbit on the wall by a dexterous interlacement of fingers and thumbs – and certainly this shadow, in the momentary glance she had of it, appeared to have a large moustache. She could make nothing whatever out of that, except to suppose that just as fingers and thumbs became a rabbit, so his nose became a moustache, for he could not have grown one since he came back from golf . . .

* * *

She was out early for her shopping next morning, for there were some delicacies to be purchased for her bridge party, more particularly some little chocolate cakes she had lately discovered which looked very small and innocent, but were in reality of so cloying and substantial a nature, that the partaker thereof would probably not feel capable of making any serious inroads into other provisions. Naturally she was much on the alert today, for it was more than possible that Diva's dress was finished and in evidence. What colour it would be she did not know, but a large quantity of rosebuds would, even at a distance, make identification easy. Diva was certainly not at her window this morning, so it seemed more than probable that they would soon meet.

Far away, just crossing the High Street at the further end, she caught sight of a bright patch of purple, very much of the required shape. There was surely a pink border round the skirt and a pink panel on the collar, and just as surely Mrs Bartlett, recognizable for her gliding mouse-like walk, was moving in its fascinating wake. Then the purple patch vanished into a shop, and Miss Mapp, all smiles and poppies, went with her basket up the street. Presently she encountered Evie, who, also all smiles, seemed to have some communication to make, but only got as far as 'Have you seen' – when she gave a little squeal of laughter, quite inexplicable, and glided into some dark entry. A minute afterwards, the purple patch suddenly appeared from a shop and almost collided with her. It was not Diva at all, but Diva's Janet.

The shock was so indescribably severe that Miss Mapp's smile was frozen, so to speak, as by some sudden congealment on to her face, and did not thaw off it till she had reached the sharp turn at the end of the street, where she leaned heavily on the railing and breathed through her nose. A light autumnal mist overlay the miles of marsh, but the sun was already drinking it up, promising the Tillingites another golden day. The tidal river was at the flood, and the bright water lapped the bases of the turf-covered banks that kept it within its course. Beyond that was the tram station towards which presently Major Benjy and Captain Puffin would be hurrying to catch the tram that would take them out to the golf links. The straight road across the marsh was visible, and the railway bridge. All these things were pitilessly unchanged, and Miss Mapp noted them blankly, until rage began to restore the numbed current of her mental processes.

*   *   *

If the records of history contained any similar instance of such treachery and low cunning as was involved in this plot of Diva's to dress Janet in the rosebud chintz, Miss Mapp would have liked to be told clearly and distinctly what it was. She could trace the workings of Diva's base mind with absolute accuracy, and if all the archangels in the hierarchy of heaven had assured her that Diva had originally intended the rosebuds for Janet, she would have scorned them for their clumsy perjury. Diva had designed and executed that dress for herself, and just because Miss Mapp's ingenuity (inspired by the two rosebuds that had fluttered out of the window) had forestalled her, she had taken this fiendish revenge. It was impossible to pervade the High Street covered with chintz poppies when a parlourmaid was being equally pervasive in chintz rosebuds, and what was to be done with this frock executed with such mirth and malice by Withers, Mary and herself she had no idea. She might just as well give it Withers, for she could no longer wear it herself, or tear the poppies from the hem and bestrew the High Street with them.

Miss Mapp's face froze into immobility again, for here, trundling swiftly towards her, was Diva herself.

Diva appeared not to see her till she got quite close.

'Morning, Elizabeth,' she said. 'Seen my Janet anywhere?'

'No,' said Miss Mapp.

Janet (no doubt according to instructions received) popped out of a shop, and came towards her mistress.

'Here she is,' said Diva. 'All right, Janet. You go home. I'll see to the other things.'

'It's a lovely day,' said Miss Mapp, beginning to lash her tail. 'So bright.'

'Yes. Pretty trimming of poppies,' said Diva. 'Janet's got rosebuds.'

This was too much.

'Diva, I didn't think it of you,' said Miss Mapp in a shaking voice. 'You saw my new frock yesterday, and you were filled with malice and envy, Diva, just because I had thought of using flowers off an old chintz as well as you, and came out first with it. You had meant to wear that purple frock yourself – though I must say it fits Janet perfectly – and just because I was first in the field you did this. You gave Janet that frock, so that I should be dressed in the same style as your parlourmaid, and you've got a black heart, Diva!'

'That's nonsense,' said Diva firmly. 'Heart's as red as anybody's, and talking of black hearts doesn't become *you*, Elizabeth. You knew I was cutting out roses from my curtains –'

Miss Mapp laughed shrilly.

'Well, if I happen to notice that you've taken your chintz curtains down,' she said with an awful distinctness that showed the wisdom teeth of which Diva had got three at the most, 'and pink bunches of roses come flying out of your window into the High Street, even my poor wits, small as they are, are equal to drawing the conclusion that you are cutting roses out of curtains. Your well-known fondness for dress did the rest. With your permission, Diva, I intend to draw exactly what conclusions I please on every occasion, including this one.'

'Ho! That's how you got the idea then,' said Diva. 'I knew you had cribbed it from me.'

'Cribbed?' asked Miss Mapp, in ironical ignorance of what so vulgar and slangy an expression meant.

'Cribbed means taking what isn't yours,' said Diva. 'Even then, if you had only acted in a straightforward manner – '

Miss Mapp, shaken as with palsy, regretted that she had let slip, out of pure childlike joy, in irony, the manner in which she had obtained the poppy notion, but in a quarrel regrets are useless, and she went on again.

'And would you very kindly explain how or when I have acted in a manner that was not straightforward,' she asked with laborious politeness. 'Or do I understand that a monopoly of cutting up chintz curtains for personal adornment has been bestowed on you by Act of Parliament?'

'You knew I was meaning to make a frock with chintz roses on it,' said Diva. 'You stole my idea. Worked night and day to be first. Just like you. Mean behaviour.'

'It was meaner to give that frock to Janet,' said Miss Mapp.

'You can give yours to Withers,' snapped Diva.

'Much obliged, Mrs Plaistow,' said Miss Mapp.

*　　*　　*

Diva had been watching Janet's retreating figure, and feeling that though revenge was sweet, revenge was also strangely expensive, for she had sacrificed one of the most strikingly successful frocks she had ever made on that smoking altar. Now her revenge was gratified, and deeply she regretted the frock. Miss Mapp's heart was similarly wrung by torture: revenge too had been hers (general revenge on Diva for existing), but this dreadful counter-stroke had made it quite impossible for her to enjoy the use of this frock any more, for she could not habit herself like a housemaid. Each, in fact, had, as matters at present stood, completely wrecked the other, like two express trains meeting in top-speed collision, and, since the quarrel had clearly risen to its utmost height, there was no further joy of battle to be anticipated, but only the melancholy task of counting the corpses. So they paused, breathing very quickly and trembling, while both sought for some way out. Besides Miss

Mapp had a bridge party this afternoon, and if they parted now in this extreme state of tension, Diva might conceivably not come, thereby robbing herself of her bridge and spoiling her hostess's table. Naturally any permanent quarrel was not contemplated by either of them, for if quarrels were permanent in Tilling, nobody would be on speaking terms any more with anyone else in a day or two, and (hardly less disastrous) there could be no fresh quarrels with anybody, since you could not quarrel without words. There might be songs without words, as Mendelssohn had proved, but not rows without words. By what formula could this deadly antagonism be bridged without delay?

Diva gazed out over the marsh. She wanted desperately to regain her rosebud frock, and she knew that Elizabeth was starving for further wearing of her poppies. Perhaps the wide, serene plain below inspired her with a hatred of littleness. There would be no loss of dignity in making a proposal that her enemy, she felt sure, would accept: it merely showed a Christian spirit, and set an example to Elizabeth, to make the first move. Janet she did not consider.

'If you are in a fit state to listen to reason, Elizabeth,' she began.

Miss Mapp heaved a sigh of relief. Diva had thought of something. She swallowed the insult at a gulp.

'Yes, dear,' she said.

'Got an idea. Take away Janet's frock, and wear it myself. Then you can wear yours. Too pretty for parlourmaids. Eh?'

A heavenly brightness spread over Miss Mapp's face.

'Oh, how wonderful of you to have thought of that, Diva,' she said. 'But how shall we explain it all to everybody?'

Diva clung to her rights. Though clearly Christian, she was human.

'Say I thought of tacking chintz on and told you,' she said.

'Yes, darling,' said Elizabeth. 'That's beautiful, I agree. But poor Janet!'

'I'll give her some other old thing,' said Diva. 'Good sort, Janet. Wants me to win.'

'And about her having been seen wearing it?'

'Say she hasn't ever worn it. Say they're mad,' said Diva.

Miss Mapp felt it better to tear herself away before she began distilling all sorts of acidities that welled up in her fruitful mind. She could, for instance, easily have agreed that nothing was more probable than that Janet had been mistaken for her mistress . . .

'*Au reservoir* then, dear,' she said tenderly. 'See you at about four? And will you wear your pretty rosebud frock?'

This was agreed to, and Diva went home to take it away from Janet.

* * *

The reconciliation of course was strictly confined to matters relating to chintz and did not include such extraneous subjects as coal strike or food hoarding, and even in the first glowing moments of restored friendliness, Diva began wondering whether she would have the opportunity that afternoon of testing the truth of her conjecture about the cupboard in the garden room. Cudgel her brains as she might she could think of no other cache that could contain the immense amount of provisions that Elizabeth had probably accumulated, and she was all on fire to get to practical grips with the problem. As far as tins of corned beef and tongues went, Elizabeth might possibly have buried them in her garden in the manner of a dog, but it was not likely that a hoarder would limit herself to things in tins. No: there was a cupboard somewhere ready to burst with strong supporting foods . . .

Diva intentionally arrived a full quarter of an hour on the hither side of punctuality, and was taken by Withers out into the garden room, where tea was laid, and two card tables were in readiness. She was, of course, the first of the guests, and the moment Withers withdrew to tell her mistress that she had come, Diva stealthily glided to the cupboard, from in front of which the bridge table had been removed, feeling the shrill joy of some romantic treasure hunter. She found the catch, she pressed it, she pulled open the door and the whole of the damning profusion of provisions burst upon her delighted eyes. Shelf after shelf was crowded with eatables; there were tins of corned beef and tongues (that she knew already), there was a sack of flour, there were tubes of Bath Oliver biscuits, bottles of Bovril, the yield of a thousand condensed Swiss cows, jars of prunes . . . All these were in the front row, flush with the door, and who knew to what depth the cupboard extended?

Even as she feasted her eyes on this incredible store, some package on the top shelf wavered and toppled, and she had only just time to shut the door again, in order to prevent it falling out on to the floor. But this displacement prevented the door from wholly closing, and push and shove as Diva might, she could not get the catch to click home, and the only result of her energy and efforts was to give rise to a muffled explosion from within, just precisely as if something made of cardboard had burst. That mental image was so vivid that to her fevered imagination it seemed to be real. This was followed by certain faint taps from within against 'Elegant Extracts' and 'Astronomy'.

Diva grew very red in the face, and said 'Drat it' under her breath. She did not dare open the door again in order to push things back, for fear of an uncontrollable stream of 'things' pouring out. Some nicely balanced equilibrium had clearly been upset in those capacious shelves, and it was impossible to tell, without looking, how deep and how extensive the disturbance was. And in order to look, she had to open the bookcase again . . . Luckily the pressure against the door was not sufficiently heavy to cause it to swing wide, so the best she could do was to leave it just ajar with temporary quiescence inside. Simultaneously she heard Miss Mapp's step, and had no more than time to trundle at the utmost speed of her whirling feet across to the window, where she stood looking out, and appeared quite unconscious of her hostess's entry.

'Diva darling, how sweet of you to come so early!' she said. 'A little cosy chat before the others arrive.'

Diva turned round, much startled.

'Hello!' she said. 'Didn't hear you. Got Janet's frock you see.'

('What makes Diva's face so red?' thought Miss Mapp.)

'So I see, darling,' she said. 'Lovely rose garden. How well it suits you, dear! Did Janet mind?'

'No. Promised her a new frock at Christmas.'

'That will be nice for Janet,' said Elizabeth enthusiastically. 'Shall we pop into the garden, dear, till my guests come?'

Diva was glad to pop into the garden and get away from the immediate vicinity of the cupboard, for though she had planned and looked forward to the exposure of Elizabeth's hoarding, she had not meant it to come, as it now probably would, in crashes of tins and bursting of Bovril bottles. Again she had intended to have opened that door quite casually and innocently while she was being dummy, so that everyone could see how accidental the exposure was, and to have gone poking about the cupboard in Elizabeth's absence was a shade too professional, so to speak, for the usual detective work of Tilling. But the fuse was set now. Sooner or later the explosion must come. She wondered as they went out to commune with Elizabeth's sweet flowers till the other guests arrived how great a torrent would be let loose. She did not repent her exploration – far from it – but her pleasurable anticipations were strongly diluted with suspense.

Miss Mapp had found such difficulty in getting eight players together today, that she had transgressed her principles and asked Mrs Poppit as well as Isabel, and they, with Diva, the two Bartletts, and the Major and the Captain, formed the party. The moment Mrs Poppit appeared, Elizabeth hated her more than ever, for she put up her glasses, and began to give her patronizing advice about her garden, which she had not been allowed to see before.

'You have quite a pretty little piece of garden, Miss Mapp,' she said, 'though, to be sure, I fancied from what you said that it was more extensive. Dear me, your roses do not seem to be doing very well. Probably they are old plants and want renewing. You must send your gardener round – you keep a gardener? – and I will let you have a dozen vigorous young bushes.'

Miss Mapp licked her dry lips. She kept a kind of gardener: two days a week.

'Too good of you,' she said, 'but that rose bed is quite sacred, dear Mrs Poppit. Not all the vigorous young bushes in the world would tempt me. It's my "Friendship's Border": some dear friend gave me each of my rose trees.'

Mrs Poppit transferred her gaze to the wistaria that grew over the steps up to the garden room. Some of the dear friends she thought must be centenarians.

'Your wistaria wants pruning sadly,' she said. 'Your gardener does not understand wistarias. That corner there was made, I may say, for fuchsias. You should get a dozen choice fuchsias.'

Miss Mapp laughed.

'Oh, you must excuse me,' she said with a glance at Mrs Poppit's brocaded silk. 'I can't bear fuchsias. They always remind me of overdressed women. Ah, there's Mr Bartlett. How-de-do, Padre. And dear Evie!'

Dear Evie appeared fascinated by Diva's dress.

'Such beautiful rosebuds,' she murmured, 'and what a lovely shade of purple. And Elizabeth's poppies too, quite a pair of you. But surely this morning, Diva, didn't I see your good Janet in just such another dress, and I thought at the time how odd it was that – '

'If you saw Janet this morning,' said Diva quite firmly, 'you saw her in her print dress.'

'And here's Major Benjy,' said Miss Mapp, who had made her slip about his Christian name yesterday, and had been duly entreated to continue slipping. 'And Captain Puffin. Well, that is nice! Shall we go into my little garden shed, dear Mrs Poppit, and have our tea?'

Major Flint was still a little lame, for his golf today had been of the nature of gardening, and he hobbled up the steps behind the ladies, with that little cock-sparrow sailor following him and telling the Padre how badly and yet how successfully he himself had played.

'Pleasantest room in Tilling, I always say, Miss Elizabeth,' said he, diverting his mind from a mere game to the fairies.

'My dear little room,' said Miss Mapp, knowing that it was much larger than anything in Mrs Poppit's house. 'So tiny!'

'Oh, not a bad-sized little room,' said Mrs Poppit encouragingly 'Much the same proportions, on a very small scale, as the throne room at Buckingham Palace.'

'That beautiful throne room!' exclaimed Miss Mapp. 'A cup of tea, dear Mrs Poppit? None of that naughty redcurrant fool, I am afraid. And a little chocolate cake?'

These substantial chocolate cakes soon did their fell work of producing the sense of surfeit, and presently Elizabeth's guests dropped off gorged from the tea table. Diva fortunately remembered their consistency in time, and nearly cleared a plate of jumbles instead, which the hostess had hoped would form a pleasant accompaniment to her dessert at her supper this evening, and was still crashingly engaged on them when the general drifting movement towards the two bridge tables set in. Mrs Poppit, with her glasses up, followed by Isabel, was employed in making a tour of the room, in case, as Miss Mapp had already determined, she never saw it again, examining the quality of the carpet, the curtains, the chair backs with the air of a doubtful purchaser.

'And quite a quantity of books, I see,' she announced as she came opposite the fatal cupboard. 'Look, Isabel, what a quantity of books. There is something strange about them, though; I do not believe they are real.'

She put out her hand and pulled at the back of one of the volumes of 'Elegant Extracts'. The door swung open, and from behind it came a noise of rattling, bumping and clattering. Something soft and heavy thumped on to the floor, and a cloud of floury dust arose. A bottle of Bovril embedded itself quietly there without damage, and a tin of Bath Oliver biscuits beat a fierce tattoo on one of corned beef. Innumerable dried apricots from the burst package flew about like shrapnel, and tapped at the tins. A jar of prunes, breaking its fall on the flour, rolled merrily out into the middle of the floor.

The din was succeeded by complete silence. The Padre had said 'What ho, i' fegs?' during the tumult, but his voice had been drowned by the rattling of the dried apricots. The Member of the Order of the British Empire stepped free of the provisions that bumped round her, and examined them through her glasses. Diva crammed the last jumble into her mouth and disposed of it with the utmost rapidity. The birthday of her life had come, as Miss Rossetti said.

'Dear Elizabeth!' she exclaimed. 'What a disaster! All your little stores in case of the coal strike. Let me help to pick them up. I do not think anything is broken. Isn't that lucky?'

Evie hurried to the spot.

'Such a quantity of good things,' she said rapidly under her breath. 'Tinned meats and Bovril and prunes, and ever so many apricots. Let me pick them all up, and with a little dusting . . . Why, what a big cupboard, and such a quantity of good things.'

Miss Mapp had certainly struck a streak of embarrassments. What with naked Mr Hopkins, and Janet's frock and this unveiling of her hoard, life seemed at the moment really to consist of nothing else than beastly situations. How on earth that catch of the door had come undone, she had no idea, but much as she would have liked to suspect foul play from somebody, she was bound to conclude that Mrs Poppit with her prying hands had accidentally pressed it. It was like Diva, of course, to break the silence with odious allusions to hoarding, and bitterly she wished that she had not started the topic the other day, but had been content to lay in her stores without so pointedly affirming that she was doing nothing of the kind. But this was no time for vain laments, and restraining a natural impulse to scratch and beat Mrs Poppit, she exhibited an admirable inventiveness and composure. Though she knew it would deceive nobody, everybody had to pretend he was deceived.

'Oh, my poor little Christmas presents for your needy parishioners, Padre,' she said. 'You've seen them before you were meant to, and you must forget all about them. And so little harm done, just an apricot or two. Withers will pick them all up, so let us get to our bridge.'

Withers entered the room at this moment to clear away tea, and Miss Mapp explained it all over again.

'All our little Christmas presents have come tumbling out, Withers,' she said. 'Will you put as many as you can back in the cupboard and take the rest indoors? Don't tread on the apricots.'

It was difficult to avoid doing this, as the apricots were everywhere, and their colour on the brown carpet was wonderfully protective. Miss Mapp herself had already stepped on two, and their adhesive stickiness was hard to get rid of. In fact, for the next few minutes the coal shovel was in strong request for their removal from the soles of shoes, and the fender was littered with their squashed remains . . . The party generally was distinctly thoughtful as it sorted itself out into two tables, for every single member of it was trying to assimilate the amazing proposition that Miss Mapp had, halfway through September, loaded her cupboard with Christmas presents on a scale that staggered belief. The feat required thought: it required a faith so childlike as to verge on the imbecile. Conversation during deals had an awkward tendency towards discussion of the coal strike. As often as it drifted there the subject was changed very abruptly, just as if there was some occult reason for not speaking of so natural a topic. It concerned everybody, but it was rightly felt to concern Miss Mapp the most . . .

CHAPTER FIVE

It was the Major's turn to entertain his friend, and by half-past nine, on a certain squally October evening, he and Puffin were seated by the fire in the diary room, while the rain volleyed at the windows and occasional puffs of stinging smoke were driven down the chimney by the gale that squealed and buffeted round the house. Puffin, by way of keeping up the comedy of Roman roads, had brought a map of the district across from his house, but the more essential part of his equipment for this studious evening was a bottle of whisky. Originally the host had provided whisky for himself and his guest at these pleasant chats, but there were undeniable objections to this plan, because the guest always proved unusually thirsty, which tempted his host to keep pace with him, while if they both drank at their own expense, the causes of economy and abstemiousness had a better chance. Also, while the Major took his drinks short and strong in a small tumbler, Puffin enriched his with lemons and sugar in a large one, so that nobody could really tell if equality as well as fraternity was realized. But if each brought his own bottle . . .

It had been a trying day, and the Major was very lame. A drenching storm had come up during their golf, while they were far from the clubhouse, and Puffin, being three up, had very naturally refused to accede to his opponent's suggestion to call the match off. He was perfectly willing to be paid his half-crown and go home, but Major Flint, remembering that Puffin's game usually went to pieces if it rained, had rejected this proposal with the scorn that it deserved. There had been other disagreeable incidents as well. His driver, slippery from rain, had flown out of the Major's hands on the twelfth tee, and had 'shot like a streamer of the northern morn', and landed in a pool of brackish water left by an unusually high tide. The ball had gone into another pool nearer the tee. The ground was greasy with moisture, and three holes further on Puffin had fallen flat on his face instead of lashing his fifth shot home on to the green, as he had intended. They had given each other stymies, and each had holed his opponent's ball by mistake; they had wrangled over the correct procedure if you lay in a rabbit scrape or on the tram lines; the Major had lost a new ball; there was a mushroom on one of the greens between Puffin's ball and the hole . . . All these untoward incidents had come crowding in together, and from the Major's point of view, the worst of them all had been the collective incident that Puffin, so far from being put off by the rain, had, in spite of mushroom and falling down, played with a steadiness of which he was usually quite incapable. Consequently Major Flint was lame and his wound troubled him, while Puffin, in spite of his obvious reasons for complacency, was growing irritated with his companion's ill-temper, and was half blinded by wood smoke.

He wiped his streaming eyes.

'You should get your chimney swept,' he observed.

Major Flint had put his handkerchief over his face to keep the wood smoke out of his eyes. He blew it off with a loud, indignant puff.

'Oh! Ah! Indeed!' he said.

Puffin was rather taken aback by the violence of these interjections; they dripped with angry sarcasm.

'Oh, well! No offence,' he said.

'A man,' said the Major impersonally, 'makes an offensive remark, and says "No offence." If your own fireside suits you better than mine, Captain Puffin, all I can say is that you're at liberty to enjoy it!'

This was all rather irregular: they had indulged in a good stiff breeze this afternoon, and it was too early to ruffle the calm again. Puffin plucked and proffered an olive branch.

'There's your handkerchief,' he said, picking it up. 'Now let's have one of our comfortable talks. Hot glass of grog and a chat over the fire: that's the best thing after such a wetting as we got this afternoon. I'll take a slice of lemon, if you'll be so good as to give it me, and a lump of sugar.'

The Major got up and limped to his cupboard. It struck him precisely at that moment that Puffin scored considerably over lemons and sugar, because he was supplied with them gratis every other night; whereas he himself, when Puffin's guest, took nothing off his host but hot water. He determined to ask for some biscuits, anyhow, tomorrow . . .

'I hardly know whether there's a lemon left,' he grumbled. 'I must lay in a store of lemons. As for sugar – '

Puffin chose to disregard this suggestion.

'Amusing incident the other day,' he said brightly, 'when Miss Mapp's cupboard door flew open. The old lady didn't like it. Don't suppose the poor of the parish will see much of that corned beef.'

The Major became dignified.

'Pardon me,' he said. 'When an esteemed friend like Miss Elizabeth tells me that certain provisions are destined for the poor of the parish, I take it that her statement is correct. I expect others of my friends, while they are in my presence, to do the same. I have the honour to give you a lemon, Captain Puffin, and a slice of sugar. I should say a lump of sugar. Pray make yourself comfortable.'

This dignified and lofty mood was often one of the after effects of an unsuccessful game of golf. It generally yielded quite quickly to a little stimulant. Puffin filled his glass from the bottle and the kettle, while his friend put his handkerchief again over his face.

'Well, I shall just have my grog before I turn in,' he observed, according to custom. 'Aren't you going to join me, Major?'

'Presently, sir,' said the Major.

Puffin knocked out the consumed cinders in his pipe against the edge of the fender. Major Flint apparently was waiting for this, for he withdrew his handkerchief and closely watched the process. A minute piece of ash fell from Puffin's pipe on to the hearthrug, and he jumped to his feet and removed it very carefully with the shovel.

'I have your permission, I hope?' he said witheringly.

'Certainly, certainly,' said Puffin. 'Now get your glass, Major. You'll feel better in a minute or two.'

Major Flint would have liked to have kept up this magnificent attitude, but the smell of Puffin's steaming glass beat dignity down, and after glaring at him, he limped back to the cupboard for his whisky bottle. He gave a lamentable cry when he beheld it.

'But I got that bottle in only the day before yesterday,' he shouted, 'and there's hardly a drink left in it.'

'Well, you did yourself pretty well last night,' said Puffin. 'Those small glasses of yours, if frequently filled up, empty a bottle quicker than you seem to realize.'

Motives of policy prevented the Major from receiving this with the resentment that was proper to it, and his face cleared. He would get quits over these incessant lemons and lumps of sugar.

'Well, you'll have to let me borrow from you tonight,' he said genially, as he poured the rest of the contents of his bottle into the glass. 'Ah, that's more the ticket! A glass of whisky a day keeps the doctor away.'

The prospect of sponging on Puffin was most exhilarating, and he put his large slippered feet on to the fender.

'Yes, indeed, that was a highly amusing incident about Miss Mapp's cupboard,' he said. 'And wasn't Mrs Plaistow down on her like a knife about it? Our fair friends, you know, have a pretty sharp eye for each other's little failings. They've no sooner finished one squabble than they begin another, the pert little fairies. They can't sit and enjoy themselves like two old cronies I could tell you of, and feel at peace with all the world.'

He finished his glass at a gulp, and seemed much surprised to find it empty.

'I'll be borrowing a drop from you, old friend,' he said.

'Help yourself, Major,' said Puffin, with a keen eye as to how much he took.

'Very obliging of you. I feel as if I caught a bit of a chill this afternoon. My wound.'

'Be careful not to inflame it,' said Puffin.

'Thank ye for the warning. It's this beastly climate that touches it up. A winter in England adds years on to a man's life unless he takes care of himself. Take care of yourself, old boy. Have some more sugar.'

Before long the Major's hand was moving slowly and instinctively towards Puffin's whisky bottle again.

'I reckon that big glass of yours, Puffin,' he said, 'holds between three and a half times to four times what my little tumbler holds. Between three and a half and four I should reckon. I may be wrong.'

'Reckoning the water in, I dare say you're not far out, Major,' said he. 'And according to my estimate you mix your drink somewhere about three and a half times to four stronger than I mix mine.'

'Oh, come, come!' said the Major.

'Three and a half to four times, *I* should say,' repeated Puffin. 'You won't find I'm far out.'

He replenished his big tumbler, and instead of putting the bottle back on the table, absently deposited it on the floor on the far side of his chair. This second tumbler usually marked the most convivial period of the evening, for the first would have healed whatever unhappy discords had marred the harmony of the day, and, those being disposed of, they very contentedly talked through their hats about past prowesses, and took a rosy view of the youth and energy which still beat in their vigorous pulses. They would begin, perhaps, by extolling each other: Puffin, when informed that his friend would be fifty-four next birthday, flatly refused (without offence) to believe it, and, indeed, he was quite right in so doing, because the Major was in reality fifty-six. In turn, Major Flint would say that his friend had the figure of a boy of twenty, which caused Puffin presently to feel a little cramped and to wander negligently in front of the big looking glass between the windows, and find this compliment much easier to swallow than the Major's age. For the next half-hour they would chiefly talk about themselves in a pleasant glow of self-satisfaction. Major Flint, looking at the various implements and trophies that adorned the room, would suggest putting a sporting challenge in *The Times*.

''Pon my word, Puffin,' he would say, 'I've half a mind to do it. Retired Major of His Majesty's Forces – the King, God bless him!' (and he took a substantial sip); '"Retired Major, aged fifty-four, challenges any gentleman of fifty years or over."'

'Forty,' said Puffin sycophantically, as he thought over what he would say about himself when the old man had finished.

'Well, we'll halve it, we'll say forty-five, to please you, Puffin – let's see, where had I got to? – "Retired Major challenges any gentleman of forty-five years or over to – to a shooting match in the morning, followed by half a dozen rounds with four-ounce gloves, a game of golf, eighteen holes, in the afternoon, and a billiard match of two hundred up after tea." Ha! ha! I shouldn't feel much anxiety as to the result.'

'My confounded leg!' said Puffin. 'But I know a retired captain from His Majesty's merchant service – the King, God bless him! – aged fifty – '

'Ho! ho! Fifty, indeed!' said the Major, thinking to himself that a dried-up little man like Puffin might be as old as an Egyptian mummy. Who can tell the age of a kipper? . . .

'Not a day less, Major. "Retired Captain, aged fifty, who'll take on all comers of forty-two and over, at a steeplechase, round of golf, billiard match, hopping match, gymnastic competition, swinging Indian clubs – " No objection, gentlemen? Then carried *nem. con.*'

This gaseous mood, athletic, amatory or otherwise (the amatory ones were the worst), usually faded slowly, like the light from the setting sun or an exhausted coal in the grate, about the end of Puffin's second tumbler, and the gentlemen after that were usually somnolent, but occasionally laid the foundation for some disagreement next day, which they were too sleepy to go into now. Major Flint by this time would have had some five small glasses of whisky (equivalent, as he bitterly observed, to one in pre-war days), and as he measured his next with extreme care and a slightly jerky movement, would announce it as being his nightcap, though you would have thought he had plenty of nightcaps on already. Puffin correspondingly took a thimbleful more (the thimble apparently belonging to some housewife of Anak), and after another half-hour of sudden single snores and startings awake again, of pipes frequently lit and immediately going out, the guest, still perfectly capable of coherent speech and voluntary motion in the required direction, would stumble across the dark cobbles to his house, and doors would be very carefully closed for fear of attracting the attention of the lady who at this period of the evening was usually known as 'Old Mappy'. The two were perfectly well aware of the sympathetic interest that Old Mappy took in all that concerned them, and that she had an eye on their evening séances was evidenced by the frequency with which the corner of her blind in the window of the garden room was raised between, say, half-past nine and eleven at night. They had often watched with giggles the pencil of light that escaped, obscured at the lower end by the outline of Old Mappy's head, and occasionally drank to the 'Guardian Angel'. Guardian Angel, in answer to direct enquiries, had been told by Major Benjy during the last month that he worked at his diaries on three nights in the week and went to bed early on the others, to the vast improvement of his mental grasp.

'And on Sunday night, dear Major Benjy?' asked Old Mappy in the character of Guardian Angel.

'I don't think you knew my beloved, my revered mother, Miss Elizabeth,' said Major Benjy. 'I spend Sunday evening as – Well, well.'

The very next Sunday evening Guardian Angel had heard the sound of singing. She could not catch the words, and only fragments of the tune, which reminded her of 'The roseate morn hath passed away'. Brimming with emotion, she sang it softly to herself as she undressed, and blamed herself very much for ever having thought that dear Major Benjy – She peeped out of her window when she had extinguished her light, but fortunately the singing had ceased.

* * *

Tonight, however, the epoch of Puffin's second big tumbler was not accompanied by harmonious developments. Major Benjy was determined to make the most of this unique opportunity of drinking his friend's whisky, and whether Puffin put the bottle on the further side of him, or under his chair, or under the table, he came padding round in his slippers and standing near the ambush while he tried to interest his friend in tales of love or tiger-shooting so as to distract his attention. When he mistakenly thought he had done so, he hastily refilled his glass, taking unusually stiff doses for fear of not getting another opportunity, and altogether omitting to ask Puffin's leave for these maraudings. When this had happened four or five times, Puffin, acting on the instinct of the polar bear who eats her babies for fear that anybody else should get them, surreptitiously poured the rest of his bottle into his glass, and filled it up to the top with hot water, making a mixture of extraordinary power.

Soon after this Major Flint came rambling round the table again. He was not sure whether Puffin had put the bottle by his chair or behind the coal scuttle, and was quite ignorant of the fact that wherever it was, it was empty. Amorous reminiscences tonight had been the accompaniment to Puffin's second tumbler.

'Devilish fine woman she was,' he said, 'and that was the last that Benjamin Flint ever saw of her. She went up to the hills next morning – '

'But the last you saw of her just now was on the deck of the P&O at Bombay,' objected Puffin. 'Or did she go up to the hills on the deck of the P&O? Wonderful line!'

'No, sir,' said Benjamin Flint, 'that was Helen, *la belle Hélène*. It was *la belle Hélène* whom I saw off at the Apollo Bunder. I don't know if I told you – By Gad, I've kicked the bottle over. No idea you'd put it there. Hope the cork's in.'

'No harm if it isn't,' said Puffin, beginning on his third most fiery glass. The strength of it rather astonished him.

'You don't mean to say it's empty?' asked Major Flint. 'Why just now there was close on a quarter of a bottle left.'

'As much as that?' asked Puffin. 'Glad to hear it.'

'Not a drop less. You don't mean to say – Well, if you can drink that and can say hippopotamus afterwards, I should put that among your challenges, to men of four hundred and two: I should say forty-two. It's a fine thing to have a strong head, though if I drank what you've got in your glass, I should be tipsy, sir.'

Puffin laughed in his irritating falsetto manner.

'Good thing that it's in my glass then, and not your glass,' he said. 'And lemme tell you, Major, in case you don't know it, that when I've drunk every drop of this and sucked the lemon, you'll have had far more out of my bottle this evening than I have. My usual twice and – and my usual nightcap, as you say, is what's my ration, and I've had no more than my ration. Eight Bells.'

'And a pretty good ration you've got there,' said the baffled Major. 'Without your usual twice.'

Puffin was beginning to be aware of that as he swallowed the fiery mixture, but nothing in the world would now have prevented his drinking every single drop of it. It was clear to him, among so much that was dim owing to the woodsmoke, that the Major would miss a good many drives tomorrow morning.

'And whose whisky is it?' he said, gulping down the fiery stuff.

'I know whose it's going to be,' said the other.

'And I know whose it is now,' retorted Puffin, 'and I know whose whisky it is that's filled you up ti' as a drum. Tight as a drum,' he repeated very carefully.

Major Flint was conscious of an unusual activity of brain, and, when he spoke, of a sort of congestion and entanglement of words. It pleased him to think that he had drunk so much of somebody else's whisky, but he felt that he ought to be angry.

'That's a very unmentionable sor' of thing to say,' he remarked. 'An' if it wasn't for the sacred claims of hospitality, I'd make you explain just what you mean by that, and make you eat your words. Pologise, in fact.'

Puffin finished his glass at a gulp, and rose to his feet.

'Pologies be blowed,' he said. 'Hittopopamus!'

'And were you addressing that to me?' asked Major Flint with deadly calm.

'Of course, I was. Hippot – same animal as before. Pleasant old boy. And as for the lemon you lent me, well, I don't want it any more. Have a suck at it, ole fellow! I don't want it any more.'

The Major turned purple in the face, made a course for the door like a knight's move at chess (a long step in one direction and a short one at right angles to the first) and opened it. The door thus served as an aperture from the room and a support to himself. He spoke no word of any sort or kind: his silence spoke for him in a far more dignified manner than he could have managed for himself.

Captain Puffin stood for a moment wreathed in smiles, and fingering the slice of lemon, which he had meant playfully to throw at his friend. But his smile faded, and by some sort of telepathic perception he realized how much more decorous it was to say (or, better, to indicate) good night in a dignified manner than to throw lemons about. He walked in dots and dashes like a Morse code out of the room, bestowing a naval salute on the Major as he passed. The latter returned it with a military salute and a suppressed hiccup. Not a word passed.

Then Captain Puffin found his hat and coat without much difficulty, and marched out of the house, slamming the door behind him with a bang that echoed down the street and made Miss Mapp dream about a thunderstorm. He let himself into his own house, and bent down before his expired fire, which he tried to blow into life again. This was unsuccessful, and he breathed in a quantity of wood ash.

He sat down by his table and began to think things out. He told himself that he was not drunk at all, but that he had taken an unusual quantity of whisky, which seemed to produce much the same effect as intoxication. Allowing for that, he was conscious that he was extremely angry about something, and had a firm idea that the Major was very angry too.

'But woz'it all been about?' he vainly asked himself. 'Woz'it all been about?'

He was roused from his puzzling over this unanswerable conundrum by the clink of the flap in his letter box. Either this was the first post in the morning, in which case it was much later than he thought, and wonderfully dark still, or it was the last post at night, in which case it was much earlier than he thought. But, whichever it was, a letter had been slipped into his box, and he brought it in. The gum on the envelope was still wet, which saved trouble in opening it. Inside was a half-sheet containing but a few words. This curt epistle ran as follows:

Sir – My seconds will wait on you in the course of tomorrow morning.

Your faithful obedient servant,

Benjamin Flint

Captain Puffin.

Puffin felt as calm as a tropic night, and as courageous as a captain. Somewhere below his courage and his calm was an appalling sense of misgiving. That he successfully stifled.

'Very proper,' he said aloud. 'Qui' proper. Insults. Blood. Seconds won't have to wait a second. Better get a good sleep.'

He went up to his room, fell on to his bed and instantly began to snore.

* * *

It was still dark when he awoke, but the square of his window was visible against the blackness, and he concluded that though it was not morning yet, it was getting on for morning, which seemed a pity. As he turned over on to his side his hand came in contact with his coat, instead of a sheet, and he became aware that he had all his clothes on. Then, as with a crash of cymbals and the beating of a drum in his brain, the events of the evening before leaped into reality and significance. In a few hours now arrangements would have been made for a deadly encounter. His anger was gone, his whisky was gone, and in particular his courage was gone. He expressed all this compendiously by moaning 'Oh, God!'

He struggled to a sitting position, and lit a match at which he kindled his candle. He looked for his watch beside it, but it was not there. What could have happened – then he remembered that it was in its accustomed place in his waistcoat pocket. A consultation of it followed by holding it to his ear only revealed the fact that it had stopped at half-past five. With the lucidity that was growing brighter in his brain, he concluded that this stoppage was due to the fact that he had not wound it up . . . It was after half-past five then, but how much later only the Lords of Time knew – Time which bordered so closely on Eternity.

He felt that he had no use whatever for Eternity but that he must not waste Time. Just now, that was far more precious.

From somewhere in the Cosmic Consciousness there came to him a thought, namely, that the first train to London started at half-past six in the morning. It was a slow train, but it got there, and in any case it went away from Tilling. He did not trouble to consider how that thought came to him: the important point was that it had come. Coupled with that was the knowledge that it was now an undiscoverable number of minutes after half-past five.

There was a Gladstone bag under his bed. He had brought it back from the clubhouse only yesterday, after that game of golf which had been so full of disturbances and wet stockings, but which now wore the shimmering security of peaceful, tranquil days long past. How little, so he thought to himself, as he began swiftly storing shirts, ties, collars and other useful things into his bag, had he appreciated the sweet amenities of life, its pleasant conversations and companionships, its topped drives, and mush-rooms and incalculable incidents. Now they wore a glamour and a preciousness that was bound up with life itself. He starved for more of them, not knowing while they were his how sweet they were.

The house was not yet astir, when ten minutes later he came downstairs with his bag. He left on his sitting-room table, where it would catch the eye of his housemaid, a sheet of paper on which he wrote 'Called away' (he shuddered as he traced the words). 'Forward no letters. Will communicate . . .' (Somehow the telegraphic form seemed best to suit the urgency of the situation.) Then very quietly he let himself out of his house.

He could not help casting an apprehensive glance at the windows of his quondam friend and prospective murderer. To his horror he observed that there was a light behind the blind of the Major's bedroom, and pictured him writing to his seconds – he wondered who the 'seconds' were going to be – or polishing up his pistols. All the rumours and hints of the Major's duels and affairs of honour, which he had rather scorned before, not wholly believing them, poured like a red torrent into his mind, and he found that now he believed them with a passionate sincerity. Why had he ever attempted (and with such small success) to call this fire-eater a hippopotamus?

The gale of the night before had abated, and thick chilly rain was falling from a sullen sky as he tiptoed down the hill. Once round the corner and out of sight of the duellist's house, he broke into a limping run, which was accelerated by the sound of an engine whistle from the station. It was mental suspense of the most agonizing kind not to know how long it was after his watch had stopped that he had awoke, and the sound of that whistle, followed by several short puffs of steam, might prove to be the six-thirty bearing away to London, on business or pleasure, its secure and careless pilgrims. Splashing through puddles, lopsidedly weighted by his bag, with his mackintosh flapping against his legs, he gained the sanctuary of the waiting room and booking office, which was lighted by a dim expiring lamp, and scrutinized the face of the murky clock . . .

With a sob of relief he saw that he was in time. He was, indeed, in exceptionally good time, for he had a quarter of an hour to wait. An anxious internal debate followed as to whether or not he should take a return ticket. Optimism, that is to say, the hope that he would return to Tilling in peace and safety before the six months for which the ticket was available inclined him to the larger expense, but in these disquieting circumstances, it was difficult to be optimistic and he purchased a first-class single, for on such a morning, and on such a journey, he must get what comfort he could from looking glasses, padded seats and coloured photographs of places of interest on the line. He formed no vision at all of the future: that was a dark well into which it was dangerous to peer. There was no bright speck in its unplumbable depths: unless Major Flint died suddenly without revealing the challenge he had sent last night, and the promptitude with which its recipient had disappeared rather than face his pistol, he could not frame any grouping of events which would make it possible for him to come back to Tilling again, for he would either have to fight (and this he was quite determined not to do) or be pointed at by the finger of scorn as the man who had refused to do so, and this was nearly as unthinkable as the other. Bitterly he blamed himself for having made a friend (and worse than that, an enemy) of one so obsolete and old-fashioned as to bring duelling into modern life . . . As far as he could be glad of anything he was glad that he had taken a single, not a return ticket.

He turned his eyes away from the blackness of the future and let his mind dwell on the hardly less murky past. Then, throwing up his hands, he buried his face in them with a hollow groan. By some miserable forgetfulness he had left the challenge on his chimney piece, where his housemaid would undoubtedly find and read it. That would explain his absence far better than the telegraphic instructions he had left on his table. There was no time to go back for it now, even if he could have faced the risk of being seen by the Major, and in an hour or two the whole story, via Withers, Janet, etc., would be all over Tilling.

It was no use then thinking of the future nor of the past, and in order to anchor himself to the world at all and preserve his sanity he had to confine himself to the present. The minutes, long though each tarried, were slipping away and provided his train was punctual, the passage of five more of these laggards would see him safe. The newsboy took down the shutters of his stall, a porter quenched the expiring lamp, and Puffin began to listen for the rumble of the approaching train. It stayed three minutes here: if up to time it would be in before a couple more minutes had passed.

There came from the station yard outside the sound of heavy footsteps running. Some early traveller like himself was afraid of missing the train. The door burst open, and, streaming with rain and panting for breath, Major Flint stood at the entry. Puffin looked wildly round to see whether he could escape, still perhaps unobserved, on to the platform, but it was too late, for their eyes met.

In that instant of abject terror, two things struck Puffin. One was that the Major looked at the open door behind him as if meditating retreat, the second that he carried a Gladstone bag. Simultaneously Major Flint spoke, if indeed that reverberating thunder of scornful indignation can be called speech.

'Ha! I guessed right then,' he roared. 'I guessed, sir, that you might be meditating flight, and I – in fact, I came down to see whether you were running away. I was right. You are a coward, Captain Puffin! But relieve your mind, sir. Major Flint will not demean himself to fight with a coward.'

Puffin gave one long sigh of relief, and then, standing in front of his own Gladstone bag, in order to conceal it, burst into a cackling laugh.

'Indeed!' he said. 'And why, Major, was it necessary for you to pack a Gladstone bag in order to stop me from running away? I'll tell you what has happened. You were running away, and you know it. I guessed you would. I came to stop you, you, you quaking runaway. Your wound troubled you, hey? Didn't want another, hey?'

There was an awful pause, broken by the entry from behind the Major of the outside porter, panting under the weight of a large portmanteau.

'You had to take your portmanteau, too,' observed Puffin witheringly, 'in order to stop me. That's a curious way of stopping me. You're a coward, sir! But go home. You're safe enough. This will be a fine story for tea parties.'

Puffin turned from him in scorn, still concealing his own bag. Unfortunately the flap of his coat caught it, precariously perched on the bench, and it bumped to the ground.

'What's that?' said Major Flint.

They stared at each other for a moment and then simultaneously burst into peals of laughter. The train rumbled slowly into the station, but neither took the least notice of it, and only shook their heads and broke out again when the station master urged them to take their seats. The only thing that had power to restore Captain Puffin to gravity was the difficulty of getting the money for his ticket refunded, while the departure of the train with his portmanteau in it did the same for the Major.

*   *   *

The events of that night and morning, as may easily be imagined, soon supplied Tilling with one of the most remarkable conundrums that had ever been forced upon its notice. Puffin's housemaid, during his absence at the station, found and read not only the notice intended for her eyes, but the challenge which he had left on the chimney piece. She conceived it to be her duty to take it down to Mrs Gashly, his cook, and while they were putting the bloodiest construction on these inscriptions, their conference was interrupted by the return of Captain Puffin in the highest spirits, who, after a vain search for the challenge, was quite content, as its purport was no longer fraught with danger and death, to suppose that he had torn it up. Mrs Gashly, therefore, after preparing breakfast at this unusually early hour, went across to the back door of the Major's house, with the challenge in her hand, to borrow a nutmeg grater, and gleaned the information that Mrs Dominic's employer (for master he could not be called) had gone off in a great hurry to the station early that morning with a Gladstone bag and a portmanteau, the latter of which had been seen no more, though the Major had returned. So Mrs Gashly produced the challenge, and having watched Miss Mapp off to the High Street at half-past ten, Dominic and Gashly went together to her house, to see if Withers could supply anything of importance, or, if not, a nutmeg grater. They were forced to be content with the grater, but pored over the challenge with Withers, and she having an errand to Diva's house, told Janet, who without further ceremony bounded upstairs to tell her mistress. Hardly had Diva heard, than she plunged into the

High Street, and, with suitable additions, told Miss Mapp, Evie, Irene and the Padre under promise, in each case, of the strictest secrecy. Ten minutes later Irene had asked the defenceless Mr Hopkins, who was being Adam again, what he knew about it, and Evie, with her mouse-like gait that looked so rapid and was so deliberate, had the mortification of seeing Miss Mapp outdistance her and be admitted into the Poppits' house, just as she came in view of the front door. She rightly conjectured that, after the affair of the store cupboard in the garden room, there could be nothing of lesser importance than 'the duel' which could take that lady through those abhorred portals. Finally, at ten minutes past eleven, Major Flint and Captain Puffin were seen by one or two fortunate people (the morning having cleared up) walking together to the tram, and, without exception, everybody knew that they were on their way to fight their duel in some remote hollow of the sand dunes.

Miss Mapp had gone straight home from her visit to the Poppits just about eleven, and stationed herself in the window where she could keep an eye on the houses of the duellists. In her anxiety to outstrip Evie and be the first to tell the Poppits, she had not waited to hear that they had both come back and knew only of the challenge and that they had gone to the station. She had already formed a glorious idea of her own as to what the history of the duel (past or future) was, and intoxicated with emotion had retired from the wordy fray to think about it, and, as already mentioned, to keep an eye on the two houses just below. Then there appeared in sight the Padre, walking swiftly up the hill, and she had barely time under cover of the curtain to regain the table where her sweet chrysanthemums were pining for water when Withers announced him. He wore a furrowed brow and quite forgot to speak either Scotch or Elizabethan English. A few rapid words made it clear that they both had heard the main outlines.

'A terrible situation,' said the Padre. 'Duelling is in direct contravention of all Christian principles, and, I believe, of the civil law. The discharge of a pistol, in unskilful hands, may lead to deplorable results. And Major Flint, so one has heard, is an experienced duellist . . . That, of course, makes it even more dangerous.'

It was at this identical moment that Major Flint came out of his house and *quai-hai*ed cheerily to Puffin. Miss Mapp and the Padre, deep in these bloody possibilities, neither saw nor heard them. They passed together down the road and into the High Street, unconscious that their every look and action was being more commented on than the Epistle to the Hebrews. Inside the garden room Miss Mapp sighed, and bent her eyes on her chrysanthemums.

'Quite terrible!' she said. 'And in our peaceful, tranquil Tilling!'

'Perhaps the duel has already taken place, and – and they've missed,' said the Padre. 'They were both seen to return to their houses early this morning.'

'By whom?' asked Miss Mapp jealously. She had not heard that.

'By Hopkins,' said he. 'Hopkins saw them both return.'

'I shouldn't trust that man too much,' said Miss Mapp. 'Hopkins may not be telling the truth. I have no great opinion of his moral standard.'

'Why is that?'

This was no time to discuss the nudity of Hopkins and Miss Mapp put the question aside.

'That does not matter now, dear Padre,' she said. 'I only wish I thought the duel had taken place without accident. But Major Benjy's – I mean Major Flint's – portmanteau has not come back to his house. Of that I'm sure. What if they have sent it away to some place where they are unknown, full of pistols and things?'

'Possible – terribly possible,' said the Padre. 'I wish I could see my duty clear. I should not hesitate to – well, to do the best I could to induce them to abandon this murderous project. And what do you imagine was the root of the quarrel?'

'I couldn't say, I'm sure,' said Miss Mapp. She bent her head over the chrysanthemums.

'Your distracting sex,' said he with a moment's gallantry, 'is usually the cause of quarrel. I've noticed that they both seemed to admire Miss Irene very much.'

Miss Mapp raised her head and spoke with great animation.

'Dear, quaint Irene, I'm sure, has nothing whatever to do with it,' she said with perfect truth. 'Nothing whatever!'

There was no mistaking the sincerity of this, and the Padre, Tillingite to the marrow, instantly concluded that Miss Mapp knew what (or who) was the cause of all this unique disturbance. And as she bent her head again over the chrysanthemums, and quite distinctly grew brick-red in the face, he felt that delicacy prevented his enquiring any further.

'What are you going to do, dear Padre?' she asked in a low voice, choking with emotion. 'Whatever you decide will be wise and Christian. Oh, these violent men! Such babies, too!'

The Padre was bursting with curiosity, but since his delicacy forbade him to ask any of the questions which effervesced like sherbet round his tongue, he propounded another plan.

'I think my duty is to go straight to the Major,' he said, 'who seems to be the principal in the affair, and tell him that I know all – and guess the rest,' he added.

'Nothing that I have said,' declared Miss Mapp in great confusion, 'must have anything to do with your guesses. Promise me that, Padre.'

This intimate and fruitful conversation was interrupted by the sound of two pairs of steps just outside, and before Withers had had time to say 'Mrs Plaistow,' Diva burst in.

'They have both taken the eleven-twenty tram,' she said, and sank into the nearest chair.

'Together?' asked Miss Mapp, feeling a sudden chill of disappointment at the thought of a duel with pistols trailing off into one with golf clubs.

'Yes, but that's a blind,' panted Diva. 'They were talking and laughing together. Sheer blind! Duel among the sand dunes!'

'Padre, it is your duty to stop it,' said Miss Mapp faintly.

'But if the pistols are in a portmanteau – ' he began.

'What portmanteau?' screamed Diva, who hadn't heard about that.

'Darling, I'll tell you presently,' said Miss Mapp. 'That was only a guess of mine, Padre. But there's no time to lose.'

'But there's no tram to catch,' said the Padre. 'It has gone by this time.'

'A taxi then, Padre! Oh, lose no time!'

'Are you coming with me?' he said in a low voice. 'Your presence – '

'Better not,' she said. 'It might – Better not,' she repeated.

He skipped down the steps and was observed running down the street.

'What about the portmanteau?' asked the greedy Diva.

* * *

It was with strong misgivings that the Padre started on his Christian errand, and had not the sense of adventure spiced it, he would probably have returned to his sermon instead, which was Christian, too. To begin with, there was the ruinous expense of taking a taxi out to the golf links, but by no other means could he hope to arrive in time to avert an encounter that might be fatal. It must be said to his credit that, though this was an errand distinctly due to his position as the spiritual head of Tilling, he rejected, as soon as it occurred to him, the idea of charging the hire of the taxi to Church Expenses, and as he whirled along the flat road across the marsh, the thing that chiefly buoyed up his drooping spirits and annealed his courage was the romantic nature of his mission. He no longer, thanks to what Miss Mapp had so clearly refrained from saying, had the slightest doubt that she, in some manner that scarcely needed conjecture, was the cause of the duel he was attempting to avert. For years it had been a matter of unwearied and confidential discussion as to whether and when she would marry either Major Flint or Captain Puffin, and it was superfluous to look for any other explanation. It was true that she, in popular parlance, was 'getting on', but so, too, and at exactly the same rate, were the representatives of the United Services, and the sooner that two out of the three of them 'got on' permanently, the better. No doubt some crisis had arisen, and inflamed with love . . . He intended to confide all this to his wife on his return.

On his return! The unspoken words made his heart sink. What if he never did return? For he was about to place himself in a position of no common danger. His plan was to drive past the clubhouse, and then on foot, after discharging the taxi, to strike directly into the line of tumbled sand dunes which, remote and undisturbed and full of large convenient hollows, stretched along the coast above the flat beach. Any of those hollows, he knew, might prove to contain the duellists in the very act of firing, and over the rim of each he had to pop his unprotected head. He (if in time) would have to separate the combatants, and who knew whether, in their very natural chagrin at being interrupted, they might not turn their combined pistols on him first, and settle with each other afterwards? One murder the more made little difference to desperate men. Other shocks, less deadly but extremely unnerving, might await him. He might be too late, and pop his head over the edge of one of these craters, only to discover it full of bleeding if not mangled bodies. Or there might be only one mangled body, and the other, unmangled, would pursue him through the sand dunes and offer him life at the price of silence. That, he painfully reflected, would be a very difficult decision to make. Luckily, Captain Puffin (if he proved to be the survivor) was lame . . .

With drawn face and agonized prayers on his lips, he began a systematic search of the sand dunes. Often his nerve nearly failed him, and he would sink panting among the prickly bents before he dared to peer into the hollow up the sides of which he had climbed. His ears shuddered at the anticipation of hearing from near at hand the report of pistols, and once a backfire from a motor passing along the road caused him to leap high in the air. The sides of these dunes were steep, and his shoes got so full of sand, that from time to time, in spite of the urgency of his errand, he was forced to pause in order to empty them out. He stumbled in rabbit holes, he caught his foot and once his trousers in strands of barbed wire, the remnant of coast defences in the Great War, he crashed among potsherds and abandoned kettles; but with a thoroughness that did equal credit to his wind and his Christian spirit, he searched a mile of perilous dunes from end to end, and peered into every important hollow. Two hours later, jaded and torn and streaming with perspiration, he came, in the vicinity of the clubhouse, to the end of his fruitless search.

He staggered round the corner of it and came in view of the eighteenth green. Two figures were occupying it, and one of these was in the act of putting. He missed. Then he saw who the figures were: it was Captain Puffin who had just missed his putt, it was Major Flint who now expressed elated sympathy.

'Bad luck, old boy,' he said. 'Well, a jolly good match and we halve it. Why, there's the Padre. Been for a walk? Join us in a round this afternoon, Padre! Blow your sermon!'

CHAPTER SIX

The same delightful prospect at the end of the High Street, over the marsh, which had witnessed not so long ago the final encounter in the Wars of the Roses and the subsequent armistice, was, of course, found to be peculiarly attractive that morning to those who knew (and who did not?) that the combatants had left by the eleven-twenty steam tram to fight among the sand dunes, and that the intrepid Padre had rushed after them in a taxi. The Padre's taxi had returned empty, and the driver seemed to know nothing whatever about anything, so the only thing for everybody to do was to put off lunch and wait for the arrival of the next tram, which occurred at one thirty-seven. In consequence, all the doors in Tilling flew open like those of cuckoo clocks at ten minutes before that hour, and this pleasant promenade was full of those who so keenly admired autumn tints.

From here the progress of the tram across the plain was in full view; so, too, was the shed-like station across the river, which was the terminus of the line, and expectation, when the two-waggoned little train approached the end of its journey, was so tense that it was almost disagreeable. A couple of hours had elapsed since, like the fishers who sailed away into the West and were seen no more till the corpses lay out on the shining sand, the three had left for the sand dunes, and a couple of hours, so reasoned the Cosmic Consciousness of Tilling, gave ample time for a duel to be fought, if the Padre was not in time to stop it, and for him to stop it if he was. No surgical assistance, as far as was known, had been summoned, but the reason for that might easily be that a surgeon's skill was no longer, alas! of any avail for one, if not both, of the combatants. But if such was the case, it was nice to hope that the Padre had been in time to supply spiritual aid to anyone whom first aid and probes were powerless to succour.

The variety of *denouements* which the approaching tram, that had now cut off steam, was capable of providing was positively bewildering. They whirled through Miss Mapp's head like the autumn leaves which she admired so much, and she tried in vain to catch them all, and, when caught, to tick them off on her fingers. Each, moreover, furnished diverse and legitimate conclusions. For instance (taking the thumb):

I If nobody of the slightest importance arrived by the tram, that might be because
    (a) Nothing had happened, and they were all playing golf.
    (b) The worst had happened, and, as the Padre had feared, the duellists had first shot him and then each other.
    (c) The next worst had happened, and the Padre was arranging for the reverent removal of the corpse of
        (i) Major Benjy, or
        (ii) Captain Puffin, or those of
        (iii) Both.

Miss Mapp let go of her thumb and lightly touched her forefinger.

II The Padre might arrive alone.
    In that case anything or nothing might have happened to either or both of the others, and the various contingencies hanging on this arrival were so numerous that there was not time to sort them out.
III The Padre might arrive with two limping figures whom he assisted.
    Here it must not be forgotten that Captain Puffin always limped, and the Major occasionally. Miss Mapp did not forget it.
IV The Padre might arrive with a stretcher. Query – Whose?
V The Padre might arrive with two stretchers.
VI Three stretchers might arrive from the shining sands, at the town where the women were weeping and wringing their hands.

In that case Miss Mapp saw herself busily employed in strengthening poor Evie, who now was running about like a mouse from group to group picking up crumbs of Cosmic Consciousness.

Miss Mapp had got as far as sixthly, though she was aware she had not exhausted the possibilities, when the tram stopped. She furtively took out from her pocket (she had focused them before she put them in) the opera glasses through which she had watched the station yard on a day which had been very much less exciting than this. After one glance she put them back again, feeling vexed and disappointed with herself, for the *dénouement* which they had so unerringly disclosed was one that had not entered her mind at all. In that moment she had seen that out of the tram there stepped three figures and no stretcher. One figure, it is true, limped, but in a manner so natural, that she scorned to draw any deductions from that halting gait. They proceeded, side by side, across the bridge over the river towards the town.

It is no use denying that the Cosmic Consciousness of the ladies of Tilling was aware of a disagreeable anticlimax to so many hopes and fears. It had, of course, hoped for the best, but it had not expected that the best would be quite as bad as this. The best, to put it frankly, would have been a bandaged arm, or something of that kind. There was still room for the more hardened optimist to hope that something of some sort had occurred, or that something of some sort had been averted, and that the whole affair was not, in the delicious new slang phrase of the Padre's, which was spreading like wildfire through Tilling, a 'washout'. Pistols might have been innocuously discharged for all that was known to the contrary. But it looked bad.

Miss Mapp was the first to recover from the blow, and took Diva's podgy hand.

'Diva, darling,' she said, 'I feel so deeply thankful. What a wonderful and beautiful end to all our anxiety!'

There was a subconscious regret with regard to the anxiety. The anxiety was, so to speak, a dear and beloved departed . . . And Diva did not feel so sure that the end was so beautiful and wonderful. Her grandfather, Miss Mapp had reason to know, had been a butcher, and probably some inherited indifference to slaughter lurked in her tainted blood.

'There's the portmanteau still,' she said hopefully. 'Pistols in the portmanteau. Your idea, Elizabeth.'

'Yes, dear,' said Elizabeth; 'but thank God I must have been very wrong about the portmanteau. The outside porter told me that he brought it up from the station to Major Benjy's house half an hour ago. Fancy your not knowing that! I feel sure he is a truthful man, for he attends the Padre's confirmation class. If there had been pistols in it, Major Benjy and Captain Puffin would have gone away too. I am quite happy about that now. It went away and it has come back. That's all about the portmanteau.'

She paused a moment.

'But what does it contain, then?' she said quickly, more as if she was thinking aloud than talking to Diva. 'Why did Major Benjy pack it and send it to the station this morning? Where has it come back from? Why did it go there?'

She felt that she was saying too much, and pressed her hand to her head.

'Has all this happened this morning?' she said. 'What a full morning, dear! Lovely autumn leaves! I shall go home and have my lunch and rest. *Au reservoir*, Diva.'

Miss Mapp's eternal *reservoir*s had begun to get on Diva's nerves, and as she lingered here a moment more a great idea occurred to her, which temporarily banished the disappointment about the duellists. Elizabeth, as all the world knew, had accumulated a great reservoir of provisions in the false bookcase in her garden room, and Diva determined that, if she could think of a neat phrase, the very next time Elizabeth said *au reservoir* to her, she would work in an allusion to Elizabeth's own reservoir of corned beef, tongue, flour, Bovril, dried apricots and condensed milk. She would have to frame some stinging rejoinder which would 'escape her' when next Elizabeth used that stale old phrase: it would have to be short, swift and spontaneous, and therefore required careful thought. It would be good to bring 'pop' into it also. 'Your reservoir in the garden room hasn't gone "pop" again, I hope, darling?' was the first draft that occurred to her, but that was not sufficiently condensed. 'Pop goes the reservoir,' on the analogy of the weasel, was better. And, better than either, was there not some sort of corn called popcorn, which Americans ate? . . . 'Have you any popcorn in your reservoir?' That would be a nasty one . . .

But it all required thinking over, and the sight of the Padre and the duellists crossing the field below, as she still lingered on this escarpment of the hill, brought the duel back to her mind. It would have been considered inquisitive even at Tilling to put direct questions to the combatants, and (still hoping for the best) ask them point-blank 'Who won?' or something of that sort; but until she arrived at some sort of information, the excruciating pangs of curiosity that must be endured could be likened only to some acute toothache of the mind with no dentist to stop or remove the source of the trouble. Elizabeth had already succumbed to these pangs of surmise and excitement, and had frankly gone home to rest, and her absence, the fact that for the next hour or two she could not, except by some extraordinary feat on the telephone, get hold of anything which would throw light on the whole prodigious situation, inflamed Diva's brain to the highest pitch of inventiveness. She knew that she was Elizabeth's inferior in point of reconstructive imagination, and the present moment, while the other was recuperating her energies for fresh assaults on the unknown, was Diva's opportunity. The one person who might be presumed to know more than anybody else was the Padre, but while he was with the duellists, it was as impossible to ask him what had happened as to ask the duellists who had won. She must, while Miss Mapp rested, get hold of the Padre without the duellists.

Even as Athene sprang full grown and panoplied from the brain of Zeus, so from Diva's brain there sprang her plan complete. She even resisted the temptation to go on admiring autumn tints, in order to see how the interesting trio 'looked' when, as they must presently do, they passed close to where she stood, and hurried home, pausing only to purchase, pay for, and carry away with her from the provision shop a large and expensively dressed crab, a dainty of which the Padre was inordinately fond. Ruinous as this was, there was a note of triumph in her voice when, on arrival, she called loudly for Janet, and told her to lay another place at the luncheon table. Then putting a strong constraint on herself, she waited three minutes by her watch, in order to give the Padre time to get home, and then rang him up and reminded him that he had promised to lunch with her that day. It was no use asking him to lunch in such a way that he might refuse: she employed without remorse this pitiless *force majeure*.

The engagement was short and brisk. He pleaded that not even now could he remember even having been asked (which was not surprising), and said that he and wee wifie had begun lunch. On which Diva unmasked her last gun, and told him that she had ordered a crab on purpose. That silenced further argument, and he said that he and wee wifie would be round in a jiffy, and rang off. She did not particularly want wee wifie, but there was enough crab.

Diva felt that she had never laid out four shillings to better purpose, when, a quarter of an hour later, the Padre gave her the full account of his fruitless search among the sand dunes, so deeply impressive was his sense of being buoyed up to that incredibly fatiguing and perilous excursion by some Power outside himself. It never even occurred to her to think that it was an elaborate practical joke on the part of the Power outside himself, to spur him on to such immense exertions to no purpose at all. He had only got as far as this over his interrupted lunch with wee wifie, and though she, too, was in agonized suspense as to what happened next, she bore the repetition with great equanimity, only making small mouse-like noises of impatience which nobody heard. He was quite forgetting to speak either Scotch or Elizabethan English, so obvious was the absorption of his hearers, without these added aids to command attention.

'And then I came round the corner of the clubhouse,' he said, 'and there were Captain Puffin and the Major finishing their match on the eighteenth hole.'

'Then there's been no duel at all,' said Diva, scraping the shell of the crab.

'I feel sure of it. There wouldn't have been time for a duel and a round of golf, in addition to the impossibility of playing golf immediately after a duel. No nerves could stand it. Besides, I asked one of their caddies. They had come straight from the tram to the clubhouse, and from the clubhouse to the first tee. They had not been alone for a moment.'

'Washout,' said Diva, wondering whether this had been worth four shillings, so tame was the conclusion.

Mrs Bartlett gave a little squeak which was her preliminary to speech.

'But I do not see why there may not be a duel yet, Kenneth,' she said. 'Because they did not fight this morning – excellent crab, dear Diva, so good of you to ask us – there's no reason why there shouldn't be a duel this afternoon. Oh dear me, and cold beef as well: I shall be quite stuffed. Depend upon it a man doesn't take the trouble to write a challenge and all that, unless he means business.'

The Padre held up his hand. He felt that he was gradually growing to be the hero of the whole affair. He had certainly looked over the edge of numberless hollows in the sand dunes with vivid anticipations of having a bullet whizz by him on each separate occasion. It behoved him to take a sublime line.

'My dear,' he said, 'business is hardly a word to apply to murder. That within the last twenty-four hours there was the intention of fighting a duel, I don't deny. But something has decidedly happened which has averted that deplorable calamity. Peace and reconciliation is the result of it, and I have never seen two men so unaffectedly friendly.'

Diva got up and whirled round the table to get the port for the Padre, so pleased was she at a fresh idea coming to her while still dear Elizabeth was resting. She attributed it to the crab

'We've all been on a false scent,' she said. 'Peace and reconciliation happened before they went out to the sand dunes at all. It happened at the station. They met at the station, you know. It is proved that Major Flint went there. Major wouldn't send the portmanteau off alone. And it's proved that Captain Puffin went there too, because the note which his housemaid found on the table before she saw the challenge from the Major, which was on the chimney piece, said that he had been called away very suddenly. No: they both went to catch the early train in order to go away before they could be stopped, and kill each other. But why didn't they go? What happened? Don't suppose the outside porter showed them how wicked they were, confirmation class or no confirmation class. Stumps me. Almost wish Elizabeth was here. She's good at guessing.'

The Padre's eye brightened. Reaction after the perils of the morning, crab and port combined to make a man of him.

'Eh, 'tis a bonny wee drappie of port whatever, Mistress Plaistow,' he said. 'And I dinna ken that ye're far wrang in jaloosing that Mistress Mapp might have a wee bitty word to say aboot it a', 'gin she had the mind.'

'She was wrong about the portmanteau,' said Diva. 'Confessed she was wrong.'

'Hoots! I'm not mindin' the bit pochmantie,' said the Padre.

'What else does she know?' asked Diva feverishly.

There was no doubt that the Padre had the fullest attention of the two ladies again, and there was no need to talk Scotch any more.

'Begin at the beginning,' he said. 'What do we suppose was the cause of the quarrel?'

'Anything,' said Diva. 'Golf, tigerskins, coal strike, summertime.'

He shook his head.

'I grant you words may pass on such subjects,' he said. 'We feel keenly, I know, about summertime in Tilling, though we shall all be reconciled over that next Sunday, when real time, God's time, as I am venturing to call it in my sermon, comes in again.'

Diva had to bite her tongue to prevent herself bolting off on this new scent. After all, she had invested in crab to learn about duelling, not about summertime.

'Well?' she said.

'We may have had words on that subject,' said the Padre, booming as if he was in the pulpit already, 'but we should, I hope, none of us go so far as to catch the earliest train with pistols, in defence of our conviction about summertime. No, Mrs Plaistow, if you are right, and there is something to be said for your view, in thinking that they both went to such lengths as to be in time for the early train, in order to fight a duel undisturbed, you must look for a more solid cause than that.'

Diva vainly racked her brains to think of anything more worthy of the highest pitches of emotion than this. If it had been she and Miss Mapp who had been embroiled, hoarding and dress would have occurred to her. But as it was, no one in his senses could dream that the Captain and the Major were sartorial rivals, unless they had quarrelled over the question as to which of them wore the snuffiest old clothes.

'Give it up,' she said. 'What did they quarrel about?'

'Passion!' said the Padre, in those full, deep tones in which next Sunday he would allude to God's time. 'I do not mean anger, but the flame that exalts man to heaven or – or does exactly the opposite!'

'But whomever for?' asked Diva, quite thrown off her bearings. Such a thing had never occurred to her, for, as far as she was aware, passion, except in the sense of temper, did not exist in Tilling. Tilling was far too respectable.

The Padre considered this a moment.

'I am betraying no confidence,' he said, 'because no one has confided in me. But there certainly is a lady in this town – I do not allude to Miss Irene – who has long enjoyed the Major's particular esteem. May not some deprecating remark – '

Wee wifie gave a much louder squeal than usual.

'He means poor Elizabeth,' she said in a high, tremulous voice. 'Fancy, Kenneth!'

Diva, a few seconds before, had seen no reason why the Padre should drink the rest of her port, and was now in the act of drinking some of that unusual beverage herself. She tried to swallow it, but it was too late, and next moment all the openings in her face were fountains of that delicious wine. She choked and she gurgled, until the last drop had left her windpipe – under the persuasion of pattings on the back from the others – and then she gave herself up to loud, hoarse laughter, through which there shrilled the staccato squeaks of wee wifie. Nothing, even if you are being laughed at yourself, is so infectious as prolonged laughter, and the Padre felt himself forced to join it. When one of them got a little better, a relapse ensued by reason of infection from the others, and it was not till exhaustion set in, that this triple volcano became quiescent again.

'Only fancy!' said Evie faintly. 'How did such an idea get into your head, Kenneth?'

His voice shook as he answered.

'Well, we were all a little worked up this morning,' he said. 'The idea – really, I don't know what we have all been laughing at – '

'I do,' said Diva. 'Go on. About the idea – '

A feminine, a diabolical inspiration flared within wee wifie's mind.

'Elizabeth suggested it herself,' she squealed.

Naturally Diva could not help remembering that she had found Miss Mapp and the Padre in earnest conversation together when she forced her way in that morning with the news that the duellists had left by the 11.20 tram. Nobody could be expected to have so short a memory as to have forgotten *that*. Just now she forgave Elizabeth for anything she had ever done. That might have to be reconsidered afterwards, but at present it was valid enough.

'Did she suggest it?' she asked.

The Padre behaved like a man, and lied like Ananias.

'Most emphatically she did not,' he said.

The disappointment would have been severe, had the two ladies believed this confident assertion, and Diva pictured a delightful interview with Elizabeth, in which she would suddenly tell her the wild surmise the Padre had made with regard to the cause of the duel, and see how she looked then. Just see how she looked then: that was all – self-consciousness and guilt would fly their colours . . .

* * *

Miss Mapp had been tempted when she went home that morning, after enjoying the autumn tints, to ask Diva to lunch with her, but remembered in time that she had told her cook to broach one of the tins of corned beef which no human wizard could coax into the storecupboard again, if he shut the door after it. Diva would have been sure to say something acid and allusive, to remark on its excellence being happily not wasted on the poor people in the hospital, or, if she had not said anything at all about it, her silence as she ate a great deal would have had a sharp flavour. But Miss Mapp would have liked, especially when she went to take her rest afterwards on the big sofa in the garden room, to have had somebody to talk to, for her brain seethed with conjectures as to what had happened, was happening and would happen, and discussion was the best method of simplifying a problem, of narrowing it down to the limits of probability, whereas when she was alone now with her own imaginings, the most fantastic of them seemed plausible. She had, however, handed a glorious suggestion to the Padre, the one, that is, which concerned the cause of the duel, and it had been highly satisfactory to observe the sympathy and respect with which he had imbibed it. She had, too, been so discreet about it; she had not come within measurable distance of asserting that the challenge had been in any way connected with her. She had only been very emphatic on the point of its not being connected with poor dear Irene, and then occupied herself with her sweet flowers. That had been sufficient, and she felt in her bones and marrow that he inferred what she had meant him to infer . . .

The vulture of surmise ceased to peck at her for a few moments as she considered this, and followed up a thread of gold . . . Though the Padre would surely be discreet, she hoped that he would 'let slip' to dear Evie in the course of the vivid conversation they would be sure to have over lunch, that he had a good guess as to the cause which had led to that savage challenge. Upon which dear Evie would be certain to ply him with direct squeaks and questions, and when she 'got hot' (as in animal, vegetable and mineral) his reticence would lead her to make a good guess too. She might be incredulous, but there the idea would be in her mind, while if she felt that these stirring days were no time for scepticism, she could hardly fail to be interested and touched. Before long (how soon Miss Mapp was happily not aware) she would 'pop in' to see Diva, or Diva would 'pop in' to see her, and, Evie observing a discretion similar to that of the Padre and herself, would soon enable dear Diva to make a good guess too. After that, all would be well, for dear Diva ('such a gossiping darling') would undoubtedly tell everybody in Tilling, under vows of secrecy (so that she should have the pleasure of telling everybody herself), just what her good guess was. Thus, very presently, all Tilling would know exactly that which Miss Mapp had not said to the dear Padre, namely, that the duel which had been fought (or which hadn't been fought) was 'all about' her. And the best of it was, that though everybody knew, it would still be a great and beautiful secret, reposing inviolably in every breast or chest, as the case might be. She had no anxiety about anybody asking direct questions of the duellists, for if duelling, for years past, had been a subject which no delicately minded person alluded to purposely in Major Benjy's presence, how much more now after this critical morning would that subject be taboo? That certainly was a good thing, for the duellists if closely questioned might have a different explanation, and it would be highly inconvenient to have two contradictory stories going about. But, as it was, nothing could be nicer: the whole of the rest of Tilling, under promise of secrecy, would know, and even if under further promises of secrecy they communicated their secret to each other, there would be no harm done . . .

After this excursion into Elysian fields, poor Miss Mapp had to get back to her vulture again, and the hour's rest that she had felt was due to herself as the heroine of a duel became a period of extraordinary cerebral activity. Puzzle as she might, she could make nothing whatever of the portmanteau and the excursion to the early train, and she got up long before her hour was over, since she found that the more she thought, the more invincible were the objections to any conclusion that she drowningly grasped at. Whatever attack she made on this mystery, the garrison failed to march out and surrender but kept their flag flying, and her conjectures were woefully blasted by the forces of the most elementary reasons. But as the agony of suspense, if no fresh topic of interest intervened, would be frankly unendurable, she determined to concentrate no more on it, but rather to commit it to the ice house or safe of her subconscious mind, from which at will, when she felt refreshed and reinvigorated, she could unlock it and examine it again. The whole problem was more superlatively baffling than any that she could remember having encountered in all these inquisitive years, just as the subject of it was more majestic than any, for it concerned not hoarding, nor visits of the Prince of Wales, nor poppy-trimmed gowns, but life and death and firing of deadly pistols. And should love be added to this august list? Certainly not by her, though Tilling might do what it liked. In fact Tilling always did.

She walked across to the bow window from which she had conducted so many exciting and successful investigations. But today the view seemed as stale and unprofitable as the world appeared to Hamlet, even though Mrs Poppit at that moment went waddling down the street and disappeared round the corner where the dentist and Mr Wyse lived. With a sense of fatigue Miss Mapp recalled the fact that she had seen the housemaid cleaning Mr Wyse's windows yesterday – ('Children dear, was it yesterday?') – and had noted her industry, and drawn from it the irresistible conclusion that Mr Wyse was probably expected home. He usually came back about mid-October, and let slip allusions to his enjoyable visits in Scotland and his *villeggiatura* (so he was pleased to express it) with his sister the Contessa di Faraglione at Capri. That Contessa Faraglione was rather a mythical personage to Miss Mapp's mind: she was certainly not in a medieval copy of *Who's Who?* which was the only accessible handbook in matters relating to noble and notable personages, and though Miss Mapp would not have taken an oath that she did not exist, she saw no strong reason for supposing that she did. Certainly she had never been to Tilling, which was strange as her brother lived there, and there was nothing but her brother's allusions to certify her. About Mrs Poppit now: had she gone to see Mr Wyse or had she gone to the dentist? One or other it must be, for apart from them that particular street contained nobody who counted, and at the bottom it simply conducted you out into the uneventful country. Mrs Poppit was all dressed up, and she would never walk in the country in such a costume. It would do either for Mr Wyse or the dentist, for she was the sort of woman who would like to appear grand in the dentist's chair, so that he might be shy of hurting such a fine lady. Then again, Mrs Poppit had wonderful teeth, almost too good to be true, and before now she had asked who lived at that pretty little house just round the corner, as if to show that she didn't know where the dentist lived! Or had she found out by some underhand means that Mr Wyse had come back, and had gone to call on him and give him the first news of the duel, and talk to him about Scotland? Very likely they had neither of them been to Scotland at all: they conspired to say that they had been to Scotland and stayed at shooting lodges (keepers' lodges more likely) in order to impress Tilling with their magnificence . . .

Miss Mapp sat down on the central-heating pipes in her window, and fell into one of her reconstructive musings. Partly, if Mr Wyse was back, it was well just to run over his record; partly she wanted to divert her mind from the two houses just below, that of Major Benjy on the one side and that of Captain Puffin on the other, which contained the key to the great, insoluble mystery, from conjecture as to which she wanted to obtain relief. Mr Wyse, anyhow, would serve as a mild opiate, for she had never lost an angry interest in him. Though he was for eight months of the year, or thereabouts, in Tilling, he was never, for a single hour, *of* Tilling. He did not exactly invest himself with an air of condescension and superiority – Miss Mapp did him that justice – but he made other people invest him with it, so that it came to the same thing: he was invested. He did not drag the fact of his sister being the Contessa Faraglione into conversation, but if talk turned on sisters, and he was asked about his, he confessed to her nobility. The same phenomenon appeared when the innocent county of Hampshire was mentioned, for it turned out that he knew the county well, being one of the Wyses of Whitchurch. You couldn't say he talked about it, but he made other people talk about it . . . He was quite impervious to satire on such points, for when, goaded to madness, Miss Mapp had once said that she was one of the Mapps of Maidstone, he had merely bowed and said: 'A very old family, I believe,' and when the conversation branched off on to old families he had rather pointedly said 'we' to Miss Mapp. So poor Miss Mapp was sorry she had been satirical . . . But for some reason, Tilling never ceased to play up to Mr Wyse, and there was not a tea party or a bridge party given during the whole period of his residence there to which he was not invited. Hostesses always started with him, sending him round a note with 'To await answer', written in the top left-hand corner, since he had clearly stated that he considered the telephone an undignified instrument only fit to be used for household purposes, and had installed his in the kitchen, in the manner of the Wyses of Whitchurch. That alone, apart from Mr Wyse's old-fashioned notions on the subject, made telephoning impossible, for your summons was usually answered by his cook, who instantly began scolding the butcher irrespective and disrespectful of whom you were. When her mistake was made known to her, she never apologized, but grudgingly said she would call Mr Figgis, who was Mr Wyse's valet. Mr Figgis always took a long time in coming, and when he came he sneezed or did something disagreeable and said: 'Yes, yes; what is it?' in a very testy manner. After explanations he would consent to tell his master, which took another long time, and even then Mr Wyse did not come himself, and usually refused the proffered invitation. Miss Mapp had tried the expedient of sending Withers to the telephone when she wanted to get at Mr Wyse, but this had not succeeded, for Withers and Mr Wyse's cook quarrelled so violently before they got to business that Mr Figgis had to calm the cook and Withers to complain to Miss Mapp . . . This, in brief, was the general reason why Tilling sent notes to Mr Wyse. As for chatting through the telephone, which was the main use of telephones, the thing was quite out of the question.

Miss Mapp revived a little as she made this piercing analysis of Mr Wyse, and the warmth of the central-heating pipes, on this baffling day of autumn tints, was comforting . . . No one could say that Mr Wyse was not punctilious in matters of social etiquette, for though he refused three-quarters of the invitations which were showered on him, he invariably returned the compliment by an autograph note hoping that he might have the pleasure of entertaining you at lunch on Thursday next, for he always gave a small luncheon party on Thursday. These invitations were couched in Chesterfield terms: Mr Wyse said that he had met a mutual friend just now who had informed him that you were in residence, and had encouraged him to hope that you might give him the pleasure of your company, etc. This was alluring diction: it presented the image of Mr Wyse stepping briskly home again, quite heartened up by this chance encounter, and no longer the prey to melancholy at the thought that you might not give him the joy. He was encouraged to hope . . . These polite expressions were traced in a neat upright hand on paper which, when he had just come back from Italy, often bore a coronet on the top with 'Villa Faraglione, Capri' printed on the right-hand top corner and 'Amelia' (the name of his putative sister) in sprawling gilt on the left, the whole being lightly erased. Of course he was quite right to filch a few sheets, but it threw rather a lurid light on his character that they should be such grand ones.

Last year only, in a fit of passion at Mr Wyse having refused six invitations running on the plea of other engagements, Miss Mapp had headed a movement, the object of which was that Tilling should not accept any of Mr Wyse's invitations unless he accepted its. This had met with theoretical sympathy; the Bartletts, Diva, Irene, the Poppits had all agreed – rather absently – that it would be a very proper thing to do, but the very next Thursday they had all, including the originator, met on Mr Wyse's doorstep for a luncheon party, and the movement then and there collapsed.

Though they all protested and rebelled against such a notion, the horrid fact remained that everybody basked in Mr Wyse's effulgence whenever it was disposed to shed itself on them. Much as they distrusted the information they dragged out of him, they adored hearing about the Villa Faraglione, and dressed themselves in their very best clothes to do so. Then again there was the quality of the lunch itself: often there was caviare, and it was impossible (though the interrogator who asked whether it came from Twemlow's feared the worst) not to be mildly excited to know, when Mr Wyse referred the question to Figgis, that the caviare had arrived from Odessa that morning. The haunch of roe deer came from Perthshire; the wine, on the subject of which the Major could not be silent, and which often made him extremely talkative, was from 'my brother-in-law's vineyard'. And Mr Wyse would taste it with the air of a connoisseur and say: 'Not quite as good as last year: I must tell the Cont – I mean my sister.'

Again when Mr Wyse did condescend to honour a tea party or a bridge party, Tilling writhed under the consciousness that their general deportment was quite different from that which they ordinarily practised among themselves. There was never any squabbling at Mr Wyse's table, and such squabbling as took place at the other tables was conducted in low hissings and whispers, so that Mr Wyse should not hear. Diva never haggled over her gains or losses when he was there, the Padre never talked Scotch or Elizabethan English. Evie never squeaked like a mouse, no shrill recriminations or stately sarcasms took place between partners, and if there happened to be a little disagreement about the rules, Mr Wyse's decision, though he was not a better player than any of them, was accepted without a murmur. At intervals for refreshment, in the same way, Diva no longer filled her mouth and both hands with nougat chocolate; there was no scrambling or jostling, but the ladies were waited on by the gentlemen, who then refreshed themselves. And yet Mr Wyse in no way asserted himself, or reduced them all to politeness by talking about the polished manners of Italians; it was Tilling itself which chose to behave in this unusual manner in his presence. Sometimes Diva might forget herself for a moment, and address something withering to her partner, but the partner never replied in suitable terms, and Diva became honey-mouthed again. It was, indeed, if Mr Wyse had appeared at two or three parties, rather a relief not to find him at the next, and breathe freely in less rarefied air. But whether he came or not he always returned the invitation by one to a Thursday luncheon party, and thus the high circles of Tilling met every week at his house.

Miss Mapp came to the end of this brief retrospect, and determined, when once it was proved that Mr Wyse had arrived, to ask him to tea on Tuesday. That would mean lunch with him on Thursday, and it was unnecessary to ask anybody else unless Mr Wyse accepted. If he refused, there would be no tea party . . . But, after the events of the last twenty-four hours, there was no vividness in these plans and reminiscences, and her eye turned to the profile of the Colonel's house.

'The portmanteau,' she said to herself. . . No: she must take her mind off that subject. She would go for a walk, not into the High Street, but into the quiet level country, away from the turmoil of passion (in the Padre's sense) and quarrels (in her own), where she could cool her curiosity and her soul with contemplation of the swallows and the white butterflies (if they had not all been killed by the touch of frost last night) and the autumn tints of which there were none whatever in the treeless marsh . . . Decidedly the shortest way out of the town was that which led past Mr Wyse's house. But before leaving the garden room she practised several faces at the looking glass opposite the door, which should suitably express, if she met anybody to whom the cause of the challenge was likely to have spread, the bewildering emotion which the unwilling cause of it must feel. There must be a wistful wonder, there must be a certain pride, there must be the remains of romantic excitement, and there must be deep womanly anxiety. The carriage of the head 'did' the pride, the wide-open eyes 'did' the wistful wonder and the romance, the deep womanly anxiety lurked in the tremulous smile, and a violent rubbing of the cheeks produced the colour of excitement. In answer to any impertinent questions, if she encountered such, she meant to give an absent answer, as if she had not understood. Thus equipped she set forth.

It was rather disappointing to meet nobody, but as she passed Mr Wyse's bow window she adjusted the chrysanthemums she wore, and she had a good sight of his profile and the back of Mrs Poppit's head. They appeared deep in conversation, and Miss Mapp felt that the tiresome woman was probably giving him a very incomplete account of what had happened. She returned late for tea, and broke off her apologies to Withers for being such a trouble because she saw a note on the hall table. There was a coronet on the back of the envelope, and it was addressed in the neat, punctilious hand which so well expressed its writer. Villa Faraglione, Capri, a coronet and Amelia all lightly crossed out headed the page, and she read:

Dear Miss Mapp – It is such a pleasure to find myself in our little Tilling again, and our mutual friend Mrs Poppit, MBE, tells me you are in residence, and encourages me to hope that I may induce you to take *déjeuner* with me on Thursday, at one o'clock. May I assure you, with all delicacy, that you will not meet here anyone whose presence could cause you the slightest embarrassment?

Pray excuse this hasty note. Figgis will wait for your answer if you are in.

Yours very sincerely,
Algernon Wyse

Had not Withers been present, who might have misconstrued her action, Miss Mapp would have kissed the note; failing that, she forgave Mrs Poppit for being an MBE.

'The dear woman!' she said. 'She has heard, and has told him.'

Of course she need not ask Mr Wyse to tea now . . .

CHAPTER SEVEN

A white frost on three nights running and a terrible blackening of dahlias, whose reputation was quite gone by morning, would probably have convinced the ladies of Tilling that it was time to put summer clothing in camphor and winter clothing in the back yard to get aired, even if the Padre had not preached that remarkable sermon on Sunday. It was so remarkable that Miss Mapp quite forgot to note grammatical lapses and listened entranced.

The text was, 'He made summer and winter', and after repeating the words very impressively, so that there might be no mistake about the origin of the seasons, the Padre began to talk about something quite different – namely, the unhappy divisions which exist in Christian communities. That did not deceive Miss Mapp for a moment: she saw precisely what he was getting at over his oratorical fences. He got at it . . .

Ever since summertime had been inaugurated a few years before, it had been one of the chronic dissensions of Tilling. Miss Mapp, Diva and the Padre flatly refused to recognize it, except when they were going by train or tram, when principle must necessarily go to the wall, or they would never have succeeded in getting anywhere, while Miss Mapp, with the halo of martyrdom round her head, had once arrived at a summertime party an hour late, in order to bear witness to the truth, and, in consequence, had got only dregs of tea and the last faint strawberry. But the Major and Captain Puffin used the tram so often, that they had fallen into the degrading habit of dislocating their clocks and watches on the first of May, and dislocating them again in the autumn, when they were forced into uniformity with properly minded people. Irene was flippant on the subject, and said that any old time would do for her. The Poppits followed convention, and Mrs Poppit, in naming the hour for a party to the stalwarts, wrote '4.30 (your 3.30)'. The King, after all, had invited her to be decorated at a particular hour, summertime, and what was good enough for the King was good enough for Mrs Poppit.

The sermon was quite uncompromising. There was summer and winter, by Divine ordinance, but there was nothing said about summertime and wintertime. There was but one Time, and even as Life only stained the white radiance of eternity, as the gifted but, alas! infidel poet remarked, so, too, did Time. But ephemeral as Time was, noon in the Bible clearly meant twelve o'clock, and not one o'clock: towards even, meant towards even, and not the middle of a broiling afternoon. The sixth hour similarly was the Roman way of saying twelve. Wintertime, in fact, was God's time, and though there was nothing wicked (far from it) in adopting strange measures, yet the simple, the childlike, clung to the sacred tradition, which they had received from their fathers and forefathers at their mother's knee. Then followed a long and eloquent passage, which recapitulated the opening about unhappy divisions, and contained several phrases, regarding the lengths to which such divisions might go, which were strikingly applicable to duelling. The peroration recapitulated the recapitulation, in case anyone had missed it, and the coda, the close itself, in the fall noon of the winter sun, was full of joy at the healing of all such unhappy divisions. And now . . . The rain rattling against the windows drowned the Doxology.

The doctrine was so much to her mind that Miss Mapp gave a shilling to the offertory instead of her usual sixpence, to be devoted to the organist and choir fund. The Padre, it is true, had changed the hour of services to suit the heresy of the majority, and this for a moment made her hand falter. But the hope, after this convincing sermon, that next year morning service would be at the hour falsely called twelve decided her not to withdraw this handsome contribution.

Frosts and dead dahlias and sermons then were together overwhelmingly convincing, and when Miss Mapp went out on Monday morning to do her shopping, she wore a tweed skirt and jacket, and round her neck a long woollen scarf to mark the end of the summer. Mrs Poppit, alone in her disgusting ostentation, had seemed to think two days ago that it was cold enough for furs, and she presented a truly ridiculous aspect in an enormous sable coat, under the weight of which she could hardly stagger, and stood rooted to the spot when she stepped out of the Royce. Brisk walking and large woollen scarves saved the others from feeling the cold and from being unable to move, and this morning the High Street was dazzling with the shifting play of bright colours. There was quite a group of scarves at the corner, where Miss Mapp's street debouched into the High Street: Irene was there (for it was probably too cold for Mr Hopkins that morning), looking quainter than ever in corduroys and mauve stockings with an immense orange scarf bordered with pink. Diva was there, wound up in so delicious a combination of rose-madder and Cambridge blue, that Miss Mapp, remembering the history of the rose-madder, had to remind herself how many things there were in the world more important than worsted. Evie was there in vivid green with a purple border, the Padre had a knitted magenta waistcoat, and Mrs Poppit that great sable coat which almost prevented movement. They were all talking together in a very animated manner when first Miss Mapp came in sight, and if, on her approach, conversation seemed to wither, they all wore, besides their scarves, very broad, pleasant smiles. Miss Mapp had a smile, too, as good as anybody's.

'Good morning, all you dear things,' she said. 'How lovely you all look – just like a bed of delicious flowers! Such nice colours! My poor dahlias are all dead.'

Quaint Irene uttered a hoarse laugh, and, swinging her basket, went quickly away. She often did abrupt things like that. Miss Mapp turned to the Padre.

'Dear Padre, what a delicious sermon!' she said. 'So glad you preached it! Such a warning against all sorts of divisions!'

The Padre had to compose his face before he responded to these compliments.

'I'm reecht glad, fair lady,' he replied, 'that my bit discourse was to your mind. Come, wee wifie, we must be stepping.'

Quite suddenly all the group, with the exception of Mrs Poppit, melted away. Wee wifie gave a loud squeal, as if to say something, but her husband led her firmly off, while Diva, with rapidly revolving feet, sped like an arrow up the centre of the High Street.

'Such a lovely morning!' said Miss Mapp to Mrs Poppit, when there was no one else to talk to. 'And everyone looks so pleased and happy, and all in such a hurry, busy as bees, to do their little businesses. Yes.'

Mrs Poppit began to move quietly away with the deliberate, tortoise-like progression necessitated by the fur coat. It struck Miss Mapp that she, too, had intended to take part in the general breaking up of the group, but had merely been unable to get under way as fast as the others.

'Such a lovely fur coat,' said Miss Mapp sycophantically. 'Such beautiful long fur! And what is the news this morning? Has a little bird been whispering anything?'

'Nothing,' said Mrs Poppit very decidedly, and having now sufficient way on to turn, she went up the street down which Miss Mapp had just come. The latter was thus left all alone with her shopping basket and her scarf.

With the unerring divination which was the natural fruit of so many years of ceaseless conjecture, she instantly suspected the worst. All that busy conversation which her appearance had interrupted, all those smiles which her presence had seemed but to render broader and more hilarious, certainly concerned her. They could not still have been talking about that fatal explosion from the cupboard in the garden room, because the duel had completely silenced the last echoes of that, and she instantly put her finger on the spot. Somebody had been gossiping (and how she hated gossip); somebody had given voice to what she had been so studiously careful not to say. Until that moment, when she had seen the rapid breaking up of the group of her friends all radiant with merriment, she had longed to be aware that somebody had given voice to it, and that everybody (under seal of secrecy) knew the unique queenliness of her position, the overwhelmingly interesting role that the violent passions of men had cast her for. She had not believed in the truth of it herself, when that irresistible seizure of coquetry took possession of her as she bent over her sweet chrysanthemums; but the Padre's respectful reception of it had caused her to hope that everybody else might believe in it. The character of the smiles, however, that wreathed the faces of her friends did not quite seem to give fruition to that hope. There were smiles and smiles, respectful smiles, sympathetic smiles, envious and admiring smiles, but there were also smiles of hilarious and mocking incredulity. She concluded that she had to deal with the latter variety.

'Something,' thought Miss Mapp, as she stood quite alone in the High Street, with Mrs Poppit labouring up the hill, and Diva already a rose-madder speck in the distance, 'has got to be done,' and it only remained to settle what. Fury with the dear Padre for having hinted precisely what she meant, intended and designed that he should hint, was perhaps the paramount emotion in her mind; fury with everybody else for not respectfully believing what she did not believe herself made an important pendant.

'What am I to do?' said Miss Mapp aloud, and had to explain to Mr Hopkins, who had all his clothes on, that she had not spoken to him. Then she caught sight again of Mrs Poppit's sable coat hardly further off than it had been when first this thunderclap of an intuition deafened her, and still reeling from the shock, she remembered that it was almost certainly Mrs Poppit who was the cause of Mr Wyse writing her that exquisitely delicate note with regard to Thursday. It was a herculean task, no doubt, to plug up all the fountains of talk in Tilling which were spouting so merrily at her expense, but a beginning must be made before she could arrive at the end. A short scurry of nimble steps brought her up to the sables.

'Dear Mrs Poppit,' she said, 'if you are walking by my little house, would you give me two minutes' talk? And – so stupid of me to forget just now – will you come in after dinner on Wednesday for a little rubber? The days are closing in now; one wants to make the most of the daylight, and I think it is time to begin our pleasant little winter evenings.'

This was a bribe, and Mrs Poppit instantly pocketed it, with the effect that two minutes later she was in the garden room, and had deposited her sable coat on the sofa ('Quite shook the room with the weight of it,' said Miss Mapp to herself while she arranged her plan).

She stood looking out of the window for a moment, writhing with humiliation at having to be suppliant to the Member of the British Empire. She tried to remember Mrs Poppit's Christian name, and was even prepared to use that, but this crowning ignominy was saved her, as she could not recollect it.

'Such an annoying thing has happened,' she said, though the words seemed to blister her lips. 'And you, dear Mrs Poppit, as a woman of the world, can advise me what to do. The fact is that somehow or other, and I can't think how, people are saying that the duel last week, which was so happily averted, had something to do with poor little me. So absurd! But you know what gossips we have in our dear little Tilling.'

Mrs Poppit turned on her a fallen and disappointed face.

'But hadn't it?' she said. 'Why, when they were all laughing about it just now' ('I was right, then,' thought Miss Mapp, 'and what a tactless woman!'), 'I said I believed it. And I told Mr Wyse.'

Miss Mapp cursed herself for her frankness. But she could obliterate that again, and not lose a rare (goodness knew how rare!) believer.

'I am in such a difficult position,' she said. 'I think I ought to let it be understood that there is no truth whatever in such an idea, however much truth there may be. And did dear Mr Wyse believe – in fact, I know he must have, for he wrote me, oh, such a delicate, understanding note. He, at any rate, takes no notice of all that is being said and hinted.'

Miss Mapp was momentarily conscious that she meant precisely the opposite of this. Dear Mr Wyse *did* take notice, most respectful notice, of all that was being said and hinted, thank goodness! But a glance at Mrs Poppit's fat and interested face showed her that the verbal discrepancy had gone unnoticed, and that the luscious flavour of romance drowned the perception of anything else. She drew a handkerchief out, and buried her thoughtful eyes in it a moment, rubbing them with a stealthy motion, which Mrs Poppit did not perceive, though Diva would have.

'My lips are sealed,' she continued, opening them very wide, 'and I can say nothing, except that I want this rumour to be contradicted. I dare say those who started it thought it was true, but, true or false, I must say nothing. I have always led a very quiet life in my little house, with my sweet flowers for my companions, and if there is one thing more than another that I dislike, it is that my private affairs should be made matters of public interest. I do no harm to anybody, I wish everybody well, and nothing – nothing will induce me to open my lips upon this subject. I will not,' cried Miss Mapp, 'say a word to defend or justify myself. What is true will prevail. It comes in the Bible.'

Mrs Poppit was too much interested in what she said to mind where it came from.

'What can I do?' she asked.

'Contradict, dear, the rumour that I have had anything to do with the terrible thing which might have happened last week. Say on my authority that it is so. I tremble to think' – here she trembled very much – 'what might happen if the report reached Major Benjy's ears, and he found out who had started it. We must have no more duels in Tilling. I thought I should never survive that morning.'

'I will go and tell Mr Wyse instantly – dear,' said Mrs Poppit.

That would never do. True believers were so scarce that it was wicked to think of unsettling their faith.

'Poor Mr Wyse!' said Miss Mapp with a magnanimous smile. 'Do not think, dear, of troubling him with these little trumpery affairs. He will not take part in these little tittle-tattles. But if you could let dear Diva and quaint Irene and sweet Evie and the good Padre know that I laugh at all such nonsense – '

'But they laugh at it, too,' said Mrs Poppit.

That would have been baffling for anyone who allowed herself to be baffled, but that was not Miss Mapp's way.

'Oh, that bitter laughter!' she said. 'It hurt me to hear it. It was envious laughter, dear, scoffing, bitter laughter. I heard! I cannot bear that the dear things should feel like that. Tell them that I say how silly they are to believe anything of the sort. Trust me, I am right about it. I wash my hands of such nonsense.'

She made a vivid dumb show of this, and after drying them on an imaginary towel, let a sunny smile peep out the eyes which she had rubbed.

'All gone!' she said; 'and we will have a dear little party on Wednesday to show we are all friends again. And we meet for lunch at dear Mr Wyse's the next day? Yes? He will get tired of poor little me if he sees me two days running, so I shall not ask him. I will just try to get two tables together, and nobody shall contradict dear

Diva, however many shillings she says she has won. I would sooner pay them all myself than have any more of our unhappy divisions. You will have talked to them all before Wednesday, will you not, dear?'

As there were only four to talk to, Mrs Poppit thought that she could manage it, and spent a most interesting afternoon. For two years now she had tried to unfreeze Miss Mapp, who, when all was said and done, was the centre of the Tilling circle, and who, if any attempt was made to shove her out towards the circumference, always gravitated back again. And now, on these important errands she was Miss Mapp's accredited ambassador, and all the terrible business of the opening of the storecupboard and her decoration as MBE was quite forgiven and forgotten. There would be so much walking to be done from house to house, that it was impossible to wear her sable coat unless she had the Royce to take her about . . .

The effect of her communications would have surprised anybody who did not know Tilling. A less subtle society, when assured from a first-hand, authoritative source that a report which it had entirely refused to believe was false, would have prided itself on its perspicacity, and said that it had laughed at such an idea, as soon as ever it heard it, as being palpably (look at Miss Mapp!) untrue. Not so Tilling. The very fact that, by the mouth of her ambassador, she so uncompromisingly denied it, was precisely why Tilling began to wonder if there was not something in it, and from wondering if there was not something in it, surged to the conclusion that there certainly was. Diva, for instance, the moment she was told that Elizabeth (for Mrs Poppit remembered her Christian name perfectly) utterly and scornfully denied the truth of the report, became intensely thoughtful.

'Say there's nothing in it?' she observed. 'Can't understand that.'

At that moment Diva's telephone bell rang, and she hurried out and in.

'Party at Elizabeth's on Wednesday,' she said. 'She saw me laughing. Why ask me?'

Mrs Poppit was full of her sacred mission.

'To show how little she minds your laughing,' she suggested.

'As if it wasn't true, then. Seems like that. Wants us to think it's not true.'

'She was very earnest about it,' said the ambassador.

Diva got up, and tripped over the outlying skirts of Mrs Poppit's fur coat as she went to ring the bell.

'Sorry,' she said. 'Take it off and have a chat. Tea's coming. Muffins!'

'Oh, no, thanks!' said Mrs Poppit. 'I've so many calls to make.'

'What? Similar calls?' asked Diva. 'Wait ten minutes. Tea, Janet. Quickly.'

She whirled round the room once or twice, all corrugated with perplexity, beginning telegraphic sentences, and not finishing them: 'Says it's not true – laughs at notion of – And Mr Wyse believes – The Padre believed. After all, the Major – Little cock sparrow Captain Puffin – Or t'other way round, do you think? – No other explanation, you know – Might have been blood – '

She buried her teeth in a muffin.

'Believe there's something in it,' she summed up.

She observed her guest had neither tea nor muffin.

'Help yourself,' she said. 'Want to worry this out.'

'Elizabeth absolutely denies it,' said Mrs Poppit. 'Her eyes were full of – '

'Oh, anything,' said Diva. 'Rubbed them. Or pepper if it was at lunch. That's no evidence.'

'But her solemn assertion – ' began Mrs Poppit, thinking that she was being a complete failure as an ambassador. She was carrying no conviction at all.

'Saccharine!' observed Diva, handing her a small phial. 'Haven't got more than enough sugar for myself. I expect Elizabeth's got plenty – well, never mind that. Don't you see? If it wasn't true she would try to convince us that it was. Seemed absurd on the face of it. But if she tries to convince us that it isn't true – well, something in it.'

There was the gist of the matter, and Mrs Poppit proceeding next to the Padre's house, found more muffins and incredulity. Nobody seemed to believe Elizabeth's assertion that there was 'nothing in it'. Evie ran round the room with excited squeaks, the Padre nodded his head, in confirmation of the opinion which, when he first delivered it, had been received with mocking incredulity over the crab. Quaint Irene, intent on Mr Hopkins's left knee in the absence of the model, said, 'Good old Mapp: better late than never.' Utter incredulity, in fact, was the ambassador's welcome . . . and all the incredulous were going to Elizabeth's party on Wednesday.

Mrs Poppit had sent the Royce home for the last of her calls, and staggered up the hill past Elizabeth's house. Oddly enough, just as she passed the garden room, the window was thrown up.

'Cup of tea, dear Susan?' said Elizabeth. She had found an old note of Mrs Poppit's among the waste paper for the firing of the kitchen oven fully signed.

'Just two minutes' talk, Elizabeth,' she promptly responded.

* * *

The news that nobody in Tilling believed her left Miss Mapp more than calm, on the bright side of calm, that is to say. She had a few indulgent phrases that tripped readily off her tongue for the dear things who hated to be deprived of their gossip, but Susan certainly did not receive the impression that this playful magnanimity was attained with an effort. Elizabeth did not seem really to mind: she was very gay. Then, skilfully changing the subject, she mourned over her dead dahlias.

Though Tilling with all its perspicacity could not have known it, the intuitive reader will certainly have perceived that Miss Mapp's party for Wednesday night had, so to speak, further irons in its fire. It had originally been a bribe to Susan Poppit, in order to induce her to spread broadcast that that ridiculous rumour (whoever had launched it) had been promptly denied by the person whom it most immediately concerned. It served a second purpose in showing that Miss Mapp was too high above the mire of scandal, however interesting, to know or care who might happen to be wallowing in it, and for this reason she asked everybody who had done so. Such loftiness of soul had earned her an amazing bonus, for it had induced those who sat in the seat of the scoffers before to come hastily off, and join the thin but unwavering ranks of the true believers, who up till then had consisted only of Susan and Mr Wyse. Frankly, so blest a conclusion had never occurred to Miss Mapp: it was one of those unexpected rewards that fall like ripe plums into the lap of the upright. By denying a rumour she had got everybody to believe it, and when on Wednesday morning she went out to get the chocolate cakes which were so useful in allaying the appetites of guests, she encountered no broken conversations and gleeful smiles, but sidelong glances of respectful envy.

But what Tilling did not and could not know was that this, the first of the autumn after-dinner bridge parties, was destined to look on the famous tea gown of kingfisher blue, as designed for Mrs Trout. No doubt other ladies would have hurried up their new gowns, or at least have camouflaged their old ones, in honour of the annual inauguration of evening bridge, but Miss Mapp had no misgivings about being outshone. And once again here she felt that luck waited on merit, for though when she dressed that evening she found she had not anticipated that artificial light would cast a somewhat pale (though not ghastly) reflection from the vibrant blue on to her features, similar in effect to (but not so marked as) the light that shines on the faces of those who lean over the burning brandy and raisins of 'snapdragon', this interesting pallor seemed very aptly to bear witness to all that she had gone through. She did not look ill – she was satisfied as to that – she looked gorgeous and a little wan.

The bridge tables were not set out in the garden room, which entailed a scurry over damp gravel on a black, windy night, but in the little square parlour above her dining room, where Withers, in the intervals of admitting her guests, was laying out plates of sandwiches and the chocolate cakes, reinforced when the interval for refreshments came with hot soup, whisky and syphons, and a jug of 'cup' prepared according to an ancestral and economical recipe, which Miss Mapp had taken a great deal of trouble about. A single bottle of white wine, with suitable additions of ginger, nutmeg, herbs and soda water, was the mother of a gallon of a drink that seemed aflame with fiery and probably spirituous ingredients. Guests were very careful how they partook of it, so stimulating it seemed.

Miss Mapp was reading a book on gardening upside down (she had taken it up rather hurriedly) when the Poppits arrived, and sprang to her feet with a pretty cry at being so unexpectedly but delightfully disturbed.

'Susan! Isabel!' she said. 'Lovely of you to have come! I was reading about flowers, making plans for next year.'

She saw the four eyes riveted to her dress. Susan looked quite shabby in comparison, and Isabel did not look anything at all.

'My dear, too lovely!' said Mrs Poppit slowly.

Miss Mapp looked brightly about, as if wondering what was too lovely: at last she guessed.

'Oh, my new frock?' she said. 'Do you like it, dear? How sweet of you. It's just a little nothing that I talked over with that nice Miss Greele in the High Street. We put our heads together, and invented something quite cheap and simple. And here's Evie and the dear Padre. So kind of you to look in.'

Four more eyes were riveted on it.

'Enticed you out just once, Padre,' went on Miss Mapp. 'So sweet of you to spare an evening. And here's Major Benjy and Captain Puffin. Well, that is nice!'

This was really tremendous of Miss Mapp. Here was she meeting without embarrassment or awkwardness the two, who if the duel had not been averted, would have risked their very lives over some dispute concerning her. Everybody else, naturally, was rather taken aback for the moment at this situation, so deeply dyed in the dramatic. Should either of the gladiators have heard that it was the Padre who undoubtedly had spread the rumour concerning their hostess, Mrs Poppit was afraid that even his cloth might not protect him. But no such deplorable calamity occurred, and only four more eyes were riveted to the kingfisher blue.

'Upon my word,' said the Major, 'I never saw anything more beautiful than that gown, Miss Elizabeth. Straight from Paris, eh? Paris in every line of it.'

'Oh, Major Benjy,' said Elizabeth. 'You're all making fun of me and my simple little frock. I'm getting quite shy. Just a bit of old stuff that I had. But so nice of you to like it. I wonder where Diva is. We shall have to scold her for being late. Ah – she shan't be scolded. Diva, darl – '

The endearing word froze on Miss Mapp's lips and she turned deadly white. In the doorway, in equal fury and dismay, stood Diva, dressed in precisely the same staggeringly lovely costume as her hostess. Had Diva and Miss Greele put their heads together too? Had Diva got a bit of old stuff . . . ?

Miss Mapp pulled herself together first and moistened her dry lips.

'So sweet of you to look in, dear,' she said. 'Shall we cut?'

Naturally the malice of cards decreed that Miss Mapp and Diva should sit next each other as adversaries at the same table, and the combined effect of two lots of kingfisher blue was blinding. Complete silence on every subject connected, however remotely, with dress was, of course, the only line for correct diplomacy to pursue, but then Major Benjy was not diplomatic, only gallant.

'Never saw such stunning gowns, eh, Padre?' he said. 'Dear me, they are very much alike too, aren't they? Pair of exquisite sisters.'

It would be hard to say which of the two found this speech the more provocative of rage, for while Diva was four years younger than Miss Mapp, Miss Mapp was four inches taller than Diva. She cut the cards to her sister with a hand that trembled so much that she had to do it again, and Diva could scarcely deal.

* * *

Mr Wyse frankly confessed the next day when, at one o'clock, Elizabeth found herself the first arrival at his house, that he had been very self-indulgent.

'I have given myself a treat, dear Miss Mapp,' he said. 'I have asked three entrancing ladies to share my humble meal with me, and have provided – is it not shocking of me? – nobody else to meet them. Your pardon, dear lady, for my greediness.'

Now this was admirably done. Elizabeth knew very well why two out of the three men in Tilling had not been asked (very gratifying, that reason was), and with the true refinement of which Mr Wyse was so amply possessed, here he was taking all the blame on himself, and putting it so prettily. She bestowed her widest smile on him.

'Oh, Mr Wyse,' she said. 'We shall all quarrel over you.'

Not until Miss Mapp had spoken did she perceive how subtle her words were. They seemed to bracket herself and Mr Wyse together: all the men (two out of the three, at any rate) had been quarrelling over her, and now there seemed a very fair prospect of three of the women quarrelling over Mr Wyse . . .

Without being in the least effeminate, Mr Wyse this morning looked rather like a modern troubadour. He had a velveteen coat on, a soft, fluffy, mushy tie which looked as if made of Shirley poppies, very neat knickerbockers, brown stockings with blobs, like the fruit of plane trees, dependent from elaborate 'tops', and shoes with a cascade of leather frilling covering the laces. He might almost equally well be about to play golf over putting holes on the lawn as the guitar. He made a gesture of polished, polite dissent, not contradicting, yet hardly accepting this tribute, remitting it perhaps, just as the King when he enters the City of London touches the sword of the Lord Mayor and tells him to keep it . . .

'So pleasant to be in Tilling again,' he said. 'We shall have a cosy, busy winter, I hope. You, I know, Miss Mapp, are always busy.'

'The day is never long enough for me,' said Elizabeth enthusiastically. 'What with my household duties in the morning, and my garden, and our pleasant little gatherings, it is always bedtime too soon. I want to read a great deal this winter, too.'

Diva (at the sight of whom Elizabeth had to make a strong effort of self-control) here came in, together with Mrs Poppit, and the party was complete. Elizabeth would have been willing to bet that, in spite of the warmness of the morning, Susan would have on her sable coat, and though, technically, she would have lost, she more than won morally, for Mr Wyse's repeated speeches about his greediness were hardly out of his mouth when she discovered that she had left her handkerchief in the pocket of her sable coat, which she had put over the back of a conspicuous chair in the hall. Figgis, however, came in at the moment to say that lunch was ready, and she delayed them all very much by a long, ineffectual search for it, during which Figgis, with a visible effort, held up the sable coat, so that it was displayed to the utmost advantage. And then, only fancy, Susan discovered that it was in her sable muff all the time!

All three ladies were on tenterhooks of anxiety as to who was to be placed on Mr Wyse's right, who on his left, and who would be given only the place between two other women. But his tact was equal to anything.

'Miss Mapp,' he said, 'will you honour me by taking the head of my table and be hostess for me? Only I must have that vase of flowers removed, Figgis; I can look at my flowers when Miss Mapp is not here. Now, what have we got for breakfast – lunch, I should say?'

The macaroni which Mr Wyse had brought back with him from Naples naturally led on to Italian subjects, and the general scepticism about the Contessa di Faraglione had a staggering blow dealt it.

'My sister,' began Mr Wyse (and by a swift sucking motion, Diva drew into her mouth several serpents of dependent macaroni in order to be able to listen better without this agitating distraction), 'my sister, I hope, will come to England this winter, and spend several weeks with me.' (Sensation.)

'And the Count?' asked Diva, having swallowed the serpents.

'I fear not; Cecco – Francesco, you know – is a great stay-at-home. Amelia is looking forward very much to seeing Tilling. I shall insist on her making a long stay here, before she visits our relations at Whitchurch.'

Elizabeth found herself reserving judgement. She would believe in the Contessa Faraglione – no one more firmly – when she saw her, and had reasonable proofs of her identity.

'Delightful!' she said, abandoning with regret the fruitless pursuit with a fork of the few last serpents that writhed on her plate. 'What an addition to our society! We shall all do our best to spoil her, Mr Wyse. When do you expect her?'

'Early in December. You must be very kind to her, dear ladies. She is an insatiable bridge player. She has heard much of the great players she will meet here.'

That decided Mrs Poppit. She would join the correspondence class conducted by 'Little Slam', in 'Cosy Corner'. Little Slam, for the sum of two guineas, payable in advance, engaged to make first-class players of anyone with normal intelligence. Diva's mind flew off to the subject of dress, and the thought of the awful tragedy concerning the tea gown of kingfisher blue, combined with the endive salad, gave a wry twist to her mouth for a moment.

'I, as you know,' continued Mr Wyse, 'am no hand at bridge.'

'Oh, Mr Wyse, you play beautifully,' interpolated Elizabeth.

'Too flattering of you, Miss Mapp. But Amelia and Cecco do

not agree with you. I am never allowed to play when I am at the Villa Faraglione, unless a table cannot be made up without me. But I shall look forward to seeing many well-contested games.'

The quails and the figs had come from Capri, and Miss Mapp, greedily devouring each in turn, was so much incensed by the information that she had elicited about them, that, though she joined in the general Lobgesang, she was tempted to enquire whether the ice had not been brought from the South Pole by some Antarctic expedition. Her mind was not, like poor Diva's, taken up with obstinate questionings about the kingfisher-blue tea gown, for she had already determined what she was going to do about it. Naturally it was impossible to contemplate fresh encounters like that of last night, but another gown, crimson lake, the colour of Mrs Trout's toilet for the second evening of the Duke of Hampshire's visit, as *Vogue* informed her, had completely annihilated Newport with its splendour. She had already consulted Miss Greele about it, who said that if the kingfisher blue was bleached first the dye of crimson lake would be brilliant and pure . . . The thought of that, and the fact that Miss Greele's lips were professionally sealed, made her able to take Diva's arm as they strolled about the garden afterwards. The way in which both Diva and Susan had made up to Mr Wyse during lunch was really very shocking, though it did not surprise Miss Mapp, but she supposed their heads had been turned by the prospect of playing bridge with a countess. Luckily she expected nothing better of either of them, so their conduct was in no way a blow or a disappointment to her.

This companionship with Diva was rather prolonged, for the adhesive Susan, staggering about in her sables, clung close to their host and simulated a clumsy interest in chrysanthemums; and whatever the other two did, manoeuvred herself into a strong position between them and Mr Wyse, from which, operating on interior lines, she could cut off either assailant. More depressing yet (and throwing a sad new light on his character), Mr Wyse seemed to appreciate rather than resent the appropriation of himself, and instead of making a sortie through the beleaguering sables, would beg Diva and Elizabeth, who were so fond of fuchsias and knew about them so well, to put their heads together over an afflicted bed of these flowers in quite another part of the garden, and tell him what was the best treatment for their anaemic condition. Pleasant and proper though it was to each of them that Mr Wyse should pay so little attention to the other, it was bitter as the endive salad to both that he should tolerate, if not enjoy, the companionship which the forwardness of Susan forced on him, and while they absently stared at the fuchsias, the fire kindled, and Elizabeth spake with her tongue.

'How very plain poor Susan looks today,' she said. 'Such a colour, though to be sure I attribute that more to what she ate and drank than to anything else. Crimson. Oh, those poor fuchsias! I think I should throw them away.'

The common antagonism, Diva felt, had drawn her and Elizabeth into the most cordial of understandings. For the moment she felt nothing but enthusiastic sympathy with Elizabeth, in spite of her kingfisher-blue gown . . . What on earth, in parenthesis, was she to do with hers? She could not give it to Janet: it was impossible to contemplate the idea of Janet walking about the High Street in a tea gown of kingfisher blue just in order to thwart Elizabeth . . .

'Mr Wyse seems taken with her,' said Diva. 'How he can! Rather a snob. MBE. She's always popping in here. Saw her yesterday going round the corner of the street.'

'What time, dear?' asked Elizabeth, nosing the scent.

'Middle of the morning.'

'And I saw her in the afternoon,' said Elizabeth. 'That great lumbering Rolls-Royce went tacking and skidding round the corner below my garden room.'

'Was she in it?' asked Diva.

This appeared rather a slur on Elizabeth's reliability in observation.

'No, darling, she was sitting on the top,' she said, taking the edge off the sarcasm, in case Diva had not intended to be critical, by a little laugh. Diva drew the conclusion that Elizabeth had actually seen her inside.

'Think it's serious?' she said. 'Think he'll marry her?'

The idea of course, repellent and odious as it was, had occurred to Elizabeth, so she instantly denied it.

'Oh, you busy little matchmaker,' she said brightly. 'Such an idea never entered my head. You shouldn't make such fun of dear

Susan. Come, dear, I can't look at fuchsias any more. I must be getting home and must say goodbye – *au reservoir*, rather – to Mr Wyse, if Susan will allow me to get a word in edgeways.'

Susan seemed delighted to let Miss Mapp get this particular word in edgewise, and after a little speech from Mr Wyse, in which he said that he would not dream of allowing them to go yet, and immediately afterwards shook hands warmly with them both, hoping that the reservoir would be a very small one, the two were forced to leave the artful Susan in possession of the field . . .

It all looked rather black. Miss Mapp's vivid imagination altogether failed to picture what Tilling would be like if Susan succeeded in becoming Mrs Wyse and the sister-in-law of a countess, and she sat down in her garden room and closed her eyes for a moment, in order to concentrate her power of figuring the situation. What dreadful people these climbers were! How swiftly they swarmed up the social ladder with their Rolls-Royces and their redcurrant fool, and their sables! A few weeks ago she herself had never asked Susan into her house, while the very first time she came she unloosed the sluices of the storecupboard, and now, owing to the necessity of getting her aid in stopping that mischievous rumour, which she herself had been so careful to set on foot, regarding the cause of the duel, Miss Mapp had been positively obliged to flatter and to 'Susan' her. And if Diva's awful surmise proved to be well founded, Susan would be in a position to patronize them all, and talk about counts and countesses with the same air of unconcern as Mr Wyse. She would be bidden to the Villa Faraglione, she would play bridge with Cecco and Amelia, she would visit the Wyses of Whitchurch . . .

What was to be done? She might head another movement to put Mr Wyse in his proper place; this, if successful, would have the agreeable result of pulling down Susan a rung or two should she carry out her design. But the failure of the last attempt and Mr Wyse's eminence did not argue well for any further manoeuvre of the kind. Or should she poison Mr Wyse's mind with regard to Susan? . . . Or was she herself causelessly agitated?

Or –

Curiosity rushed like a devastating tornado across Miss Mapp's mind, rooting up all other growths, buffeting her with the necessity of knowing what the two whom she had been forced to leave in the garden were doing now, and snatching up her opera glasses she glided upstairs, and let herself out through the trap door on to the roof. She did not remember if it was possible to see Mr Wyse's garden or any part of it from that watch tower, but there was a chance . . .

Not a glimpse of it was visible. It lay quite hidden behind the redbrick wall which bounded it, and not a chrysanthemum or a fuchsia could she see. But her blood froze as, without putting the glasses down, she ran her eye over such part of the house wall as rose above the obstruction. In his drawing-room window on the first floor were seated two figures. Susan had taken her sables off: it was as if she intended remaining there for ever, or at least for tea . . .

CHAPTER EIGHT

The hippopotamus quarrel over their whisky between Major Flint and Captain Puffin, which culminated in the challenge and all the shining sequel, had had the excellent effect of making the United Services more united than ever. They both knew that, had they not severally run away from the encounter, and, so providentially, met at the station, very serious consequences might have ensued. Had not both but only one of them been averse from taking or risking life, the other would surely have remained in Tilling, and spread disastrous reports about the bravery of the refugee; while if neither of them had had scruples on the sacredness of human existence there might have been one if not two corpses lying on the shining sands. Naturally the fact that they both had taken the very earliest opportunity of averting an encounter by flight, made it improbable that any future quarrel would be proceeded with to violent extremes, but it was much safer to run no risks, and not let verbal disagreements rise to hippopotamus-pitch again. Consequently when there was any real danger of such savagery as was implied in sending challenges, they hastened, by mutual concessions, to climb down from these perilous places, where loss of balance might possibly occur. For which of them could be absolutely certain that next time the other of them might not be more courageous? . . .

They were coming up from the tram station one November evening, both fizzing and fuming a good deal, and the Major was extremely lame, lamer than Puffin. The rattle of the tram had made argument impossible during the transit from the links, but they had both in this enforced silence thought of several smart repartees, supposing that the other made the requisite remarks to call them out, and on arrival at the Tilling station they went on at precisely the same point at which they had broken off on starting from the station by the links.

'Well, I hope I can take a beating in as English a spirit as anybody,' said the Major.

This was lucky for Captain Puffin: he had thought it likely that he would say just that, and had got a stinger for him.

'And it worries you to find that your hopes are doomed to disappointment,' he swiftly said.

Major Flint stepped in a puddle which cooled his foot but not his temper.

'Most offensive remark,' he said. 'I wasn't called Sporting Benjy in the regiment for nothing. But never mind that. A worm cast – '

'It wasn't a worm cast,' said Puffin. 'It was sheep's dung!'

Luck had veered here: the Major had felt sure that Puffin would reiterate that utterly untrue contention.

'I can't pretend to be such a specialist as you in those matters,' he said, 'but you must allow me sufficient power of observation to know a worm cast when I see it. It was a worm cast, sir, a cast of a worm, and you had no right to remove it. If you will do me the favour to consult the rules of golf – ?'

'Oh, I grant you that you are more a specialist in the rules of golf, Major, than in the practice of it,' said Puffin brightly.

Suddenly it struck Sporting Benjy that the red signals of danger danced before his eyes, and though the odious Puffin had scored twice to his once, he called up all his powers of self-control, for if his friend was anything like as exasperated as himself, the breeze of disagreement might develop into a hurricane. At the moment he was passing through a swing gate which led to a short cut back to the town, but before he could take hold of himself he had slammed it back in his fury, hitting Puffin, who was following him, on the knee. Then he remembered he was a sporting Christian gentleman, and no duellist.

'I'm sure I beg your pardon, my dear fellow,' he said, with the utmost solicitude. 'Uncommonly stupid of me. The gate flew out of my hand. I hope I didn't hurt you.'

Puffin had just come to the same conclusion as Major Flint: magnanimity was better than early trains, and ever so much better than bullets. Indeed there was no comparison . . .

'Not hurt a bit, thank you, Major,' he said, wincing with the shrewdness of the blow, silently cursing his friend for what he felt sure was no accident, and limping with both legs. 'It didn't touch me. Ha! What a brilliant sunset. The town looks amazingly picturesque.'

'It does indeed,' said the Major. 'Fine subject for Miss Mapp.'

Puffin shuffled alongside.

'There's still a lot of talk going on in the town,' he said, 'about that duel of ours. Those fairies of yours are all agog to know what it was about. I am sure they all think that there was a lady in the case. Just like the vanity of the sex. If two men have a quarrel, they think it must be because of their silly faces.'

Ordinarily the Major's gallantry would have resented this view, but the reconciliation with Puffin was too recent to risk just at present.

'Poor little devils,' he said. 'It makes an excitement for them. I wonder who they think it is. It would puzzle me to name a woman in Tilling worth catching an early train for.'

'There are several who'd be surprised to hear you say that, Major,' said Puffin archly.

'Well, well,' said the other, strutting and swelling, and walking without a sign of lameness . . .

They had come to where their houses stood opposite each other on the steep cobbled street, fronted at its top end by Miss Mapp's garden room. She happened to be standing in the window, and the Major made a great flourish of his cap, and laid his hand on his heart.

'And there's one of them,' said Puffin, as Miss Mapp acknowledged these florid salutations with a wave of her hand, and tripped away from the window.

'Poking your fun at me,' said the Major. 'Perhaps she was the cause of our quarrel, hey? Well, I'll step across, shall I, about half-past nine, and bring my diaries with me?'

'I'll expect you. You'll find me at my Roman roads.'

The humour of this joke never staled, and they parted with hoots and guffaws of laughter.

It must not be supposed that duelling, puzzles over the portmanteau, or the machinations of Susan had put out of Miss

Mapp's head her amiable interest in the hour at which Major Benjy went to bed. For some time she had been content to believe, on direct information from him, that he went to bed early and worked at his diaries on alternate evenings, but maturer consideration had led her to wonder whether he was being quite as truthful as a gallant soldier should be. For though (on alternate evenings) his house would be quite dark by half-past nine, it was not for twelve hours or more afterwards that he could be heard *quai-haï*ng for his breakfast, and unless he was in some incipient stage of sleeping sickness, such hours provided more than ample slumber for a growing child, and might be considered excessive for a middle-aged man. She had a mass of evidence to show that on the other set of alternate nights his diaries (which must, in parenthesis, be of extraordinary fullness) occupied him into the small hours, and to go to bed at half-past nine on one night and after one o'clock on the next implied a complicated kind of regularity which cried aloud for elucidation. If he had only breakfasted early on the mornings after he had gone to bed early, she might have allowed herself to be weakly credulous, but he never *quai-hai*ed earlier than half-past nine, and she could not but think that to believe blindly in such habits would be a triumph not for faith but for foolishness. 'People,' said Miss Mapp to herself, as her attention refused to concentrate on the evening paper, 'don't do it. I never heard of a similar case.'

She had been spending the evening alone, and even the conviction that her cold apple tart had suffered diminution by at least a slice, since she had so much enjoyed it hot at lunch, failed to occupy her mind for long, for this matter had presented itself with a clamouring insistence that drowned all other voices. She had tried, when, at the conclusion of her supper, she had gone back to the garden room, to immerse herself in a book, in an evening paper, in the portmanteau problem, in a jigsaw puzzle, and in Patience, but none of these supplied the stimulus to lead her mind away from Major Benjy's evenings, or the narcotic to dull her unslumbering desire to solve a problem that was rapidly becoming one of the greater mysteries.

Her radiator made a seat in the window agreeably warm, and a chink in the curtains gave her a view of the Major's lighted window. Even as she looked, the illumination was extinguished. She had expected this, as he had been at his diaries late – quite naughtily late – the evening before, so this would be a night of infant slumber for twelve hours or so.

Even as she looked, a chink of light came from his front door, which immediately enlarged itself into a full oblong. Then it went completely out. 'He has opened the door, and has put out the hall light,' whispered Miss Mapp to herself . . . 'He has gone out and shut the door . . . (Perhaps he is going to post a letter.) . . . He has gone into Captain Puffin's house without knocking. So he is expected.'

Miss Mapp did not at once guess that she held in her hand the key to the mystery. It was certainly Major Benjy's night for going to bed early . . . Then a fierce illumination beat on her brain. Had she not, so providentially, actually observed the Major cross the road, unmistakable in the lamplight, and had she only looked out of her window after the light in his was quenched, she would surely have told herself that good Major Benjy had gone to bed. But good Major Benjy, on ocular evidence, she now knew to have done nothing of the kind: he had gone across to see Captain Puffin . . . He was not good.

She grasped the situation in its hideous entirety. She had been deceived and hoodwinked. Major Benjy never went to bed early at all: on alternate nights he went and sat with Captain Puffin. And Captain Puffin, she could not but tell herself, sat up on the other set of alternate nights with the Major, for it had not escaped her observation that when the Major seemed to be sitting up, the Captain seemed to have gone to bed. Instantly, with strong conviction, she suspected orgies. It remained to be seen (and she would remain to see it) to what hour these orgies were kept up.

About eleven o'clock a little mist had begun to form in the street, obscuring the complete clarity of her view, but through it there still shone the light from behind Captain Puffin's red blind, and the mist was not so thick as to be able wholly to obscure the figure of Major Flint when he should pass below the gas lamp again into his house. But no such figure passed. Did he then work at his diaries every evening? And what price, to put it vulgarly, Roman roads?

Every moment her sense of being deceived grew blacker, and

every moment her curiosity as to what they were doing became more unbearable. After a spasm of tactical thought she glided back into her house from the garden room, and, taking an envelope in her hand, so that she might, if detected, say that she was going down to the letter box at the corner to catch the early post, she unbolted her door and let herself out. She crossed the street and tiptoed along the pavement to where the red light from Captain Puffin's window shone like a blurred danger signal through the mist.

From inside came a loud duet of familiar voices: sometimes they spoke singly, sometimes together. But she could not catch the words: they sounded blurred and indistinct, and she told herself that she was very glad that she could not hear what they said, for that would have seemed like eavesdropping. The voices sounded angry. Was there another duel pending? And what was it about this time?

Quite suddenly, from so close at hand that she positively leaped off the pavement into the middle of the road, the door was thrown open and the duet, louder than ever, streamed out into the street. Major Benjy bounced out on to the threshold, and stumbled down the two steps that led from the door.

'Tell you it was a worm cast,' he bellowed, 'Think I don't know a worm cast when I see a worm cast?'

Suddenly his tone changed: this was getting too near a quarrel.

'Well, good night, old fellow,' he said. 'Jolly evening.'

He turned and saw, veiled and indistinct in the mist, the female figure in the roadway. Undying coquetry, as Mr Stevenson so finely remarked, awoke, for the topic preceding the worm cast had been 'the sex'.

'Bless me,' he crowed, 'if there isn't an unprotected lady all 'lone here in the dark, and lost in the fog. 'Llow me to 'scort you home, madam. Lemme introduce myself and friend – Major Flint, that's me, and my friend Captain Puffin.'

He put up his hand and whispered an aside to Miss Mapp: 'Revolutionized the theory of navigation.'

Major Benjy was certainly rather gay and rather indistinct, but his polite gallantry could not fail to be attractive. It was naughty of him to have said that he went to bed early on alternate nights, but really . . . Still, it might be better to slip away unrecognized, and, thinking it would be nice to scriggle by him and disappear in the mist, she made a tactical error in her scriggling, for she scriggled full into the light that streamed from the open door where Captain Puffin was standing.

He gave a shrill laugh.

'Why, it's Miss Mapp,' he said in his high falsetto. 'Blow me, if it isn't our mutual friend Miss Mapp. What a 'strordinary coincidence.'

Miss Mapp put on her most winning smile. To be dignified and at the same time pleasant was the proper way to deal with this situation. Gentlemen often had a glass of grog when they thought the ladies had gone upstairs. That was how, for the moment, she summed things up.

'Good evening,' she said. 'I was just going down to the pillar box to post a letter,' and she exhibited her envelope. But it dropped out of her hand, and the Major picked it up for her.

'I'll post it for you,' he said very pleasantly. 'Save you the trouble. Insist on it. Why, there's no stamp on it! Why, there's no address on it! I say, Puffie, here's a letter with no address on it. Forgotten the address, Miss Mapp? Think they'll remember it at the post office? Well, that's one of the mos' comic things I ever came across. An, an anonymous letter, eh?'

The night air began to have a most unfortunate effect on Puffin. When he came out it would have been quite unfair to have described him as drunk. He was no more than gay and ready to go to bed. Now he became portentously solemn, as the cold mist began to do its deadly work.

'A letter,' he said impressively, 'without an address is an uncommonly dangerous thing. Hic! Can't tell into whose hands it may fall. I would sooner go 'bout with a loaded pistol than with a letter without any address. Send it to the bank for safety. Send for the police. Follow my advice and send for the p'lice. Police!'

Miss Mapp's penetrating mind instantly perceived that that dreadful Captain Puffin was drunk, and she promised herself that Tilling should ring with the tale of his excesses tomorrow. But Major Benjy, whom, if she mistook not, Captain Puffin had been trying, with perhaps some small success, to lead astray, was a gallant gentleman still, and she conceived the brilliant but madly mistaken idea of throwing herself on his protection.

'Major Benjy,' she said, 'I will ask you to take me home. Captain Puffin has had too much to drink – '

'Woz that?' asked Captain Puffin, with an air of great interest.

Miss Mapp abandoned dignity and pleasantness, and lost her temper.

'I said you were drunk,' she said with great distinctness. 'Major Benjy, will you – '

Captain Puffin came carefully down the two steps from the door on to the pavement.

'Look here,' he said, 'this all needs 'splanation. You say I'm drunk, do you? Well, I say you're drunk, going out like this in mill' of the night to post letter with no 'dress on it. Shamed of yourself, mill'aged woman going out in the mill' of the night in the mill' of Tilling. Very shocking thing. What do you say, Major?'

Major Benjy drew himself up to his full height, and put on his hat in order to take it off to Miss Mapp.

'My fren' Cap'n Puffin,' he said, 'is a man of strictly 'stemious habits. Boys together. Very serious thing to call a man of my fren's character drunk. If you call him drunk, why shouldn't he call you drunk? Can't take away man's character like that.'

'Abso – ' began Captain Puffin. Then he stopped and pulled himself together.

'Absolooly,' he said without a hitch.

'Tilling shall hear of this tomorrow,' said Miss Mapp, shivering with rage and sea mist.

Captain Puffin came a step closer.

'Now I'll tell you what it is, Miss Mapp,' he said. 'If you dare to say that I was drunk, Major and I, my fren' the Major and I will say you were drunk. Perhaps you think my fren' the Major's drunk too. But sure's I live, I'll say we were taking lil' walk in the moonlight and found you trying to post a letter with no 'dress on it, and couldn't find the slit to put it in. But 'slong as you say nothing, I say nothing. Can't say fairer than that. Liberal terms. Mutual Protection Society. Your lips sealed, our lips sealed. Strictly private. All trespassers will be prosecuted. By order. Hic!'

Miss Mapp felt that Major Benjy ought instantly to have

challenged his ignoble friend to another duel for this insolent suggestion, but he did nothing of the kind, and his silence, which had some awful quality of consent about it, chilled her mind, even as the sea mist, now thick and cold, made her certain that her nose was turning red. She still boiled with rage, but her mind grew cold with odious apprehensions: she was like an ice pudding with scalding sauce . . . There they all stood, veiled in vapours, and outlined by the red light that streamed from the still-open door of the intoxicated Puffin, getting colder every moment.

'Yessorno,' said Puffin, with chattering teeth.

Bitter as it was to accept those outrageous terms, there really seemed, without the Major's support, to be no way out of it.

'Yes,' said Miss Mapp.

Puffin gave a loud crow.

'The ayes have it, Major,' he said. 'So we're all frens again. Goonight everybody.'

* * *

Miss Mapp let herself into her house in an agony of mortification. She could scarcely realize that her little expedition, undertaken with so much ardent and earnest curiosity only a quarter of an hour ago, had ended in so deplorable a surfeit of sensation. She had gone out in obedience to an innocent and, indeed, laudable desire to ascertain how Major Benjy spent those evenings on which he had deceived her into imagining that, owing to her influence, he had gone ever so early to bed, only to find that he sat up ever so late and that she was fettered by a promise not to breathe to a soul a single word about the depravity of Captain Puffin, on pain of being herself accused out of the mouth of two witnesses of being equally depraved herself. More wounding yet was the part played by her Major Benjy in these odious transactions, and it was only possible to conclude that he put a higher value on his fellowship with his degraded friend than on chivalry itself . . . And what did his silence imply? Probably it was a defensive one; he imagined that he, too, would be included in the stories that Miss Mapp proposed to sow broadcast upon the fruitful fields of Tilling, and, indeed, when she called to mind his bellowing about worm casts, his general instability of speech and equilibrium, she told herself that he had ample cause for such a supposition. He, when his lights were out, was abetting, assisting and perhaps joining Captain Puffin. When his window was alight on alternate nights she made no doubt now that Captain Puffin was performing a similar role. This had been going on for weeks under her very nose, without her having the smallest suspicion of it.

Humiliated by all that had happened, and flattened in her own estimation by the sense of her blindness, she penetrated to the kitchen and lit a gas ring to make herself some hot cocoa, which would at least comfort her physical chatterings. There was a letter for Withers, slipped sideways into its envelope, on the kitchen table, and mechanically she opened and read it by the bluish flame of the burner. She had always suspected Withers of having a young man, and here was proof of it. But that he should be Mr Hopkins of the fish shop!

There is known to medical science a pleasant device known as a counter-irritant. If the patient has an aching and rheumatic joint he is counselled to put some hot burning application on the skin, which smarts so agonizingly that the ache is quite extinguished. Metaphorically, Mr Hopkins was thermogene to Miss Mapp's outraged and aching consciousness, and the smart occasioned by the knowledge that Withers must have encouraged Mr Hopkins (else he could scarcely have written a letter so familiar and amorous), and thus be contemplating matrimony, relieved the aching humiliation of all that had happened in the sea mist. It shed a new and lurid light on Withers, it made her mistress feel that she had nourished a serpent in her bosom, to think that Withers was contemplating so odious an act of selfishness as matrimony. It would be necessary to find a new parlourmaid, and all the trouble connected with that would not nearly be compensated for by being able to buy fish at a lower rate. That was the least that Withers could do for her, to insist that Mr Hopkins should let her have dabs and plaice exceptionally cheap. And ought she to tell Withers that she had seen Mr Hopkins . . . no, that was impossible: she must write it, if she decided (for Withers's sake) to make this fell communication.

Miss Mapp turned and tossed on her uneasy bed, and her mind went back to the Major and the Captain and that fiasco in the fog. Of course she was perfectly at liberty (having made her promise under practical compulsion) to tell everybody in Tilling what had occurred, trusting to the chivalry of the men not to carry out their counter-threat, but looking at the matter quite dispassionately, she did not think it would be wise to trust too much to chivalry. Still, even if they did carry out their unmanly menace, nobody would seriously believe that she had been drunk. But they might make a very disagreeable joke of pretending to do so, and, in a word, the prospect frightened her. Whatever Tilling did or did not believe, a residuum of ridicule would assuredly cling to her, and her reputation of having perhaps been the cause of the quarrel which, so happily, did not end in a duel, would be lost for ever. Evie would squeak, quaint Irene would certainly burst into hoarse laughter when she heard the story. It was very inconvenient that honesty should be the best policy.

Her brain still violently active switched off for a moment on to the eternal problem of the portmanteau. Why, so she asked herself for the hundredth time, if the portmanteau contained the fatal apparatus of duelling, did not the combatants accompany it? And if (the only other alternative) it did not – ?

An idea so luminous flashed across her brain that she almost thought the room had leaped into light. The challenge distinctly said that Major Benjy's seconds would wait upon Captain Puffin in the course of the morning. With what object then could the former have gone down to the station to catch the early train? There could be but one object, namely to get away as quickly as possible from the dangerous vicinity of the challenged Captain. And why did Captain Puffin leave that note on his table to say that he was suddenly called away, except in order to escape from the ferocious neighbourhood of his challenger?

'The cowards!' ejaculated Miss Mapp. 'They both ran away from each other! How blind I've been!'

The veil was rent. She perceived how, carried away with the notion that a duel was to be fought among the sand dunes, Tilling had quite overlooked the significance of the early train. She felt sure that she had solved everything now, and gave herself up to a rapturous consideration of what use she would make of the precious solution. All regrets for the impossibility of ruining the character of Captain Puffin with regard to intoxicants were gone, for she had an even deadlier blacking to hand. No faintest hesitation at ruining the reputation of Major Benjy as well crossed her mind; she gloried in it, for he had not only caused her to deceive herself about the early hours on alternate nights, but by his infamous willingness to back up Captain Puffin's bargain, he had shown himself imperviously waterproof to all chivalrous impulses. For weeks now the sorry pair of them had enjoyed the spurious splendours of being men of blood and valour, when all the time they had put themselves to all sorts of inconvenience in catching early trains and packing bags by candlelight in order to escape the hot impulses of quarrel that, as she saw now, were probably derived from drained whisky bottles. That mysterious holloaing about worm casts was just such another disagreement. And, crowning rapture of all, her own position as cause of the projected duel was quite unassailed. Owing to her silence about drink, no one would suspect a mere drunken brawl: she would still figure as heroine, though the heroes were terribly dismantled. To be sure, it would have been better if their ardour about her had been such that one of them, at the least, had been prepared to face the ordeal, that they had not both preferred flight, but even without that she had much to be thankful for. 'It will serve them both,' said Miss Mapp (interrupted by a sneeze, for she had been sitting up in bed for quite a considerable time), 'right'

To one of Miss Mapp's experience, the first step of her new and delightful strategic campaign was obvious, and she spent hardly any time at all in the window of her garden room after breakfast next morning, but set out with her shopping basket at an unusually early hour. She shuddered as she passed between the front doors of her miscreant neighbours, for the chill of last night's mist and its dreadful memories still lingered there, but her present errand warmed her soul even as the tepid November day comforted her body. No sign of life was at present evident in those bibulous abodes, no *quai-hai*s had indicated breakfast, and she put her utmost irony into the reflection that the United Services slept late after their protracted industry last night over diaries and Roman roads. By a natural revulsion, violent in proportion to the depth of her previous regard for Major Benjy, she hugged herself more closely on the prospect of exposing him than on that of exposing the other. She had had daydreams about Major Benjy and the conversion of these into nightmares annealed her softness into the semblance of some red-hot stone, giving vengeance a concentrated sweetness as of saccharine contrasted with ordinary lump sugar. This sweetness was of so powerful a quality that she momentarily forgot all about the contents of Withers's letter on the kitchen table, and tripped across to Mr Hopkins's with an oblivious smile for him.

'Good morning, Mr Hopkins,' she said. 'I wonder if you've got a nice little dab for my dinner today? Yes? Will you send it up then, please? What a mild morning, like May!'

The opening move, of course, was to tell Diva about the revelation that had burst on her the night before. Diva was incomparably the best disseminator of news: she walked so fast, and her telegraphic style was so brisk and lucid. Her terse tongue, her revolving feet! Such a gossip!

'Diva, darling, I had to look in a moment,' said Elizabeth, pecking her affectionately on both cheeks. 'Such a bit of news!'

'Oh, Contessa di Faradidleony,' said Diva sarcastically. 'I heard yesterday. Journey put off.'

Miss Mapp just managed to stifle the excitement which would have betrayed that this was news to her.

'No, dear, not that,' she said. 'I didn't suspect you of not knowing that. Unfortunate though, isn't it, just when we were all beginning to believe that there was a Contessa di Faradidleony! What a sweet name! For my part I shall believe in her when I see her. Poor Mr Wyse!'

'What's the news then?' asked Diva.

'My dear, it all came upon me in a flash,' said Elizabeth. 'It explains the portmanteau and the early train and the duel.'

Diva looked disappointed. She thought this was to be some solid piece of news, not one of Elizabeth's ideas only.

'Drive ahead,' she said.

'They ran away from each other,' said Elizabeth, mouthing her words as if speaking to a totally deaf person who understood lip-reading. 'Never mind the cause of the duel: that's another affair. But whatever the cause – ' here she dropped her eyes ' – the Major having sent the challenge packed his portmanteau. He ran away, dear Diva, and met Captain Puffin at the station running away too.'

'But did – ' began Diva.

'Yes, dear, the note on Captain Puffin's table to his housekeeper said he was called away suddenly. What called him away? Cowardice, dear! How ignoble it all is. And we've all been thinking how brave and wonderful they were. They fled from each other, and came back together and played golf. I never thought it was a game for men. The sand dunes where they were supposed to be fighting! They might lose a ball there, but that would be the utmost. Not a life. Poor Padre! Going out there to stop a duel, and only finding a game of golf. But I understand the nature of men better now. What an eye-opener!'

Diva by this time was trundling away round the room, and longing to be off in order to tell everybody. She could find no hole in Elizabeth's arguments; it was founded as solidly as a Euclidean proposition.

'Ever occurred to you that they drink?' she asked. 'Believe in Roman roads and diaries? I don't.'

Miss Mapp bounded from her chair. Danger flags flapped and crimsoned in her face. What if Diva went flying round Tilling, suggesting that in addition to being cowards those two men were drunkards? They would, as soon as any hint of the further exposure reached them, conclude that she had set the idea on foot, and then –

'No, Diva darling,' she said, 'don't dream of imagining such a thing. So dangerous to hint anything of the sort. Cowards they may be, and indeed are, but never have I seen anything that leads me to suppose that they drink. We must give them their due, and stick to what we know; we must not launch accusations wildly about other matters, just because we know they are cowards. A coward need not be a drunkard, thank God! It is all miserable enough, as it is!'

Having averted this danger, Miss Mapp, with her radiant, excited face, seemed to be bearing all the misery very courageously, and as Diva could no longer be restrained from starting on her morning round they plunged together into the maelstrom of the High Street, riding and whirling in its waters with the solution of the portmanteau and the early train for life buoy. Very little shopping was done that morning, for every permutation and combination of Tilling society (with the exception, of course, of the cowards) had to be formed on the pavement with a view to the amplest possible discussion. Diva, as might have been expected, gave proof of her accustomed perfidy before long, for she certainly gave the Padre to understand that the chain of inductive reasoning was of her own welding and Elizabeth had to hurry after him to correct this grabbing impression; but the discovery in itself was so great, that small false notes like these could not spoil the glorious harmony. Even Mr Wyse abandoned his usual neutrality with regard to social politics and left his tall malacca cane in the chemist's, so keen was his gusto, on seeing Miss Mapp on the pavement outside, to glean any fresh detail of evidence.

By eleven o'clock that morning, the two duellists were universally known as 'the cowards', the Padre alone demurring, and being swampingly outvoted. He held (sticking up for his sex) that the Major had been brave enough to send a challenge (on whatever subject) to his friend, and had, though he subsequently failed to maintain that high level, shown courage of a high order, since, for all he knew, Captain Puffin might have accepted it. Miss Mapp was spokesman for the mind of Tilling on this too indulgent judgement.

'Dear Padre,' she said, 'you are too generous altogether. They both ran away: you can't get over that. Besides you must remember that, when the Major sent the challenge, he knew Captain Puffin, oh so well, and quite expected he would run away – '

'Then why did he run away himself?' asked the Padre.

This was rather puzzling for a moment, but Miss Mapp soon thought of the explanation.

'Oh, just to make sure,' she said, and Tilling applauded her ready irony.

And then came the climax of sensationalism, when at about ten minutes past eleven the two cowards emerged into the High Street on their way to catch the eleven-twenty tram out to the links. The day threatened rain, and they both carried bags which contained a change of clothes. Just round the corner of the High Street was the group which had applauded Miss Mapp's quickness, and the cowards were among the breakers. They glanced at each other, seeing that Miss Mapp was the most towering of the breakers, but it was too late to retreat, and they made the usual salutations.

'Good morning,' said Diva, with her voice trembling. 'Off to catch the early train together – I mean the tram.'

'Good morning, Captain Puffin,' said Miss Mapp with extreme sweetness. 'What a nice little travelling bag! Oh, and the Major's got one too! H'm!'

A certain dismay looked from Major Flint's eyes, Captain Puffin's mouth fell open, and he forgot to shut it.

'Yes; change of clothes,' said the Major. 'It looks a threatening morning.'

'Very threatening,' said Miss Mapp. 'I hope you will do nothing rash or dangerous.'

There was a moment's silence, and the two looked from one face to another of this fell group. They all wore fixed, inexplicable smiles.

'It will be pleasant among the sand dunes,' said the Padre, and his wife gave a loud squeak.

'Well, we shall be missing our tram,' said the Major. '*Au – au reservoir*, ladies.'

Nobody responded at all, and they hurried off down the street, their bags bumping together very inconveniently.

'Something's up, Major,' said Puffin, with true Tilling perspicacity, as soon as they had got out of hearing . . .

* * *

Precisely at the same moment Miss Mapp gave a little cooing laugh. 'Now I must run and do my bittie shopping, Padre,' she said, and kissed her hand all round . . . The curtain had to come down for a little while on so dramatic a situation. Any discussion, just then, would be an anticlimax.

CHAPTER NINE

Captain Puffin found but a sombre diarist when he came over to study his Roman roads with Major Flint that evening, and indeed he was a sombre antiquarian himself. They had pondered a good deal during the day over their strange reception in the High Street that morning and the recondite allusions to bags, sand dunes and early trains, and the more they pondered the more probable it became that not only was something up, but, as regards the duel, everything was up. For weeks now they had been regarded by the ladies of Tilling with something approaching veneration, but there seemed singularly little veneration at the back of the comments this morning. Following so closely on the encounter with Miss Mapp last night, this irreverent attitude was probably due to some atheistical manoeuvre of hers. Such, at least, was the Major's view, and when he held a view he usually stated it, did Sporting Benjy.

'We've got you to thank for this, Puffin,' he said. 'Upon my soul, I was ashamed of you for saying what you did to Miss Mapp last night. Utter absence of any chivalrous feeling hinting that if she said you were drunk you would say she was. She was as sober and lucid last night as she was this morning. And she was devilish lucid, to my mind, this morning.'

'Pity you didn't take her part last night,' said Puffin. 'You thought that was a very ingenious idea of mine to make her hold her tongue.'

'There are finer things in this world, sir, than ingenuity,' said the Major. 'What your ingenuity has led to is this public ridicule. You may not mind that yourself – you may be used to it – but a man should regard the consequences of his act on others . . . My status in Tilling is completely changed. Changed for the worse, sir.'

Puffin emitted his fluty, disagreeable laugh.

'If your status in Tilling depended on a reputation for bloodthirsty bravery,' he said, 'the sooner it was changed the better. We're in the same boat: I don't say I like the boat, but there we are. Have a drink, and you'll feel better. Never mind your status.'

'I've a good mind never to have a drink again,' said the Major, pouring himself out one of his stiff little glasses, 'if a drink leads to this sort of thing.'

'But it didn't,' said Puffin. 'How it all got out, I can't say, nor for that matter can you. If it hadn't been for me last night, it would have been all over Tilling that you and I were tipsy as well. That wouldn't have improved our status that I can see.'

'It was in consequence of what you said to Mapp – ' began the Major.

'But, good Lord, where's the connection?' asked Puffin. 'Produce the connection! Let's have a look at the connection! There ain't any connection! Duelling wasn't as much as mentioned last night.'

Major Flint pondered this in gloomy, sipping silence.

'Bridge party at Mrs Poppit's the day after tomorrow,' he said. 'I don't feel as if I could face it. Suppose they all go on making allusions to duelling and early trains and that? I shan't be able to keep my mind on the cards for fear of it. More than a sensitive man ought to be asked to bear.'

Puffin made a noise that sounded rather like 'Fudge!'

'Your pardon?' said the Major haughtily.

'Granted by all means,' said Puffin. 'But I don't see what you're in such a taking about. We're no worse off than we were before we got a reputation for being such fire-eaters. Being fire-eaters is a washout, that's all. Pleasant while it lasted, and now we're as we were.'

'But we're not,' said the Major. 'We're detected frauds! That's not the same as being a fraud; far from it. And who's going to rub it in, my friend? Who's been rubbing away for all she's worth? Miss Mapp, to whom, if I may say so without offence, you behaved like a cur last night.'

'And another cur stood by and wagged his tail,' retorted Puffin. This was about as far as it was safe to go, and Puffin hastened to say something pleasant about the hearthrug, to which his friend had a suitable rejoinder. But after the affair last night, and the dark sayings in the High Street this morning, there was little content or cosiness about the session. Puffin's brazen optimism was but a tinkling cymbal, and the Major did not feel like tinkling at all. He but snorted and glowered, revolving in his mind how to square Miss Mapp. Allied with her, if she could but be won over, he felt he could face the rest of Tilling with indifference, for hers would be the most penetrating shafts, the most stinging pleasantries. He had more too, so he reflected, to lose than Puffin, for till the affair of the duel the other had never been credited with deeds of bloodthirsty gallantry, whereas he had enjoyed no end of a reputation in amorous and honourable affairs. Marriage no doubt would settle it satisfactorily, but this bachelor life, with plenty of golf and diaries, was not to be lightly exchanged for the unknown. Short of that . . .

A light broke, and he got to his feet, following the gleam and walking very lame out of general discomfiture.

'Tell you what it is, Puffin,' he said. 'You and I, particularly you, owe that estimable lady a very profound apology for what happened last night. You ought to withdraw every word you said, and I every word that I didn't say.'

'Can't be done,' said Puffin. 'That would be giving up my hold over your lady friend. We should be known as drunkards all over the shop before you could say winkie. Worse off than before.'

'Not a bit of it. If it's Miss Mapp, and I'm sure it is, who has been spreading these – these damaging rumours about our duel, it's because she's outraged and offended, quite rightly, at your conduct to her last night. Mine, too, if you like. Ample apology, sir, that's the ticket.'

'Dog-ticket,' said Puffin. 'No thanks.'

'Very objectionable expression,' said Major Flint. 'But you shall do as you like. And so, with your permission, shall I. I shall apologize for my share in that sorry performance, in which, thank God, I only played a minor role. That's my view, and if you don't like it, you may dislike it.'

Puffin yawned.

'Mapp's a cat,' he said. 'Stroke a cat and you'll get scratched.

Shy a brick at a cat, and she'll spit at you and skedaddle. You're poor company tonight, Major, with all these qualms.'

'Then, sir, you can relieve yourself of my company,' said the Major, 'by going home.'

'Just what I was about to do. Good night, old boy. Same time tomorrow for the tram, if you're not too badly mauled.'

Miss Mapp, sitting by the hot-water pipes in the garden room, looked out not long after to see what the night was like. Though it was not yet half-past ten the cowards' sitting rooms were both dark, and she wondered what precisely that meant. There was no bridge party anywhere that night, and apparently there were no diaries or Roman roads either. Why this sober and chastened darkness? . . .

The Major *quai-hai*ed for his breakfast at an unusually early hour next morning, for the courage of this resolve to placate, if possible, the hostility of Miss Mapp had not, like that of the challenge, oozed out during the night. He had dressed himself in his frock coat, seen last on the occasion when the Prince of Wales proved not to have come by the six thirty-seven, and no female breast however furious could fail to recognize the compliment of such a formality. Dressed thus, with top hat and patent-leather boots, he was clearly observed from the garden room to emerge into the street just when Captain Puffin's hand thrust the sponge on to the window sill of his bathroom. Probably he too had observed this apparition, for his fingers prematurely loosed hold of the sponge, and it bounded into the street. Wild surmises flashed into Miss Mapp's active brain, the most likely of which was that Major Benjy was going to propose to Mrs Poppit, for if he had been going up to London for some ceremonial occasion, he would be walking down the street instead of up it. And then she saw his agitated finger press the electric bell of her own door. So he was not on his way to propose to Mrs Poppit. . .

She slid from the room and hurried across the few steps of garden to the house just in time to intercept Withers, though not with any idea of saying that she was out. Then Withers, according to instructions, waited till Miss Mapp had tiptoed upstairs, and conducted the Major to the garden room, promising that she would 'tell' her mistress. This was unnecessary, as her mistress knew. The Major pressed a half-crown into her astonished hand, thinking it was a florin. He couldn't precisely account for that impulse, but general propitiation was at the bottom of it.

Miss Mapp meantime had sat down on her bed, and firmly rejected the idea that his call had anything to do with marriage. During all these years of friendliness he had not got so far as that, and, whatever the future might hold, it was not likely that he would begin now at this moment when she was so properly punishing him for his unchivalrous behaviour. But what could the frock coat mean? (There was Captain Puffin's servant picking up the sponge. She hoped it was covered with mud.) It would be a very just continuation of his punishment to tell Withers she would not see him, but the punishment which that would entail on herself would be more than she could bear, for she would not know a moment's peace while she was ignorant of the nature of his errand. Could he be on his way to the Padre's to challenge him for that very stinging allusion to sand dunes yesterday, and was he come to give her fair warning, so that she might stop a duel? It did not seem likely. Unable to bear the suspense any longer, she adjusted her face in the glass to an expression of frozen dignity and threw over her shoulders the cloak trimmed with blue in which, on the occasion of the Prince's visit, she had sat down in the middle of the road. That matched the Major's frock coat.

She hummed a little song as she mounted the few steps to the garden room, and stopped just after she had opened the door. She did not offer to shake hands.

'You wish to see me, Major Flint?' she said, in such a voice as icebergs might be supposed to use when passing each other by night in the Arctic seas.

Major Flint certainly looked as if he hated seeing her, instead of wishing it, for he backed into a corner of the room and dropped his hat.

'Good morning, Miss Mapp,' he said. 'Very good of you. I – I called.'

He clearly had a difficulty in saying what he had come to say, but if he thought that she was proposing to give him the smallest assistance, he was in error.

'Yes, you called,' said she. 'Pray be seated.'

He did so; she stood; he got up again.

'I called,' said the Major, 'I called to express my very deep regret at my share, or, rather, that I did not take a more active share – I allowed, in fact, a friend of mine to speak to you in a manner that did equal discredit – '

Miss Mapp put her head on one side, as if trying to recollect some trivial and unimportant occurrence.

'Yes?' she said. 'What was that?'

'Captain Puffin,' began the Major.

Then Miss Mapp remembered it all.

'I hope, Major Flint,' she said, 'that you will not find it necessary to mention Captain Puffin's name to me. I wish him nothing but well, but he and his are ho concern of mine. I have the charity to suppose that he was quite drunk on the occasion to which I imagine you allude. Intoxication alone could excuse what he said. Let us leave Captain Puffin out of whatever you have come to say to me.'

This was adroit; it compelled the Major to begin all over again.

'I come entirely on my own account,' he began.

'I understand,' said Miss Mapp, instantly bringing Captain Puffin in again. 'Captain Puffin, now I presume sober, has no regret for what he said when drunk. I quite see, and I expected no more and no less from him. Yes, I am afraid I interrupted you.'

Major Flint threw his friend overboard like ballast from a bumping balloon.

'I speak for myself,' he said. 'I behaved, Miss Mapp, like a – ha – worm. Defenceless lady, insolent fellow drunk – I allude to Captain P—. I'm very sorry for my part in it.'

Up till this moment Miss Mapp had not made up her mind whether she intended to forgive him or not; but here she saw how crushing a penalty she might be able to inflict on Puffin if she forgave the erring and possibly truly repentant Major. He had already spoken strongly about his friend's offence, and she could render life supremely nasty for them both – particularly Puffin – if she made the Major agree that he could not, if truly sorry, hold further intercourse with him. There would be no more golf, no more diaries. Besides, if she was observed to be friendly with the Major again and to cut Captain Puffin, a very natural interpretation would be that she had learned that in the original quarrel the Major had been defending her from some odious tongue to the extent of a challenge, even though he subsequently ran away. Tilling was quite clever enough to make that inference without any suggestion from her . . . But if she forgave neither of them, they would probably go on boozing and golfing together, and saying quite dreadful things about her, and not care very much whether she forgave them or not. Her mind was made up, and she gave a wan smile.

'Oh, Major Flint,' she said, 'it hurt me so dreadfully that you should have stood by and heard that man – if he is a man – say those awful things to me and not take my side. It made me feel so lonely. I had always been such good friends with you, and then you turned your back on me like that. I didn't know what I had done to deserve it. I lay awake ever so long.'

This was affecting, and he violently rubbed the nap of his hat the wrong way . . . Then Miss Mapp broke into her sunniest smile.

'Oh, I'm so glad you came to say you were sorry!' she said. 'Dear Major Benjy, we're quite friends again.'

She dabbed her handkerchief on her eyes.

'So foolish of me!' she said. 'Now sit down in my most comfortable chair and have a cigarette.'

Major Flint made a peck at the hand she extended to him, and cleared his throat to indicate emotion. It really was a great relief to think that she would not make awful allusions to duels in the middle of bridge parties.

'And since you feel as you do about Captain Puffin,' she said, 'of course, you won't see anything more of him. You and I are quite one, aren't we, about that? You have dissociated yourself from him completely. The fact of your being sorry does that.'

It was quite clear to the Major that this condition was involved in his forgiveness, though that fact, so obvious to Miss Mapp, had not occurred to him before. Still, he had to accept it, or go unhoused again. He could explain to Puffin, under cover of night, or perhaps in deaf-and-dumb alphabet from his window . . .

'Infamous, unforgivable behaviour!' he said. 'Pah!'

'So glad you feel that,' said Miss Mapp, smiling till he saw the entire row of her fine teeth. 'And oh, may I say one little thing more? I feel this: I feel that the dreadful shock to me of being insulted like that was quite a lovely little blessing in disguise, now that the effect has been to put an end to your intimacy with him. I never liked it, and I liked it less than ever the other night. He's not a fit friend for you. Oh, I'm so thankful!'

Major Flint saw that for the present he was irrevocably committed to this clause in the treaty of peace. He could not face seeing it torn up again, as it certainly would be, if he failed to accept it in its entirety, nor could he imagine himself leaving the room with a renewal of hostilities. He would lose his game of golf today as it was, for apart from the fact that he would scarcely have time to change his clothes (the idea of playing golf in a frock coat and top hat was inconceivable) and catch the 11.20 tram, he could not be seen in Puffin's company at all. And, indeed, in the future, unless Puffin could be induced to apologize and Miss Mapp to forgive, he saw, if he was to play golf at all with his friend, that endless deceptions and subterfuges were necessary in order to escape detection. One of them would have to set out ten minutes before the other, and walk to the tram by some unusual and circuitous route; they would have to play in a clandestine and furtive manner, parting company before they got to the clubhouse; disguises might be needful; there was a peck of difficulties ahead. But he would have to go into these later; at present he must be immersed in the rapture of his forgiveness.

'Most generous of you, Miss Elizabeth,' he said. 'As for that – well, I won't allude to him again.'

Miss Mapp gave a happy little laugh, and having made a further plan, switched away from the subject of captains and insults with alacrity.

'Look!' she said. 'I found these little rosebuds in flower still, though it is the end of November. Such brave little darlings, aren't they? One for your buttonhole, Major Benjy? And then I must do my little shoppings or Withers will scold me – Withers is so severe with me, keeps me in such order! If you are going into the town, will you take me with you? I will put on my hat.'

Requests for the present were certainly commands, and two minutes later they set forth. Luck, as usual, befriended ability, for there was Puffin at his door, itching for the Major's return (else they would miss the tram); and lo! there came stepping along Miss Mapp in her blue-trimmed cloak, and the Major attired as for marriage – top hat, frock coat and buttonhole. She did not look at Puffin and cut him; she did not seem (with the deceptiveness of appearances) to see him at all, so eager and agreeable was her conversation with her companion. The Major, so Puffin thought, attempted to give him some sort of dazed and hunted glance; but he could not be certain even of that, so swiftly had it to be transformed into a genial interest in what Miss Mapp was saying, and Puffin stared open-mouthed after them, for they were terrible as an army with banners. Then Diva, trundling swiftly out of the fish shop, came, as well she might, to a dead halt, observing this absolutely inexplicable phenomenon.

'Good morning, Diva darling,' said Miss Mapp. 'Major Benjy and I are doing our little shopping together. So kind of him, isn't it? and very naughty of me to take up his time. I told him he ought to be playing golf. Such a lovely day! *Au reservoir,* sweet! Oh, and there's the Padre, Major Benjy! How quickly he walks! Yes, he sees us! And there's Mrs Poppit; everybody is enjoying the sunshine. What a beautiful fur coat, though I should think she found it very heavy and warm. Good morning, dear Susan! You shopping, too, like Major Benjy and me? How is your dear Isabel?'

Miss Mapp made the most of that morning; the magnanimity of her forgiveness earned her incredible dividends. Up and down the High Street she went, with Major Benjy in attendance, buying grocery, stationery, gloves, eau-de-Cologne, bootlaces, the 'Literary Supplement' of *The Times*, dried camomile flowers, and every conceivable thing that she might possibly need in the next week, so that her shopping might be as protracted as possible. She allowed him (such was her firmness in 'spoiling' him) to carry her shopping basket, and when that was full, she decked him like a sacrificial ram with little parcels hung by loops of string. Sometimes she took him into a shop in case there might be someone there who had not seen him yet on her leash; sometimes she left him on the pavement in a prominent position, marking, all the time, just as if she had been a clinical thermometer, the feverish curiosity that was burning in Tilling's veins. Only yesterday she had spread the news of his cowardice broadcast; today their comradeship was of the chattiest and most genial kind. There he was, carrying her basket, and wearing frock coat and top hat and hung with parcels like a Christmas tree, spending the entire morning with her instead of golfing with Puffin. Miss Mapp positively shuddered as she tried to realize what her state of mind would have been, if she had seen him thus coupled with Diva. She would have suspected (rightly in all probability) some loathsome intrigue against herself. And the cream of it was that until she chose, nobody could possibly find out what had caused this metamorphosis so paralysing to enquiring intellects, for Major Benjy would assuredly never tell anyone that there was a reconciliation, due to his apology for his rudeness, when he had stood by and permitted an intoxicated Puffin to suggest disgraceful bargains. Tilling – poor Tilling – would go crazy with suspense as to what it all meant.

Never had there been such a shopping! It was nearly lunchtime when, at her front door, Major Flint finally stripped himself of her parcels and her companionship and hobbled home, profusely perspiring, and lame from so much walking on pavements in tight patent-leather shoes. He was weary and footsore; he had had no golf, and, though forgiven, was but a wreck. She had made him ridiculous all the morning with his frock coat and top hat and his porterages, and if forgiveness entailed any more of these nightmare sacraments of friendliness, he felt that he would be unable to endure the fatiguing accessories of the regenerate state. He hung up his top hat and wiped his wet and throbbing head; he kicked off his shoes and shed his frock coat, and furiously *quai-hai*ed for a whisky and soda and lunch.

His physical restoration was accompanied by a quickening of dismay at the general prospect. What (to put it succinctly) was life worth, even when unharassed by allusions to duels, without the solace of golf, quarrels and diaries in the companionship of Puffin? He hated Puffin – no one more so – but he could not possibly get on without him, and it was entirely due to Puffin that he had spent so outrageous a morning, for Puffin, seeking to silence Miss Mapp by his intoxicated bargain, had been the prime cause of all this misery. He could not even, for fear of that all-seeing eye in Miss Mapp's garden room, go across to the house of the unforgiven sea captain, and by a judicious recital of his woes induce him to beg Miss Mapp's forgiveness instantly. He would have to wait till the kindly darkness fell . . . 'Mere slavery!' he exclaimed with passion.

A tap at his sitting-room door interrupted the chain of these melancholy reflections, and his permission to enter was responded to by Puffin himself. The Major bounced from his seat.

'You mustn't stop here,' he said in a low voice, as if afraid that he might be overheard. 'Miss Mapp may have seen you come in.'

Puffin laughed shrilly.

'Why, of course she did,' he gaily assented. 'She was at her window all right. Ancient lights, I shall call her. What's this all about now?'

'You must go back,' said Major Flint agitatedly. 'She must see you go back. I can't explain now. But I'll come across after dinner when it's dark. Go; don't wait.'

He positively hustled the mystified Puffin out of the house, and Miss Mapp's face, which had grown sharp and pointed with doubts and suspicions when she observed him enter Major Benjy's house, dimpled, as she saw him return, into her sunniest smiles. 'Dear Major Benjy,' she said, 'he has refused to see him,' and she cut the string of the large cardboard box which had just arrived from the dyer's with the most pleasurable anticipations . . .

Well, it was certainly very magnificent, and Miss Greele was quite right, for there was not the faintest tinge to show that it had originally been kingfisher blue. She had not quite realized how brilliant crimson-lake was in the piece; it seemed almost to cast a ruddy glow on the very ceiling, and the fact that she had caused the orange chiffon with which the neck and sleeves were trimmed to be dyed black (following the exquisite taste of Mrs Titus Trout) only threw the splendour of the rest into more dazzling radiance. Kingfisher blue would appear quite ghostly and corpse-like in its neighbourhood; and painful though that would be for Diva, it would, as all her well-wishers must hope, be a lesson to her not to indulge in such garishness. She should be taught her lesson (D.V.), thought Miss Mapp, at Susan's bridge party tomorrow evening. Captain Puffin was being taught a lesson, too, for we are never too old to learn, or, for that matter, to teach.

Though the night was dark and moonless, there was an inconveniently brilliant gas lamp close to the Major's door, and that strategist, carrying his round roll of diaries, much the shape of a bottle, under his coat, went about half-past nine that evening to look at the rain-gutter which had been weeping into his yard, and let himself out of the back door round the corner. From there he went down past the fishmonger's, crossed the road, and doubled back again up Puffin's side of the street, which was not so vividly illuminated, though he took the precaution of making himself little with bent knees, and of limping. Puffin was already warming himself over the fire and imbibing Roman roads, and was disposed to be hilarious over the Major's shopping.

'But why top hat and frock coat, Major?' he asked. 'Another visit of the Prince of Wales, I asked myself, or the Voice that breathed o'er Eden? Have a drink – one of mine, I mean? I owe you a drink for the good laugh you gave me.'

Had it not been for this generosity and the need of getting on the right side of Puffin, Major Flint would certainly have resented such clumsy levity, but this double consideration caused him to take it with unwonted good humour. His attempt to laugh, indeed, sounded a little hollow, but that is the habit of self-directed merriment.

'Well, I allow it must have seemed amusing,' he said. 'The fact was that I thought she would appreciate my putting a little ceremony into my errand of apology, and then she whisked me off shopping before I could go and change.'

'Kiss and friends again, then?' asked Puffin.

The Major grew a little stately over this.

'No such familiarity passed,' he said. 'But she accepted my regrets with – ha – the most gracious generosity. A fine-spirited woman, sir; you'll find the same.'

'I might if I looked for it,' said Puffin. 'But why should I want to make it up? You've done that, and that prevents her talking about duelling and early trains. She can't mock at me because of you. You might pass me back my bottle, if you've taken your drink.'

The Major reluctantly did so.

'You must please yourself, old boy,' he said. 'It's your business, and no one's ever said that Benjy Flint interfered in another man's affairs. But I trust you will do what good feeling indicates. I hope you value our jolly games of golf and our pleasant evenings sufficiently highly.'

'Eh! how's that?' asked Puffin. 'You going to cut me too?'

The Major sat down and put his large feet on the fender. 'Tact and diplomacy, Benjy, my boy,' he reminded himself.

'Ha! That's what I like,' he said, 'a good fire and a friend, and the rest of the world may go hang. There's no question of cutting, old man; I needn't tell you that – but we must have one of our good talks. For instance, I very unceremoniously turned you out of my house this afternoon, and I owe you an explanation of that. I'll give it you in one word: Miss Mapp saw you come in. She didn't see me come in here this evening – ha! ha! – and that's why I can sit at my ease. But if she knew – '

Puffin guessed.

'What has happened, Major, is that you've thrown me over for Miss Mapp,' he observed.

'No, sir, I have not,' said the Major with emphasis. 'Should I be sitting here and drinking your whisky if I had? But this morning, after that lady had accepted my regret for my share in what occurred the other night, she assumed that since I condemned my own conduct unreservedly, I must equally condemn yours. It really was like a conjuring trick; the thing was done before I knew anything about it. And before I'd had time to say, "Hold on a bit," I was being led up and down the High Street, carrying as much merchandise as a drove of camels. God, sir, I suffered this morning; you don't seem to realize that I suffered; I couldn't stand any more mornings like that: I haven't the stamina.'

'A powerful woman,' said Puffin reflectively.

'You may well say that,' observed Major Flint. 'That is finely said. A powerful woman she is, with a powerful tongue, and able to be powerful nasty, and if she sees you and me on friendly terms again, she'll turn the full hose on to us both unless you make it up with her.'

'H'm, yes. But as likely as not she'll tell me and my apologies to go hang.'

'Have a try, old man,' said the Major encouragingly.

Puffin looked at his whisky bottle.

'Help yourself, Major,' he said. 'I think you'll have to help me out, you know. Go and interview her: see if there's a chance of my favourable reception.'

'No, sir,' said the Major firmly, 'I will not run the risk of another morning's shopping in the High Street.'

'You needn't. Watch till she comes back from her shopping tomorrow.'

Major Benjy clearly did not like the prospect at all, but Puffin grew firmer and firmer in his absolute refusal to lay himself open to rebuff, and presently, they came to an agreement that the Major was to go on his ambassadorial errand next morning. That being settled, the still undecided point about the worm cast gave rise to a good deal of heat, until, it being discovered that the window was open, and that their voices might easily carry as far as the garden room, they made malignant rejoinders to each other in whispers. But it was impossible to go on quarrelling for long in so confidential a manner, and the disagreement was deferred to a more convenient occasion. It was late when the Major left, and after putting out the light in Puffin's hall, so that he should not be silhouetted against it, he slid into the darkness, and reached his own door by a subtle detour.

Miss Mapp had a good deal of division of her swift mind, when, next morning, she learned the nature of Major Benjy's second errand. If she, like Mr Wyse, was to encourage Puffin to hope that she would accept his apologies, she would be obliged to remit all further punishment of him, and allow him to consort with his friend again. It was difficult to forgo the pleasure of his chastisement, but, on the other hand, it was just possible that the Major might break away, and, whether she liked it or not (and she would not), refuse permanently to give up Puffin's society. That would be awkward since she had publicly paraded her reconciliation with him. What further inclined her to clemency, was that this very evening the crimson-lake tea gown would shed its effulgence over Mrs Poppit's bridge party, and Diva would never want to hear the word 'kingfisher' again. That was enough to put anybody in a good temper. So the diplomatist returned to the miscreant with the glad tidings that Miss Mapp would hear his supplication with a favourable ear, and she took up a stately position in the garden room, which she selected as audience chamber, near the bell so that she could ring for Withers if necessary.

*　　*　　*

Miss Mapp's mercy was largely tempered with justice, and she proposed, in spite of the leniency which she would eventually exhibit, to give Puffin 'what for', first. She had not for him, as for Major Benjy, that feminine weakness which had made it a positive luxury to forgive him: she never even thought of Puffin as Captain Dicky, far less let the pretty endearment slip off her tongue accidentally, and the luxury which she anticipated from the interview was that of administering a quantity of hard slaps. She had appointed half-past twelve as the hour for his suffering, so that he must go without his golf again.

She put down the book she was reading when he appeared, and gazed at him stonily without speech. He limped into the middle of the room. This might be forgiveness, but it did not look like it, and he wondered whether she had got him here on false pretences.

'Good morning,' said he.

Miss Mapp inclined her head. Silence was gold.

'I understood from Major Flint – ' began Puffin.

Speech could be gold too.

'If,' said Miss Mapp, 'you have come to speak about Major Flint you have wasted your time. And mine!'

(How different from Major Benjy, she thought. What a shrimp!)

The shrimp gave a slight gasp. The thing had got to be done, and the sooner he was out of range of this powerful woman the better.

'I am extremely sorry for what I said to you the other night,' he said.

'I am glad you are sorry,' said Miss Mapp.

'I offer you my apologies for what I said,' continued Puffin.

The whip whistled.

'When you spoke to me on the occasion to which you refer,' said Miss Mapp, 'I saw of course at once that you were not in a condition to speak to anybody. I instantly did you that justice, for I am just to everybody. I paid no more attention to what you said than I should have paid to any tipsy vagabond in the slums. I dare say you hardly remember what you said, so that before I hear your expression of regret, I will remind you of it. You threatened, unless I promised to tell nobody in what a disgusting condition you were, to say that I was tipsy. Elizabeth Mapp tipsy! That was what you said, Captain Puffin.'

Captain Puffin turned extremely red. ('Now the shrimp's being boiled,' thought Miss Mapp.)

'I can't do more than apologize,' said he. He did not know whether he was angrier with his ambassador or her.

'Did you say you couldn't do "more"?' said Miss Mapp with an air of great interest. 'How curious! I should have thought you couldn't have done less.'

'Well, what more can I do?' asked he.

'If you think,' said Miss Mapp, 'that you hurt me by your conduct that night, you are vastly mistaken. And if you think you can do no more than apologize, I will teach you better. You can make an effort, Captain Puffin, to break with your deplorable habits, to try to get back a little of the self-respect, if you ever had any, which you have lost. You can cease trying, oh, so unsuccessfully, to drag Major Benjy down to your level. That's what you can do.'

She let these withering observations blight him.

'I accept your apologies,' she said. 'I hope you will do better in the future, Captain Puffin, and I shall look anxiously for signs of improvement. We will meet with politeness and friendliness when we are brought together and I will do my best to wipe all remembrance of your tipsy impertinence from my mind. And you must do your best too. You are not young, and engrained habits are difficult to get rid of. But do not despair, Captain Puffin. And now I will ring for Withers and she will show you out.'

She rang the bell, and gave a sample of her generous oblivion.

'And we meet, do we not, this evening at Mrs Poppit's?' she said, looking not at him, but about a foot above his head. 'Such pleasant evenings one always has there, I hope it will not be a wet evening, but the glass is sadly down. Oh, Withers, Captain Puffin is going. Good morning, Captain Puffin. Such a pleasure!'

Miss Mapp hummed a rollicking little tune as she observed him totter down the street.

'There!' she said, and had a glass of Burgundy for lunch as a treat.

CHAPTER TEN

The news that Mr Wyse was to be of the party that evening at Mrs Poppit's and was to dine there first, *en famille* (as he casually let slip in order to air his French), created a disagreeable impression that afternoon in Tilling. It was not usual to do anything more than 'have a tray' for your evening meal, if one of these winter bridge parties followed, and there was, to Miss Mapp's mind, a deplorable tendency to ostentation in this dinner-giving before a party. Still, if Susan was determined to be extravagant, she might have asked Miss Mapp as well, who resented this want of hospitality. She did not like, either, this hole-and-corner *en famille* work with Mr Wyse; it indicated a pushing familiarity to which, it was hoped, Mr Wyse's eyes were open.

There was another point: the party, it had been ascertained, would in all number ten, and if, as was certain, there would be two bridge tables, that seemed to imply that two people would have to cut out. There were often nine at Mrs Poppit's bridge parties (she appeared to be unable to count), but on those occasions Isabel was generally told by her mother that she did not care for bridge, and so there was no cutting out, but only a pleasant book for Isabel. But what would be done with ten? It was idle to hope that Susan would sit out: as hostess she always considered it part of her duties to play solidly the entire evening. Still, if the cutting of cards malignantly ordained that Miss Mapp was ejected, it was only reasonable to expect that after her magnanimity to the United Services, either Major Benjy or Captain Puffin would be so obdurate in his insistence that she must play instead of him, that it would be only ladylike to yield.

She did not, therefore, allow this possibility to dim the pleasure she anticipated from the discomfiture of darling Diva, who would be certain to appear in the kingfisher-blue tea gown, and find herself ghastly and outshone by the crimson lake which was the colour of Mrs Trout's second toilet, and Miss Mapp, after prolonged thought as to her most dramatic moment of entrance in the crimson lake, determined to arrive when she might expect the rest of the guests to have already assembled. She would risk, it is true, being out of a rubber for a little, since bridge might have already begun, but play would have to stop for a minute of greetings when she came in, and she would beg everybody not to stir, and would seat herself quite, quite close to Diva, and openly admire her pretty frock, 'like one I used to have . . . !'

It was, therefore, not much lacking of ten o'clock when, after she had waited a considerable time on Mrs Poppit's threshold, Boon sulkily allowed her to enter, but gave no answer to her timid enquiry of: 'Am I very late, Boon?' The drawing-room door was a little ajar, and as she took off the cloak that masked the splendour of the crimson lake, her acute ears heard the murmur of talk going on, which indicated that bridge had not yet begun, while her acute nostrils detected the faint but certain smell of roast grouse, which showed what Susan had given Mr Wyse for dinner, probably telling him that the birds were a present to her from the shooting lodge where she had stayed in the summer. Then, after she had thrown herself a glance in the mirror, and put on her smile, Boon preceded her, slightly shrugging his shoulders, to the drawing-room door, which he pushed open, and grunted loudly, which was his manner of announcing a guest. Miss Mapp went tripping in, almost at a run, to indicate how vexed she was with herself for being late, and there, just in front of her, stood Diva, dressed not in kingfisher blue at all, but in the crimson lake of Mrs Trout's second toilet. Perfidious Diva had had her dress dyed too . . .

Miss Mapp's courage rose to the occasion. Other people, majors and tipsy captains, might be cowards, but not she. Twice now (omitting the matter of the Wars of the Roses) had Diva by some cunning, which it was impossible not to suspect of a diabolical origin, clad her odious little roundabout form in splendours identical with Miss Mapp's, but now, without faltering even when she heard Evie's loud squeak, she turned to her hostess, who wore the Order of MBE on her ample breast, and made her salutations in a perfectly calm voice.

'Dear Susan, don't scold me for being so late,' she said, 'though I know I deserve it. So sweet of you! Isabel darling and dear Evie! Oh, and Mr Wyse! Sweet Irene! Major Benjy and Captain Puffin! Had a nice game of golf? And the Padre! . . .'

She hesitated a moment wondering, if she could, without screaming or scratching, seem aware of Diva's presence. Then she soared, lambent as flame.

'Diva darling!' she said, and bent and kissed her, even as St Stephen in the moment of martyrdom prayed for those who stoned him. Flesh and blood could not manage more, and she turned to Mr Wyse, remembering that Diva had told her that the Contessa Faradiddleony's arrival was postponed.

'And your dear sister has put off her journey, I understand,' she said. 'Such a disappointment! Shall we see her at Tilling at all, do you think?'

Mr Wyse looked surprised.

'Dear lady,' he said, 'you're the second person who has said that to me. Mrs Plaistow asked me just now – '

'Yes; it was she who told me,' said Miss Mapp in case there was a mistake. 'Isn't it true?'

'Certainly not. I told my housekeeper that the Contessa's maid was ill, and would follow her, but that's the only foundation I know of for this rumour. Amelia encourages me to hope that she will be here early next week.'

'Oh, no doubt that's it!' said Miss Mapp in an aside so that Diva could hear. 'Darling Diva's always getting hold of the most erroneous information. She must have been listening to servants' gossip. So glad she's wrong about it.'

Mr Wyse made one of his stately inclinations of the head.

'Amelia will regret very much not being here tonight,' he said, 'for I see all the great bridge players are present.'

'Oh, Mr Wyse!' said she. 'We shall all be humble learners compared with the Contessa, I expect.'

'Not at all!' said Mr Wyse. 'But what a delightful idea of yours and Mrs Plaistow's to dress alike in such lovely gowns. Quite like sisters.'

Miss Mapp could not trust herself to speak on this subject, and showed all her teeth, not snarling but amazingly smiling. She had no occasion to reply, however, for Captain Puffin joined them, eagerly deferential.

'What a charming surprise you and Mrs Plaistow have given us, Miss Mapp,' he said, 'in appearing again in the same beautiful dresses. Quite like – '

Miss Mapp could not bear to hear what she and Diva were like, and wheeled about, passionately regretting that she had forgiven Puffin. This manoeuvre brought her face to face with the Major.

'Upon my word, Miss Elizabeth,' he said, 'you look magnificent tonight.'

He saw the light of fury in her eyes, and guessed, mere man as he was, what it was about. He bent to her and spoke low.

'But, by Jove!' he said with supreme diplomacy, 'somebody ought to tell our good Mrs Plaistow that some women can wear a wonderful gown and others – ha!'

'Dear Major Benjy,' said she. 'Cruel of you to poor Diva.'

But instantly her happiness was clouded again, for the Padre had a very ill-inspired notion.

'What ho! fair Madam Plaistow,' he humorously observed to Miss Mapp. 'Ah! *Peccavi!* I am in error. It is Mistress Mapp. But let us to the cards! Our hostess craves thy presence at yon table.'

Contrary to custom Mrs Poppit did not sit firmly down at a table, nor was Isabel told that she had an invincible objection to playing bridge. Instead she bade everybody else take their seats, and said that she and Mr Wyse had settled at dinner that they much preferred looking on and learning to playing. With a view to enjoying this incredible treat as fully as possible, they at once seated themselves on a low sofa at the far end of the room where they could not look or learn at all, and engaged in conversation. Diva and Elizabeth, as might have been expected from the malignant influence which watched over their attire, cut in at the same table and were partners, so that they had, in spite of the deadly antagonism of identical tea gowns, a financial interest in common, while a further bond between them was the eagerness with which they strained their ears to overhear anything that their hostess and Mr Wyse were saying to each other.

Miss Mapp and Diva alike were perhaps busier when they were being dummy than when they were playing the cards. Over the background of each mind was spread a hatred of the other, red as their tea gowns, and shot with black despair as to what on earth they should do now with those ill-fated pieces of pride. Miss Mapp was prepared to make a perfect chameleon of hers, if only she could get away from Diva's hue, but what if, having changed, say, to purple, Diva became purple too? She could not stand a third coincidence, and besides, she much doubted whether any gown that had once been of so pronounced a crimson lake, could successfully attempt to appear of any other hue except perhaps black. If Diva died, she might perhaps consult Miss Greele as to whether black would be possible, but then if Diva died, there was no reason for not wearing crimson lake for ever, since it would be an insincerity of which Miss Mapp humbly hoped she was incapable, to go into mourning for Diva just because she died.

In front of this lurid background of despair moved the figures which would have commanded all her attention, have aroused all the feelings of disgust and pity of which she was capable, had only Diva stuck to kingfisher blue. There they sat on the sofa, talking in voices which it was impossible to overhear, and if ever a woman made up to a man, and if ever a man was taken in by shallow artifices, 'they', thought Miss Mapp, 'are the ones'. There was no longer any question that Susan was doing her utmost to inveigle Mr Wyse into matrimony, for no other motive, not politeness, not the charm of conversation, not the low, comfortable seat by the fire could possibly have had force enough to keep her for a whole evening from the bridge table. That dinner *en famille*, so Miss Mapp sarcastically reflected – what if it was the first of hundreds of similar dinners *en famille*? Perhaps, when safely married, Susan would ask her to one of the family dinners, with a glassful of foam which she called champagne, and the leg of a crow which she called game from the shooting lodge . . . There was no use in denying that Mr Wyse seemed to be swallowing flattery and any other form of bait as fast as they were supplied him; never had he been so made up to since the day, now two years ago, when Miss Mapp herself wrote him down as uncapturable. But now, on this awful evening of crimson lake, it seemed only prudent to face the prospect of his falling into the nets which were spread for him . . . Susan the sister-in-law of a Contessa. Susan the wife of the man whose urbanity made all Tilling polite to each other, Susan a Wyse of Whitchurch! It made Miss Mapp feel positively weary of earth . . .

Nor was this the sum of Miss Mapp's mental activities, as she sat being dummy to Diva, for, in addition to the rage, despair and disgust with which these various topics filled her, she had narrowly to watch Diva's play, in order, at the end, to point out to her with lucid firmness all the mistakes she had made, while with snorts and sniffs and muttered exclamations and jerks of the head and pullings-out of cards and puttings of them back with amazing assertions that she had not quitted them, she wrestled with the task she had set herself of getting two no-trumps. It was impossible to count the tricks that Diva made, for she had a habit of putting her elbow on them after she had raked them in, as if in fear that her adversaries would filch them when she was not looking, and Miss Mapp, distracted with other interests, forgot that no-trumps had been declared and thought it was hearts, of which Diva played several after their adversaries' hands were quite denuded of them. She often did that 'to make sure'.

'Three tricks,' she said triumphantly at the conclusion, counting the cards in the cache below her elbow.

Miss Mapp gave a long sigh, but remembered that Mr Wyse was present.

'You could have got two more,' she said, 'if you hadn't played those hearts, dear. You would have been able to trump Major Benjy's club and the Padre's diamond, and we should have gone out. Never mind, you played it beautifully otherwise.'

'Can't trump when it's no-trumps,' said Diva, forgetting that Mr Wyse was there. 'That's nonsense. Got three tricks. Did go out. Did you think it was hearts? Wasn't.'

Miss Mapp naturally could not demean herself to take any notice of this.

'Your deal, is it, Major Benjy?' she asked. 'Me to cut?'

Diva had remembered just after her sharp speech to her partner that Mr Wyse was present, and looked towards the sofa to see if there were any indications of pained surprise on his face which might indicate that he had heard. But what she saw there

– or, to be more accurate, what she failed to see there – forced her to give an exclamation which caused Miss Mapp to look round in the direction where Diva's bulging eyes were glued . . . There was no doubt whatever about it: Mrs Poppit and Mr Wyse were no longer there. Unless they were under the sofa they had certainly left the room together and altogether. Had she gone to put on her sable coat on this hot night? Was Mr Wyse staggering under its weight as he fitted her into it? Miss Mapp rejected the supposition; they had gone to another room to converse more privately. This looked very black indeed, and she noted the time on the clock in order to ascertain, when they came back, how long they had been absent.

The rubber went on its wild way, relieved from the restraining influence of Mr Wyse, and when, thirty-nine minutes afterwards, it came to its conclusion and neither the hostess nor Mr Wyse had returned, Miss Mapp was content to let Diva muddle herself madly, adding up the score with the assistance of her fingers, and went across to the other table till she should be called back to check her partner's figures. They would be certain to need checking.

'Has Mr Wyse gone away already, dear Isabel?' she said. 'How early!'

('And four makes nine,' muttered Diva, getting to her little finger.)

Isabel was dummy, and had time for conversation.

'I think he has only gone with Mamma into the conservatory,' she said – 'no more diamonds, partner? – to advise her about the orchids.'

Now the conservatory was what Miss Mapp considered a potting shed with a glass roof, and the orchids were one anaemic odonto-glossum, and there would scarcely be room besides that for Mrs Poppit and Mr Wyse. The potting shed was visible from the drawing-room window, over which curtains were drawn.

'Such a lovely night,' said Miss Mapp. 'And while Diva is checking the score may I have a peep at the stars, dear? So fond of the sweet stars.'

She glided to the window (conscious that Diva was longing to glide too, but was preparing to quarrel with the Major's score) and took her peep at the sweet stars. The light from the hall shone full into the potting shed, but there was nobody there. She made quite sure of that.

Diva had heard about the sweet stars, and for the first time in her life made no objection to her adversaries' total.

'You're right, Major Flint, eighteen-pence,' she said. 'Stupid of me: I've left my handkerchief in the pocket of my cloak. I'll pop out and get it. Back in a minute. Cut again for partners.'

She trundled to the door and popped out of it before Miss Mapp had the slightest chance of intercepting her progress. This was bitter, because the dining room opened out of the hall, and so did the book cupboard with a window which dear Susan called her boudoir. Diva was quite capable of popping into both of these apartments. In fact, if the truants were there, it was no use bothering about the sweet stars any more, and Diva would already have won . . .

There was a sweet moon as well, and just as baffled Miss Mapp was turning away from the window, she saw that which made her positively glue her nose to the cold window-pane, and tuck the curtain in, so that her silhouette should not be visible from outside. Down the middle of the garden path came the two truants, Susan in her sables and Mr Wyse close beside her with his coat collar turned up. Her ample form with the small round head on the top looked like a short-funnelled locomotive engine, and he like the driver on the footplate. The perfidious things had said they were going to consult over the orchid. Did orchids grow on the lawn? It was news to Miss Mapp if they did.

They stopped, and Mr Wyse quite clearly pointed to some celestial object, moon or star, and they both gazed at it. The sight of two such middle-aged people behaving like this made Miss Mapp feel quite sick, but she heroically continued a moment more at her post. Her heroism was rewarded, for immediately after the inspection of the celestial object, they turned and inspected each other. And Mr Wyse kissed her.

Miss Mapp 'scriggled' from behind the curtain into the room again.

'Aldebaran!' she said. 'So lovely!'

Simultaneously Diva re-entered with her handkerchief, thwarted and disappointed, for she had certainly found nobody either in the boudoir or in the dining room. But there was going to be a sit-down supper, and as Boon was not there, she had taken a *marron glacé.*

Miss Mapp was flushed with excitement and disgust, and almost forgot about Diva's gown.

'Found your hanky, dear?' she said. 'Then shall we cut for partners again? You and me, Major Benjy. Don't scold me if I play wrong.'

She managed to get a seat that commanded a full-face view of the door, for the next thing was to see how 'the young couple' (as she had already labelled them in her sarcastic mind) 'looked' when they returned from their amorous excursion to the orchid that grew on the lawn. They entered, most unfortunately, while she was in the middle of playing a complicated hand, and her brain was so switched off from the play by their entrance that she completely lost the thread of what she was doing, and threw away two tricks that simply required to be gathered up by her, but now lurked below Diva's elbow. What made it worse was that no trace of emotion, no heightened colour, no coy and downcast eye betrayed a hint of what had happened on the lawn. With brazen effrontery Susan informed her daughter that Mr Wyse thought a little leaf-mould . . .

'What a liar!' thought Miss Mapp, and triumphantly put her remaining trump on to her dummy's best card. Then she prepared to make the best of it.

'We've lost three, I'm afraid, Major Benjy,' she said. 'Don't you think you overbid your hand just a little wee bit?'

'I don't know about that, Miss Elizabeth,' said the Major. 'If you hadn't let those two spades go, and hadn't trumped my best heart – '

Miss Mapp interrupted with her famous patter.

'Oh, but if I had taken the spades,' she said quickly, 'I should have had to lead up to Diva's clubs, and then they would have got the rough in diamonds, and I should have never been able to get back into your hand again. Then at the end if I hadn't trumped your heart, I should have had to lead the losing spade and Diva would have over-trumped; and brought in her club, and we should have gone down two more. If you follow me, I think you'll agree that I was right to do that. But all good players overbid their hands sometimes, Major Benjy. Such fun!'

The supper was unusually ostentatious, but Miss Mapp saw the reason for that; it was clear that Susan wanted to impress poor Mr Wyse with her wealth, and probably when it came to settlements, he would learn some very unpleasant news. But there were agreeable little circumstances to temper her dislike of this extravagant display, for she was hungry, and Diva, always a gross feeder, spilt some hot chocolate sauce on the crimson lake, which, if indelible, might supply a solution to the problem of what was to be done now about her own frock. She kept an eye, too, on Captain Puffin, to see if he showed any signs of improvement in the direction she had indicated to him in her interview, and was rejoiced to see that one of these glances was clearly the cause of his refusing a second glass of port. He had already taken the stopper out of the decanter when their eyes met . . . and then he put it back again. Improvement already!

Everything else (pending the discovery as to whether chocolate on crimson lake spelt ruin) now faded into a middle distance, while the affairs of Susan and poor Mr Wyse occupied the entire foreground of Miss Mapp's consciousness. Mean and cunning as Susan's conduct must have been in entrapping Mr Wyse when others had failed to gain his affection, Miss Mapp felt that it would be only prudent to continue on the most amicable of terms with her, for as future sister-in-law to a countess, and wife to the man who by the mere exercise of his presence could make Tilling sit up and behave, she would doubtless not hesitate about giving Miss Mapp some nasty ones back if retaliation demanded. It was dreadful to think that this audacious climber was so soon to belong to the Wyses of Whitchurch, but since the moonlight had revealed that such was Mr Wyse's intention, it was best to be friends with the Mammon of the British Empire. Poppit-cum-Wyse was likely to be a very important centre of social life in Tilling, when not in Scotland or Whitchurch or Capri, and Miss Mapp wisely determined that even the announcement of the engagement should not induce her to give voice to the very proper sentiments which it could not help inspiring.

After all she had done for Susan, in letting the door of high life in

Tilling swing open for her when she could not possibly keep it shut any longer, it seemed only natural that, if she only kept on good terms with her now, Susan would insist that her dear Elizabeth must be the first to be told of the engagement. This made her pause before adopting the obvious course of setting off immediately after breakfast next morning, and telling all her friends, under promise of secrecy, just what she had seen in the moonlight last night. Thrilling to the narrator as such an announcement would be, it would be even more thrilling, provided only that Susan had sufficient sense of decency to tell her of the engagement before anybody else, to hurry off to all the others and inform them that she had known of it ever since the night of the bridge party.

It was important, therefore, to be at home whenever there was the slightest chance of Susan coming round with her news, and Miss Mapp sat at her window the whole of that first morning, so as not to miss her, and hardly attended at all to the rest of the pageant of life that moved within the radius of her observation. Her heart beat fast when, about the middle of the morning, Mr Wyse came round the dentist's corner, for it might be that the bashful Susan had sent him to make the announcement, but, if so, he was bashful too, for he walked by her house without pause. He looked rather worried, she thought (as well he might), and passing on he disappeared round the church corner, clearly on his way to his betrothed. He carried a square parcel in his hand, about as big as some jewel case that might contain a tiara. Half an hour afterwards, however, he came back, still carrying the tiara. It occurred to her that the engagement might have been broken off . . . A little later, again with a quickened pulse, Miss Mapp saw the Royce lumber down from the church corner. It stopped at her house, and she caught a glimpse of sables within. This time she felt certain that Susan had come with her interesting news, and waited till Withers, having answered the door, came to enquire, no doubt, whether she would see Mrs Poppit. But, alas, a minute later the Royce lumbered on, carrying the additional weight of the Christmas number of *Punch*, which Miss Mapp had borrowed last night and had not, of course, had time to glance at yet.

Anticipation is supposed to be pleasanter than any fulfilment, however agreeable, and if that is the case, Miss Mapp during the next day or two had more enjoyment than the announcement of fifty engagements could have given her, so constantly (when from the garden room she heard the sound of the knocker on her front door) did she spring up in certainty that this was Susan, which it never was. But however enjoyable it all might be, she appeared to herself at least to be suffering tortures of suspense, through which by degrees an idea, painful and revolting in the extreme, yet strangely exhilarating, began to insinuate itself into her mind. There seemed a deadly probability of the correctness of the conjecture, as the week went by without further confirmation of that kiss, for, after all, who knew anything about the character and antecedents of Susan? As for Mr Wyse, was he not a constant visitor to the fierce and fickle South, where, as everyone knew, morality was wholly extinct? And how, if it was all too true, should Tilling treat this hitherto unprecedented situation? It was terrible to contemplate this moral upheaval, which might prove to be a social upheaval also. Time and again, as Miss Mapp vainly waited for news, she was within an ace of communicating her suspicions to the Padre. He ought to know, for Christmas (as was usual in December) was daily drawing nearer . . .

There came some halfway through that month a dark and ominous afternoon, the rain falling sad and thick, and so unusual a density of cloud dwelling in the upper air that by three o'clock Miss Mapp was quite unable, until the street lamp at the corner was lit, to carry out the minor duty of keeping an eye on the houses of Captain Puffin and Major Benjy. The Royce had already lumbered by her door since lunchtime, but so dark was it that, peer as she might, it was lost in the gloom before it came to the dentist's corner, and Miss Mapp had to face the fact that she really did not know whether it had turned into the street where Susan's lover lived or had gone straight on. It was easier to imagine the worst, and she had already pictured to herself a clandestine meeting between those passionate ones, who under cover of this darkness were imperviously concealed from any observation (beneath an umbrella) from her house roof. Nothing but a powerful searchlight could reveal what was going on in the drawing-room window of Mr Wyse's house, and apart from the fact that she had not got a powerful searchlight, it was strongly improbable that anything of a very intimate nature was going on there . . . it was not likely that they would choose the drawing-room window. She thought of calling on Mr Wyse and asking for the loan of a book, so that she would see whether the sables were in the hall, but even then she would not really be much further on. Even as she considered this a sea mist began to creep through the street outside, and in a few minutes it was blotted from view. Nothing was visible, and nothing audible but the hissing of the shrouded rain.

Suddenly from close outside came the sound of a door knocker imperiously plied, which could be no other than her own. Only a telegram or some urgent errand could bring anyone out on such a day, and unable to bear the suspense of waiting till Withers had answered it, she hurried into the house to open the door herself. Was the news of the engagement coming to her at last? Late though it was, she would welcome it even now, for it would atone, in part at any rate . . . It was Diva.

'Diva dear!' said Miss Mapp enthusiastically, for Withers was already in the hall. 'How sweet of you to come round. Anything special?'

'Yes,' said Diva, opening her eyes very wide, and spreading a shower of moisture as she whisked off her mackintosh. 'She's come.'

This could not refer to Susan . . .

'Who?' asked Miss Mapp.

'Faradiddleony,' said Diva.

'No!' said Miss Mapp very loud, so much interested that she quite forgot to resent Diva's being the first to have the news. 'Let's have a comfortable cup of tea in the garden room. Tea, Withers.'

Miss Mapp lit the candles there, for, lost in meditation, she had been sitting in the dark, and with reckless hospitality poked the fire to make it blaze.

'Tell me all about it,' she said. That would be a treat for Diva, who was such a gossip.

'Went to the station just now,' said Diva. 'Wanted a new timetable. Besides the Royce had just gone down. Mr Wyse and Susan on the platform.'

'Sables?' asked Miss Mapp parenthetically, to complete the picture.

'Swaddled. Talked to them. Train came in. Woman got out. Kissed Mr Wyse. Shook hands with Susan. Both hands. While luggage was got out.'

'Much?' asked Miss Mapp quickly.

'Hundreds. Covered with coronets and Fs. Two cabs.'

Miss Mapp's mind, on a hot scent, went back to the previous telegraphic utterance.

'Both hands did you say, dear?' she asked. 'Perhaps that's the Italian fashion.'

'Maybe. Then what else do you think? Faradiddleony kissed Susan! Mr Wyse and she must be engaged. I can't account for it any other way. He must have written to tell his sister. Couldn't have told her then at the station. Must have been engaged some days and we never knew. They went to look at the orchid. Remember? That was when.'

It was bitter, no doubt, but the bitterness could be transmuted into an amazing sweetness.

'Then now I can speak,' said Miss Mapp with a sigh of great relief. 'Oh, it has been so hard keeping silence, but I felt I ought to. I knew all along, Diva dear, all, all along.'

'How?' asked Diva with a fallen crest.

Miss Mapp laughed merrily.

'I looked out of the window, dear, while you went for your hanky and peeped into dining room and boudoir, didn't you? There they were on the lawn, and they kissed each other. So I said to myself: "Dear Susan has got him! Perseverance rewarded!"'

'H'm. Only a guess of yours. Or did Susan tell you?'

'No, dear, she said nothing. But Susan was always secretive.'

'But they might not have been engaged at all,' said Diva with a brightened eye. 'Man doesn't always marry a woman he kisses!'

Diva had betrayed the lowness of her mind now by hazarding that which had for days dwelt in Miss Mapp's mind as almost certain. She drew in her breath with a hissing noise as if in pain.

'Darling, what a dreadful suggestion,' she said. 'No such idea ever occurred to me. Secretive I thought Susan might be, but immoral, never. I must forget you ever thought that. Let's talk about something less painful. Perhaps you would like to tell me more about the Contessa.'

Diva had the grace to look ashamed of herself, and to take refuge in the new topic so thoughtfully suggested.

'Couldn't see clearly,' she said. 'So dark. But tall and lean. Sneezed.'

'That might happen to anybody, dear,' said Miss Mapp, 'whether tall or short. Nothing more?'

'An eyeglass,' said Diva after thought.

'A single one?' asked Miss Mapp. 'On a string? How strange for a woman.'

That seemed positively the last atom of Diva's knowledge, and though Miss Mapp tried on the principles of psychoanalysis to disinter something she had forgotten, the catechism led to no results whatever. But Diva had evidently something else to say, for after finishing her tea she whizzed backwards and forwards from window to fireplace with little grunts and whistles, as was her habit when she was struggling with utterance. Long before it came out, Miss Mapp had, of course, guessed what it was. No wonder Diva found difficulty in speaking of a matter in which she had behaved so deplorably . . .

'About that wretched dress,' she said at length. 'Got it stained with chocolate first time I wore it, and neither I nor Janet can get it out.'

('Hurrah,' thought Miss Mapp.)

'Must have it dyed again,' continued Diva. 'Thought I'd better tell you. Else you might have yours dyed the same colour as mine again. Kingfisher blue to crimson lake. All came out of *Vogue* and Mrs Trout. Rather funny, you know, but expensive. You should have seen your face, Elizabeth, when you came in to Susan's the other night.'

'Should I, dearest?' said Miss Mapp, trembling violently.

'Yes. Wouldn't have gone home with you in the dark for anything. Murder.'

'Diva dear,' said Miss Mapp anxiously, 'you've got a mind which likes to put the worst construction on everything. If Mr Wyse kisses his intended you think things too terrible for words; if I look surprised you think I'm full of hatred and malice. Be more generous, dear. Don't put evil constructions on all you see.'

'Ho!' said Diva with a world of meaning.

'I don't know what you intend to convey by ho,' said Miss Mapp, 'and I shan't try to guess. But be kinder, darling, and it will make you happier. Thinketh no evil, you know! Charity!'

Diva felt that the limit of what was tolerable was reached when Elizabeth lectured her on the need of charity, and she would no doubt have explained tersely and unmistakably exactly what she meant by 'Ho!' had not Withers opportunely entered to clear away tea. She brought a note with her, which Miss Mapp opened. 'Encourage me to hope,' were the first words that met her eye: Mrs Poppit had been encouraging him to hope again.

'To dine at Mr Wyse's tomorrow,' she said. 'No doubt the announcement will be made then. He probably wrote it before he went to the station. Yes, a few friends. You going, dear?'

Diva instantly got up.

'Think I'll run home and see,' she said. 'By the by, Elizabeth, what about the – the tea gown, if I go? You or I?'

'If yours is all covered with chocolate, I shouldn't think you'd like to wear it,' said Miss Mapp.

'Could tuck it away,' said Diva, 'just for once. Put flowers. Then send it to dyer's. You won't see it again. Not crimson lake, I mean.'

Miss Mapp summoned the whole of her magnanimity. It had been put to a great strain already and was tired out, but it was capable of one more effort.

'Wear it then,' she said. 'It'll be a treat to you. But let me know if you're not asked. I dare say Mr Wyse will want to keep it very small. Goodbye, dear; I'm afraid you'll get very wet going home.'

CHAPTER ELEVEN

The sea mist and the rain continued without intermission next morning, but shopping with umbrellas and mackintoshes was unusually brisk, for there was naturally a universally felt desire to catch sight of a Contessa with as little delay as possible. The foggy conditions perhaps added to the excitement, for it was not possible to see more than a few yards, and thus at any moment anybody might almost run into her. Diva's impressions, meagre though they were, had been thoroughly circulated, but the morning passed, and the ladies of Tilling went home to change their wet things and take a little ammoniated quinine as a precaution after so long and chilly an exposure, without a single one of them having caught sight of the single eyeglass. It was disappointing, but the disappointment was bearable since Mr Wyse, so far from wanting his party to be very small, had been encouraged by Mrs Poppit to hope that it would include all his world of Tilling with one exception. He had hopes with regard to the Major and the Captain, and the Padre and wee wifie, and Irene and Miss Mapp, and of course Isabel. But apparently he despaired of Diva.

She alone therefore was absent from this long, wet shopping, for she waited indoors, almost pen in hand, to answer in the affirmative the invitation which had at present not arrived. Owing to the thickness of the fog, her absence from the street passed unnoticed, for everybody supposed that everybody else had seen her, while she, biting her nails at home, waited and waited and waited. Then she waited. About a quarter-past one she gave it up, and duly telephoned, according to promise, via Janet and Withers, to Miss Mapp to say that Mr Wyse had not yet hoped. It was very unpleasant to let them know, but if she had herself rung up and been answered by Elizabeth, who usually rushed to the telephone, she felt that she would sooner have choked than have delivered this message. So Janet telephoned and Withers said she would tell her mistress. And did.

Miss Mapp was steeped in pleasant conjectures. The most likely of all was that the Contessa had seen that roundabout little busybody in the station, and taken an instant dislike to her through her single eyeglass. Or she might have seen poor Diva inquisitively inspecting the luggage with the coronets and the Fs on it, and have learned with pain that this was one of the ladies of Tilling. 'Algernon,' she would have said (so said Miss Mapp to herself), 'who is that queer little woman? Is she going to steal some of my luggage?' And then Algernon would have told her that this was poor Diva, quite a decent sort of little body. But when it came to Algernon asking his guests for the dinner party in honour of his betrothal and her arrival at Tilling, no doubt the Contessa would have said, 'Algernon, I beg . . .' Or if Diva – poor Diva – was right in her conjectures that the notes had been written before the arrival of the train, it was evident that Algernon had torn up the one addressed to Diva, when the Contessa heard whom she was to meet the next evening . . . Or Susan might easily have insinuated that they would have two very pleasant tables of bridge after dinner without including Diva, who was so wrong and quarrelsome over the score. Any of these explanations were quite satisfactory, and since Diva would not be present, Miss Mapp would naturally don the crimson lake. They would all see what crimson lake looked like when it decked a suitable wearer and was not parodied on the other side of a card table. How true, as dear Major Benjy had said, that one woman could wear what another could not. . . And if there was a woman who could not wear crimson lake it was Diva . . . Or was Mr Wyse really ashamed to let his sister see Diva in the crimson lake? It would be just like him to be considerate of Diva, and not permit her to make a guy of herself before the Italian aristocracy. No doubt he would ask her to lunch someday, quite quietly. Or had . . . Miss Mapp bloomed with pretty conjectures, like some Alpine meadow when smitten into flower by the spring, and enjoyed her lunch very much indeed.

The anxiety and suspense of the morning, which, instead of being relieved, had ended in utter gloom, gave Diva a headache, and she adopted her usual strenuous methods of getting rid of it. So, instead of lying down and taking aspirin and dozing, she set out after lunch to walk it off. She sprinted and splashed along the miry roads, indifferent as to whether she stepped in puddles or not, and careless how wet she got. She bit on the bullet of her omission from the dinner party this evening, determining not to mind one atom about it, but to look forward to a pleasant evening at home instead of going out (like this) in the wet. And never – never under any circumstances would she ask any of the guests what sort of an evening had been spent, how Mr Wyse announced the news, and how the Faradiddleony played bridge. (She said that satirical word aloud, mouthing it to the puddles and the dripping hedgerows.) She would not evince the slightest interest in it all; she would cover it with spadefuls of oblivion, and when next she met Mr Wyse she would, whatever she might feel, behave exactly as usual. She plumed herself on this dignified resolution, and walked so fast that the hedgerows became quite transparent. That was the proper thing to do; she had been grossly slighted, and, like a true lady, would be unaware of that slight; whereas poor Elizabeth, under such circumstances, would have devised a hundred petty schemes for rendering Mr Wyse's life a burden to him. But if – if (she only said 'if') she found any reason to believe that Susan was at the bottom of this, then probably she would think of something worthy not so much of a true lady but of a true woman. Without asking any questions, she might easily arrive at information which would enable her to identify Susan as the culprit, and she would then act in some way which would astonish Susan. What that way was she need not think yet, and so she devoted her entire mind to the question all the way home.

Feeling better and with her headache quite gone, she arrived in Tilling again drenched to the skin. It was already after teatime, and she abandoned tea altogether, and prepared to console herself for her exclusion from gaiety with a 'good blow-out' in the shape of regular dinner, instead of the usual muffin now and a tray later. To add dignity to her feast, she put on the crimson lake tea gown for the last time that it would be crimson-lake (though the same tea gown still), since tomorrow it would be sent to the dyer's to go into perpetual mourning for its vanished glories. She had meant to send it today, but all this misery and anxiety had put it out of her head.

Having dressed thus, to the great astonishment of Janet, she sat down to divert her mind from trouble by Patience. As if to reward her for her stubborn fortitude, the malignity of the cards relented, and she brought out an intricate matter three times running. The clock on her mantelpiece chiming a quarter to eight, surprised her with the lateness of the hour, and recalled to her with a stab of pain that it was dinner time at Mr Wyse's, and at this moment some seven pairs of eager feet were approaching the door. Well, she was dining at a quarter to eight, too; Janet would enter presently to tell her that her own banquet was ready, and gathering up her cards, she spent a pleasant though regretful minute in looking at herself and the crimson-lake for the last time in her long glass. The tremendous walk in the rain had given her an almost equally high colour. Janet's foot was heard on the stairs, and she turned away from the glass. Janet entered.

'Dinner?' said Diva.

'No, ma'am, the telephone,' said Janet. 'Mr Wyse is on the telephone, and wants to speak to you very particularly.'

'Mr Wyse himself?' asked Diva, hardly believing her ears, for she knew Mr Wyse's opinion of the telephone.

'Yes, ma'am.'

Diva walked slowly, but reflected rapidly. What must have happened was that somebody had been taken ill at the last moment – was it Elizabeth? – and that he now wanted her to fill the gap . . . She was torn in two. Passionately as she longed to dine at Mr Wyse's, she did not see how such a course was compatible with dignity. He had only asked her to suit his own convenience; it was not out of encouragement to hope that he invited her now. No; Mr Wyse should want. She would say that she had friends dining with her; that was what the true lady would do.

She took up the earpiece and said, 'Hello!'

It was certainly Mr Wyse's voice that spoke to her, and it seemed to tremble with anxiety.

'Dear lady,' he began, 'a most terrible thing has happened – '

(Wonder if Elizabeth's very ill, thought Diva.)

'Quite terrible,' said Mr Wyse. 'Can you hear?'

'Yes,' said Diva, hardening her heart.

'By the most calamitous mistake the note which I wrote you yesterday was never delivered. Figgis has just found it in the pocket of his overcoat. I shall certainly dismiss him unless you plead for him. Can you hear?'

'Yes,' said Diva excitedly.

'In it I told you that I had been encouraged to hope that you would dine with me tonight. There was such a gratifying response to my other invitations that I most culpably and carelessly, dear lady, thought that everybody had accepted. Can you hear?'

'Of course I can!' shouted Diva.

'Well, I come on my knees to you. Can you possibly forgive the joint stupidity of Figgis and me, and honour me after all? We will put dinner off, of course. At what time, in case you are ever so kind and indulgent as to come, shall we have it? Do not break my heart by refusing. Su – Mrs Poppit will send her car for you.'

'I have already dressed for dinner,' said Diva proudly. 'Very pleased to come at once.'

'You are too kind; you are angelic,' said Mr Wyse. 'The car shall start at once; it is at my door now.'

'Right,' said Diva.

'Too good – too kind,' murmured Mr Wyse. 'Figgis, what do I do next?'

Diva clapped the instrument into place.

'Powder,' she said to herself, remembering what she had seen in the glass, and whizzed upstairs. Her fish would have to be degraded into kedgeree, though plaice would have done just as well as sole for that; the cutlets could be heated up again, and perhaps the whisking for the apple meringue had not begun yet, and could still be stopped.

'Janet!' she shouted. 'Going out to dinner! Stop the meringue.'

She dashed an interesting pallor on to her face as she heard the hooting of the Royce, and coming downstairs, stepped into its warm luxuriousness, for the electric lamp was burning. There were Susan's sables there – it was thoughtful of Susan to put them in, but ostentatious – and there was a carriage rug, which she was convinced was new, and was very likely a present from Mr Wyse. And soon there was the light streaming out from Mr Wyse's open door, and Mr Wyse himself in the hall to meet and greet and thank and bless her. She pleaded for the contrite Figgis, and was conducted in a blaze of triumph into the drawing room, where all Tilling was awaiting her. She was led up to the Contessa, with whom Miss Mapp, wreathed in sycophantic smiles, was eagerly conversing.

The crimson lakes . . .

* * *

There were embarrassing moments during dinner; the Contessa, confused by having so many people introduced to her in a lump, got all their names wrong, and addressed her neighbours as Captain Flint and Major Puffin, and thought that Diva was Mrs Mapp. She seemed vivacious and good-humoured, dropped her eyeglass into her soup, talked with her mouth full, and drank a good deal of wine, which was a very bad example for Major Puffin. Then there were many sudden and complete pauses in the talk, for Diva's news of the kissing of Mrs Poppit by the Contessa had spread like wildfire through the fog this morning, owing to Miss Mapp's dissemination of it, and now, whenever Mr Wyse raised his voice ever so little, everybody else stopped talking, in the expectation that the news was about to be announced. Occasionally, also, the Contessa addressed some remark to her brother in shrill and voluble Italian, which rather confirmed the gloomy estimate of her table manners in the matter of talking with her mouth full, for to speak in Italian was equivalent to whispering, since the purport of what she said could not be understood by anybody except him . . . Then also, the sensation of dining with a countess produced a slight feeling of strain, which, in addition to the correct behaviour which Mr Wyse's presence always induced, almost congealed correctness into stiffness. But as dinner went on her evident enjoyment of herself made itself felt, and her eccentricities, though carefully observed and noted by Miss Mapp, were not succeeded by silences and hurried bursts of conversation.

'And is your ladyship making a long stay in Tilling?' asked the (real) Major, to cover the pause which had been caused by Mr Wyse saying something across the table to Isabel.

She dropped her eyeglass with quite a splash into her gravy, pulled it out again by the string as if landing a fish and sucked it.

'That depends on you gentlemen,' she said with greater audacity than was usual in Tilling. 'If you and Major Puffin and that sweet little Scotch clergyman all fall in love with me, and fight duels about me, I will stop for ever . . .'

The Major recovered himself before anybody else.

'Your ladyship may take that for granted,' he said gallantly, and a perfect hubbub of conversation rose to cover this awful topic.

She laid her hand on his arm.

'You must not call me ladyship, Captain Flint,' she said. 'Only servants say that. Contessa, if you like. And you must blow away this fog for me. I have seen nothing but bales of cotton wool out of the window. Tell me this, too: why are those ladies dressed alike? Are they sisters? Mrs Mapp, the little round one, and her sister, the big round one?'

The Major cast an apprehensive eye on Miss Mapp seated just opposite, whose acuteness of hearing was one of the terrors of Tilling . . . His apprehensions were perfectly well founded, and Miss Mapp hated and despised the Contessa from that hour.

'No, not sisters,' said he, 'and your la – you've made a little error about the names. The one opposite is Miss Mapp, the other Mrs Plaistow.'

The Contessa moderated her voice.

'I see; she looks vexed, your Miss Mapp. I think she must have heard, and I will be very nice to her afterwards. Why does not one of you gentlemen marry her? I see I shall have to arrange that. The sweet little Scotch clergyman now; little men like big wives. Ah! Married already is he to the mouse? Then it must be you, Captain Flint. We must have more marriages in Tilling.'

Miss Mapp could not help glancing at the Contessa, as she made this remarkable observation. It must be the cue, she thought, for the announcement of that which she had known so long . . . In the space of a wink the clever Contessa saw that she had her attention, and spoke rather loudly to the Major.

'I have lost my heart to your Miss Mapp,' she said. 'I am jealous of you, Captain Flint. She will be my great friend in Tilling, and if you marry her, I shall hate you, for that will mean that she likes you best.'

Miss Mapp hated nobody at that moment, not even Diva, off whose face the hastily applied powder was crumbling, leaving little red marks peeping out like the stars on a fine evening. Dinner came to an end with roasted chestnuts brought by the Contessa from Capri.

'I always scold Amelia for the luggage she takes with her,' said Mr Wyse to Diva. 'Amelia dear, you are my hostess tonight' – everybody saw him look at Mrs Poppit – 'you must catch somebody's eye.'

'I will catch Miss Mapp's,' said Amelia, and all the ladies rose as if connected with some hidden mechanism which moved them simultaneously . . . There was a great deal of pretty diffidence at the door, but the Contessa put an end to that.

'Eldest first,' she said, and marched out, making Miss Mapp, Diva and the mouse feel remarkably young. She might drop her eyeglass and talk with her mouth full, but really such tact . . . They all determined to adopt this pleasing device in the future. The disappointment about the announcement of the engagement was sensibly assuaged, and Miss Mapp and Susan, in their eagerness to be younger than the Contessa, and yet take precedence of all the rest, almost stuck in the doorway. They rebounded from each other, and Diva whizzed out between them. Quaint Irene went in her right place – last. However quaint Irene was, there was no use in pretending that she was not the youngest.

However hopelessly Amelia had lost her heart to Miss Mapp, she did not devote her undivided attention to her in the drawing room, but swiftly established herself at the card table, where she proceeded, with a most complicated sort of Patience and a series of cigarettes, to while away the time till the gentlemen joined them. Though the ladies of Tilling had plenty to say to each other, it was all about her, and such comments could not conveniently be made in her presence. Unless, like her, they talked some language unknown to the subject of their conversation, they could not talk at all, and so they gathered round her table, and watched the lightning rapidity with which she piled black knaves on red queens in some packs and red knaves on black queens in others. She had taken off all her rings in order to procure a greater freedom of finger, and her eyeglass continued to crash on to a glittering mass of magnificent gems. The rapidity of her motions was only equalled by the swift and surprising monologue that poured from her mouth.

'There, that odious king gets in my way,' she said. 'So like a man to poke himself in where he isn't wanted. *Bacco!* No, not that: I have a cigarette. I hear all you ladies are terrific bridge players: we will have a game presently, and I shall sink into the earth with terror at your Camorra! *Dio!* there's another king, and that's his own queen whom he doesn't want at all. He is *amoroso* for that black queen, who is quite covered up, and he would like to be covered up with her. Susan, my dear' (that was interesting, but they all knew it already), 'kindly ring the bell for coffee. I expire if I do not get my coffee at once, and a toothpick. Tell me all the scandal of Tilling, Miss Mapp, while I play – all the dreadful histories of that Major and that Captain. Such a grand air has the Captain – no, it is the Major, the one who does not limp. Which of all you ladies do they love most? It is Miss Mapp, I believe: that is why she does not answer me. Ah! here is the coffee, and the other king: three lumps of sugar, dear Susan, and then stir it up well, and hold it to my mouth, so that I can drink without interruption. Ah, the ace! He is the intervener, or is it the King's Proctor? It would be nice to have a proctor who told you all the love affairs that were going on. Susan, you must get me a proctor: you shall be my proctor. And here are the men – the wretches, they have been preferring wine to women, and we will have our bridge, and if anybody scolds me, I shall cry, Miss Mapp, and Captain Flint will hold my hand and comfort me.'

She gathered up a heap of cards and rings, dropped them on the floor, and cut with the remainder.

Miss Mapp was very lenient with the Contessa, who was her partner, and pointed out the mistakes of her and their adversaries with the most winning smile and eagerness to explain things clearly. Then she revoked heavily herself, and the Contessa, so far from being angry with her, burst into peals of unquenchable merriment. This way of taking a revoke was new to Tilling, for the right thing was for the revoker's partner to sulk and be sarcastic for at least twenty minutes after. The Contessa's laughter continued to spurt out at intervals during the rest of the rubber, and it was all very pleasant; but at the end she said she was not up to Tilling standards at all, and refused to play any more. Miss Mapp, in the highest good humour, urged her not to despair.

'Indeed, dear Contessa,' she said, 'you play very well. A little overbidding of your hand, perhaps, do you think? but that is a tendency we are all subject to: I often overbid my hand myself. Not a little wee rubber more? I'm sure I should like to be your partner again. You must come and play at my house some afternoon. We will have tea early, and get a good two hours. Nothing like practice.'

The evening came to an end without the great announcement being made, but Miss Mapp, as she reviewed the events of the party, sitting next morning in her observation window, found the whole evidence so overwhelming that it was no longer worth while to form conjectures, however fruitful, on the subject, and she diverted her mind to pleasing reminiscences and projects for the future. She had certainly been distinguished by the Contessa's marked regard, and her opinion of her charm and ability was of the very highest . . . No doubt her strange remark about duelling at dinner had been humorous in intention, but many a true word is spoken in jest, and the Contessa – perspicacious woman – had seen at once that Major Benjy and Captain Puffin were just the sort of men who might get to duelling (or, at any rate, challenging) about a woman. And her asking which of the ladies the men were most in love with, and her saying that she believed it was Miss Mapp! Miss Mapp had turned nearly as red as poor Diva when that came out, so lightly and yet so acutely . . .

Diva! It had, of course, been a horrid blow to find that Diva had been asked to Mr Wyse's party in the first instance, and an even shrewder one when Diva entered (with such unnecessary fussing and apology on the part of Mr Wyse) in the crimson lake. Luckily, it would be seen no more, for Diva had promised – if you could trust Diva – to send it to the dyer's; but it was a great puzzle to know why Diva had it on at all, if she was preparing to spend a solitary evening at home. By eight o'clock she ought by rights to have already had her tray, dressed in some old thing; but within three minutes of her being telephoned for she had appeared in the crimson lake, and eaten so heartily that it was impossible to imagine, greedy though she was, that she had already consumed her tray . . . But in spite of Diva's adventitious triumph, the main feeling in Miss Mapp's mind was pity for her. She looked so ridiculous in that dress with the powder peeling off her red face. No wonder the dear Contessa stared when she came in.

There was her bridge party for the Contessa to consider. The Contessa would be less nervous, perhaps, if there was only one table: that would be more homey and cosy, and it would at the same time give rise to great heartburnings and indignation in the breasts of those who were left out. Diva would certainly be one of the spurned, and the Contessa would not play with Mr Wyse . . . Then there was Major Benjy, he must certainly be asked, for it was evident that the Contessa delighted in him . . .

Suddenly Miss Mapp began to feel less sure that Major Benjy must be of the party. The Contessa, charming though she was, had said several very tropical, Italian things to him. She had told him that she would stop here for ever if the men fought duels about her. She had said 'you dear darling' to him at bridge when, as adversary, he failed to trump her losing card, and she had asked him to ask her to tea ('with no one else, for I have a great deal to say to you'), when the general *macédoine* of sables, *au reservoirs*, and thanks for such a nice evening took place in the hall. Miss Mapp was not, in fact, sure, when she thought it over, that the Contessa was a nice friend for Major Benjy. She did not do him the injustice of imagining that he would ask her to tea alone; the very suggestion proved that it must be a piece of the Contessa's Southern extravagance of expression. But, after all, thought Miss Mapp to herself, as she writhed at the idea, her other extravagant expressions were proved to cover a good deal of truth. In fact, the Major's chance of being asked to the select bridge party diminished swiftly towards vanishing point.

It was time (and indeed late) to set forth on morning marketings, and Miss Mapp had already determined not to carry her capacious basket with her today, in case of meeting the Contessa in the High Street. It would be grander and Wysier and more magnificent to go basket-less, and direct that the goods should be sent up, rather than run the risk of encountering the Contessa with a basket containing a couple of mutton cutlets, a ball of wool and some tooth-powder. So she put on her Prince of Wales's cloak, and, postponing further reflection over the bridge party till a less busy occasion, set forth in unencumbered gentility for the morning gossip. At the corner of the High Street, she ran into Diva.

'News,' said Diva. 'Met Mr Wyse just now. Engaged to Susan. All over the town by now. Everybody knows. Oh, there's the Padre for the first time.'

She shot across the street, and Miss Mapp, shaking the dust of Diva off her feet, proceeded on her chagrined way. Annoyed as she was with Diva, she was almost more annoyed with Susan. After all she had done for Susan, Susan ought to have told her long ago, pledging her to secrecy. But to be told like this by that common Diva, without any secrecy at all, was an affront that she would find it hard to forgive Susan for. She mentally reduced by a half the sum that she had determined to squander on Susan's wedding present. It should be plated, not silver, and if Susan was not careful, it shouldn't be plated at all.

She had just come out of the chemist's, after an indignant interview about precipitated chalk. He had deposited the small packet on the counter, when she asked to have it sent up to her house. He could not undertake to deliver small packages. She left the precipitated chalk lying there. Emerging, she heard a loud, foreign sort of scream from close at hand. There was the Contessa, all by herself, carrying a marketing basket of unusual size and newness. It contained a bloody steak and a crab.

'But where is your basket, Miss Mapp?' she exclaimed. 'Algernon told me that all the great ladies of Tilling went marketing in the morning with big baskets, and that if I aspired to be *du monde*, I must have my basket, too. It is the greatest fun, and I have already written to Cecco to say I am just going marketing with my basket. Look, the steak is for Figgis, and the crab is for Algernon and me, if Figgis does not get it. But why are you not *du monde*? Are you *du demi-monde*, Miss Mapp?'

She gave a croak of laughter and tickled the crab . . .

'Will he eat the steak, do you think?' she went on. 'Is he not lively? I went to the shop of Mr Hopkins, who was not there, because he was engaged with Miss Coles. And was that not Miss Coles last night at my brother's? The one who spat in the fire when nobody but I was looking? You are enchanting at Tilling. What is Mr Hopkins doing with Miss Coles? Do they kiss? But your market basket: that disappoints me, for Algernon said you had the biggest market basket of all. I bought the biggest I could find: is it as big as yours?'

Miss Mapp's head was in a whirl. The Contessa said in the loudest possible voice all that everybody else only whispered; she displayed (in her basket) all that everybody else covered up with thick layers of paper. If Miss Mapp had only guessed that the Contessa would have a market basket, she would have paraded the High Street with a leg of mutton protruding from one end and a pair of Wellington boots from the other . . . But who could have suspected that a Contessa . . .

Black thoughts succeeded. Was it possible that Mr Wyse had been satirical about the affairs of Tilling? If so, she wished him nothing worse than to be married to Susan. But a playful face must be put, for the moment, on the situation.

'Too lovely of you, dear Contessa,' she said. 'May we go marketing together tomorrow, and we will measure the size of our baskets? Such fun I have, too, laughing at the dear people in Tilling. But what thrilling news this morning about our sweet Susan and your dear brother, though of course I knew it long ago.'

'Indeed! how was that?' said the Contessa quite sharply.

Miss Mapp was 'nettled' at her tone.

'Oh, you must allow me two eyes,' she said, since it was merely tedious to explain how she had seen them from behind a curtain kissing in the garden. 'Just two eyes.'

'And a nose for scent,' remarked the Contessa very genially.

This was certainly coarse, though probably Italian. Miss Mapp's opinion of the Contessa fluctuated violently like a barometer before a storm and indicated 'Changeable'.

'Dear Susan is such an intimate friend,' she said.

The Contessa looked at her very fixedly for a moment, and then appeared to dismiss the matter.

'My crab, my steak,' she said. 'And where does your nice Captain, no, Major Flint live? I have a note to leave on him, for he has asked me to tea all alone, to see his tigerskins. He is going to be my flirt while I am in Tilling, and when I go he will break his heart, but I will have told him who can mend it again.'

'Dear Major Benjy!' said Miss Mapp, at her wits' end to know how to deal with so feather-tongued a lady. 'What a treat it will be to him to have you to tea. Today, is it?'

The Contessa quite distinctly winked behind her eyeglass, which she had put up to look at Diva, who whirled by on the other side of the street.

'And if I said "Today",' she remarked, 'you would – what is it that that one says' – and she indicated Diva – 'yes, you would pop in, and the good Major would pay no attention to me. So if I tell you I shall go today, you will know that is a lie, you clever Miss Mapp, and so you will go to tea with him tomorrow and find me there. *Bene!* Now where is his house?'

This was a sort of scheming that had never entered into Miss Mapp's life, and she saw with pain how shallow she had been all these years. Often and often she had, when inquisitive questions were put her, answered them without any strict subservience to truth, but never had she thought of confusing the issues like this. If she told Diva a lie, Diva probably guessed it was a lie, and acted accordingly, but she had never thought of making it practically impossible to tell whether it was a lie or not. She had no more idea when she walked back along the High Street with the Contessa swinging her basket by her side, whether that lady was going to tea with Major Benjy today or tomorrow or when, than she knew whether the crab was going to eat the beef steak.

'There's his house,' she said, as they paused at the dentist's corner, 'and there's mine next it, with the little bow window of my garden room looking out on to the street. I hope to welcome you there, dear Contessa, for a tiny game of bridge and some tea one of these days very soon. What day do you think? Tomorrow?'

(Then she would know if the Contessa was going to tea with Major Benjy tomorrow . . . unfortunately the Contessa appeared to know that she would know it, too.)

'My flirt!' she said. 'Perhaps I may be having tea with my flirt tomorrow.'

Better anything than that.

'I will ask him, too, to meet you,' said Miss Mapp, feeling in some awful and helpless way that she was playing her adversary's game. 'Adversary?' did she say to herself? She did. The inscrutable Contessa was 'up to' that too.

'I will not amalgamate my treats,' she said. 'So that is his house! What a charming house! How my heart flutters as I ring the bell!'

Miss Mapp was now quite distraught. There was the possibility that the Contessa might tell Major Benjy that it was time he married, but on the other hand she was making arrangements to go to tea with him on an unknown date, and the hero of amorous adventures in India and elsewhere might lose his heart again to somebody quite different from one whom he could hope to marry. By daylight the dear Contessa was undeniably plain: that was something, but in these short days, tea would be conducted by artificial light, and by artificial light she was not so like a rabbit. What was worse was that by any light she had a liveliness which might be mistaken for wit, and a flattering manner which might be taken for sincerity. She hoped men were not so easily duped as that, and was sadly afraid that they were. Blind fools!

* * *

The number of visits that Miss Mapp made about teatime in this week before Christmas to the postbox at the corner of the High Street, with an envelope in her hand containing Mr Hopkins's bill for fish (and a postal order enclosed), baffles computation. Naturally, she did not intend, either by day or night, to risk being found again with a blank unstamped envelope in her hand, and the one enclosing Mr Hopkins's bill and the postal order would have passed scrutiny for correctness, anywhere. But fair and calm as was the exterior of that envelope, none could tell how agitated was the hand that carried it backwards and forwards until the edges got crumpled and the inscription clouded with much fingering. Indeed, of all the tricks that Miss Mapp had compassed for others, none was so sumptuously contrived as that in which she had now entangled herself.

For these December days were dark, and in consequence not only would the Contessa be looking her best (such as it was) at teatime, but from Miss Mapp's window it was impossible to tell whether she had gone to tea with him on any particular afternoon, for there had been a strike at the gasworks, and the lamp at the corner, which, in happier days, would have told all, told nothing whatever. Miss Mapp must therefore trudge to the letter box

with Mr Hopkins's bill in her hand as she went out, and (after
a feint of posting it) with it in her pocket as she came back, in
order to gather from the light in the windows, from the sound
of conversation that would be audible as she passed close beneath
them, whether the Major was having tea there or not, and with
whom. Should she hear that ringing laugh which had sounded so
pleasant when she revoked, but now was so sinister, she had quite
determined to go in and borrow a book or a tigerskin – anything.
The Major could scarcely fail to ask her to tea, and, once there,
wild horses should not drag her away until she had outstayed the
other visitor. Then, as her malady of jealousy grew more feverish,
she began to perceive, as by the ray of some dreadful dawn, that
lights in the Major's room and sounds of elfin laughter were not
completely trustworthy as proofs that the Contessa was there. It
was possible, awfully possible, that the two might be sitting in the
firelight, that voices might be hushed to amorous whisperings, that
pregnant smiles might be taking the place of laughter. On one such
afternoon, as she came back from the letter box with patient Mr
Hopkins's overdue bill in her pocket, a wild certainty seized her,
when she saw how closely the curtains were drawn, and how still it
seemed inside his room, that firelight dalliance was going on.

She rang the bell, and imagined she heard whisperings inside
while it was being answered. Presently the light went up in the hall,
and the Major's Mrs Dominic opened the door.

'The Major is in, I think, isn't he, Mrs Dominic?' said Miss
Mapp, in her most insinuating tones.

'No, miss; out,' said Dominic uncompromisingly. (Miss Mapp
wondered if Dominic drank.)

'Dear me! How tiresome, when he told me – ' said she, with
playful annoyance. 'Would you be very kind, Mrs Dominic, and just
see for certain that he is not in his room? He may have come in.'

'No, miss, he's out,' said Dominic, with the parrotlike utterance
of the determined liar. 'Any message?'

Miss Mapp turned away, more certain than ever that he was in
and immersed in dalliance. She would have continued to be quite
certain about it, had she not, glancing distractedly down the street,
caught sight of him coming up with Captain Puffin.

Meantime she had twice attempted to get up a cosy little party of four (so as not to frighten the Contessa) to play bridge from tea till dinner, and on both occasions the Faradiddleony (for so she had become) was most unfortunately engaged. But the second of these disappointing replies contained the hope that they would meet at their marketings tomorrow morning, and though poor Miss Mapp was really getting very tired with these innumerable visits to the postbox, whether wet or fine, she set forth next morning with the hopes anyhow of finding out whether the Contessa had been to tea with Major Flint, or on what day she was going . . . There she was, just opposite the post office, and there – oh, shame! – was Major Benjy on his way to the tram, in light-hearted conversation with her. It was a slight consolation that Captain Puffin was there too.

Miss Mapp quickened her steps to a little tripping run.

'Dear Contessa, so sorry I am late,' she said. 'Such a lot of little things to do this morning. (Major Benjy! Captain Puffin!) Oh, how naughty of you to have begun your shopping without me!'

'Only been to the grocer's,' said the Contessa. 'Major Benjy has been so amusing that I haven't got on with my shopping at all. I have written to Cecco to say that there is no one so witty.'

(Major Benjy! thought Miss Mapp bitterly, remembering how long it had taken her to arrive at that. 'And witty.' She had not arrived at that yet.)

'No, indeed!' said the Major. 'It was the Contessa, Miss Mapp, who has been so entertaining.'

'I'm sure she would be,' said Miss Mapp, with an enormous smile. 'And, oh, Major Benjy, you'll miss your tram unless you hurry, and get no golf at all, and then be vexed with us for keeping you. You men always blame us poor women.'

'Well, upon my word, what's a game of golf compared with the pleasure of being with the ladies?' asked the Major, with a great fat bow.

'I want to catch that tram,' said Puffin quite distinctly, and Miss Mapp found herself more nearly forgetting his inebriated insults than ever before.

'You poor Captain Puffin,' said the Contessa, 'you shall catch it. Be off, both of you, at once. I will not say another word to either of you. I will never forgive you if you miss it. But tomorrow afternoon, Major Benjy.'

He turned round to bow again, and a bicycle luckily (for the rider) going very slowly, butted softly into him behind.

'Not hurt?' called the Contessa. 'Good! Ah, Miss Mapp, let us get to our shopping! How well you manage those men! How right you are about them! They want their golf more than they want us, whatever they may say. They would hate us, if we kept them from their golf. So sorry not to have been able to play bridge with you yesterday, but an engagement. What a busy place Tilling is. Let me see! Where is the list of things that Figgis told me to buy? That Figgis! A roller towel for his pantry, and some blacking for his boots, and some flannel I suppose for his fat stomach. It is all for Figgis. And there is that swift Mrs Plaistow. She comes like a train with a red light in her face and wheels and whistlings. She talks like a telegram – Good morning, Mrs Plaistow.'

'Enjoyed my game of bridge, Contessa,' panted Diva. 'Delightful game of bridge yesterday.'

The Contessa seemed in rather a hurry to reply. But long before she could get a word out Miss Mapp felt she knew what had happened . . .

'So pleased,' said the Contessa quickly. 'And now for Figgis's towels, Miss Mapp. Ten and sixpence apiece, he says. What a price to give for a towel! But I learn housekeeping like this, and Cecco will delight in all the economies I shall make. Quick, to the draper's, lest there should be no towels left.'

In spite of Figgis's list, the Contessa's shopping was soon over, and Miss Mapp having seen her as far as the corner, walked on, as if to her own house, in order to give her time to get to Mr Wyse's, and then fled back to the High Street. The suspense was unbearable: she had to know without delay when and where Diva and the Contessa had played bridge yesterday. Never had her eye so rapidly scanned the movement of passengers in that entrancing thoroughfare in order to pick Diva out, and learn from her precisely what had happened . . . There she was, coming out of the dyer's with her basket completely filled by a bulky package, which it needed no ingenuity to identify as the late crimson lake. She would have to be pleasant with Diva, for much as that perfidious woman might enjoy telling her where this furtive bridge party had taken place, she might enjoy even more torturing her with uncertainty. Diva could, if put to it, give no answer whatever to a direct question, but, skilfully changing the subject, talk about something utterly different.

'The crimson lake,' said Miss Mapp, pointing to the basket. 'Hope it will turn out well, dear.'

There was rather a wicked light in Diva's eyes.

'Not crimson lake,' she said. 'Jet black.'

'Sweet of you to have it dyed again, dear Diva,' said Miss Mapp. 'Not very expensive, I trust?'

'Send the bill in to you, if you like,' said Diva.

Miss Mapp laughed very pleasantly.

'That would be a good joke,' she said. 'How nice it is that the dear Contessa takes so warmly to our Tilling ways. So amusing she was about the commissions Figgis had given her. But a wee bit satirical, do you think?'

This ought to put Diva in a good temper, for there was nothing she liked so much as a few little dabs at somebody else. (Diva was not very good-natured.)

'She is rather satirical,' said Diva.

'Oh, tell me some of her amusing little speeches!' said Miss Mapp enthusiastically. 'I can't always follow her, but you are so quick! A little coarse too, at times, isn't she? What she said the other night when she was playing Patience, about the queens and kings, wasn't quite – was it? And the toothpick.'

'Yes. Toothpick,' said Diva.

'Perhaps she has bad teeth,' said Miss Mapp; 'it runs in families, and Mr Wyse's, you know – We're lucky, you and I.'

Diva maintained a complete silence, and they had now come nearly as far as her door. If she would not give the information that she knew Miss Mapp longed for, she must be asked for it, with the uncertain hope that she would give it then.

'Been playing bridge lately, dear?' asked Miss Mapp.

'Quite lately,' said Diva.

'I thought I heard you say something about it to the Contessa. Yesterday, was it? Whom did you play with?'

Diva paused, and, when they had come quite to her door, made up her mind.

'Contessa, Susan, Mr Wyse, me,' she said.

'But I thought she never played with Mr Wyse,' said Miss Mapp.

'Had to get a four,' said Diva. 'Contessa wanted her bridge. Nobody else.'

She popped into her house.

There is no use in describing Miss Mapp's state of mind, except by saying that for the moment she quite forgot that the Contessa was almost certainly going to tea with Major Benjy tomorrow.

CHAPTER TWELVE

'Peace on earth and mercy mild,' sang Miss Mapp, holding her head back with her uvula clearly visible. She sat in her usual seat close below the pulpit, and the sun streaming in through a stained-glass window opposite made her face of all colours, like Joseph's coat. Not knowing how it looked from outside, she pictured to herself a sort of celestial radiance coming from within, though Diva, sitting opposite, was reminded of the iridescent hues observable on cold boiled beef. But then, Miss Mapp had registered the fact that Diva's notion of singing alto was to follow the trebles at the uniform distance of a minor third below, so that matters were about square between them. She wondered between the verses if she could say something very tactful to Diva, which might before next Christmas induce her not to make that noise . . .

Major Flint came in just before the first hymn was over, and held his top hat before his face by way of praying in secret, before he opened his hymn book. A piece of loose holly fell down from the window ledge above him on the exact middle of his head, and the jump that he gave was, considering his baldness, quite justifiable. Captain Puffin, Miss Mapp was sorry to see, was not there at all. But he had been unwell lately with attacks of dizziness, one of which had caused him, in the last game of golf that he had played, to fall down on the eleventh green and groan. If these attacks were not due to his lack of perseverance, no right-minded person could fail to be very sorry for him.

There was a good deal more peace on earth as regards Tilling than might have been expected considering what the week immediately before Christmas had been like. A picture by Miss Coles (who had greatly dropped out of society lately, owing to her odd ways) called 'Adam', which was certainly Mr Hopkins (though no one could have guessed) had appeared for sale in the window of a dealer in pictures and curios, but had been withdrawn from public view at Miss Mapp's personal intercession and her revelation of whom, unlikely as it sounded, the picture represented. The unchivalrous dealer had told the artist the history of its withdrawal, and it had come to Miss Mapp's ears (among many other things) that quaint Irene had imitated the scene of intercession with such piercing fidelity that her servant, Lucy-Eve, had nearly died of laughing. Then there had been clandestine bridge at Mr Wyse's house on three consecutive days, and on none of these occasions was Miss Mapp asked to continue the instruction which she had professed herself perfectly willing to give to the Contessa. The Contessa, in fact – there seemed to be no doubt about it – had declared that she would sooner not play bridge at all than play with Miss Mapp, because the effort of not laughing would put an unwarrantable strain on those muscles which prevented you from doing so . . . Then the Contessa had gone to tea quite alone with Major Benjy, and though her shrill and senseless monologue was clearly audible in the street as Miss Mapp went by to post her letter again, the Major's Dominic had stoutly denied that he was in, and the notion that the Contessa was haranguing all by herself in his drawing room was too ridiculous to be entertained for a moment . . . And Diva's dyed dress had turned out so well that Miss Mapp gnashed her teeth at the thought that she had not had hers dyed instead. With some green chiffon round the neck, even Diva looked quite distinguished – for Diva.

Then, quite suddenly, an angel of Peace had descended on the distracted garden room, for the Poppits, the Contessa and Mr Wyse all went away to spend Christmas and the New Year with the Wyses of Whitchurch. It was probable that the Contessa would then continue a round of visits with all that coronetted luggage, and leave for Italy again without revisiting Tilling. She had behaved as if that was the case, for taking advantage of a fine afternoon, she had borrowed the Royce and whirled round the town on a series of calls, leaving p.p.c. calling cards everywhere, and saying only (so Miss Mapp gathered from Withers), 'Your mistress not in? So sorry,' and had driven away before Withers could get out the information that her mistress was very much in, for she had a bad cold.

But there were the p.p.c. cards, and the Wyses with their future connections were going to Whitchurch, and after a few hours of rage against all that had been going on, without revenge being now possible, and of reaction after the excitement of it, a different reaction set in. Odd and unlikely as it would have appeared a month or two earlier, when Tilling was seething with duels, it was a fact that it was possible to have too much excitement. Ever since the Contessa had arrived, she had been like an active volcano planted down among dangerously inflammable elements, and the removal of it was really a matter of relief. Miss Mapp felt that she would be dealing again with materials whose properties she knew, and since, no doubt, the strain of Susan's marriage would soon follow, it was a merciful dispensation that the removal of the volcano granted Tilling a short restorative pause. The young couple would be back before long, and with Susan's approaching elevation certainly going to her head, and making her talk in a manner wholly intolerable about the grandeur of the Wyses of Whitchurch, it was a boon to be allowed to recuperate for a little, before settling to work afresh to combat Susan's pretensions. There was no fear of being dull: for plenty of things had been going on in Tilling before the Contessa flared on the High Street, and plenty of things would continue to go on after she had taken her explosions elsewhere.

By the time that the second lesson was being read the sun had shifted from Miss Mapp's face, and enabled her to see how ghastly dear Evie looked when focused under the blue robe of Jonah, who was climbing out of the whale. She had had her disappointments to contend with, for the Contessa had never really grasped at all who she was. Sometimes she mistook her for Irene, sometimes she did not seem to see her, but never had she appeared fully to identify her as Mr Bartlett's wee wifey. But then, dear Evie was very insignificant even when she squeaked her loudest. Her best friends, among whom was Miss Mapp, would not deny that. She had been wilted by non-recognition; she would recover again, now that they were all left to themselves.

The sermon contained many repetitions and a quantity of split infinitives. The Padre had once openly stated that Shakespeare was good enough for him, and that Shakespeare was guilty of many split infinitives. On that occasion there had nearly been a breach between him and Mistress Mapp, for Mistress Mapp had said, 'But then you are not Shakespeare, dear Padre.' And he could find nothing better to reply than 'Hoots!'. . . There was nothing more of interest about the sermon.

At the end of the service Miss Mapp lingered in the church looking at the lovely decorations of holly and laurel, for which she was so largely responsible, until her instinct assured her that everybody else had shaken hands and was wondering what to say next about Christmas. Then, just then, she hurried out.

They were all there, and she came like the late and honoured guest (poor Diva).

'Diva, darling,' she said. 'Merry Christmas! And Evie! And the Padre. Padre dear, thank you for your sermon! And Major Benjy! Merry Christmas, Major Benjy. What a small company we are, but not the less Christmassy. No Mr Wyse, no Susan, no Isabel. Oh, and no Captain Puffin. Not quite well again, Major Benjy? Tell me about him. Those dreadful fits of dizziness. So hard to understand.'

She beautifully succeeded in detaching the Major from the rest. With the peace that had descended on Tilling, she had forgiven him for having been made a fool of by the Contessa.

'I'm anxious about my friend Puffin,' he said. 'Not at all up to the mark. Most depressed. I told him he had no business to be depressed. It's selfish to be depressed, I said. If we were all depressed it would be a dreary world, Miss Elizabeth. He's sent for the doctor. I was to have had a round of golf with Puffin this afternoon, but he doesn't feel up to it. It would have done him much more good than a host of doctors.'

'Oh, I wish I could play golf, and not disappoint you of your round, Major Benjy,' said she.

Major Benjy seemed rather to recoil from the thought. He did not profess, at any rate, any sympathetic regret.

'And we were going to have had our Christmas dinner together tonight,' he said, 'and spend a jolly evening afterwards.'

'I'm sure quiet is the best thing for Captain Puffin with his dizziness,' said Miss Mapp firmly.

A sudden audacity seized her. Here was the Major feeling lonely as regards his Christmas evening: here was she delighted that he should not spend it 'jollify' with Captain Puffin . . . and there was plenty of plum pudding.

'Come and have your dinner with me,' she said. 'I'm alone too.'

He shook his head.

'Very kind of you, I'm sure, Miss Elizabeth,' he said, 'but I think I'll hold myself in readiness to go across to poor old Puffin, if he feels up to it. I feel lost without my friend Puffin.'

'But you must have no jolly evening, Major Benjy,' she said. 'So bad for him. A little soup and a good night's rest. That's the best thing. Perhaps he would like me to go in and read to him. I will gladly. Tell him so from me. And if you find he doesn't want anybody, not even you, well, there's a slice of plum pudding at your neighbour's, and such a warm welcome.'

She stood on the steps of her house, which in summer were so crowded with sketchers, and would have kissed her hand to him had not Diva been following close behind, for even on Christmas Day poor Diva was capable of finding something ill-natured to say about the most tender and womanly action . . . and Miss Mapp let herself into her house with only a little wave of her hand . . .

Somehow the idea that Major Benjy was feeling lonely and missing the quarrelsome society of his debauched friend was not entirely unpleasing to her. It was odd that there should be anybody who missed Captain Puffin. Who would not sooner play golf all alone (if that was possible) than with him, or spend an evening alone rather than with his companionship? But if Captain Puffin had to be missed, she would certainly have chosen Major Benjy to be the person who missed him. Without wishing Captain Puffin any unpleasant experience, she would have borne with equanimity the news of his settled melancholia, or his permanent dizziness, for Major Benjy with his bright robustness was not the sort of man to prove a willing comrade to a chronically dizzy or melancholic friend. Nor would it be right that he should be so. Men in the prime of life were not meant for that. Nor were they meant to be the victims of designing women, even though Wyses of Whitchurch . . . He was saved from that by their most opportune departure.

In spite of her readiness to be interrupted at any moment, Miss Mapp spent a solitary evening. She had pulled a cracker with

Withers, and severely jarred a tooth over a threepenny-piece in the plum pudding, but there had been no other events. Once or twice, in order to see what the night was like, she had gone to the window of the garden room, and been aware that there was a light in Major Benjy's house, but when half-past ten struck, she had despaired of company and gone to bed. A little carol singing in the streets gave her a Christmas feeling, and she hoped that the singers got a nice supper somewhere.

Miss Mapp did not feel as genial as usual when she came down to breakfast next day, and omitted to say good morning to her rainbow of piggies. She had run short of wool for her knitting, and Boxing Day appeared to her a very ill-advised institution. You would have imagined, thought Miss Mapp, as she began cracking her egg, that the tradespeople had had enough relaxation on Christmas Day, especially when, as on this occasion, it was immediately preceded by Sunday, and would have been all the better for getting to work again. She never relaxed her efforts for a single day in the year, and why –

An overpowering knocking on her front door caused her to stop cracking her egg. That imperious summons was succeeded by but a moment of silence, and then it began again. She heard the hurried step of Withers across the hall, and almost before she could have been supposed to reach the front door, Diva burst into the room.

'Dead!' she said. 'In his soup. Captain Puffin. Can't wait!'

She whirled out again and the front door banged.

Miss Mapp ate her egg in three mouthfuls, had no marmalade at all, and putting on the Prince of Wales's cloak tripped down into the High Street. Though all shops were shut, Evie was there with her market basket, eagerly listening to what Mrs Brace, the doctor's wife, was communicating. Though Mrs Brace was not, strictly speaking, 'in society', Miss Mapp waived all social distinctions, and pressed her hand with a mournful smile.

'Is it all too terribly true?' she asked.

Mrs Brace did not take the smallest notice of her, and, dropping her voice, spoke to Evie in tones so low that Miss Mapp could not catch a single syllable except the word soup, which seemed to imply that Diva had got hold of some correct news at last. Evie gave a shrill little scream at the concluding words, whatever they were, as Mrs Brace hurried away.

Miss Mapp firmly cornered Evie, and heard what had happened. Captain Puffin had gone up to bed last night, not feeling well, without having any dinner. But he had told Mrs Gashly to make him some soup, and he would not want anything else. His parlourmaid had brought it to him, and had soon afterwards opened the door to Major Flint, who, learning that his friend had gone to bed, went away. She called her master in the morning, and found him sitting, still dressed, with his face in the soup which he had poured out into a deep soup plate. This was very odd, and she had called Mrs Gashly. They settled that he was dead, and rang up the doctor, who agreed with them. It was clear that Captain Puffin had had a stroke of some sort, and had fallen forward into the soup which he had just poured out . . .

'But he didn't die of his stroke,' said Evie in a strangled whisper. 'He was drowned.'

'Drowned, dear?' said Miss Mapp.

'Yes. Lungs were full of ox-tail, oh, dear me! A stroke first, and he fell forward with his face in his soup plate and got his nose and mouth quite covered with the soup. He was drowned. All on dry land and in his bedroom. Too terrible. What dangers we are all in!'

She gave a loud squeak and escaped, to tell her husband.

*   *   *

Diva had finished calling on everybody, and approached rapidly.

'He must have died of a stroke,' said Diva. 'Very much depressed lately. That precedes a stroke.'

'Oh, then, haven't you heard, dear?' said Miss Mapp. 'It is all too terrible! On Christmas Day, too!'

'Suicide?' asked Diva. 'Oh, how shocking!'

'No, dear. It was like this . . .'

*   *   *

Miss Mapp got back to her house long before she usually left it. Her cook came up with the proposed bill of fare for the day.

'That will do for lunch,' said Miss Mapp. 'But not soup in the evening. A little fish from what was left over yesterday, and some toasted cheese. That will be plenty. Just a tray.'

Miss Mapp went to the garden room and sat at her window.

'All so sudden,' she said to herself.

She sighed.

'I dare say there may have been much that was good in Captain Puffin,' she thought, 'that we knew nothing about.'

She wore a wintry smile.

'Major Benjy will feel very lonely,' she said.

EPILOGUE

Miss Mapp went to the garden room and sat at her window . . .

It was a warm, bright day of February, and a butterfly was enjoying itself in the pale sunshine on the other window, and perhaps (so Miss Mapp sympathetically interpreted its feelings) was rather annoyed that it could not fly away through the pane. It was not a white butterfly, but a tortoiseshell, very pretty, and in order to let it enjoy itself more, she opened the window and it fluttered out into the garden. Before it had flown many yards, a starling ate most of it up, so the starling enjoyed itself too.

Miss Mapp fully shared in the pleasure first of the tortoiseshell and then of the starling, for she was enjoying herself very much too, though her left wrist was terribly stiff. But Major Benjy was so cruel: he insisted on her learning that turn of the wrist which was so important in golf.

'Upon my word, you've got it now, Miss Elizabeth,' he had said to her yesterday, and then made her do it all over again fifty times more. ('Such a bully!') Sometimes she struck the ground, sometimes she struck the ball, sometimes she struck the air. But he had been very much pleased with her. And she was very much pleased with him. She forgot about the butterfly and remembered the starling.

It was idle to deny that the last six weeks had been a terrific strain, and the strain on her left wrist was nothing to them. The worst tension of all, perhaps, was when Diva had bounced in with the news that the Contessa was coming back. That was so like Diva: the only foundation for the report proved to be that Figgis had said to her Janet that Mr Wyse was coming back, and either Janet had misunderstood Figgis, or Diva (far more probably) had misunderstood Janet, and Miss Mapp only hoped that Diva had not done so on purpose, though it looked like it. Stupid as poor Diva undoubtedly was, it was hard for Charity itself to believe that she had thought that Janet really said that. But when this report proved to be totally unfounded, Miss Mapp rose to the occasion, and said that Diva had spoken out of stupidity and not out of malice towards her . . .

Then in due course Mr Wyse had come back and the two Poppits had come back, and only three days ago one Poppit had become a Wyse, and they had all three gone for a motor tour on the Continent in the Royce. Very likely they would go as far south as Capri, and Susan would stay with her new grand Italian connections. What she would be like when she got back Miss Mapp forbore to conjecture, since it was no use anticipating trouble; but Susan had been so grandiose about the Wyses, multiplying their incomes and their acreage by fifteen or twenty, so Miss Mapp conjectured, and talking so much about county families, that the liveliest imagination failed to picture what she would make of the Faragliones. She already alluded to the Count as 'my brother-in-law Cecco Faraglione', but had luckily heard Diva say 'Faradiddleony' in a loud aside, which had made her a little more reticent. Susan had taken the insignia of the Member of the British Empire with her, as she at once conceived the idea of being presented to the Queen of Italy by Amelia, and going to a court ball, and Isabel had taken her manuscript book of Malaprops and Spoonerisms. If she put down all the Italian malaprops that Mrs Wyse would commit, it was likely that she would bring back two volumes instead of one.

Though all these grandeurs were so rightly irritating, the departure of the 'young couple' and Isabel had left Tilling, already shocked and shattered by the death of Captain Puffin, rather flat and purposeless. Miss Mapp alone refused to be flat, and had never been so full of purpose. She felt that it would be unpardonably selfish of her if she regarded for a moment her own loss, when there was one in Tilling who suffered so much more keenly, and she set herself with admirable singleness of purpose to restore Major Benjy's zest in life, and fill the gap. She wanted no assistance from others in this: Diva, for instance, with her jerky ways would be only too apt to jar on him, and her black dress might remind him of his loss if Miss Mapp had asked her to go shares in the task of making the Major's evenings less lonely. Also the weather, during the whole of January, was particularly inclement, and it would have been too much to expect of Diva to come all the way up the hill in the wet, while it was but a step from the Major's door to her own. So there was little or nothing in the way of winter bridge as far as Miss Mapp and the Major were concerned. Piquet with a single sympathetic companion who did not mind being rubiconned at threepence a hundred was as much as he was up to at present.

With the end of the month a balmy foretaste of spring (such as had encouraged the tortoiseshell butterfly to hope) set in, and the Major used to drop in after breakfast and stroll round the garden with her, smoking his pipe. Miss Mapp's sweet snowdrops had begun to appear, and green spikes of crocuses pricked the black earth, and the sparrows were having such fun in the creepers. Then one day the Major, who was going out to catch the 11.20 tram, had a 'golf stick', as Miss Mapp so foolishly called it, with him, and a golf ball, and after making a dreadful hole in her lawn, she had hit the ball so hard that it rebounded from the brick wall, which was quite a long way off, and came back to her very feet, as if asking to be hit again by the golf stick – no, golf club. She learned to keep her wonderfully observant eye on the ball and bought one of her own. The Major lent her a mashie – and before anyone would have thought it possible, she had learned to propel her ball right over the bed where the snowdrops grew, without beheading any of them in its passage. It was the turn of the wrist that did that, and Withers cleaned the dear little mashie afterwards, and put it safely in the corner of the garden room.

Today was to be epoch-making. They were to go out to the real links by the 11.20 tram (consecrated by so many memories), and he was to call for her at eleven. He had *quai-hai*ed for porridge fully an hour ago.

After letting out the tortoiseshell butterfly from the window looking into the garden, she moved across to the post of observation on the street, and arranged snowdrops in a little glass vase. There were a few over when that was full, and she saw that a reel of cotton was close at hand, in case she had an idea of what to do with the remainder. Eleven o'clock chimed from the church, and on the stroke she saw him coming up the few yards of street that separated his door from hers. So punctual! So manly!

Diva was careering about the High Street as they walked along it, and Miss Mapp kissed her hand to her.

'Off to play golf, darling,' she said. 'Is that not grand? *Au reservoir.*'

Diva had not missed seeing the snowdrops in the Major's buttonhole, and stood stupefied for a moment at this news. Then she caught sight of Evie, and shot across the street to communicate her suspicions. Quaint Irene joined then and the Padre.

'Snowdrops, i'fegs!' said he . . .

MAPP AND
LUCIA

CHAPTER ONE

Though it was nearly a year since her husband's death, Emmeline Lucas (universally known to her friends as Lucia) still wore the deepest and most uncompromising mourning. Black certainly suited her very well, but that had nothing to do with this continued use of it, whatever anybody said. Peppino and she had been the most devoted couple for over twenty-five years, and her grief at his loss was heartfelt: she missed him constantly and keenly. But months ago now, she, with her very vital and active personality, had felt a most natural craving to immerse herself again in all those thrilling interests which made life in this Elizabethan village of Riseholme so exciting a business, and she had not yet been able to make up her mind to take the plunge she longed for. Though she had not made a luxury out of the tokens of grief, she had perhaps made, ever so slightly, a stunt of them.

For instance. There was that bookshop on the green, Ye Signe of Ye Daffodil, under the imprint of which Peppino had published his severely limited edition of *Fugitive Lyrics* and *Pensieri Persi*. A full six months after his death Lucia had been walking past it with Georgie Pillson, and had seen in the window a book she would have liked to purchase. But next to it, on the shelf, was the thin volume of Peppino's *Pensieri Persi*, and, frankly, it had been rather stuntish of her to falter on the threshold and, with eyes that were doing their best to swim, to say to Georgie: 'I can't quite face going in, Georgie. Weak of me, I know, but there it is. Will you please just pop in, *caro*, and ask them to send me *Beethoven's Days of Boyhood*? I will stroll on.'

So Georgie had pressed her hand and done this errand for her, and of course he had repeated this pathetic little incident to others. Tasteful embroideries had been tacked on to it, and it was soon known all over Riseholme that poor Lucia had gone into Ye Signe of Ye Daffodil to buy the book about Beethoven's boyhood, and had been so sadly affected by the sight of Peppino's poems in their rough brown linen cover with dark green tape to tie them up with (although she constantly saw the same volume in her own house), that she had quite broken down. Some said that sal volatile had been administered.

Similarly, she had never been able to bring herself to have a game of golf, or to resume her Dante readings, and having thus established the impression that her life had been completely smashed up it had been hard to decide that on Tuesday or Wednesday next she would begin to glue it together again. In consequence she had remained in as many pieces as before. Like a sensible woman she was very careful of her physical health, and since this stunt of mourning made it impossible for her to play golf or take brisk walks, she sent for a very illuminating little book, called *An Ideal System of Callisthenics For Those No Longer Young*, and in a secluded glade of her garden she exposed as much of herself as was proper to the invigorating action of the sun, when there was any, and had long bouts of skipping, and kicked, and jerked, and swayed her trunk, gracefully and vigorously, in accordance with the instructions laid down. The effect was most satisfactory, and at the very, very back of her mind she conceived it possible that some day she might conduct callisthenic classes for those ladies of Riseholme who were no longer young.

Then there was the greater matter of the Elizabethan fête to be held in August next, when Riseholme would be swarming with tourists. The idea of it had been entirely Lucia's, and there had been several meetings of the fête committee (of which, naturally, she was president) before Peppino's death. She had planned the great scene in it: this was to be Queen Elizabeth's visit to the *Golden Hind*, when, on the completion of Francis Drake's circumnavigation of the world, Her Majesty went to dine with him on board his ship at Deptford and knighted him. The *Golden Hind* was to be moored in the pond on the village green; or, more accurately, a platform on piles was to be built there, in the shape of a ship's deck, with masts and rudder and cannons and bulwarks, and banners and ancients, particularly ancients. The pond would be an admirable stage, for rows of benches would be put up all round it, and everybody would see beautifully. The Queen's procession with trumpeters and men-at-arms and ladies of the Court was planned to start from The Hurst, which was Lucia's house, and make its glittering and melodious way across the green to Deptford to the sound of madrigals and medieval marches. Lucia would impersonate the Queen, Peppino following her as Raleigh, and Georgie would be Francis Drake. But at an early stage of these incubations Peppino had died, and Lucia had involved herself in this inextricable widowhood. Since then the reins of government had fallen into Daisy Quantock's podgy little hands, and she, in this as in all other matters, had come to consider herself quite the Queen of Riseholme, until Lucia could get a move on again and teach her better.

One morning in June, some seven weeks before the date fixed for the fête, Mrs Quantock telephoned from her house a hundred yards away to say that she particularly wanted to see Lucia, if she might pop over for a little talk. Lucia had heard nothing lately about the preparations for the fête, for the last time that it had been mentioned in her presence, she had gulped and sat with her hand over her eyes for a moment overcome with the memory of how gaily she had planned it. But she knew that the preparations for it must by this time be well in hand, and now she instantly guessed that it was on this subject that Daisy wanted to see her. She had premonitions of that kind sometimes, and she was sure that this was one of them. Probably Daisy wanted to address a moving appeal to her that, for the sake of Riseholme generally, she should make this fête the occasion of her emerging from her hermetic widowhood. The idea recommended itself to Lucia, for before the date fixed for it, she would have been a widow for over a year, and she reflected that her dear Peppino would never have wished her to make this permanent suttee of herself: also there was the prestige of Riseholme to be considered. Besides, she was really itching to get back into the saddle again, and depose Daisy from her awkward, clumsy seat there, and this would be an admirable opportunity. So, as was usual now with her, she first sighed into the telephone, said rather faintly that she would be delighted to see dear Daisy, and then sighed again. Daisy, very stupidly, hoped she had not got a cough, and was reassured on that point.

Lucia gave a few moments' thought as to whether she would be found at the piano, playing the funeral march from Beethoven's Sonata in A flat which she now knew by heart, or be sitting out in Perdita's garden, reading Peppino's poems. She decided on the latter, and putting on a shady straw hat with a crêpe bow on it, and taking a copy of the poems from the shelf, hurried out into Perdita's garden. She also carried with her a copy of today's *Times*, which she had not yet read.

Perdita's garden requires a few words of explanation. It was a charming little square plot in front of the timbered façade of The Hurst, surrounded by yew hedges and intersected with paths of crazy pavement, carefully smothered in stone crop, which led to the Elizabethan sundial from Wardour Street in the centre. It was gay in spring with those flowers (and no others) on which Perdita doted. There were 'violets dim', and primroses and daffodils, which came before the swallow dared and took the winds (usually of April) with beauty. But now in June the swallow had dared long ago, and when spring and the daffodils were over, Lucia always allowed Perdita's garden a wider, though still strictly Shakespearian scope. There was eglantine (Penzance briar) in full flower now, and honeysuckle and gillyflowers and plenty of pansies for thoughts, and yards of rue (more than usual this year), and so Perdita's garden was gay all the summer.

Here then, this morning, Lucia seated herself by the sundial, all in black, on a stone bench on which was carved the motto 'Come thou north wind, and blow thou south, that my garden spices may flow forth.' Sitting there with Peppino's poems and *The Times* she obscured about one-third of this text, and fat little Daisy would obscure the rest . . . It was rather annoying that the tapes which tied the covers of Peppino's poems had got into a hard knot, which she was quite unable to unravel, for she had meant that Daisy should come up, unheard by her, in her absorption, and find her reading Peppino's lyric called 'Loneliness'. But she could not untie the tapes, and as soon as she heard Daisy's footsteps she became lost in reverie with the book lying shut on her lap, and the famous faraway look in her eyes.

It was a very hot morning. Daisy, like many middle-aged women who enjoyed perfect health, was always practising some medical regime of a hygienic nature, and just now she was a devoted slave to the eliminative processes of the body. The pores of the skin were the most important of these agencies, and, after her drill of physical jerks by the open window of her bedroom, she had trotted in all this heat across the green to keep up the elimination. She mopped and panted for a little.

'Made quite a new woman of me,' she said. 'You should try it, dear Lucia. But so good of you to see me, and I'll come to the point at once. The Elizabethan fête, you know. You see it won't be till August. Can't we persuade you, as they say, to come among us again? We all want you: such a fillip you'd give it.'

Lucia made no doubt that this request implied the hope that she might be induced to take the part of Queen Elizabeth, and under the spell of the exuberant sunshine that poured in upon Perdita's garden, she felt the thrill and the pulse of life bound in her veins. The fête would be an admirable occasion for entering the arena of activities again, and, as Daisy had hinted (delicately for Daisy), more than a year of her widowhood would have elapsed by August. It was self-sacrificing, too, of Daisy to have suggested this herself, for she knew that according to present arrangements Daisy was to take the part of the Virgin Queen, and Georgie had told her weeks ago (when the subject of the fête had been last alluded to) that she was already busy pricking her fingers by sewing a ruff to go round her fat little neck, and that she had bought a most sumptuous string of Woolworth pearls. Perhaps dear Daisy had realized what a very ridiculous figure she would present as Queen, and was anxious for the sake of the fête to retire from so laughable a role. But, however that might be, it was nice of her to volunteer abdication.

Lucia felt that it was only proper that Daisy should press her a little. She was being asked to sacrifice her personal feelings which so recoiled from publicity, and for the sake of Riseholme to rescue the fête from being a farce. She was most eager to do so, and a very little pressing would be sufficient. So she sighed again, she stroked the cover of Peppino's poems, but she spoke quite briskly.

'Dear Daisy,' she said, 'I don't think I could face it. I cannot imagine myself coming out of my house in silks and jewels to take my place in the procession without my Peppino. He was to have been

Raleigh, you remember, and to have walked immediately behind me. The welcome, the shouting, the rejoicing, the madrigals, the Morris dances and me with my poor desolate heart! But perhaps I ought to make an effort. My dear Peppino, I know, would have wished me to. You think so, too, and I have always respected the soundness of your judgement.'

A slight change came over Daisy's round red face. Lucia was getting on rather too fast and too far.

'My dear, none of us ever thought of asking you to be Queen Elizabeth,' she said. 'We are not so unsympathetic, for of course that would be far too great a strain on you. You must not think of it. All that I was going to suggest was that you might take the part of Drake's wife. She only comes forward just for a moment, and makes her curtsey to me – I mean to the Queen – and then walks backwards again into the chorus of ladies-in-waiting and halberdiers and things.'

Lucia's beady eyes dwelt for a moment on Daisy's rather anxious face with a glance of singular disdain. What a fool poor Daisy was to think that she, Lucia, could possibly consent to take any subordinate part in tableaux or processions or anything else at Riseholme where she had been Queen so long! She had decided in her own mind that with a very little judicious pressing she would take the part of the Queen, and thus make her superb entry into Riseholme life again, but all the pressure in the world would not induce her to impersonate anyone else, unless she could double it with the Queen. Was there ever anything so tactless as Daisy's tact? . . .

She gave a wintry smile, and stroked the cover of Peppino's poems again.

'Sweet of you to suggest it, dear,' she said, 'but indeed it would be quite too much for me. I was wrong to entertain the idea even for a moment. Naturally I shall take the greatest, the *very* greatest interest in it all, and I am sure you will understand if I do not even feel equal to coming to it, and read about it instead in the *Worcestershire Herald*.' She paused. Perhaps it would be more in keeping with her empty heart to say nothing more about the fête. On the other hand, she felt a devouring curiosity to know how they were getting on. She sighed.

'I must begin to interest myself in things again,' she said. 'So tell me about it all, Daisy, if you would like to.'

Daisy was much relieved to know that even the part of Drake's wife was too much for Lucia. She was safe now from any risk of having the far more arduous part of the Queen snatched from her.

'All going splendidly,' she said. 'Revels on the green to open with, and madrigals and Morris dances. Then comes the scene on the *Golden Hind* which was entirely your idea. We've only elaborated it a little. There will be a fire on the poop of the ship, or is it the prow?'

'It depends, dear, which end of the ship you mean,' said Lucia.

'The behind part, the stern. Poop, is it? Well, there will be a fire on the poop for cooking. Quite safe, they say, if the logs are laid on a sheet of iron. Over the fire we shall have an Elizabethan spit, and roast a sheep on it.'

'I wouldn't,' said Lucia, feeling the glamour of these schemes glowing in her. 'Half of it will be cinders and the rest blood.'

'No, dear,' said Daisy. 'It will really be roasted first at the Ambermere Arms, and then just hung over the fire on the *Golden Hind*.'

'Oh, yes: just to get a little kippered in the smoke,' said Lucia.

'Not to matter. Of course I shan't really eat any, because I never touch meat of any sort now: I shall only pretend to. But there'll be the scene of cooking going on for the Queen's dinner on the deck of the *Golden Hind*, just to fill up, while the Queen's procession is forming. Oh, I wonder if you would let us start the procession from your house rather than mine. The route would be so much more in the open: everyone will see it better. I would come across to dress, if you would let me, half an hour before.'

Lucia of course knew perfectly well that Daisy was to be the Queen, but she wanted to make her say so.

'Certainly start from here,' said Lucia. 'I am only too happy to help. And dress here yourself. Let me see: what are you going to be?'

'They've all insisted that I should be Queen Elizabeth,' said Daisy hurriedly. 'Where had we got to? Oh yes: as the procession is forming, the cooking will be going on. Songs of course, a chorus of cooks. Then the procession will cross the green to the *Golden Hind*, then dinner, and then I knight Drake. Such a lovely sword.'

Then Elizabethan games, running, jumping, wrestling and so on. We thought of baiting a bear, one out of some menagerie that could be trusted not to get angry, but we've given that up. If it didn't get angry, it wouldn't be baited, and if it did get angry it would be awful.'

'Very prudent,' said Lucia.

'Then I steal away into the Ambermere Arms which is quite close, and change into a riding dress. There'll be a white palfrey at the door, the one that draws the milk cart. Oh, I forgot. While I'm dressing, before the palfrey comes round, a rider gallops in from Plymouth on a horse covered with soapsuds to say that the Spanish Armada has been sighted. I think we must have a megaphone for that, or no one will hear. So I come out, and mount my palfrey, and make my speech to my troops at Tilbury. A large board, you know, with Tilbury written up on it like a station. That's quite in the Shakespearian style. I shall have to learn it all by heart, and just have Raleigh standing by the palfrey with a copy of my speech to prompt me if I forget.'

The old familiar glamour glowed brighter and brighter to Lucia as Daisy spoke. She wondered if she had made a mistake in not accepting the ludicrous part of Drake's wife, just in order to get a footing in these affairs again and attend committees, and, gradually ousting Daisy from her supremacy, take the part of the Queen herself. She felt that she must think it all over, and settle whether, in so advanced a stage of the proceedings, it could be done. At present, till she had made up her mind, it was wiser, in order to rouse no suspicions, to pretend that these things were all very remote. She would take a faint though kindly interest in them, as if some elderly person was watching children at play, and smiling pensively at their pretty gambols. But as for watching the fête when the date arrived, that was unthinkable. She would either be Queen Elizabeth herself, or not be at Riseholme at all. That was that.

'Well, you have got your work cut out for you, dear Daisy,' she said, giving a surreptitious tug at the knotted tape of Peppino's poems. 'What fun you will have, and, dear me, how far away it all seems!'

Daisy wrenched her mind away from the thought of the fête.

'It won't always, dear,' she said, making a sympathetic little dab at Lucia's wrist. 'Your joy in life will revive again. I see you've got Peppino's poems there. Won't you read me one?'

Lucia responded to this gesture with another dab.

'Do you remember the last one he wrote?' she said. 'He called it "Loneliness". I was away in London at the time. Beginning:

"The spavined storm-clouds limp down the ruinous sky,
    While I sit alone.
Thick through the acid air the dumb leaves fly . . .".

But I won't read it you now. Another time.'

Daisy gave one more sympathetic poke at her wrist, and rose to go.

'Must be off,' she said. 'Won't you come round and dine quietly tonight?'

'I can't, many thanks. Georgie is dining with me. Any news in Riseholme this morning?'

Daisy reflected for a moment.

'Oh, yes,' she said. 'Mrs Antrobus's got a wonderful new apparatus. Not an ear trumpet at all. She just bites on a small leather pad, and hears everything perfectly. Then she takes it out of her mouth and answers you, and puts it back again to listen.'

'No!' said Lucia excitedly. 'All wet?'

'Quite dry. Just between her teeth. No wetter anyhow than a pen you put in your mouth, I assure you.'

Daisy hurried away to do some more exercises and drink pints and pints of hot water before lunch. She felt that she had emerged safely from a situation which might easily have become menacing, for without question Lucia, in spite of her sighs and her wistful stroking of the covers of Peppino's poems, and her great crêpe bow, was beginning to show signs of her old animation. She had given Daisy a glance or two from that beady eye which had the qualities of a gimlet about it, she had shown eager interest in such topics as the roasting of the sheep and Mrs Antrobus's gadget, which a few weeks ago would not have aroused the slightest response from her stricken mind, and it was lucky, Daisy thought, that Lucia had given her the definite assurance that even the part of Drake's wife in the fête would be too much for her. For goodness only knew, when once Lucia settled to be on the mend, how swift her recuperation might be, or what mental horsepower in the way of schemings and domination she might not develop after this fallow period of quiescence. There was a new atmosphere about her today: she was like some spring morning when, though winds might still be chilly and the sun still of tepid and watery beams, the air was pregnant with the imminent birth of new life. But evidently she meant to take no hand in the fête, which at present completely filled Daisy's horizon. 'She may do what she likes afterwards,' thought Daisy, breaking into a trot, 'but I will be Queen Elizabeth.'

Her house, with its mulberry tree in front and its garden at the back, stood next Georgie Pillson's on the edge of the green, and as she passed through it and out on to the lawn behind, she heard from the other side of the paling that tap-tap of croquet mallet and ball which now almost without cessation punctuated the hours of any fine morning. Georgie had developed a craze for solitary croquet: he spent half the day practising all by himself, to the great neglect of his watercolour painting and his piano playing. He seemed indeed, apart from croquet, to be losing his zest for life; he took none of his old interest in the thrilling topics of Riseholme. He had not been a bit excited at Daisy's description of Mrs Antrobus's new apparatus, and the prospect of impersonating Francis Drake at the forthcoming fête aroused only the most tepid enthusiasm in him. A book of Elizabethan costumes, full of sumptuous coloured plates, had roused him for a while from his lethargy, and he had chosen a white satin tunic with puffed sleeves slashed with crimson, and a cloak of rose-coloured silk, on the reproduction of which his peerless parlourmaid Foljambe was at work, but he didn't seem to have any keenness about him. Of course he had had some rather cruel blows of Fate to contend against lately: Miss Olga Bracely the prima donna to whom he had been so devoted had left Riseholme a month ago for a year's operatic tour in the United States and Australia, and that was a desolate bereavement for him, while Lucia's determination not to do any of all these things which she had once enjoyed so much had deprived him of all the duets they used to play together. Moreover, it was believed in Riseholme (though only whispered at present) that Foljambe, that paragon of parlourmaids, in whom the smoothness and comfort of his domestic life was centred, was walking out with Cadman, Lucia's chauffeur. It might not mean anything, but if it did, if Foljambe and he intended to get married and Foljambe left Georgie, and if Georgie had got wind of this, then indeed there would be good cause for that lack of zest, that air of gloom and apprehension which was now so often noticeable in him. All these causes, the blows Fate had already rained on him, and the anxiety concerning this possible catastrophe in the future, probably contributed to the eclipsed condition of his energies.

Daisy sat down on a garden bench, and began to do a little deep breathing, which was a relic of the days when she had studied Yoga. It was important to concentrate (otherwise the deep breathing did no good at all), or rather to attain a complete blankness of mind and exclude from it all mundane interests which were Maya, or illusion. But this morning she found it difficult: regiments of topics grew up like mushrooms. Now she congratulated herself on having made certain that Lucia was not intending to butt into the fête, now she began to have doubts – these were disconcerting mushrooms – as to whether that was so certain, for Lucia was much brisker today than she had been since Peppino's death, and if that continued, her reawakened interest in life would surely seek for some outlet. Then the thought of her own speech to her troops at Tilbury began to leak into her mind: would she ever get it so thoroughly by heart that she could feel sure that no attack of nervousness or movement on the part of her palfrey would put it out of her head? Above all there was that disturbing tap-tap going on from Georgie's garden, and however much she tried to attain blankness of mind, she found herself listening for the next tap . . . It was no use and she got up.

'Georgie, are you there?' she called out.

'Yes,' came his voice, trembling with excitement. 'Wait a minute. I've gone through nine hoops and – Oh, how tarsome, I missed quite an easy one. What is it? I rather wish you hadn't called me just then.'

Georgie was tall, and he could look over the paling. Daisy pulled her chair up to it, and mounted on it, so that they could converse with level heads.

'So sorry, Georgie,' she said, 'I didn't know you were making such a break. Fancy! Nine! I wanted to tell you I've been to see Lucia.'

'Is that all? I knew that because I saw you,' said Georgie. 'I was polishing my bibelots in the drawing room. And you sat in Perdita's garden.'

'And there's a change,' continued Daisy, who had kept her mouth open, in order to go on again as soon as Georgie stopped. 'She's better. Distinctly. More interested, and not so faint and die-away. Sarcastic about the roast sheep for instance.'

'What? Did she talk about the fête again?' asked Georgie. 'That is an improvement.'

'That was what I went to talk about. I asked her if she wouldn't make an effort to be Drake's wife. But she said it would be too great a strain.'

'My dear, you didn't ask her to be Drake's wife?' said Georgie incredulously. 'You might as well have asked her to be a confused noise within. What can you have been thinking of?'

'Anyhow, she said she couldn't be anything at all,' said Daisy. 'I have her word for that. But if she is recovering, and I'm sure she is, her head will be full of plans again. I'm not quite happy about it.'

'What you mean is that you're afraid she may want to be the Queen,' observed Georgie acutely.

'I won't give it up,' said Daisy very firmly, not troubling to confirm so obvious an interpretation. 'I've had all the trouble of it, and very nearly learned the speech to the troops, and made my ruff and bought a rope of pearls. It wouldn't be fair, Georgie. So don't encourage her, will you? I know you're dining with her tonight.'

'No, I won't encourage her,' said he. 'But you know what Lucia is, when she's in working order. If she wants a thing, she gets it somehow. It happens. That's all you can say about it.'

'Well, this one shan't happen,' said Daisy, dismounting from her basket chair which was beginning to sag. 'It would be too mean. And I wish you would come across now and let us practise that scene where I knight you. We must get it very slick.'

'Not this morning,' said Georgie. 'I know my bit: I've only got to kneel down. You can practise on the end of a sofa. Besides, if Lucia is really waking up, I shall take some duets across this evening, and I must have a go at some of them. I've not touched my piano for weeks. And my shoulder's sore where you knighted me so hard the other day. Quite a bruise.'

Daisy suddenly remembered something more.

'And Lucia repeated me several lines out of one of Peppino's last poems,' she said. 'She couldn't possibly have done that a month ago without breaking down. And I believe she would have read one to me when I asked her to, but I'm pretty sure she couldn't undo one of those tapes that the book is tied up with. A hard knot. She was picking at it . . .'

'Oh, she must be better,' said he. 'Ever so much.'

So Georgie went in to practise some of the old duets in case Lucia felt equal to evoking the memories of happier days at the piano, and Daisy hit the end of her sofa some half-dozen times with her umbrella bidding it rise Sir Francis Drake. She still wondered if Lucia had some foul scheme in her head, but though there had ticked by some minutes, directly after their talk in Perdita's garden, which might have proved exceedingly dangerous to her own chance of being the Queen, these, by the time that she was knighting the sofa, had passed. For Lucia, still meditating whether she should not lay plots for ousting Daisy, had, in default of getting that knotted tape undone, turned to her unread *Times*, and scanned its columns with a rather absent eye. There was no news that could interest anybody, and her glance wandered up and down the lists of situations vacant and wanted, of the sailings of steamers, and finally of houses to be let for summer months. There was a picture of one with a plain pleasant Queen Anne front looking on to a cobbled street. It was highly attractive, and below it she read that Miss Mapp sought a tenant for her house in Tilling, called Mallards, for the months of August and September. Seven bedrooms, four sitting rooms, h. & c, and an old-world garden. At that precise psychological moment Daisy's prospects of being Queen Elizabeth became vastly rosier, for this house to let started an idea in Lucia's mind which instantly took precedence of other schemes. She must talk to Georgie about it this evening: till then it should simmer. Surely also the name of Miss Mapp aroused faint echoes of memory in her mind: she seemed to remember a large woman with a wide smile who had stayed at the Ambermere Arms a few years ago, and had been very agreeable but slightly superior. Georgie would probably remember her . . . But the sun had become extremely powerful, and Lucia picked up her *Times* and her book of poems and went indoors to the cool lattice-paned parlour where her piano stood. By it was a bookcase with volumes of bound-up music, and she drew from it one which contained the duets over which Georgie and she used to be so gay and so industrious. These were Mozart quartets arranged for four hands, delicious, rippling airs: it was months since she had touched them, or since the music room had resounded to anything but the most sombre and pensive strains. Now she opened the book and put it on the music rest. '*Uno, due, tre,*' she said to herself and began practising the treble part which was the more amusing to play.

*   *   *

Georgie saw the difference in her at once when he arrived for dinner that evening. She was sitting outside in Perdita's garden and for the first time hailed him as of old in brilliant Italian.

'*Buona sera, caro,*' she said. '*Come sta?*'

'*Molto bene,*' he answered, 'and what a *caldo* day. I've brought a little music across with me in case you felt inclined. Mozartino.'

'What a good idea! We will have *un po' di musica* afterwards, but I've got *tanto, tanto* to talk to you about. Come in: dinner will be ready. Any news?'

'Let me think,' he said. 'No, I don't think there's much. I've got rather a bruised shoulder where Daisy knighted me the other day – '

'Dear Daisy!' said Lucia. 'A little heavy-handed sometimes, don't you find? Not a light touch. She was in here this morning talking about the fête. She urged me to take part in it. What part do you think she suggested, Georgie? You'll never guess.'

'I never should have, if she hadn't told me,' he said. 'The most ludicrous thing I ever heard.'

Lucia sighed.

'I'm afraid not much more ludicrous than her being Queen Elizabeth,' she said. 'Daisy on a palfrey addressing her troops! Georgie dear, think of it! It sounds like that rather vulgar game called "Consequences". Daisy, I am afraid, has got tipsy with excitement at the thought of being a queen. She is running amok, and she will make a deplorable exhibition of herself, and Riseholme will become the laughing stock of all those American tourists who come here in August to see our lovely Elizabethan village. The village will be all right, but what of Elizabeth? *Tacete un momento*, Georgie. *Le domestiche.*'

Georgie's Italian was rusty after so much disuse, but he managed to translate this sentence to himself, and unerringly inferred that Lucia did not want to pursue the subject while Grosvenor, the parlourmaid, and her colleague were in the room.

'*Sicuro*,' he said, and made haste to help himself to his fish. The *domestiche* thereupon left the room again, to be summoned back by the stroke of a silver bell in the shape of a pomander which nestled among pepper- and mustard-pots beside Lucia. Almost before the door had closed on their exit, Lucia began to speak again.

'Of course after poor Daisy's suggestion I shall take no part myself in this fête,' she said; 'and even if she besought me on her knees to play Queen Elizabeth, I could not dream of doing so. She cannot deprive me of what I may call a proper pride, and since she has thought good to offer me the role of Drake's wife, who, she hastened to explain, only came on for one moment and curtseyed to her, and then retired into the ranks of men-at-arms and ladies-in-waiting again, my sense of dignity, of which I have still some small fragments left, would naturally prevent me from taking any part in the performance, even at the end of a barge pole. But I am sorry for Daisy, since she knows her own deficiencies so little, and I shall mourn for Riseholme if the poor thing makes such a mess of the whole affair as she most indubitably will if she is left to organize it herself. That's all.'

It appeared, however, that there was a little more, for Lucia quickly finished her fish, and continued at once.

'So after what she said to me this morning, I cannot myself offer to help her, but if you like to do so, Georgie, you can tell her – not from me, mind, but from your own impression – that you think I should be perfectly willing to coach her and make the best I can of her as the embodiment of great Queen Bess. Something might be done with her. She is short, but so was the Queen. She has rather bad teeth, but that doesn't matter, for the Queen had the same. Again she is not quite a lady, but the Queen also had a marked strain of vulgarity and bourgeoisie. There was a coarse fibre in the Tudors, as I have always maintained. All this, dear Georgie, is to the good. If dear Daisy will only not try to look tall, and if she will smile a good deal, and behave naturally, these are advantages, real advantages. But in spite of them Daisy will merely make herself and Riseholme silly if she does not manage to get hold of some semblance of dignity and queenship. Little gestures, little turnings of the head, little graciousnesses; all that acting means. I thought it out in those dear old days when we began to plan it, and, as I say, I shall be happy to give poor Daisy all the hints I can, if she will come and ask me to do so. But mind, Georgie, the suggestion must not come from me. You are at liberty to say that you think I possibly might help her, but nothing more than that. *Capite?*'

This Italian word, not understanded of the people, came rather late, for already Lucia had struck the bell, as, unconsciously, she was emphasizing her generous proposal, and Grosvenor and her satellite had been in the room quite a long time. Concealment from *le domestiche* was therefore no longer possible. In fact both Georgie and Lucia had forgotten about the *domestiche* altogether.

'That's most kind of you, Lucia,' said Georgie. 'But you know what Daisy is. As obstinate as – '

'As a palfrey,' interrupted Lucia.

'Yes, quite. Certainly I'll tell her what you say, or rather suggest what you might say if she asked you to coach her, but I don't believe it will be any use. The whole fête has become an awful bore. There are six weeks yet before it's held, and she wants to practise knighting me every day, and has processions up and down her garden, and she gets all the tradesmen in the place to walk before her as halberdiers and sea captains, when they ought to be attending to their businesses and chopping meat and milking cows. Everyone's sick of it. I wish you would take it over, and be Queen yourself. Oh, I forgot, I promised Daisy I wouldn't encourage you. Dear me, how awful!'

Lucia laughed, positively laughed. This was an enormous improvement on the pensive smiles.

'Not awful at all, *Georgino mio*,' she said. 'I can well imagine poor Daisy's feverish fear that I should try to save her from being ridiculous. She loves being ridiculous, dear thing; it's a complex with her – that wonderful new book of Freud's which I must read – and subconsciously she pines to be ridiculous on as large a scale as possible. But as for my taking it over, that's quite out of the question. To begin with, I don't suppose I shall be here. Twelfth of August isn't it? Grouse-shooting opens in Scotland and bear-baiting at Riseholme.'

'No, that was given up,' said Georgie. 'I opposed it throughout on the committee. I said that even if we could get a bear at all, it wouldn't be baited if it didn't get angry – '

Lucia interrupted.

'And that if it did get angry it would be awful,' she put in.

'Yes. How did you know I said that?' asked Georgie. 'Rather neat, wasn't it?'

'Very neat indeed, *caro*,' said she. 'I knew you said it because Daisy told me she had said it herself.'

'What a cheat!' said Georgie indignantly.

Lucia looked at him wistfully.

'Ah, you mustn't think hardly of poor dear Daisy,' she said. 'Cheat is too strong a word. Just a little envious, perhaps, of bright clever things that other people say, not being very quick herself.'

'Anyhow, I shall tell her that I know she has bagged my joke,' said he.

'My dear, not worth while. You'll make quantities of others. All so trivial, Georgie, not worth noticing. Beneath you.'

Lucia leaned forward with her elbows on the table, quite in the old braced way, instead of drooping.

'But we've got far more important things to talk about than Daisy's little pilferings,' she said. 'Where shall I begin?'

'From the beginning,' said Georgie greedily. He had not felt so keen about the affairs of daily life since Lucia had buried herself in her bereavement.

'Well, the real beginning was this morning,' she said, 'when I saw something in *The Times*.'

'More than I did,' said Georgie. 'Was it about Riseholme or the fête? Daisy said she was going to write a letter to *The Times* about it.'

'I must have missed that,' said Lucia, 'unless by any chance they didn't put it in. No, not about the fête, nor about Riseholme. Very much not about Riseholme. Georgie, do you remember a woman who stayed at the Ambermere Arms one summer called Miss Mapp?'

Georgie concentrated.

'I remember the name, because she was rather globular, like a map of the world,' he said. 'Oh, wait a moment: something's coming back to me. Large, with a great smile. Teeth.'

'Yes, that's the one,' cried Lucia. 'There's telepathy going on, Georgie. We're suggesting to each other . . . Rather like a hyena, a handsome hyena. Not hungry now but might be.'

'Yes. And talked about a place called Tilling, where she had a Queen Anne house. We rather despised her for that. Oh, yes, and she came to a garden party of mine. And I know when it was too. It was that summer when you invented saying "*Au reservoir*" instead of "*Au revoir*". We all said it for about a week and then got tired of it. Miss Mapp came here just about then, because she picked it up at my garden party. She stopped quite to the end, eating quantities of redcurrant fool, and saying that she had inherited a recipe from her grandmother which she would send me. She did, too, and my cook said it was rubbish. Yes: it was the *au reservoir* year, because she said *au reservoir* to everyone as they left, and told me she would take it back to Tilling. That's the one. Why?'

'Georgie, your memory's marvellous,' said Lucia. 'Now about the advertisement I saw in *The Times*. Miss Mapp is letting her Queen Anne house called Mallards, h. & c. and old-world garden, for August and September. I want you to drive over with me tomorrow and see it. I think that very likely, if it's at all what I hope, I shall take it.'

'No!' cried Georgie. 'Why of course I'll drive there with you tomorrow. What fun! But it will be too awful if you go away for two months. What shall I do? First there's Olga not coming back for a year, and now you're thinking of going away, and there'll be nothing left for me except my croquet and being Drake.'

Lucia gave him one of those glances behind which lurked so much purpose, which no doubt would be disclosed at the proper time. The bees were astir once more in the hive, and presently they would stream out for swarmings or stingings or honey-harvesting

. . . It was delightful to see her looking like that again.

'Georgie, I want change,' she said, 'and though I'm much touched at the idea of your missing me, I think I must have it. I want to get roused up again and shaken and made to tick. Change of air, change of scene, change of people. I don't suppose anyone alive has been more immersed than I in the spacious days of Elizabeth, or more devoted to Shakespearian tradition and environment – perhaps I ought to except Sir Sidney Lee, isn't it? – than I, but I want for the present anyhow to get away from it, especially when poor Daisy is intending to make this deplorable public parody of all that I have held sacred so long.'

Lucia swallowed three or four strawberries as if they had been pills and took a gulp of water.

'I don't think I could bear to be here for all the rehearsals,' she said; 'to look out from the rue and honeysuckle of my sweet garden and see her on her palfrey addressing her lieges of Riseholme, and making them walk in procession in front of her. It did occur to me this morning that I might intervene, take the part of the Queen myself, and make a pageant such as I had planned in those happy days, which would have done honour to the great age and credit to Riseholme, but it would spoil the dream of Daisy's life, and one must be kind. I wash my hands of it all, though of course I shall allow her to dress here, and the procession to start from my house. She wanted that, and she shall have it, but of course she must state on the programmes that the procession starts from Mrs Philip Lucas's house. It would be too much that the visitors, if there are any, should think that my beautiful Hurst belongs to Daisy. And, as I said, I shall be happy to coach her, and see if I can do anything with her. But I won't be here for the fête, and I must be somewhere and that's why I'm thinking of Tilling.'

They had moved into the music room where the bust of Shakespeare stood among its vases of flowers, and the picture of Lucia by Tancred Sigismund, looking like a chessboard with some arms and legs and eyes sticking out of it, hung on the wall. There were Georgie's sketches there, and the piano was open, and *Beethoven's Days of Boyhood* was lying on the table with the paperknife stuck between its leaves, and there was animation about the room once more.

Lucia seated herself in the chair that might so easily have come from Anne Hathaway's cottage, though there was no particular reason for supposing that it did.

'Georgie, I am beginning to feel alive again,' she said. 'Do you remember what wonderful Alfred says in *Maud?* "My life hath crept so long on a broken wing." That's what my life has been doing, but now I'm not going to creep any more. And just for the time, as I say, I'm "off" the age of Elizabeth, partly poor Daisy's fault, no doubt. But there were other ages, Georgie, the age of Pericles, for instance. Fancy sitting at Socrates' feet or Plato's, and hearing them talk while the sun set over Salamis or Pentelicus. I must rub up my Greek, Georgie. I used to know a little Greek at one time, and if I ever manage any tableaux again, we must have the death of Agamemnon. And then there's the age of Anne. What a wonderful time, Pope and Addison! So civilized, so cultivated. Their routs and their tea parties and rapes of the lock. With all the greatness and splendour of the Elizabethan age, there must have been a certain coarseness and crudity about them. No one reveres it more than I, but it is a mistake to remain in the same waters too long. There comes a tide in the affairs of men, which, if you don't nip it in the bud, leads on to boredom.'

'My dear, is that yours?' said Georgie. 'And absolutely impromptu like that! You're too brilliant.'

It was not quite impromptu, for Lucia had thought of it in her bath. But it would be meticulous to explain that.

'Wicked of me, I'm afraid,' she said. 'But it expresses my feelings just now. I do want a change, and my happening to see this notice of Miss Mapp's in *The Times* seems a very remarkable coincidence. Almost as if it was sent: what they call a leading. Anyhow, you and I will drive over to Tilling tomorrow and see it. Let us make a jaunt of it, Georgie, for it's a long way, and stay the night at an inn there. Then we shall have plenty of time to see the place.'

This was rather a daring project, and Georgie was not quite sure if it was proper. But he knew himself well enough to be certain that no passionate impulse of his would cause Lucia to regret that she had made so intimate a proposal.

'That'll be the greatest fun,' he said. 'I shall take my painting things. I haven't sketched for weeks.'

'*Cattivo ragazzo!*' said Lucia. 'What have you been doing with yourself?'

'Nothing. There's been no one to play the piano with, and no one, who knows, to show my sketches to. Hours of croquet, just killing the time. Being Drake. How that fête bores me!'

''Oo poor thing!' said Lucia, using again the baby talk in which she and Georgie used so often to indulge. 'But me's back again now, and me will scold 'oo vewy vewy much if 'oo does not do your lessons.'

'And me vewy glad to be scolded again,' said Georgie. 'Me idle boy! Dear me, how nice it all is!' he exclaimed enthusiastically.

The clock on the old oak dresser struck ten, and Lucia jumped up.

'Georgie, ten o'clock already,' she cried. 'How time has flown. Now I'll write out a telegram to be sent to Miss Mapp first thing tomorrow to say we'll get to Tilling in the afternoon, to see her house, and then ickle *musica*. There was a Mozart duet we used to play. We might wrestle with it again.'

She opened the book that stood on the piano. Luckily that was the very one Georgie had been practising this morning. (So too had Lucia.)

'That will be lovely,' he said. 'But you mustn't scold me if I play vewy badly. Months since I looked at it.'

'Me too,' said Lucia. 'Here we are! Shall I take the treble? It's a little easier for my poor fingers. Now: *Uno, due, tre!* Off we go!'

CHAPTER TWO

They arrived at Tilling in the middle of the afternoon, entering it from the long level road that ran across the reclaimed marshland to the west. Blue was the sky overhead, complete with larks and small white clouds; the town lay basking in the hot June sunshine, and its narrow streets abounded in red-brick houses with tiled roofs, that shouted Queen Anne and George I in Lucia's enraptured ears, and made Georgie's fingers itch for his sketching tools.

'Dear Georgie, perfectly enchanting!' exclaimed Lucia. 'I declare I feel at home already. Look, there's another lovely house. We must just drive to the end of this street, and then we'll enquire where Mallards is. The people, too, I like their looks. Faces full of interest. It's as if they expected us.'

The car had stopped to allow a dray to turn into the High Street from a steep cobbled way leading to the top of the hill. On the pavement at the corner was standing quite a group of Tillingites: there was a clergyman, there was a little round bustling woman dressed in a purple frock covered with pink roses which looked as if they were made of chintz, there was a large military-looking man with a couple of golf clubs in his hand, and there was a hatless girl with hair closely cropped, dressed in a fisherman's jersey and knickerbockers, who spat very neatly in the roadway.

'We must ask where the house is,' said Lucia, leaning out of the window of her Rolls-Royce. 'I wonder if you would be so good as to tell me – '

The clergyman sprang forward.

'It'll be Miss Mapp's house you're seeking,' he said in a broad Scotch accent. 'Straight up the street, to yon corner, and it's right there is Mistress Mapp's house.'

The odd-looking girl gave a short hoot of laughter, and they all stared at Lucia. The car turned with difficulty and danced slowly up the steep narrow street.

'Georgie, he told me where it was before I asked,' said Lucia. 'It must be known in Tilling that I was coming. What a strange accent that clergyman had! A little tipsy, do you think, or only Scotch? The others too! All most interesting and unusual. Gracious, here's an enormous car coming down. Can we pass, do you think?'

By means of both cars driving on to the pavement on each side of the cobbled roadway, the passage was effected, and Lucia caught sight of a large woman inside the other, who in spite of the heat of the day wore a magnificent sable cloak. A small man with a monocle sat eclipsed by her side. Then, with glimpses of more red-brick houses to right and left, the car stopped at the top of the street opposite a very dignified door. Straight in front where the street turned at a right angle, a room with a large bow window faced them; this, though slightly separate from the house, seemed to belong to it. Georgie thought he saw a woman's face peering out between half-drawn curtains, but it whisked itself away.

'Georgie, a dream,' whispered Lucia, as they stood on the doorstep waiting for their ring to be answered. 'That wonderful chimney, do you see, all crooked. The church, the cobbles, the grass and dandelions growing in between them . . , Oh, is Miss Mapp in? Mrs Lucas. She expects me.'

They had hardly stepped inside, when Miss Mapp came hurrying in from a door in the direction of the bow window where Georgie had thought he had seen a face peeping out.

'Dear Mrs Lucas,' she said. 'No need for introductions, which makes it all so happy, for how well I remember you at Riseholme, your lovely Riseholme. And Mr Pillson! Your wonderful garden party! All so vivid still. Red-letter days! Fancy your having driven all this way to see my little cottage! Tea at once, Withers, please. In the garden room. Such a long drive but what a heavenly day for it. I got your telegram at breakfast time this morning. I could have clapped my hands for joy at the thought of possibly having such a tenant as Mrs Lucas of Riseholme. But let us have a cup of tea first. Your chauffeur? Of course he will have his tea here, too. Withers: Mrs Lucas's chauffeur. Mind you take care of him.'

Miss Mapp took Lucia's cloak from her, and still keeping up an effortless flow of hospitable monologue, led them through a small panelled parlour which opened on to the garden. A flight of eight steps with a canopy of wistaria overhead led to the garden room.

'My little plot,' said Miss Mapp. 'Very modest, as you see, three-quarters of an acre at the most, but well screened. My flower-beds: sweet roses, tortoiseshell butterflies. Rather a nice clematis. My Little Eden I call it, so small, but so well beloved.'

'Enchanting!' said Lucia, looking round the garden before mounting the steps up to the garden-room door. There was a very green and well-kept lawn, set in bright flower-beds. A trellis at one end separated it from a kitchen garden beyond, and round the rest ran high brick walls, over which peered the roofs of other houses. In one of these walls was cut a curved archway with a della Robbia head above it.

'Shall we just pop across the lawn,' said Miss Mapp, pointing to this, 'and peep in there while Withers brings our tea? Just to stretch the – the limbs, Mrs Lucas, after your long drive. There's a wee little plot beyond there which is quite a pet of mine. And here's sweet Puss-Cat come to welcome my friends. Lamb! Lovebird!'

Lovebird's welcome was to dab rather crossly at the caressing hand which its mistress extended, and to trot away to ambush itself beneath some fine hollyhocks, where it regarded them with singular disfavour.

'My little secret garden,' continued Miss Mapp as they came to the archway. 'When I am in here and shut the door, I mustn't be disturbed for anything less than a telegram. A rule of the house: I am very strict about it. The tower of the church keeping watch, as I always say over my little nook, and taking care of me. Otherwise not overlooked at all. A little paved walk round it, you see, flower-beds, a pocket handkerchief of a lawn, and in the middle a pillar with a bust of good Queen Anne. Picked it up in a shop here for a song. One of my lucky days.'

'Oh Georgie, isn't it too sweet?' cried Lucia. '*Un giardino segreto. Molto bello!*'

Miss Mapp gave a little purr of ecstasy.

'How lovely to be able to talk Italian like that,' she said. 'So pleased you like my little . . . *giardino segreto*, was it? Now shall we have our tea, for I'm sure you want refreshment, and see the house afterwards? Or would you prefer a little whisky and soda, Mr Pillson? I shan't be shocked. Major Benjy – I should say Major Flint – often prefers a small whisky and soda to tea on a hot day after his game of golf, when he pops in to see me and tell me all about it.'

The intense interest in humankind, so strenuously cultivated at Rischolme, obliterated for a moment Lucia's appreciation of the secret garden.

'I wonder if it was he whom we saw at the corner of the High Street,' she said. 'A big soldier-like man, with a couple of golf clubs.'

'How you hit him off in a few words,' said Miss Mapp admiringly. 'That can be nobody else but Major Benjy. Going off no doubt by the steam tram (most convenient, lands you close to the links) for a round of golf after tea. I told him it would be far too hot to play earlier. I said I should scold him if he was naughty and played after lunch. He served for many years in India. Hindustani is quite a second language to him. Calls "*Quai-hai*" when he wants his breakfast. Volumes of wonderful diaries, which we all hope to see published some day. His house is next to mine down the street. Lots of tigerskins. A rather impetuous bridge player: quite wicked sometimes. You play bridge of course, Mrs Lucas. Plenty of that in Tilling. Some good players.'

They had strolled back over the lawn to the garden room where Withers was laying tea. It was cool and spacious, one window was shaded with the big leaves of a fig tree, through which, unseen, Miss Mapp so often peered out to see whether her gardener was idling. Over the big bow window looking on to the street one curtain was half-drawn, a grand piano stood near it, bookcases half-lined the walls, and above them hung many watercolour sketches of the sort that proclaims a domestic origin. Their subjects also betrayed them, for there was one of the front of Miss Mapp's house, and one of the secret garden, another of the crooked chimney, and several of the church tower looking over the house roofs on to Miss Mapp's lawn.

Though she continued to spray on her visitors a perpetual shower of flattering and agreeable trifles, Miss Mapp's inner attention was wrestling with the problem of how much a week, when it came to the delicate question of terms for the rent of her house, she should ask Lucia. The price had not been mentioned in her advertisement in *The Times*, and though she had told the local house agent to name twelve guineas a week, Lucia was clearly more than delighted with what she had seen already, and it would be a senseless Quixotism to let her have the house for twelve, if she might, all the time, be willing to pay fifteen. Moreover, Miss Mapp (from behind the curtain where Georgie had seen her) was aware that Lucia had a Rolls-Royce car, so that a few additional guineas a week would probably be of no significance to her. Of course, if Lucia was not enthusiastic about the house as well as the garden, it might be unwise to ask fifteen, for she might think that a good deal, and would say something tiresome about letting Miss Mapp hear from her when she got safe away back to Riseholme, and then it was sure to be a refusal. But if she continued to rave and talk Italian about the house when she saw over it, fifteen guineas should be the price. And not a penny of that should Messrs Woolgar & Pipstow, the house agents, get for commission, since Lucia had said definitely that she saw the advertisement in *The Times*. That was Miss Mapp's affair: nothing to do with Woolgar & Pipstow. Meantime she begged Georgie not to look at those watercolours on the walls.

'Little daubs of my own,' she said, most anxious that this should be known. 'I should sink into the ground with shame, dear Mr Pillson, if you looked at them, for I know what a great artist you are yourself. And Withers has brought us our tea . . . You like the one of my little *giardino segreto*? (I must remember that beautiful phrase.) How kind of you to say so! Perhaps it isn't quite so bad as the others, for the subject inspired me, and it's so important, isn't it, to love your subject? Major Benjy likes it too. Cream, Mrs Lucas? I see Withers has picked some strawberries for us from my little plot. Such a year for strawberries! And Major Benjy was chatting with friends I'll be bound, when you passed him.'

'Yes, a clergyman,' said Lucia, 'who kindly directed us to your house. In fact he seemed to know we were going there before I said so, didn't he, Georgie? A broad Scotch accent.'

'Dear Padre!' said Miss Mapp. 'It's one of his little ways to talk Scotch, though he came from Birmingham. A very good bridge player when he can spare time as he usually can. Reverend Kenneth

Bartlett. Was there a teeny little thin woman with him like a mouse? It would be his wife.'

'No, not thin, at all,' said Lucia thoroughly interested. 'Quite the other way round: in fact round. A purple coat and a skirt covered with pink roses that looked as if they were made of chintz.'

Miss Mapp nearly choked over her first sip of tea, but just saved herself.

'I declare I'm quite frightened of you, Mrs Lucas,' she said. 'What an eye you've got. Dear Diva Plaistow, whom we're all devoted to. Christened Godiva! Such a handicap! And they *were* chintz roses, which she cut out of an old pair of curtains and tacked them on. She's full of absurd delicious fancies like that. Keeps us all in fits of laughter. Anyone else?'

'Yes, a girl with no hat and an Eton crop. She was dressed in a fisherman's jersey and knickerbockers.'

Miss Mapp looked pensive.

'Quaint Irene,' she said. 'Irene Coles. Just a touch of unconventionality, which sometimes is very refreshing, but can be rather embarrassing. Devoted to her art. She paints strange pictures, men and women with no clothes on. One has to be careful to knock when one goes to see quaint Irene in her studio. But a great original.'

'And then when we turned up out of the High Street,' said Georgie eagerly, 'we met another Rolls-Royce. I was afraid we shouldn't be able to pass it.'

'So was I,' said Miss Mapp unintentionally betraying the fact that she had been watching from the garden room. 'That car is always up and down this street here.'

'A large woman in it,' said Lucia. 'Wrapped in sables on this broiling day. A little man beside her.'

'Mr and Mrs Wyse,' said Miss Mapp. 'Lately married. She was Mrs Poppit, MBE. Very worthy, and such a crashing snob.'

As soon as tea was over and the inhabitants of Tilling thus plucked and roasted, the tour of the house was made. There were charming little panelled parlours with big windows letting in a flood of air and sunshine and vases of fresh flowers on the tables. There was a broad staircase with shallow treads, and every moment Lucia became more and more enamoured of the plain well-shaped rooms. It all looked so white and comfortable, and, for one wanting a change, so different from The Hurst with its small latticed windows, its steep irregular stairs, its single steps, up or down, at the threshold of every room. People of the age of Anne seemed to have a much better idea of domestic convenience, and Lucia's Italian exclamations grew gratifyingly frequent. Into Miss Mapp's own bedroom she went alone with the owner, leaving Georgie on the landing outside, for delicacy would not permit his looking on the scene where Miss Mapp nightly disrobed herself, and the bed where she nightly disposed herself. Besides, it would be easier for Lucia to ask that important point-blank question of terms, and for herself to answer it if they were alone.

'I'm charmed with the house,' said Lucia. 'And what exactly, how much I mean, for a period of two months – '

'Fifteen guineas a week,' said Miss Mapp without pause. 'That would include the use of my piano. A sweet instrument by Blumenfelt.'

'I will take it for August and September,' said Lucia.

'And I'm sure I hope you'll be as pleased with it,' said Miss Mapp, 'as I'm sure I shall be with my tenant.'

A bright idea struck her, and she smiled more widely than ever.

'That would not include, of course, the wages of my gardener, such a nice steady man,' she said, 'or garden produce. Flowers for the house by all means, but not fruit or vegetables.'

At that moment Lucia, blinded by passion for Mallards, Tilling and the Tillingites, would have willingly agreed to pay the water rate as well. If Miss Mapp had guessed that, she would certainly have named this unusual condition.

Miss Mapp, as requested by Lucia, had engaged rooms for her and Georgie at a pleasant hostelry near by, called the Trader's Arms, and she accompanied them there with Lucia's car following, like an empty carriage at a funeral, to see that all was ready for them. There must have been some misunderstanding of the message, for Georgie found that a double bedroom had been provided for them. Luckily Lucia had lingered outside with Miss Mapp, looking at the view over the marsh, and Georgie with embarrassed blushes explained at the bureau that this would not do at all, and the palms of his hands got cold and wet until the mistake was erased and remedied. Then Miss Mapp left them and they went out to wander about the town. But Mallards was the magnet for Lucia's enamoured eye, and presently they stole back towards it. Many houses apparently were to be let furnished in Tilling just now, and Georgie too grew infected with the desire to have one. Riseholme would be very dismal without Lucia, for the moment the fête was over he felt sure that an appalling reaction after the excitement would settle on it; he might even miss being knighted. He had sketched everything sketchable, there would be nobody to play duets with, and the whole place would stagnate again until Lucia's return, just as it had stagnated during her impenetrable widowhood. Whereas here there were innumerable subjects for his brush, and Lucia would be installed in Mallards with a Blumenfelt in the garden room, and, as was already obvious, a maelstrom of activities whirling in her brain. Major Benjy interested her, so did quaint Irene and the Padre, all the group, in fact, which had seen them drive up with such pre-knowledge, so it seemed, of their destination.

The wall of Miss Mapp's garden, now known to them from inside, ran up to where they now stood, regarding the front of Mallards, and Georgie suddenly observed that just beside them was the sweetest little gabled cottage with the board announcing that it was to be let furnished.

'Look, Lucia,' he said. 'How perfectly fascinating! If it wasn't for that blasted fête, I believe I should be tempted to take it, if I could get it for the couple of months when you are here.'

Lucia had been waiting just for that. She was intending to hint something of the sort before long unless he did, and had made up her mind to stand treat for a bottle of champagne at dinner, so that when they strolled about again afterwards, as she was quite determined to do, Georgie, adventurous with wine, might find the light of the late sunset glowing on Georgian fronts in the town and on the levels of the surrounding country, quite irresistible. But how wise to have waited, so that Georgie should make the suggestion himself.

'My dear, what a delicious idea!' she said. 'Are you really thinking of it? Heavenly for me to have a friend here instead of being planted among strangers. And certainly it is a darling little house. It doesn't seem to be occupied, no smoke from any of the chimneys. I think we might really peep in through the windows and get some idea of what it's like.'

They had to stand on tiptoe to do this, but by shading their eyes from the westerly sun they could get a very decent idea of the interior.

'This must be the dining room,' said Georgie, peering in.

'A lovely open fireplace,' said Lucia. 'So cosy.'

They moved on sideways like crabs.

'A little hall,' said Lucia. 'Pretty staircase going up out of it.'

More crab-like movements.

'The sitting room,' said Georgie. 'Quite charming, and if you press your nose close you can see out of the other window into a tiny garden beyond. The wooden paling must be that of your kitchen garden.'

They stepped back into the street to get a better idea of the topography, and at this moment Miss Mapp looked out of the bow window of her garden room and saw them there. She was as intensely interested in this as they in the house.

'And three bedrooms I should think upstairs,' said Lucia, 'and two attics above. Heaps.'

'I shall go and see the agent tomorrow morning,' said Georgie. 'I can imagine myself being very comfortable there!'

They strolled off into the disused graveyard round the church. Lucia turned to have one more look at the front of Mallards, and Miss Mapp made a low swift curtsey, remaining down so that she disappeared completely.

'About that old fête,' said Georgie, 'I don't want to throw Daisy over, because she'll never get another Drake.'

'But you can go down there for the week,' said Lucia who had thought it all out, 'and come back as soon as it's over. You know how to be knighted by now. You needn't go to all those endless rehearsals. Georgie, look at that wonderful clock on the church.'

'Lovely,' said Georgie absently. 'I told Daisy I simply would not be knighted every day. I shall have no shoulder left.'

'And I think that must be the town hall,' said Lucia. 'Quite right about not being knighted so often. What a perfect sketch you could do of that.'

'Heaps of room for us all in the cottage,' said Georgie. 'I hope there's a servants' sitting room.'

'They'll be in and out of Mallards all day,' said Lucia. 'A lovely servants' hall there.'

'If I can get it, I will,' said Georgie. 'I shall try to let my house at Riseholme, though I shall take my bibelots away. I've often had applications for it in other years. I hope Foljambe will like Tilling. She will make me miserable if she doesn't. Tepid water, fluff on my clothes.'

It was time to get back to their inn to unpack, but Georgie longed for one more look at his cottage, and Lucia for one at Mallards. Just as they turned the corner that brought them in sight of these there was thrust out of the window of Miss Mapp's garden room a hand that waved a white handkerchief. It might have been samite.

'Georgie, what can that be?' whispered Lucia. 'It must be a signal of some sort. Or was it Miss Mapp waving us good night?'

'Not very likely,' said he. 'Let's wait one second.'

He had hardly spoken when Miss Coles, followed by the breathless Mrs Plaistow, hurried up the three steps leading to the front door of Mallards and entered.

'Diva and quaint Irene,' said Lucia. 'It must have been a signal '

'It might be a coincidence,' said Georgie. To which puerile suggestion Lucia felt it was not worth while to reply.

Of course it was a signal and one long prearranged, for it was a matter of the deepest concern to several householders in Tilling, whether Miss Mapp found a tenant for Mallards, and she had promised Diva and quaint Irene to wave a handkerchief from the window of the garden room at six o'clock precisely, by which hour it was reasonable to suppose that her visitors would have left her. These two ladies, who would be prowling about the street below, on the look-out, would then hasten to hear the best or the worst.

Their interest in the business was vivid, for if Miss Mapp succeeded in letting Mallards, she had promised to take Diva's house, Wasters, for two months at eight guineas a week (the house being much smaller) and Diva would take Irene's house, Taormina (smaller still) at five guineas a week, and Irene would take a four-roomed labourer's cottage (unnamed) just outside the town at two guineas a week, and the labourer, who, with his family would be harvesting in August and hop-picking in September, would live in some sort of shanty and pay no rent at all. Thus from top to bottom of this ladder of lessors and lessees they all scored, for they all received more than they paid, and all would enjoy the benefit of a change without the worry and expense of travel and hotels. Each of these ladies would wake in the morning in an unfamiliar room, would sit in unaccustomed chairs, read each other's books (and possibly letters), look at each other's pictures, imbibe all the stimulus of new surroundings, without the wrench of leaving Tilling at all. No true Tillingite was ever really happy away from her town; foreigners were very queer untrustworthy people, and if you did not like the food it was impossible to engage another cook for a hotel of which you were not the proprietor. Annually in the summer this sort of ladder of house-letting was set up in Tilling and was justly popular. But it all depended on a successful letting of Mallards, for if Elizabeth Mapp did not let Mallards, she would not take Diva's Wasters nor Diva Irene's Taormina.

Diva and Irene therefore hurried to the garden room where they would hear their fate; Irene forging on ahead with that long masculine stride that easily kept pace with Major Benjy's, the short-legged Diva with that twinkle of feet that was like the scudding of a thrush over the lawn.

'Well, Mapp, what luck?' asked Irene.

Miss Mapp waited till Diva had shot in.

'I think I shall tease you both,' said she playfully with her widest smile.

'Oh, hurry up,' said Irene. 'I know perfectly well from your face that you've let it. Otherwise it would be all screwed up.'

Miss Mapp, though there was no question about her being the social queen of Tilling, sometimes felt that there were ugly Bolshevistic symptoms in the air, when quaint Irene spoke to her like that. And Irene had a dreadful gift of mimicry, which was a very low weapon, but formidable. It was always wise to be polite to mimics.

'Patience, a little patience, dear,' said Miss Mapp soothingly. 'If you know I've let it, why wait?'

'Because I should like a cocktail,' said Irene. 'If you'll just send for one, you can go on teasing.'

'Well, I've let it for August and September,' said Miss Mapp, preferring to abandon her teasing than give Irene a cocktail. 'And I'm lucky in my tenant. I never met a sweeter woman than dear Mrs Lucas.'

'Thank God,' said Diva, drawing up her chair to the still uncleared table. 'Give me a cup of tea, Elizabeth. I could eat nothing till I knew.'

'How much did you stick her for it?' asked Irene.

'Beg your pardon, dear?' asked Miss Mapp, who could not be expected to understand such a vulgar expression.

'What price did you screw her up to? What's she got to pay you?' said Irene impatiently. 'Damage: dibs.'

'She instantly closed with the price I suggested,' said Miss Mapp. 'I'm not sure, quaint one, that anything beyond that is what might be called your business.'

'I disagree about that,' said the quaint one. 'There ought to be a sliding scale. If you've made her pay through the nose, Diva ought to make you pay through the nose for her house, and I ought to make her pay through the nose for mine. Equality, Fraternity, Nosality.'

Miss Mapp bubbled with disarming laughter and rang the bell for Irene's cocktail, which might stop her pursuing this subject, for the sliding scale of twelve, eight and five guineas a week had been the basis of previous calculations. Yet if Lucia so willingly consented to pay more, surely that was nobody's affair but that of the high contracting parties. Irene, soothed by the prospect of her cocktail, pursued the dangerous topic no further, but sat down at Miss Mapp's piano and picked out God Save the King, with one uncertain finger. Her cocktail arrived just as she finished it.

'Thank you, dear,' said Miss Mapp. 'Sweet music.'

'Cheerio!' said Irene. 'Are you charging Lucas anything extra for use of a fine old instrument?'

Miss Mapp was goaded into a direct and emphatic reply.

'No, darling, I am not,' she said, 'as you are so interested in matters that don't concern you.'

'Well, well, no offence meant,' said Irene. 'Thanks for the

cocktail. Look in tomorrow between twelve and one at my studio, if you want to see far the greater part of a well-made man. I'll be off now to cook my supper. *Au reservoir.*'

Miss Mapp finished the few strawberries that Diva had spared and sighed.

'Our dear Irene has a very coarse side to her nature, Diva,' she said. 'No harm in her, but just common. Sad! Such a contrast to dear Mrs Lucas. So refined: scraps of Italian beautifully pronounced. And so delighted with everything.'

'Ought we to call on her?' asked Diva. 'Widow's mourning, you know.'

Miss Mapp considered this. One plan would be that she should take Lucia under her wing (provided she was willing to go there), another to let it be known in Tilling (if she wasn't) that she did not want to be called upon. That would set Tilling's back up, for if there was one thing it hated it was anything that (in spite of widow's weeds) might be interpreted into superiority. Though Lucia would only be two months in Tilling, Miss Mapp did not want her to be too popular on her own account, independently. She wanted . . . she wanted to have Lucia in her pocket, to take her by the hand and show her to Tilling, but to be in control. It all had to be thought out.

'I'll find out when she comes,' she said. 'I'll ask her, for indeed I feel quite an old friend already.'

'And who's the man?' asked Diva.

'Dear Mr Georgie Pillson. He entertained me so charmingly when I was at Riseholme for a night or two some years ago. They are staying at the Trader's Arms, and off again tomorrow.'

'What? Staying there together?' asked Diva.

Miss Mapp turned her head slightly aside as if to avoid some faint unpleasant smell.

'Diva dear,' she said, 'Old friends as we are, I should be sorry to have a mind like yours. Horrid. You've been reading too many novels. If widow's weeds are not a sufficient protection against such innuendoes, a baby girl in its christening robe wouldn't be safe.'

'Gracious me, I made no innuendo,' said the astonished Diva. 'I only meant it was rather a daring thing to do. So it is. Anything more came from your mind, Elizabeth, not mine. I merely ask you not to put it on to me, and then say I'm horrid.'

Miss Mapp smiled her widest.

'Of course I accept your apology, dear Diva,' she said. 'Fully, without back thought of any kind.'

'But I haven't apologized and I won't,' cried Diva. 'It's for you to do that.'

To those not acquainted with the usage of the ladies of Tilling, such bitter plain-speaking might seem to denote a serious friction between old friends. But neither Elizabeth nor Diva had any such feeling: they would both have been highly surprised if an impartial listener had imagined anything so absurd. Such breezes, even if they grew far stronger than this, were no more than bracing airs that disposed to energy, or exercises to keep the mind fit. No malice.

'Another cup of tea, dear?' said Miss Mapp earnestly.

That was so like her, thought Diva: that was Elizabeth all over. When logic and good feeling alike had produced an irresistible case against her, she swept it all away, and asked you if you would have some more cold tea or cold mutton, or whatever it was.

Diva gave up. She knew she was no match for her and had more tea.

'About our own affairs then,' she said, 'if that's all settled – '

'Yes, dear: so sweetly, so harmoniously,' said Elizabeth.

Diva swallowed a regurgitation of resentment, and went on as if she had not been interrupted.

' – Mrs Lucas takes possession on the first of August,' she said. 'That's to say, you would like to get into Wasters that day.'

'Early that day, Diva, if you can manage it,' said Elizabeth, 'as I want to give my servants time to clean and tidy up. I would pop across in the morning, and my servants follow later. All so easy to manage.'

'Then there's another thing,' said Diva. 'Garden produce. You're leaving yours, I suppose.'

Miss Mapp gave a little trill of laughter.

'I shan't be digging up all my potatoes and stripping the beans and the fruit trees,' she said. 'And I thought – correct me if I am wrong – that my eight guineas a week for your little house included garden produce, which is all that really concerns you and me. I think we agreed as to that.'

Miss Mapp leaned forward with an air of imparting luscious secret information, as that was settled.

'Diva: something thrilling,' she said. 'I happened to be glancing out of my window just by chance a few minutes before I waved to you, and there were Mrs Lucas and Mr Pillson peering, positively peering into the windows of Mallards Cottage. I couldn't help wondering if Mr Pillson is thinking of taking it. They seemed to be so absorbed in it. It is to let, for Isabel Poppit has taken that little brown bungalow with no proper plumbing out by the golf links.'

'Thrilling!' said Diva. 'There's a door in the paling between that little back yard at Mallards Cottage and your garden. They could unlock it – '

She stopped, for this was a development of the trend of ideas for which neither of them had apologized.

'But even if Mr Pillson is thinking of taking it, what next, Elizabeth?' she asked.

Miss Mapp bent to kiss the roses in that beautiful vase of flowers which she had cut this morning in preparation for Lucia's visit.

'Nothing particular, dear,' she said. 'Just one of my madcap notions. You and I might take Mallards Cottage between us, if it appealed to you. Sweet Isabel is only asking four guineas a week for it. If Mr Pillson happens – it's only a speculation – to want it, we might ask, say, six. So cheap at six.'

Diva rose.

'Shan't touch it,' she said. 'What if Mr Pillson doesn't want it? A pure speculation.'

'Perhaps it would be rather risky,' said Miss Mapp. 'And now I come to think of it, possibly, possibly rather stealing a march – don't they call it – on my friends.'

'Oh, decidedly,' said Diva. 'No "possibly possibly" about it.'

Miss Mapp winced for a moment under this smart rap, and changed the subject.

'I shall have little more than a month, then, in my dear house,' she said, 'before I'm turned out of it. I must make the most of it, and have a quantity of little gaieties for you all.'

* * *

Georgie and Lucia had another long stroll through the town after their dinner. The great celestial signs behaved admirably; it was as if the spirit of Tilling had arranged that sun, moon and stars alike should put forth their utmost arts of advertisement on its behalf, for scarcely had the fires of sunset ceased to blaze on its red walls and roofs and to incarnadine the thin skeins of mist that hung over the marsh, than a large punctual moon arose in the east and executed the most wonderful nocturnes in black and silver.

They found a great grey Norman tower keeping watch seaward, an Edwardian gate with drum towers looking out landward: they found a belvedere platform built out on a steep slope to the east of the town, and the odour of the flowering hawthorns that grew there was wafted to them as they gazed at a lighthouse winking in the distance. In another street there stood Elizabethan cottages of brick and timber, very picturesque, but of no interest to those who were at home in Riseholme. Then there were human interests as well: quaint Irene was sitting, while the sunset flamed, on a camp stool in the middle of a street, hatless and trousered, painting a most remarkable picture, apparently of the Day of Judgement, for the whole world was enveloped in fire. Just as they passed her her easel fell down, and in a loud angry voice she said, 'Damn the beastly thing.' Then they saw Diva scuttling along the High Street carrying a birdcage. She called up to an open window very lamentably, 'Oh, Dr Dobbie, please! My canary's had a fit!' From another window, also open and unblinded, positively inviting scrutiny, there came a baritone voice singing 'Will ye no' come back again?' and there, sure enough, was the Padre from Birmingham, with the little grey mouse tinkling on the piano. They could not tear themselves away (indeed there was quite a lot of people listening) till the song was over, and then they stole up the street, at the head of which stood Mallards, and from the house just below it came a muffled cry of '*Quai-hai*' and Lucia's lips formed the syllables 'Major Benjy. At his diaries.' They tiptoed on past Mallards itself, for the garden-room window was open wide, and so past Mallards Cottage, till they were out of sight.

'Georgie, entrancing,' said Lucia. 'They're all being themselves, and all so human and busy – '

'If I don't get Mallards Cottage,' said Georgie, 'I shall die.'

'But you must. You shall. Now it's time to go to bed, though I could wander about for ever. We must be up early in order to get to the house agents' as soon as it's open. Woggles & Pickstick, isn't it?'

'Now you've confused me,' said Georgie. 'Rather like it, but not quite.'

They went upstairs to bed: their rooms were next each other, with a communicating door. There was a bolt on Georgie's side of it, and he went swiftly across to this and fastened it. Even as he did so, he heard a key quietly turned from the other side of it. He undressed with the stealth of a burglar prowling about a house, for somehow it was shy work that he and Lucia should be going to bed so close to each other; he brushed his teeth with infinite precaution and bent low over the basin to eject (spitting would be too noisy a word) the water with which he had rinsed his mouth, for it would never do to let a sound of these intimate manoeuvres penetrate next door. When half-undressed he remembered that the house agents' name was Woolgar & Pipstow, and he longed to tap at Lucia's door and proclaim it, but the silence of the grave reigned next door, and perhaps Lucia was asleep already. Or was she, too, being as stealthy as he? Whichever it was (particularly if it was the last) he must not let a betrayal of his presence reach her.

He got into bed and clicked out his light. That could be done quite boldly: she might hear that, for it only betokened that all was over. Then, in spite of this long day in the open air, which should have conduced to drowsiness, he felt terribly wide awake, for the subject which had intermittently occupied his mind, shadowing it with dim apprehension, ever since Peppino's death, presented itself in the most garish colours. For years, by a pretty Riseholme fantasy, it had always been supposed that he was the implacably Platonic but devout lover of Lucia: somehow that interesting fiction had grown up, and Lucia had certainly abetted it as well as himself. She had let it be supposed that he was, and that she accepted this chaste fervour. But now that her year of widowhood was nearly over, there loomed in front of Georgie the awful fact that very soon there could be no earthly reason why he should not claim his reward for these years of devotion and exchange his passionate celibacy for an even more passionate matrimony. It was an unnerving thought that he might have the right before the summer was over, to tap at some door of communication like that which he had so carefully bolted (and she locked) and say, 'May I come in, darling?' He felt that the words would freeze on his tongue before he could utter them.

Did Lucia expect him to ask to marry her? There was the crux and his imagination proceeded to crucify him upon it. They had posed for years as cherishing for each other a stainless devotion, but what if, with her, it had been no pose at all, but a dreadful reality? Had he been encouraging her to hope, by coming down to stay at this hotel in this very compromising manner? In his ghastly midnight musing, it seemed terribly likely. He had been very rash to come, and all this afternoon he had been pursuing his foolhardy career. He had said that life wasn't worth living if he could not get hold of Mallards Cottage, which was less than a stone's throw (even he could throw a stone as far as that) from the house she was to inhabit alone. Really it looked as if it was the proximity to her that made the cottage so desirable. If she only knew how embarrassing her proximity had been just now when he prepared himself for bed! . . .

And Lucia always got what she wanted. There was a force about her he supposed (so different from poor Daisy's violent yappings and scufflings), which caused things to happen in the way she wished. He had fallen in with all her plans with a zest which it was only reasonable she should interpret favourably: only an hour or two ago he had solemnly affirmed that he must take Mallards Cottage, and the thing already was as good as done, for they were to breakfast tomorrow morning at eight, in order to be at the house agents' (Woggle & Pipsqueak, was it? He had forgotten again), as soon as it opened. Things happened like that for her: she got what she wanted. 'But never, never,' thought Georgie, 'shall she get me. I couldn't possibly marry her, and I won't. I want to live quietly and do my sewing and my sketching, and see lots of Lucia, and play any amount of duets with her, but not marry her. Pray God, she doesn't want me to!'

Lucia was lying awake, too, next door, and if either of them could have known what the other was thinking about, they would both instantly have fallen into a refreshing sleep, instead of tossing and turning as they were doing. She, too, knew that for years she and Georgie had let it be taken for granted that they were mutually devoted, and had both about equally encouraged that impression. There had been an interlude, it is true, when that wonderful Olga Bracely had shone (like evening stars singing) over Riseholme, but she was to be absent from England for a year; besides she was married, and even if she had not been would certainly not have married Georgie. 'So we needn't consider Olga,' thought Lucia. 'It's all about Georgie and me. Dear Georgie: he was so terribly glad when I began to be myself again, and how he jumped at the plan of coming to Tilling and spending the night here! And how he froze on to the idea of taking Mallards Cottage as soon as he knew I had got Mallards! I'm afraid I've been encouraging him to hope. He knows that my year of widowhood is almost over, and on the very eve of its accomplishment, I take him off on this solitary expedition with me. Dear me: it looks as if I was positively asking for it. How perfectly horrible!'

Though it was quite dark, Lucia felt herself blushing.

'What on earth am I to do?' continued these disconcerting reflections. 'If he asks me to marry him, I must certainly refuse, for I couldn't do so: quite impossible. And then when I say no, he has every right to turn on me, and say I've been leading him on. I've been taking moonlight walks with him, I'm at this moment staying alone with him in an hotel. Oh dear! Oh dear!'

Lucia sat up in bed and listened. She longed to hear sounds of snoring from the next room, for that would show that the thought of the fulfilment of his long devotion was not keeping him awake, but there was no sound of any kind.

'I must do something about it tomorrow,' she said to herself, 'for if I allow things to go on like this, these two months here with him will be one series of agitating apprehensions. I must make it quite clear that I won't before he asks me. I can't bear to think of hurting Georgie, but it will hurt him less if I show him beforehand he's got no chance. Something about the beauty of a friendship untroubled with passion. Something about the tranquillity that comes with age . . . There's that eternal old church clock striking three. Surely it must be fast.'

Lucia lay down again: at last she was getting sleepy.

'Mallards,' she said to herself. 'Quaint Irene . . . Woffles and . . . Georgie will know. Certainly Tilling is fascinating . . . Intriguing, too . . . characters of strong individuality to be dealt with . . . A great variety, but I think I can manage them . . . And what about Miss Mapp? . . . Those wide grins . . . We shall see about that . . .'

Lucia awoke herself from a doze by giving a loud snore, and for one agonized moment thought it was Georgie, whom she had hoped to hear snoring, in alarming proximity to herself. That nightmare spasm was quickly over, and she recognized that it was she that had done it. After all her trouble in not letting a sound of any sort penetrate through that door!

Georgie heard it. He was getting sleepy, too, in spite of his uneasy musings, but he was just wide awake enough to realize where that noise had come from.

'And if she snores as well . . .' he thought, and dozed off.

CHAPTER THREE

It was hardly nine o'clock in the morning when they set out for the house agents', and the upper circles of Tilling were not yet fully astir. But there was a town-crier in a blue frock coat ringing a bell in the High Street and proclaiming that the water supply would be cut off that day from twelve noon till three in the afternoon. It was difficult to get to the house agents', for the street where it was situated was being extensively excavated and they had chosen the wrong side of the road, and though they saw it opposite them when halfway down the street, a long detour must be made to reach it.

'But so characteristic, so charming,' said Lucia. 'Naturally there is a town crier in Tilling, and naturally the streets are up. Do not be so impatient, Georgie. Ah, we can cross here.'

There was a further period of suspense.

'The occupier of Mallards Cottage,' said Mr Woolgar (or it might have been Mr Pipstow), 'is wanting to let for three months, July, August and September. I'm not so sure that she would entertain – '

'Then will you please ring her up,' interrupted Georgie, 'and say you've had a firm offer for two months.'

Mr Woolgar turned round a crank like that used for starting rather old-fashioned motor cars, and when a bell rang, he gave a number, and got into communication with the brown bungalow without proper plumbing.

'Very sorry, sir,' he said, 'but Miss Poppit has gone out for her sun-bath among the sand dunes. She usually takes about three hours if fine.'

'But we're leaving again this morning,' said Georgie. 'Can't her servant, or whoever it is, search the sand dunes and ask her?'

'I'll enquire, sir,' said Mr Woolgar sympathetically. 'But there are about two miles of sand dunes, and she may be anywhere.'

'Please enquire,' said Georgie.

There was an awful period, during which Mr Woolgar kept on saying 'Quite', 'Just so', 'I see', 'Yes, dear', with the most tedious monotony, in answer to unintelligible quacking noises from the other end.

'Quite impossible, I am afraid,' he said at length. 'Miss Poppit only keeps one servant, and she's got to look after the house. Besides, Miss Poppit likes . . . likes to be private when she's enjoying the sun.'

'But how tarsome,' said Georgie. 'What am I to do?'

'Well, sir, there's Miss Poppit's mother you might get hold of. She is Mrs Wyse now. Lately married. A beautiful wedding. The house you want is her property.'

'I know,' broke in Lucia. 'Sables and a Rolls-Royce. Mr Wyse has a monocle.'

'Ah, if you know the lady, madam, that will be all right, and I can give you her address. Starling Cottage, Porpoise Street. I will write it down for you.'

'Georgie, Porpoise Street!' whispered Lucia in an entranced aside. '*Com' e bello e molto characteristuoso!*'

While this was being done, Diva suddenly blew in, beginning to speak before she was wholly inside the office. A short tempestuous interlude ensued.

' – morning, Mr Woolgar,' said Diva, 'and I've let Wasters, so you can cross it off your books; such a fine morning.'

'Indeed, madam,' said Mr Woolgar. 'Very satisfactory. And I hope your dear little canary is better.'

'Still alive and in less pain, thank you, pip,' said Diva, and plunged through the excavations outside sooner than waste time in going round.

Mr Woolgar apparently understood that 'pip' was not a salutation but a disease of canaries, and did not say 'So long' or 'Pip pip'. Calm returned again.

'I'll ring up Mrs Wyse to say you will call, madam,' he said. 'Let me see: what name? It has escaped me for the moment.'

As he had never known it, it was difficult to see how it could have escaped.

'Mrs Lucas and Mr Pillson,' said Lucia. 'Where is Porpoise Street?'

'Two minutes' walk from here, madam. As if you were going up to Mallards, but first turning to the right just short of it.'

'Many thanks,' said Lucia, 'I know Mallards.'

'The best house in Tilling, madam,' said Mr Woolgar, 'if you were wanting something larger than Mallards Cottage. It is on our books, too.'

The pride of proprietorship tempted Lucia for a moment to say 'I've got it already,' but she refrained. The complications which might have ensued, had she asked the price of it, were endless . . .

'A great many houses to let in Tilling,' she said.

'Yes, madam, a rare lot of letting goes on about this time of year,' said Mr Woolgar, 'but they're all snapped up very quickly. Many ladies in Tilling like a little change in the summer.'

It was impossible (since time was so precious, and Georgie so feverishly apprehensive, after this warning, that somebody else would secure Mallards Cottage before him, although the owner was safe in the sand dunes for the present) to walk round the excavations in the street, and like Diva they made an intrepid short cut among gas pipes and water mains and braziers and bricks to the other side. A sad splash of mud hurled itself against Georgie's fawn-coloured trousers as he stepped in a puddle, which was very tarsome, but it was useless to attempt to brush it off till it was dry. As they went up the now familiar street towards Mallards they saw quaint Irene leaning out of the upper window of a small house, trying to take down a board that hung outside it which advertised that this house, too, was to let: the fact of her removing it seemed to indicate that from this moment it was to let no longer. Just as they passed, the board, which was painted in the most amazing colours, slipped from her hand and crashed on to the pavement, narrowly missing Diva who simultaneously popped out of the front door. It broke into splinters at her feet, and she gave a shrill cry of dismay. Then perceiving Irene she called up, 'No harm done, dear,' and Irene, in a voice of fury, cried, 'No harm? My beautiful board's broken to smithereens. Why didn't you catch it, silly?'

A snort of infinite contempt was the only proper reply, and Diva trundled swiftly away into the High Street again.

'But it's like a game of general post, Georgie,' said Lucia excitedly, 'and we're playing too. Are they all letting their houses to each other? Is that it?'

'I don't care whom they're letting them to,' said Georgie, 'so long as I get Mallards Cottage. Look at this tarsome mud on my trousers, and I daren't try to brush it off. What will Mrs Wyse think? Here's Porpoise Street anyhow, and there's Starling Cottage. Elizabethan again.'

The door was of old oak, without a handle, but with a bobbin in the strictest style, and there was a thickly patinated green bronze chain hanging close by, which Georgie rightly guessed to be the bell pull, and so he pulled it. A large bronze bell, which he had not perceived, hanging close to his head, thereupon broke into a clamour that might have been heard not only in the house but all over Tilling, and startled him terribly. Then bobbins and gadgets were manipulated from within and they were shown into a room in which two very diverse tastes were clearly exhibited. Oak beams crossed the ceiling, oak beams made a criss-cross on the walls: there was a large open fireplace of grey Dutch bricks, and on each side of the grate an inglenook with a section of another oak beam to sit down upon. The windows were latticed and had antique levers for their control: there was a refectory table and a spice chest and some pewter mugs and a Bible box and a coffin stool. All this was one taste, and then came in another, for the room was full of beautiful objects of a very different sort. The refectory table was covered with photographs in silver frames: one was of a man in uniform and many decorations signed 'Cecco Faraglione', another of a lady in Court dress with a quantity of plumes on her head signed 'Amelia Faraglione'. Another was of the King of Italy, another of a man in a frock coat signed 'Wyse'. In front of these, rather prominent, was an open purple morocco box in which reposed the riband and cross of a Member of the Order of the British Empire. There was a cabinet of china in one corner with a malachite vase above it: there was an occasional table with a marble mosaic top: there was a satinwood piano draped with a piece of embroidery: a palm tree: a green velvet sofa over the end of which lay a sable coat, and all these things spoke of post-Elizabethan refinements.

Long before Lucia had time to admire them all, there came a jingling from a door over which hung a curtain of reeds and beads, and Mrs Wyse entered.

'So sorry to keep you waiting, Mrs Lucas,' she said, 'but they thought I was in the garden, and I was in my boudoir all the time. And you must excuse my deshabille, just my shopping frock. And Mr Pillson, isn't it? So pleased. Pray be seated.'

She heaved the sable coat off the end of the sofa on to the window seat.

'We've just been to see the house agent,' said Georgie in a great hurry, as he turned his muddied leg away from the light, 'and he told us that you might help me.'

'Most happy I am sure, if I can. Pray tell me,' said Mrs Wyse, in apparent unconsciousness of what she could possibly help him about.

'Mallards Cottage,' said Georgie. 'There seems to be no chance of getting hold of Miss Poppit and we've got to leave before she comes back from her sun-bath. I so much want to take it for August and September.'

Mrs Wyse made a little cooing sound.

'Dear Isabel!' she said. 'My daughter. Out in the sand dunes all morning! What if a tramp came along? I say to her. But no use: she calls it the Browning Society, and she must not miss a meeting. So quick and clever! Browning, not the poet but the action of the sun.'

'Most amusing!' said Georgie. 'With regard to Mallards Cottage – '

'The little house is mine, as no doubt Mr Woolgar told you,' said Mrs Wyse, forgetting she had been in complete ignorance of these manoeuvres, 'but you must certainly come and see over it, before anything is settled . . . Ah, here is Mr Wyse. Algernon: Mrs Lucas and Mr Pillson. Mr Pillson wants to take Mallards Cottage.'

Lucia thought she had never seen anyone so perfectly correct and polite as Mr Wyse. He gave little bows and smiles to each as he spoke to them, and that in no condescending manner, nor yet cringingly, but as one consorting with his high-bred equals.

'From your beautiful Riseholme, I understand,' he said to Lucia (bowing to Riseholme as well). 'And we are all encouraging ourselves to hope that for two months at the least the charm of our picturesque – do you not find it so? – little Tilling will give Susan and myself the inestimable pleasure of being your neighbours. We shall look forward to August with keen anticipation. Remind me, dear Susan, to tell Amelia what is in store for us.' He bowed to August, Susan and Amelia and continued – 'And now I hear that Mr Pillson' (he bowed to Georgie and observed the drying spot of mud) 'is "after" as they say, after Mallards Cottage. This will indeed be a summer for Tilling.'

Georgie, during this pretty speech which Mr Wyse delivered in the most finished manner, was taking notes of his costume and appearance. His clean-shaven face, with abundant grey hair brushed back from his forehead, was that of an actor who has seen his best days, but who has given command performances at Windsor. He wore a brown velveteen coat, a Byronic collar and a tie strictured with a cameo ring: he wore brown knickerbockers and stockings to match, he wore neat golfing shoes. He looked as if he might be going to play golf, but somehow it didn't seem likely . . .

Georgie and Lucia made polite deprecating murmurs.

'I was telling Mr Pillson he must certainly see over it first,' said Mrs Wyse. 'There are the keys of the cottage in my boudoir, if you'll kindly fetch them, Algernon. And the Royce is at the door, I see, so if Mrs Lucas will allow us, we will all drive up there together, and show her and Mr Pillson what there is.'

While Algernon was gone, Mrs Wyse picked up the photograph signed Amelia Faraglione.

'You recognize, no doubt, the family likeness,' she said to Lucia. 'My husband's sister Amelia who married the Conte di Faraglione, of the old Neapolitan nobility. That is he.'

'Charming,' said Lucia. 'And so like Mr Wyse. And that Order? What is that?'

Mrs Wyse hastily shut the morocco box.

'So like servants to leave that about,' she said. 'But they seem proud of it. Graciously bestowed upon me. Member of the British Empire. Ah, here is Algernon with the keys. I was showing Mrs Lucas, dear, the photograph of Amelia. She recognized the likeness at once. Now let us all pack in. A warm morning, is it not? I don't think I shall need my furs.'

The total distance to be traversed was not more than a hundred yards, but Porpoise Street was very steep, and the cobbles which must be crossed very unpleasant to walk on, so Mrs Wyse explained. They had to wait some little while at the corner, twenty yards away from where they started, for a van was coming down the street from the direction of Mallards, and the Royce could not possibly pass it, and then they came under fire of the windows of Miss Mapp's garden room. As usual at this hour she was sitting there with the morning paper in her hand in which she could immerse herself if anybody passed whom she did not wish to see, but was otherwise intent on the movements of the street.

Diva Plaistow had looked in with the news that she had seen Lucia and Georgie at the house agents', and that her canary still lived. Miss Mapp professed her delight to hear about the canary, but was secretly distrustful of whether Diva had seen the visitors or not. Diva was so imaginative; to have seen a man and a woman who were strangers was quite enough to make her believe she had seen Them. Then the Royce heaved into sight round the corner below, and Miss Mapp became much excited.

'I think, Diva,' she said, 'that this is Mrs Lucas's beautiful car coming. Probably she is going to call on me about something she wants to know. If you sit at the piano you will see her as she gets out. Then we shall know whether you really – '

The car came slowly up, barked loudly and instead of stopping at the front door of Mallards, turned up the street in the direction of Mallards Cottage. Simultaneously Miss Mapp caught sight of that odious chauffeur of Mrs Wyse's. She could not see more than people's knees in the car itself (that was the one disadvantage of the garden-room window being so high above the street), but there were several pairs of them.

'No, it's only Susan's great lumbering bus,' she said, 'filling up the street as usual. Probably she has found out that Mrs Lucas is staying at the Trader's Arms, and has gone to leave cards. Such a woman to shove herself in where she's not wanted I never saw. Luckily I told Mrs Lucas what a dreadful snob she was.'

'A disappointment to you, dear, when you thought Mrs Lucas

was coming to call,' said Diva. 'But I did see them this morning at Woolgar's and it's no use saying I didn't!'

Miss Mapp uttered a shrill cry.

'Diva, they've stopped at Mallards Cottage. They're getting out. Susan first – so like her – and . . . it's Them. She's got hold of them somehow . . . There's Mr Wyse with the keys, bowing . . . They're going in . . . I was right, then, when I saw them peering in through the windows yesterday. Mr Pillson's come to see the house, and the Wyses have got hold of them. You may wager they know by now about the Count and Countess Faradiddleone, and the Order of the British Empire. I really didn't think Mrs Lucas would be so easily taken in. However, it's no business of mine.'

There could not have been a better reason for Miss Mapp being violently interested in all that happened. Then an idea struck her and the agitated creases in her face faded out.

'Let us pop in to Mallards Cottage, Diva, while they are still there,' she said. 'I should hate to think that Mrs Lucas should get her ideas of the society she will meet in Tilling from poor common Susan. Probably they would like a little lunch before their long drive back to Riseholme.'

The inspection of the cottage had taken very little time. The main point in Georgie's mind was that Foljambe should be pleased, and there was an excellent bedroom for Foljambe, where she could sit when unoccupied. The rooms that concerned him had been viewed through the windows from the street the evening before. Consequently Miss Mapp had hardly had time to put on her garden hat, and trip up the street with Diva, when the inspecting party came out.

'Sweet Susan!' she said. 'I saw your car go by . . . Dear Mrs Lucas, good morning, I just popped across – this is Mrs Plaistow – to see if you would not come and have an early lunch with me before you drive back to your lovely Riseholme. Any time would suit me, for I never have any breakfast. Twelve, half-past twelve? A little something?'

'So kind of you,' said Lucia, 'but Mrs Wyse has just asked us to lunch with her.'

'I see,' said Miss Mapp, grinning frightfully. 'Such a pity. I had hoped – but there it is.'

Clearly it was incumbent on sweet Susan to ask her to join them at this early lunch, but sweet Susan showed no signs of doing anything of the sort. Off went Lucia and Georgie to the Trader's Arms to pack their belongings and leave the rest of the morning free, and the Wyses, after vainly trying to persuade them to drive there in the Royce, got into it themselves and backed down the street till it could turn in the slightly wider space opposite Miss Mapp's garden room. This took a long time, and she was not able to get to her own front door till the manoeuvre was executed, for as often as she tried to get round the front of the car it took a short run forward, and it threatened to squash her flat against the wall of her own room if she tried to squeeze round behind it.

But there were topics to gloat over which consoled her for this act of social piracy on the part of the Wyses. It was a noble stroke to have let Mallards for fifteen guineas a week without garden produce, and an equally brilliant act to have got Diva's house for eight with garden produce, for Diva had some remarkably fine plum trees, the fruit of which would be ripe during her tenancy, not to mention apples: Miss Mapp foresaw a kitchen cupboard the doors of which could not close because of the jam pots within. Such reflections made a happy mental background as she hurried out into the town, for there were businesses to be transacted without delay. She first went to the house agents' and had rather a job to convince Mr Woolgar that the letting of Mallards was due to her own advertisement in *The Times*, and that therefore she owed no commission to his firm, but her logic proved irresistible. Heated but refreshed by that encounter, she paid a visit to her greengrocer and made a pleasant arrangement for the sale of the produce of her own kitchen garden at Mallards during the months of August and September. This errand brought her to the east end of the High Street, and there was Georgie already established on the belvedere busy sketching the Landgate, before he went to breakfast (as those Wyses always called lunch) in Porpoise Street. Miss Mapp did not yet know whether he had taken Mallards Cottage or not, and that must be instantly ascertained.

She leaned on the railing close beside him, and moved a little, rustled a little, till he looked up.

'Oh, Mr Pillson, how ashamed of myself I am!' she said. 'But I couldn't help taking a peep at your lovely little sketch. So rude of me: just like an inquisitive stranger in the street. Never meant to interrupt you, but to steal away again when I'd had my peep. Every moment's precious to you, I know, as you're off this afternoon after your early lunch. But I must ask you whether your hotel was comfortable. I should be miserable if I thought that I had recommended it, and that you didn't like it.'

'Very comfortable indeed, thank you,' said Georgie.

Miss Mapp sidled up to the bench where he sat.

'I will just perch here for a moment before I flit off again,' she said, 'if you'll promise not to take any notice of me, but go on with your picky, as if I was not here. How well you've got the perspective! I always sit here for two or three minutes every morning to feast my eyes on the beauty of the outlook. What a pity you can't stay longer here! You've only had a glimpse of our sweet Tilling.'

Georgie held up his drawing.

'Have I got the perspective right, do you think?' he said. 'Isn't it tarsome when you mean to make a road go downhill and it will go up instead?'

'No fear of that with you!' ejaculated Miss Mapp. 'If I was a little bolder I should ask you to send your drawing to our Art Society here. We have a little exhibition every summer. Could I persuade you?'

'I'm afraid I shan't be able to finish it this morning,' said Georgie.

'No chance then of your coming back?' she asked.

'In August, I hope,' said he, 'for I've taken Mallards Cottage for two months.'

'Oh, Mr Pillson, that is good news!' cried Miss Mapp. 'Lovely! All August and September. Fancy!'

'I've got to be away for a week in August,' said Georgie, 'as we've got an Elizabethan fête at Riseholme. I'm Francis Drake.'

That was a trove for Miss Mapp and must be published at once. She prepared to flit off.

'Oh how wonderful!' she said. 'Dear me, I can quite see you. The *Golden Hind!* Spanish treasure! All the pomp and majesty. I wonder if I could manage to pop down to see it. But I won't interrupt you any more. So pleased to think it's only *au reservoir* and not goodbye.'

She walked up the street again, bursting with her budget of news. Only the Wyses could possibly know that Georgie had taken Mallards Cottage, and nobody that he was going to impersonate Francis Drake . . . There was the Padre talking to Major Benjy, no doubt on his way to the steam tram, and there were Diva and Irene a little further on.

'Good morning, Padre: good morning, Major Benjy,' said she.

'Good morrow, Mistress Mapp,' said the Padre. 'An' hoo's the time o' day wi' ye? 'Tis said you've a fair tenant for yon Mallards.'

Miss Mapp fired off her news in a broadside.

'Indeed, I have, Padre,' she said. 'And there's Mallards Cottage, too, about which you won't have heard. Mr Pillson has taken that, though he won't be here all the time as he's playing Francis Drake in a fête at Riseholme for a week.'

Major Benjy was not in a very good temper. It was porridge morning with him, and his porridge had been burned. Miss Mapp already suspected something of the sort, for there had been loud angry sounds from within as she passed his dining-room window.

'That fellow whom I saw with Mrs Lucas this morning with a cape over his arm?' he said scornfully. 'Not much of a hand against the Spaniards, I should think. Ridiculous! Tea parties with a lot of old cats more in his line. Pshaw!' And away he went to the tram, shovelling passengers off the pavement.

'Porridge burned, I expect,' said Miss Mapp, thoughtfully, 'though I couldn't say for certain. Morning, dear Irene. Another artist is coming to Tilling for August and September.'

'Hoot awa', woman,' said Irene, in recognition of the Padre's presence. 'I ken that fine, for Mistress Wyse told me half an hour agone.'

'But he'll be away for a week, though of course you know that, too,' said Miss Mapp, slightly nettled. 'Acting Francis Drake in a fête at Riseholme.'

Diva trundled up.

'I don't suppose you've heard, Elizabeth,' she said in a great hurry, 'that Mr Pillson has taken Mallards Cottage.'

Miss Mapp smiled pityingly.

'Quite correct, dear Diva,' she said. 'Mr Pillson told me himself hours ago. He's sketching the Landgate now – a sweet picky – and insisted that I should sit down and chat to him while he worked.'

'Lor! How you draw them all in, Mapp,' said quaint Irene. 'He looks a promising young man for his age, but it's time he had his hair dyed again. Grey at the roots.'

The Padre tore himself away; he had to hurry home and tell wee wifie.

'Aweel, I mustn't stand daffing here,' he said, 'I've got my sermon to think on.'

Miss Mapp did a little more shopping, hung about on the chance of seeing Lucia again, and then went back to Mallards, to attend to her sweet flowers. Some of the beds wanted weeding, and now as she busied herself with that useful work and eradicated groundsel, each plant as she tore it up and flung it into her basket might have been Mr and Mrs Wyse. It was very annoying that they had stuck their hooks (so the process represented itself to her vigorous imagery) into Lucia, for Miss Mapp had intended to have no one's hook there but her own. She wanted to run her, to sponsor her, to arrange little parties for her, and cause Lucia to arrange little parties at her dictation, and, while keeping her in her place, show her off to Tilling. Providence, or whatever less beneficent power ruled the world, had not been considerate of her clear right to do this, for it was she who had been put to the expense of advertising Mallards in *The Times*, and it was entirely owing to that that Lucia had come down here, and wound up that pleasant machine of sub-letting houses, so that everybody scored financially as well as got a change. But there was nothing to be done about that for the present: she must wait till Lucia arrived here, and then be both benignant and queenly. A very sweet woman, up till now, was her verdict, though possibly lacking in fine discernment, as witnessed by her having made friends with the Wyses. Then there was Georgie: she was equally well disposed towards him for the present, but he, like Lucia, must be good, and recognize that she was the arbiter of all things social in Tilling. If he behaved properly in that regard she would propose him as an honorary member of the Tilling Art Society, and, as member of the hanging committee, see that his work had a conspicuous place on the walls of the exhibition, but

it was worth remembering (in case he was not good) that quaint
Irene had said that his hair was dyed, and that Major Benjy thought
that he would have been very little use against the Spaniards.

But thinking was hungry work, and weeding was dirty work,
and she went indoors to wash her hands for lunch after this exciting
morning.

There was a dreadful block in Porpoise Street when Lucia's car
came to pick up her and Georgie after their breakfast at Starling
Cottage, for Mrs Wyse's Royce was already drawn up there. The
two purred and backed and advanced foot by foot, they sidled
and stood on pavements meant for pedestrians, and it was not till
Lucia's car had gone backwards again round the corner below Miss
Mapp's garden room, and Mrs Wyse's forward towards the High
Street, that Lucia's could come to the door, and the way down
Porpoise Street lie open for their departure to Riseholme. As long
as they were in sight, Susan stood waving her hand, and Algernon
bowing.

Often during the drive Lucia tried, but always in vain, to start
the subject which had kept them both awake last night, and tell
Georgie that never would she marry again, but the moment she
got near the topic of friendship, or even wondered how long
Mrs Plaistow had been a widow or whether Major Benjy would
ever marry, Georgie saw a cow or a rainbow or something out
of the window and violently directed attention to it. She could
not quite make out what was going on in his mind. He shied
away from such topics as friendship and widowhood, and she
wondered if that was because he was not feeling quite ready yet,
but was screwing himself up. If he only would let her develop
those topics she could spare him the pain of a direct refusal, and
thus soften the blow. But she had to give it up, determining,
however, that when he came to dine with her that evening, she
would not be silenced by his irrelevances: she would make it quite
clear to him, before he embarked on his passionate declaration
that, with all her affection for him, she could never marry him
. . . Poor Georgie!

She dropped him at his house, and as soon as he had told
Foljambe about his having taken the house at Tilling (for that must
be done at once), he would come across to The Hurst.

'I hope she will like the idea,' said Georgie very gravely, as he got out, 'and there is an excellent room for her, isn't there?'

Foljambe opened the door to him.

'A pleasant outing, I hope, sir,' said she.

'Very indeed, thank you, Foljambe,' said Georgie. 'And I've got great news. Mrs Lucas has taken a house at Tilling for August and September, and so have I. Quite close to hers. You could throw a stone.'

'That'll be an agreeable change,' said Foljambe.

'I think you'll like it. A beautiful bedroom for you.'

'I'm sure I shall,' said Foljambe.

Georgie was immensely relieved, and, as he went gaily across to The Hurst, he quite forgot for the time about this menace of matrimony.

'She likes the idea,' he said before he had opened the gate into Perdita's garden, where Lucia was sitting.

'Georgie, the most wonderful thing,' cried she. 'Oh, Foljambe's pleased, is she? So glad. An excellent bedroom. I knew she would. But I've found a letter from Adele Brixton; you know, Lady Brixton who always goes to America when her husband comes to England, and the other way about, so that they only pass each other on the Atlantic; she wants to take The Hurst for three months. She came down here for a Sunday, don't you remember, and adored it. I instantly telephoned to say I would let it.'

'Well, that is luck for you,' said Georgie. 'But three months; what will you do for the third?'

'Georgie, I don't know, and I'm not going to think,' she said. 'Something will happen: it's sure to. My dear, it's perfect rapture to feel the great tide of life flowing again. How I'm going to set to work on all the old interests and the new ones as well. Tilling, the age of Anne, and I shall get a translation of Pope's *Iliad* and of Plato's *Symposium* till I can rub up my Greek again. I have been getting lazy, and I have been getting – let us go into dinner – narrow. I think you have been doing the same. We must open out, and receive new impressions, and adjust ourselves to new conditions!'

This last sentence startled Georgie very much, though it might only apply to Tilling, but Lucia did not seem to notice his faltering step as he followed her into the panelled dining room with the refectory table, below which it was so hard to adjust the feet with any comfort, owing to the foot rail.

'Those people at Tilling,' she said, 'how interesting it will all be. They seemed to me very much alive, especially the women, who appear to have got their majors and their padres completely under their thumbs. Delicious, isn't it, to think of the new interchange of experience which awaits us. Here, nothing happens. Our dear Daisy gets a little rounder and Mrs Antrobus a little deafer. We're in a rut: Riseholme is in a rut. We want, both of us, to get out of it, and now we're going to. Fresh fields and pastures new, Georgie . . . Nothing on your mind, my dear? You were so *distrait* as we drove home.'

Some frightful revivification, thought poor Georgie, had happened to Lucia. It had been delightful, only a couple of days ago, to see her returning to her normal interests, but this repudiation of Riseholme and the craving for the *Iliad* and Tilling and the *Symposium* indicated an almost dangerous appetite for novelty. Or was it only that having bottled herself up for a year, it was natural that, the cork being now out, she should overflow in these ebullitions? She seemed to be lashing her tail, goading herself to some further revelation of her mental or spiritual needs. He shuddered at the thought of what further novelty might be popping out next. The question perhaps.

'I'm sorry I was *distrait*,' said he. 'Of course I was anxious about how Foljambe might take the idea of Tilling.'

Lucia struck the pomander, and it was a relief to Georgie to know that Grosvenor would at once glide in . . . She laughed and laid her hand affectionately on his.

'Georgie, dear, you are' – she took refuge in Italian as Grosvenor appeared – 'you are *una vecchia signorina*.' (That means 'old maid', thought Georgie.) 'Wider horizons, Georgie: that is what you want. Put the rest of the food on the table, Grosvenor, and we'll help ourselves. Coffee in the music room when I ring.'

This was ghastly: Lucia, with all this talk of his being an old maid and needing to adapt himself to new conditions, was truly alarming. He almost wondered if she had been taking monkey gland during her seclusion. Was she going to propose to him in the middle of dinner? Never, in all the years of his friendship with her, had he felt himself so strangely alien. But he was still the master of his fate (at least he hoped so), and it should not be that.

'Shall I give you some strawberry fool?' he asked miserably.

Lucia did not seem to hear him.

'Georgie, we must have ickle talk, before I ring for coffee,' she said. 'How long have you and I been dear friends? Longer than either of us care to think.'

'But all so pleasant,' said Georgie, rubbing his cold moist hands on his napkin . . . He wondered if drowning was anything like this.

'My dear, what do the years matter, if they have only deepened and broadened our friendship? Happy years, Georgie, bringing their sheaves with them. That lovely scene in Esmondi; Winchester Cathedral! And now we're both getting on. You're rather alone in the world, and so am I, but people like us with this dear strong bond of friendship between us can look forward to old age – can't we? – without any qualms. Tranquillity comes with years, and that horrid thing which Freud calls sex is expunged. We must read some Freud, I think; I have read none at present. That was one of the things I wanted to say all the time that you would show me cows out of the window. Our friendship is just perfect as it is.'

Georgie's relief when he found that Foljambe liked the idea of Tilling was nothing, positively nothing, to the relief he felt now.

'My dear, how sweet of you to say that,' he said. 'I, too, find the quality of our friendship perfect in every way. Quite impossible, in fact, to think of – I mean, I quite agree with you. As you say, we're getting on in years, I mean I am. You're right a thousand times.'

Lucia saw the sunlit dawn of relief in Georgie's face, and though she had been quite sincere in hoping that he would not be terribly hurt when she hinted to him that he must give up all hopes of being more to her than he was, she had not quite expected this effulgence. It was as if instead of pronouncing his sentence, she had taken from him some secret burden of terrible anxiety. For the moment her own satisfaction at having brought this off without paining him was swallowed up in surprise that he was so far from being pained. Was it possible that all his concern to interest her in cows and rainbows was due to apprehension that she might be leading up, *via* the topics of friendship and marriage, to something exceedingly different from the disclosure which had evidently gratified him rather than the reverse?

She struck the pomander quite a sharp blow.

'Let us go and have our coffee then,' she said. 'It is lovely that we are of one mind. Lovely! And there's another subject we haven't spoken about at all. Miss Mapp. What do you make of Miss Mapp? There was a look in her eye when she heard we were going to lunch with Mrs Wyse that amazed me. She would have liked to bite her or scratch her. What did it mean? It was as if Mrs Wyse – she asked me to call her Susan by the way, but I'm not sure that I can manage it just yet without practising – as if Mrs Wyse had pocketed something of hers. Most extraordinary. I don't belong to Miss Mapp. Of course it's easy to see that she thinks herself very much superior to all the rest of Tilling. She says that all her friends are angels and lambs, and then just crabs them a little. *Marcate mie parole, Georgino!* I believe she wants to run me. I believe Tilling is seething with intrigue. But we shall see. How I hate all that sort of thing! We have had a touch of it now and then in Riseholme. As if it mattered who took the lead! We should aim at being equal citizens of a noble republic, where art and literature and all the manifold interests of the world are our concern. Now let us have a little music.'

*   *   *

Whatever might be the state of affairs at Tilling, Riseholme during this month of July boiled and seethed with excitements. It was just like old times, and all circled, as of old, round Lucia. She had taken the plunge; she had come back (though just now for so brief a space before her entering upon Mallards) into her native centrality. Gradually, and in increasing areas, grey and white and violet invaded the unrelieved black in which she had spent the year of her widowhood; one day she wore a white belt, another there were grey panels in her skirt, another her garden hat had a violet riband on it. Even Georgie, who had a great eye for female attire, could not accurately follow these cumulative changes: he could not be sure whether she had worn a grey cloak before, or whether she had had white gloves in church last Sunday. Then, instead of letting her hair droop in slack and mournful braids over her ears, it resumed its old polished and corrugated appearance, and on her pale cheeks (ashen with grief) there bloomed a little brown rouge, which made her look as if she had been playing golf again, and her lips certainly were ruddier. It was all intensely exciting, a series of subtle changes at the end of which, by the middle of July, her epiphany in church without anything black about her, and with the bloom of her vitality quite restored, passed almost unremarked.

These outward and visible signs were duly representative of what had taken place within. Time, the great healer, had visited her sickroom, laid his hand on her languid brow, and the results were truly astonishing. Lucia became as good as new, or as good as old. Mrs Antrobus and her tall daughters, Piggy and Goosie, Georgie and Daisy and her husband, greedy Robert, Colonel Boucher and his wife, and the rest were all bidden to dinner at The Hurst once more, and sometimes Lucia played to them the slow movement of the 'Moonlight Sonata', and sometimes she instructed them in such elements of contract bridge as she had mastered during the day. She sketched, she played the organ in church in the absence of the organist who had measles, she sang a solo, 'O for the wings of a Dove' when he recovered and the leading chorister got chickenpox, she had lessons in bookbinding at Ye Signe of Ye Daffodil, she sat in Perdita's garden, not reading Shakespeare, but Pope's *Iliad*, and murmured half-forgotten fragments of Greek irregular verbs as she went to sleep. She had a plan for visiting Athens in the spring ('"the violet-crowned", is not that a lovely epithet, Georgie?') and in compliment to Queen Anne regaled her guests with rich thick chocolate. The hounds of spring were on the winter traces of her widowhood, and snapped up every fragment of it, and indeed spring seemed truly to have returned to her, so various and so multicoloured were the blossoms that were unfolding. Never at all had Riseholme seen Lucia in finer artistic and intellectual fettle, and it was a long time since she had looked so gay. The world, or at any rate Riseholme, which at Riseholme came to much the same thing, had become her parish again.

Georgie, worked to the bone with playing duets, with consulting Foljambe as to questions of linen and plate (for it appeared that Isabel Poppit, in pursuance of the simple life, slept between blankets in the back yard, and ate uncooked vegetables out of a wooden bowl like a dog), with learning Vanderbilt conventions, with taking part in royal processions across the green, with packing his bibelots and sending them to the bank, with sketching, so that he might be in good form when he began to paint at Tilling with a view to exhibiting in the Art Society, wondered what was the true source of these stupendous activities of Lucia's, whether she was getting fit, getting in training, so to speak, for a campaign at Tilling. Somehow it seemed likely, for she would hardly think it worth while to run the affairs of Riseholme with such energy, when she was about to disappear from it for three months. Or was she intending to let Riseholme see how dreadfully flat everything would become when she left them? Very likely both these purposes were at work; it was like her to kill two birds with one stone. Indeed, she was perhaps killing three birds with one stone, for multifarious as were the interests in which she was engaged there was one, now looming large in Riseholme, namely the Elizabethan fête, of which she seemed strangely unconscious. Her drive, her powers of instilling her friends with her own fervour, never touched that: she did not seem to know that a fête was being contemplated at all, though now a day seldom passed without a procession of some sort crossing the green or a Morris dance getting entangled with the choristers practising madrigals, or a crowd of soldiers and courtiers being assembled near the front entrance of the Ambermere Arms, while Daisy harangued them from a chair put on the top of a table, pausing occasionally because she forgot her words, or in order to allow them to throw up their hats and cry 'God Save the Queen's Grace', 'To hell with Spain', and other suitable ejaculations. Daisy, occasionally now in full dress, ruff and pearls and all, came across to the gate of The Hurst, to wait for the procession to join her, and Lucia sitting in Perdita's garden would talk to her about Tilling or the importance of being prudent if you were vulnerable at contract, apparently unaware that Daisy was dressed up at all. Once Lucia came out of the Ambermere Arms when Daisy was actually mounting the palfrey that drew the milk cart for a full-dress rehearsal, and she seemed to be positively palfrey-blind. She merely said, 'Don't forget that you and Robert are dining with me tonight. Half-past seven, so that we shall get a good evening's bridge,' and went on her way . . . Or she would be passing the pond on which the framework of the *Golden Hind* was already constructed, and on which Georgie was even then kneeling down to receive the accolade amid the faint cheers of Piggy and Goosie, and she just waved her hand to Georgie and said: '*Musica* after lunch, Georgie?' She made no sarcastic comments to anybody, and did not know that they were doing anything out of the ordinary.

Under this pointed unconsciousness of hers, a species of blight spread over the scheme to which Riseholme ought to have been devoting its most enthusiastic energies. The courtiers were late for rehearsals, they did not even remove their cigarettes when they bent to kiss the Queen's hand, Piggy and Goosie made steps of Morris dances when they ought to have been holding up Elizabeth's train, and Georgie snatched up a cushion, when the accolade was imminent, to protect his shoulder. The choirboys droned their way through madrigals, sucking peppermints, there was no life, no keenness about it all, because Lucia, who was used to inspire all Riseholme's activities, was unaware that anything was going on.

One morning when only a fortnight of July was still to run, Drake was engaged on his croquet lawn tapping the balls about and trying to tame his white satin shoes which hurt terribly. From the garden next door came the familiar accents of the Queen's speech to her troops.

'And though I am only a weak woman,' declaimed Daisy who was determined to go through the speech without referring to her book. 'Though I am only a weak woman, a weak woman – ' she repeated. 'Yet I have the heart of a prince,' shouted Drake with the friendly intention of prompting her.

'Thank you, Georgie. Or ought it to be princess, do you think?'

'No: prince,' said Georgie.

'Prince,' cried Daisy. 'Though I am only a weak woman, yet I have the heart of a prince . . . Let me see . . . prince.'

There was silence.

'Georgie,' said Daisy in her ordinary voice. 'Do stop your croquet a minute and come to the paling. I want to talk.'

'I'm trying to get used to these shoes,' said Georgie. 'They hurt frightfully. I shall have to take them to Tilling and wear them there. Oh, I haven't told you, Lady Brixton came down yesterday evening – '

'I know that,' said Daisy.

' – and she thinks that her brother will take my house for a couple of months, as long as I don't leave any servants. He'll be here for the fête, if he does, so I wonder if you could put me up. How's Robert's cold?'

'Worse,' she said. 'I'm worse too. I can't remember half of what I knew by heart a week ago. Isn't there some memory system?'

'Lots, I believe,' said Georgie. 'But it's rather late. They don't improve your memory all in a minute. I really think you had better read your speech to the troops, as if it was the opening of Parliament.'

'I won't,' said Daisy, taking off her ruff. 'I'll learn it if it costs me the last breath of blood in my body – I mean drop.'

'Well, it will be very awkward if you forget it all,' said Georgie. 'We can't cheer nothing at all. Such a pity, because your voice carries perfectly now. I could hear you while I was breakfasting.'

'And it's not only that,' said Daisy. 'There's no life in the thing. It doesn't look as if it was happening.'

'No, that's true,' said Georgie. 'These tarsome shoes of mine are real enough, though!'

'I begin to think we ought to have had a producer,' said Daisy. 'But it was so much finer to do it all ourselves, like – like Oberammergau. Does Lucia ever say anything about it? I think it's too mean for words of her to take no interest in it.'

'Well, you must remember that you asked her only to be my wife,' said Georgie. 'Naturally she wouldn't like that.'

'She ought to help us instead of going about as if we were all invisible,' exclaimed Daisy.

'My dear, she did offer to help you. At least, I told you ages ago, that I felt sure she would if you asked her to.'

'I feel inclined to chuck the whole thing,' said Daisy.

'But you can't. Masses of tickets have been sold. And who's to pay for the *Golden Hind* and the roast sheep and all the costumes?' asked Georgie. 'Not to mention all our trouble. Why not ask her to help, if you want her to?'

'Georgie, will you ask her?' said Daisy.

'Certainly not,' said Georgie very firmly. 'You've been managing it from the first. It's your show. If I were you, I would ask her at once. She'll be over here in a few minutes, as we're going to have a music. Pop in.'

A melodious cry of 'Georgino mio!' resounded from the open window of Georgie's drawing room, and he hobbled away down the garden walk. Ever since that beautiful understanding they had arrived at, that both of them shrank, as from a cup of hemlock, from the idea of marriage, they had talked Italian or baby language to a surprising extent from mere lightness of heart.

'Me tummin',' he called. ''Oo very good girl, Lucia, 'oo molto punctuate.'

(He was not sure about that last word, nor was Lucia, but she understood it.)

'Georgino! Che curiose scalpe!' said Lucia, leaning out of the window.

'Don't be so cattiva. They are cattivo enough,' said Georgie. 'But Drake did have shoes exactly like these.'

The mere mention of Drake naturally caused Lucia to talk about something else. She did not understand any allusion to Drake.

'Now for a good practice,' she said, as Georgie limped into the drawing room. 'Foljambe beamed at me. How happy it all is! I hope you said you were at home to nobody. Let us begin at once. Can you manage the sostenuto pedal in those odd shoes?'

Foljambe entered.

'Mrs Quantock, sir,' she said.

'Daisy darling,' said Lucia effusively. 'Come to hear our little practice? We must play our best, Georgino.'

Daisy was still in queenly costume, except for the ruff. Lucia seemed as usual to be quite unconscious of it.

'Lucia, before you begin – ' said Daisy.

'So much better than interrupting,' said Lucia. 'Thank you, dear. Yes?'

'About this fête. Oh, for gracious' sake don't go on seeming to know nothing about it. I tell you there is to be one. And it's all nohow. Can't you help us?'

Lucia sprang from the music stool. She had been waiting for this moment, not impatiently, but ready for it if it came, as she knew it must, without any scheming on her part. She had been watching from Perdita's garden the straggling procession smoking cigarettes, the listless halberdiers not walking in step, the courtiers yawning in Her Majesty's face, the languor and the looseness arising from the lack of an inspiring mind. The scene on the *Golden Hind* and that of Elizabeth's speech to her troops were equally familiar to her, for though she could not observe them from under her garden hat close at hand, her husband had been fond of astronomy and there were telescopes great and small, which brought these scenes quite close. Moreover, she had that speech which poor Daisy found so elusive by heart. So easy to learn, just the sort of cheap bombast that Elizabeth would indulge in: she had found it in a small history of England, and had committed it to memory, just in case . . .

'But I'll willingly help you, dear Daisy,' she said. 'I seem to remember you told me something about it. You as Queen Elizabeth, was it not, a roast sheep on the *Golden Hind*, a speech to the troops, Morris dances, bear-baiting, no, not bear-baiting. Isn't it all going beautifully?'

'No! It isn't,' said Daisy in a lamentable voice. 'I want you to help us, will you? It's all like dough.'

Great was Lucia. There was no rubbing in: there was no hesitation, there was nothing but helpful sunny cordiality in response to this SOS.

'How you all work me!' she said, 'but I'll try to help you if I can. Georgie, we must put off our practice, and get to grips with all this, if the fête is to be a credit to Riseholme. *Addio, caro Mozartino* for the present. Now begin, Daisy, and tell me all the trouble.'

For the next week Mozartino and the *Symposium* and contract bridge were non-existent and rehearsals went on all day. Lucia demonstrated to Daisy how to make her first appearance, and, when the trumpeters blew a fanfare, she came out of the door of The Hurst, and without the slightest hurry majestically marched down the crazy pavement. She did not fumble at the gate as Daisy always did, but with a swift imperious nod to Robert Quantock, which made him pause in the middle of a sneeze, she caused him to fly forward, open it, and kneel as she passed through. She made a wonderful curtsey to her lieges and motioned them to close up in front of her. And all this was done in the clothes of today, without a ruff or a pearl to help her.

'Something like that, do you think, dear Daisy, for the start of the procession?' she said to her. 'Will you try it like that and see how it goes? And a little more briskness, gentlemen, from the halberdiers. Would you form in front of me now, while Mrs Quantock goes into the house . . . Ah, that has more snap, hasn't it? Excellent. Quite like guardsmen. Piggy and Goosie, my dears, you must remember that you are Elizabethan countesses. Very stately, please, and countesses never giggle. Sweep two low curtseys, and while still down pick up the Queen's train. You opened the gate very properly, Robert. Very nice indeed. Now may we have that all over again. Queen, please,' she called to Daisy.

Daisy came out of the house in all the panoply of majesty, and with the idea of not hurrying came so slowly that her progress resembled that of a queen following a hearse. ('A little quicker, dear,' called Lucia encouragingly. 'We're all ready.') Then she tripped over a piece of loose crazy pavement. Then she sneezed, for she had certainly caught Robert's cold. Then she forgot to bow to her lieges, until they had closed up in procession in front of her, and then bobbed to their backs.

'Hey ho, nonny, nonny,' sang Lucia to start the chorus. 'Off we go! Right, left – I beg your pardon, how stupid of me – Left, right. Crescendo, choir. Sing out, please. We're being Merrie England. Capital!'

Lucia walked by the side of the procession across the green, beating time with her parasol, full of encouragement and enthusiasm. Sometimes she ran on in front and observed their progress, sometimes she stood still to watch them go by.

'Open out a little, halberdiers,' she cried, 'so that we can get a glimpse of the Queen from in front. Hey nonny! Hold that top G, choirboys! Queen, dear, don't attempt to keep step with the halberdiers. Much more royal to walk as you choose. The train a little higher, Piggy and Goosie. Hey nonny, nonny HEY!'

She looked round as they got near the *Golden Hind*, to see if the cooks were basting the bolster that did duty for the sheep, and that Drake's sailors were dancing their hornpipes.

'Dance, please, sailors,' she shrieked. 'Go on basting, cooks, until the procession stops, and then begins the chorus of sailors on the last "nonny Hey". Cooks must join in, too, or we shan't get enough body of sound. Open out, halberdiers, leave plenty of room for the Queen to come between you. Slowly, Elizabeth! "When the storm winds blow and the surges sweep." Louder! Are you ready, Georgie? No; don't come off the *Golden Hind*. You receive the Queen on the deck. A little faster, Elizabeth, the chorus will be over before you get here.' Lucia clapped her hands.

'A moment, please,' she said. 'A wonderful scene. But just one suggestion. May I be Queen for a minute and show you the effect I want to get, dear Daisy? Let us go back, procession, please, twenty yards. Halberdiers still walking in front of Queen. Sailors' chorus all over again. Off we go! Now, halberdiers, open out. Half right and left turn respectively. Two more steps and halt, making an avenue.'

It was perfectly timed. Lucia moved forward up the avenue of halberdiers, and just as the last 'Yo ho' was yelled by cooks, courtiers and sailors, she stepped with indescribable majesty on to the deck of the *Golden Hind*. She stood there a moment quite still, and whispered to Georgie, 'Kneel and kiss my hand, Georgie. Now, everybody together! "God save the Queen." "Hurrah." Hats in the air. Louder, louder! Now die away! There!'

Lucia had been waving her own hat, and shrilly cheering herself, and now she again clapped her hands for attention, as she scrutinized the deck of the *Golden Hind*. 'But I don't see Drake's wife,' she said.

'Drake's wife, please.' Drake's wife was certainly missing. She was also the grocer's wife, and as she had only to come forward for one moment, curtsey and disappear, she was rather slack at her attendance of rehearsals.

'It doesn't matter,' said Lucia. 'I'll take Drake's wife, just for this rehearsal. Now we must have that over again. It's one of the most important moments, this Queen's entry on to the *Golden Hind*. We must make it rich in romance, in majesty, in spaciousness. Will the procession, please, go back, and do it over again?'

This time poor Daisy was much too early. She got to the *Golden Hind* long before the cooks and the chorus were ready for her. But there was a murmur of applause when Mrs Drake (so soon to be Lady Drake) ran forward and threw herself at the Queen's feet in an ecstasy of loyalty, and having kissed her hand walked backwards from the Presence with head bent low, as if in adoration.

'Now step to the Queen's left, Georgie,' said Lucia, 'and take her left hand, holding it high, and lead her to the banquet. Daisy dear, you *must* mind your train. Piggy and Goosie will lay it down as you reach the deck, and then you must look after it yourself. If you're not careful you'll tread on it and fall into the Thames. You've got to move so that it follows you when you turn round.'

'May I kick it?' asked Daisy.

'No, it can be done without. You must practise that.'

The whole company now, sailors, soldiers, courtiers and all were eager as dogs are to be taken out for a walk by their mistress, and Lucia reluctantly consented to come and look at the scene of the review at Tilbury. Possibly some little idea, she diffidently said, might occur to her; fresh eyes sometimes saw something, and if they all really wanted her she was at their disposal. So off they went to the rendezvous in front of the Ambermere Arms, and the fresh eyes perceived that according to the present grouping of soldiers and populace no spectator would see anything of the Queen at all. So that was rectified, and the mob was drilled to run into its proper places with due eagerness, and Lucia sat where the front row of spectators would be to hear the great speech. When it was over she warmly congratulated the Queen.

'Oh, I'm so glad you liked it,' said the Queen. 'Is there anything that strikes you?'

Lucia sat for a while in pensive silence.

'Just one or two little tiny things, dear,' she said, thoughtfully. 'I couldn't hear very well. I wondered sometimes what the mob was cheering about. And would it perhaps be safer to read the speech? There was a good deal of prompting that was quite audible. Of course there are disadvantages in reading it. It won't seem so spontaneous and inspiring if you consult a paper all the time. Still, I dare say you'll get it quite by heart before the time comes. Indeed, the only real criticism I have to make is about your gestures, your movements. Not quite, quite majestic enough, not inspiring enough. Too much as if you were whisking flies away. More breadth!'

Lucia sighed, she appeared to be lost in meditation.

'What kind of breadth?' asked Daisy.

'So difficult to explain,' said Lucia. 'You must get more variety, more force, both in your gestures and your voice. You must be fierce sometimes, the great foe of Spain, you must be tender, the mother of your people. You must be a Tudor. The daughter of that glorious cad, King Hal. Coarse and kingly. Shall I show you for a moment the sort of thing I mean? So much easier to show than to explain.'

Daisy's heart sank: she was full of vague apprehensions. But having asked for help, she could hardly refuse this generous granting of it, for indeed Lucia was giving up her whole morning.

'Very good of you,' she said.

'Lend me your copy of the speech, then,' said Lucia, 'and might I borrow your ruff, just to encourage myself. Now let me read through the speech to myself. Yes . . . yes . . . crescendo, and flare up then . . . pause again; a touch of tenderness . . . Well, as you insist on it I'll try to show you what I mean. Terribly nervous, though.'

Lucia advanced and spoke in the most ingratiating tones to her army and the mob.

'Please have patience with me, ladies and gentlemen,' she said, 'while I go through the speech once more. Wonderful words, aren't they? I know I shan't do them justice. Let me see: the palfrey with the Queen will come out from the garden of the Ambermere Arms, will it not? Then will the whole mob, please, hurry into the garden and then come out romping and cheering and that sort of thing in front of me. When I get to where the table is, that is to say, where the palfrey will stand as I make my speech, some of the mob must fall back, and the rest sit on the grass, so that the spectators may see. Now, please.'

Lucia stalked in from the garden, joining the mob now and then to show them how to gambol, and nimbly vaulted (thanks to callisthenics) on to the table on which was the chair where she sat on horseback.

Then with a great sweep of her arm she began to speak. The copy of the speech which she carried flew out of her hand, but that made no difference, for she had it all by heart, and without pause, except for the bursts of cheering from the mob, when she pointed at them, she declaimed it all, her voice now rising, now falling, now full of fire, now tender and motherly. Then she got down from the table, and passed along the line of her troops, beckoned to the mob – which in the previous scene had been cooks and sailors and all sorts of things – to close up behind her with shouts and cheers and gambollings, and went off down the garden path again.

'That sort of thing, dear Daisy, don't you think?' she said to the Queen, returning her ruff. 'So crude and awkwardly done I know, but perhaps that may be the way to put a little life into it. Ah, there's your copy of the speech. Quite familiar to me, I found. I dare say I learned it when I was at school. Now, I really must be off. I wish I could think that I had been any use.'

Next morning Lucia was too busy to superintend the rehearsal: she was sure that Daisy would manage it beautifully, and she was indeed very busy watching through a field glass in the music room the muddled and anaemic performance. The halberdiers strolled along with their hands in their pockets. Piggy and Goosie sat down on the grass, and Daisy knew less of her speech than ever. The collective consciousness of Riseholme began to be aware that nothing could be done without Lucia, and conspiratorial groups conferred stealthily, dispersing or dropping their voices as Queen Elizabeth approached and forming again when she had gone by. The choir which had sung so convincingly when Lucia was there with her loud 'Hey nonny nonny', never bothered about the high G at all, but simply left it out; the young Elizabethans who had gambolled like intoxicated lambkins under her stimulating eye sat down and chewed daisies; the cooks never attempted to baste the bolster; and the Queen's speech to her troops was received with the most respectful tranquillity.

Georgie, in Drake's shoes which were becoming less agonizing with use, lunched with Colonel and Mrs Boucher. Mrs Boucher was practically the only Riseholmite who was taking no part in the fête, because her locomotion was confined to the wheels of a bath chair. But she attended every rehearsal and had views which were as strong as her voice.

'You may like it or not,' she said very emphatically, 'but the only person who can pull you through is Lucia.'

'Nobody can pull poor Daisy through,' said Georgie. 'Hopeless!'

'That's what I mean,' said she. 'If Lucia isn't the Queen, I say give it all up. Poor Daisy's bitten off, if you won't misunderstand me, as we're all such friends of hers, more than she can chew. My kitchen cat, and I don't care who knows it, would make a better Queen.'

'But Lucia's going off to Tilling, next week,' said Georgie. 'She won't be here even.'

'Well, beg and implore her not to desert Riseholme,' said Mrs Boucher. 'Why, everybody was muttering about it this morning, army and navy and all. It was like a revolution. There was Mrs Antrobus; she said to me, "Oh dear, oh dear, it will never do at all," and there was poor Daisy standing close beside her; and we all turned red. Most awkward. And it's up to you, Georgie, to go down on your knees to Lucia and say "Save Riseholme!" There!'

'But she refused to have anything to do with it, after Daisy asked her to be my wife,' said Georgie Drake.

'Naturally she would be most indignant. An insult. But you and Daisy must implore her. Perhaps she could go to Tilling and settle herself in and then come back for the fête, for she doesn't need any rehearsals. She could act every part herself if she could be a crowd.'

'Marvellous woman!' said Colonel Boucher. 'Every word of the Queen's speech by heart, singing with the choir, basting with the cooks, dancing with the sailors. That's what I call instinct, eh? You'd have thought she had been studying it all the time. I agree with my wife, Georgie. The difficulty is Daisy. *Would* she give it up?'

Georgie brightened.

'She did say that she felt inclined to chuck the whole thing, a few days ago,' he said.

'There you are, then,' said Mrs Boucher. 'Remind her of what she said. You and she go to Lucia before you waste time over another rehearsal without her, and implore her. Implore! I shouldn't a bit wonder if she said yes. Indeed, if you ask me, I believe that she's been keeping out of it all until you saw you couldn't do without her. Then she came to help at a rehearsal, and you all saw what you could do when she was there. Why, I burst out cheering myself when she said she had the heart of a prince. Then she retires again as she did this morning, and more than ever you see you can't do without her. I say she's waiting to be asked. It would be like her, you know.'

That was an illuminating thought; it certainly seemed tremendously like Lucia at her very best.

'I believe you're right. She's cleverer than all of us put together,' said Georgie. 'I shall go over to Daisy at once and sound her. Thank God, my shoes are better.'

It was a gloomy queen that Georgie found, a Queen of Sheba with no spirit left in her, but only a calmness of despair.

'It went worse than ever this morning,' she remarked. 'And I dare say we've not touched bottom yet. Georgie, what is to be done?'

It was more delicate to give Daisy the chance of abdicating herself.

'I'm sure I don't know,' said he. 'But something's got to be done. I wish I could think what.'

Daisy was rent with pangs of jealousy and of consciousness of her supreme impotence. She took half a glass of port, which her regime told her was deadly poison.

'Georgie! Do you think there's the slightest chance of getting Lucia to be the Queen and managing the whole affair?' she asked quaveringly.

'We might try,' said Georgie. 'The Bouchers are for it, and everybody else as well, I think.'

'Well, come quick then, or I may repent,' said Daisy.

* * *

Lucia had seen them coming, and sat down at her piano. She had not time to open her music, and so began the first movement of the 'Moonlight Sonata'.

'Ah, how nice!' she said. 'Georgie, I'm going to practise all afternoon. Poor fingers so rusty! And did you have a lovely rehearsal this morning? Speech going well, Daisy? I'm sure it is.'

'Couldn't remember a word,' said Daisy. 'Lucia, we all want to turn the whole thing over to you, Queen and all. Will you – '

'Please, Lucia,' said Georgie.

Lucia looked from one to the other in amazement.

'But, dear things, how can I?' she said. 'I shan't be here to begin with, I shall be at Tilling. And then all the trouble you've been taking, Daisy. I couldn't. Impossible. Cruel.'

'We can't do it at all without you,' said Daisy firmly. 'So that's impossible too. Please, Lucia.'

Lucia seemed quite bewildered by these earnest entreaties.

'Can't you come back for the fête?' said Georgie. 'Rehearse all day, every day, till the end of the month. Then go to Tilling, and you and I will return just for the week of the fête.'

Lucia seemed to be experiencing a dreadful struggle with herself.

'Dear Georgie, dear Daisy, you're asking a great sacrifice of me,' she said. 'I had planned my days here so carefully. My music, my Dante: all my lessons! I shall have to give them all up, you know, if I'm to get this fête into any sort of shape. No time for anything else.'

A miserable two-part fugue of 'Please, Lucia. It's the only chance. We can't do it unless you're Queen,' suddenly burst into the happy strains of 'It *is* good of you. Oh, thank you, Lucia,' and the day was won.

Instantly she became extremely businesslike.

'No time to waste then,' she said. 'Let us have a full rehearsal at three, and after that I'll take the Morris dancers and the halberdiers. You and Georgie must be my lieutenants, dear Daisy. We shall all have to pull together. By the way, what will you be now?'

'Whatever you like,' said Daisy recklessly.

Lucia looked at her fixedly with that gimlet eye, as if appraising, at their highest, her possibilities.

'Then let us see, dear Daisy,' she said, 'what you can make of Drake's wife. Quite a short part, I know, but so important. You have to get into that one moment all the loyalty, all the devotion of the women of England to the Queen.'

She rose. 'Let us begin working at once,' she said. 'This is the *Golden Hind*: I have just stepped on to it. Now go behind the piano, and then come tripping out, full of awe, full of reverence . . . Oh, dear me, that will never do. Shall I act it for you once more?' . . .

CHAPTER FOUR

Lucia had come back to Tilling last night from the fêteful week at Riseholme, and she was sitting next morning after breakfast at the window of the garden room in Miss Mapp's house. It was a magic casement to anyone who was interested in life, as Lucia certainly was, and there was a tide every morning in the affairs of Tilling which must be taken at the flood. Mrs Wyse's Royce had lurched down the street, Diva had come out with her market basket from quaint Irene's house, of which she was now the tenant, Miss Mapp's (she was already by special request 'Elizabeth') gardener had wheeled off to the greengrocer his daily barrowful of garden produce. Elizabeth had popped in to welcome her on her return from Riseholme and congratulate her on the fête of which the daily illustrated papers had been so full, and, strolling about the garden with her, had absently picked a few roses (Diva's had greenfly); the Padre passing by the magic casement had wished her, 'Good morrow, Mistress Lucas,' and finally Major Benjy had come out of his house on the way to catch the tram to the golf links. Lucia called '*Quai-hai*' to him in silvery tones, for they had made great friends in the days she had already spent at Tilling, and reminded him that he was dining with her that night. With great gallantry he had taken off his cap, and bawled out that this wasn't the sort of engagement he was in any danger of forgetting, *au reservoir*.

The tide had ebbed now, and Lucia left the window. There was so much to think about that she hardly knew where to begin. First her eyes fell on the piano which was no longer the remarkable Blumenfelt belonging to Elizabeth on which she had been granted the privilege to play, but one which she had hired from Brighton. No doubt it was quite true that, as Elizabeth had said, her Blumenfelt had been considered a very fine instrument, but nobody, for the last twenty years or so, could have considered it anything but a remarkable curiosity. Some notes sounded like the chirping of canaries (Diva's canary was quite well again after its pip), others did not sound at all, and the *sostenuto* pedal was a thing of naught. So Lucia had hired a new piano, and had put the canary piano in the little telephone room off the hall. It filled it up, but it was still possible to telephone if you went in sideways. Elizabeth had shown traces of acidity about this when she discovered the substitution, and had rather pensively remarked that her piano had belonged to her dearest mamma, and she hoped the telephone room wasn't damp. It seemed highly probable that it had been her mother's if not her grandmother's, but after all Lucia had not promised to play on it.

So much for the piano. There lay on it now a china bowl full of press cuttings, and Lucia glanced at a few, recalling the triumphs of the past week. The fête, favoured by brilliant weather and special trains from Worcester and Gloucester and Birmingham, had been a colossal success. The procession had been cinematographed, so too had the scene on the *Golden Hind*, and the click of cameras throughout the whole performance had been like the noise of cicadas in the south. The Hurst had been the target for innumerable lenses (Lucia was most indulgent) and she was photographed at her piano and in Perdita's garden and musing in an arbour, as Queen Elizabeth and as herself, and she had got one of those artists to take (rather reluctantly) a special photograph of Drake's poor wife. That had not been a success, for Daisy had moved, but Lucia's intention was of the kindest. And throughout, to photographers and interviewers alike, Lucia (knowing that nobody would believe it) had insisted that all the credit was due to Drake's wife, who had planned everything (or nearly) and had done all the spadework.

There had nearly been one dreadful disaster. In fact there had been the disaster, but the amazing Lucia, quite impromptu, had wrung a fresh personal triumph out of it. It was on the last day of the fête, when the green would hardly contain the influx of visitors, and another tier of benches had been put up round the pond where the *Golden Hind* lay, that this excruciating moment had occurred. Queen Elizabeth had just left the deck where she had feasted on a plateful of kippered cinders, and the procession was escorting her

away, when the whole of the stern of the *Golden Hind*, on which
was the fire and the previously roasted sheep and a mast, streaming
with ancients and the crowd of cheering cooks, broke off, and with
a fearful splash and hiss fell into the water. Before anyone could
laugh, Lucia (remembering that the water was only three feet deep
at the most and so there was no danger of anyone drowning) broke
into a ringing cry. 'Zounds and Zooks,' she shouted. 'Thus will I
serve the damned galleons of Spain,' and with a magnificent gesture
of disdain at the cooks standing waist-high in the water, she swept
on with her procession. The reporters singled out for special notice
this wonderful piece of symbolism. A few of the most highbrow
deemed it not quite legitimate business, but none questioned
the superb dramatic effect of the device, for it led on with such
perfect fitness to the next topic, namely the coming of the Armada.
The cooks waded ashore, rushed home to change their clothes,
and were in time to take their places in the mob that escorted her
white palfrey. Who would mind a ducking in the service of such a
resourceful Queen? Of all Lucia's triumphs during the week that
inspired moment was the crown, and she could not help wondering
what poor Daisy would have done, if she had been on the throne
that day. Probably she would have said: 'Oh dear, oh dear, they've
all fallen into the water. We must stop.'

No wonder Riseholme was proud of Lucia, and Tilling which
had been greedily devouring the picture papers was proud too.
There was one possible exception, she thought, and that was
Elizabeth, who in her visit of welcome just now had said, 'How
dreadful all this publicity must be for you, dear! How you must
shrink from it!'

But Lucia, as usual, had been quite up to the mark.

'Sweet of you to be so sympathetic, Elizabeth,' she had said.
'But it was my duty to help dear Riseholme, and I mustn't regard
the consequences to myself.'

That put the lid on Elizabeth: she said no more about the fête.

* * *

Lucia, as these random thoughts suggested by that stack of press
cuttings flitted through her brain, felt that she would have soon
to bring it to bear on Elizabeth, for she was becoming something

of a problem. But first, for this was an immediate concern, she must concentrate on Georgie. Georgie at the present moment, unconscious of his doom, and in a state of the highest approbation with life generally, was still at Riseholme, for Adele Brixton's brother, Colonel Cresswell, had taken his house for two months and there were many bits of things, embroidery and sketches and little bottles with labels, 'For outward application only', which he must put away. He had been staying with Daisy for the fête, for Foljambe and the rest of his staff had come to Tilling at the beginning of August and it was not worth while taking them all back, though it would be difficult to get on without Foljambe for a week. Then he had stopped on for this extra day with Daisy after the fête was over, to see that everything was tidy and discreet and Lucia expected him back this morning.

She had very upsetting news for him: ghastly in fact. The vague rumours which had been rife at Riseholme were all too true, and Cadman, her chauffeur, had come to Lucia last night with the bombshell that he and Foljambe were thinking of getting married. She had seen Foljambe as well, and Foljambe had begged her to break the news to Georgie.

'I should take it very kind of you, ma'am, if you would,' Foljambe had said, 'for I know I could never bring myself to do it, and he wouldn't like to feel that I had made up my mind without telling him. We're in no hurry, me and Cadman, we shouldn't think of being married till after we got back to Riseholme in the autumn, and that'll give Mr Georgie several months to get suited. I'm sure you'll make him see it the right way, if anybody can.'

This handsome tribute to her tact had had its due weight, and Lucia had promised to be the messenger of these dismal tidings. Georgie would arrive in time for lunch today, and she was determined to tell him at once. But it was dreadful to think of poor Georgie on his way now, full of the pleasantest anticipations for the future (since Foljambe had expressed herself more than pleased with her bedroom) and rosy with the remarkable success of his Drake, and the very substantial rent for which he had let his house for two months, with this frightful blow so soon to be dealt him by her hand. Lucia had no idea how he would take it, except that he was certain to be terribly upset. So, leaving the garden room and establishing herself in the pleasant shade on the lawn outside, she thought out quite a quantity of bracing and valuable reflections.

She turned her thoughts towards Elizabeth Mapp. During those ten days before Lucia had gone to Riseholme for the fête, she had popped in every single day: it was quite obvious that Elizabeth was keeping her eye on her. She always had some glib excuse: she wanted a hot-water bottle, or a thimble or a screwdriver that she had forgotten to take away, and declining all assistance would go to look for them herself, feeling sure that she could put her hand on them instantly without troubling anybody. She would go into the kitchen wreathed in smiles and pleasant observations for Lucia's cook, she would pop into the servants' hall and say something agreeable to Cadman, and pry into cupboards to find what she was in search of. (It was during one of these expeditions that she had discovered her dearest mamma's piano in the telephone room.) Often she came in without knocking or ringing the bell, and then if Lucia or Grosvenor heard her clandestine entry, and came to see who it was, she scolded herself for her stupidity in not remembering that for the present, this was not her house. So forgetful of her.

On one of these occasions she had popped out into the garden, and found Lucia eating a fig from the tree that grew against the garden room, and was covered with fruit.

'Oh you dear thief.' she said. 'What about garden produce?'

Then seeing Lucia's look of blank amazement, she had given a pretty peal of laughter.

'Lulu, dear! Only my joke,' she cried. 'Poking a little fun at Queen Elizabeth. You may eat every fig in my garden, and I wish there were more of them.'

On another occasion Elizabeth had found Major Benjy having tea with Lucia, and she had said, 'Oh, how disappointed I am! I had so hoped to introduce you to each other, and now someone else has taken that treat from me. Who was the naughty person?' But perhaps that was a joke too. Lucia was not quite sure that she liked Elizabeth's jokes, any more than she liked her informal visits.

This morning, Lucia cast an eye over her garden. The lawn badly wanted cutting, the flower-beds wanted weeding, the box-edgings to them wanted clipping, and it struck her that the gardener, whose wages she paid, could not have done an hour's work here since she left. He was never in this part of the garden at all, she seemed to remember, but was always picking fruit and vegetables in the kitchen garden, or digging over the asparagus bed, or potting chrysanthemums, or doing other jobs that did not concern her own interests but Elizabeth's. There he was now, a nice genial man, preparing a second basketful of garden produce to take to the greengrocer's, from whom eventually Lucia bought it. An enquiry must instantly be held.

'Good morning, Coplen,' she said. 'I want you to cut the lawn today. It's got dreadfully long.'

'Very sorry, ma'am,' said he. 'I don't think I can find time today myself. I could get a man in perhaps to do it.'

'I should prefer that you should,' said Lucia. 'You can get a man in to pick those vegetables.'

'It's not only them,' he said. 'Miss Mapp she told me to manure the strawberry beds today.'

'But what has Miss Mapp got to do with it?' said she. 'You're in my employment.'

'Well, that does only seem fair,' said the impartial Coplen. 'But you see, ma'am, my orders are to go to Miss Mapp every morning and she tells me what she wants done.'

'Then for the future please come to me every morning and see what I want done,' she said. 'Finish what you're at now, and then start on the lawn at once. Tell Miss Mapp by all means that I've given you these instructions. And no strawberry bed shall be manured today, nor indeed until my garden looks less like a tramp who hasn't shaved for a week.'

Supported by an impregnable sense of justice but still dangerously fuming, Lucia went back to her garden room, to tranquillize herself with an hour's practice on the new piano. Very nice tone; she and Georgie would be able to start their musical hours again now. This afternoon, perhaps, if he felt up to it after the tragic news, a duet might prove tonic. Not a note had she played during that triumphant week at Riseholme. Scales first then, and presently she was working away at a new Mozart, which she and Georgie would subsequently read over together.

There came a tap at the door of the garden room. It opened a chink, and Elizabeth in her sweetest voice said: 'May I pop in once more, dear?'

Elizabeth was out of breath. She had hurried up from the High Street.

'So sorry to interrupt your sweet music, *Lucia mia*,' she said. 'What a pretty tune! What fingers you have! But my good Coplen has come to me in great perplexity. So much better to clear it up at once, I thought, so I came instantly though rather rushed today. A little misunderstanding, no doubt. Coplen is not clever.'

Elizabeth seemed to be labouring under some excitement which might account for this loss of wind. So Lucia waited till she was more controlled.

' – And your new piano, dear?' asked Elizabeth. 'You like it? It sounded so sweet, though not quite the tone of dearest mamma's. About Coplen then?'

'Yes, about Coplen,' said Lucia.

'He misunderstood, I am sure, what you said to him just now. So distressed he was. Afraid I should be vexed with him. I said I would come to see you and make it all right.'

'Nothing easier, dear,' said Lucia. 'We can put it all right in a minute. He told me he had not time to cut the lawn today because he had to manure your strawberry beds, and I said "The lawn please, at once," or words to that effect. He didn't quite grasp, I think, that he's in my employment, so naturally I reminded him of it. He understands now, I hope.'

Elizabeth looked rather rattled at these energetic remarks, and Lucia saw at once that this was the stuff to give her.

'But my garden produce, you know, dear Lulu,' said Elizabeth. 'It is not much use to me if all those beautiful pears are left to rot on the trees till the wasps eat them.'

'No doubt that is so,' said Lucia; 'but Coplen, whose wages I pay, is no use to me if he spends his entire time in looking after your garden produce. I pay for his time, dear Elizabeth, and I intend to have it. He also told me he took his orders every morning from you. That won't do at all. I shan't permit that for a moment. If I had engaged your cook as well as your gardener, I should not allow her to spend her day in roasting mutton for you. So that's all settled.'

It was borne in upon Elizabeth that she hadn't got a leg to stand upon and she sat down.

'Lulu,' she said, 'anything would be better than that I should have a misunderstanding with such a dear as you are. I won't argue, I won't put my point of view at all. I yield. There! If you can spare Coplen for an hour in the morning to take my little fruits and vegetables to the greengrocer's I should be glad.'

'Quite impossible, I'm afraid, dear Elizabeth,' said Lucia with the greatest cordiality. 'Coplen has been neglecting the flower garden dreadfully, and for the present it will take him all his time to get it tidy again. You must get someone else to do that.'

Elizabeth looked quite awful for a moment: then her face was wreathed in smiles again.

'Precious one!' she said. 'It shall be exactly as you wish. Now I must run away. *Au reservoir.* You're not free, I suppose, this evening to have a little dinner with me? I would ask Major Benjy to join us, and our beloved Diva, who has a passion, positively a passion for you. Major Benjy indeed too. He raves about you. Wicked woman, stealing all the hearts of Tilling.'

Lucia felt positively sorry for the poor thing. Before she left for Riseholme last week, she had engaged Diva and Major Benjy to dine with her tonight, and it was quite incredible that Elizabeth, by this time, should not have known that.

'Sweet of you,' she said, 'but I have a tiny little party myself tonight. Just one or two, dropping in.'

Elizabeth lingered a moment yet, and Lucia said to herself that the thumbscrew and the rack would not induce her to ask Elizabeth, however long she lingered.

Lucia and she exchanged kissings of the hand as Elizabeth emerged from the front door, and tripped down the street. 'I see I must be a little firm with her,' thought Lucia, 'and when I've taught her her place, then it will be time to be kind. But I won't ask her to dinner just yet. She must learn not to ask me when she knows I'm engaged. And she shall not pop in without ringing. I must tell Grosvenor to put the door on the chain.'

Lucia returned to her practice, but shovelled the new Mozart out of sight, when, in one of her glances out of the open window, she observed Georgie coming up the street, on his way from the station. He had a light and airy step, evidently he was in the best of spirits and he waved to her as he caught sight of her.

'Just going to look in at the cottage one second,' he called out, 'to see that everything's all right, and then I'll come and have a chat before lunch. Heaps to tell you.'

'So have I,' said Lucia, ruefully thinking what one of those things was. 'Hurry up, Georgie.'

He tripped along up to the cottage, and Lucia's heart was wrung for him, for all that gaiety would soon suffer a total eclipse, and she was to be the darkener of his day. Had she better tell him instantly, she wondered, or hear his news first, and outline the recent Manoeuvres of Mapp. These exciting topics might prove tonic, something to fall back on afterwards. Whereas, if she stabbed him straight away, they would be of no service as restoratives. Also there was stewed lobster for lunch, and Georgie who adored it would probably not care a bit about it if the blow fell first.

Georgie began to speak almost before he opened the door.

'All quite happy at the cottage,' he said, 'and Foljambe ever so pleased with Tilling. Everything in spick-and-span order and my paintbox cleaned up and the hole in the carpet mended quite beautifully. She must have been busy while I was away.'

('Dear, oh dear, she has,' thought Lucia.)

'And everything settled at Riseholme,' continued poor Georgie. 'Colonel Cresswell wants my house for three months, so I said yes, and now we're both homeless for October, unless we keep on our houses here. I had to put on my Drake clothes again yesterday, for the *Birmingham Gazette* wanted to photograph me. My dear, what a huge success it all was, but I'm glad to get away, for everything will be as flat as ditch water now, all except Daisy. She began to buck up at once the moment you left, and I positively heard her say how quickly you picked up the part of the Queen after watching her once or twice.'

'No! Poor thing!' said Lucia with deep compassion.

'Now tell me all about Tilling,' said Georgie, feeling he must play fair.

'Things are beginning to move, Georgie,' said she, forgetting for the time the impending tragedy. 'Night marches, Georgie, manoeuvres. Elizabeth, of course. I'm sure I was right, she wants to run me, and if she can't (if!) she'll try to fight me. I can see glimpses of hatred and malice in her.'

'And you'll fight her?' asked Georgie eagerly.

'Nothing of the kind, my dear,' said Lucia. 'What do you take me for? Every now and then, when necessary, I shall just give her two or three hard slaps. I gave her one this morning: I did indeed. Not a very hard one, but it stung.'

'No! Do tell me,' said Georgie.

Lucia gave a short but perfectly accurate description of the gardener crisis.

'So I stopped that,' she said, 'and there are several other things I shall stop. I won't have her, for instance, walking into my house without ringing. So I've told Grosvenor to put up the chain. And she calls me Lulu which makes me sick. Nobody's ever called me Lulu and they shan't begin now. I must see if calling her Liblib will do the trick. And then she asked me to dinner tonight, when she must have known perfectly well that Major Benjy and Diva are dining with me. You're dining too, by the way.'

'I'm not sure if I'd better,' said Georgie. 'I think Foljambe might expect me to dine at home the first night I get back. I know she wants to go through the linen and plate with me.'

'No, Georgie, quite unnecessary,' said she. 'I want you to help me to give the others a jolly comfortable evening. We'll play bridge and let Major Benjy lay down the law. We'll have a genial evening, make them enjoy it. And tomorrow I shall ask the Wyses and talk about countesses. And the day after I shall ask the Padre and his wife and talk Scotch. I want you to come every night. It's new in Tilling I find, to give little dinners. Tea is the usual entertainment. And I shan't ask Liblib at all till next week.'

'But my dear, isn't that war?' asked Georgie. (It did look rather like it.)

'Not the least. It's benevolent neutrality. We shall see if she learns sense. If she does, I shall be very nice to her again and ask her to several pleasant little parties. I am giving her every chance. Also Georgie . . .' Lucia's eyes assumed that gimlet-like expression which betokened an earnest purpose, 'I want to understand her and be fair to her. At present I can't understand her. The idea of her giving orders to a gardener to whom I give wages! But that's all done with. I can hear the click of the mowing machine on the lawn now. Just two or three things I won't stand. I won't be patronized by Liblib, and I won't be called Lulu, and I won't have her popping in and out of my house like a cuckoo clock.'

Lunch drew to an end. There was Georgie looking so prosperous and plump, with his chestnut-coloured hair no longer in the least need of a touch of dye, and his beautiful clothes. Already Major Benjy, who had quickly seen that if he wanted to be friends with Lucia he must be friends with Georgie too, had pronounced him to be the best-dressed man in Tilling, and Lucia, who invariably passed on dewdrops of this kind, had caused Georgie the deepest gratification by repeating this. And now she was about to plunge a dagger in his heart. She put her elbows on the table, so as to be ready to lay a hand of sympathy on his.

'Georgie, I've got something to tell you,' she said.

'I'm sure I shall like it,' said he. 'Go on.'

'No, you won't like it at all,' she said.

It flashed through his mind that Lucia had changed her mind about marrying him, but it could not be that, for she would never have said he wouldn't like it at all. Then he had a flash of intuition.

'Something about Foljambe,' he said in a quavering voice.

'Yes. She and Cadman are going to marry.'

Georgie turned on her a face from which all other expression except hopeless despair had vanished, and her hand of sympathy descended on his, firmly pressing it.

'When?' he said, after moistening his dry lips.

'Not for the present. Not till we get back to Riseholme.'

Georgie pushed away his untasted coffee.

'It's the most dreadful thing that's ever happened to me,' he said. 'It's quite spoiled all my pleasure. I didn't think Foljambe was so selfish. She's been with me fifteen years, and now she goes and breaks up my home like this.'

'My dear, that's rather an excessive statement,' said Lucia. 'You can get another parlourmaid. There are others.'

'If you come to that, Cadman could get another wife,' said Georgie, 'and there isn't another parlourmaid like Foljambe. I have suspected something now and then, but I never thought it would come to this. What a fool I was to leave her here when I went back to Riseholme for the fête! Or if only we had driven back there with Cadman instead of going by train. It was madness. Here they were with nothing to do but make plans behind our backs. No one will ever look after my clothes as she does. And the silver. You'll miss Cadman, too.'

'Oh, but I don't think he means to leave me,' said Lucia in some alarm. 'What makes you think that? He said nothing about it.'

'Then perhaps Foljambe doesn't mean to leave me,' said Georgie, seeing a possible dawn on the wreck of his home.

'That's rather different,' said Lucia. 'She'll have to look after his house, you see, by day, and then at night he'd – he'd like her to be there.'

'Horrible to think of,' said Georgie bitterly. 'I wonder what she can see in him. I've got a good mind to go and live in a hotel. And I had left her five hundred pounds in my will.'

'Georgie, that was very generous of you. Very,' put in Lucia, though Georgie would not feel the loss of that large sum after he was dead.

'But now I shall certainly add a codicil to say "if still in my service",' said Georgie rather less generously. 'I didn't think it of her.'

Lucia was silent a moment. Georgie was taking it very much to heart indeed, and she racked her ingenious brain.

'I've got an idea,' she said at length. 'I don't know if it can be worked, but we might see. Would you feel less miserable about it if Foljambe would consent to come over to your house say at nine in the morning and be there till after dinner? If you were dining out as you so often are, she could go home earlier. You see Cadman's at The Hurst all day, for he does odd jobs as well, and his cottage at Riseholme is quite close to your house. You would have to give them a charwoman to do the housework.'

'Oh, that is a good idea,' said Georgie, cheering up a little. 'Of course I'll give her a charwoman or anything else she wants if she'll only look after me as before. She can sleep wherever she likes. Of course there may be periods when she'll have to be away, but I shan't mind that as long as I know she's coming back. Besides, she's rather old for that, isn't she?'

It was no use counting the babies before they were born, and

Lucia glided along past this slightly indelicate subject with Victorian eyes.

'It's worth while seeing if she'll stay with you on these terms,' she said.

'Rather. I shall suggest it at once,' said Georgie. 'I think I shall congratulate her very warmly, and say how pleased I am, and then ask her. Or would it be better to be very cold and preoccupied and not talk to her at all? She'd hate that, and then when I ask her after some days whether she'll stop on with me, she might promise anything to see me less unhappy again.'

Lucia did not quite approve of this Machiavellian policy.

'On the other hand, it might make her marry Cadman instantly, in order to have done with you,' she suggested. 'You'd better be careful.'

'I'll think it over,' said Georgie. 'Perhaps it would be safer to be very nice to her about it and appeal to her better nature, if she's got one. But I know I shall never manage to call her Cadman. She must keep her maiden name, like an actress.'

* * *

Lucia duly put in force her disciplinary measures for the reduction of Elizabeth. Major Benjy, Diva and Georgie dined with her that night, and there was a plate of nougat chocolates for Diva, whose inordinate passion for them was known all over Tilling, and a fiery curry for the Major to remind him of India, and a dish of purple figs bought at the greengrocer's but plucked from the tree outside the garden room. She could not resist giving Elizabeth ever so gentle a little slap over this, and said that it was rather a roundabout process to go down to the High Street to buy the figs which Coplen plucked from the tree in the garden, and took down with other garden produce to the shop: she must ask dear Elizabeth to allow her to buy them, so to speak, at the pit mouth. But she was genuinely astonished at the effect this little joke had on Diva. Hastily she swallowed a nougat chocolate entire and turned bright red.

'But doesn't Elizabeth give you garden produce?' she asked in an incredulous voice.

'Oh no,' said Lucia, 'Just flowers for the house. Nothing else.'

'Well, I never!' said Diva. 'I fully understood, at least I thought I did – '

Lucia got up. She must be magnanimous and encourage no public exposure, whatever it might be, of Elizabeth's conduct, but for the pickling of the rod of discipline she would like to hear about it quietly.

'Let's go into the garden room and have a chat,' she said. 'Look after Major Benjy, Georgie, and don't sit too long in bachelordom, for I must have a little game of bridge with him. I'm terribly frightened of him, but he and Mrs Plaistow must be kind to beginners like you and me.'

The indignant Diva poured out her tale of Elizabeth's iniquities in a turgid flood.

'So like Elizabeth,' she said. 'I asked her if she gave you garden produce, and she said she wasn't going to dig up her potatoes and carry them away. Well, of course I thought that meant she did give it you. So like her. Bismarck, wasn't it, who told the truth in order to deceive? And so of course I gave her my garden produce and she's selling one and eating the other. I wish I'd known I ought to have distrusted her.'

Lucia smiled that indulgent Sunday-evening smile which meant she was thinking hard on weekday subjects.

'I like Elizabeth so much,' she said, 'and what do a few figs matter?'

'No, but she always scores,' said Diva, 'and sometimes it's hard to bear. She got my house with garden produce thrown in for eight guineas a week and she lets her own without garden produce for twelve.'

'No dear, I pay fifteen,' said Lucia.

Diva stared at her open-mouthed.

'But it was down in Woolgar's books at twelve,' she said. 'I saw it myself. She is a one: isn't she?'

Lucia maintained her attitude of high nobility, but this information added a little more pickling.

'Dear Elizabeth!' she said. 'So glad that she was sharp enough to get a few more guineas. I expect she's very clever, isn't she? And here come the gentlemen. Now for a jolly little game of bridge.'

Georgie was astonished at Lucia. She was accustomed to lay

down the law with considerable firmness, and instruct partners and opponents alike, but tonight a most unusual humility possessed her. She was full of diffidence about her own skill and of praise for her partner's: she sought advice, even once asking Georgie what she ought to have played, though that was clearly a mistake, for next moment she rated him. But for the other two she had nothing but admiring envy at their declarations and their management of the hand, and when Diva revoked she took all the blame on herself for not having asked her whether her hand was bare of the suit. Rubber after rubber they played in an amity hitherto unknown in the higher gambling circles of Tilling; and when, long after the incredible hour of twelve had struck, it was found on the adjustment of accounts that Lucia was the universal loser, she said she had never bought experience so cheaply and pleasantly.

Major Benjy wiped the foam of his third (surreptitious and hastily consumed) whisky and soda from his walrus moustache.

'Most agreeable evening of bridge I've ever spent in Tilling,' he said. 'Bless me, when I think of the scoldings I've had in this room for some little slip, and the friction there's been . . . Mrs Plaistow knows what I mean.'

'I should think I did,' said Diva, beginning to simmer again at the thought of garden produce. 'Poor Elizabeth! Lessons in self-control are what she wants and after that a few lessons on the elements of the game wouldn't be amiss. Then it would be time to think about telling other people how to play.'

This very pleasant party broke up, and Georgie, hurrying home to Mallards Cottage, thought he could discern in these comments the key to Lucia's unwonted humility at the card table. For herself she had only kind words on the subject of Elizabeth as befitted a large-hearted woman, but Diva and Major Benjy could hardly help contrasting brilliantly to her advantage, the charming evening they had spent with the vituperative scenes which usually took place when they played bridge in the garden room. 'I think Lucia has begun,' thought Georgie to himself as he went noiselessly upstairs so as not to disturb the slumbers of Foljambe.

It was known, of course, all over Tilling the next morning that there had been a series of most harmonious rubbers of bridge last night at Mallards till goodness knew what hour, for Diva spent half the morning in telling everybody about it, and the other half in advising them not to get their fruit and vegetables at the shop which dealt in the garden produce of the Bismarckian Elizabeth. Equally well known was it that the Wyses were dining at Mallards tonight, for Mrs Wyse took care of that, and at eight o'clock that evening the Royce started from Porpoise Street, and arrived at Mallards at precisely one minute past. Georgie came on foot from the cottage thirty yards away in the other direction, in the highest spirits, for Foljambe after consultation with her Cadman had settled to continue on day duty after the return to Riseholme. So Georgie did not intend at present to execute that vindictive codicil to his will. He told the Wyses whom he met on the doorstep of Mallards about the happy termination of this domestic crisis, while Mrs Wyse took off her sables and disclosed the fact that she was wearing the order of the MBE on her ample bosom; and he observed that Mr Wyse had a soft crinkly shirt with a low collar, and velveteen dress clothes: this pretty costume caused him to look rather like a conjurer. There followed very polite conversations at dinner, full of bows from Mr Wyse; first he talked to his hostess, and when Lucia tried to produce general talk and spoke to Georgie, he instantly turned his head to the right, and talked most politely to his wife about the weather and the news in the evening paper till Lucia was ready for him again.

'I hear from our friend Miss Mapp,' he said to her, 'that you speak the most beautiful and fluent Italian.'

Lucia was quite ready to oblige.

'*Ah, che bella lingua!*' said she. '*Ma ho dimenticato tutto, non parla nessuno* in Riseholme.'

'But I hope you will have the opportunity of speaking it before long in Tilling,' said Mr Wyse. 'My sister Amelia, Contessa Faraglione, may possibly be with us before long and I shall look forward to hearing you and she talk together. A lovely language to listen to, though Amelia laughs at my poor efforts when I attempt it.'

Lucia smelled danger here. There had been a terrible occasion once at Riseholme when her bilingual reputation had been shattered by her being exposed to the full tempest of Italian volleyed at her by a native, and she had been unable to understand anything that he said. But Amelia's arrival was doubtful and at present remote, and it would be humiliating to confess that her knowledge was confined to a chosen though singularly limited vocabulary.

'Georgie, we must rub up our Italian again,' she said. 'Mr Wyse's sister may be coming here before long. What an opportunity for us to practise!'

'I do not imagine that you have much need of practice,' said Mr Wyse, bowing to Lucia. 'And I hear your Elizabethan fête' (he bowed to Queen Elizabeth) 'was an immense success. We so much want somebody at Tilling who can organize and carry through schemes like that. My wife does all she can, but she sadly needs someone to help, or indeed direct her. The hospital for instance, terribly in need of funds. She and I were talking as to whether we could not get up a garden fête with some tableaux or something of the sort to raise money. She has designs on you, I know, when she can get you alone, for indeed there is no one in Tilling with ability and initiative.'

Suddenly it struck Lucia that though this was very gratifying to herself, it had another purpose, namely to depreciate somebody else, and surely that could only be one person. But that name must not escape her lips.

'My services, such as they are, are completely at Mrs Wyse's disposal,' she said, 'as long as I am in Tilling. This garden for instance. Would that be a suitable place for something of the sort?'

Mr Wyse bowed to the garden.

'The ideal spot,' said he. 'All Tilling would flock here at your bidding. Never yet in my memory has the use of it been granted for such a purpose; we have often lamented it.'

There could no longer be much doubt as to the sub-current in such remarks, but the beautiful smooth surface must not be broken.

'I quite feel with you,' said Lucia. 'If one is fortunate enough, even for a short time, to possess a pretty little garden like this, it should be used for the benefit of charitable entertainment. The hospital: what more deserving object could we have? Some tableaux, you suggested. I'm sure Mr Pillson and I would be only too glad to repeat a scene or two from our fête at Riseholme.'

Mr Wyse bowed so low that his large loose tie nearly dipped itself in an ice pudding.

'I was trying to summon my courage to suggest exactly that,' he said. 'Susan, Mrs Lucas encourages us to hope that she will give you a favourable audience about the project we talked over.'

The favourable audience began as soon as the ladies rose, and was continued when Georgie and Mr Wyse followed them. Already it had been agreed that the Padre might contribute an item to the entertainment, and that was very convenient, for he was to dine with Lucia the next night.

'His Scotch stories,' said Susan. 'I can never hear them too often, for though I've not got a drop of Scotch blood myself, I can appreciate them. Not a feature of course, Mrs Lucas, but just to fill up pauses. And then there's Mrs Plaistow. How I laugh when she does the seasick passenger with an orange, though I doubt if you can get oranges now. And Miss Coles. A wonderful mimic. And then there's Major Benjy. Perhaps he would read us portions of his diary.'

A pause followed. Lucia had one of those infallible presentiments that a certain name hitherto omitted would follow. It did.

'And if Miss Mapp would supply the refreshment department with fruit from her garden here, that would be a great help,' said Mrs Wyse.

Lucia caught in rapid succession the respective eyes of all her guests, each of whom in turn looked away. 'So Tilling knows all about the garden produce already,' she thought to herself.

Bridge followed, and here she could not be as humble as she had been last night, for both the Wyses abased themselves before she had time to begin.

'We know already,' said Algernon, 'of the class of player that you are, Mrs Lucas,' he said. 'Any hints you will give Susan and me will be so much appreciated. We shall give you no game at all I am afraid, but we shall have a lesson. There is no one in Tilling who has any pretensions of being a player. Major Benjy and Mrs Plaistow and we sometimes have a well-fought rubber on our own level, and the Padre does not always play a bad game. But otherwise the less said about our bridge the better. Susan, my dear, we must do our best.'

Here indeed was a reward for Lucia's humility last night. The winners had evidently proclaimed her consummate skill, and was that, too, a reflection on somebody else, only once hitherto named, and that in connection with garden produce? Tonight Lucia's hands dripped with aces and kings: she denuded her adversaries of all their trumps, and then led one more for safety's sake, after which she poured forth a galaxy of winners. Whoever was her partner was in luck, and tonight it was Georgie who had to beg for change for a ten-shilling note and leave the others to adjust their portions. He recked nothing of this financial disaster, for Foljambe was not lost to him. When the party broke up Mrs Wyse begged him to allow her to give him a lift in the Royce, but as this would entail a turning of that majestic car, which would take at least five minutes followed by a long drive for them round the church square and down into the High Street and up again to Porpoise Street, he adventured forth on foot for his walk of thirty yards and arrived without undue fatigue.

* * *

Georgie and Lucia started their sketching next morning. Like charity, they began at home, and their first subjects were each other's houses. They put their camp stools side by side, but facing in opposite directions, in the middle of the street halfway between Mallards and Mallards Cottage; and thus, by their having different objects to portray, they avoided any sort of rivalry, and secured each other's companionship.

'So good for our drawing,' said Georgie. 'We were getting to do nothing but trees and clouds which needn't be straight.'

'I've got the crooked chimney,' said Lucia proudly. 'That one beyond your house. I think I shall put it straight. People might think I had done it crooked by accident. What do you advise?'

'I think I wouldn't,' said he. 'There's character in its crookedness. Or you might make it rather more crooked than it is: then there won't be any doubt . . . Here comes the Wyses' car. We shall have to move on to the pavement. Tarsome.'

A loud hoot warned them that that was the safer course, and the car lurched towards them. As it passed, Mr Wyse saw whom he had disturbed, stopped the Royce (which had so much better a right to the road than the artists) and sprang out, hat in hand.

'A thousand apologies,' he cried. 'I had no idea who it was, and for what artistic purpose, occupying the roadway. I am indeed distressed, I would instantly have retreated and gone round the other way had I perceived in time. May I glance? Exquisite! The crooked chimney! Mallards Cottage! The west front of the church!' He bowed to them all.

There followed that evening the third dinner party when the Padre and wee wifie made the quartet. The Royce had called for him that day to take him to lunch in Porpoise Street (Lucia had seen it go by), and it was he who now introduced the subject of the proposed entertainment on behalf of the hospital, for he knew all about it and was ready to help in any way that Mistress Lucas might command. There were some Scottish stories which he would be happy to narrate, in order to fill up intervals between the tableaux, and he had ascertained that Miss Coles (dressed as usual as a boy) would give her most amusing parody of 'The boy stood on the burning deck', and that Mistress Diva said she thought that an orange or two might be procured. If not, a ripe tomato would serve the purpose. He would personally pledge himself for the services of the church choir to sing catches and glees and madrigals, whenever required. He suggested also that such members of the workhouse as were not bedridden might be entertained to tea, in which case the choir would sing grace before and after buns.

'As to the expense of that, if you approve,' he said, 'put another baubee on the price of admission, and there'll be none in Tilling to grudge the extra expense wi' such entertainment as you and the other leddies will offer them.'

'Dear me, how quickly it is all taking shape,' said Lucia, finding that almost without effort on her part she had been drawn into the place of prime mover in all this, and that still a sort of conspiracy of silence prevailed with regard to Miss Mapp's name, which hitherto had only been mentioned as a suitable provider of fruit for the refreshment department. 'You must form a little committee, Padre, for putting all the arrangements in hand at once. There's Mr Wyse who really thought of the idea, and you – '

'And with yourself,' broke in the Padre, 'that will make three. That's sufficient for any committee that is going to do its work without any argle-bargle.'

There flashed across Lucia's mind a fleeting vision of what

Elizabeth's face would be like when she picked up, as she would no doubt do next morning, the news of all that was becoming so solid.

'I think I had better not be on the committee,' she said, quite convinced that they would insist on it. 'It should consist of real Tillingites who take the lead among you in such things. I am only a visitor here. They will all say I want to push myself in.'

'Ah, but we can't get on wi'out ye, Mistress Lucas,' said the Padre. 'You must consent to join us. An' three, as I say, makes the perfect committee.'

Mrs Bartlett had been listening to all this with a look of ecstatic attention on her sharp but timid little face. Here she gave vent to a series of shrill minute squeaks which expressed a mouse-like merriment, quite unexplained by anything that had been actually said, but easily accounted for by what had not been said. She hastily drank a sip of water and assured Lucia that a crumb of something (she was eating a peach) had stuck in her throat and made her cough. Lucia rose when the peach was finished.

'Tomorrow we must start working in earnest,' she said. 'And to think that I planned to have a little holiday in Tilling! You and Mr Wyse are regular slave-drivers, Padre.'

Georgie waited behind that night after the others had gone, and bustled back to the garden room after seeing them off.

'My dear, it's getting too exciting,' he said. 'But I wonder if you're wise to join the committee.'

'I know what you mean,' said Lucia, 'but there really is no reason why I should refuse, because they won't have Elizabeth. It's not me, Georgie, who is keeping her out. But perhaps you're right, and I think tomorrow I'll send a line to the Padre and say that I am really too busy to be on the committee, and beg him to ask Elizabeth instead. It would be kinder. I can manage the whole thing just as well without being on the committee. She'll hear all about the entertainment tomorrow morning, and know that she's not going to be asked to do anything, except supply some fruit.'

'She knows a good deal about it now,' said Georgie. 'She came to tea with me today.'

'No! I didn't know you had asked her.'

'I didn't,' said Georgie. 'She came.'

'And what did she say about it?'

'Not very much, but she's thinking hard what to do. I could see that. I gave her the little sketch I made of the Landgate when we first came down here, and she wants me to send in another picture for the Tilling Art Exhibition. She wants you to send something too.'

'Certainly she shall have my sketch of Mallards Cottage and the crooked chimney,' said Lucia. 'That will show goodwill. What else did she say?'

'She's getting up a jumble sale in aid of the hospital,' said Georgie. 'She's busy, too.'

'Georgie, that's copied from us.'

'Of course it is; she wants to have a show of her own, and I'm sure I don't wonder. And she knows all about your three dinner parties.'

Lucia nodded. 'That's all right then,' she said. 'I'll ask her to the next. We'll have some duets that night, Georgie. Not bridge I think, for they all say she's a perfect terror at cards. But it's time to be kind to her.'

Lucia rose.

'Georgie, it's becoming a frightful rush already,' she said. 'This entertainment which they insist on my managing will make me very busy, but when one is appealed to like that, one can't refuse. Then there's my music, and sketching, and I haven't begun to rub up my Greek . . . And don't forget to send for your Drake clothes. Good night, my dear. I'll call to you over the garden paling tomorrow if anything happens.'

'I feel as if it's sure to,' said Georgie with enthusiasm.

CHAPTER FIVE

Lucia was writing letters in the window of the garden room next morning. One, already finished, was to Adele Brixton asking her to send to Mallards the Queen Elizabeth costume for the tableaux: a second, also finished, was to the Padre, saying that she found she would not have time to attend committees for the hospital fête, and begging him to co-opt Miss Mapp. She would, however, do all in her power to help the scheme, and make any little suggestions that occurred to her. She added that the chance of getting fruit gratis for the refreshment department would be far brighter if the owner of it was on the board.

The third letter, firmly beginning 'Dearest Liblib' (and to be signed very large, LUCIA), asking her to dine in two days' time, was not quite done when she saw dearest Liblib, with a fixed and awful smile, coming swiftly up the street. Lucia, sitting sideways to the window, could easily appear absorbed in her letter and unconscious of Elizabeth's approach, but from beneath half-lowered eyelids she watched her with the intensest interest. She was slanting across the street now, making a beeline for the door of Mallards ('And if she tries to get in without ringing the bell, she'll find the chain on the door,' thought Lucia).

The abandoned woman, disdaining the bell, turned the handle and pushed. It did not yield to her intrusion, and she pushed more strongly. There was the sound of jingling metal, audible even in the garden room, as the hasp that held the end of the chain gave way; the door flew open wide, and with a few swift and nimble steps she just saved herself from falling flat on the floor of the hall.

Lucia, pale with fury, laid down her pen and waited for the situation to develop. She hoped she would behave like a lady, but was quite sure it would be a firm sort of lady. Presently up the steps to the garden room came that fairy tread, the door was opened an inch, and that odious voice said: 'May I come in, dear?'

'Certainly,' said Lucia brightly.

'Lulu dear,' said Elizabeth, tripping across the room with little brisk steps. 'First I must apologize: so humbly. Such a stupid accident. I tried to open your front door, and gave it a teeny little push and your servants had forgotten to take the chain down. I am afraid I broke something. The hasp must have been rusty.'

Lucia looked puzzled. 'But didn't Grosvenor come to open the door when you rang?' she asked.

'That was just what I forgot to do, dear,' said Elizabeth. 'I thought I would pop in to see you without troubling Grosvenor. You and I such friends, and so difficult to remember that my dear little Mallards – Several things to talk about!'

Lucia got up.

'Let us first see what damage you have done,' she said with an icy calmness, and marched straight out of the room, followed by Elizabeth. The sound of the explosion had brought Grosvenor out of the dining room, and Lucia picked up the dangling hasp and examined it.

'No, no sign of rust,' she said. 'Grosvenor, you must go down to the ironmonger and get them to come up and repair this at once. The chain must be made safer and you must remember always to put it on, day and night. If I am out, I will ring.'

'So awfully sorry, dear Lulu,' said Elizabeth, slightly cowed by this firm treatment. 'I had no idea the chain could be up. We all keep our doors on the latch in Tilling. Quite a habit.'

'I always used to in Riseholme,' said Lucia. 'Let us go back to the garden room, and you will tell me what you came to talk about.'

'Several things,' said Elizabeth when they had settled themselves. 'First, I am starting a little jumble sale for the hospital, and I wanted to look out some old curtains and rugs, laid away in cupboards, to give to it. May I just go upstairs and downstairs and poke about to find them?'

'By all means,' said Lucia. 'Grosvenor shall go round with you as soon as she has come back from the ironmonger's.'

'Thank you, dear,' said Elizabeth, 'though there's no need to trouble Grosvenor. Then another thing. I persuaded Mr Georgie to send me a sketch for our picky exhibition. Promise me that you'll send me one too. Wouldn't be complete without something by you. How you get all you do into the day is beyond me; your sweet music, your sketching, and your dinner parties every evening.'

Lucia readily promised, and Elizabeth then appeared to lose herself in reverie.

'There *is* one more thing,' she said at last. 'I have heard a little gossip in the town both today and yesterday about a fête which it is proposed to give in my garden. I feel sure it is mere tittle-tattle, but I thought it would be better to come up here to know from you that there is no foundation for it.'

'But I hope there is a great deal,' said Lucia. 'Some tableaux, some singing, in order to raise funds for the hospital. It would be so kind of you if you would supply the fruit for the refreshment booth from your garden. Apropos I should be so pleased to buy some of it every day myself. It would be fresher than if, as at present, it is taken down to the greengrocer and brought up again.'

'Anything to oblige you, dear Lulu,' said Elizabeth. 'But that would be difficult to arrange. I have contracted to send all my garden produce to Twistevant's – such a quaint name, is it not? – for these months, and for the same reason I should be unable to supply this fête which I have heard spoken of. The fruit is no longer mine.'

Lucia had already made up her mind that, after this affair of the chain, nothing would induce her to propose that Elizabeth should take her place on the committee. She would cling to it through storm and tempest.

'I see,' she said. 'Perhaps then you could let us have some fruit from Diva's garden, unless you have sold that also.'

Elizabeth came to the point, disregarding so futile a suggestion.

'The fête itself, dear one,' she said, 'is what I must speak about. I cannot possibly permit it to take place in my garden. The ragtag and bobtail of Tilling passing through my hall and my sweet little sitting room and spending the afternoon in my garden! All my carpets soiled and my flower-beds trampled on! And how do I know that they will not steal upstairs and filch what they can find?'

Lucia's blood had begun to boil: nobody could say that she was preserving a benevolent neutrality. In consequence she presented an icy demeanour, and if her voice trembled at all, it was from excessive cold.

'There will be no admission to the rooms in the house,' she said. 'I will lock all the doors, and I am sure that nobody in Tilling will be so ill bred as to attempt to force them open.'

That was a nasty one. Elizabeth recoiled for a moment from the shock, but rallied. She opened her mouth very wide to begin again, but Lucia got in first.

'They will pass straight from the front door into the garden,' she said, 'where we undertake to entertain them, presenting their tickets of admission or paying at the door. As for the carpet in your sweet little sitting room, there isn't one. And I have too high an opinion of the manners of Tilling in general to suppose that they will trample on your flower-beds.'

'Perhaps you would like to hire a menagerie,' said Elizabeth, completely losing her self-control, 'and have an exhibition of tigers and sharks in the garden room.'

'No: I should particularly dislike it,' said Lucia earnestly. 'Half of the garden room would have to be turned into a sea-water tank for the sharks and my piano would be flooded. And the rest would have to be full of horseflesh for the tigers. A most ridiculous proposal, and I cannot entertain it.'

Elizabeth gave a dreadful gasp as if she was one of the sharks and the water had been forgotten. She adroitly changed the subject.

'Then again, there's the rumour – of course it's only rumour – that there is some idea of entertaining such inmates of the workhouse as are not bedridden. Impossible.'

'I fancy the Padre is arranging that,' said Lucia. 'For my part, I'm delighted to give them a little treat.'

'And for my part,' said Miss Mapp, rising (she had become Miss Mapp again in Lucia's mind), 'I will not have my little home sanctuary invaded by the ragtag – '

'The tickets will be half a crown,' interposed Lucia.

' – and bobtail of Tilling,' continued Miss Mapp.

'As long as I am tenant here,' said Lucia, 'I shall ask here whom I please, and when I please, and – and how I please. Or do you wish me to send you a list of the friends I ask to dinner for your sanction?'

Miss Mapp, trembling very much, forced her lips to form the syllables: 'But, dear Lulu – '

'Dear Elizabeth, I must beg you not to call me Lulu,' she said. 'Such a detestable abbreviation – '

Grosvenor had appeared at the door of the garden room.

'Yes, Grosvenor, what is it?' asked Lucia in precisely the same voice.

'The ironmonger is here, ma'am,' she said, 'and he says that he'll have to put in some rather large screws, as they're pulled out – '

'Whatever is necessary to make the door safe,' said Lucia. 'And Miss Mapp wants to look into cupboards and take some things of her own away. Go with her, please, and give her every facility.'

Lucia, quite in the grand style, turned to look out of the window in the direction of Mallards Cottage, in order to give Miss Mapp the opportunity of a discreet exit. She threw the window open.

'Georgino! Georgino!' she called, and Georgie's face appeared above the paling.

'Come round and have ickle talk, Georgie,' she said. 'Sumfin' I want to tell you. *Presto!*'

She kissed her hand to Georgie and turned back into the room. Miss Mapp was still there, but now invisible to Lucia's eye. She hummed a gay bar of Mozartino, and went back to her table in the bow window where she tore up the letter of resignation and recommendation she had written to the Padre, and the half-finished note to Miss Mapp, which so cordially asked her to dinner, saying that it was so long since they had met, for they had met again now. When she looked up she was alone, and there was Georgie tripping up the steps by the front door. Though it was standing open (for the ironmonger was already engaged on the firm restoration of the chain) he very properly rang the bell and was admitted.

'There you are,' said Lucia brightly as he came in. 'Another lovely day.'

'Perfect. What has happened to your front door?'

Lucia laughed.

'Elizabeth came to see me,' she said gaily. 'The chain was on the door, as I have ordered it always shall be. But she gave the door such a biff that the hasp pulled out. It's being repaired.'

'No!' said Georgie, 'and did you give her what for?'

'She had several things she wanted to see me about,' said Lucia, keeping an intermittent eye on the front door. 'She wanted to get out of her cupboards some stuff for the jumble sale she is getting up in aid of the hospital, and she is at it now under Grosvenor's superintendence. Then she wanted me to send a sketch for the picture exhibition, I said I would be delighted. Then she said she could not manage to send any fruit for our fête here. She did not approve of the fête at all, Georgie. In fact, she forbade me to give it. We had a little chat about that.'

'But what's to be done then?' asked Georgie.

'Nothing that I know of, except to give the fête,' said Lucia. 'But it would be no use asking her to be on the committee for an object of which she disapproved, so I tore up the letter I had written to the Padre about it.'

Lucia suddenly focused her eyes and her attention on the front door, and a tone of warm human interest melted the deadly chill of her voice.

'Georgie, there she goes,' she said. 'What a quantity of things! There's an old kettle and a boot jack, and a rug with a hole in it, and one stair rod. And there's a shaving from the front door where they are putting in bigger screws, stuck to her skirt . . . And she's dropped the stair rod . . . Major Benjy's picking it up for her.'

Georgie hurried to the window to see these exciting happenings, but Miss Mapp, having recovered the stair rod, was already disappearing.

'I wish I hadn't given her my picture of the Landgate,' said he. 'It was one of my best. But aren't you going to tell me all about your interview? Properly, I mean: everything.'

'Not worth speaking of,' said Lucia. 'She asked me if I would like to have a menagerie and keep tigers and sharks in the garden room. That sort of thing. Mere raving. Come out, Georgie. I want to do a little shopping. Coplen told me there were some excellent greengages from the garden which he was taking down to Twistevant's.'

It was the hour when the collective social life of Tilling was at its briskest. The events of the evening before, tea parties and games of bridge had become known and were under discussion, as the ladies of the place with their baskets on their arms collided with each other as they popped in and out of shops and obstructed the pavements. Many parcels were being left at Wasters which Miss Mapp now occupied, for jumble sales on behalf of deserving objects were justly popular, since everybody had a lot of junk in their houses, which they could not bear to throw away, but for which they had no earthly use. Diva had already been back from Taormina to her own house (as Elizabeth to hers) and had disinterred from a cupboard of rubbish a pair of tongs, the claws of which twisted round if you tried to pick up a lump of coal and dropped it on the carpet, but which were otherwise perfect. Then there was a scuttle which had a hole in the bottom, through which coal dust softly dribbled, and a candlestick which had lost one of its feet, and a glass inkstand once handsome, but now cracked. These treasures, handsome donations to a jumble sale, but otherwise of no particular value, she carried to her own hall, where donors were requested to leave their offerings, and she learned from Withers, Miss Mapp's parlour-maid, the disagreeable news that the jumble sale was to be held here. The thought revolted her; all the ragtag and bobtail of Tilling would come wandering about her house, soiling her carpets and smudging her walls. At this moment Miss Mapp herself came in carrying the tea kettle and the boot jack and the other things. She had already thought of half a dozen withering retorts she might have made to Lucia.

'Elizabeth, this will never do,' said Diva. 'I can't have the jumble sale held here. They'll make a dreadful mess of the place.'

'Oh no, dear,' said Miss Mapp, with searing memories of a recent interview in her mind. 'The people will only come into your hall where you see there's no carpet, and make their purchases. What a beautiful pair of tongs! For my sale? Fancy! Thank you, dear Diva.'

'But I forbid the jumble sale to be held here,' said Diva. 'You'll be wanting to have a menagerie here next.'

This was amazing luck.

'No, dear, I couldn't dream of it,' said Miss Mapp. 'I should hate to have tigers and sharks all over the place. Ridiculous!'

'I shall put up a merry-go-round in quaint Irene's studio at Taormina,' said Diva.

'I doubt if there's room, dear,' said Miss Mapp, scoring heavily again, 'but you might measure. Perfectly legitimate, of course, for if my house may be given over to parties for paupers, you can surely have a merry-go-round in quaint Irene's and I a jumble sale in yours.'

'It's not the same thing,' said Diva. 'Providing beautiful tableaux in your garden is quite different from using my panelled hall to sell kettles and coal scuttles with holes in them.'

'I dare say I could find a good many holes in the tableaux,' said Miss Mapp.

Diva could think of no adequate verbal retort to such coruscations, so for answer she merely picked up the tongs, the coal scuttle, the candlestick and the inkstand, and put them back in the cupboard from which she had just taken them, and left her tenant to sparkle by herself.

*　*　*

Most of the damaged objects for the jumble sale must have arrived by now, and after arranging them in tasteful groups Miss Mapp sat down in a rickety basket chair presented by the Padre for fell meditation. Certainly it was not pretty of Diva (no one could say that Diva was pretty) to have withdrawn her treasures, but that was not worth thinking about. What did demand her highest mental activities was Lucia's conduct. How grievously different she had turned out to be from that sweet woman for whom she had originally felt so warm an affection, whom she had planned to take so cosily under her wing, and administer in small doses as treats to Tilling society! Lucia had turned upon her and positively bitten the caressing hand. By means of showy little dinners and odious flatteries, she had quite certainly made Major Benjy and the Padre and the Wyses and poor Diva think that she was a very remarkable and delightful person and in these manoeuvres Miss Mapp saw a shocking and sinister attempt to set herself up as the Queen of Tilling society. Lucia had given dinner parties on three consecutive nights since her return, she had put herself on the committee for this fête, which (however much Miss Mapp might say she could not possibly permit it) she had not the slightest idea how to stop, and though Lucia was only a temporary resident here, these weeks would be quite intolerable if she continued to inflate herself in this presumptuous manner. It was certainly time for Miss Mapp to reassert herself before this rebel made more progress, and though dinner-giving was unusual in Tilling, she determined to give one or two most amusing ones herself, to none of which, of course, she would invite Lucia. But that was not nearly enough: she must administer some frightful snub (or snubs) to the woman. Georgie was in the same boat and must suffer too, for Lucia would not like that. So she sat in this web of crippled fire irons and napless rugs like a spider, meditating reprisals. Perhaps it was a pity, when she needed allies, to have quarrelled with Diva, but a dinner would set that right. Before long she got up with a pleased expression. 'That will do to begin with: she won't like that at all,' she said to herself and went out to do her belated marketing.

She passed Lucia and Georgie, but decided not to see them, and, energetically waving her hand to Mrs Bartlett, she popped into Twistevant's, from the door of which they had just come out. At that moment quaint Irene, after a few words with the Padre, caught sight of Lucia, and hurried across the street to her. She was hatless, as usual, and wore a collarless shirt and knickerbockers unlike any other lady of Tilling, but as she approached Lucia her face assumed an acid and awful smile, just like somebody else's, and then she spoke in a cooing velvety voice that was quite unmistakable.

'The boy stood on the burning deck, Lulu,' she said. 'Whence all but he had fled, dear. The flames that lit the battle-wreck, sweet one, shone round him – '

Quaint Irene broke off suddenly, for within a yard of her at the door of Twistevant's appeared Miss Mapp. She looked clean over all their heads, and darted across the street to Wasters, carrying a small straw basket of her own delicious greengages.

'Oh, lor!' said Irene. 'The Mapp's in the fire, so that's done. Yes. I'll recite for you at your fête. Georgie, what a saucy hat! I was just going to Taormina to rout out some old sketches of mine for the Art Show, and then this happens. I wouldn't have had it not happen for a hundred pounds.'

'Come and dine tonight,' said Lucia warmly, breaking all records in the way of hospitality.

'Yes, if I needn't dress, and you'll send me home afterwards. I'm half a mile out of the town and I may be tipsy, for Major Benjy says you've got jolly good booze, "*quai-hai*", the King, God bless him! Goodbye.'

* * *

'Most original!' said Lucia. 'To go on with what I was telling you, Georgie, Liblib said she would not have her little home sanctuary – Good morning, Padre. Miss Mapp shoved her way into Mallards this morning without ringing, and broke the chain which was on the door, such a hurry was she in to tell me that she will not have her little home sanctuary, as I was just saying to Georgie, invaded by the ragtag and bobtail of Tilling.'

'Hoots awa!' said the Padre. 'What in the world has Mistress Mapp got to do with it? An' who's holding a jumble sale in Mistress Plaistow's? I keeked in just now wi' my bit o' rubbish and never did I see such a mess. Na, na! Fair play's a jool, an' we'll go richt ahead. Excuse me, there's wee wifie wanting me.'

'It's war,' said Georgie as the Padre darted across to the Mouse, who was on the other side of the street, to tell her what had happened.

'No, I'm just defending myself,' said Lucia. 'It's right that people should know she burst my door chain.'

'Well, I feel like the fourth of August, 1914,' said Georgie. 'What do you suppose she'll do next?'

'You may depend upon it, Georgie, that I shall be ready for her whatever it is,' said Lucia. 'I shan't raise a finger against her, if she behaves. But she *shall* ring the bell and I *won't* be dictated to and I *won't* be called Lulu. However, there's no immediate danger of that. Come, Georgie, let us go home and finish our sketches. Then we'll have them framed and send them to Liblib for the picture exhibition. Perhaps that will convince her of my general goodwill, which I assure you is quite sincere.'

* * *

The jumble sale opened next day, and Georgie, having taken his picture of Lucia's house and her picture of his to be framed in a very handsome manner, went on to Wasters with the idea of buying anything that could be of the smallest use for any purpose, and thus showing more goodwill towards the patroness. Miss Mapp was darting to and fro with lures for purchasers, holding the kettle away from the light so that the hole in its bottom should not be noticed, and she gave him a smile that looked rather like a snarl, but after all very like the smile she had for others. Georgie selected a hearth brush, some curtain rings and a kettle holder.

Then in a dark corner he came across a large cardboard tray, holding miscellaneous objects with the label 'All 6d. Each'. There were thimbles, there were photographs with slightly damaged frames, there were chipped china ornaments and corkscrews, and there was the picture of the Landgate which he had painted himself and given Miss Mapp. Withers, Miss Mapp's parlourmaid, was at a desk for the exchange of custom by the door, and he exhibited his purchases for her inspection.

'Ninepence for the hearth brush and threepence for the curtain rings,' said Georgie in a trembling voice, 'and sixpence for the kettle holder. Then there's this little picture out of the sixpenny tray, which makes just two shillings.'

Laden with these miscellaneous purchases he went swiftly up the street to Mallards. Lucia was at the window of the garden room, and her gimlet eye saw that something had happened. She threw the sash up.

'I'm afraid the chain is on the door, Georgie,' she called out. 'You'll have to ring. What is it?'

'I'll show you,' said Georgie.

He deposited the hearth brush, the curtain rings and the kettle holder in the hall, and hurried out to the garden room with the picture.

'The sketch I gave her,' he said. 'In the sixpenny tray. Why, the frame cost a shilling.'

Lucia's face became a flint.

'I never heard of such a thing, Georgie,' said she. 'The monstrous woman!'

'It may have got there by mistake,' said Georgie, frightened at this Medusa countenance.

'Rubbish, Georgie,' said Lucia.

* * *

Pictures for the annual exhibition of the Art Society of which Miss Mapp was president had been arriving in considerable numbers at Wasters, and stood stacked round the walls of the hall where the jumble sale had been held a few days before, awaiting the judgement of the hanging committee which consisted of the president, the treasurer and the secretary: the two latter were Mr and Mrs Wyse. Miss Mapp had sent in half a dozen watercolours, the treasurer a study in still life of a tea cup, an orange and a wallflower, the secretary a pastel portrait of the King of Italy, whom she had seen at a distance in Rome last spring. She had reinforced the vivid impression he had made on her by photographs. All these, following the precedent of the pictures of Royal Academicians at Burlington House, would be hung on the line without dispute, and there could not be any friction concerning them. But quaint Irene had sent some at which Miss Mapp felt lines must be drawn. They were, as usual, very strange and modern: there was one, harmless but insane, that purported to be Tilling church by moonlight: a bright green pinnacle all crooked (she supposed it was a pinnacle) rose up against a strip of purple sky and the whole of the rest of the canvas was black. There was the back of somebody with no clothes on lying on an emerald-green sofa: and, worst of all, there was a picture called *Women Wrestlers*, from which Miss Mapp hurriedly averted her eyes. A proper regard for decency alone, even if Irene had not mimicked her reciting 'The boy stood on the burning deck', would have made her resolve to oppose, tooth and nail, the exhibition of these shameless athletes. Unfortunately Mr Wyse had the most unbounded admiration for quaint Irene's work, and if she had sent in a picture of mixed wrestlers he would probably have said, 'Dear me, very powerful!' He was a hard man to resist, for if he and Miss Mapp had a very strong difference of opinion concerning any particular canvas he broke off and fell into fresh transports of admiration at her own pictures and this rather disarmed opposition.

The meeting of the hanging committee was to take place this morning at noon. Half an hour before that time, an errand boy arrived at Wasters from the frame-maker's bringing, according to the order he had received, two parcels which contained Georgie's picture of Mallards and Lucia's picture of Mallards Cottage: they had the cards of their perpetrators attached. 'Rubbishy little daubs,' thought Miss Mapp to herself, 'but I suppose those two Wyses will insist.' Then an imprudent demon of revenge suddenly took complete possession of her, and she called back the boy, and said she had a further errand for him.

At a quarter before twelve the boy arrived at Mallards and rang the bell. Grosvenor took down the chain and received from him a thin square parcel labelled 'With care'. One minute afterwards he delivered a similar parcel to Foljambe at Mallards Cottage, and had discharged Miss Mapp's further errand. The two maids conveyed these to their employers, and Georgie and Lucia, tearing off the wrappers, found themselves simultaneously confronted with their own pictures. A typewritten slip accompanied each, conveying to them the cordial thanks of the hanging committee and its regrets that the limited wall space at its disposal would not permit of these works of art being exhibited.

Georgie ran out into his little yard and looked over the paling of Lucia's garden. At the same moment Lucia threw open the window of the garden room which faced towards the paling.

'Georgie, have you received –' she called.

'Yes,' said Georgie.

'So have I.'

'What are you going to do?' he asked.

Lucia's face assumed an expression eager and pensive, the faraway look with which she listened to Beethoven. She thought intently for a moment.

'I shall take a season ticket for the exhibition,' she said, 'and constantly –'

'I can't quite hear you,' said Georgie.

Lucia raised her voice.

'I shall buy a season ticket for the exhibition,' she shouted, 'and go there every day. Believe me, that's the only way to take it. They don't want our pictures, but we mustn't be small about it. Dignity, Georgie.'

There was nothing to add to so sublime a declaration and Lucia went across to the bow window, looking down the street. At that moment the Wyses' Royce lurched out of Porpoise Street, and turned down towards the High Street. Lucia knew they were both on the hanging committee which had just rejected one of her own most successful sketches (for the crooked chimney had turned out beautifully), but she felt not the smallest resentment towards them. No doubt they had acted quite conscientiously and she waved her hand in answer to a flutter of sables from the interior of the car. Presently she went down herself to the High Street to hear the news of the morning, and there was the Wyses' car drawn up in front of Wasters. She remembered then that the hanging committee met this morning, and a suspicion, too awful to be credible, flashed through her mind. But she thrust it out, as being unworthy of entertainment by a clean mind. She did her shopping and on her return took down a pale straw-coloured sketch by Miss Mapp that hung in the garden room, and put in its place her picture of Mallards Cottage and the crooked chimney. Then she called to mind that powerful platitude, and said to herself that time would show . . .

* * *

Miss Mapp had not intended to be present at the desecration of her garden by paupers from the workhouse and such low haunts. She had consulted her solicitor, about her power to stop the entertainment, but he assured her that there was no known statute in English law, which enabled her to prevent her tenant giving a party. So she determined, in the manner of Lucia and the Elizabethan fête at Riseholme, to be unaware of it, not to know that any fête was contemplated, and never afterwards to ask a single question about it. But as the day approached she suspected that the hot tide of curiosity, rapidly rising in her, would probably end by swamping and submerging her principles. She had seen the Padre dressed in a long black cloak, and carrying an axe of enormous size, entering Mallards; she had seen Diva come out in a white satin gown and scuttle down the street to Taormina, and those two prodigies taken together suggested that the execution of Mary Queen of Scots was in hand. (Diva as the Queen!) She had seen boards and posts carried in by the garden door and quantities of red cloth, so there was perhaps to be a stage for these tableaux. More intriguing yet was the apparition of Major Benjy carrying a cardboard crown glittering with gold paper. What on earth did that portend? Then there was her fruit to give an eye to: those choirboys, scampering all over the garden in the intervals between their glees, would probably pick every pear from the tree. She starved to know what was going on, but since she avoided all mention of the fête herself, others were most amazingly respectful to her reticence. She knew nothing, she could only make these delirious guesses, and there was *that* Lucia, being the centre of executioners and queens and choirboys, instead of in her proper place, made much of by kind Miss Mapp, and enjoying such glimpses of Tilling society as she chose to give her. 'A fortnight ago,' thought kind Miss Mapp, 'I was popping in and out of the house, and she was Lulu. Anyhow, that was a nasty one she got over her picture, and I must bear her no grudge. I shall go to the fête because I can't help it, and I shall be very cordial to her and admire her tableaux. We're all Christians together, and I despise smallness.'

It was distressing to be asked to pay half a crown for admittance to her own Mallards, but there seemed positively no other way to get past Grosvenor. Very distressing, too, it was, to see Lucia in full fig as Queen Elizabeth, graciously receiving newcomers on the edge of the lawn, precisely as if this was her party and these people who had paid half a crown to come in, her invited guests. It was a bitter thought that it ought to be herself who (though not dressed in all that flummery, so unconvincing by daylight) welcomed the crowd; for to whom, pray, did Mallards belong, and who had allowed it (since she could not stop it) to be thrown open? At the bottom of the steps into the garden room was a large placard 'Private', but of course that would not apply to her. Through the half-opened door, as she passed, she caught a glimpse of a familiar figure, though sadly travestied, sitting in a robe and a golden crown and pouring something into a glass: no doubt then the garden room was the green room of performers in the tableaux, who, less greedy of publicity than Lulu, hid themselves here till the time of their exposure brought them out. She would go in there presently, but her immediate duty, bitter but necessary, was to greet her hostess. With a very happy inspiration she tripped up to Lucia and dropped a low curtsey.

'Your Majesty's most obedient humble servant,' she said, and then trusting that Lucia had seen that this obeisance was made in a mocking spirit, abounded in geniality.

'My dear, what a love of a costume!' she said. 'And what a lovely day for your fête! And what a crowd! How the half-crowns have been pouring in! All Tilling seems to be here, and I'm sure I don't wonder.'

Lucia rivalled these cordialities with equal fervour and about as much sincerity.

'Elizabeth! How nice of you to look in!' she said. '*Ecco, le due Elizabethe!* And you like my frock? Sweet of you! Yes. Tilling has indeed come to the aid of the hospital! And your jumble sale too was a wonderful success, was it not? Nothing left, I am told.'

Miss Mapp had a moment's hesitation as to whether she should not continue to stand by Lucia and shake hands with new arrivals and give them a word of welcome, but she decided she could do more effective work if she made herself independent and played hostess by herself. Also this mention of the jumble sale made her slightly uneasy. Withers had told her that Georgie had bought his own picture of the Landgate from the sixpenny tray, and Lucia (for all her cordiality) might be about to spring some horrid trap on her about it.

'Yes, indeed,' she said. 'My little sale room was soon as bare as Mother Hubbard's cupboard. But I mustn't monopolize you, dear, or I shall be lynched. There's a whole *queue* of people waiting to get a word with you. How I shall enjoy the tableaux! Looking forward to them so!'

She sidled off into the crowd. There were those dreadful old wretches from the workhouse, snuffy old things, some of them smoking pipes on her lawn and scattering matches, and being served with tea by Irene and the Padre's curate.

'So pleased to see you all here,' she said, 'sitting in my garden and enjoying your tea. I must pick a nice nosegay for you to take back home. How de do, Mr Sturgis. Delighted you could come and help to entertain the old folks for us. Good afternoon, Mr Wyse; yes, my little garden is looking nice, isn't it? Susan, dear! Have you noticed my bed of delphiniums? I must give you some seed. Oh, there is the town crier ringing his bell! I suppose that means we must take our places for the tableaux. What a good stage! I hope the posts will not have made very big holes in my lawn. Oh, one of those naughty choirboys is hovering about my fig tree. I cannot allow that.'

She hurried off to stop any possibility of such depredation, and had made some telling allusions to the eighth commandment when on a second peal of the town-crier's bell, the procession of mummers came down the steps of the garden room and advancing across the lawn disappeared behind the stage. Poor Major Benjy (so weak of him to allow himself to be dragged into this sort of thing) looked a perfect guy in his crown (who could he be meant for?) and as for Diva – Then there was Georgie (Drake indeed!), and last of all Queen Elizabeth with her train held up by two choirboys. Poor Lucia! Not content with a week of mumming at Riseholme she had to go on with her processions and dressings-up here. Some people lived on limelight.

Miss Mapp could not bring herself to take a seat close to the stage, and be seen applauding – there seemed to be some hitch with the curtain: no, it righted itself, what a pity! – and she hung about on the outskirts of the audience. Glees were interposed between the tableaux; how thin were the voices of those little boys out of doors! Then Irene, dressed like a sailor, recited that ludicrous parody. Roars of laughter. Then Major Benjy was King Cophetua: that was why he had a crown. Oh dear, oh dear! It was sad to reflect that an elderly, sensible man (for when at his best, he was that) could be got hold of by a pushing woman. The final tableau, of course (anyone might have guessed that), was the knighting of Drake by Queen Elizabeth. Then amid sycophantic applause the procession of guys returned and went back into the garden room. Mr and Mrs Wyse followed them, and it seemed pretty clear that they were going to have a private tea there. Doubtless she would be soon sought for among the crowd with a message from Lucia to hope that she would join them in her own garden room, but as nothing of the sort came, she presently thought that it would be only kind to Lucia to do so, and add her voice to the general chorus of congratulation that was no doubt going on. So with a brisk little tap on the door, and the enquiry 'May I come in?' she entered.

There they all were, as pleased as children with dressing-up.

King Cophetua still wore his crown, tilted slightly to one side like a forage cap, and he and Queen Elizabeth and Queen Mary were seated round the tea table and calling each other your Majesty. King Cophetua had a large whisky and soda in front of him and Miss Mapp felt quite certain it was not his first. But though sick in soul at these puerilities she pulled herself together and made a beautiful curtsey to the silly creatures. And the worst of it was that there was no one left of her own intimate circle to whom she could in private express her disdain, for they were all in it, either actively or, like the Wyses, truckling to Lucia.

Lucia for the moment seemed rather surprised to see her, but she welcomed her and poured her out a cup of rather tepid tea, nasty to the taste. She must truckle, too, to the whole lot of them, though that tasted nastier than the tea.

'How I congratulate you all,' she cried. 'Padre, you looked too cruel as executioner, your mouth so fixed and stern. It was quite a relief when the curtain came down. Irene, quaint one, how you made them laugh! Diva, Mr Georgie, and above all our wonderful Queen Lucia. What a treat it has all been! The choir! Those beautiful glees. A thousand pities, Mr Wyse, that the Contessa was not here.'

There was still Susan to whom she ought to say something pleasant, but positively she could not go on, until she had eaten something solid. But Lucia chimed in.

'And your garden, Elizabeth,' she said. 'How they are enjoying it. I believe if the truth was known they are all glad that our little tableaux are over, so that they can wander about and admire the flowers. I must give a little party some night soon with Chinese lanterns and fairy lights in the beds.'

'Upon my word, your Majesty is spoiling us all,' said Major Benjy. 'Tilling's never had a month with so much pleasure provided for it. Glorious.'

Miss Mapp had resolved to stop here if it was anyhow possible, till these sycophants had dispersed, and then have one private word with Lucia to indicate how ready she was to overlook all the little frictions that had undoubtedly arisen. She fully meant, without eating a morsel of humble pie herself, to allow Lucia to eat proud pie, for she saw that just for the present she herself was nowhere and Lucia everywhere. So Lucia should glut herself into a sense of complete superiority, and then it would be time to begin fresh manoeuvres. Major Benjy and Diva soon took themselves off: she saw them from the garden window going very slowly down the street, ever so pleased to have people staring at them, and Irene, at the Padre's request, went out to dance a hornpipe on the lawn in her sailor clothes. But the two Wyses (always famous for sticking) remained and Georgie.

Mr Wyse got up from the tea table and passed round behind Miss Mapp's chair. Out of the corner of her eye she could see he was looking at the wall where a straw-coloured picture of her own hung. He always used to admire it, and it was pleasant to feel that he was giving it so careful and so respectful a scrutiny. Then he spoke to Lucia.

'How well I remember seeing you painting that,' he said, 'and how long I took to forgive myself for having disturbed you in my blundering car. A perfect little masterpiece, Mallards Cottage and the crooked chimney. To the life.'

Susan heaved herself up from the sofa and joined in the admiration.

'Perfectly delightful,' she said. 'The lights, the shadows. Beautiful! What a touch!'

Miss Mapp turned her head slowly as if she had a stiff neck, and verified her awful conjecture that it was no longer a picture of her own that hung there, but the very picture of Lucia's which had been rejected for the art exhibition. She felt as if no picture but a bomb hung there, which might explode at some chance word, and blow her into a thousand fragments. It was best to hurry from this perilous neighbourhood.

'Dear Lucia,' she said, 'I must be off. Just one little stroll, if I may, round my garden, before I go home. My roses will never forgive me, if I go away without noticing them.'

She was too late.

'How I wish I had known it was finished!' said Mr Wyse. 'I should have begged you to allow us to have it for our art exhibition. It would have been the gem of it. Cruel of you, Mrs Lucas!'

'But I sent it in to the hanging committee,' said Lucia. 'Georgie sent his, too, of Mallards. They were both sent back to us.'

Mr Wyse turned from the picture to Lucia with an expression of incredulous horror, and Miss Mapp quietly turned to stone.

'But impossible,' he said. 'I am on the hanging committee myself, and I hope you cannot think I should have been such an imbecile. Susan is on the committee too: so is Miss Mapp. In fact, we are the hanging committee. Susan, that gem, that little masterpiece never came before us.'

'Never,' said Susan. 'Never. Never, never.'

Mr Wyse's eye transferred itself to Miss Mapp. She was still stone and her face was as white as the wall of Mallards Cottage in the masterpiece. Then for the first time in the collective memory of Tilling Mr Wyse allowed himself to use slang.

'There has been some hanky-panky,' he said. 'That picture never came before the hanging committee.'

The stone image could just move its eyes and they looked, in a glassy manner, at Lucia. Lucia's met them with one short gimlet thrust, and she whisked round to Georgie. Her face was turned away from the others, and she gave him a prodigious wink, as he sat there palpitating with excitement.

'*Georgino mio*,' she said. 'Let us recall exactly what happened. The morning, I mean, when the hanging committee met. Let me see: let me see. Don't interrupt me: I will get it all clear.'

Lucia pressed her hands to her forehead. 'I have it,' she said. 'It is perfectly vivid to me now. You had taken our little pictures down to the framer's, Georgie, and told him to send them in to Elizabeth's house direct. That was it. The errand boy from the framer's came up here that very morning, and delivered mine to Grosvenor, and yours to Foljambe. Let me think exactly when that was. What time was it, Mr Wyse, that the hanging committee met?'

'At twelve, precisely,' said Mr Wyse.

'That fits in perfectly,' said Lucia. 'I called to Georgie out of the window here, and we told each other that our pictures had been rejected. A moment later, I saw your car go down to the High Street and when I went down there soon afterwards, it was standing in front of Miss – I mean Elizabeth's house. Clearly what happened was that the framer misunderstood Georgie's instructions, and returned the pictures to us before the hanging committee sat at all.

So you never saw them, and we imagined all the time – did we not, Georgie? – that you had simply sent them back.'

'But what must you have thought of us?' said Mr Wyse, with a gesture of despair.

'Why, that you did not conscientiously think very much of our art,' said Lucia. 'We were perfectly satisfied with your decision. I felt sure that my little picture had a hundred faults and feeblenesses.'

Miss Mapp had become unpetrified. Could it be that by some miraculous oversight she had not put into those parcels the formal, typewritten rejection of the committee? It did not seem likely, for she had a very vivid remembrance of the gratification it gave her to do so, but the only alternative theory was to suppose a magnanimity on Lucia's part which seemed even more miraculous. She burst into speech.

'How we all congratulate ourselves,' she cried, 'that it has all been cleared up! Such a stupid errand boy! What are we to do next, Mr Wyse? Our exhibition must secure Lucia's sweet picture, and of course Mr Pillson's too. But how are we to find room for them? Everything is hung.'

'Nothing easier,' said Mr Wyse. 'I shall instantly withdraw my paltry little piece of still life, and I am sure that Susan – '

'No, that would never do,' said Miss Mapp, currying favour all round. 'That beautiful wallflower, I could almost smell it: that King of Italy. Mine shall go: two or three of mine. I insist on it.'

Mr Wyse bowed to Lucia and then to Georgie.

'I have a plan better yet,' he said. 'Let us put – if we may have the privilege of securing what was so nearly lost to our exhibition – let us put these two pictures on easels as showing how deeply we appreciate our good fortune in getting them.'

He bowed to his wife, he bowed – was it quite a bow? – to Miss Mapp, and had there been a mirror, he would no doubt have bowed to himself.

'Besides,' he said, 'our little sketches will not thus suffer so much from their proximity to – ' and he bowed to Lucia. 'And if Mr Pillson will similarly allow us – ' he bowed to Georgie.

Georgie, following Lucia's lead, graciously offered to go round to the cottage and bring back his picture of Mallards, but Mr Wyse would not hear of such a thing. He and Susan would go off in

the Royce now, with Lucia's masterpiece, and fetch Georgie's from
Mallards Cottage, and the sun should not set before they both
stood on their distinguished easels in the enriched exhibition. So off
they went in a great hurry to procure the easels before the sun went
down and Miss Mapp, unable alone to face the reinstated victims
of her fraud, scurried after them in a tumult of mixed emotions.
Outside in the garden Irene, dancing hornpipes, was surrounded
by both sexes of the enraptured youth of Tilling, for the boys knew
she was a girl, and the girls thought she looked so like a boy. She
shouted out 'Come and dance, Mapp,' and Elizabeth fled from her
own sweet garden as if it had been a plague-stricken area, and never
spoke to her roses at all.

The Queen and Drake were left alone in the garden room.

'Well, I never!' said Georgie. 'Did you? She sent them back all
by herself.'

'I'm not the least surprised,' said Lucia. 'It's like her.'

'But why did you let her off?' he asked. 'You ought to have
exposed her and have done with her.'

Lucia showed a momentary exultation, and executed a few steps
from a Morris dance.

'No, Georgie, that would have been a mistake,' she said. 'She
knows that we know, and I can't wish her worse than that. And I
rather think, though he makes me giddy with so much bowing,
that Mr Wyse has guessed. He certainly suspects something of the
sort.'

'Yes, he said there had been some hanky-panky,' said Georgie.
'That was a strong thing for him to say. All the same – '

Lucia shook her head.

'No, I'm right,' she said. 'Don't you see I've taken the moral
stuffing out of that woman far more completely than if I had
exposed her?'

'But she's a cheat,' cried Georgie. 'She's a liar, for she sent back
our pictures with a formal notice that the committee had rejected
them. She hasn't got any moral stuffing to take out.'

Lucia pondered this.

'That's true, there doesn't seem to be much,' she said. 'But
even then, think of the moral stuffing that I've put into myself. A
far greater score, Georgie, than to have exposed her, and it must

be quite agonizing for her to have that hanging over her head. Besides, she can't help being deeply grateful to me if there are any depths in that poor shallow nature. There may be: we must try to discover them. Take a broader view of it all, Georgie . . . Oh, and I've thought of something fresh! Send round to Mr Wyse for the exhibition your picture of the Landgate, which poor Elizabeth sold. He will certainly hang it and she will see it there. That will round everything off nicely.'

Lucia moved across to the piano and sat down on the treble music stool.

'Let us forget all about these *piccoli disturbi*, Georgie,' she said, 'and have some music to put us in tune with beauty again. No, you needn't shut the door: it is so hot, and I am sure that no one else will dream of passing that notice of "Private", or come in here unasked. Ickle bit of divine Mozartino?'

Lucia found the duet at which she had worked quietly at odd moments.

'Let us try this,' she said, 'though it looks rather diffy. Oh, one thing more, Georgie. I think you and I had better keep those formal notices of rejection from the hanging committee just in case. We might need them some day, though I'm sure I hope we shan't. But one must be careful in dealing with that sort of woman. That's all I think. Now let us breathe harmony and loveliness again. *Uno, due* . . . pom.'

CHAPTER SIX

It was a mellow morning of October, the season, as Lucia reflected, of mists and mellow fruitfulness, wonderful John Keats. There was no doubt about the mists, for there had been several sea fogs in the English Channel, and the mellow fruitfulness of the garden at Mallards was equally indisputable. But now the fruitfulness of that sunny plot concerned Lucia far more than it had done during August and September, for she had taken Mallards for another month (Adele Brixton having taken The Hurst, Riseholme, for three), not on those original Shylock terms of fifteen guineas a week, and no garden produce – but of twelve guineas a week, and all the garden produce. It was a wonderful year for tomatoes: there were far more than a single widow could possibly eat, and Lucia, instead of selling them, constantly sent little presents of them to Georgie and Major Benjy. She had sent one basket of them to Miss Mapp, but these had been returned and Miss Mapp had written an effusive note saying that they would be wasted on her. Lucia had applauded that; it showed a very proper spirit.

The chain of consequences, therefore, of Lucia's remaining at Mallards was far-reaching. Miss Mapp took Wasters for another month at a slightly lower rent, Diva extended her lease of Taormina, and Irene still occupied the four-roomed labourer's cottage outside Tilling, which suited her so well, and the labourer and his family remained in the hop-picker's shanty. It was getting chilly of nights in the shanty, and he looked forward to the time when, Adele having left The Hurst, his cottage could be restored to him. Nor did the chain of consequences end here, for Georgie could not go back to Riseholme without Foljambe, and Foljambe would not go back there and leave her Cadman, while Lucia remained at Mallards. So Isabel Poppit continued to inhabit her bungalow by the sea, and Georgie remained in Mallards Cottage. With her skin turned black with all those sun-baths, and her hair spiky and wiry with so many sea-baths, Isabel resembled a cross between a kipper and a sea urchin.

September had been full of events. The art exhibition had been a great success, and quantities of the pictures had been sold. Lucia had bought Georgie's picture of Mallards, Georgie had bought Lucia's picture of Mallards Cottage, Mr Wyse had bought his wife's pastel of the King of Italy, and sent it as a birthday present to Amelia, and Susan Wyse had bought her husband's tea cup and wallflower and kept them herself. But the greatest gesture of all had been Lucia's purchase of one of Miss Mapp's six exhibits, and this had practically forced Miss Mapp, so powerful was the suggestion hidden in it, to buy Georgie's picture of the Landgate, which he had given her, and which she had sold (not even for her own benefit but for that of the hospital) for sixpence at her jumble sale. She had had to pay a guinea to regain what had once been hers, so that in the end the revengeful impulse which had prompted her to put it in the sixpenny tray had been cruelly expensive. But she had still felt herself to be under Lucia's thumb in the whole matter of the exhibition (as indeed she was) and this purchase was of the nature of a propitiatory act. They had met one morning at the show, and Lucia had looked long at this sketch of Georgie's and then, looking long at Elizabeth, she had said it was one of the most charming and exquisite of his watercolours. Inwardly raging, yet somehow impotent to resist, Elizabeth had forked up. But she was now busily persuading herself that this purchase had something to do with the hospital, and that she need not make any further contributions to its funds this year: she felt there was a very good chance of persuading herself about this. No one had bought quaint Irene's pictures, and she had turned the women wrestlers into men.

Since then Miss Mapp had been very busy with the conversion of the marvellous crop of apples, plums and redcurrants in Diva's garden into jam and jelly. Her cook could not tackle so big a job alone, and she herself spent hours a day in the kitchen, and the most delicious odours of boiling preserves were wafted out of the windows into the High Street. It could not be supposed that they would escape Diva's sharp nose, and there had been words about it. But garden produce (Miss Mapp believed) meant what it said, or would dear Diva prefer that she let the crop rot on the trees, and be a portion for wasps. Diva acknowledged that she would. And when the fruit was finished Miss Mapp proposed to turn her attention to the vegetable marrows, which, with a little ginger, made a very useful preserve for the household. She would leave a dozen of these pots for Diva.

But the jam-making was over now and Miss Mapp was glad of that, for she had scalded her thumb: quite a blister. She was even gladder that the art exhibition was over. All the important works of the Tilling school (except the pastel of the King of Italy) remained in Tilling, she had made her propitiatory sacrifice about Georgie's sketch of the Landgate, and she had no reason to suppose that Lucia had ever repented of that moment of superb magnanimity in the garden room, which had averted an exposure of which she still occasionally trembled to think. Lucia could not go back on that now, it was all over and done with like the jam-making (though, like the jam-making, it had left a certain seared and sensitive place behind) and having held her tongue then, Lucia could not blab afterwards. Like the banns in church, she must for ever hold her peace. Miss Mapp had been deeply grateful for that clemency at the time, but no one could go on being grateful indefinitely. You were grateful until you had paid your debt of gratitude, and then you were free. She would certainly be grateful again, when this month was over and Lucia and Georgie left Tilling, never, she hoped, to return, but for the last week or two she had felt that she had discharged in full every groat of gratitude she owed Lucia, and her mind had been busier than usual over plots and plans and libels and inductions with regard to her tenant who, with those cheese-paring ways so justly abhorred by Miss Mapp, had knocked down the rent to twelve guineas a week and grabbed the tomatoes.

But Miss Mapp did not yet despair of dealing Lucia some nasty blow, for the fact of the matter was (she felt sure of it) that Tilling generally was growing a little restive under Lucia's autocratic ways. She had been taking them in hand, she had been patronizing them, which Tilling never could stand, she had been giving them treats, just like that! She had sent out cards for an evening party (not dinner at all) with '*un po' di musica*' written in the left-hand corner. Even Mr Wyse, that notorious sycophant, had raised his eyebrows over this, and had allowed that this was rather an unusual inscription: '*musica*' (he thought) would have been more ordinary, and he would ask Amelia when she came. That had confirmed a secret suspicion which Miss Mapp had long entertained that Lucia's Italian (and, of course, Georgie's too) was really confined to such words as '*ecco*' and '*bon giorno*' and '*bello*' and she was earnestly hoping that Amelia would come before October was over, and they would all see what these great talks in Italian, to which Mr Wyse was so looking forward, would amount to.

And what an evening that 'po-di-mu' (as it was already referred to with faint little smiles) had been! It was a wet night and in obedience to her command (for at that time Lucia was at the height of the ascendancy she had acquired at the hospital fête), they had all put mackintoshes over their evening clothes, and galoshes over their evening shoes, and slopped up to Mallards through the pouring rain. A couple of journeys of Lucia's car could have brought them all in comfort and dryness, but she had not offered so obvious a convenience. Mrs Wyse's Royce was being overhauled, so they had to walk too, and a bedraggled and discontented company had assembled. They had gone into the garden room dripped on by the wistaria, and an interminable po-di-mu ensued. Lucia turned off all the lights in the room except one on the piano, so that they saw her profile against a black background, like the head on a postage stamp, and first she played the slow movement out of the 'Moonlight Sonata'. She stopped once, just after she had begun, because Diva coughed, and when she had finished there was a long silence. Lucia sighed and Georgie sighed, and everyone said 'Thank you' simultaneously. Major Benjy said he was devoted to Chopin and Lucia playfully told him that she would take his musical education in hand.

Then she had allowed the lights to be turned up again, and there was a few minutes' pause to enable them to conquer the poignancy of emotion aroused by that exquisite rendering of the 'Moonlight Sonata', to disinfect it so to speak with cigarettes, or drown it, as Major Benjy did, in rapid whiskies and sodas, and when they felt braver the po-di-mu began again, with a duet, between her and Georgie, of innumerable movements by Mozart, who must indeed have been a most prolific composer if he wrote all that. Diva fell quietly asleep, and presently there were indications that she would soon be noisily asleep. Miss Mapp hoped that she would begin to snore properly, for that would be a good set-down for Lucia, but Major Benjy poked her stealthily on the knee to rouse her. Mr Wyse began to stifle yawns, though he sat as upright as ever, with his eyes fixed rather glassily on the ceiling, and ejaculated 'Charming' at the end of every movement. When it was all over there were some faintly murmured requests that Lucia would play to them again, and without any further pressing, she sat down. Her obtuseness was really astounding.

'How you all work me!' she said. 'A fugue by Bach then, if you insist on it, and if Georgie will promise not to scold me if I break down.'

Luckily amid suppressed sighs of relief, she did break down, and though she was still perfectly willing to try again, there was a general chorus of unwillingness to take advantage of her great good nature, and after a wretched supper, consisting largely of tomato-salad, they trooped out into the rain, cheered by the promise of another musical evening next week when she would have that beautiful fugue by heart.

It was not the next week but the same week that they had all been bidden to a further evening of harmony, and symptoms of revolt, skilfully fomented by Miss Mapp, were observable. She had just received her note of invitation one morning, when Diva trundled in to Wasters.

'Another po-di-mu already,' said she sarcastically. 'What are you – '

'Isn't it unfortunate?' interrupted Elizabeth, 'for I hope, dear Diva, you have not forgotten that you promised to come in that very night – Thursday, isn't it – and play piquet with me.'

Diva returned Elizabeth's elaborate wink. 'So I did,' she said. 'Anyhow, I do.'

'Consequently we shall have to refuse dear Lucia's invitation,' said Elizabeth regretfully. 'Lovely, wasn't it, the other night? And so many movements of Mozart. I began to think he must have discovered the secret of perpetual motion, and that we should be stuck there till Doomsday.'

Diva was fidgeting about the room in her restless manner. ('Rather like a spinning top,' thought Miss Mapp, 'bumping into everything. I wish it would die.')

'I don't think she plays bridge very well,' said Diva. 'She began, you know; by saying she was so anxious to learn, and that we all played marvellously, but now she lays down the law like anything, telling us what we ought to have declared, and how we ought to have played. It's quite like – '

She was going to say 'It's quite like playing with you,' but luckily stopped in time.

'I haven't had the privilege of playing with her. Evidently I'm not up to her form,' said Elizabeth, 'but I hear, only report, mind, that she doesn't know the elements of the game.'

'Well, not much more,' said Diva. 'And she says she will start a bridge class if we like.'

'She spoils us! And who will the pupils be?' asked Elizabeth.

'I know one who won't,' said Diva darkly.

'And one and one make two,' observed Elizabeth. 'A pity that she sets herself up like that. Saying the other night that she would take Major Benjy's musical education in hand! I always thought education began at home, and I'm sure I never heard so many wrong notes in my life.'

Diva ruminated a moment, and began spinning again. 'She offered to take the choir practices in church, only the Padre wouldn't hear of it,' she said. 'And there's talk of a class to read Homer in Pope's translation.'

'She has every accomplishment,' said Elizabeth, 'including push.'

Diva bumped into another topic.

'I met Mr Wyse just now,' she said. 'Countess Amelia Faraglione is coming tomorrow.'

Miss Mapp sprang up.

'Not really?' she cried. 'Why, she'll be here for Lucia's po-di-mu on Thursday. And the Wyses will be going, that's certain, and they are sure to ask if they may bring the Faradidleone with them. Diva, dear, we must have our piquet another night. I wouldn't miss that for anything.'

'Why?' asked Diva.

'Just think what will happen! She'll be forced to talk Italian, for Mr Wyse has often said what a treat it will be to hear them talk it together, and I'm sure Lucia doesn't know any. I must be there.'

'But if she does know it, it will be rather a sell,' said Diva. 'We shall have gone there for nothing except to hear all that Mozart over again and to eat tomatoes. I had heartburn half the night afterwards.'

'Trust me, Diva,' said Elizabeth. 'I swear she doesn't know any Italian. And how on earth will she be able to wriggle out of talking it? With all her ingeniousness, it can't be done. She can't help being exposed.'

'Well, that would be rather amusing,' said Diva. 'Being put down a peg or two certainly wouldn't hurt her. All right. I'll say I'll come.'

Miss Mapp's policy was now of course the exact reverse of what she had first planned. Instead of scheming to get all Tilling to refuse Lucia's invitation to listen to another po-di-mu, her object was to encourage everyone to go, in order that they might listen not so much to Mozart as to her rich silences or faltering replies when challenged to converse in the Italian language. She found that the Padre and Mrs Bartlett had hurriedly arranged a choir practice and a meeting of the girl guides respectively to take place at the unusual hour of half-past nine in the evening in order to be able to decline the po-di-mu, but Elizabeth, throwing economy to the winds, asked them both to dine with her on the fatal night, and come on to Lucia's delicious music afterwards. This added inducement prevailed, and off they scurried to tell choirboys and girl guides that the meetings were cancelled and would be held at the usual hour the day after. The curate needed no persuasion, for he thought that Lucia had a wonderful touch on the piano, and was already looking forward to more; Irene similarly had developed a violent *schwarm* for Lucia and had accepted, so that Tilling, thanks to Elizabeth's friendly offices, would now muster in force to hear Lucia play duets and fugues and not speak Italian. And when, in casual conversation with Mr Wyse, Elizabeth learned that he had (as she had anticipated) ventured to ask Lucia if she would excuse the presumption of one of her greatest admirers, and allow him to bring his sister Amelia to her *soirée* and that Lucia had sent him her most cordial permission to do so, it seemed that nothing could stand in the way of the fulfilment of Elizabeth's romantic revenge on that upstart visitor for presuming to set herself up as Queen of the social life of Tilling.

It was, as need hardly be explained, this aspect of the affair which so strongly appealed to the sporting instincts of the place. Miss Mapp had long been considered by others as well as herself the first social citizen of Tilling, and though she had often been obliged to fight desperately for her position, and had suffered from time to time manifold reverses, she had managed to maintain it, because there was no one else of so commanding and unscrupulous a character. Then, this alien from Riseholme had appeared and had not so much challenged her as just taken her sceptre and her crown and worn them now for a couple of months. At present all attempts to recapture them had failed, but Lucia had grown a little arrogant, she had offered to take choir practice, she had issued her invitations (so thought Tilling) rather as if they had been commands, and Tilling would not have been sorry to see her suffer some setback. Nobody wanted to turn out in the evening to hear her play Mozart (except the curate), no one intended to listen to her read Pope's translation of Homer's *Iliad*, or to be instructed how to play bridge, and though Miss Mapp was no favourite, they would have liked to see her score. But there was little partisanship; it was the sporting instinct which looked forward to witnessing an engagement between two well-equipped Queens, and seeing whether one really could speak Italian or not, even if they had to listen to all the fugues of Bach first. Everyone, finally, except Miss Mapp, wherever their private sympathies might lie, regretted that now in less than a month, Lucia would have gone back to her own kingdom of Riseholme, where it appeared she had no rival of any sort, for these encounters were highly stimulating to students of human nature and haters of Miss Mapp. Never before had Tilling known so exciting a season.

*   *   *

On this mellow morning, then, of October, Lucia, after practising her fugue for the coming po-di-mu, and observing Coplen bring into the house a wonderful supply of tomatoes, had received that appalling note from Mr Wyse, conveyed by the Royce, asking if he might bring Contessa Amelia di Faraglione to the musical party to which he so much looked forward. The gravity of the issue was instantly clear to Lucia, for Mr Wyse had made no secret about the pleasure it would give him to hear his sister and herself mellifluously converse in the Italian tongue, but without hesitation she sent back a note by the chauffeur and the Royce, that she would be charmed to see the Contessa. There was no getting out of that, and she must accept the inevitable before proceeding irresistibly to deal with it. From the window she observed the Royce backing and advancing and backing till it managed to turn and went round the corner to Porpoise Street.

Lucia closed the piano, for she had more cosmic concerns to think about than the fingerings of a fugue. Her party of course (that required no consideration) would have to be cancelled, but that was only one point in the problem that confronted her. For that baleful bilinguist the Contessa di Faraglione was not coming to Tilling (all the way from Italy) for one night but she was to stay here, so Mr Wyse's note had mentioned, for 'about a week', after which she would pay visits to her relations the Wyses of Whitchurch and others. So for a whole week (or about) Lucia would be in perpetual danger of being called upon to talk Italian. Indeed, the danger was more than mere danger, for if anything in this world was certain, it was that Mr Wyse would ask her to dinner during this week, and exposure would follow. Complete disappearance from Tilling during the Contessa's sojourn here was the only possible plan, yet how was that to be accomplished? Her house at Riseholme was let, but even if it had not been, she could not leave Tilling tomorrow, when she had invited everybody to a party in the evening.

The clock struck noon: she had meditated for a full half-hour, and now she rose.

'I can only think of influenza,' she said to herself. 'But I shall consult Georgie. A man might see it from another angle.'

He came at once to her SOS.

'*Georgino mio*,' began Lucia, but then suddenly corrected herself. 'Georgie,' she said. 'Something very disagreeable. The Contessa Thingummy is coming to the Wyses tomorrow, and he's asked me if he may bring her to our *musica*. I had to say yes; no way out of it.'

Georgie was often very perceptive. He saw what this meant at once.

'Good Lord,' he said. 'Can't you put it off? Sprain your thumb.'

The man's angle was not being of much use so far.

'Not a bit of good,' she said. 'She'll be here about a week, and naturally I have to avoid meeting her altogether. The only thing I can think of is influenza.'

Georgie never smoked in the morning, but the situation seemed to call for a cigarette.

'That would do it,' he said. 'Rather a bore for you, but you could live in the secret garden a good deal. It's not overlooked.'

He stopped: the unusual tobacco had stimulated his perceptive powers.

'But what about me?' he said.

'I'm sure I don't know,' said Lucia.

'You're not looking far enough,' said Georgie. 'You're not taking the long view which you so often talk to me about. I can't have influenza too, it would be too suspicious. So I'm bound to meet the Faraglione and she'll see in a minute I can't talk Italian.'

'Well?' said Lucia in a very selfish manner, as if he didn't matter at all.

'Oh, I'm not thinking about myself only,' said Georgie in self-defence. 'Not so at all. It'll react on you. You and I are supposed to talk Italian together, and when it's obvious I can't say more than three things in it, the fat's in the fire, however much influenza you have. How are you going to be supposed to jabber away in Italian to me when it's seen that I can't understand a word of it?'

Here indeed was the male angle, and an extremely awkward angle it was. For a moment Lucia covered her face with her hands.

'Georgie, what are we to do?' she asked in a stricken voice.

Georgie was a little ruffled at having been considered of such absolute unimportance until he pointed out to Lucia that her fate was involved with his, and it pleased him to echo her words.

'I'm sure I don't know,' he said stiffly.

Lucia hastened to smooth his smart.

'My dear, I'm so glad I thought of consulting you,' she said. 'I knew it would take a man's mind to see all round the question, and how right you are! I never thought of that.'

'Quite,' said Georgie. 'It's evident you haven't grasped the situation at all.'

She paced up and down the garden room in silence, recoiling once from the window, as she saw Elizabeth go by and kiss her hand with that awful hyena grin of hers.

'Georgie, 'oo not cross with poor Lucia?' she said, resorting to the less dangerous lingo which they used in happier days. This softened Georgie.

'I was rather,' said Georgie, 'but never mind that now. What am I to do? *Che faro*, in fact.'

Lucia shuddered.

'Oh, for goodness' sake, don't talk Italian,' she said. 'It's that we've got to avoid. It's odd that we have to break ourselves of the habit of doing something we can't do . . . And you can't have influenza too. It would be too suspicious if you began simultaneously with me tomorrow. I've often wondered, now I come to think of it, if that woman, that Mapp, hasn't suspected that our Italian was a fake, and if we both had influenza exactly as the Faraglione arrived, she might easily put two and two together. Her mind is horrid enough for anything.'

'I know she suspects,' said Georgie. 'She said some word in Italian to me the other day, which meant paperknife, and she looked surprised when I didn't understand, and said it in English. Of course, she had looked it out in a dictionary: it was a trap.'

A flood of horrid light burst in on Lucia. 'Georgie,' she cried. 'She tried me with the same word. I've forgotten it again, but it did mean paperknife. I didn't know it either, though I pretended it was her pronunciation that puzzled me. There's no end to her craftiness. But I'll get the better of her yet. I think you'll have to go away, while the Faraglione is here and I have influenza.'

'But I don't want to go away,' began Georgie. 'Surely we can think of – '

Lucia paid no heed to this attempt at protest: it is doubtful if she even heard it, for the spark was lit now, and it went roaring through her fertile brain like a prairie fire in a high gale.

'You must go away tomorrow,' she said. 'Far better than

influenza, and you must stop away till I send you a telegram, that the Faraglione has left. It will be very dull for me because I shall be entirely confined to the house and garden all the time you are gone. I think the garden will be safe. I cannot remember that it is overlooked from any other house and I shall do a lot of reading, though even the piano won't be possible . . . Georgie, I see it all. You have not been looking very well lately (my dear, you're the picture of health really, I have never seen you looking younger or better) and so you will have gone off to have a week at Folkestone or Littlestone, whichever you prefer. Sea air; you needn't bathe. And you can take my car, for I shan't be able to use it, and why not take Foljambe as well to valet you, as you often do when you go for a jaunt? She'll have her Cadman: we may as well make other people happy, Georgie, as it all seems to fit in so beautifully. And one thing more: this little jaunt of yours is entirely undertaken for my sake, and I must insist on paying it all. Go to a nice hotel and make yourself thoroughly comfortable; half a bottle of champagne whenever you want it in the evening, and what extras you like, and I will telephone to you to say when you can come back. You must start tomorrow morning before the Faraglione gets here.'

Georgie knew it was useless to protest when Lucia got that loud, inspired, gabbling ring in her voice; she would cut through any opposition, as a steam saw buzzes through the most solid oak board till, amid a fountain of flying sawdust, it has sliced its way. He did not want to go away, but when Lucia exhibited that calibre of determination that he should, it was better to yield at once than to collapse later in a state of wretched exhaustion. Besides, there were bright points in her scheme. Foljambe would be delighted at the plan, for it would give her and Cadman leisure to enjoy each other's society; and it would not be disagreeable to stay for a week at some hotel in Folkestone and observe the cargoes of travellers from abroad arriving at the port after a billowy passage. Then he might find some bibelots in the shops, and he would listen to a municipal band, and have a bathroom next his bedroom, and do some sketches, and sit in a lounge in a series of those suits which had so justly earned him the title of the best-dressed man in Tilling. He would have a fine Rolls-Royce in the hotel garage, and a smart chauffeur coming to ask for orders every morning, and he would be seen, an interesting and opulent figure, drinking his half-bottle of champagne every evening and he would possibly pick up an agreeable acquaintance or two. He had no hesitation whatever in accepting Lucia's proposal to stand the charges of this expedition, for, as she had most truly said, it was undertaken in her interests, and naturally she paid (besides, she was quite rich) for its equipment.

The main lines of this defensive campaign being thus laid down, Lucia, with her Napoleonic eye for detail, plunged into minor matters. She did not, of course, credit 'that Mapp' with having procured the visit of the Faraglione, but a child could see that if she herself met the Faraglione during her stay here the grimmest exposure of her ignorance of the language she talked in such admired snippets must inevitably follow. 'That Mapp' would pounce on this, and it was idle to deny that she would score heavily and horribly. But Georgie's absence (cheap at the cost) and her own invisibility by reason of influenza made a seemingly unassailable position and it was with a keen sense of exhilaration in the coming contest that she surveyed the arena.

Lucia sent for the trusty Grosvenor and confided in her sufficiently to make her a conspirator. She told her that she had a great mass of arrears to do in reading and writing, and that for the next week she intended to devote herself to them, and lead the life of a hermit. She wanted no callers, and did not mean to see anyone, and the easiest excuse was to say that she had influenza. No doubt there would be many enquiries, and so day by day she would issue to Grosvenor her own official bulletin. Then she told Cadman that Mr Georgie was far from well, and she had bundled him off with the car to Folkestone for about a week: he and Foljambe would accompany him. Then she made a careful survey of the house and garden to ascertain what freedom of movement she could have during her illness. Playing the piano, except very carefully with the soft pedal down, would be risky, but by a judicious adjustment of the curtains in the garden-room window, she could refresh herself with very satisfactory glances at the world outside. The garden, she was pleased to notice, was quite safe, thanks to its encompassing walls, from any prying eyes in the houses round: the top of the church tower alone overlooked it, and that might be disregarded, for only tourists ascended it.

Then forth she went for the usual shoppings and chats in the High Street and put in some further fine work. The morning tide was already on the ebb, but by swift flirtings this way and that she managed to have a word with most of those who were coming to her po-di-mu tomorrow, and interlarded all she said to them with brilliant scraps of Italian. She just caught the Wyses as they were getting back into the Royce and said how *molto amabile* it was of them to give her the *gran' piacere* of seeing the Contessa next evening: indeed she would be a welcome guest, and it would be another *gran' piacere* to talk *la bella lingua* again. Georgie, alas, would not be there for he was *un po' ammalato*, and was going to spend a *settimana* by the *mare per stabilirsi*. Never had she been so fluent and idiomatic, and she accepted with *mille grazie* Susan's invitation to dine the evening after her music and renew the conversations to which she so much looked forward. She got almost tipsy with Italian . . . Then she flew across the street to tell the curate that she was going to shut herself up all afternoon in order to get the Bach fugue more worthy of his critical ear, she told Diva to come early to her party in order that they might have a little chat first, and she just managed by a flutelike 'Cooee' to arrest Elizabeth as she was on the very doorstep of Wasters. With glee she learned that Elizabeth was entertaining the Padre and his wife and Major Benjy to dinner before she brought them on to her party, and then, remembering the trap which that woman had laid for her and Georgie over the Italian paperknife, she could not refrain from asking her to dine and play bridge on the third night of her coming illness. Of course she would be obliged to put her off, and that would be about square . . . This half-hour's active work produced the impression that, however little pleasure Tilling anticipated from tomorrow's po-di-mu, the musician herself looked forward to it enormously, and was thirsting to talk Italian.

From the window of her bedroom next morning Lucia saw Georgie and Cadman and Foljambe set off for Folkestone, and it was with a Lucretian sense of pleasure in her own coming tranquillity that she contemplated the commotion and general upset of plans which was shortly to descend on Tilling. She went to the garden room, adjusted the curtains and brewed the tempest which she now sent forth in the shape of a series of notes charged with the bitterest regrets. They were written in pencil (the consummate artist) as if from bed, and were traced in a feeble hand not like her usual firm script. 'What a disappointment!' she wrote to Mrs Wyse. 'How cruel to have got the influenza – where could she have caught it? – on the very morning of her party, and what a blow not to be able to welcome the Contessa today or to dine with dear Susan tomorrow!' There was another note to Major Benjy, and others to Diva and quaint Irene and the curate and the Padre and Elizabeth. She still hoped that possibly she might be well enough for bridge and dinner the day after tomorrow, but Elizabeth must remember how infectious influenza was, and again she herself might not be well enough. That seemed pretty safe, for Elizabeth had a frantic phobia of infection, and Wasters had reeked of carbolic all the time the jumble sale was being held, for fear of some bit of rubbish having come in contact with tainted hands. Lucia gave these notes to Grosvenor for immediate delivery and told her that the bulletin for the day in answer to callers was that there was no anxiety, for the attack though sharp was not serious, and only demanded warmth and complete quiet. She then proceeded to get both by sitting in this warm October sun in her garden, reading Pope's translation of the *Iliad* and seeing what the Greek for it was.

Three impregnable days passed thus. From behind the adjusted curtains of the garden room she observed the coming of many callers and Grosvenor's admirable demeanour to them. The Royce lurched up the street, and there was Susan in her sables, and, sitting next her, a vivacious gesticulating woman with a monocle, who looked the sort of person who could talk at the most appalling rate. This without doubt was the fatal Contessa, and Lucia felt that to see her thus was like observing a lion at large from behind the bars of a comfortable cage. Miss Mapp on the second day came twice, and each time she glanced piercingly at the curtains, as if she knew that trick, and listened as if hoping to hear the sound of the piano. The Padre sent a note almost entirely in Highland dialect, the curate turned away from the door with evident relief in his face at the news he had received, and whistled the Bach fugue rather out of tune.

On the fifth day of her illness new interests sprang up for Lucia that led her to neglect Pope's *Iliad* altogether. By the first post there came a letter from Georgie, containing an enclosure which Lucia saw (with a slight misgiving) was written in Italian. She turned first to Georgie's letter.

* * *

The most wonderful thing has happened [wrote Georgie] and you will be pleased . . . There's a family here with whom I've made friends, an English father, an Italian mother and a girl with a pigtail. Listen! The mother teaches the girl Italian, and sets her little themes to write on some subject or other, and then corrects them and writes a fair copy. Well, I was sitting in the lounge this morning while the girl was having her lesson, and Mrs Brocklebank (that's her name) asked me to suggest a subject for the theme, and I had the most marvellous idea. I said 'Let her write a letter to an Italian Countess whom she has never seen before, and say how she regretted having been obliged to put off her musical party to which she had asked the Countess and her brother, because she had caught influenza. She was so sorry not to meet her, and she was afraid that as the Countess was only staying a week in the place, she would not have the pleasure of seeing her at all.' Mrs B. thought that would do beautifully for a theme, and I repeated it over again to make sure. Then the girl wrote it, and Mrs B. corrected it and made a fair copy. I begged her to give it me, because I adored Italian (though I couldn't speak it) and it was so beautifully expressed. I haven't told this very well, because I'm in a hurry to catch the post, but I enclose Mrs B.'s Italian letter, and you just see whether it doesn't do the trick too marvellously. I'm having quite a gay time, music and drives and seeing the Channel boat come in, and aren't I clever?

Your devoted,

Georgie

Foljambe and Cadman have had a row, but I'm afraid they've made it up.

* * *

Lucia, with her misgivings turned to joyful expectation, seized and read the enclosure. Indeed it was a miraculous piece of manna to one whom the very sight of it made hungry. It might have been the result of telepathy between Mrs Brocklebank and her own subconscious self, so aptly did that lady grasp her particular unspoken need. It expressed in the most elegant idiom precisely what met the situation, and she would copy out and send it today, without altering a single word. And how clever of Georgie to have thought of it. He deserved all the champagne he could drink.

Lucia used her highest art in making a copy (on Mallard paper) of this document, as if writing hastily in a familiar medium. Occasionally she wrote a word (it did not matter what), erased it so as to render it illegible to the closest scrutiny, and then went on with Mrs Brocklebank's manuscript; occasionally she omitted a word of it and then inserted it with suitable curves of direction above. No one receiving her transcript could imagine that it was other than her own extempore scribble. Mrs Brocklebank had said that in two or three days she hoped to be able to see her friends again, and that fitted beautifully, because in two or three days now the Contessa's visit would have come to an end, and Lucia could get quite well at once.

The second post arrived before Lucia had finished this thoughtful copy. There was a letter in Lady Brixton's handwriting, and hastily scribbling the final florid salutations to the Contessa, she opened this, and thereupon forgot Georgie and Mrs Brocklebank and everything else in the presence of the tremendous question which was brought for her decision. Adele had simply fallen in love with Riseholme; she affirmed that life was no longer worth living without a house there, and, of all houses, she would like best to purchase, unfurnished, The Hurst. Failing that there was another that would do, belonging to round red little Mrs Quantock, who, she had ascertained, might consider selling it. Could darling Lucia therefore let her know with the shortest possible delay whether she would be prepared to sell The Hurst? If she had no thought of doing so Adele would begin tempting Mrs Quantock at once. But if she had, let genteel indications about price be outlined at once.

There are certain processes of mental solidification which take place with extraordinary rapidity, because the system is already soaked and super-saturated with the issues involved. It was so now with Lucia. Instantly, on the perusal of Adele's enquiries her own mind solidified. She had long been obliquely contemplating some such step as Adele's letter thrust in front of her, and she was surprised to find that her decision was already made. Riseholme, once so vivid and significant, had during these weeks at Tilling been fading like an ancient photograph exposed to the sun, and all its features, foregrounds and backgrounds had grown blurred and dim. If she went back to Riseholme at the end of the month, she would find there nothing to occupy her energies, or call out her unique powers of self-assertion. She had so swept the board with her management of the Elizabethan fête that no further progress was possible. Poor dear Daisy might occasionally make some minute mutinies, but after being Drake's wife (what a lesson for her!) there would be no real fighting spirit left in her. It was far better, while her own energies still bubbled within her, to conquer this fresh world of Tilling than to smoulder at Riseholme. Her work there was done, whereas here, as this week of influenza testified, there was a very great deal to do. Elizabeth Mapp was still in action and capable of delivering broadsides; innumerable crises might still arise, volcanoes smoked, thunderclouds threatened, there were hostile and malignant forces to be thwarted. She had never been better occupied and diverted, the place suited her, and it bristled with opportunities. She wrote to Adele at once saying that dear as Riseholme (and especially The Hurst) was to her, she was prepared to be tempted, and indicated a sum before which she was likely to fall.

* * *

Miss Mapp by this fifth day of Lucia's illness was completely baffled. She did not yet allow herself to despair of becoming unbaffled, for she was certain that there was a mystery here, and every mystery had an explanation if you only worked at it enough. The coincidence of Lucia's illness with the arrival of the Contessa and Georgie's departure, supported by the trap she had laid about the paperknife, was far too glaring to be overlooked by any constructive mind, and there must be something behind it. Only a foolish ingenuous child (and Elizabeth was anything but that) could have considered these as isolated phenomena. With a faith that would have removed mountains, she believed that Lucia was perfectly well, but all she had been able to do at present was to recite her creed to Major Benjy and Diva and others, and eagerly wait for any shred of evidence to support it. Attempts to pump Grosvenor and lynxlike glances at the window of the garden room had yielded nothing, and her anxious enquiry addressed to Dr Dobbie, the leading physician of Tilling, had yielded a snub. She did not know who Lucia's doctor was, so with a view to ascertaining that, and possibly getting other information, she had approached him with her most winning smile, and asked how the dear patient at Mallards was.

'I am not attending any dear patient at Mallards,' had been his unpromising reply, 'and if I was I need hardly remind you that, as a professional man, I should not dream of answering any enquiry about my patients without their express permission to do so. Good morning.'

'A very rude man,' thought Miss Mapp, 'but perhaps I had better not try to get at it that way.'

She looked up at the church, wondering if she would find inspiration in that beautiful grey tower, which she had so often sketched, outlined against the pellucid blue of the October sky. She found it instantly, for she remembered that the leads at the top of it which commanded so broad a view of the surrounding country commanded also a perfectly wonderful view of her own little secret garden. It was a small chance, but no chance however small must be neglected in this famine of evidence, and it came to her in a flash that there could be no more pleasant way of spending the morning than making a sketch of the green, green marsh and the line of the blue, blue sea beyond. She hurried back to Wasters, pausing only at Mallards to glance at the garden room where the curtains were adjusted in the most exasperatingly skilful manner, and to receive Grosvenor's assurance that the patient's temperature was quite normal today.

'Oh, that is good news,' said Miss Mapp. 'Then tomorrow perhaps she will be about again.'

'I couldn't say, miss,' said Grosvenor, holding on to the door.

'Give her my fondest love,' said Miss Mapp, 'and tell her how rejoiced I am, please, Grosvenor.'

'Yes, miss,' said Grosvenor, and before Miss Mapp could step from the threshold, she heard the rattle of the chain behind the closed door.

She was going to lunch that day with the Wyses, a meal which Mr Wyse, in his absurd affected fashion, always alluded to as breakfast, especially when the Contessa was staying with them. Breakfast was at one, but there was time for an hour at the top of the church tower first. In order to see the features of the landscape better, she took up an opera glass with her sketching things. She first put a blue watery wash on her block for the sky and sea, and a green one for the marsh, and while these were drying she examined every nook of her garden with the opera glass. No luck, and she picked up her sketch again on which the sky was rapidly inundating the land.

Lucia had learned this morning *via* Grosvenor and her cook and Figgis, Mr Wyse's butler, that the week of the Contessa's stay here was to be curtailed by one day and that the Royce would convey her to Whitchurch next morning on her visit to the younger but ennobled branch of the family. Further intelligence from the same source made known that the breakfast today to which Miss Mapp was bidden was a Belshazzar breakfast, eight if not ten. This was good news: the period of Lucia's danger of detection would be over in less than twenty-four hours, and about the time that Miss Mapp at the top of the tower of Tilling church was hastily separating the firmament from the dry land, Lucia wrote out a telegram to Georgie that he might return the following day and find all clear. Together with that she sent a request to Messrs Woolgar & Pipstow that they should furnish her with an order to view a certain house she had seen just outside Tilling, near quaint Irene's cottage, which she had observed was for sale.

She hesitated about giving Grosvenor the envelope addressed to Contessa di Faraglione, which contained the transcript, duly signed, of Mrs Brocklebank's letter to a countess, and decided, on the score of dramatic fitness, to have it delivered shortly after one o'clock when Mrs Wyse's breakfast would be in progress, with orders that it should be presented to the Contessa at once.

Lucia was feeling the want of vigorous exercise, and bethought herself of the *Ideal System of Callisthenics For Those No Longer Young*. For five days she had been confined to house and garden, and the craving to skip took possession of her. Skipping was an exercise highly recommended by the ideal system, and she told

Grosvenor to bring back for her, with the order to view from Messrs Woolgar & Pipstow, a simple skipping rope from the toyshop in the High Street. While Grosvenor was gone this desire for free active movement in the open air awoke a kindred passion for the healthful action of the sun on the skin, and she hurried up to her sick-room, changed into a dazzling bathing suit of black and yellow, and, putting on a very smart dressing gown gay with ribands, was waiting in the garden room when Grosvenor returned, recalling to her mind the jerks and swayings which had kept her in such excellent health when grief forbade her to play golf.

The hour was a quarter to one when Lucia tripped into the secret garden, shed her dressing gown and began skipping on the little lawn with the utmost vigour. The sound of the church clock immediately below Miss Mapp's eyrie on the tower warned her that it was time to put her sketching things away, deposit them at Wasters and go out to breakfast. During the last half-hour she had cast periodical but fruitless glances at her garden, and had really given it up as a bad job. Now she looked down once more, and there close beside the bust of good Queen Anne was a gay striped figure of waspish colours skipping away like mad. She dropped her sketch, she reached out a trembling hand for her opera glasses, the focus of which was already adjusted to a nicety, and by their aid she saw that this athletic wasp who was skipping with such exuberant activity was none other than the invalid.

Miss Mapp gave a shrill crow of triumph. All came to him who waited, and if she had known Greek she would undoubtedly have exclaimed 'Eureka': as it was she only crowed. It was all too good to be true, but it was all too distinct not to be. 'Now I've got her,' she thought. 'The whole thing is as clear as daylight. I was right all the time. She has not had influenza any more than I, and I'll tell everybody at breakfast what I have seen.' But the sight still fascinated her. What shameless vigour, when she should have been languid with fever! What abysses of falsehood, all because she could not talk Italian! What expense to herself in that unnecessary dinner to the Padre and Major Benjy! There was no end to it . . .

Lucia stalked about the lawn with a high prancing motion when she had finished her skipping. Then she skipped again, and then she made some odd jerks, as if she was being electrocuted. She took long deep breaths, she lifted her arms high above her head as if to dive, she lay down on the grass and kicked, she walked on tiptoe like a ballerina, she swung her body round from the hips. All this had for Miss Mapp the fascination that flavours strong disgust and contempt. Eventually, just as the clock struck one, she wrapped herself in her dressing gown, the best was clearly over. Miss Mapp was already late, and she must hurry straight from the tower to her breakfast, for there was no time to go back to Wasters first. She would be profuse in pretty apologies for her lateness; the view from the church tower had been so entrancing (this was perfectly true) that she had lost all count of time. She could not show her sketch to the general company, because the firmament had got dreadfully muddled up with the waters which were below it, but instead she would tell them something which would muddle up Lucia.

The breakfast party was all assembled in Mrs Wyse's drawing room with its dark oak beams and its silver-framed photographs and its morocco case containing the order of the MBE, still negligently open. Everybody had been waiting, everybody was rather grumpy at the delay, and on her entry the Contessa had clearly said 'Ecco! Now at last!'

They would soon forgive her when they learned what had really made her late, but it was better to wait for a little before imparting her news, until breakfast had put them all in a more appreciative mood. She hastened on this desired moment by little compliments all round: what a wonderful sermon the Padre had preached last Sunday: how well dear Susan looked: what a delicious dish these eggs à la Capri were, she must really be greedy and take a teeny bit more. But these dewdrops were only interjected, for the Contessa talked in a loud continuous voice as usual, addressing the entire table, and speaking with equal fluency whether her mouth was full or empty.

At last the opportunity arrived. Figgis brought in a note on an immense silver (probably plated) salver, and presented it to the Contessa: it was to be delivered at once. Amelia said 'Scusi' which everybody understood – even Lucia might have understood that – and was silent for a space as she tore it open and began reading it.

Miss Mapp decided to tantalize and excite them all before actually making her revelation.

'I will give anybody three guesses as to what I have seen this morning,' she said. 'Mr Wyse, Major Benjy, Padre, you must all guess. It is about someone whom we all know, who is still an invalid. I was sketching this morning at the top of the tower, and happened to glance down into my pet little secret garden. And there was Lucia in the middle of the lawn. How was she dressed, and what was she doing? Three guesses each, shall it be?'

Alas! The introductory tantalization had been too long, for before anybody could guess anything the Contessa broke in again.

'But never have I read such a letter!' she cried. 'It is from Mrs Lucas. All in Italian, and such Italian! Perfect. I should not have thought that any foreigner could have had such command of idiom and elegance. I have lived in Italy for ten years, but my Italian is a bungle compared to this. I have always said that no foreigner ever can learn Italian perfectly, and Cecco too, but we were wrong. This Mrs Lucas proves it. It is composed by the ear, the spoken word on paper. *Dio mio!* What an escape I have had, Algernon! You had a plan to bring me and your Mrs Lucas together to hear us talk. But she would smile to herself, and I should know what she was thinking, for she would be thinking how very poorly I talk Italian compared with herself. I will read her letter to you all, and though you do not know what it means you will recognize a fluency, a music . . .'

The Contessa proceeded to do so, with renewed exclamations of amazement, and all that bright edifice of suspicion, so carefully reared by the unfortunate Elizabeth, that Lucia knew no Italian, collapsed like a house built of cards when the table is shaken. Elizabeth had induced everybody to accept invitations to the second po-di-mu in order that all Tilling might hear Lucia's ignorance exposed by the Contessa, and when she had wriggled out of that, Elizabeth's industrious efforts had caused the gravest suspicions to be entertained that Lucia's illness was feigned in order to avoid any encounter with one who did know Italian, and now not only was not one pane of that Crystal Palace left unshattered, but the Contessa was congratulating herself on her own escape.

Elizabeth stirred feebly below the ruins: she was not quite crushed.

'I'm sure it sounds lovely,' she said when the recitation was over. 'But did not you yourself, dear Mr Wyse, think it odd that anyone who knew Italian should put *un po' di musica* on her invitation card?'

'Then he was wrong,' said the Contessa. 'No doubt that phrase is a little humorous quotation from something I do not know. Rather like you ladies of Tilling who so constantly say "*au reservoir*". It is not a mistake: it is a joke.'

Elizabeth made a final effort.

'I wonder if dear Lucia wrote that note herself,' she said pensively.

'Pish! Her parlourmaid, doubtless,' said the Contessa. 'For me, I must spend an hour this afternoon to see if I can answer that letter in a way that will not disgrace me.'

There seemed little more to be said on that subject and Elizabeth hastily resumed her tantalization.

'Nobody has tried to guess yet what I saw from the church tower,' she said. 'Major Benjy, you try! It was Lucia, but how was she dressed and what was she doing?'

There was a coldness about Major Benjy. He had allowed himself to suspect, owing to Elizabeth's delicate hints, that there was perhaps some Italian mystery behind Lucia's influenza, and now he must make amends.

'Couldn't say, I'm sure,' he said. 'She was sure to have been very nicely dressed from what I know of her.'

'I'll give you a hint then,' said she. 'I've never seen her dressed like that before.'

Major Benjy's attention completely wandered. He made no attempt to guess but sipped his coffee.

'You then, Mr Wyse, if Major Benjy gives up,' said Elizabeth, getting anxious. Though the suspected cause of Lucia's illness was disproved, it still looked as if she had never had influenza at all, and that was something.

'My ingenuity, I am sure, will not be equal to the occasion,' said Mr Wyse very politely. 'You will be obliged to tell me. I give up.'

Elizabeth emitted a shrill little titter.

'A dressing gown,' she said. 'A bathing costume. And she was skipping! Fancy! With influenza!'

There was a dreadful pause. No babble of excited enquiry and comment took place at all. The Contessa put up her monocle, focused Elizabeth for a moment, and this pause somehow was like the hush that succeeds some slight *gaffe*, some small indelicacy that had better have been left unsaid. Her host came to her rescue.

'That is indeed good news,' said Mr Wyse. 'We may encourage ourselves to hope that our friend is well on the road to convalescence. Thank you for telling us that, Miss Mapp.'

Mrs Bartlett gave one of her little mouse-like squeals, and Irene said: 'Hurrah! I shall try to see her this afternoon. I am glad.'

That again was an awful thought. Irene no doubt, if admitted, would give an account of the luncheon party which would lose nothing in the telling, and she was such a ruthless mimic. Elizabeth felt a sinking feeling.

'Would that be wise, dear?' she said. 'Lucia is probably not yet free from infection, and we mustn't have you down with it. I wonder where she caught it, by the way?'

'But your point is that she's never had influenza at all,' said Irene with that dismal directness of hers.

Choking with this monstrous dose of fiasco, Elizabeth made for the present no further attempt to cause her friends to recoil from the idea of Lucia's skippings, for they only rejoiced that she was sufficiently recovered to do so. The party presently dispersed, and she walked away with her sketching things and Diva, and glanced up the street towards her house. Irene was already standing by the door, and Elizabeth turned away with a shudder, for Irene waved her hand to them and was admitted.

'It's all very strange, dear Diva, isn't it?' she said. 'It's impossible to believe that Lucia's been ill, and it's useless to try to do so. Then there's Mr Georgie's disappearance. I never thought of that before.'

Diva interrupted.

'If I were you, Elizabeth,' she said, 'I should hold my tongue about it all. Much wiser.'

'Indeed?' said Elizabeth, beginning to tremble.

'Yes. I tell you so as a friend,' continued Diva firmly. 'You got hold of a false scent. You made us think that Lucia was avoiding the

Faraglione. All wrong from beginning to end. One of your worst shots. Give it up.'

'But there is something queer,' said Elizabeth wildly. 'Skipping –'

'If there is,' said Diva, 'you're not clever enough to find it out. That's my advice. Take it or leave it. I don't care. *Au reservoir.*'

CHAPTER SEVEN

Had Miss Mapp been able to hear what went on in the garden room that afternoon, as well as she had been able to see what had gone on that morning in the garden, she would never have found Irene more cruelly quaint. Her account of this luncheon party was more than graphic, for so well did she reproduce the Contessa's fervid monologue and poor Elizabeth's teasings over what she wanted them all to guess, that it positively seemed to be illustrated. Almost more exasperating to Miss Mapp would have been Lucia's pitiful contempt for the impotence of her malicious efforts.

'Poor thing!' she said. 'Sometimes I think she is a little mad. *Una pazza: un po' pazza* . . . But I regret not seeing the Contessa. Nice of her to have approved of my scribbled note, and I dare say I should have found that she talked Italian very well indeed. Tomorrow – for after my delicious exercise on the lawn this morning, I do not feel up to more today – tomorrow I should certainly have hoped to call – in the afternoon – and have had a chat with her. But she is leaving in the morning, I understand.'

Lucia, looking the picture of vigour and vitality, swept across to the curtained window and threw back those screenings with a movement that made the curtain rings chime together.

'Poor Elizabeth!' she repeated. 'My heart aches for her, for I am sure all that carping bitterness makes her wretched. I dare say it is only physical: liver perhaps, or acidity. The. ideal system of callisthenics might do wonders for her. I cannot, as you will readily understand, dear Irene, make the first approaches to her after her conduct to me, and the dreadful innuendoes she has made, but I should like her to know that I bear her no malice at all. Do convey that to her sometime. Tactfully, of course. Women like her who do all they can on every possible occasion to hurt and injure others are usually very sensitive themselves, and I would not add to the poor creature's other chagrins. You must all be kind to her.'

'My dear, you're too wonderful!' said Irene, in a sort of ecstasy. 'What a joy you are! But, alas, you're leaving us so soon. It's too unkind of you to desert us.'

Lucia had dropped on to the music stool by the piano which had so long been dumb, except for a few timorous chords muffled by the *unsustenuto* pedal, and dreamily recalled the first bars of the famous slow movement.

Irene sat down on the cold hot-water pipes and yearned at her.

'You can do everything,' she said. 'You play like an angel, and you can knock out Mapp with your little finger, and you can skip and play bridge, and you've got such a lovely nature that you don't bear Mapp the slightest grudge for her foul plots. You are adorable! Won't you ask me to come and stay with you at Riseholme sometime?'

Lucia, still keeping perfect time with her triplets while this recital of her perfections was going on, considered whether she should not tell Irene at once that she had practically determined not to desert them. She had intended to tell Georgie first, but she would do that when he came back tomorrow, and she wanted to see about getting a house here without delay. She played a nimble arpeggio on the chord of C sharp minor and closed the piano.

'Too sweet of you to like me, dear,' she said, 'but as for your staying with me at Riseholme, I don't think I shall ever go back there myself. I have fallen in love with this dear Tilling, and I fully expect I shall settle here for good.'

'Angel!' said Irene.

'I've been looking about for a house that might suit me,' she continued when Irene had finished kissing her, 'and the house agents have just sent me the order to view one which particularly attracts me. It's that white house on the road that skirts the marsh, half a mile away. A nice garden sheltered from the north wind. Right down on the level, it is true, but such a divine view. Broad, tranquil! A dyke and a bank just across the road, keeping back the high tides in the river.'

'But of course I know it; you mean Grebe,' cried Irene. 'The cottage I am in now adjoins the garden. Oh, do take it! While you're settling in, I'll let Diva have Taormina, and Diva will let Mapp have Wasters, and Mapp will let you have Mallards till Grebe's ready for you. And I shall be at your disposal all day to help you with your furniture.'

Lucia decided that there was no real danger of meeting the Contessa if she drove out there: besides the Contessa now wanted to avoid her for fear of showing how inferior was her Italian.

'It's such a lovely afternoon,' she said, 'that I think a little drive would not hurt me. Unfortunately Georgie, who comes back tomorrow, has got my car. I lent it him for his week by the sea.'

'Oh, how like you!' cried Irene. 'Always unselfish!'

'Dear Georgie! So pleased to give him a little treat,' said Lucia. 'I'll ring up the garage and get them to send me something closed. Come with me, dear, if you have nothing particular to do, and we'll look over the house.'

Lucia found much to attract her in Grebe. Though it was close to the road it was not overlooked, for a thick hedge of hornbeam made a fine screen: besides, the road did not lead anywhere particular. The rooms were of good dimensions, there was a hall and dining room on the ground floor, with a broad staircase leading up to the first floor where there were two or three bedrooms and a long admirable sitting room with four windows looking across the road to the meadows and the high bank bounding the river. Beyond that lay the great empty levels of the marsh, with the hill of Tilling rising out of it half a mile away to the west. Close behind the house was the cliff which had once been the coastline before the marshes were drained and reclaimed, and this would be a rare protection against northerly and easterly winds. All these pleasant rooms looked south, and all had this open view away seawards; they had character and dignity, and at once Lucia began to see herself living here. The kitchen and offices were in a wing by themselves, and here again there was character, for the kitchen had evidently been a coach house, and still retained the big double doors appropriate to such. There had once been a road from it to the end of the kitchen garden, but with its disuse as a coach house, the road had been replaced by a broad cinder path now bordered with beds of useful vegetables.

'*Ma molto conveniente*,' said Lucia more than once, for it was now perfectly safe to talk Italian again, since the Contessa, no less than she, was determined to avoid a duet in that language. *'Mi piace molto. E un bel giardino.'*

'How I love hearing you talk Italian,' ejaculated Irene, 'especially since I know it's the very best. Will you teach it me? Oh, I am so pleased you like the house.'

'But I am charmed with it,' said Lucia. 'And there's a garage with a very nice cottage attached which will do beautifully for Cadman and Foljambe.'

She broke off suddenly, for in the fervour of her enthusiasm for the house, she had not thought about the awful, catastrophe which must descend on Georgie, if she decided to live at Tilling. She had given no direct thought to him, and now for the first time she realized the cruel blow that would await him, when he came back tomorrow, all bronzed from his week at Folkestone. He had been a real *Deus ex machina* to her: his stroke of genius had turned a very hazardous moment into a blaze of triumph, and now she was going to plunge a dagger into his domestic heart by the news that she and therefore Cadman and therefore Foljambe were not coming back to Riseholme at all . . .

'Oh, are they going to marry?' asked Irene. 'Or do you mean they just live together? How interesting!'

'Dear Irene, do not be so modern,' said Lucia, quite sharply. 'Marriage of course, and banns first. But never mind that for the present. I like those great double doors to the kitchen. I shall certainly keep them.'

'How ripping that you're thinking about kitchen doors already,' said Irene. 'That really sounds as if you did mean to buy the house. Won't Mapp have a fit when she hears it! I must be there when she's told. She'll say "Darling Lulu, what a joy," and then fall down and foam at the mouth.'

Lucia gazed out over the marsh where the level rays of sunset turned a few low-lying skeins of mist to rose and gold. The tide was high and the broad channel of the river running out to sea was brimming from edge to edge. Here and there, where the banks were low, the water had overflowed on to adjacent margins of land; here and there, spread into broad lakes, it lapped the confining dykes. There were sheep cropping the meadows, there were seagulls floating in the water, and half a mile away to the west the red roofs of Tilling glowed as if molten not only with the soft brilliance of the evening light, but (to the discerning eye) with the intensity of the interests that burned beneath them . . . Lucia hardly knew what gave her the most satisfaction, the magic of the marsh, her resolve to live here, or the recollection of the complete discomfiture of Elizabeth.

Then again the less happy thought of Georgie recurred, and she wondered what arguments she could use to induce him to leave Riseholme and settle here. Tilling with all its manifold interests would be incomplete without him, and how dismally incomplete Riseholme would be to him without herself and Foljambe. Georgie had of late taken his painting much more seriously than ever before, and he had often during the summer put off dinner to an unheard-of lateness in order to catch a sunset, and had risen at most inconvenient hours to catch a sunrise. Lucia had strongly encouraged this zeal, she had told him that if he was to make a real career as an artist he had no time to waste. Appreciation and spurring on was what he needed: perhaps Irene could help.

She pointed to the glowing landscape. 'Irene, what would life be without sunsets?' she asked. 'And to think that this miracle happens every day, except when it's very cloudy!'

Irene looked critically at the view. 'Generally speaking, I don't like sunsets,' she said. 'The composition of the sky is usually childish. But good colouring about this one.'

'There are practically no sunsets at Riseholme,' said Lucia. 'I suppose the sun goes down, but there's a row of hills in the way. I often think that Georgie's development as an artist is starved there. If he goes back there he will find no one to make him work. What do you think of his painting, dear?'

'I don't think of it at all,' said Irene.

'No? I am astonished. Of course your own is so different in character. Those wrestlers! Such movement! But personally I find very great perception in Georgie's work. A spaciousness, a calmness! I wish you would take an interest in it and encourage him. You can find beauty anywhere if you look for it.'

'Of course I'll do my best if you want me to,' said Irene. 'But it will be hard work to find beauty in Georgie's little valentines.'

'Do try. Give him some hints. Make him see what you see. All that boldness and freedom. That's what he wants . . . Ah, the sunset is fading. *Buona notte, bel sole! We* must be getting home too. *Addio, mia bella casa.* But Georgie must be the first to know, Irene, do not speak of it until I have told him. Poor Georgie: I hope it will not be a terrible blow to him.'

*   *   *

Georgie came straight to Mallards on his arrival next morning from Folkestone with Cadman and Foljambe. His recall, he knew, meant that the highly dangerous Contessa had gone, and his admission by Grosvenor, after the door had been taken off the chain, that Lucia's influenza was officially over. He looked quite bronzed, and she gave him the warmest welcome.

'It all worked without a hitch,' she said as she told him of the plots and counter-plots which had woven so brilliant a tapestry of events. 'And it was that letter of Mrs Brocklebank's which you sent me that clapped the lid on Elizabeth. I saw at once what I could make of it. Really, Georgie, I turned it into a stroke of genius.'

'But it was a stroke of genius already,' said Georgie. 'You only had to copy it out and send it to the Contessa.'

Lucia was slightly ashamed of having taken the supreme credit for herself: the habit was hard to get rid of.

'My dear, all the credit shall be yours then,' she said handsomely. 'It was your stroke of genius. I copied it out very carelessly as if I had scribbled it off without thought. That was a nice touch, don't you think? The effect? Colossal, so Irene tells me, for I could not be there myself. That was only yesterday. A few desperate wriggles from Elizabeth, but of course no good. I do not suppose there was a more thoroughly thwarted woman in all Sussex than she.'

Georgie gave a discreet little giggle.

'And what's so terribly amusing is that she was right all the time about your influenza and your Italian and everything,' he said. 'Perfectly maddening for her.'

Lucia sighed pensively.

'Georgie, she was malicious,' she observed, 'and that never pays.'

'Besides, it serves her right for spying on you,' Georgie continued.

'Yes, poor thing. But I shall begin now at once to be kind to her again. She shall come to lunch tomorrow, and you of course. By the way, Georgie, Irene takes so much interest in your painting. It was news to me, for her style is so different from your beautiful, careful work.'

'No! That's news to me too,' said Georgie. 'She never seemed to see my sketches before: they might have been blank sheets of paper. Does she mean it? She's not pulling my leg?'

'Nothing of the sort. And I couldn't help thinking it was a great opportunity for you to learn something about more modern methods. There is something you know in those fierce canvases of hers.'

'I wish she had told me sooner,' said Georgie. 'We've only got a fortnight more here. I shall be very sorry when it's over, for I felt terribly pleased to be getting back to Tilling this morning. It'll be dull going back to Riseholme. Don't you feel that too? I'm sure you must. No plots: no competition.'

Lucia had just received a telegram from Adele concerning the purchase of The Hurst, and it was no use putting off the staggering moment. She felt as if she was Zeus about to discharge a thunderbolt on some unhappy mortal.

'Georgie, I'm not going back to Riseholme at all,' she said. 'I have sold The Hurst: Adele Brixton has bought it. And, practically, I've bought that white house with the beautiful garden, which we admired so much, and that view over the marsh (how I thought of you at sunset yesterday), and really charming rooms with character.'

Georgie sat open-mouthed, and all expression vanished from his face. It became as blank as a piece of sunburnt paper. Then slowly, as if he was coming round from an anaesthetic while the surgeon was still carving dexterously at living tissue, a look of intolerable anguish came into his face.

'But Foljambe, Cadman!' he cried. 'Foljambe can't come back here every night from Riseholme. What am I to do? Is it all irrevocable?'

Lucia bridled. She was quite aware that this parting (if there was to be one) between him and Foljambe would be a dagger; but it was surprising, to say the least, that the thought of the parting between herself and him should not have administered him the first shock. However, there it was. Foljambe first by all means.

'I knew parting from Foljambe would be a great blow to you,' she said, with an acidity that Georgie could hardly fail to notice. 'What a pity that row you told me about came to nothing! But I am afraid that I can't promise to live in Riseholme for ever in order that you may not lose your parlourmaid.'

'But it's not only that,' said Georgie, aware of this acidity and hastening to sweeten it. 'There's you as well. It will be ditch water at Riseholme without you.'

'Thank you, Georgie,' said Lucia. 'I wondered if and when, as the lawyers say, you would think of that. No reason why you should, of course.'

Georgie felt that this was an unjust reproach.

'Well, after all, you settled to live in Tilling,' he retorted, 'and said nothing about how dull it would be without me. And I've got to do without Foljambe as well.'

Lucia had recourse to the lowest artifice.

'Georgie-orgie, 'oo not cwoss with me?' she asked in an innocent, childish voice.

Georgie was not knocked out by this sentimental stroke below the belt. It was like Lucia to settle everything in exactly the way that suited her best, and then expect her poor pawns to be stricken at the thought of losing their queen. Besides, the loss of Foljambe *had* occurred to him first. Comfort, like charity, began at home.

'No, I'm not cross,' he said, utterly refusing to adopt baby talk which implied surrender. 'But I've got every right to be hurt with you for settling to live in Tilling and not saying a word about how you would miss me.'

'My dear, I knew you would take that for granted,' began Lucia.

'Then why shouldn't you take it for granted about me?' he observed.

'I ought to have,' she said. 'I confess it, so that's all right. But why don't you leave Riseholme too and settle here, Georgie? Foljambe, me, your career, now that Irene is so keen about your pictures, and this marvellous sense of not knowing what's going to happen next. Such stimulus, such stuff to keep the soul awake.

And you don't want to go back to Riseholme: you said so yourself. You'd moulder and vegetate there.'

'It's different for you,' said Georgie. 'You've sold your house and I haven't sold mine. But there it is: I shall go back, I suppose, without Foljambe or you – I mean you or Foljambe. I wish I had never come here at all. It was that week when we went back for the fête, leaving Cadman and her here, which did all the mischief.'

There was no use in saying anything more at present, and Georgie, feeling himself the victim of an imperious friend and of a faithless parlourmaid, went sadly back to Mallards Cottage. Lucia had settled to leave Riseholme without the least thought of what injury she inflicted on him by depriving him at one fell blow of Foljambe and her own companionship. He was almost sorry he had sent her that wonderful Brocklebank letter, for she had been in a very tight place, especially when Miss Mapp had actually seen her stripped and skipping in the garden as a cure for influenza; and had he not, by his stroke of genius, come to her rescue, her reputation here might have suffered an irretrievable eclipse, and they might all have gone back to Riseholme together. As it was, he had established her on the most exalted pinnacle and her thanks for that boon were expressed by dealing this beastly blow at him.

He threw himself down, in deep dejection, on the sofa in the little parlour of Mallards Cottage, in which he had been so comfortable. Life at Tilling had been full of congenial pleasures, and what a spice all these excitements had added to it! He had done a lot of painting, endless subjects still awaited his brush, and it had given him a thrill of delight to know that quaint Irene, with all her modern notions about art, thought highly of his work. Then there was the diversion of observing and nobly assisting in Lucia's campaign for the sovereignty, and her wars, as he knew, were far from won yet, for Tilling certainly had grown restive under her patronizings and acts of autocracy, and there was probably life in the old dog (meaning Elizabeth Mapp) yet. It was dreadful to think that he would not witness the campaign that was now being planned in those Napoleonic brains. These few weeks that remained to him here would be blackened by the thought of the wretched future that awaited him, and there would be no savour in them, for in so short a time now he would go back to

Riseholme in a state of the most pitiable widowerhood, deprived
of the ministering care of Foljambe, who all these years had made
him so free from household anxieties, and of the companion who
had spurred him on to ambitions and activities. Though he had
lain awake shuddering at the thought that perhaps Lucia expected
him to marry her, he felt he would almost sooner have done that
than lose her altogether. 'It may be better to have loved and lost,'
thought Georgie, 'than never to have loved at all, but it's very poor
work not having loved and also to have lost' . . .

There was Foljambe singing in a high buzzing voice as she
unpacked his luggage in his room upstairs, and though it was a
rancid noise, how often had it filled him with the liveliest satisfaction,
for Foljambe seldom sang, and when she did, it meant that she was
delighted with her lot in life and was planning fresh efforts for his
comfort. Now, no doubt, she was planning all sorts of pleasures
for Cadman, and not thinking of him at all. Then there was Lucia:
through his open window he could already hear the piano in the
garden room, and that showed a horrid callousness to his miserable
plight. She didn't care; she was rolling on like the moon or the car
of Juggernaut. It was heartless of her to occupy herself with those
gay tinkling tunes, but the fact was that she was odiously selfish,
and cared about nothing but her own successes . . . He abstracted
himself from those painful reflections for a moment and listened
more attentively. It was clearly Mozart that she was practising, but
the melody was new to him. 'I bet,' thought Georgie, 'that this
evening or tomorrow, she'll ask me to read over a new Mozart, and
it'll be that very piece that she's practising now.'

His bitterness welled up within him again, as that pleasing
reflection faded from his mind, and almost involuntarily he began
to revolve how he could pay her back for her indifference to him.
A dark but brilliant thought (like a black pearl) occurred to him.
What if he dismissed his own chauffeur, Dickie, at present in the
employment of his tenant at Riseholme, and, by a prospect of a rise
in wages, seduced Cadman from Lucia's service, and took him and
Foljambe back to Riseholme? He would put into practice the plan
that Lucia herself had suggested, of establishing them in a cottage
of their own, with a charwoman, so that Foljambe's days should be
his, and her nights Cadman's. That would be a nasty one for Lucia,

and the idea was feasible, for Cadman didn't think much of Tilling, and might easily fall in with it. But hardly had this devilish device occurred to him than his better nature rose in revolt against it. It would serve Lucia right, it is true, but it was unworthy of him. 'I should be descending to her level,' thought Georgie very nobly, 'if I did such a thing. Besides, how awful it would be if Cadman said no, and then told her that I had tempted him. She would despise me for doing it, as much as I despise her, and she would gloat over me for having failed. It won't do. I must be more manly about it all somehow. I must be like Major Benjy and say "Damn the woman! Faugh!" and have a drink. But I feel sick at the idea of going back to Riseholme alone . . . I wish I had eyebrows like a paste brush, and could say damn properly.'

With a view to being more manly he poured himself out a very small whisky and soda, and his eye fell on a few letters lying for him on the table, which must have come that morning. There was one with the Riseholme postmark, and the envelope was of that very bright blue which he always used. His own stationery evidently, of which he had left a supply, without charge, for the use of his tenant. He opened it, and behold there was dawn breaking on his dark life, for Colonel Cresswell wanted to know if he had any thoughts of selling his house. He was much taken by Riseholme, his sister had bought The Hurst, and he would like to be near her. Would Georgie therefore let him have a line about this as soon as possible, for there was another house, Mrs Quantock's, about which he would enter into negotiations, if there was no chance of getting Georgie's . . .

The revulsion of feeling was almost painful. Georgie had another whisky and soda at once, not because he was depressed, but because he was so happy. 'But I mustn't make a habit of it,' he thought, as he seized his pen.

Georgie's first impulse when he had written his letter to Colonel Cresswell was to fly round to Mallards with this wonderful news, but now he hesitated. Some hitch might arise, the price Colonel Cresswell proposed might not come up to his expectations, though – God knew – he would not dream of haggling over any reasonable offer. Lucia would rejoice at the chance of his staying in Tilling but she did not deserve to have such a treat of pleasurable expectation for the present. Besides, though he had been manly enough to reject with scorn the wiles of the devil who had suggested the seduction of Cadman, he thought he would tease her a little even if his dream came true. He had often told her that if he was rich enough he would have a flat in London, and now, if this sale of his house came off, he would pretend that he was not meaning to live in Tilling at all, but would live in town, and he would see how she would take that. It would be her turn to be hurt, and serve her right. So instead of interrupting the roulades of Mozart that were pouring from the window of the garden room, he walked briskly down to the High Street to see how Tilling was taking the news that it would have Lucia always with it, if her purchase of Grebe had become public property. If not, he would have the pleasure of disseminating it.

There was a hint of seafaring about Georgie's costume as befitted one who had lately spent so much time on the pier at Folkestone. He had a very nautical-looking cap, with a black shining brim, a dark blue double-breasted coat, white trousers and smart canvas shoes: really he might have been supposed to have come up to Tilling in his yacht, and have landed to see the town . . . A piercing whistle from the other side of the street showed him that his appearance had at once attracted attention, and there was Irene planted with her easel in the middle of the pavement, and painting a row of flayed carcasses that hung in the butcher's shop. Rembrandt had better look out . . .

'Avast there, Georgie,' she cried. 'Home is the sailor, home from sea. Come and talk.'

This was rather more attention than Georgie had anticipated, but as Irene was quite capable of shouting nautical remarks after him if he pretended not to hear, he tripped across the street to her.

'Have you seen Lucia, Commodore?' she said. 'And has she told you?'

'About her buying Grebe?' asked Georgie. 'Oh, yes.'

'That's all right then. She told me not to mention it till she'd seen you. Mapp's popping in and out of the shops, and I simply must be the first to tell her. Don't cut in in front of me, will you? Oh, by the way, have you done any sketching at Folkestone?'

'One or two,' said Georgie. 'Nothing very much.'

'Nonsense. Do let me come and see them. I love your handling. Just cast your eye over this and tell me what's wrong with – There she is. Hi! Mapp!'

Elizabeth, like Georgie, apparently thought it more prudent to answer that summons and avoid further public proclamation of her name, and came hurrying across the street.

'Good morning, Irene mine,' she said. 'What a beautiful picture! All the poor skinned piggies in a row, or are they sheep? Back again, Mr Georgie? How we've missed you. And how do you think dear Lulu is looking after her illness?'

'Mapp, there's news for you,' said Irene, remembering the luncheon party yesterday. 'You must guess: I shall tease you. It's about your Lulu. Three guesses.'

'Not a relapse, I hope?' said Elizabeth brightly.

'Quite wrong. Something much nicer. You'll enjoy it tremendously.'

'Another of those beautiful musical parties?' asked Elizabeth. 'Or has she skipped a hundred times before breakfast?'

'No, much nicer,' said Irene. 'Heavenly for us all.'

A look of apprehension had come over Elizabeth's face, as an awful idea occurred to her.

'Dear one, give over teasing,' she said. 'Tell me.'

'She's not going away at the end of the month,' said Irene. 'She's bought Grebe.'

Blank dismay spread over Elizabeth's face.

'Oh, what a joy!' she said. 'Lovely news.'

She hurried off to Wasters, too much upset even to make Diva, who was coming out of Twistevant's, a partner in her joy. Only this morning she had been consulting her calendar and observing that there were only fifteen days more before Tilling was quit of Lulu, and now at a moderate estimate there might be at least fifteen years of her. Then she found she could not bear the weight of her joy alone and sped back after Diva.

'Diva dear, come in for a minute,' she said. 'I've heard something.'

Diva looked with concern at that lined and agitated face.

'What's the matter?' she said. 'Nothing serious?'

'Oh no, lovely news,' she said with bitter sarcasm. 'Tilling will rejoice. *She's* not going away. *She's* going to stop here for ever.'

There was no need to ask who 'she' was. For weeks Lucia had been 'she'. If you meant Susan Wyse, or Diva or Irene, you said so. But 'she' was Lucia.

'I suspected as much,' said Diva. 'I know she had an order to view Grebe.'

Elizabeth, in a spasm of exasperation, banged the door of Wasters so violently after she and Diva had entered, that the house shook and a note leaped from the wire letter box on to the floor.

'Steady on with my front door,' said Diva, 'or there'll be some dilapidations to settle.'

Elizabeth took no notice of this petty remark, and picked up the note. The handwriting was unmistakable, for Lucia's study of Homer had caused her (subconsciously or not) to adopt a modified form of Greek script, and she made her 'a' like alpha and her 'e' like epsilon. At the sight of it Elizabeth suffered a complete loss of self-control, she held the note on high as if exposing a relic to the gaze of pious worshippers, and made a low curtsey to it.

'And this is from Her,' she said. 'Oh, how kind of Her Majesty to write to me in her own hand with all those ridiculous twiddles. Not content with speaking Italian quite perfectly, she must also write in Greek. I dare say she talks it beautifully too.'

'Come, pull yourself together, Elizabeth,' said Diva.

'I am not aware that I am coming to bits, dear,' said Elizabeth, opening the note with the very tips of her fingers, as if it had been written by someone infected with plague or at least influenza. 'But let me see what Her Majesty says . . . "Dearest Liblib" . . . the impertinence of it! Or is it Riseholme humour?'

'Well, you call her Lulu,' said Diva. 'Do get on.'

Elizabeth frowned with the difficulty of deciphering this crabbed handwriting.

' "Now that I am quite free of infection," ' she read – (Infection indeed. She never had flu at all) – ' "of infection, I can receive my friends again, and hope so much you will lunch with me tomorrow. I hasten also to tell you of my change of plans, for I have so fallen in love with your delicious Tilling that I have bought a house here – (Stale news!) – and shall settle into it next month. An awful wrench, as you may imagine, to leave my dear Riseholme – (Then why wrench yourself?) – . . . and poor Georgie is in despair, but Tilling and all you dear people have wrapped yourselves round my heart – (Have we? The same to you!) – and it is no use my struggling to get free. I wonder therefore if you would consider letting me take your beautiful Mallards at the same rent for another month, while Grebe is being done up, and my furniture being installed? I should be so grateful if this is possible, otherwise I shall try to get Mallards Cottage when my Georgie – (My!) – goes back to Riseholme. Could you, do you think, let me know about this tomorrow, if, as I hope, you will send me *un amabile 'si'* – (What in the world is an *amabile si*?) – and come to lunch? *Tanti saluti*, Lucia." '

'I understand,' said Diva. 'It means "an amiable yes", about going to lunch.'

'Thank you, Diva. You are quite an Italian scholar too,' said Elizabeth. 'I call that a thoroughly heartless letter. And all of us, mark you, must serve her convenience. I can't get back into Mallards, because She wants it, and even if I refused, She would be next door at Mallards Cottage. I've never been so long out of my own house before.'

Both ladies felt that it would be impossible to keep up any semblance of indignation that Lucia was wanting to take Mallards for another month, for it suited them both so marvellously well.

'You are in luck,' said Diva, 'getting another month's let at that price. So am I too, if you want to stop here, for Irene is certain to let me stay on at her house, because her cottage is next to Grebe and she'll be in and out all day – '

'Poor Irene seems to be under a sort of spell,' said Elizabeth in parenthesis. 'She can think about nothing except that woman. Her painting has fallen off terribly. Coarsened . . . Yes, dear, I think I will give the Queen of the Italian language an *amabile si* about Mallards. I don't know if you would consider taking rather a smaller rent for November. Winter prices are always lower.'

'Certainly not,' said Diva. 'You're going to get the same as before for Mallards.'

'That's my affair, dear,' said Elizabeth.

'And this is mine,' said Diva firmly. 'And will you go to lunch with her tomorrow?'

Elizabeth, now comparatively calm, sank down in the window

seat, which commanded so good a view of the High Street.

'I suppose I shall have to,' she said. 'One must be civil, whatever has happened. Oh, there's Major Benjy. I wonder if he's heard.'

She tapped at the window and threw it open. He came hurrying across the street and began to speak in a loud voice before she could get in a word.

'That amusing guessing game of yours, Miss Elizabeth,' he said, just like Irene. 'About Mrs Lucas. I'll give you three – '

'One's enough: we all know,' said Elizabeth. 'Joyful news, isn't it?'

'Indeed, it is delightful to know that we are not going to lose one who – who has endeared herself to us all so much,' said he very handsomely.

He stopped. His tone lacked sincerity; there seemed to be something in his mind which he left unsaid. Elizabeth gave him a piercing and confidential look.

'Yes, Major Benjy?' she suggested.

He glanced round like a conspirator to see there was no one eavesdropping.

'Those parties, you know,' he said. 'Those entertainments which we've all enjoyed so much. Beautiful music. But Grebe's a long way off on a wet winter night. Not just round the corner. Now if she was settling in Mallards – '

He saw at once what an appalling interpretation might be put on this, and went on in a great hurry.

'You'll have to come to our rescue, Miss Elizabeth,' he said, dropping his voice so that even Diva could not hear. 'When you're back in your own house again, you'll have to look after us all as you always used to. Charming woman, Mrs Lucas, and most hospitable, I'm sure, but in the winter, as I was saying, that long way out of Tilling, just to hear a bit of music, and have a tomato, if you see what I mean.'

'Why, of course I see what you mean,' murmured Elizabeth. 'The dear thing, as you say, is so hospitable. Lovely music and tomatoes, but we must make a stand.'

'Well, you can have too much of a good thing,' said Major Benjy, 'and for my part a little Mozart lasts me a long time, especially if it's a long way on a wet night. Then I'm told there's an idea of callisthenic classes, though no doubt they would be for ladies only – '

'I wouldn't be too sure about that,' said Elizabeth. 'Our dear friend has got enough – shall we call it self-confidence? – to think herself capable of teaching anybody anything. If you aren't careful, Major Benjy, you'll find yourself in a skipping match on the lawn at Grebe, before you know what you're doing. You've been King Cophetua already, which I, for one, never thought to see.'

'That was just once in a way,' said he. 'But when it comes to callisthenic classes – '

Diva, in an agony at not being able to hear what was going on, had crept up behind Elizabeth, and now crouched close to her as she stood leaning out of the window. At this moment, Lucia, having finished her piano practice, came round the corner from Mallards into the High Street. Elizabeth hastily withdrew from the window and bumped into Diva.

'So sorry: didn't know you were there, dear,' she said. 'We must put our heads together another time, Major Benjy. *Au reservoir.*'

She closed the window.

'Oh, do tell me what you're going to put your heads together about,' said Diva. 'I only heard just the end.'

It was important to get allies: otherwise Elizabeth would have made a few well-chosen remarks about eavesdroppers.

'It is sad to find that just when Lucia has settled never to leave us any more,' she said, 'that there should be so much feeling in Tilling about being told to do this and being made to listen to that. Major Benjy – I don't know if you heard that part, dear – spoke very firmly, and I thought sensibly about it. The question really is if England is a free country or not, and whether we're going to be trampled upon. We've been very happy in Tilling all these years, going our own way, and living in sweet harmony together, and I for one, and Major Benjy for another, don't intend to put our necks under the yoke. I don't know how you feel about it. Perhaps you like it, for after all you were Mary Queen of Scots just as much as Major Benjy was King Cophetua.'

'I won't go to any po-di-mus, after dinner at Grebe,' said Diva. 'I shouldn't have gone to the last, but you persuaded us all to go. Where was your neck then, Elizabeth? Be fair.'

'Be fair yourself, Diva,' said Elizabeth with some heat. 'You know perfectly well that I wanted you to go in order that you might all get your necks from under her yoke, and hear that she couldn't speak a word of Italian.'

'And a nice mess you made of that,' said Diva. 'But never mind. She's established now as a perfect Italian linguist, and there it is. Don't meddle with that again, or you'll only prove that she can talk Greek too.'

Elizabeth rose and pointed at her like one of Raphael's Sibyls.

'Diva, to this day I don't believe she can talk Italian. It was a conjuring trick, and I'm no conjurer but a plain woman, and I can't tell you how it was done. But I will swear it was a trick. Besides, answer me this! Why doesn't she offer to give us Italian lessons if she knows it? She has offered to teach us bridge and Homer and callisthenics and take choir practices and arranged tableaux. Why not Italian?'

'That's curious,' said Diva thoughtfully.

'Not the least curious. The reason is obvious. Everyone snubbed me and scolded me, you among others, at that dreadful luncheon party, but I know I'm right, and some day the truth will come out. I can wait. Meantime what she means to do is to take us all in hand, and I won't be taken in hand. What is needed from us all is a little firmness.'

Diva went home thrilled to the marrow of her bones at the thought of the rich entertainment that these next months promised to provide. Naturally she saw through Elizabeth's rodomontade about yokes and free countries: what she meant was that she intended to assert herself again, and topple Lucia over. Two could not reign in Tilling, as everybody could see by this time. 'All most interesting,' said Diva to herself. 'Elizabeth's got hold of Major Benjy for the present, and Lucia's going to lose Georgie, but then men don't count for much in Tilling: it's brains that do it. There'll be more bridge parties and teas this winter than ever before. Really, I don't know which of them I would back. Hello, there's a note from her. Lunch tomorrow, I expect . . . I thought so.'

Lucia's luncheon party next day was to be of the nature of a banquet to celebrate the double event of her recovery and of the fact that Tilling, instead of mourning her approaching departure, was privileged to retain her, as Elizabeth had said, for ever and ever. The whole circle of her joyful friends would be there, and she meant to give them to eat of the famous dish of lobster *à la Riseholme*, which she had provided for Georgie, a few weeks ago, to act as a buffer to break the shock of Foljambe's engagement. It had already produced a great deal of wild surmise in the minds of the housewives at Tilling, for no one could conjecture how it was made, and Lucia had been deaf to all requests for the recipe: Elizabeth had asked her twice to give it her, but Lucia had merely changed the subject without attempt at transition: she had merely talked about something quite different. This secretiveness was considered unamiable, for the use of Tilling was to impart its culinary mysteries to friends, so that they might enjoy their favourite dishes at each other's houses, and lobster *à la Riseholme* had long been an agonizing problem to Elizabeth. She had made an attempt at it herself, but the result was not encouraging. She had told Diva and the Padre that she felt sure she had 'guessed it', and, when bidden to come to lunch and partake of it, they had both anticipated a great treat. But Elizabeth had clearly guessed wrong, for lobster *à la Riseholme à la Mapp* had been found to consist of something resembling lumps of india-rubber (so tough that the teeth positively bounced away from them on contact) swimming in a dubious pink gruel, and both of them left a great deal on their plates, concealed as far as possible under their knives and forks, though their hostess continued manfully to chew, till her jaw muscles gave out. Then Elizabeth had had recourse to underhand methods. Lucia had observed her more than once in the High Street, making herself suspiciously pleasant to her cook, and from the window of the garden room just before her influenza, she had seen her at the back door of Mallards again in conversation with the lady of the kitchen. On this occasion, with an unerring conviction in her mind, she had sent for her cook and asked her what Miss Mapp wanted. It was even so: Elizabeth's ostensible enquiry was for an egg whisk, which she had left by mistake at Mallards three months ago, but then she had unmasked her batteries, and, actually fingering a bright half-crown, had asked point-blank for the recipe of this lobster *à la Riseholme*. The cook had given her a polite but firm refusal, and Lucia was now more determined than ever that Elizabeth should never know the exquisite secret. She naturally felt that it was beneath her to take the slightest notice of this low and paltry attempt to obtain by naked bribery a piece of private knowledge, and she never let Elizabeth know that she was cognisant of it.

During the morning before Lucia's luncheon party a telegram had come for Georgie from Colonel Cresswell making a firm and very satisfactory offer for his house at Riseholme, unfurnished. That had made him really busy: first he had to see Foljambe and tell her (under seal of secrecy, for he had his little plot of teasing Lucia in mind) that he was proposing to settle in Tilling. Foljambe was very pleased to hear it, and in a burst of most unusual feeling, had said that it would have gone to her heart to leave his service, after so many harmonious years, when he went back to Riseholme, and that she was very glad to adopt the plan, which she had agreed to, when it was supposed that they would all go back to Riseholme together. She would do her work all day in Georgie's house, and retire in the evening to the connubialities of the garage at Grebe. When this affecting interview was over, she went back to her jobs, and again Georgie heard her singing as she cleaned the silver. 'So that's beautiful,' he said to himself, 'and the cloud has passed for ever. Now I must instantly see about getting a house here.'

He hurried out. There was still an hour before he was due at the lobster lunch. Though he had left the seaside twenty-four hours ago, he put on his yachtsman's cap and, walking on air, set off for the house agents'. Of all the houses in the place which he had seen, he was sure that none would suit him as well as this dear little Mallards Cottage which he now occupied; he liked it, Foljambe liked it, they all liked it, but he had no idea whether he could get a lease from kippered Isabel. As he crossed the High Street, a wild hoot from a motor horn just behind him gave him a dreadful fright, but he jumped nimbly for the pavement, reached it unhurt, and though his cap fell off and landed in a puddle, he was only thankful to have escaped being run down by Isabel Poppit on her motorcycle. Her hair was like a twisted mop, her skin incredibly tanned, and mounted on her cycle she looked like a sort of modernized Valkyrie in rather bad repair . . . Meeting her just at this moment, when he was on his way to enquire about Mallards Cottage, seemed a good omen to Georgie, and he picked up his cap and ran back across the street, for in her natural anxiety to avoid killing him she had swerved into a baker's cart, and had got messed up in the wheels.

'I do apologize, Miss Poppit,' he said. 'Entirely my fault for not looking both ways before I crossed.'

'No harm done,' said she. 'Oh, your beautiful cap. I am sorry. But after all the wonderful emptiness and silence among the sand dunes, a place like a town seems to me a positive nightmare.'

'Well, the emptiness and silence does seem to suit you,' said Georgie, gazing in astonishment at her mahogany face. 'I never saw anybody looking so well.'

Isabel, with a tug of her powerful arms, disentangled her cycle.

'It's the simple life,' said she, shaking her hair out of her eyes. 'Never again will I live in a town. I have taken the bungalow I am in now for six months more, and I only came in to Tilling to tell the house agent to get another tenant for Mallards Cottage, as I understand that you're going back to Riseholme at the end of this month.'

Georgie had never felt more firmly convinced that a wise and beneficent Providence looked after him with the most amiable care.

'And I was also on my way to the house agents',' he said, 'to see if I could get a lease of it.'

'Gracious! What a good thing I didn't run over you just now,' said Isabel, with all the simplicity derived from the emptiness and silence of sand dunes. 'Come on to the agents'.'

Within half an hour the whole business was as good as settled. Isabel held a lease from her mother of Mallards Cottage, which had five years yet to run, and she agreed to transfer this to Georgie, and store her furniture. He had just time to change into his new mustard-coloured suit with its orange tie and its topaz tie pin, and arrived at the luncheon party in the very highest spirits. Besides, there was his talk with Lucia when other guests had gone, to look forward to. How he would tease her about settling in London!

Though Tilling regarded the joyful prospect of Lucia's never going away again with certain reservations, and, in the case of Elizabeth, with nothing but reservations, her guests vied with each other in the fervency of their self-congratulations, and Elizabeth outdid them all, as she took into her mouth small fragments of lobster, in the manner of a wine-taster, appraising subtle flavours. There was cheese, there were shrimps, there was cream: there were so many things that she felt like Adam giving names to the innumerable procession of different animals. She had helped herself so largely that when the dish came to Georgie there was nothing left but a little pink juice, but he hardly minded, at all, so happy had the events of the morning made him. Then when Elizabeth felt that she would choke if she said anything more in praise of Lucia, Mr Wyse took it up, and Georgie broke in and said it was cruel of them all to talk about the delicious busy winter they would have, when they all knew that he would not be here any longer but back at Riseholme. In fact, he rather overdid his lamentations, and Lucia, whose acute mind detected the grossest insincerity in Elizabeth's raptures, began to wonder whether Georgie for some unknown reason was quite as woeful as he professed to be. Never had he looked more radiant, not a shadow of disappointment had come over his face when he inspected the casserole that had once contained his favourite dish, and found nothing left for him. There was something up – what on earth could it be? Had Foljambe jilted Cadman? – and just as Elizabeth was detecting flavours in the mysterious dish, so Lucia was trying to arrive at an analysis of the gay glad tones in which Georgie expressed his misery.

'It's too tarsome of you all to go on about the lovely things you're going to do,' he said. 'Callisthenic classes and Homer and bridge, and poor me far away. I shall tell myself every morning that I hate Tilling; I shall say like Coué, "Day by day in every way, I dislike it more and more," until I've convinced myself that I shall be glad to go.'

Mr Wyse made him a beautiful bow.

'We too shall miss you very sadly, Mr Pillson,' he said, 'and for my part I shall be tempted to hate Riseholme for taking from us one who has so endeared himself to us.'

'I ask to be allowed to associate myself with those sentiments,' said Major Benjy, whose contempt for Georgie and his sketches and his needlework had been intensified by the sight of his yachting cap, which he had pronounced to be only fit for a popinjay. It had been best to keep on good terms with him while Lucia was at Mallards, for he might poison her mind about himself, and now that he was going, there was no harm in these handsome remarks. Then the

Padre said something Scotch and sympathetic and regretful, and Georgie found himself, slightly to his embarrassment, making bows and saying 'thank you' right and left in acknowledgement of these universal expressions of regret that he was so soon about to leave them. It was rather awkward, for within a few hours they would all know that he had taken Mallards Cottage unfurnished for five years, which did not look like an immediate departure. But this little deception was necessary if he was to bring off his joke against Lucia, and make her think that he meant to settle in London. And after all, since everybody seemed so sorry that (as they imagined) he was soon to leave Tilling, they ought to be very much pleased to find that he was doing nothing of the kind.

The guests dispersed soon after lunch and Georgie, full of mischief and naughtiness, lingered with his hostess in the garden room. All her gimlet glances during lunch had failed to fathom his high good humour: here was he on the eve of parting with his Foljambe and herself, and yet his face beamed with content. Lucia was in very good spirits also, for she had seen Elizabeth's brow grow more and more furrowed as she strove to find a formula for the lobster.

'What a lovely luncheon party, although I got no lobster at all,' said Georgie, as he settled himself for his teasing. 'I did enjoy it. And Elizabeth's rapture at your stopping here! She must have an awful blister on her tongue.'

Lucia sighed.

'Sapphira must look to her laurels, poor thing,' she observed pensively. 'And how sorry they all were that you are going away.'

'Wasn't it nice of them?' said Georgie. 'But never mind that now: I've got something wonderful to tell you. I've never felt happier in my life, for the thing I've wanted for so many years can be managed at last. You will be pleased for my sake.'

Lucia laid a sympathetic hand on his. She felt that she had shown too little sympathy with one who was to lose his parlour-maid and his oldest friend so soon. But the gaiety with which he bore his double stroke was puzzling . . .

'Dear Georgie,' she said, 'anything that makes you happy makes me happy. I am rejoiced that something of the sort has occurred. Really rejoiced. Tell me what it is instantly.'

Georgie drew a long breath. He wanted to give it out all in a burst of triumph like a fanfare.

'Too lovely,' he said. 'Colonel Cresswell has bought my house at Riseholme – such a good price – and now at last I shall be able to settle in London. I was just as tired of Riseholme as you, and now I shall never see it again or Tilling either. Isn't it a dream? Riseholme, stuffy little Mallards Cottage, all things of the past! I shall have a nice little home in London, and you must promise to come up and stay with me sometimes. How I looked forward to telling you! Orchestral concerts at Queen's Hall, instead of our fumbling little arrangements of Mozartino for four hands. Pictures, a club if I can afford it, and how nice to think of you so happy down at Tilling! As for all the fuss I made yesterday about losing Foljambe, I can't think why it seemed to me so terrible.'

Lucia gave him one more gimlet glance, and found she did not believe a single word he was saying except as regards the sale of his house at Riseholme. All the rest must be lies, for the Foljambe wound could not possibly have healed so soon. But she instantly made up her mind to pretend to believe him, and clapped her hands for pleasure.

'Dear Georgie! What splendid news!' she said. 'I am pleased. I've always felt that you, with all your keenness and multifarious interests in life, were throwing your life away in these little backwaters like Riseholme and Tilling. London is the only place for you! Now, tell me: are you going to get a flat or a house? And where is it to be? If I were you I should have a house!'

This was not quite what Georgie had expected. He had thought that Lucia would suggest that now that he was quit of Riseholme he positively must come to Tilling, but not only did she fail to do that, but she seemed delighted that no such thought had entered into his head.

'I haven't really thought about that yet,' he said. 'There's something to be said for a flat.'

'No doubt. It's more compact, and then there's no bother about rates and taxes. And you'll have your car, I suppose. And will your cook go with you? What does she say to it all?'

'I haven't told her yet,' said Georgie, beginning to get a little pensive.

'Really? I should have thought you would have done that at once. And isn't Foljambe pleased that you are so happy again?'

'She doesn't know yet,' said Georgie. 'I thought I would tell you first.'

'Dear Georgie, how sweet of you,' said Lucia. 'I'm sure Foljambe will be as pleased as I am. You'll be going up to London, I suppose, constantly now till the end of this month, so that you can get your house or your flat, whichever it is, ready as soon as possible. How busy you and I will be, you settling into London and I into Tilling. Do you know, supposing you had thought of living permanently here, now that you've got rid of your house at Riseholme, I should have done my best to persuade you not to, though I know in my selfishness that I did suggest that yesterday. But it would never do, Georgie. It's all very well for elderly women like me, who just want a little peace and quietness, or for retired men like Major Benjy or for dilettantes like Mr Wyse, but for you, a thousand times no. I am sure of it.'

Georgie got thoughtfuller and thoughtfuller. It had been rather a mistake to try to tease Lucia, for so far from being teased she was simply pleased. The longer she went on like this, and there seemed no end to her expressions of approval, the harder it would be to tell her.

'Do you really think that?' he said.

'Indeed I do. You would soon be terribly bored with Tilling. Oh, Georgie, I am so pleased with your good fortune and your good sense. I wonder if the agents here have got any houses or flats in London on their books. Let's go down there at once and see. We might find something. I'll run and put on my hat.'

Georgie threw in his hand. As usual Lucia had come out on top.

'You're too tarsome,' he said. 'You don't believe a single word I've been telling you of my plans.'

'My dear, of course I don't,' said Lucia brightly. 'I never heard such a pack of rubbish. Ananias is not in it. But it is true about selling your Riseholme house, I hope?'

'Yes, that part is,' said Georgie.

'Then of course you're going to live here,' said she. 'I meant you to do that all along. Now how about Mallards Cottage? I saw that Yahoo in the High Street this morning, and she told me she wanted to let it for the winter. Let's go down to the agents' as I suggested, and see.'

'I've done that already,' said Georgie, 'for I met her too, and she nearly knocked me down. I've got a five years' lease of it.'

It was not in Lucia's nature to crow over anybody. She proved her quality and passed on to something else.

'Perfect!' she said. 'It has all come out just as I planned, so that's all right. Now, if you've got nothing to do, let us have some music.'

She got out the new Mozart which she had been practising.

'This looks a lovely duet,' she said, 'and we haven't tried it yet. I shall be terribly rusty, for all the time I had influenza, I hardly dared to play the piano at all.'

Georgie looked at the new Mozart.

'It does look nice,' he said. 'Tum-ti-tum. Why, that's the one I heard you practising so busily yesterday morning.'

Lucia took not the slightest notice of this.

'We begin together,' she said, 'on the third beat. Now . . . *Uno, due, TRE!*'

CHAPTER EIGHT

The painting and decorating of Grebe began at once. Irene offered to do all the painting with her own hands, and recommended as a scheme for the music room, a black ceiling and four walls of different colours, vermilion, emerald green, ultramarine and yellow. It would take a couple of months or so to execute, and the cost would be considerable as lapis lazuli must certainly be used for the ultramarine wall, but she assured Lucia that the result would be unique and marvellously stimulating to the eye, especially if she would add a magenta carpet and a nickel-plated mantelpiece.

'It sounds too lovely, dear,' said Lucia, contemplating the sample of colours which Irene submitted to her, 'but I feel sure I shan't be able to afford it. Such a pity! Those beautiful hues!'

Then Irene besought her to introduce a little variety into the shape of the windows. It would be amusing to have one window egg-shaped, and another triangular, and another with five or six or seven irregular sides, so that it looked as if it was a hole in the wall made by a shell. Or how about a front door that, instead of opening sideways, let down like a portcullis?

Irene rose to more daring conceptions yet. One night she had dined on a pot of strawberry jam and half a pint of very potent cocktails, because she wanted her eye for colour to be at its keenest round about eleven o'clock when the moon would rise over the marsh, and she hoped to put the lid for ever on Whistler's naïve old-fashioned attempts to paint moonlight. After this salubrious meal she had come round to Mallards, waiting for the moon to rise and sat for half an hour at Lucia's piano, striking random chords, and asking Lucia what colour they were. These musical rainbows suggested a wonderful idea, and she shut down the piano with a splendid purple bang.

'Darling, I've got a new scheme for Grebe,' she said. 'I want you to furnish a room sideways, if you understand what I mean.'

'I don't think I do,' said Lucia.

'Why, like this,' said Irene very thoughtfully. 'You would open the door of the room and find you were walking about on wallpaper with pictures hanging on it. (I'll do the pictures for you.) Then one side of the room where the window is would be whitewashed as if it was a ceiling and the window would be the skylight. The opposite side would be the floor; and you would have the furniture screwed on to it. The other walls, including the one which would be the ceiling in an ordinary room, would be covered with wallpaper and more pictures and a bookcase. It would all be sideways, you see: you'd enter through the wall, and the room would be at right angles to you; ceiling on the left, floor on the right, or vice versa. It would give you a perfectly new perception of the world. You would see everything from a new angle, which is what we want so much in life nowadays. Don't you think so?'

Irene's speech was distinct and clear cut, she walked up and down the garden room with a firm unwavering step, and Lucia put from her the uneasy suspicion that her dinner had gone to her head.

'It would be most delightful,' she said, 'but slightly too experimental for me.'

'And then, you see,' continued Irene, 'how useful it would be if somebody tipsy came in. It would make him sober at once, for tipsy people see everything crooked, and so your sideways room, being crooked, would appear to him straight, and so he would be himself again. Just like that.'

'That would be splendid,' said Lucia, 'but I can't provide a room where tipsy people could feel sober again. The house isn't big enough.'

Irene sat down by her, and passionately clasped one of her hands.

'Lucia, you're too adorable,' she said. 'Nothing defeats you. I've been talking the most abject nonsense, though I do think that there may be something in it, and you remain as calm as the moon which I hope will rise over the marsh before long, unless the almanac in which I looked it out is last year's. Don't tell anybody else about the sideways room, will you, or they might think I was drunk. Let it be our secret, darling.'

Lucia wondered for a moment if she ought to allow Irene to spend the night on the marsh, but she was perfectly capable of coherent speech and controlled movements, and possibly the open air might do her good.

'Not a soul shall know, dear,' she said. 'And now if you're really going to paint the moon, you had better start. You feel quite sure you can manage it, don't you?'

'Of course I can manage the moon,' said Irene stoutly. 'I've managed it lots of times. I wish you would come with me. I always hate leaving you. Or shall I stop here, and paint you instead? Or do you think Georgie would come? What a lamb, isn't he? Pass the mint sauce please, or shall I go home?'

'Perhaps that would be best,' said Lucia. 'Paint the moon another night.'

* * *

Lucia next day hurried up the firm to which she had entrusted the decoration of Grebe, in case Irene had some new schemes, and halfway through November, the house was ready to receive her furniture from Riseholme. Georgie simultaneously was settling into Mallards Cottage, and in the course of it went through a crisis of the most agitating kind. Isabel had assured him that by noon on a certain day men would arrive to take her furniture to the repository where it was to be stored, and as the vans with his effects from Riseholme had arrived in Tilling the night before, he induced the foreman to begin moving everything out of the house at nine next morning and bring his furniture in. This was done, and by noon all Isabel's tables and chairs and beds and crockery were standing out in the street ready for her van. They completely blocked it for wheeled traffic, though pedestrians could manage to squeeze by in single file. Tilling did not mind this little inconvenience in the least, for it was all so interesting, and tradesmen's carts coming down the street were cheerfully backed into the churchyard again and turned round in order to make a more circuitous route, and those coming up were equally obliging, while foot passengers, thrilled with having the entire contents of a house exposed for their inspection, were unable to tear themselves away from so intimate an exhibition. Then Georgie's furniture was moved in, and there were dazzling and fascinating objects for inspection, pictures that he had painted, screens and bedspreads that he had worked, very pretty woollen pyjamas for the winter and embroidered covers for hot-water bottles. These millineries roused Major Benjy's manliest indignation, and he was nearly late for the tram to take him out to play golf, for he could not tear himself away from the revolting sight. In a few hours Georgie's effects had passed into the house, but still there was no sign of anyone coming to remove Isabel's from the street, and, by dint of telephoning, it was discovered that she had forgotten to give any order at all about them, and the men from the repository were out on other jobs. It then began to rain rather heavily, and though Georgie called heaven and earth to witness that all this muddle was not his fault he felt compelled, out of mere human compassion, to have Isabel's furniture moved back into his house again. In consequence the rooms and passages on the ground floor were completely blocked with stacks of cupboards and tables piled high with books and crockery and saucepans, the front door would not shut, and Foljambe, caught upstairs by the rising tide, could not come down. The climax of intensity arrived when she let down a string from an upper window, and Georgie's cook attached a small basket of nourishing food to it. Diva was terribly late for lunch at the Wyses, for she was rooted to the spot, though it was raining heavily, till she was sure that Foljambe would not be starved.

But by the time that the month of November was over, the houses of the newcomers were ready to receive them, and a general post of owners back to their homes took place after a remunerative let of four months. Elizabeth returned to Mallards from Wasters, bringing with her, in addition to what she had taken there, a cargo of preserves made from Diva's garden of such bulk that Coplen had to make two journeys with her large wheelbarrow. Diva returned to Wasters from Taormina, quaint Irene came back to Taormina from the labourer's cottage with a handcart laden with striking canvases including that of the women wrestlers who had become men, and the labourer and his family were free to trek to their own abode from the hop-picker's shanty which they had inhabited so much longer than they had intended.

There followed several extremely busy days for most of the returning emigrants. Elizabeth in particular was occupied from morning till night in scrutinizing every corner of Mallards and making out a list of dilapidations against Lucia. There was a tea cup missing, the men who removed Lucia's hired piano from the garden room had scraped a large piece of paint off the wall, Lucia had forgotten to replace dearest mamma's piano which still stood in the telephone room, and there was no sign of a certain egg whisk. Simultaneously Diva was preparing a similar list for Elizabeth which would astonish her, but was pleased to find that the tenant had left an egg whisk behind; while the wife of the labourer, not being instructed in dilapidations, was removing from the whitewashed wall of her cottage the fresco which Irene had painted there in her spare moments. It wasn't fit to be seen, that it wasn't, but a scrubbing brush and some hot water made short work of all those naked people. Irene, for her part, was frantically searching among her canvases for a picture of Adam and Eve with quantities of the sons of God shouting for joy: an important work. Perhaps she had left it at the cottage, and then remembering that she had painted it on the wall, she hurried off there in order to varnish it against the inclemencies of weather. But it was already too late, for the last of the sons of God was even then disappearing under the strokes of the scrubbing brush.

Gradually, though not at once, these claims and counter-claims were (with the exception of the fresco) adjusted to the general dissatisfaction. Lucia acknowledged the charge for the re-establishment of dearest mamma's piano in the garden room, but her cook very distinctly remembered that on the day when Miss Mapp tried to bribe her to impart the secret of lobster *à la Riseholme*, she took away the egg whisk, which had formed the gambit of Miss Mapp's vain attempt to corrupt her. So Lucia reminded Elizabeth that not very long ago she had called at the back door of Mallards and had taken it away herself. Her cook believed that it was in two if not three pieces. So Miss Mapp, having made certain it had not got put by mistake among the pots of preserves she had brought from Wasters, went to see if she had left it there, and found not it alone, but a preposterous list of claims against her from Diva. But by degrees these billows, which were of annual occurrence, subsided, and apart from Elizabeth's chronic grievance against Lucia for her hoarding the secret of the lobster, they and other differences in the past faded away and Tilling was at leisure to turn its attention again to the hardly more important problems and perplexities of life and the menaces that might have to be met in the future.

* * *

Elizabeth, on this morning of mid-December, was quite settled into Mallards again, egg-whisk and all, and the window of her garden room was being once more used by the rightful owner for the purpose of taking observations. It had always been a highly strategic position; it commanded, for instance, a perfect view of the front door of Taormina, which at the present moment quaint Irene was painting in stripes of salmon pink and azure. She had tried to reproduce the lost fresco on it, but there had been earnest remonstrances from the Padre, and also the panels on the door broke it up and made it an unsuitable surface for such a cartoon. She therefore was contenting herself with brightening it up. Then Elizabeth could see the mouth of Porpoise Street and register all the journeys of the Royce. These, after a fortnight's intermission, had become frequent again, for the Wyses had just come back from 'visiting friends in Devonshire', and though Elizabeth had strong reason to suspect that friends in Devonshire denoted nothing more than an hotel in Torquay, they had certainly taken the Royce with them, and during its absence the streets of Tilling had been far more convenient for traffic. Then there was Major Benjy's house as before, under her very eye, and now Mallards Cottage as well was a point that demanded frequent scrutiny. She had never cared what that distraught Isabel Poppit did, but with Georgie there it was different, and neither Major Benjy nor he (nor anybody else visiting them) could go in or out of either house without instant detection. The two most important men in Tilling, in fact, were powerless to evade her observation.

Nothing particular was happening at the moment, and Elizabeth was making a mental retrospect rather as if she was the King preparing his speech for the opening of Parliament. Her relations with foreign powers were excellent, and though during the last six months there had been disquieting incidents, there was nothing immediately threatening . . . Then round the corner of the High Street came Lucia's car and the King's speech was put aside.

The car stopped at Taormina. Quaint Irene instantly put down her painting paraphernalia on the pavement, and stood talking into the window of the car for quite a long time. Clearly therefore Lucia, though invisible, was inside it. Eventually Irene leaned her head forward into the car, exactly as if she was kissing something, and stepping back again upset one of her paint pots. This was pleasant, but not of first-rate importance compared with what the car would do next. It turned down into Porpoise Street: naturally there was no telling for certain what happened to it there, for it was out of sight, but a tyro could conjecture that it had business at the Wyses', even if he had been so deaf as not to hear the clanging of that front-door bell. Then it came backing out again, went through the usual manoeuvres of turning, and next stopped at Major Benjy's. Lucia was still invisible, but Cadman got down and delivered a note. The tyro could therefore conjecture by this time that invitations were coming from Grebe.

She slid her chair a little further back behind the curtain, feeling sure that the car would stop next at her own door. But it turned the corner below the window without drawing up, and Elizabeth got a fleeting glance into the interior, where Lucia was sitting with a large book open in her lap. Next it stopped at Mallards Cottage: no note was delivered there, but Cadman rang the bell, and presently Georgie came out. Like Irene, he talked for quite a long time into the window of the car, but, unlike her, did not kiss anything at the conclusion of the interview. The situation was therefore perfectly clear: Lucia had asked Irene and Major Benjy and Georgie and probably the Wyses to some entertainment, no doubt the house-warming of which there had been rumours, but had not asked her. Very well. The relations with foreign powers therefore had suddenly become far from satisfactory.

Elizabeth quitted her seat in the window, for she had observed enough to supply her with plenty of food for thought, and went back, in perfect self-control, to the inspection of her household books; adding up figures was a purely mechanical matter, which allowed the intenser emotions full play. Georgie would be coming in here presently, for he was painting a sketch of the interior of the garden room; this was to be his Christmas present to Lucia (a surprise, about which she was to know nothing), to remind her of the happy days she had spent in it. He usually left his sketch here, for it was not worth while to take it backwards and forwards, and there it stood, propped up on the bookcase. He had first tried an Irene-ish technique, but he had been obliged to abandon that, since the garden room with this handling persisted in looking like Paddington Station in a fog, and he had gone back to the style he knew, in which bookcases, chairs and curtains were easily recognizable. It needed a few mornings' work yet, and now the idea of destroying it, and, when he arrived, of telling him that she was quite sure he had taken it back with him yesterday darted unbidden into Elizabeth's mind. But she rejected it, though it would have been pleasant to deprive Lucia of her Christmas present . . . and she did not believe for a moment that she had ordered a dozen eggs on Tuesday and a dozen more on Thursday. The butcher's bill seemed to be correct, though extortionate, and she must find out as soon as possible whether the Padre and his wife and Diva were asked to Grebe too. If they were – but she banished the thought of what was to be done if they were: it was difficult enough to know what to do even if they weren't.

The books were quickly done, and Elizabeth went back to finish reading the morning paper in the window. Just as she got there Georgie, with his little cape over his shoulders and his paintbox in his hand, came stepping briskly along from Mallards Cottage. Simultaneously Lucia's great bumping car returned round the corner by the churchyard, in the direction of Mallards.

An inspiration of purest ray serene seized Elizabeth. She waited till Georgie had rung the front-door bell, at which psychological moment Lucia's car was straight below the window. Without a second's hesitation Elizabeth threw up the sash, and, without appearing to see Lucia at all, called out to Georgie in a high cheerful voice, using baby language.

''Oo is very naughty boy, Georgie!' she cried. 'Never ring

Elizabeth's belly-pelly. 'Oo walk straight in always, and sing out for her. There's no chain up.'

Georgie looked round in amazement. Never had Elizabeth called him Georgie before, or talked to him in the language consecrated for his use and Lucia's. And there was Lucia's car close to him. She must have heard this affectionate welcome, and what would she think? But there was nothing to do but to go in.

Still without seeing (far less cutting) Lucia, Elizabeth closed the window again, positively dazzled by her own brilliance. An hour's concentrated thought could not have suggested to her anything that Lucia would dislike more thoroughly than hearing that gay little speech, which parodied her and revealed such playful intimacy with Georgie. Georgie came straight out to the garden room, saying 'Elizabeth, Elizabeth' to himself below his breath, in order to get used to it, for he must return this token of friendship in kind.

'Good morning, Elizabeth,' he said firmly (and the worst was over until such time as he had to say it again in Lucia's presence).

'Good morning, Georgie,' she said by way of confirmation. 'What a lovely light for your painting this morning. Here it is ready for you, and Withers will bring you out your glass of water. How you've caught the feel of my dear little room!'

Another glance out of the window as she brought him his sketch was necessary, and she gasped. There was Cadman on the doorstep just handing Withers a note. In another minute she came into the garden room.

'From Mrs Lucas,' she said. 'She forgot to leave it when she went by before.'

'That's about the house-warming, I'm sure,' said Georgie, getting his paintbox ready.

What was done, was done, and there was no use in thinking about that. Elizabeth tore the note open.

'A house-warming?' she said. 'Dear Lucia! What a treat that will be. Yes, you're quite right.'

'She's sending her car up for the Padre and his wife and Irene and Mrs Plaistow,' said Georgie, 'and asked me just now if I would bring you and Major Benjy. Naturally I will.'

Elizabeth's brilliant speech out of the window had assumed the aspect of a gratuitous act of war. But she could not have guessed that Lucia had merely forgotten to leave her invitation. The most charitable would have assumed that there was no invitation to leave.

'How kind of you!' she said. 'Tomorrow night, isn't it? Rather short notice. I must see if I'm disengaged.'

As Lucia had asked the whole of the elite of Tilling, this proved to be the case. But Elizabeth still pondered as to whether she should accept or not. She had committed one unfriendly act in talking baby language to Georgie, with a pointed allusion to the door chain, literally over Lucia's head, and it was a question whether, having done that, it would not be wise to commit another (while Lucia, it might be guessed, was still staggering) by refusing to go to the house-warming. She did not doubt that there would be war before long: the only question was if she was ready now.

As she was pondering Withers came in to say that Major Benjy had called. He would not come out into the garden room, but he would like to speak to her a minute.

'Evidently he has heard that Georgie is here,' thought Elizabeth to herself as she hurried into the house. 'Dear me, how men quarrel with each other, and I only want to be on good terms with everybody. No doubt he wants to know if I'm going to the house-warming – Good morning, Major Benjy.'

'Thought I wouldn't come out,' said this bluff fellow, 'as I heard your Miss Milliner Michael-Angelo, ha, was with you – '

'Oh Major Benjy, fie!' said Elizabeth. 'Cruel of you.'

'Well, leave it at that. Now about this party tomorrow. I think I shall make a stand straight away, for I'm not going to spend the whole of the winter evenings tramping through the mud to Grebe. To be sure it's dinner this time, which makes a difference.'

Elizabeth found that she longed to see what Lucia had made of Grebe, and what she had made of her speech from the window.

'I quite agree in principle,' she said, 'but a house-warming, you know. Perhaps it wouldn't be kind to refuse. Besides, Georgie – '

'Eh?' said the Major.

'Mr Pillson, I mean,' said Elizabeth, hastily correcting herself, 'has offered to drive us both down.'

'And back?' asked he suspiciously.

'Of course. So just for once, shall we?'

'Very good. But none of those after-dinner musicals, or lessons in bridge for me.'

'Oh, Major Benjy!' said Elizabeth. 'How can you talk so? As if poor Lucia would attempt to teach *you* bridge.'

This could be taken in two ways, one interpretation would read that he was incapable of learning, the other that Lucia was incapable of teaching. He took the more obvious one.

'Upon my soul she did, at the last game I had with her,' said he. 'Laid out the last three tricks and told me how to play them. Beyond a joke. Well, I won't keep you from your dressmaker.'

'O fie!' said Elizabeth again. '*Au reservoir.*'

* * *

Lucia, meantime, had driven back to Grebe with that mocking voice still ringing in her ears, and a series of most unpleasant images, like some diabolical film, displaying themselves before her inward eye. Most probably Elizabeth had seen her when she called out to Georgie like that, and was intentionally insulting her. Such conduct called for immediate reprisals and she must presently begin to think these out. But the alternative, possible though not probable, that Elizabeth had not seen her, was infinitely more wounding, for it implied that Georgie was guilty of treacheries too black to bear looking at. Privately, when she herself was not present, he was on Christian name terms with that woman, and permitted and enjoyed her obvious mimicry of herself. And what was Georgie doing popping in to Mallards like this, and being scolded in baby voice for ringing the bell instead of letting himself in, with allusions of an absolutely unmistakable kind to that episode about the chain? Did they laugh over that together: did Georgie poke fun at his oldest friend behind her back? Lucia positively writhed at the thought. In any case, whether or not he was guilty of this monstrous infidelity, he must be in the habit of going into Mallards, and now she remembered that he had his paintbox in his hand. Clearly then he was going there to paint, and in all their talks when he so constantly told her what he had been doing, he had never breathed a word of that. Perhaps he was painting Elizabeth, for in this winter weather he could never be painting in the garden. Just now too, when she called at Mallards Cottage, and they had

had a talk together, he had refused to go out and drive with her, because he had some little jobs to do indoors, and the moment he had got rid of her – no less than that – he had hurried off to Mallards with his paintbox. With all this evidence, things looked very dark indeed, and the worst and most wounding of these two alternatives began to assume probability.

Georgie was coming to tea with her that afternoon, and she must find out what the truth of the matter was. But she could not imagine herself saying to him: 'Does she really call you Georgie, and does she imitate me behind my back, and are you painting her?' Pride absolutely forbade that: such humiliating enquiries would choke her. Should she show him an icy aloof demeanour, until he asked her if anything was the matter? But that wouldn't do, for either she must say that nothing was the matter, which would not help, or she must tell him what the matter was, which was impossible. She must behave to him exactly as usual, and he would probably do the same. 'So how am I to find out?' said the bewildered Lucia quite aloud.

Another extremely uncomfortable person in tranquil Tilling that morning was Georgie himself. As he painted this sketch of the garden room for Lucia, with Elizabeth busying herself with dusting her piano and bringing in chrysanthemums from her greenhouse, and making bright little sarcasms about Diva who was in ill odour just now, there painted itself in his mind, in colours growing ever more vivid, a most ominous picture of Lucia. If he knew her at all, and he was sure he did, she would say nothing whatever about that disconcerting scene on the doorstep. Awkward as it would be, he would be obliged to protest his innocence, and denounce Elizabeth. Most disagreeable, and who could foresee the consequences? For Lucia (if he knew her) would see red, and there would be war. Bloody war of the most devastating sort. 'But it will be rather exciting too,' thought he, 'and I back Lucia.'

Georgie could not wait for tea time, but set forth on his uncomfortable errand soon after lunch. Lucia had seen him coming up the garden, and abandoned her musings and sat down hastily at the piano. Instantly on his entry she sprang up again, and plunged into mixed Italian and baby talk.

'*Ben arrivato, Georgino*,' she cried. 'How early you are, and so we can have cosy ickle chat-chat before tea. Any newsy-pewsy?'

Georgie took the plunge.

'Yes,' he said.

'Tell Lucia, *presto*. 'Oo think me like it?'

'It'll interest you,' said Georgie guardedly. 'Now! When I was standing on Mallards doorstep this morning, did you hear what that old witch called to me out of the garden-room window?'

Lucia could not repress a sigh of relief. The worst could not be true. Then she became herself again.

'Let me see now!' she said. 'Yes. I think I did. She called you Georgie, didn't she: she scolded you for ringing. Something of that sort.'

'Yes. And she talked baby talk like you and me,' interrupted Georgie, 'and she said the door wasn't on the chain. I want to tell you straight off that she never called me Georgie before, and that we've never talked baby talk together in my life. I owe it to myself to tell you that.'

Lucia turned her piercing eye on to Georgie. There seemed to be a sparkle in it that boded ill for somebody.

'And you think she saw me, Georgie?' she asked.

'Of course she did. Your car was directly below her window.'

'I am afraid there is no doubt about it,' said Lucia. 'Her remarks, therefore, seem to have been directed at me. A singularly ill-bred person. There's one thing more. You were taking your paintbox with you – '

'Oh, that's all right,' said he. 'I'm doing a sketch of the garden room. You'll know about that in time. And what are you going to do?' he asked greedily.

Lucia laughed in her most musical manner.

'Well, first of all I shall give her a very good dinner tomorrow, as she has not had the decency to say she was engaged. She telephoned to me just now telling me what a joy it would be, and how she was looking forward to it. And mind you call her Elizabeth.'

'I've done that already,' said Georgie proudly. 'I practised saying it to myself.'

'Good. She dines here then tomorrow night, and I shall be her hostess and shall make the evening as pleasant as I can to all my guests. But apart from that, Georgie, I shall take steps to teach her manners if she's not too old to learn. She will be sorry; she will wish she had not been so rude. And I can't see any objection to our other friends in Tilling knowing what occurred this morning, if you feel inclined to speak of it. I shan't, but there's no reason why you shouldn't.'

'Hurrah, I'm dining with the Wyses tonight,' said Georgie. 'They'll soon know.'

Lucia knitted her brows in profound thought.

'And then there's that incident about our pictures, yours and mine, being rejected by the hanging committee of the Art Club,' said she. 'We have both kept the forms we received saying that they regretted having to return them, and I think, Georgie, that while you are on the subject of Elizabeth Mapp, you might show yours to Mr Wyse. He is a member, so is Susan, of the committee, and I think they have a right to know that our pictures were rejected on official forms without ever coming before the committee at all. I behaved towards our poor friend with a magnanimity that now appears to me excessive, and since she does not appreciate magnanimity we will try her with something else. That would not be amiss.' Lucia rose.

'And now let us leave this very disagreeable subject for the present,' she said, 'and take the taste of it out of our mouths with a little music. Beethoven, noble Beethoven, don't you think? The fifth symphony, Georgie, for four hands. Fate knocking at the door.'

Georgie rather thought that Lucia smacked her lips as she said, 'this very disagreeable subject', but he was not certain, and presently Fate was knocking at the door with Lucia's firm fingers, for she took the treble.

They had a nice long practice, and when it was time to go home Lucia detained him.

'I've got one thing to say to you, Georgie,' she said, 'though not about that paltry subject. I've sold The Hurst, I've bought this new property, and so I've made a new will. I've left Grebe and all it contains to you, and also, well, a little sum of money. I should like you to know that.'

Georgie was much touched.

'My dear, how wonderful of you,' he said. 'But I hope it will be ages and ages before – '

'So do I, Georgie,' she said in her most sincere manner.

* * *

Tilling had known tensions before and would doubtless know them again. Often it had been on a very agreeable rack of suspense, as when, for instance, it had believed (or striven to believe) that Major Benjy might be fighting a duel with that old crony of his, Captain Puffin, lately deceased. Now there was a suspense of a more intimate quality (for nobody would have cared at all if Captain Puffin had been killed, nor much, if Major Benjy), for it was as if the innermost social guts of Tilling were attached to some relentless windlass, which, at any moment now, might be wound, but not relaxed. The High Street next morning, therefore, was the scene of almost painful excitement. The Wyses' Royce, with Susan smothered in sables, went up and down, until she was practically certain that she had told everybody that she and Algernon had retired from the hanging committee of the Art Club, pending explanations which they had requested Miss (no longer Elizabeth) Mapp to furnish, but which they had no hope of receiving. Susan was perfectly explicit about the cause of this step, and Algernon who, at a very early hour, had interviewed the errand boy at the frame shop, was by her side, to corroborate all she said. His high-bred reticence, indeed, had been even more weighty than Susan's volubility. 'I am afraid it is all too true,' was all that could be got out of him. Two hours had now elapsed since their resignations had been sent in, and still no reply had come from Mallards.

But that situation was but an insignificant fraction of the prevalent suspense, for the exhibition had been open and closed months before, and if Tilling was to make a practice of listening to such posthumous revelations, life would cease to have any poignant interest, but be wholly occupied in retrospective retributions. Thrilling therefore as was the past, as revealed by the stern occupants of the Royce, what had happened only yesterday on the doorstep of Mallards was far more engrossing. The story of that, by 11.30 a.m., already contained several remarkable variants. The Padre affirmed that Georgie had essayed to enter Mallards without knocking, and that Miss Mapp (the tendency to call her Miss Mapp was spreading) had seen Lucia in her motor just below the window of the garden room, and had called out, 'Turn in, *Georgino mio*, no tarsome chains now that Elizabeth has got back to her own housie-pousie.' Diva had reason to believe that Elizabeth (she still stuck to that) had not seen Lucia in her motor, and had called out of the window to Georgie 'Ring the belly-pelly, dear, for I'm afraid the chain is on the door.' Mrs Bartlett (she was no use at all) said, 'All so distressing and exciting and Christmas Day next week, and very little goodwill, oh dear me!' Irene had said, 'That old witch will get what for.'

Again, it was known that Major Benjy had called at Mallards soon after the scene, whatever it was, had taken place, and had refused to go into the garden room, when he heard that Georgie was painting Elizabeth's portrait. Withers was witness (she had brought several pots of jam to Diva's house that morning, not vegetable marrow at all, but raspberry, which looked like a bribe) that the Major had said 'Faugh!' when she told him that Georgie was there. Major Benjy himself could not be cross-examined because he had gone out by the eleven o'clock tram to play golf. Lucia had not been seen in the High Street at all, nor had Miss Mapp, and Georgie had only passed through it in his car, quite early, going in the direction of Grebe. This absence of the principals, in these earlier stages of development, was felt to be in accordance with the highest rules of dramatic technique, and everybody, as far as was known, was to meet that very night at Lucia's house-warming. Opinion as to what would happen then was as divergent as the rumours of what had happened already. Some said that Miss Mapp had declined the invitation on the plea that she was engaged to dine with Major Benjy. This was unlikely, because he never had anybody to dinner. Some said that she had accepted, and that Lucia no doubt intended to send out a message that she was not expected, but that Georgie's car would take her home again. So sorry. All this, however, was a matter of pure conjecture, and it was work enough to sift out what had happened, without wasting time (for time was precious) in guessing what would happen.

The church clock had hardly struck half-past eleven (winter time) before the first of the principals appeared on the stage of the High Street. This was Miss Mapp, wreathed in smiles, and occupied in her usual shopping errands. She trotted about from grocer to butcher, and butcher to general stores, where she bought a mousetrap, and was exceedingly affable to tradespeople. She nodded to her friends, she patted Mr Woolgar's dog on the head, she gave a penny to a ragged individual with a lugubrious baritone voice who was singing 'The Last Rose of Summer', and said 'Thank you for your sweet music.' Then after pausing for a moment on the pavement in front of Wasters, she rang the bell. Diva, who had seen her from the window, flew to open it.

'Good morning, Diva dear,' she said. 'I just looked in. Any news?'

'Good gracious, it's I who ought to ask you that,' said Diva. 'What *did* happen really?'

Elizabeth looked very much surprised.

'How? When? Where?' she asked.

'As if you didn't know,' said Diva, fizzing with impatience. 'Mr Georgie, Lucia, paintboxes, no chain on the door, you at the garden-room window, belly-pelly. Etcetera. Yesterday morning.'

Elizabeth put her finger to her forehead, as if trying to recall some dim impression. She appeared to succeed.

'Dear gossipy one,' she said, 'I believe I know what you mean. Georgie came to paint in the garden room, as he so often does – '

'Do you call him Georgie?' asked Diva in an eager parenthesis.

'Yes, I fancy that's his name, and he calls me Elizabeth.'

'No!' said Diva.

'Yes,' said Elizabeth. 'Do not interrupt me, dear . . . I happened to be at the window as he rang the bell, and I just popped my head out, and told him he was a naughty boy not to walk straight in.'

'In baby talk?' asked Diva. 'Like Lucia?'

'Like any baby you chance to mention,' said Elizabeth. 'Why not?'

'But with her sitting in her car just below?'

'Yes, dear, it so happened that she was just coming to leave an invitation on me for her house-warming tonight. Are you going?'

'Yes, of course, everybody is. But how could you do it?'

Elizabeth sat wrapped in thought.

'I'm beginning to see what you mean,' she said at length. 'But

what an absurd notion. You mean, don't you, that dear Lulu thinks
– goodness, how ridiculous – that I was mimicking her.'

'Nobody knows what she thinks,' said Diva. 'She's not been
seen this morning.'

'But gracious goodness me, what have I done?' asked Elizabeth.
'Why this excitement? Is there a law that only Mrs Lucas of Grebe
may call Georgie, Georgie? So ignorant of me if there is. Ought
I to call him Frederick? And pray, why shouldn't I talk baby talk?
Another law perhaps. I must get a book of the laws of England.'

'But you knew she was in the car just below you and must have
heard.'

Elizabeth was now in possession of what she wanted to know.
Diva was quite a decent barometer of Tilling weather, and the
weather was stormy.

'Rubbish, darling,' she said. 'You are making mountains out of
molehills. If Lulu heard – and I don't know that she did, mind –
what cause of complaint has she? Mayn't I say Georgie? Mayn't I
say "vewy naughty boy"? Let us hear no more about it. You will see
this evening how wrong you all are. Lulu will be just as sweet and
cordial as ever. And you will hear with your own ears how Georgie
calls me Elizabeth.'

These were brave words, and they very fitly represented the
stout heart that inspired them. Tilling had taken her conduct to
be equivalent to an act of war, exactly as she had meant it to be,
and if anyone thought that E. M. was afraid they were wrong . . .
Then there was that matter of Mr Wyse's letter, resigning from the
hanging committee. She must tap the barometer again.

'I think everybody is a shade mad this morning,' she observed,
'and I should call Mr Wyse, if anybody asked me to be candid,
a raving lunatic. There was a little misunderstanding months and
months ago – I am vague about it – concerning two pictures that
Lulu and Georgie sent in to the art exhibition in the summer.
I thought it was all settled and done with. But I did act a little
irregularly. Technically I was wrong, and when I have been wrong
about a thing, as you very well know, dear Diva, I am not ashamed
to confess it.'

'Of course you were wrong,' said Diva cordially, 'if Mr Wyse's
account of it is correct. You sent the pictures back, such beauties,

too, with a formal rejection from the hanging committee when they had never seen them at all. So rash, too: I wonder at you.'

These unfavourable comments did not make the transaction appear any the less irregular.

'I said I was wrong, Diva,' remarked Elizabeth with some asperity, 'and I should have thought that was enough. And now Mr Wyse, raking bygones up again in the way he has, has written to me to say that he and Susan resign their places on the hanging committee.'

'I know: they told everybody,' said Diva. 'Awkward. What are you going to do?'

The barometer had jerked alarmingly downwards on this renewed tapping.

'I shall cry *peccavi*,' said Elizabeth, with the air of doing something exceedingly noble. 'I shall myself resign. That will show that whatever anybody else does, I am doing the best in my power to put right a technical error. I hope Mr Wyse will appreciate that, and be ashamed of the letter he wrote me. More than that, I shall regard his letter as having been written in a fit of temporary insanity, which I trust will not recur.'

'Yes; I suppose that's the best thing you can do,' said Diva. 'It will show him that you regret what you did, now that it's all found out.'

'That is not generous of you, Diva,' cried Elizabeth, 'I am sorry you said that.'

'More than I am,' said Diva. 'It's a very fair statement. Isn't it now? What's wrong with it?'

Elizabeth suddenly perceived that at this crisis it was unwise to indulge in her usual tiffs with Diva. She wanted allies.

'Diva, dear, we mustn't quarrel,' she said. 'That would never do. I felt I had to pop in to consult you as to the right course to take with Mr Wyse, and I'm so glad you agree with me. How I trust your judgement! I must be going. What a delightful evening we have in store for us. Major Benjy was thinking of declining, but I persuaded him it would not be kind. A house-warming, you know. Such a special occasion.'

The evening to which everybody had looked forward so much was, in the main, a disappointment to bellicose spirits. Nothing could exceed Lucia's cordiality to Elizabeth unless it was Elizabeth's to Lucia: they left the dining room at the end of dinner with arms and waists intertwined, a very bitter sight. They then played bridge at the same table, and so loaded each other with compliments while deploring their own errors, that Diva began to entertain the most serious fears that they had been mean enough to make it up on the sly, or that Lucia in a spirit of Christian forbearance, positively unnatural, had decided to overlook all the attacks and insults with which Elizabeth had tried to provoke her. Or did Lucia think that this degrading display of magnanimity was a weapon by which she would secure victory, by enlisting for her the sympathy and applause of Tilling? If so, that was a great mistake; Tilling did not want to witness a demonstration of forgiveness or white feathers but a combat without quarter. Again, if she thought that such nobility would soften the malevolent heart of Mapp, she showed a distressing ignorance of Mapp's nature, for she would quite properly construe this as not being nobility at all but the most ignoble cowardice. There was Georgie under Lucia's very nose, interlarding his conversation with far more 'Elizabeths' than was in the least necessary to show that he was talking to her, and she volleyed 'Georgies' at him in return. Every now and then, when these discharges of Christian names had been particularly resonant, Elizabeth caught Diva's eye with a glance of triumph as if to remind her that she had prophesied that Lulu would be all sweetness and cordiality, and Diva turned away sick at heart.

On the other hand, there were still grounds for hope, and, as the evening went on, these became more promising: they were like small caps of foam and cats'-paws of wind upon a tranquil sea. To begin with, it was only this morning that the baseness of Elizabeth in that matter concerning the art committee had come to light. Georgie, not Lucia, had been directly responsible for that damning disclosure, but it must be supposed that he had acted with her connivance, if not with her express wish, and this certainly did not look so much like forgiveness as a nasty one for Elizabeth. That was hopeful, and Diva's eagle eye espied other signs of bad weather. Elizabeth, encouraged by Lucia's compliments and humilities throughout a long rubber, began to come out more in her true colours, and to explain to her partner that she had lost a few tricks (no matter) by not taking a finesse, or a whole game by not supporting her declaration, and Diva thought she detected a certain dangerous glitter in Lucia's eye as she bent to these chastisements. Surely, too, she bit her lip when Elizabeth suddenly began to call her Lulu again. Then there was Irene's conduct to consider: Irene was fizzing and fidgeting in her chair, she cast glances of black hatred at Elizabeth, and once Diva distinctly saw Lucia frown and shake her head at her. Again, at the voluptuous supper which succeeded many rubbers of bridge, there was the famous lobster *à la Riseholme*. It had become, as all Tilling knew, a positive obsession with Elizabeth to get the secret of that delicious dish, and now, flushed with continuous victories at bridge and with Lucia's persevering pleasantness, she made another direct request for it.

'Lulu dear,' she said, 'it would be sweet of you to give me the recipe for your lobster. So good . . .'

Diva felt this to be a crucial moment: Lucia had often refused it before, but now if she was wholly Christian and cowardly she would consent. But once more she gave no reply, and asked the Padre on what day of the week Christmas fell. So Diva heaved a sigh of relief, for there was still hope,

In spite of this rebuff, it was hardly to be wondered at that Elizabeth felt in a high state of elation when the evening was over. The returning revellers changed the order of their going, and Georgie took back her and Diva. He went outside with Diva, for, during the last half-hour, Mapp (as he now mentally termed her in order to be done with Elizabeth) had grown like a mushroom in complaisance and self-confidence, and he could not trust himself, if she went on, as she would no doubt do, in the same strain, not to rap out something very sharp. 'Let her just wait,' he thought, 'she'll soon be singing a different tune.'

Georgie's precautions in going outside, well wrapped up in his cap and his fur tippet and his fur rug, were well founded, for hardly had Mapp kissed her hand for the last time to Lulu (who would come to the door to see them off), and counted over the money she had won, than she burst into staves of intolerable triumph and condescension.

'So that's that!' she said, pulling up the window. 'And if I was to ask you, dear Diva, which of us was right about how this evening would go off, I don't think there would be very much doubt about the answer. Did you ever see Lulu so terribly anxious to please me? And did you happen to hear me say Georgie and him say Elizabeth? Lulu didn't like it, I am sure, but she had to swallow her medicine, and she did so with a very good grace, I am bound to say. She just wanted a little lesson, and I think I may say I've given it her. I had no idea, I will confess, that she would take it lying down like that. I just had to lean out of the window, pretend not to see her, and talk to Georgie in that silly voice and language and the thing was done.'

Diva had been talking simultaneously for some time, but Elizabeth only paused to take breath, and went on in a slightly louder tone. So Diva talked louder too, until Georgie turned round to see what was happening. They both broke off, and smiled at him, and then both began again.

'If you would allow me to get a word in edgeways,' said Diva, who had some solid arguments to produce, and, had she not been a lady, could have slapped Mapp's face in impotent rage –

'I don't think,' said Elizabeth, 'that we shall have much more trouble with her and her queenly airs. Quite a pleasant house-warming, and there was no doubt that the house wanted it, for it was bitterly cold in the dining room, and I strongly suspect that chicken cream of being rabbit. She only had to be shown that whatever Riseholme may have stood from her in the way of condescensions and graces, she had better not try them on at Tilling. She was looking forward to teaching us, and ruling us and guiding us. Pop! Elizabeth (that's me, dear!) has a little lamb, which lives at Grebe and gives a house-warming, so you may guess who *that* is. The way she flattered and sued tonight over our cards when but a few weeks ago she was thinking of holding bridge classes – '

'You were just as bad,' shouted Diva. 'You told her she played beauti –'

'She was "all over me", to use that dreadful slang expression of Major Benjy's,' continued Mapp. 'She was like a dog that has had a scolding and begs – so prettily – to be forgiven. Mind, dear, I do not say that she is a bad sort of woman by any means, but she required to be put in her place, and Tilling ought to thank me for having done so. Dear me, here we are already at your house. How short the drive has seemed!'

'Anyhow, you didn't get the recipe for the lobster *à la Riseholme*,' said Diva, for this was one of the things she most wanted to say.

'A little final wriggle,' said Mapp. 'I have not the least doubt that she will think it over and send it me tomorrow. Good night, darling. I shall be sending out invitations for a cosy evening of bridge some time at the end of this week.'

The baffled Diva let herself into Wasters in low spirits, so convinced and lucid had been Mapp's comments on the evening. It was such a dismal conclusion to so much excitement; and all that thrilling tension, instead of snapping, had relaxed into the most depressing slackness. But she did not quite give up hope, for there had been cats'-paws and caps of foam on the tranquil sea. She fell asleep visualizing these.

CHAPTER NINE

Though Georgie had thought that the garden room would have to give him at least two more sittings before his sketch arrived at that high state of finish which he, like the Pre-Raphaelites, regarded as necessary to any work of art, he decided that he would leave it in a more impressionist state, and sent it next morning to be framed. In consequence the glass of water which Elizabeth had brought out for him in anticipation of his now usual visit at eleven o'clock remained unsullied by washings from his brush, and at twelve, Elizabeth, being rather thirsty in consequence of so late a supper the night before, drank it herself. On the second morning, a very wet one, Major Benjy did not go out for his usual round of golf, and again Georgie did not come to paint. But at a few minutes to one she observed that his car was at the door of Mallards Cottage; it passed her window, it stopped at Major Benjy's, and he got in. It was impossible not to remember that Lucia always lunched at one in the winter because a later hour for *colazione* made the afternoon so short. But it was a surprise to see Major Benjy driving away with Miss Milliner Michael-Angelo, and difficult to conjecture where else it was at all likely that they could have gone.

There was half an hour yet to her own luncheon, and she wrote seven postcards inviting seven friends to tea on Saturday, with bridge to follow. The Wyses, the Padres, Diva, Major Benjy and Georgie were the *destinataires* of these missives; these, with herself, made eight, and there would thus be two tables of agreeable gamblers. Lucia was not to be favoured: it would be salutary for her to be left out every now and then, just to impress upon her the lesson of which she had stood so sadly in need. She must learn to go to heel, to come when called, and to produce recipes when desired, which at present she had not done.

There had been several days of heavy rain, but early in the afternoon it cleared up, and Elizabeth set out for a brisk healthy walk. The field paths would certainly make very miry going, for she saw from the end of the High Street that there was much water lying in the marsh, and she therefore kept to that excellent road, which, having passed Grebe, went nowhere particular. She was prepared to go in and thank Lucia for her lovely house-warming, in order to make sure whether Georgie and Major Benjy had gone to lunch with her, but no such humiliating need occurred, for there in front of the house was drawn up Georgie's motor car, so (whether she liked it or not, and she didn't) *that* problem was solved. The house stood quite close to the road: a flagged pathway of half a dozen yards, flanked at the entrance gate by thick hornbeam hedges on which the leaf still lingered, separated it from the road, and just as Elizabeth passed Georgie's car drawn up there, the front door opened, and she saw Lucia and her two guests on the threshold. Major Benjy was laughing in that fat voice of his, and Georgie was giving forth his shrill little neighs like a colt with a half-cracked voice.

The temptation to know what they were laughing at was irresistible. Elizabeth moved a few steps on and, screened by the hornbeam hedge, held her breath.

Major Benjy gave another great haw-haw and spoke.

''Pon my word, did she really?' he said. 'Do it again, Mrs Lucas. Never laughed so much in my life. Infernal impertinence!'

There was no mistaking the voice and the words that followed.

''Oo is vewy naughty boy, Georgie,' said Lucia. 'Never ring Elizabeth's belly-pelly –'

Elizabeth hurried on, as she heard steps coming down that short flagged pathway. But hurry as she might, she heard a little more.

''Oo walk straight in always and sing out for her,' continued the voice, repeating word for word the speech of which she had been so proud. 'There's no chain up' – and then came loathsome parody – 'now that Liblib has *ritornata* to *Mallardino.*'

It was in a scared mood, as if she had heard or seen a ghost, that Elizabeth hastened along up the road that led nowhere in particular, before Lucia's guests could emerge from the gate. Luckily at the end of the kitchen garden the hornbeam hedge turned at right

angles, and behind this bastion she hid herself till she heard the
motor move away in the direction of Tilling, the prey of the most
agitated misgivings. Was it possible that her own speech, which she
had thought had scarified Lucia's pride, was being turned into a
mockery and a derision against herself? It seemed not only possible
but probable. And how dare Mrs Lucas invent and repeat as if
spoken by herself that rubbish about *ritornata* and *Mallardino*?
Never in her life had she said such a thing.

When the coast was clear, she took the road again, and
walked quickly on away from Tilling. The tide was very high, for
the river was swollen with rain, and the waters overbrimmed its
channel and extended in a great lake up to the foot of the bank
and dyke which bounded the road. Perturbed as she was, Miss
Mapp could not help admiring that broad expanse of water, now
lit by a gleam of sun, in front of which to the westward, the hill
of Tilling rose dark against a sky already growing red with the
winter sunset. She had just turned a corner in the road, and
now she perceived that close ahead of her somebody else was
admiring it too in a more practical manner, for there by the
roadside within twenty yards of her sat quaint Irene, with her
mouth full of paintbrushes and an easel set up in front of her.
She had not seen Irene since the night of the house-warming,
when the quaint one had not been very cordial, and so, thinking
she had walked far enough, she turned back. But Irene had quite
evidently seen her, for she shaded her eyes for a moment against
the glare, took some of the paintbrushes out of her mouth and
called to her with words that seemed to have what might be
termed a dangerous undertow.

'Hello, Mapp,' she said. 'Been lunching with Lulu?'

'What a lovely sketch, dear,' said Mapp. 'No, just a brisk little
walk. Not been lunching at Grebe today.'

Irene laughed hoarsely.

'I didn't think it was very likely, but thought I would ask,' she
said. 'Yes; I'm rather pleased with my sketch. A bloody look about
the sunlight, isn't there, as if the Day of Judgement was coming.
I'm going to send it to the winter exhibition of the Art Club.'

'Dear girlie, what do you mean?' asked Mapp. 'We don't have
winter exhibitions.'

'No, but we're going to,' said girlie. 'A new hanging committee, you see, full of pep and pop and vim. Haven't they asked you to send them something . . . Of course the space at their disposal is very limited.'

Mapp laughed, but not with any great exuberance. This undertow was tweaking at her disagreeably.

'That's news to me,' she said. 'Most enterprising of Mr Wyse and dear Susan.'

'Sweet Lulu's idea,' said Irene. 'As soon as you sent in your resignation, of course they asked her to be president.'

'That is nice for her,' said Mapp enthusiastically. 'She will like that. I must get to work on some little picky to send them.'

'There's that one you did from the church tower when Lucia had influenza,' said this awful Irene. 'That would be nice . . . Oh, I forgot. Stupid of me. It's by invitation: the committee are asking a few people to send pickies. No doubt they'll beg you for one. Such a good plan. There won't be any mistakes in the future about rejecting what is sent in.'

Mapp gave a gulp but rallied.

'I see. They'll be all Academicians together, and be hung on the line,' said she unflinchingly.

'Yes. On the line or be put on easels,' said Irene. 'Curse the light! It's fading. I must pack up. Hold these brushes, will you?'

'And then we'll walk back home together, shall we? A cup of tea with me, dear?' asked Mapp, anxious to conciliate and to know more.

'I'm going into Lucia's, I'm afraid. Wyses tummin' to play bridgey and hold a committee meeting,' said Irene.

'You are a cruel thing to imitate poor Lulu,' said Mapp. 'How well you've caught that silly baby talk of hers. Just her voice. Bye-bye.'

'Same to you,' said Irene.

*　　*　　*

There was undoubtedly, thought Mapp, as she scudded swiftly homewards alone, a sort of mocking note about quaint Irene's conversation, which she did not relish. It was full of hints and awkward allusions; it bristled with hidden menace, and even her imitation of Lucia's baby talk was not wholly satisfactory, for quaint Irene might be mimicking her imitation of Lucia, even as Lucia herself had done, and there was very little humour in that. Presently she passed the Wyses' Royce going to Grebe. She kissed her hand to a mound of sables inside, but it was too dark to see if the salute was returned. Her brisk afternoon's walk had not freshened her up; she was aware of a feeling of fatigue, of a vague depression and anxiety. And mixed with that was a hunger not only for tea but for more information. There seemed to be things going on of which she was sadly ignorant, and even when her ignorance was enlightened, they remained rather sad. But Diva (such a gossip) might know more about this winter exhibition, and she popped into Wasters. Diva was in, and begged her to wait for tea: she would be down in a few minutes.

It was a cosy little room, looking out on to the garden which had yielded her so many pots of excellent preserves during the summer, but dreadfully untidy, as Diva's house always was. There was a litter of papers on the table, notes half-thrust back into their envelopes, crossword puzzles cut out from the *Evening Standard* and partially solved: there was her own postcard to Diva sent off that morning and already delivered, and there was a sheet of paper with the stamp of Grebe upon it and Lucia's monogram, which seemed to force itself on Elizabeth's eye. The most cursory glance revealed that this was a request from the art committee that Mrs Plaistow would do them the honour to send them a couple of her sketches for the forthcoming winter exhibition. All the time there came from Diva's bedroom, directly overhead, the sound of rhythmical steps or thumps, most difficult to explain. In a few minutes these ceased, and Diva's tread on the stairs gave Elizabeth sufficient warning to enable her to snatch up the first book that came to hand, and sink into a chair by the fire. She saw, with some feeling of apprehension similar to those which had haunted her all afternoon, that this was a copy of *An Ideal System of Callisthenics For Those No Longer Young*, of which she seemed to have heard. On the title page was an inscription 'Diva from Lucia', and in brackets, like a prescription, 'Ten minutes at the exercises in Chapter I, twice a day for the present.'

Diva entered very briskly. She was redder in the face than usual, and, so Elizabeth instantly noticed, lifted her feet very high as she walked, and held her head well back and her breast out like a fat little pigeon. This time there was to be no question about getting a word in edgeways, for she began to talk before the door was fully open.

'Glad to see you, Elizabeth,' she said, 'and I shall be very pleased to play bridge on Saturday. I've never felt so well in my life, do you know, and I've only been doing them two days. Oh, I see you've got the book.'

'I heard you stamping and thumping, dear,' said Elizabeth. 'Was that them?'

'Yes, twice a day, ten minutes each time. It clears the head, too. If you sit down to a crossword puzzle afterwards you find you're much brighter than usual.'

'Callisthenics *à la Lucia?*' asked Elizabeth.

'Yes. Irene and Mrs Bartlett and I all do them, and Mrs Wyse is going to begin, but rather more gently. Hasn't Lucia told you about them?'

Here was another revelation of things happening. Elizabeth met it bravely.

'No. Dear Lulu knows my feelings about that sort of fad. A brisk walk such as I've had this afternoon is all I require. Such lovely lights of sunset and a very high tide. Quaint Irene was sketching on the road just beyond Grebe.'

'Yes. She's going to send it in and three more for the winter exhibition. Oh, perhaps you haven't heard. There's to be an exhibition directly after Christmas.'

'Such a good idea: I've been discussing it,' said Elizabeth.

Diva's eye travelled swiftly and suspiciously to the table where this flattering request to her lay on the top of the litter. Elizabeth did not fail to catch the significance of this.

'Irene told me,' she said hastily, 'I must see if I can find time to do them something.'

'Oh, then they have asked you,' said Diva with a shade of disappointment in her voice. 'They've asked me too – '

'No! Really?' said Elizabeth.

' – so of course I said yes, but I'm afraid I'm rather out of practice. Lucia is going to give an address on modern art at the opening, and then we shall all go round and look at each other's pictures.'

'What fun!' said Elizabeth cordially.

Tea had been brought in. There was a pot of greenish jam and Elizabeth loaded her buttered toast with it, and put it into her mouth. She gave a choking cry and washed it down with a gulp of tea.

'Anything wrong?' asked Diva.

'Yes, dear. I'm afraid it's fermenting,' said Elizabeth, laying down the rest of her toast. 'And I can't conceive what it's made of.'

Diva looked at the pot.

'You ought to know,' she said. 'It's one of the pots you gave me. Labelled vegetable marrow. So sorry it's not eatable. By the way, talking of food, did Lucia send you the recipe for the lobster?'

Elizabeth smiled her sweetest.

'Dear Lucia,' she said. 'She's been so busy with art and callisthenics. She must have forgotten. I shall jog her memory.'

The afternoon had been full of rather unpleasant surprises, thought Elizabeth to herself, as she went up to Mallards that evening. They were concerned with local activities, art and gymnastics, of which she had hitherto heard nothing, and they all seemed to show a common origin: there was a hidden hand directing them. This was disconcerting, especially since, only a few nights ago, she had felt so sure that that hand had been upraised to her, beseeching pardon. Now it rather looked as if that hand had spirited itself away and was very busy and energetic on its own account.

She paused on her doorstep. There was a light shining out through chinks behind the curtains in Mallards Cottage, and she thought it would be a good thing to pop in on Georgie and see if she could gather some further gleanings. She would make herself extremely pleasant: she would admire his needlework if he was at it, she would praise the beautiful specklessness of his room, for Georgie always appreciated any compliment to Foljambe, she would sing the praises of Lucia, though they blistered her tongue.

Foljambe admitted her. The door of the sitting room was ajar, and as she put down her umbrella, she heard Georgie's voice talking to the telephone.

'Saturday, half-past four,' he said. 'I've just found a postcard. Hasn't she asked you?'

Georgie, as Elizabeth had often observed, was deafer than he knew (which accounted for his not hearing all the wrong notes she played in his duets with Lucia) and he had not heard her entry, though Foljambe spoke her name quite loud. He was listening with rapt attention to what was coming through and saying 'My dear!' or 'No!' at intervals. Now, however, he turned and saw her, and with a scared expression hung up the receiver.

'Dear me, I never heard you come in!' he said. 'How nice! I was just going to tell Foljambe to bring up tea. Two cups, Foljambe.'

'I'm interrupting you,' said Elizabeth. 'I can see you were just settling down to your sewing and a cosy bachelor evening.'

'Not a bit,' said Georgie. 'Do have a chair near the fire.' It was not necessary to explain that she had already had tea with Diva, even if one mouthful of fermenting vegetable could properly be called tea, and she took the chair he pulled up for her.

'Such beautiful work,' she said, looking at Georgie's tambour of *petit point*, which lay near by. 'What eyes you must have to be able to do it.'

'Yes, they're pretty good yet,' said Georgie, slipping his spectacle case into his pocket. 'And I shall be delighted to come to tea and bridge on Saturday. Thanks so much. Just got your invitation.'

Miss Mapp knew that already.

'That's charming,' she said. 'And how I envy you your Foljambe. Not a speck of dust anywhere. You could eat your tea off the floor, as they say.'

Georgie noticed that she did not use his Christian name. This confirmed his belief that the employment of it was reserved for Lucia's presence as an annoyance to her. Then the telephone bell rang again.

'May I?' said Georgie.

He went across to it, rather nervous. It was as he thought: Lucia was at it again, explaining that somebody had cut her off. Listen as she might, Miss Mapp, from where she sat, could only hear a confused quacking noise. So to show how indifferent she was as to the conversation, she put her fingers close to her ears ready to stop them when Georgie turned round again, and listened hard to what he said.

'Yes . . . yes,' said Georgie. 'Thanks so much – lovely. I'll pick him up then, shall I? Quarter to eight, is it? Yes, her too. Yes, I've done them once today: not a bit giddy . . . I can't stop now, Lucia. Miss Ma – Elizabeth's just come in for a cup of tea . . . I'll tell her.'

Elizabeth felt she understood all this; she was an adept at telephonic reconstruction. There was evidently another party at Grebe. 'Him' and 'her' no doubt were Major Benjy and herself, whom Georgie would pick up as before. 'Them' were exercises, and Georgie's promise to tell 'her' clearly meant that he should convey an invitation. This was satisfactory: evidently Lucia was hoping to propitiate. Then Georgie turned round and saw Elizabeth smiling gaily at the fire with her hands over her ears. He moved into her field of vision and she uncorked herself.

'Finished?' she said. 'Hope you did not cut it short because of me.'

'Not at all,' said Georgie, for she couldn't (unless she was pretending) have heard him say that he had done precisely that. 'It was Lucia ringing up. She sends you her love.'

'Sweet of her, such a pet,' said Elizabeth, and waited for more about picking up and that Invitation. But Lucia's love appeared to be all, and Georgie asked her if she took sugar. She did, and tried if he in turn would take another sort of sugar, both for himself and Lucia.

'Such a lovely house-warming,' she said, 'and how we all enjoyed ourselves. Lucia seems to have time for everything, bridge, those lovely duets with you, Italian, Greek (though we haven't heard much about that lately), a winter art exhibition, and an address (how I shall look forward to it!) on modern art, callisthenics – '

'Oh, you ought to try those,' said Georgie. 'You stretch and stamp and feel ever so young afterwards. We're all doing them.'

'And does she take classes as she threat – promised to do?' asked Elizabeth.

'She will when we've mastered the elements,' said Georgie. 'We shall march round the kitchen garden at Grebe – cinder paths you know, so good in wet weather – keeping time, and then skip and flex and jerk. And if it's raining we shall do them in the kitchen.

You can throw open those double doors, and have plenty of fresh air which is so important. There's that enormous kitchen table too, to hold on to, when we're doing that swimming movement. It's like a great raft.'

Elizabeth had not the nerve to ask if Major Benjy was to be of that company. It would be too bitter to know that he, who had so sternly set his face against Lucia's domination, was in process of being sucked down in that infernal whirlpool of her energetic grabbings. Almost she wished that she had asked her to be one of her bridge party tomorrow: but it was too late now. Her seven invitations – seven against Lucia – had gone forth, and not till she got home would she know whether her two bridge tables were full.

'And this winter exhibition,' she asked. 'What a good idea! We're all so idle in the winter at dear old Tilling, and now there's another thing to work for. Are you sending that delicious picture of the garden room? How I enjoyed our lovely chatty mornings when you were painting it!'

By the ordinary rules of polite conversation, Georgie ought to have asked her what she was sending. He did nothing of the kind, but looked a little uncomfortable. Probably then, as Irene had told her, the exhibition was to consist of pictures sent by request of the committee, and at present they had not requested her. She felt that she must make sure about that, and determined to send in a picture without being asked. That would show for certain what was going on.

'Weren't those mornings pleasant?' said the evasive Georgie. 'I was quite sorry when my picture was finished.'

Georgie appeared unusually reticent: he did not volunteer any more information about the winter exhibition, nor about Lucia's telephoning, nor had he mentioned that he and Major Benjy had lunched with her today. She would lead him in the direction of that topic . . .

'How happy dear Lucia is in her pretty Grebe,' she said. 'I took my walk along the road there today. Her garden, so pleasant! A high tide this afternoon. The beautiful river flowing down to the sea, and the tide coming up to meet it. Did you notice it?'

Georgie easily saw through that: he would talk about tides with pleasure, but not lunch.

'It looked lovely,' he said, 'but they tell me that in ten days' time the spring tides are on, and they will be much higher. The water has been over the road in front of Lucia's house sometimes.'

Elizabeth went back to Mallards more uneasy than ever. Lucia was indeed busy arranging callisthenic classes and winter exhibitions and, clearly, some party at Grebe, but not a word had she said to her about any of these things, nor had she sent the recipe for lobster *à la Riseholme*. But there was nothing more to be done tonight except to take steps concerning the picture exhibition to which she had not been asked to contribute. The house was full of her sketches, and she selected quite the best of them and directed Withers to pack it up and send it, with her card, to the Committee of the Art Club, Grebe.

*   *   *

The winter bridge parties in Tilling were in their main features of a fixed and invariable pattern. An exceedingly substantial tea, including potted-meat sandwiches, was served at half-past four, and, after that was disposed of, at least three hours of bridge followed. After such a tea, nobody, as was perfectly well known, dreamed of having dinner: and though round about eight o'clock, the party broke up, with cries of astonishment at the lateness of the hour, and said it must fly back home to dress, this was a mere fashion of speech. 'A tray' was the utmost refreshment that anyone could require, and nobody dressed for a solitary tray. Elizabeth was a great upholder of the dress-and-dinner fiction, and she had been known to leave a bridge party at nine, saying that Withers would scold her for being so late, and that her cook would be furious.

So on this Saturday afternoon the party of eight (for all seven had accepted) assembled at Mallards. They were exceedingly cordial: it was as if they desired to propitiate their hostess for something presently to emerge. Also it struck that powerful observer that there was not nearly so much eaten as usual. She had provided the caviare sandwiches of which Mrs Wyse had been known absentmindedly to eat nine, she had provided the nougat chocolates of which Diva had been known to have eaten all, but though the chocolates were in front of Diva, and the caviare in front of Susan, neither of them exhibited anything resembling their usual greed. There was Scotch shortbread for the Padre, who, though he came from Birmingham, was insatiable with regard to that national form of biscuit, and there was whisky and soda for Major Benjy, who had no use for tea, and both of them, too, were mysteriously abstemious. Perhaps this wet muggy weather, thought Elizabeth, had made them all a trifle liverish, or very likely those callisthenics had taken away their appetites. It was noticeable, moreover, that throughout tea nobody mentioned the name of Lucia.

They adjourned to the garden room where two tables were set out for bridge, and till half-past six nothing momentous occurred. At that hour Elizabeth was partner to Major Benjy, and she observed with dark misgivings that when she had secured the play of the hand (at a staggering sacrifice, as it was soon to prove) he did not as usual watch her play, but got up, and standing by the fireplace indulged in some very antic movements. He bent down, apparently trying to touch his toes with his fingers and a perfect fusillade of small crackling noises from his joints (knee or hip it was impossible to tell) accompanied these athletic flexings. Then he whisked himself round to right and left as if trying to look down his back, like a parrot. This was odd and ominous conduct, this strongly suggested that he had been sucked into the callisthenic whirlpool, and what was more ominous yet was that when he sat down again he whispered to Georgie, who was at the same table, 'That makes my ten minutes, old boy.' Elizabeth did not like that at all. She knew now what the ten minutes must refer to, and that endearing form of address to Miss Milliner Michael-Angelo was a little worrying. The only consolation was that Georgie's attention was diverted from the game, and that he trumped his partner's best card. At the conclusion of the hand, Elizabeth was three tricks short of her contract, and another very puzzling surprise awaited her, for instead of Major Benjy taking her failure in very ill part, he was more than pleasant about it. What could be the matter with him?

'Very well played, Miss Elizabeth,' he said. 'I was afraid that after my inexcusable declaration we should lose more than that.'

Elizabeth began to feel more keenly puzzled as to why none of them had any appetites, and why they were all so pleasant to her. Were they rallying round her again, was their silence about Lucia a tactful approval of her absence? Or was there some hidden connection between their abstemiousness, their reticence and their unwontedly propitiatory attitude? If there was, it quite eluded her. Then as Diva dealt in her sloppy manner Lucia's name came up for the first time.

'Mr Georgie, you ought not to have led trumps,' she said. 'Lucia always says – Oh, dear me, I believe I've misdealt. Oh no, I haven't. That's all right.'

Elizabeth pondered this as she sorted her cards. Nobody enquired what Lucia said, and Diva's swift changing of the subject as if that name had slipped out by accident, looked as if possibly they none of them desired any allusion to be made to her. Had they done with her? she wondered. But if so, what about the callisthenics?

She was dummy now and was absorbed in watching Major Benjy's tragical mismanagement of the hand, for he was getting into a sadder bungle than anyone, except perhaps Lucia, could have involved himself in. Withers entered while this was going on, and gave Elizabeth a parcel. With her eye and her mind still glued to the cards, she absently unwrapped it, and took its contents from its coverings just as the last trick was being played. It was the picture she had sent to the art committee the day before and with it was a typewritten form to convey its regrets that the limited wall space at its disposal would not permit of Miss Mapp's picture being exhibited. This slip floated out on to the floor, and Georgie bent down and returned it to her. She handed it and the picture and the wrappings to Withers, and told her to put them in the cupboard. Then she leaned over the table to her partner, livid with mixed and uncontrollable emotions.

'Dear Major Benjy, what a hash!' she said. 'If you had pulled out your cards at random from your hand, you could not, bar revokes, have done worse. I think you must have been having lessons from dear Lulu. Never mind: live and unlearn.'

There was an awful pause. Even the players at the other table were stricken into immobility and looked at each other with imbecile eyes. Then the most surprising thing of all happened.

''Pon my word, partner,' said Major Benjy, 'I deserve all the scoldings you can give me. I played it like a baby. I deserve to pay all our losings. A thousand apologies.'

Elizabeth, though she did not feel like it, had to show that she was generous too. But why didn't he answer her back in the usual manner?

'Naughty Major Benjy!' she said. 'But what does it matter? It's only a game, and we all have our ups and downs. I have them myself. That's the rubber, isn't it? Not very expensive after all. Now let us have another and forget all about this one.'

Diva drew a long breath, as if making up her mind to something, and glanced at the watch set with false pearls (Elizabeth was sure) on her wrist.

'Rather late to begin again,' she said. 'I make it ten minutes to seven. I think I ought to be going to dress.'

'Nonsense, dear,' said Elizabeth. 'Much too early to leave off. Cut, Major Benjy.'

He also appeared to take his courage in his hands, not very successfully.

'Well, upon my word, do you know, really Miss Elizabeth,' he babbled, 'a rubber goes on sometimes for a very long while, and if it's close on seven now, if, you know what I mean . . . What do you say, Pillson?'

It was Georgie's turn.

'Too tarsome,' he said, 'but I'm afraid personally that I must stop. Such a delightful evening. Such good rubbers . . .'

They all got up together, as if some common mechanism controlled their movements. Diva scuttled away to the other table, without even waiting to be paid the sum of one and threepence which she had won from Elizabeth.

'I'll see how they're getting on here,' she said. 'Why they're just adding up, too.'

Elizabeth sat where she was and counted out fifteen pennies. That would serve Diva right for going at ten minutes to seven. Then she saw that the others had got up in a hurry, for Susan Wyse said to Mrs Bartlett, 'I'll pay you later on,' and her husband held up her sable coat for her.

'Diva, your winnings,' said Elizabeth, piling up the coppers.

Diva whisked round, and instead of resenting this ponderous discharge of the debt, received it with enthusiasm.

'Thank you, Elizabeth,' she said. 'All coppers: how nice! So useful for change. Good night, dear. Thanks ever so much.'

She paused a moment by the door, already open, by which Georgie was standing.

'Then you'll call for me at twenty minutes to eight,' she said to him in the most audible whisper, and Georgie with a nervous glance in Elizabeth's direction gave a silent assent. Diva vanished into the night where Major Benjy had gone. Elizabeth rose from her deserted table.

'But you're not all going too?' she said to the others. 'So early yet.'

Mr Wyse made a profound bow.

'I regret that my wife and I must get home to dress,' he said. 'But one of the most charming evenings of bridge I have ever spent, Miss Mapp. So many thanks. Come along, Susan.'

'Delicious bridge,' said Susan. 'And those caviare sandwiches. Good night, dear. You must come round and play with us some night soon.'

'A grand game of bridge, Mistress Mapp,' said the Padre. 'Ah, wee wifie's callin' for me. *Au reservoir.*'

Next moment Elizabeth was alone. Georgie had followed on the heels of the others, closing the door very carefully, as if she had fallen asleep. Instead of that she hurried to the window and peeped out between the curtains. There were three or four of them standing on the steps while the Wyses got into the Royce, and they dispersed in different directions like detected conspirators, as no doubt they were.

The odd disconnected little incidents of the evening, the lack of appetites, the propitiatory conduct to herself, culminating in this unexampled departure a full hour before bridge parties had ever been known to break up, now grouped themselves together in Elizabeth's constructive mind. They fitted on to other facts that had hitherto seemed unrelated, but now were charged with significance. Georgie, for instance, had telephoned the day and the hour of this bridge party to Lucia, he had accepted an invitation to something at a quarter to eight: he had promised to call for 'him' and 'her'. There could be no reasonable doubt that Lucia had purposely broken up Elizabeth's party at this early hour by bidding to dinner the seven guests who had just slunk away to dress . . . And her picture had been returned by the art committee, two of whom (though she did them the justice to admit that they were but the cat's-paws of a baleful intelligence) had hardly eaten any caviare sandwiches at all, for fear that they should not have good appetites for dinner. Hence also Diva's abstention from nougat chocolate, Major Benjy's from whisky, and the Padre's from shortbread. Nothing could be clearer.

Elizabeth was far from feeling unhappy or deserted, and very very far from feeling beaten. Defiance and hatred warmed her blood most pleasantly, and she spent half an hour sitting by the window, thoroughly enjoying herself. She meant to wait here till twenty minutes to eight, and if by that time she had not seen the Royce turning the corner of Porpoise Street, and Georgie's car calling at the perfidious Major Benjy's house, she would be ready to go barefoot to Grebe, and beg Lucia's pardon for having attributed to her so devilish a device. But no such humiliating pilgrimage awaited her, for all happened exactly as she knew it would. The great glaring headlights of the Royce blazed on the house opposite the turning to Porpoise Street, its raucous fog-horn sounded, and the porpoise car lurched into view scaring everybody by its lights and its odious voice, and by its size making foot passengers flatten themselves against the walls. Hardly had it cleared the corner into the High Street when Georgie's gay bugle piped out and his car came under the window of the garden room, and stopped at Major Benjy's. Elizabeth's intellect, unaided by any direct outside information, except that which she had overheard on the telephone, had penetrated this hole-and-corner business, and ringing the bell for her tray, she ate the large remainder of caviare sandwiches and nougat chocolate and fed her soul with schemes of reprisals. She could not offhand think of any definite plan of sufficiently withering a nature, and presently, tired with mental activity, she fell into a fireside doze and had a happy dream that Dr Dobbie had popped in to tell her that Lucia had developed undoubted symptoms of leprosy.

* * *

During the positively voluptuous week that followed Elizabeth's brief bridge party, no fresh development occurred of the drama on which Tilling was concentrated, except that Lucia asked Elizabeth to tea and that Elizabeth refused. The rivals therefore did not meet, and neither of them seemed aware of the existence of the other. But both Grebe and Mallards had been inordinately gay; at Grebe there had been many lunches with bridge afterwards, and the guests on several occasions had hurried back for tea and more bridge at Mallards. Indeed, Tilling had never had so much lunch and tea in its life or enjoyed so brilliant a winter season, for Diva and the Wyses and Mrs Padre followed suit in lavish hospitality, and Georgie on one notable morning remembered that he had not had lunch or tea at home for five days; this was a record that beat Riseholme all to fits.

In addition to these gaieties there were celebrated the nuptials of Foljambe and Cadman, conducted from the bride's home, and the disposition of Foljambe's time between days with Georgie and nights with Cadman was working to admiration: everybody was pleased. At Grebe there had been other entertainments as well; the callisthenic class met on alternate days and Lucia in a tunic rather like Artemis, but with a supplementary skirt and scarlet stockings, headed a remarkable procession, consisting of Diva and the Wyses and Georgie and Major Benjy and the Padres and quaint Irene, out on to the cinder path of the kitchen garden, and there they copied her jerks and flexings and whirlings of the arms and touchings of the toes to the great amazement of errand boys who came legitimately to the kitchen door, and others who peered through the hornbeam hedge. On wet days the athletes assembled in the kitchen with doors flung wide to the open air, and astonished the cook with their swimming movements, an arm and leg together, while they held on with the other hand to the great kitchen table. '*Uno, due, tre*,' counted Lucia, and they all kicked out like frogs. And quaint Irene in her knickerbockers, sometimes stood on her head, but nobody else attempted that. Lucia played them soothing music as they rested afterwards in her drawing room; she encouraged Major Benjy to learn his notes on the piano, for she would willingly teach him: she persuaded Susan to take up her singing again, and played '*La ci darem*' for her, while Susan sang it in a thin shrill voice, and Mr Wyse said '*Brava!* How I wish Amelia was here.' Sometimes Lucia read them Pope's translation of the *Iliad* as they drank their lemonade and Major Benjy his whisky and soda, and not content with these diversions (the wonderful creature) she was composing the address on modern art which she was to deliver at the opening of the exhibition on the day following Boxing Day. She made notes for it and then dictated to her secretary (Elizabeth Mapp's face was something awful to behold when Diva told her that Lucia had a secretary) who took down what she said on a typewriter. Indeed, Elizabeth's face had never been more awful when she heard that, except when Diva informed her that she was quite certain that Lucia would be delighted to let her join the callisthenic class.

But though, during these days, no act of direct aggression like that of Lucia's dinner party causing Elizabeth's bridge party to break up had been committed on either side, it was generally believed that Elizabeth was not done for yet, and Tilling was on tiptoe, expectant of some 'view halloo' call to show that the chase was astir. She had refused Lucia's invitation to tea, and if she had been done for or gone to earth she would surely have accepted. Probably she took the view that the invitation was merely a test question to see how she was getting on, and her refusal showed that she was getting on very nicely. It would be absolutely unlike Elizabeth (to adopt a further metaphor) to throw up the sponge like that, for she had not yet been seriously hurt, and the bridge-party round had certainly been won by Lucia; there would be fierce boxing in the next. It seemed likely that, in this absence of aggressive acts, both antagonists were waiting till the season of peace and goodwill was comfortably over and then they would begin again. Elizabeth would have a God-sent opportunity at the opening of the exhibition, when Lucia delivered her address. She could sit in the front row and pretend to go to sleep or suppress an obvious inclination to laugh. Tilling felt that she must have thought of that and of many other acts of reprisal unless she was no longer the Elizabeth they all knew and (within limits) respected, and (on numerous occasions) detested.

The pleasant custom of sending Christmas cards prevailed in Tilling, and most of the world met in the stationer's shop on Christmas Eve, selecting suitable salutations from the threepenny, the sixpenny and the shilling trays. Elizabeth came in rather early and had almost completed her purchases when some of her friends arrived, and she hung about looking at the backs of volumes in the lending library, but keeping an eye on what they purchased. Diva, she observed, selected nothing from the shilling tray any more than she had herself; in fact, she thought that Diva's purchases this year were made entirely from the threepenny tray. Susan, on the other hand, ignored the threepenny tray and hovered between the six pennies and the shillings and expressed an odiously opulent regret that there were not some 'choicer' cards to be obtained. The Padre and Mrs Bartlett were certainly exclusively threepenny, but that was always the case. However they, like everybody else, studied the other trays, so that when, next morning, they all received seasonable coloured greetings from their friends, a person must have a shocking memory if he did not know what had been the precise cost of all that were sent him. But Georgie and Lucia as was universally noticed, though without comment, had not been in at all, in spite of the fact that they had been seen about in the High Street together and going into other shops. Elizabeth therefore decided that they did not intend to send any Christmas cards and before paying for what she had chosen, she replaced in the threepenny tray a pretty picture of a robin sitting on a sprig of mistletoe which she had meant to send Georgie. There was no need to put back what she had chosen for Lucia, since the case did not arise.

Christmas Day dawned, a stormy morning with a strong gale from the south-west, and on Elizabeth's breakfast table was a pile of letters, which she tore open. Most of them were threepenny Christmas cards, a sixpenny from Susan, smelling of musk, and none from Lucia or Georgie. She had anticipated that, and it was pleasant to think that she had put back into the threepenny tray the one she had selected for him, before purchasing it.

The rest of her post was bills, some of which must be stoutly disputed when Christmas was over, and she found it difficult to realize the jollity appropriate to the day. Last evening various choirs of amateur riff-raffs and shrill bobtails had rendered the night hideous by repetitions of 'Good King Wenceslas' and the 'First Noel', church bells borne on squalls of wind and rain had awakened her while it was still dark and now sprigs of holly kept falling down from the picture frames where Withers had perched them. Bacon made her feel rather better, and she went to church, with a mackintosh against these driving gusts of rain, and a slightly blue nose against this boisterous wind. Diva was coming to a dinner lunch: this was an annual institution held at Wasters and Mallards alternately.

Elizabeth hurried out of church at the conclusion of the service by a side door, not feeling equal to joining in the gay group of her friends who with Lucia as their centre were gathered at the main entrance. The wind was stronger than ever, but the rain had ceased, and she battled her way round the square surrounding the church before she went home. Close to Mallards Cottage she met Georgie holding his hat on against the gale. He wished her a merry Christmas, but then his hat had been whisked off his head; something very strange happened to his hair, which seemed to have been blown off his skull, leaving a quite bare place there, and he vanished in frenzied pursuit of his hat with long tresses growing from the side of his head streaming in the wind. A violent draught eddying round the corner by the garden room propelled her into Mallards holding on to the knocker, and it was with difficulty that she closed the door. On the table in the hall stood a substantial package, which had certainly not been there when she left. Within its wrappings was a *terrine of pâté de foie gras* with a most distinguished label on it, and a card fluttered on to the floor, proclaiming that wishes for a merry Christmas from Lucia and Georgie accompanied it. Elizabeth instantly conquered the feeble temptation of sending this gift back again in the manner in which she had returned that basket of tomatoes from her own garden. Tomatoes were not *pâté*. But what a treat for Diva!

Diva arrived, and they went straight in to the banquet. The *terrine* was wrapped in a napkin, and Withers handed it to Diva. She helped herself handsomely to the truffles and the liver.

'How delicious!' she said. 'And such a monster!'

'I hope it's good,' said Elizabeth, not mentioning the donors. 'It ought to be. Paris.'

Diva suddenly caught sight of a small label pasted below the distinguished one. It was that of the Tilling grocer, and a flood of light poured in upon her.

'Lucia and Mr Georgie have sent such lovely Christmas presents to everybody,' she said. 'I felt quite ashamed of myself for only having given them threepenny cards.'

'How sweet of them,' said Elizabeth. 'What were they?'

'A beautiful box of hard chocolates for me,' said Diva. 'And a great pot of caviare for Susan, and an umbrella for the Padre – his blew inside out in the wind yesterday – and – '

'And this beautiful *pâté* for me,' interrupted Elizabeth, grasping the nettle, for it was obvious that Diva had guessed. 'I was just going to tell you.'

Diva knew that was a lie, but it was no use telling Elizabeth so, because she knew it too, and she tactfully changed the subject.

'I shall have to do my exercises three times today after such a lovely lunch,' she said, as Elizabeth began slicing the turkey. But that was not a well-chosen topic, for subjects connected with Lucia might easily give rise to discord and she tried again and again and again, bumping, in her spinning-top manner, from one impediment to another.

'Major Benjy can play the scale of C with his right hand' – (No, that wouldn't do). 'What an odd voice Susan's got: she sang an Italian song the other day at' – (Worse and worse). 'I sent two pictures to the winter exhibition' – (Worse if possible: there seemed to be no safe topic under the sun). 'A terrific gale, isn't it? There'll be three days of tremendous high tides for the wind is heaping them up. I should not wonder if the road by Grebe – ' (she gave it up: it was no use) ' – isn't flooded tomorrow.'

Elizabeth behaved like a perfect lady. She saw that Diva was doing her best to keep off disagreeable subjects on Christmas Day, but there were really no others. All topics led to Lucia.

'I hope not,' she said, 'for with all the field paths soaked from the rain it is my regular walk just now. But not very likely, dear, for after the last time that the road was flooded, they built the bank opposite – opposite that house much higher.'

They talked for quite a long while about gales and tides and dykes in complete tranquillity. Then the proletarian diversions of Boxing Day seemed safe.

'There's a new film tomorrow at the Picture Palace about tadpoles,' said Elizabeth. 'So strange to think they become toads: or is it frogs? I think I must go.'

'Lucia's giving a Christmas tree for the choirboys in the evening, in that great kitchen of hers,' said Diva.

'How kind!' said Elizabeth hastily, to show she took no offence.

'And in the afternoon there's a whist drive at the Institute,' said Diva. 'I'm letting both my servants go, and Lucia's sending all hers too. I'm not sure I should like to be quite alone in a house along that lonely road. We in the town could scream from a top window if burglars got into our houses and raise the alarm.'

'It would be a very horrid burglar who was so wicked on Boxing Day,' observed Elizabeth sententiously. 'Ah, here's the plum pudding! Blazing beautifully, Withers! So pretty!'

Diva became justifiably somnolent when lunch was over, and after half an hour's careful conversation she went off home to have a nice long nap, which she expressed by the word exercises. Elizabeth wrote two notes of gratitude to the donors of the *pâté* and sat herself down to think seriously of what she could do. She had refused Lucia's invitation to tea a few days before, thus declaring her attitude, and now it seemed to her that that was a mistake, for she had cut herself off from the opportunities of reprisals which intercourse with her might have provided. She had been unable, severed like this, to devise anything at all effective; all she could do was to lie awake at night hating Lucia, and this seemed to be quite barren of results. It might be better (though bitter) to join that callisthenic class in order to get a foot in the enemy's territory. Her note of thanks for the *pâté* would have paved the way towards such a step, and though it would certainly be eating humble pie to ask to join an affair that she had openly derided, it would be pie with a purpose. As it was, for a whole week she had had no opportunities, she had surrounded herself with a smoke cloud, she heard nothing about Lucia any more, except when clumsy Diva let out things by accident. All she knew was that Lucia, busier than any bee known to science, was undoubtedly supreme in all the social activities which she herself had been accustomed to direct, and to remain, like Achilles in his tent, did not lead to anything. Also she had an idea that Tilling expected of her some exhibition of spirit and defiance, and no one was more anxious than she to fulfil those expectations to the utmost. So she settled she would go to Grebe tomorrow, and, after thanking her in person for the *pâté*, ask to join the callisthenic class. Tilling, and Lucia too, no doubt would take that as a sign of surrender, but let them wait a while, and they should see.

'I can't fight her unless I get in touch with her,' reflected Elizabeth; 'at least I don't see how, and I'm sure I've thought enough.'

CHAPTER TEN

In pursuance of this policy Elizabeth set out early in the afternoon next day to walk out to Grebe, and there eat pie with a purpose. The streets were full of holiday folk, and by the railings at the end of the High Street, where the steep steps went down to the levels below, there was a crowd of people looking at the immense expanse of water that lay spread over the marsh. The south-westerly gale had piled up the spring tides, the continuous rains had caused the river to come down in flood, and the meeting of the two, the tide now being at its height, formed a huge lake, a mile and more wide, which stretched seawards. The gale had now quite ceased, the sun shone brilliantly from the pale blue of the winter sky, and this enormous estuary sparkled in the gleam. Far away to the south a great bank of very thick vapour lay over the horizon, showing that out in the Channel there was thick fog, but over Tilling and the flooded marsh the heavens overhead were of a dazzling radiance.

Many of Elizabeth's friends were there, the Padre and his wife (who kept exclaiming in little squeaks, 'Oh dear me, what a quantity of water!'), the Wyses who had dismounted from the Royce, which stood waiting, to look at the great sight, before they proceeded on their afternoon drive. Major Benjy was saying that it was nothing to the Jumna in flood, but then he always held up India as being far ahead of England in every way (he had even once said on an extremely frosty morning, that this was nothing to the bitterness of Bombay): Georgie was there and Diva. With them all Elizabeth exchanged the friendliest greetings, and afterwards, when the great catastrophe had happened, everyone agreed that they had never known her more cordial and pleasant, poor thing. She did not of course tell them what her errand was, for it would be rash to do that till she saw how Lucia received her, but merely said that she was going for her usual brisk walk on this lovely afternoon, and should probably pop into the Picture Palace to learn about tadpoles. With many flutterings of her hand and enough *au reservoir*s to provide water for the world, she tripped down the hill, through the Landgate, and out on to the road that led to Grebe and nowhere else particular.

She passed, as she neared Grebe, Lucia's four indoor servants and Cadman coming into the town, and, remembering that they were going to a whist drive at the Institute, wished them a merry Christmas and hoped that they would all win. (Little kindly remarks like that always pleased servants, thought Elizabeth; they showed a human sympathy with their pleasures, and cost nothing; so much better than Christmas boxes.) Her brisk pace made short work of the distance, and within quite a few minutes of her leaving her friends, she had come to the thick hornbeam hedge which shielded Grebe from the road. She stopped opposite it for a moment: there was that prodigious sheet of dazzling water now close to the top of the restraining bank to admire: there was herself to screw up to the humility required for asking Lucia if she might join her silly callisthenic class. Finally, coming from nowhere, there flashed into her mind the thought of lobster *à la Riseholme*, the recipe for which Lucia had so meanly withheld from her. Instantly that thought fructified into apples of Desire.

She gave one glance at the hornbeam hedge to make sure that she was not visible from the windows of Grebe. (Lucia used often to be seen spying from the windows of the garden room during her tenancy of Mallards, and she might be doing the same thing here.) But the hedge was quite impenetrable to human eye, as Elizabeth had often regretfully observed already, and now instead of going in at the high wooden gate which led to the front door, she passed quickly along till she came to the far corner of the hedge bordering the kitchen garden. So swift was thought to a constructive mind like hers already stung with desire, that, brisk though was her physical movement, her mind easily outstripped it, and her plan was laid before she got to the corner.

Viz.: The servants were all out – of that she had received ocular evidence but a few moments before – and the kitchen would certainly be empty. She would therefore go round to the gate at the end of the kitchen garden and approach the house that way. The cinder path, used for the prancing of the callisthenic class in fine weather, led straight to the big coach-house doors of the kitchen, and she would ascertain by the simple device of trying the handle if these were unlocked. If they were locked, there was an end to her scheme, but if they were unlocked, she would quietly pop in, and see whether the cook's book of recipes was not somewhere about. If it was she would surely find in it the recipe for lobster *à la Riseholme*. A few minutes would suffice to copy it, and then tiptoeing out of the kitchen again, with the key to the mystery in her pocket, she would go round to the front door as cool as a cucumber, and ring the bell. Should Lucia (alone in the house and possibly practising for more po-di-mus) not hear the bell, she would simply postpone the eating of her humble pie till the next day. If, by ill chance, Lucia was in the garden and saw her approaching by this unusual route, nothing was easier than to explain that, returning from her walk, she thought she would look in to thank her for the *pâté* and ask if she might join her callisthenic class. Knowing that the servants were all out (she would glibly explain) she felt sure that the main gate on to the road would be locked, and therefore she tried the back way . . . The whole formation of the scheme was instantaneous; it was as if she had switched on the lights at the door of a long gallery, and found it lit from end to end.

Without hurrying at all she walked down the cinder path and tested the kitchen door. It was unlocked, and she slipped in, closing it quietly behind her. In the centre of the kitchen, decked and ready for illumination, stood the Christmas tree designed for the delectation of the choirboys that evening, and the great kitchen table, with its broad skirting of board halfway down the legs, had been moved away and stood on its side against the dresser in order to give more room for the tree. Elizabeth hardly paused a second to admire the tapers, the reflecting glass balls, the bright tinselly decorations, for she saw a small shelf of books on the wall opposite, and swooped like a merlin on it. There were a few trashy novels, there was a hymn book and a prayer book, and there was a thick volume, with no title on the back, bound in American cloth. She opened it and saw at once that her claws had at last gripped the prey, for on one page was pasted a cutting from the daily press concerning *oeufs à l'aurore*, on the next was a recipe in manuscript for cheese straws. Rapidly she turned the leaves, and there manifest at last was the pearl of great price, lobster *à la Riseholme*. It began with the luscious words, 'Take two hen lobsters.'

Out came her pencil; that and a piece of paper in which had been wrapped a present for a choirboy was all she needed. In a couple of minutes she had copied out the mystic spell, replaced the sacred volume on its shelf, and put in her pocket the information for which she had pined so long. 'How odd,' she cynically reflected, 'that only yesterday I should have said to Diva that it must be a very horrid burglar who was so wicked as to steal things on Boxing Day. Now I'll go round to the front door.'

At the moment when this Mephistophelian thought came into her mind, she heard with a sudden stoppage of her heartbeat, a step on the crisp path outside, and the handle of the kitchen door was turned. Elizabeth took one sideways stride behind the gaudy tree and, peering through its branches, saw Lucia standing at the entrance. Lucia came straight towards her, not yet perceiving that there was a Boxing Day burglar in her own kitchen, and stood admiring her tree. Then with a startled exclamation she called out, 'Who's that?' and Elizabeth knew that she was discovered. Further dodging behind the decorated fir would be both undignified and ineffectual, however skilful her footwork.

'It's me, dear Lucia,' she said. 'I came to thank you in person for that delicious *pâté* and to ask if – '

From somewhere close outside there came a terrific roar and rush as of great water floods released. Reunited for the moment by a startled curiosity, they ran together to the open door, and saw, already leaping across the road and over the hornbeam hedge, a solid wall of water.

'The bank has given way,' cried Lucia. 'Quick, into the house through the door in the kitchen, and up the stairs.'

They fled back past the Christmas tree, and tried the door into the house. It was locked: the servants had evidently taken this precaution before going out on their pleasuring.

'We shall be drowned,' wailed Elizabeth, as the flood came foaming into the kitchen.

'Rubbish,' cried Lucia. 'The kitchen table! We must turn it upside down and get on to it.'

It was but the work of a moment to do this, for the table was already on its side, and the two stepped over the high boarding that ran round it. Would their weight be too great to allow it to float on the rushing water that now deepened rapidly in the kitchen? That anxiety was short-lived, for it rose free from the floor and bumped gently into the Christmas tree.

'We must get out of this,' cried Lucia. 'One doesn't know how much the water will rise. We may be drowned yet if the table legs come against the ceiling. Catch hold of the dresser and pull.'

But there was no need for such exertion, for the flood, eddying fiercely round the submerged kitchen, took them out of the doors that it had flung wide, and in a few minutes they were floating away over the garden and the hornbeam hedge. The tide had evidently begun to ebb before the bank gave way, and now the kitchen table, occasionally turning round in an eddy, moved off in the direction of Tilling and of the sea. Luckily it had not got into the main stream of the river but floated smoothly and swiftly along, with the tide and the torrent of the flood to carry it. Its two occupants, of course, had no control whatever over its direction, but soon, with an upspring of hope, they saw that the current was carrying it straight towards the steep slope above the Landgate, where not more than a quarter of an hour ago Elizabeth had interchanged greetings and *au reservoirs* with her friends who had been looking at the widespread waters. Little had she thought that so soon she would be involved in literal reservoirs of the most gigantic sort – but this was no time for light conceits.

The company of Tillingites was still there when the bank opposite Grebe gave way. All but Georgie had heard the rush and roar of the released waters, but his eyes were sharper than others, and he had been the first to see where the disaster had occurred.

'Look, the bank opposite Grebe has burst!' he cried. 'The road's under water, her garden's under water: the rooms downstairs must be flooded. I hope Lucia's upstairs, or she'll get dreadfully wet.'

'And that road is Elizabeth's favourite walk,' cried Diva. 'She'll be on it now.'

'But she walks so fast,' said the Padre, forgetting to speak

Scotch. 'She'll be past Grebe by now, and above where the bank has burst.'

'Oh dear, oh dear, and on Boxing Day!' wailed Mrs Bartlett.

The huge flood was fast advancing on the town, but with this outlet over the fields, it was evident that it would get no deeper at Grebe, and that, given Lucia was upstairs and that Elizabeth had walked as fast as usual, there was no real anxiety for them. All eyes now watched the progress of the water. It rose like a wave over a rock when it came to the railway line that crossed the marsh and in a couple of minutes more it was foaming over the fields immediately below the town.

Again Georgie uttered woe like Cassandra.

'There's something coming,' he cried. 'It looks like a raft with its legs in the air. And there are two people on it. Now it's spinning round and round; now it's coming straight here ever so fast. There are two women, one without a hat. It's Them! It's Lucia and Miss Mapp! What *has* happened?'

The raft, with legs sometimes madly waltzing, sometimes floating smoothly along, was borne swiftly towards the bottom of the cliff, below which the flood was pouring by. The Padre, with his new umbrella, ran down the steps that led to the road below in order to hook it in, if it approached within umbrella distance. On and on it came, now clearly recognizable as Lucia's great kitchen table upside down, until it was within a yard or two of the bank. To attempt to wade out to it, for any effective purpose, was useless: the strongest would be swept away in such a headlong torrent, and even if he reached the raft there would be three helpless people on it instead of two and it would probably sink. To hook it with the umbrella was the only chance, for there was no time to get a boat hook or a rope to throw out to the passengers. The Padre made a desperate lunge at it, slipped and fell flat into the water, and was only saved from being carried away by clutching at the iron railing alongside the lowest of the submerged steps. Then some fresh current tweaked the table and, still moving in the general direction of the flood water, it sheared off across the fields. As it receded Lucia showed the real stuff of which she was made. She waved her hand and her clear voice rang out gaily across the waste of water.

'*Au reservoir*, all of you,' she cried. 'We'll come back: just wait till we come back,' and she was seen to put her arm round the huddled form of Mapp, and comfort her.

The kitchen table was observed by the watchers to get into the main channel of the river, where the water was swifter yet. It twirled round once or twice as if waving a farewell, and then shot off towards the sea and that great bank of thick mist which hung over the horizon.

There was not yet any reason to despair. A telephone message was instantly sent to the fishermen at the port, another to the coastguards, another to the lifeboat, that a kitchen table with a cargo of ladies on it was coming rapidly down the river, and no effort must be spared to arrest its passage out to sea. But, one after the other, as the short winter afternoon waned, came discouraging messages from the coast. The flood had swept from their moorings all the fishing boats anchored at the port or drawn up on the shore above high-water mark, and a coast-guardsman had seen an unintelligible object go swiftly past the mouth of the river before the telephone message was received. He could not distinguish what it was, for the fog out in the Channel had spread to the coastline, and it had seemed to him more like the heads and necks of four sea-serpents playing together than anything else. But when interrogated as to whether it might be the legs of a kitchen table upside down he acknowledged that the short glimpse which he obtained of it before it got lost in the fog would suit a kitchen table as well as sea serpents. He had said sea serpents because it was in the sea, but it was just as like the legs of a kitchen table, which had never occurred to him as possible. His missus had just such a kitchen table – but as he seemed to be diverging into domestic reminiscences, the Mayor of Tilling, who himself conducted enquiries instead of opening the whist drive at the Institute with a short speech on the sin of gambling, cut him off. It was only too clear that this imaginative naturalist had seen – too late – the kitchen table going out to sea.

The lifeboat had instantly responded to the SOS call on its services, and the great torrent of the flood having now gone by, the crew had been able to launch the boat and had set off to search the English Channel, in the blinding fog, for the table. The tide was setting west down the coast, the flood pouring out from the river mouth was discharged east, but they had gone off to row about in every direction, where the kitchen table might have been carried. Rockets had been sent up from the station in case the ladies didn't know where they were. That, so the Mayor reflected, might conceivably show the ladies where they were, but it didn't really enable them to get anywhere else.

Dusk drew on and the friends of the missing went back to their respective houses, for there was no good in standing about in this dreadful cold fog which had now crept up from the marsh. Pneumonia wouldn't help matters. Four of them, Georgie and Major Benjy and Diva and quaint Irene, lived solitary and celibate, and the prospect of a lonely evening with only suspense and faint hopes to feed upon was perfectly ghastly. In consequence, when each of them in turn was rung up by Mr Wyse, who hoped, in a broken voice, that he might find them disengaged and willing to come round to his house for supper (not dinner), they all gladly accepted. Mr Wyse requested them not to dress as for dinner, and this was felt to show a great delicacy: not dressing would be a sort of symbol of their common anxiety. Supper would be at half-past eight, and Mr Wyse trusted that there would be encouraging news before that hour.

The Padre and Mrs Bartlett had been bidden as well, so that there was a supper party of eight. Supper began with the most delicious caviare, and on the black oak mantelpiece were two threepenny Christmas cards. Susan helped herself plentifully to the caviare. There was no use in not eating.

'Dear Lucia's Christmas present to me,' she said. 'Hers and yours I should say, Mr Georgie.'

'Lucia sent me a wonderful box of nougat chocolates,' said Diva. 'She and you, I mean, Mr Georgie.'

Major Benjy audibly gulped.

'Mrs Lucia,' he said, 'if I may call her so, sent me half a dozen bottles of pre-war whisky.'

The Padre had pulled himself together by this time, and spoke Scotch.

'I had a wee mischance wi' my umbrella two days agone,' he said, 'and Mistress Lucia, such a menseful woman, sent me a new one. An' now that's gone bobbin' out to sea.'

'You're too pessimistic, Kenneth,' said Mrs Bartlett. 'An umbrella soon gets waterlogged and sinks, I tell you. The chances are it will be picked up in the marsh tomorrow, and it'll find its way back to you, for there's that beautiful silver band on the handle with your name engraved on it.'

'Eh, 'twould be a bonnie thing to recover it,' said her husband.

Mr Wyse thought that the conversation was getting a little too much concerned with minor matters; the recovery of an umbrella, though new, was a loss that might be lamented later. Besides, the other missing lady had not been mentioned yet. He pointed to the two threepenny Christmas cards on the mantelpiece.

'Our friend Elizabeth Mapp sent those to my wife and me yesterday,' he said. 'We shall keep them always among our most cherished possessions in case – I mean in any case. Pretty designs. Roofs covered with snow. Holly. Robins. She had a very fine artistic taste. Her pictures had always something striking and original about them.'

Everybody cudgelled their brains for something appropriate to say about Elizabeth's connection with Art. The effort was quite hopeless, for her ignoble trick in rejecting Lucia's and Georgie's pictures for the last exhibition, and the rejection by the new committee of her own for the forthcoming exhibition were all that could occur to the most nimble brain, and while the artist was in direst peril on the sea, or possibly now at rest beneath it, it would be in the worst taste to recall those discordant incidents. A very long pause of silence followed, broken only by the crashing of toast in the mouths of those who had not yet finished their caviare.

Irene had eaten no caviare, nor hitherto had she contributed anything to the conversation. Now she suddenly burst into shrieks of hysterical laughter and sobs.

'What rubbish you're all talking,' she cried, wiping her eyes. 'How can you be so silly? I'm sure I beg your pardons, but there it is. I'll go home, please.'

She fled from the room and banged the front door so loudly that the house shook, and one of Miss Mapp's cards fell into the fireplace.

'Poor thing. Very excitable and uncontrolled,' said Susan. 'But I think she's better alone.'

There was a general feeling of relief that Irene had gone, and as Mrs Wyse's excellent supper progressed, with its cold turkey and its fried slices of plum pudding, its toasted cheese and its figs stuffed with almonds sent by Amelia from Capri, the general numbness caused by the catastrophe began to pass off. Consumed with anxiety as all were for the two (especially one of them) who had vanished into the Channel fogs on so unusual a vehicle, they could not fail to recognize what problems of unparalleled perplexity and interest were involved in what all still hoped might not turn out to be a tragedy. But whether it proved so or not, the whole manner of these happenings, the cause, the conditions, the circumstances which led to the two unhappy ladies whisking by on the flood must be discussed, and presently Major Benjy broke into this unnatural reticence.

'I've seen many floods on the Jumna,' he said, refilling his glass of port, 'but I never saw one so sudden and so – so fraught with enigmas. They must have been in the kitchen. Now we all know there was a Christmas tree there – '

A conversational flood equal to the largest ever seen on the Jumna was unloosed; a torrent of conjectures, and reconstruction after reconstruction of what could have occurred to produce what they had all seen, was examined and rejected as containing some inherent impossibility. And then what did the gallant Lucia's final words mean, when she said, 'Just wait till we come back'? By now discussion had become absolutely untrammelled, the rivalry between the two, Miss Mapp's tricks and pointless meannesses, Lucia's scornful victories, and, no less, her domineering ways were openly alluded to.

'But "Just wait till we come back" is what we're talking about,' cried Diva. 'We must keep to the point, Major Benjy. I believe she simply meant "Don't give up hope. We *shall* come back." And I'm sure they will.'

'No, there's more in it than that,' said Georgie, interrupting. 'I know Lucia better than any of you. She meant that she had something frightfully interesting to tell us when she did come back, as of course she will, and I'd bet it was something about Elizabeth. Some new thing she'd found her out in.'

'But at such a solemn moment,' said the Padre, again forgetting his pseudo-Highland origin, 'when they were being whirled out to sea with death staring them in the face, I hardly think that such trivialities as those which had undoubtedly before caused between those dear ladies the frictions which we all deplored – '

'Nonsense, Kenneth,' said his wife, rather to his relief, for he did not know how he was to get out of this sentence, 'you enjoyed those rows as much as anybody.'

'I don't agree with you, Padre,' said Georgie. 'To begin with, I'm sure Lucia didn't think she was facing death and even if she did, she'd still have been terribly interested in life till she went phut.'

'Thank God I live on a hill,' exclaimed Major Benjy, thinking, as usual, of himself.

Mr Wyse held up his hand. As he was the host, it was only kind to give him a chance, for he had had none as yet. 'Your pardon,' he said, 'if I may venture to suggest what may combine the ideas of our reverend friend and of Mr Pillson' – he made them two bows – 'I think Mrs Lucas felt she was facing death – who wouldn't? – but she was of that vital quality which never gives up interest in life, until, in fact (which we trust with her is not the case), all is over. But like a true Christian, she was, as we all saw, employed in comforting the weak. She could not have been using her last moments, which we hope are nothing of the sort, better. And if there had been frictions, they arose only from the contact of two highly vitalized – '

'She kissed Elizabeth too,' cried Mrs Bartlett. 'I saw her. She hasn't done that for ages. Fancy!'

'I want to get back to the kitchen,' said Diva. 'What could have taken Elizabeth to the kitchen? I've got a brilliant idea, though I don't know what you'll think of it. She knew Lucia was giving a Christmas tree to the choirboys, because I told her so yesterday – '

'I wonder what's happened to that,' said the Padre. 'If it wasn't carried away by the flood, and I think we should have seen it go by, it might be dried.'

Diva, as usual when interrupted, had held her mouth open, and went straight on.

' – and she knew the servants were out, because I'd told her that too, and she very likely wanted to see the Christmas tree. So I suggest that she went round the back way into the kitchen – that would be extremely like her, you know – in order to have a look at it, without asking a favour of – '

'Well, I do call that clever,' interrupted Georgie admiringly. 'Go on. What happened next?'

Diva had not got further than that yet, but now a blinding brilliance illuminated her and she clapped her hands.

'I see, I see,' she cried. 'In she went into the kitchen and while she was looking at it, Lucia came in too, and then the flood came in too. All three of them. That would explain what was behind her words, "Just wait till we come back." She meant that she wanted to tell us that she'd found Elizabeth in her kitchen.'

It was universally felt that Diva had hit it, and after such a stroke of reconstructive genius, any further discussion must be bathos. Instantly a sad reaction set in, and they all looked at each other much shocked to find how wildly interested they had become in these trivial affairs, while their two friends were, to put the most hopeful view of the case, on a kitchen table somewhere in the English Channel. But still Lucia had said that she and her companion were coming back, and though no news had arrived of the castaways, every one of her friends, at the bottom of their hearts, felt that these were not idle words, and that they must keep alive their confidence in Lucia. Miss Mapp alone would certainly have been drowned long ago, but Lucia, whose power of resource all knew to be unlimited, was with her. No one could suggest what she could possibly do in such difficult circumstances, but never yet had she been floored, nor failed to emerge triumphant from the most menacing situations.

Mrs Wyse's cuckoo clock struck the portentous hour of one o'clock. They all sighed, they all got up, they all said good night with melancholy faces, and groped their ways home in the cold fog. Above Georgie's head as he turned the corner by Mallards there loomed the gable of the garden room, where so often a chink of welcoming light had shone between the curtains, as the sound of Mozartino came from within. Dark and full of suspense as was the present, he could still, without the sense of something forever past from his life, imagine himself sitting at the piano again with Lucia, waiting for her *Uno*, *due*, *TRE* as they tried over for the first time the secretly familiar duets.

The whole of the next day this thick fog continued both on land and water, but no news came from seawards save the bleating and hooting of fog-horns, and as the hours passed, anxiety grew more acute. Mrs Wyse opened the picture exhibition on behalf of Lucia, for it was felt that in any case she would have wished that, but owing to the extreme inclemency of the weather only Mr Wyse and Georgie attended this inaugural ceremony. Mrs Wyse in the lamented absence of the authoress read Lucia's lecture on modern art from the typewritten copy which she had sent Georgie to look through and criticize. It lasted an hour and twenty minutes, and after Georgie's applause had died away at the end, Mr Wyse read the speech he had composed to propose a vote of thanks to Lucia for her most enthralling address. This also was rather long, but written in the most classical and urbane style. Georgie seconded this in a shorter speech, and Mrs Wyse (vice Lucia) read another longer speech of Lucia's which was appended in manuscript to her lecture, in which she thanked them for thanking her, and told them how diffident she had felt in thus appearing before them. There was more applause, and then the three of them wandered round the room and peered at each other's pictures through the dense fog. Evening drew in again, without news, and Tilling began to fear the worst.

Next morning there came a mute and terrible message from the sea. The fog had cleared, the day was of crystalline brightness, and since air and exercise would be desirable after sitting at home all the day before, and drinking that wonderful pre-war whisky, Major Benjy set off by the eleven o'clock tram to play a round of golf with the Padre. Though hope was fast expiring, neither of them said anything definitely indicating that they no longer really expected to see their friends again, but there had been talk indirectly bearing on the catastrophe; the Major had asked casually whether Mallards was a freehold, and the Padre replied that both it and Grebe were the property of their occupiers and not held on lease; he also made a distant allusion to memorial services, saying he had been to one lately, very affecting. Then Major Benjy lost his temper with the caddie, and their game assumed a more normal aspect.

They had now come to the eighth hole, the tee of which was

perched high like a pulpit on the sand dunes and overlooked the sea. The match was most exciting: hole after hole had been halved in brilliant sixes and sevens, the players were both on the top of their form, and in their keenness had quite banished from their minds the overshadowing anxiety. Here Major Benjy topped his ball into a clump of bents immediately in front of the tee, and when he had finished swearing at his caddie for moving on the stroke, the Padre put his iron shot on to the green.

'A glorious day,' he exclaimed, and, turning to pick up his clubs, gazed out seawards. The tide was low, and an immense stretch of 'shining sands' as in Charles Kingsley's poem was spread in front of him. Then he gave a gasp.

'What's that?' he said to Major Benjy, pointing with a shaking finger.

'Good God,' said Major Benjy. 'Pick up my ball, caddie.' They scrambled down the steep dunes and walked across the sands to where lay this object which had attracted the Padre's attention. It was an immense kitchen table upside down with its legs in the air, wet with brine but still in perfect condition. Without doubt it was the one which they had seen two days before whirling out to sea. But now it was by itself, no ladies were sitting upon it. The Padre bared his head.

'Shall we abandon our game, Major?' he said. 'We had better telephone from the clubhouse to the Mayor. And I must arrange to get some men to bring the table back. It's far too heavy for us to think of moving it.'

* * *

The news that the table had come ashore spread swiftly through Tilling, and Georgie, hearing that the Padre had directed that when it had passed the Custom House it should be brought to the Vicarage, went round there at once. It seemed almost unfeeling in this first shock of bereavement to think about tables, but it would save a great deal of bother afterwards to see to this now. The table surely belonged to Grebe.

'I quite understand your point of view,' he said to the Padre, 'and of course what is found on the seashore in a general way belongs to the finder, if it's a few oranges in a basket, because nobody knows who the real owner is. But we all know, at least we're afraid we do, where this came from.'

The Padre was quite reasonable.

'You mean it ought to go back to Grebe,' he said. 'Yes, I agree. Ah, I see it has arrived.'

They went out into the street, where a trolley, bearing the table, had just drawn up. Then a difficulty arose. It was late, and the bearers demurred to taking it all the way out to Grebe tonight and carrying it through the garden.

'Move it in here then for the night,' said the Padre. 'You can get it through the back yard and into the outhouse.'

Georgie felt himself bound to object to this: the table belonged to Grebe, and it looked as if Grebe, alas, belonged to him.

'I think it had better come to Mallards Cottage,' said he firmly. 'It's only just round the corner, and it can stand in my yard.'

The Padre was quite willing that it should go back to Grebe, but why should Georgie claim this object with all the painful interest attached to it? After all, he had found it.

'And so I don't quite see why you should have it,' he said a little stiffly.

Georgie took him aside.

'It's dreadful to talk about it so soon,' he said, 'but that is what I should like done with it. You see Lucia left me Grebe and all its contents. I still cling – can't help it – to the hope that neither it nor they may ever be mine, but in the interval which may elapse – '

'No! Really!' said the Padre with a sudden thrill of Tillingite interest which it was no use trying to suppress. 'I congrat – Well, well. Of course the kitchen table is yours. Very proper.'

The trolley started again and by dint of wheedlings and cunning coaxings the sad substantial relic was induced to enter the back yard of Mallards Cottage. Here for the present it would have to remain, but pickled as it was with long immersion in sea water, the open air could not possibly hurt it, and if it rained, so much the better, for it would wash the salt out.

Georgie, very tired and haggard with these harrowing arrange-ments, had a little rest on his sofa, when he had seen the table safely bestowed. His cook gave him a succulent and most nutritious dinner by way of showing her sympathy, and Foljambe waited on him with peculiar attention, constantly holding a pocket handkerchief to the end of her nose, by way of expressing her own grief. Afterwards he moved to his sitting room and took up his needlework, that 'sad narcotic exercise', and looked his loss in the face.

Indeed, it was difficult to imagine what life would be like without Lucia, but there was no need to imagine it, for he was experiencing it already. There was nothing to look forward to, and he realized how completely Lucia and her manoeuvres and her indomitable vitality and her deceptions and her greatnesses had supplied the salt to life. He had never been in the least in love with her, but somehow she had been as absorbing as any wayward and entrancing mistress. 'It will be too dull for anything,' thought he, 'and there won't be a single day in which I shan't miss her most dreadfully. It's always been like that: when she was away from Riseholme, I never seemed to care to paint or to play, except because I should show her what I had done when she came back, and now she'll never come back.'

He abandoned himself for quite a long time to despair with regard to what life would hold for him. Nobody else, not even Foljambe, seemed to matter at all. But then through the black, deep waters of his tribulation there began to appear little bubbles on the surface. It was like comparing a firefly with the huge night itself to weigh them against this all-encompassing darkness, but where for a moment each pricked the surface there was, it was idle to deny, just a spark that stood out momentarily against the blackness. The table, for instance: he would have a tablet fixed on to it, with a suitable inscription to record the tragic role it had played, a text, so to speak, as on a cenotaph. How would Lucia's last words do? 'Just wait till we come back.' But if this was a memorial table, it must record that Lucia was not coming back.

He fetched a writing pad and began again. 'This is the table – ' but that wouldn't do. It suggested 'This is the house that Jack built.' Then, 'It was upon this table on Boxing Day afternoon, 1930, that Mrs Emmeline Lucas, of Grebe, and Miss Elizabeth Mapp, of Mallards – ' that was too prolix. Then, 'In memory of Emmeline Lucas and Elizabeth Mapp. They went to sea – ' but that sounded like a nursery rhyme by Edward Lear, or it might suggest to future generations that they were sailors. Then he wondered if poetry would supply anything, and the lines, 'And may there be no sadness of farewell, when I embark,' occurred to him. But that wouldn't do: people would wonder why she had embarked on a kitchen table, and even now, when the event was so lamentably recent, nobody actually knew.

'I hadn't any idea,' thought Georgie, 'how difficult it is to write a few well-chosen and heartfelt words. I shall go and look at the tombstones in the churchyard tomorrow. Lucia would have thought of something perfect at once.'

Tiny as were these bubbles and others (larger ones) which Georgie refused to look at directly, they made a momentary, an evanescent brightness. Some of them made quite loud pops as they burst, and some presented problems. This catastrophe had conveyed a solemn warning against living in a house so low-lying, and Major Benjy had already expressed that sentiment when he gave vent to that self-centred *cri du coeur*, 'Thank God I live on a hill,' but for Georgie that question would soon become a practical one, though he would not attempt to make up his mind yet. It would be absurd to have two houses in Tilling, to be the tenant of Mallards Cottage, and the owner of Grebe. Or should he live in Grebe during the summer, when there was no fear of floods, and Mallards Cottage in the winter?

He got into bed: the sympathetic Foljambe, before going home, had made a beautiful fire, and his hot-water bottle was of such a temperature that he could not put his feet on it at all . . . If he lived at Grebe she would only have to go back across the garden to her Cadman, if Cadman remained in his service. Then there was Lucia's big car. He supposed that would be included in the contents of Grebe. Then he must remember to put a black bow on Lucia's picture in the art exhibition. Then he got sleepy . . .

CHAPTER ELEVEN

Though Georgie had thought that there would be nothing interesting left in life now that Lucia was gone, and though Tilling generally was conscious that the termination of the late rivalries would take all thrill out of existence as well as eclipsing its gaieties most dreadfully, it proved one morning when the sad days had begun to add themselves into weeks, that there was a great deal for him to do, as well as a great deal for Tilling to talk about. Lucia had employed a local lawyer over the making of her will, and today Mr Causton (*re* the affairs of Mrs Emmeline Lucas) came to see Georgie about it. He explained to him with a manner subtly compounded of sympathy and congratulation that the little sum of money to which Lucia had alluded was no less than £80,000. Georgie was, in fact, apart from certain legacies, her heir. He was much moved.

'Too kind of her,' he said. 'I had no idea – '

Mr Causton went on with great delicacy.

'It will be some months,' he said, 'before in the absence of fresh evidence, the death of my client can be legally assumed – '

'Oh, the longer, the better,' said Georgie rather vaguely, wiping his eyes, 'but what do you mean about fresh evidence?'

'The recovery, by washing ashore or other identification, of the lamented corpses,' said Mr Causton. 'In the interval the – the possibly late Mrs Lucas has left no provision for the contingency we have to face. If and when her death is proved, the staff of servants will receive their wages up to date and a month's notice. Until then the estate, I take it, will be liable for the outgoings and the upkeep of Grebe. I would see to all that, but I felt that I must get your authority first.'

'Of course, naturally,' said Georgie.

'But here a difficulty arises,' said Mr Causton. 'I have no authority for drawing on the late – or, we hope, the present Mrs Lucas's balance at the bank. There is, you see, no fund out of which the current expenses of the upkeep of the house can be paid. There is more than a month's food and wages for her servants already owing.'

George's face changed a little. A very little.

'I had better pay them myself,' he said. 'Would not that be the proper course?'

'I think, under the circumstances, that it would,' said Mr Causton. 'In fact, I don't see what else is to be done, unless all the servants were discharged at once, and the house shut up.'

'No, that would never do,' said Georgie. 'I must go down there and arrange about it all. If Mrs Lucas returns, how horrid for her to find all her servants who had been with her so long, gone. Everything must carry on as if she had only gone for a visit somewhere and forgotten to send a cheque for expenses.'

Here then, at any rate, was something to do already, and Georgie, thinking that he would like a little walk on this brisk morning, and also feeling sure that he would like a little conversation with friends in the High Street, put on his thinner cape, for a hint of spring was in the air, and there were snowdrops a-bloom in the flower border of his little garden. Lucia, he remembered, always detested snowdrops: they hung their heads and were feeble; they typified for her slack though amiable inefficiency. In order to traverse the whole length of the High Street and get as many conversations as possible he went down by Mallards and Major Benjy's house. The latter, from the window of his study, where he so often enjoyed a rest or a little refreshment before and after his game of golf, saw him pass, and beckoned him in.

'Good morning, old boy,' he said. 'I've had a tremendous slice of luck: at least that is not quite the way to put it, but what I mean is – In fact, I've just had a visit from the solicitor of our lamented friend Elizabeth Mapp, God bless her, and he told me the most surprising news. I was monstrously touched by it: hadn't a notion of it, I assure you.'

'You don't mean to say – ' began Georgie.

'Yes I do. He informed me of the provisions of that dear

woman's will. In memory of our long friendship, these were the very words – and I assure you I was not ashamed to turn away and wipe my eyes, when he told me – in memory of our long friendship she has left me that beautiful Mallards and the sum of ten thousand pounds, which I understand was the bulk of her fortune. What do you think of that?' he asked, allowing his exultation to get the better of him for the moment.

'No!' said Georgie, 'I congratulate – at least in case – '

'I know,' said Major Benjy. 'If it turns out to be too true that our friends have gone for ever, you're friendly enough to be glad that what I've told you is too true, too. Eh?'

'Quite, and I've had a visit from Mr Causton,' said Georgie, unable to contain himself any longer, 'and Lucia's left me Grebe and eighty thousand pounds.'

'My word! What a monstrous fortune,' cried the Major with a spasm of chagrin. 'I congrat – Anyhow, the same to you. I shall get a motor instead of going to my golf on that measly tram. Then there's Mallards for me to arrange about. I'm thinking of letting it furnished, servants and all. It'll be snapped up at ten guineas a week. Why, she got fifteen last summer from the other poor corpse.'

'I wouldn't,' said Georgie. 'Supposing she came back and found she couldn't get into her house for another month because you had let it?'

'God grant she may come back,' said the Major, without falling dead on the spot. 'But I see your point: it would be awkward. I'll think it over. Anyhow, of course, after a proper interval, when the tragedy is proved, I shall go and live there myself. Till then I shall certainly pay the servants' wages and the upkeep. Rather a drain, but it can't be helped. Board wages of twelve shillings a week is what I shall give them: they'll live like fighting cocks on that. By jove, when I think of that terrible sight of the kitchen table lying out there on the beach, it causes me such a sinking still. Have a drink: wonderful pre-war whisky.'

Georgie had not yet visited Grebe, and he found a thrilling though melancholy interest in seeing the starting point of the catastrophe. The Christmas tree, he ascertained, had stuck in the door of the kitchen, and the Padre had already been down to look at it, but had decided that the damage to it was irreparable.

It was lying now in the garden from which soil and plants had been swept away by the flood, but Georgie could not bear to see it there, and directed that it should be put up, as a relic, in an empty outhouse. Perhaps a tablet on that as well as on the table. Then he had to interview Grosvenor, and make out a schedule of the servants' wages, the total of which rather astonished him. He saw the cook and told her that he had the kitchen table in his yard, but she begged him not to send it back, as it had always been most inconvenient. Mrs Lucas, she told him, had had a feeling for it; she thought there was luck about it. Then she burst into tears and said it hadn't brought her mistress much luck after all. This was all dreadfully affecting, and Georgie told her that in this period of waiting during which they must not give up hope, all their wages would be paid as usual, and they must carry on as before, and keep the house in order. Then there were some unpaid bills of Lucia's, a rather appalling total, which must be discharged before long, and the kitchen must be renovated from the effects of the flood. It was after dark when he got back to Mallards Cottage again.

In the absence of what Mr Causton called further evidence in the way of corpses, and of alibis in the way of living human bodies, the Padre settled in the course of the next week to hold a memorial service, for unless one was held soon, they would all have got used to the bereavement, and the service would lose point and poignancy. It was obviously suitable that Major Benjy and Georgie, being the contingent heirs of the defunct ladies, should sit by themselves in a front pew as chief mourners, and Major Benjy ordered a black suit to be made for him without delay for use on this solemn occasion. The church bell was tolled as if for a funeral service, and the two walked in side by side after the rest of the congregation had assembled, and took their places in a pew by themselves immediately in front of the reading desk.

The service was of the usual character, and the Padre gave a most touching address on the text 'They were lovely and pleasant in their lives and in their death they were not divided.' He reminded his hearers how the two whom they mourned were as sisters, taking the lead in social activities, and dispensing to all who knew them their bountiful hospitalities. Their lives had been full of lovable energy. They had been at the forefront in all artistic and literary pursuits: indeed he might almost have taken the whole of the verse of which he had read them only the half as his text, and have added that they were swifter than eagles, they were stronger than lions. One of them had been known to them all for many years, and the name of Elizabeth Mapp was written on their hearts. The other was a newer comer, but she had wonderfully endeared herself to them in her briefer sojourn here, and it was typical of her beautiful nature that on the very day on which the disaster occurred, she had been busy with a Christmas tree for the choristers in whom she took so profound an interest.

As regards the last sad scene, he need not say much about it, for never would any of them forget that touching, that ennobling, that teaching sight of the two, gallant in the face of death as they had ever been in that of life, being whirled out to sea. Mrs Lucas in the ordeal which they would all have to face one day, giving that humorous greeting of hers, '*au reservoir*', which they all knew so well, to her friends standing in safety on the shore, and then turning again to her womanly work of comforting and encouraging her weaker sister. 'May we all,' said the Padre, with a voice trembling with emotion, 'go to meet death in that serene and untroubled spirit, doing our duty to the last. And now – '

This sermon, at the request of a few friends, he had printed in the Parish Magazine next week, and copies were sent to everybody.

* * *

It was only natural that Tilling should feel relieved when the ceremony was over, for the weeks since the stranding of the kitchen table had been like the period between a death and a funeral. The blinds were up again now, and life gradually resumed a more normal complexion. January ebbed away into February, February into March, and as the days lengthened with the returning sun, so the mirths and squabbles of Tilling grew longer and brighter.

But a certain stimulus which had enlivened them all since Lucia's advent from Riseholme was lacking. It was not wholly that there was no Lucia, nor, wholly, that there was no Elizabeth, it was the intense reactions which they had produced together that everyone missed so fearfully. Day after day those who were left met and talked in the High Street, but never was there news of that thrilling kind which since the summer had keyed existence up to so exciting a level. But it was interesting to see Major Benjy in his new motor, which he drove himself, and watch his hairbreadth escapes from collisions at sharp corners and to hear the appalling explosions of military language if any other vehicle came within a yard of his green bonnet.

'He seems to think,' said Diva to Mrs Bartlett, as they met on shopping errands one morning, 'that now he has got a motor nobody else may use the road at all.'

'A trumpery little car,' said Mrs Bartlett, 'I should have thought, with ten thousand pounds as good as in his pocket, he might have got himself something better.'

They were standing at the corner looking up towards Mallards, and Diva suddenly caught sight of a board on Major Benjy's house, announcing that it was for sale.

'Why, whatever's that?' she cried. 'That must have been put up only today. Good morning, Mr Georgie. What about Major Benjy's house?'

Georgie still wore a broad black band on his sleeve.

'Yes, he told me yesterday that he was going to move into Mallards next week,' he said. 'And he's going to have a sale of his furniture almost immediately.'

'That won't be much to write home about,' said Diva scornfully. 'A few moth-eaten tigerskins which he said he shot in India.'

'I think he wants some money,' said Georgie. 'He's bought a motor, you see, and he has to keep up Mallards as well as his own house.'

'I call that very rash,' said Mrs Bartlett. 'I call that counting your chickens before they're hatched. Oh dear me, what a thing to have said! Dreadful!'

Georgie tactfully covered this up by a change of subject.

'I've made up my mind,' he said, 'and I'm going to put up a cenotaph in the churchyard to dear Lucia and Elizabeth.'

'What? Both?' asked Diva.

'Yes, I've thought it carefully over, and it's going to be both.'

'Major Benjy ought to go halves with you then,' said Diva.

'Well, I told him I was intending to do it,' said Georgie, 'and he didn't catch on. He only said "Capital idea," and took some whisky and soda. So I shan't say any more. I would really just as soon do it all myself.'

'Well, I do think that's mean of him,' said Diva. 'He ought anyhow to bear some part of the expense, considering everything. Instead of which he buys a motor car which he can't drive. Go on about the cenotaph.'

'I saw it down at the stonemason's yard,' said Georgie, 'and that put the idea into my head. Beautiful white marble on the lines, though of course much smaller, of the one in London. It had been ordered, I found, as a tombstone, but then the man who ordered it went bankrupt, and it was on the stonemason's hands.'

'I've heard about it,' said Mrs Bartlett, in rather a superior voice. 'Kenneth told me you'd told him, and we both think that it's a lovely idea.'

'The stonemason ought to let you have it cheap then,' said Diva.

'It wasn't very cheap,' said Georgie, 'but I've bought it, and they'll put it in its place today, just outside the south transept, and the Padre is going to dedicate it. Then there's the inscription. I shall have in loving memory of them, by me, and a bit of the Padre's text at the memorial service. Just "In death they were not divided."'

'Quite right. Don't put in about the eagles and the lions,' said Diva.

'No, I thought I would leave that out. Though I like that part,' said Georgie for the sake of Mrs Bartlett.

'Talking of whisky,' said Diva, flying back, as her manner was, to a remote allusion, 'Major Benjy's finished all the pre-war whisky that Lucia gave him. At least I heard him ordering some more yesterday. Oh, and there's the notice of his sale. Old English furniture – yes, that may mean two things, and I know which of them it is. Valuable works of art. Well I never! A print of the *Monarch of the Glen* and a photograph of the *Soul's Awakening*. Rubbish! Fine tigerskins! The skins may be all right, but they're bald.'

'My dear, how severe you are,' said Georgie. 'Now I must go and see how they're getting on with the inscription. *Au reservoir.*'

Diva nodded at Evie Bartlett.

'Nice to hear that again,' she said. 'I've not heard it – well, since.'

The cenotaph with its inscription in bold leaded letters to

say that Georgie had erected it in memory of the two undivided ladies, roused much admiration, and a full-page reproduction of it appeared in the Parish Magazine for April, which appeared on the last day of March. The stonecutter had slightly miscalculated the space at his disposal for the inscription, and the words 'Elizabeth Mapp' were considerably smaller than the words 'Emmeline Lucas' in order to get them into the line. Though Tilling said nothing about that, it was felt that the error was productive of a very suitable effect, if a symbolic meaning was interpreted into it. Georgie was considered to have done it very handsomely and to be behaving in a way that contrasted most favourably with the conduct of Major Benjy, for whereas Georgie was keeping up Grebe at great expense, and restoring, all at his own charge, the havoc the flood had wrought in the garden, Major Benjy, after unsuccessfully trying to let Mallards at ten guineas a week, had moved into the house, and, with a precipitation that was as rash as it was indelicate, was already negotiating about the disposal of his own, and was to have a sale of his furniture on April the first. He had bought a motor, he had replenished the cellars of Mallards with strong wines and more pre-war whisky, he was spending money like water and on the evening of this last day of March he gave a bridge party in the garden room.

Georgie and Diva and Mrs Padre were the guests at this party: there had been dinner first, a rich elaborate dinner, and bridge afterwards up till midnight. It had been an uncomfortable evening, and before it was over they all wished they had not come, for Major Benjy had alluded to it as a house-warming, which showed that either his memory was going, or that his was a very callous nature, for no one whose perceptions were not of the commonest could possibly have used that word so soon. He had spoken of his benefactress with fulsome warmth, but it was painfully evident from what source this posthumous affection sprang. He thought of having the garden room redecorated, the house wanted brightening up a bit, he even offered each of them one of Miss Mapp's watercolour sketches, of which was a profusion on the walls, as a memento of their friend, God bless her . . . There he was straddling in the doorway with the air of a vulgar *nouveau riche* owner of an ancestral property, as they went their ways homeward into the night, and they heard him bolt and lock the door and put up the chain which Lucia in her tenancy had had repaired in order to keep out the uninvited and informal visits of Miss Mapp. 'It would serve him jolly well right,' thought Georgie, 'if she came back.'

CHAPTER TWELVE

It was a calm and beautiful night with a high tide that overflowed the channel of the river. There was spread a great sheet of moonlit water over the submerged meadows at the margin, and it came up to the foot of the rebuilt bank opposite Grebe. Between four and five of the morning of April the first, a trawler entered the mouth of the river, and just at the time when the stars were growing pale and the sky growing red with the coming dawn, it drew up at the little quay to the east of the town, and was moored to the shore. There stepped out of it two figures clad in overalls and tarpaulin jackets.

'I think we had better go straight to Mallards, dear,' said Elizabeth, 'as it's so close, and have a nice cup of tea to warm ourselves. Then you can telephone from there to Grebe, and tell them to send the motor up for you.'

'I shall ring up Georgie too,' said Lucia. 'I can't bear to think that his suspense should last a minute more than is necessary.'

Elizabeth pointed upwards.

'See, there's the sun catching the top of the church tower,' she said. 'Little did I think I should ever see dear Tilling again.'

'I never had the slightest doubt about it,' said Lucia. 'Look, there are the fields we floated across on the kitchen table. I wonder what happened to it.'

They climbed the steps at the south-east angle of the town, and up the slope to the path across the churchyard. This path led close by the south side of the church, and the white marble of the cenotaph gleamed in the early sunlight.

'What a handsome tomb,' said Elizabeth. 'It's quite new. But how does it come here? No one has been buried in the churchyard for a hundred years.'

Lucia gave a gasp as the polished lead letters caught her eye.

'But it's us!' she said.

They stood side by side in their tarpaulins, and together in a sort of chant read the inscription aloud.

THIS STONE WAS ERECTED BY

GEORGE PILLSON

IN LOVING MEMORY OF

EMMELINE LUCAS and ELIZABETH MAPP

LOST AT SEA ON BOXING DAY, 1930

'IN DEATH THEY WERE NOT DIVIDED'

'I've never heard of such a thing,' cried Lucia. 'I call it most premature of Georgie, assuming that I was dead like that. The inscription must be removed instantly. All the same it was kind of him and what a lot of money it must have cost him! Gracious me, I suppose he thought – Let us hurry, Elizabeth.'

Elizabeth was still staring at the stone.

'I am puzzled to know why my name is put in such exceedingly small letters,' she said acidly. 'You can hardly read it. As you say, dear, it was most premature of him. I should call it impertinent, and I'm very glad dear Major Benjy had nothing to do with it. There's an indelicacy about it.'

They went quickly on past Mallards Cottage where the blinds were still down, and there was the window of the garden room from which each had made so many thrilling observations, and the red-brick front, glowing in the sunlight, of Mallards itself. As they crossed the cobbled way to the front door, Elizabeth looked down towards the High Street and saw on Major Benjy's house next door the house agents' board announcing that the freehold of this desirable residence was for disposal. There were bills pasted on the walls announcing the sale of furniture to take place there that very day.

Her face turned white, and she laid a quaking hand on Lucia's arm.

'Look, Major Benjy's house is for sale,' she faltered. 'Oh, Lucia, what has happened? Have we come back from the dead, as it were, to find that it's our dear old friend instead? And to think – ' She could not complete the sentence.

'My dear, you mustn't jump at any such terrible conclusions,' said Lucia. 'He may have changed his house – '

Elizabeth shook her head; she was determined to believe the worst, and indeed it seemed most unlikely that Major Benjy who had lived in the same house for a full quarter of a century could have gone to any new abode but one. Meantime, eager to put an end to this suspense, Elizabeth kept pressing the bell and Lucia plying the knocker of Mallards.

'They all sleep on the attic floor,' said Elizabeth, 'but I think they must hear us soon if we go on. Ah, there's a step on the stairs. Someone is coming down.'

They heard the numerous bolts on the door shot back, they heard the rattle of the released chain. The door was opened and there within stood Major Benjy. He had put on his dinner jacket over his Jaeger pyjamas, and had carpet slippers on his feet. He was sleepy and bristly and very cross.

'Now what's all this about, my men,' he said, seeing two tarpaulined figures on the threshold. 'What do you mean by waking me up with that infernal – '

Elizabeth's suspense was quite over.

'You wretch,' she cried in a fury. 'What do *you* mean? Why are you in my house? Ah, I guess! He! He! He! You learned about my will, did you? You thought you wouldn't wait to step into a dead woman's shoes, but positively tear them off my living feet. My will shall be revoked this day: I promise you that . . . Now out you go, you horrid supplanter! Off to your own house with you, for you shan't spend another minute in mine.'

During this impassioned address Major Benjy's face changed to an expression of the blankest dismay, as if he had seen something much worse (as indeed he had) than a ghost. He pulled pieces of himself together.

'But, my dear Miss Elizabeth,' he said. 'You'll allow me surely to get my clothes on, and above all to say one word of my deep thankfulness that you and Mrs Lucas – it is Mrs Lucas, isn't it? – '

'Get out!' said Elizabeth, stamping her foot. 'Thankfulness indeed! There's a lot of thankfulness in your face! Go away! Shoo!'

Major Benjy had faced wounded tigers (so he said) in India, but then he had a rifle in his hand. He could not face his benefactress, and, with first one slipper and then the other dropping off his feet, he hurried down the few yards of pavement to his own house. The two ladies entered: Elizabeth banged the door and put up the chain.

'So that's that,' she observed (and undoubtedly it was). 'Ah, here's Withers. Withers, we've come back, and though you ought never to have let the Major set foot in my house, I don't blame you, for I feel sure he bullied you into it.'

'Oh, miss!' said Withers. 'Is it you? Fancy! Well, that is a surprise!'

'Now get Mrs Lucas and me a cup of tea,' said Elizabeth, 'and then she's going back to Grebe. That wretch hasn't been sleeping in my room, I trust?'

'No, in the best spare bedroom,' said Withers.

'Then get my room ready, and I shall go to bed for a few hours. We've been up all night. Then, Withers, take all Major Benjy's clothes and his horrid pipes, and all that belongs to him, and put them on the steps outside. Ring him up, and tell him where he will find them. But not one foot shall he set in *my* house again.'

Lucia went to the telephone and rang up Cadman's cottage for her motor. She heard his exclamation of 'My Gawd', she heard (what she supposed was) Foljambe's cry of astonishment, and then she rang up Georgie. He and his household were all a-bed and asleep when the telephone began its summons, but presently the persistent tinkle penetrated into his consciousness, and made him dream that he was again watching Lucia whirling down the flood on the kitchen table and ringing an enormous dinner bell as she swept by the steps. Then he became completely awake and knew it was only the telephone.

'The tarsome thing!' he muttered. 'Who on earth can it be ringing one up at this time? Go on ringing then till you're tired. I shall go to sleep again.'

In spite of these resolutions, he did nothing of the kind. So ceaseless was the summons that in a minute or two he got out of bed, and putting on his striped dressing gown (blue and yellow) went down to his sitting room.

'Yes. Who is it? What do you want?' he said crossly.

There came a little merry laugh, and then a voice, which he had thought was silent for ever, spoke in unmistakable accents.

'Georgie! *Georgino mio!*' it said.

His heart stood still. 'What? What?' he cried.

'Yes, it's Lucia,' said the voice. 'Me's turn home, Georgie.'

Eighty thousand pounds (less death duties) and Grebe seemed to sweep by him like an avalanche, and fall into the gulf of the things that might have been. But it was not the cold blast of that ruin that filled his eyes with tears.

'Oh my dear!' he cried. 'Is it really you? Lucia, where are you? Where are you talking from?'

'Mallards. Elizabeth and I – '

'What, both of you?' called Georgie. 'Then – where's Major Benjy?'

'Just gone home,' said Lucia discreetly. 'And as soon as I've had a cup of tea I'm going to Grebe.'

'But I must come round and see you at once,' said Georgie. 'I'll just put some things on.'

'Yes, do,' said Lucia. '*Presto, presto*, Georgie.'

Careless of his reputation for being the best-dressed man in Tilling, he put on his dress trousers and a pullover, and his thick brown cape, and did not bother about his *toupée*. The front door of Mallards was open, and Elizabeth's servants were laying out on the top step a curious collection of golf clubs and toothbrushes and clothes. From mere habit – everyone in Tilling had the habit – he looked up at the window of the garden room as he passed below it, and was astonished to see two mariners in sou'wester caps and tarpaulin jackets kissing their hands to him. He had only just time to wonder who these could possibly be when he guessed. He flew into Lucia's arms, then wondered if he ought to kiss Elizabeth too. But there was a slight reserve about her which caused him to refrain. He was not brilliant enough at so early an hour to guess that she had seen the smaller lettering in which her loving memory was recorded.

There was but time for a few ejaculations and a promise from Georgie to dine at Grebe that night, before Lucia's motor arrived, and the imperturbable Cadman touched his cap and said to Lucia, 'Very pleased to see you back, ma'am,' as she picked her way between the growing deposits of socks and other more intimate articles of male attire which were now being ranged on the front steps. Georgie hurried back to Mallards Cottage to dress in a manner more worthy of his reputation, and Elizabeth up to her bedroom for a few hours' sleep. Below her oilskins she still wore the ragged remains of the clothes in which she had left Tilling on Boxing Day, and now she drew out of the pocket of her frayed and sea-stained jacket, a half-sheet of discoloured paper. She unfolded it and having once more read the mystic words 'Take two hen lobsters', she stowed it safely away for future use.

Meantime Major Benjy next door had been the prey of the most sickening reflections; whichever way he turned, fate gave him some stinging blow that set him staggering and reeling in another direction. Leaning out of an upper window of his own house, he observed his clothes and boots and articles of toilet being laid out like a bird's breakfast on the steps of Mallards, and essaying to grind his teeth with rage he discovered that his upper dental plate must still be reposing in a glass of water in the best spare bedroom which he had lately quitted in such haste. To recover his personal property was the first necessity, and when from his point of observation he saw that the collection had grown to a substantial size, he crept up the pavement, seized a bundle of miscellaneous articles, as many as he could carry, then stole back again, dropping a nailbrush here and a sock suspender there, and dumped them in his house. Three times he must go on these degrading errands, before he had cleared all the bird's breakfast away; indeed he was an early bird feeding on the worms of affliction.

Tilling was beginning to awake now: the milkman came clattering down the street and, looking in amazement at his dishevelled figure, asked whether he wanted his morning supply left at his own house or at Mallards: Major Benjy turned on him so appalling a face that he left no milk at either and turned swiftly into the less alarming air of Porpoise Street. Again he had to make the passage of his Via Dolorosa to glean the objects which had dropped from his overburdened arms, and as he returned he heard a bumping noise behind him, and saw his new portmanteau hauled out by Withers rolling down the steps into the street. He emerged again when Withers had shut the door, put more gleanings into

it and pulled it into his house. There he made a swift and sorry
toilet, for there was business to be done which would not brook
delay. Already the preparations for the sale of his furniture were
almost finished; the carpet and hearthrug in his sitting room were
tied up together and labelled Lot 1; the fire irons and a fishing rod
and a rhinoceros-hide whip were Lot 2; a kitchen tray with packs
of cards, a tobacco jar, a piece of chipped *cloisonné* ware and a roll
of toilet paper formed an unappetizing Lot 3. The sale must be
stopped at once and he went down to the auctioneer's in the High
Street and informed him that owing to circumstances over which
he had no control he was compelled to cancel it. It was pointed
out to him that considerable expense had already been incurred
for the printing and display of the bills that announced it, for the
advertisements in the local press, for the time and trouble already
spent in arranging and marking the lots, but the Major bawled out:
'Damn it all, the things are mine and I won't sell one of them. Send
me in your bill.' Then he had to go to the house agents' and tell
them to withdraw his house from the market and take down his
board, and coming out of the office he ran into Irene, already on
her way to Grebe, who cried out: 'They've come back, old Benjy-
wenjy. Joy! Joy!'

The most immediate need of having a roof over his head and
a chair to sit on was now provided for, and as he had already
dismissed his own servants, taking those of Mallards, he must go
to another agency to find some sort of cook or charwoman till he
could get his establishment together again. They promised to send
an elderly lady, highly respectable though rather deaf and weak in
the legs, tomorrow if possible. Back he came to his house with such
cold comfort to cheer him, and observed on the steps of Mallards
half a dozen bottles of wine. 'My God, my cellar,' muttered the
Major, 'there are dozens and dozens of my wine and my whisky in
the house!' Again he crept up to the abhorred door and, returning
with the bottles, put a kettle on to boil, and began cutting the
strings that held the lots together. Just then the church bells burst
out into a joyful peal, and it was not difficult to conjecture the
reason for their unseemly mirth. All this before breakfast . . .

A cup of hot strong tea without any milk restored not only his
physical stability but also his mental capacity for suffering, and he

sat down to think. There was the financial side of the disaster first of all, a thing ghastly to contemplate. He had bought (but not yet paid for) a motor, some dozens of wine, a suit of new clothes, as well as the mourning habiliments in which he had attended the memorial service, quantities of stationery with the Mallards stamp on it, a box of cigars and other luxuries too numerous to mention. It was little comfort to remember that he had refused to contribute to the cenotaph; a small saving like that did not seem to signify. Then what view, he wondered, would his benefactress, when she knew all, take of his occupation of Mallards? She might find out (indeed being who she was, she would not fail to do so) that he had tried to let it at ten guineas a week and she might therefore send him in a bill on that scale for the fortnight he had spent there, together with that for her servants' wages, and for garden produce and use of her piano. Luckily he had only eaten some beetroot out of the garden, and he had had the piano tuned. But of all these staggering expenses, the only items which were possibly recoverable were the wages he had paid to the staff of Mallards between Boxing Day and the date of his tenancy: these Elizabeth might consent to set against the debits. Not less hideous than this financial débâcle that stared him in the face, was the loss of prestige in Tilling. Tilling, he knew, had disapproved of his precipitancy in entering into Mallards, and Tilling, full, like Irene, of joy, joy for the return of the lost, would simply hoot with laughter at him. He could visualize with awful clearness the chatting groups in the High Street which would vainly endeavour to suppress their smiles as he approached. The day of swank was past and done, he would have to be quiet and humble and grateful to anybody who treated him with the respect to which he had been accustomed.

He unrolled a tigerskin to lay down again in his hall: a cloud of dust and deciduous hair rose from it, pungent like snuff, and the remaining glass eye fell out of the socket. He bawled '*Quai-hai*' before he remembered that till tomorrow at least he would be alone in the house, and that even then his attendant would be deaf. He opened his front door and looked out into the street again, and there on the doorstep of Mallards was another dozen or so of wine and a walking stick. Again he stole out to recover his property with the hideous sense that perhaps Elizabeth was watching him from the garden room. His dental plate – thank God – was there too on the second step, all by itself, gleaming in the sun, and seeming to grin at him in a very mocking manner. After that throughout the morning he looked out at intervals as he rested from the awful labour of laying carpets and putting beds together, and there were usually some more bottles waiting for him, with stray golf clubs, bridge-markers and packs of cards. About one o'clock just as he was collecting what must surely be the last of these bird-breakfasts, the door of Mallards opened and Elizabeth stepped carefully over his umbrella and a box of cigars. She did not appear to see him. It seemed highly probable that she was going to revoke her will.

Georgie, as well as Major Benjy, had to do a little thinking, when he returned from his visit at dawn to Mallards. It concerned two points, the cenotaph and the kitchen table. The cenotaph had not been mentioned in those few joyful ejaculations he had exchanged with Lucia, and he hoped that the ladies had not seen it. So after breakfast he went down to the stonemason's and begged him to send a trolley and a hefty lot of men up to the churchyard at once, and remove the monument to the back yard of Mallards Cottage, which at present was chiefly occupied by the kitchen table under a tarpaulin. But Mr Marble (such was his appropriate name) shook his head over this: the cenotaph had been dedicated, and he felt sure that a faculty must be procured before it could be removed. That would never do: Georgie could not wait for a faculty, whatever that was, and he ordered that the inscription, anyhow, should be effaced without delay: surely no faculty was needed to destroy all traces of a lie. Mr Marble must send some men up to chip, and chip and chip for all they were worth till those beautiful lead letters were detached and the surface of the stone cleared of all that erroneous information.

'And then I'll tell you what,' said Georgie, with a sudden splendid thought, 'why not paint on to it (I can't afford any more cutting) the inscription that was to have been put on it when that man went bankrupt and I bought the monument instead? He'll get his monument for nothing, and I shall get rid of mine, which is just what I want . . . That's beautiful. Now you must send a trolley to my house and take a very big kitchen table, *the* one in fact, back to Grebe. It must go in through the door of the kitchen garden and be put quietly into the kitchen. And I particularly want it done today.'

All went well with these thoughtful plans. Georgie saw with his own eyes the last word of his inscription disappear in chips of marble; and he carried away all the lead letters in case they might come in useful for something, though he could not have said what: perhaps he would have 'Mallards Cottage' let into the threshold of his house for that long inscription would surely contain the necessary letters. Rather a pretty and original idea. Then he ascertained that the kitchen table had been restored to its place while Lucia slept, and he drove down at dinner time feeling that he had done his best. He wore his white waistcoat with onyx buttons for the happy occasion.

Lucia was looking exceedingly well and much sunburnt. By way of resting she had written a larger number of postcards to all her friends, both here and elsewhere, than Georgie had ever seen together in one place.

'Georgino,' she cried. 'There's so much to say that I hardly know where to begin. I think my adventures first, quite shortly, for I shall dictate a full account of them to my secretary, and have a party next week for all Tilling, and read them out to you. Two parties, I expect, for I don't think I shall be able to read it all in one evening. Now we go back to Boxing Day.

'I went into the kitchen that afternoon,' she said as they sat down to dinner, 'and there was Elizabeth. I asked her – naturally, don't you think? – why she was there, and she said, "I came to thank you for that delicious *pâté*, and to ask if – " That was as far as she got – I must return to that later – when the bank burst with a frightful roar, and the flood poured in. I was quite calm. We got on to, I should really say into the table – By the way, was the table ever washed up?'

'Yes,' said Georgie, 'it's in your kitchen now. I sent it back.'

'Thank you, my dear. We got into the kitchen table, really a perfect boat, I can't think why they don't make more like it, flew by the steps – oh, did the Padre catch a dreadful cold? Such a splash it was, and that was the only drop of water that we shipped at all.'

'No, but he lost his umbrella, the one you'd given him,' said Georgie, 'and the Padre of the Roman Catholic church found it, a week afterwards, and returned it to him. Wasn't that a coincidence? Go on. Oh no, wait a minute. What did you mean by calling out "Just wait till we get back"?'

'Why of course I wanted to tell you that I had found Elizabeth in my kitchen,' said Lucia.

'Hurrah! I guessed you meant something of the kind,' said Georgie.

'Well, out we went – I've never been so fast in a kitchen table before – out to sea in a blinding sea fog. My dear; poor Elizabeth! No nerve of any kind! I told her that if we were rescued, there was nothing to cry about, and if we weren't all our troubles would soon be over.'

Grosvenor had put some fish before Lucia. She gave an awful shudder.

'Oh, take it away,' she said. 'Never let me see fish again, particularly cod, as long as I live. Tell the cook. You'll see why presently, Georgie. Elizabeth got hysterical and said she wasn't fit to die, so I scolded her – the best plan always with hysterical people – and told her that the longer she lived, the less fit she would be, and that did her a little good. Then it got dark, and there were fog-horns hooting all round us, and we called and yelled, but they had much more powerful voices than we, and nobody heard us. One of them grew louder and louder, until I could hardly bear it, and then we bumped quite gently into it, the fog-horn's boat I mean.'

'Gracious, you might have upset,' said Georgie.

'No, it was like a liner coming up to the quay,' said Lucia. 'No shock of any kind. Then when the fog-horn stopped, they heard us shouting, and took us aboard. It was an Italian trawler on its way to the cod-fishery (that's why I never want to see cod again) on the Gallagher Banks.'

'That was lucky too,' said Georgie, 'you could make them understand a little. Better than if they had been Spanish.'

'About the same, because I'm convinced, as I told Elizabeth, that they talked a very queer Neapolitan dialect. It was rather unlucky, in fact. But as the captain understood English perfectly, it didn't matter. They were most polite, but they couldn't put us ashore, for we were miles out in the Channel by this time, and also quite lost. They hadn't an idea where the coast of England or any other coast was.'

'Wireless?' suggested Georgie.

'It had been completely smashed up by the dreadful gale the day before. We drifted about in the fog for two days, and when it cleared and they could take the sun again – a nautical expression, Georgie – we were somewhere off the coast of Devonshire. The captain promised to hail any passing vessel bound for England that he saw, but he didn't see any. So he continued his course to the Gallagher Banks, which is about as far from Ireland as it is from America, and there we were for two months. Cod, cod, cod, nothing but cod, and Elizabeth snoring all night in the cabin we shared together. Bitterly cold very often: how glad I was that I knew so many callisthenic exercises! I shall tell you all about that time at my lecture. Then we found that there was a Tilling trawler on the bank, and when it was ready to start home we transshipped – they call it – and got back, as you know, this morning. That's the skeleton.'

'It's the most wonderful skeleton I ever heard,' said Georgie. 'Do write your lecture quick.'

Lucia fixed Georgie with her gimlet eye. It had lost none of its penetrative power by being so long at sea.

'Now it's your turn for a little,' she said. 'I expect I know rather more than you think. First about that memorial service.'

'Oh, do you know about that?' he asked.

'Certainly. I found the copy of the Parish Magazine waiting for me, and read it in bed. I consider it to have been very premature. You attended it, I think.'

'We all did,' said Georgie. 'And after all, the Padre said extremely nice things about you.'

'I felt very much flattered. But all the same it was too early. And you and Major Benjy were chief mourners.'

Georgie considered for a moment.

'I'm going to make a clean breast of it,' he said. 'You told me you had left me Grebe, and a small sum of money, and your lawyer told me what that meant. My dear, I was too touched, and naturally, it was proper that I should be chief mourner. It was the same with Major Benjy. He had seen Elizabeth's will, so there we were.'

Suddenly an irresistible curiosity seized him.

'Major Benjy hasn't been seen all day,' he said. 'Do tell me what happened this morning at Mallards. You only said on the telephone that he had just gone home.'

'Yes, bag and baggage,' said Lucia. 'At least he went first and his bag and baggage followed. Socks and things, you saw some of them on the top step. Elizabeth was mad with rage, a perfect fishwife. So suitable after coming back from the Gallagher Banks. But tell me more. What was the next thing after the memorial service?'

The hope of keeping the knowledge of the cenotaph from Lucia became very dim. If Lucia had seen the February number of the Parish Magazine she had probably also seen the April number in which appeared the full-page reproduction of that monument. Besides, there was the gimlet eye.

'The next thing was that I put up a beautiful cenotaph to you and Elizabeth,' said Georgie firmly. "In loving memory of by me." But I've had the inscription erased today.'

Lucia laid her hand on his.

'Dear Georgie, I'm glad you told me,' she said. 'As a matter of fact I knew, because Elizabeth and I studied it this morning. I was vexed at first, but now I think it's rather dear of you. It must have cost a lot of money.'

'It did,' said Georgie. 'And what did Elizabeth think about it?'

'Merely furious because her name was in smaller letters than mine,' said Lucia. 'So like the poor thing.'

'Was she terribly tarsome all these months?' asked Georgie.

'Tiresome's not quite the word,' said Lucia judicially. 'Deficient rather than tiresome, except incidentally. She had no idea of the tremendous opportunities she was getting. She never rose to her chances, nor forgot our little discomforts and that everlasting smell of fish. Whereas I learned such lots of things, Georgie: the Italian for starboard and port – those are the right and left sides of the ship – and how to tie an anchor knot and a running noose, and a clove hitch, and how to splice two ends of fishing line together, and all sorts of things of the most curious and interesting kind. I shall show you some of them at my lecture. I used to go about the deck barefoot (Lucia had very pretty feet) and pull on anchors and capstans and things, and managed never to tumble out of my berth on to the floor when the ship was rolling frightfully, and not to be seasick. But poor Elizabeth was always bumping on to the floor, and sometimes being sick there. She had no spirit. Little moans and sighs and regrets that she ever came down the Tilling hill on Boxing Day.'

Lucia leaned forward and regarded Georgie steadfastly.

'I couldn't fathom her simply because she was so superficial,' she said. 'But I feel sure that there was something on her mind all the time. She used often to seem to be screwing herself up to confess something to me, and then not to be able to get it out. No courage. And though I can make no guess as to what it actually was, I believe I know its general nature.'

'How thrilling!' cried Georgie. 'Tell me!'

Lucia's eye ceased to bore, and became of far-off focus, keen still but speculative, as if she was Einstein concentrating on some cosmic deduction.

'Georgie, why did she come into my kitchen like a burglar on Boxing Day?' she asked. 'She told me she had come to thank me for that *pâté* I sent her. But that wasn't true: anyone could see that it wasn't. Nobody goes into kitchens to thank people for *pâtés*.'

'Diva guessed that she had gone there to see the Christmas tree,' said Georgie. 'You weren't on very good terms at the time. We all thought that brilliant of her.'

'Then why shouldn't she have said so?' asked Lucia. 'I believe it was something much meaner and more underhand than that. And I am convinced – I have those perceptions sometimes, as you know very well – that all through the months of our odyssey she wanted to tell me why she was there, and was ashamed of doing so. Naturally I never asked her, because if she didn't choose to tell me, it would be beneath me to force a confidence. There we were together on the Gallagher Banks, she all to bits all the time, and I should have scorned myself for attempting to worm it out of her. But the more I think of it, Georgie, the more convinced I am, that what she had to tell me and couldn't, concerned that. After all, I had unmasked every single plot she made against me before, and I knew the worst of her up till that moment. She had something on her mind, and that something was why she was in my kitchen.'

Lucia's faraway prophetic aspect cleared.

'I shall find out all right,' she said. 'Poor Elizabeth will betray herself some time. But, Georgie, how in those weeks I missed my music! Not a piano on board any of the trawlers assembled there! Just a few concertinas and otherwise nothing except cod. Let us go, in a minute, into my music room and have some Mozartino again. But first I want to say one thing.'

Georgie took a rapid survey of all he had done in his conviction that Lucia had long ago been drowned. But if she knew about the memorial service and the cenotaph there could be nothing more except the kitchen table, and that was now in its place again. She knew all that mattered. Lucia began to speak baby talk.

'Georgie,' she said. ''Oo have had dweffel disappointy – '

That was too much. Georgie thumped the table quite hard.

'I haven't,' he cried. 'How dare you say that?'

'Ickle joke, Georgie,' piped Lucia. 'Haven't had joke for so long with that melancholy Liblib. 'Pologize. 'Oo not angry wif Lucia?'

'No, but don't do it again,' said Georgie. 'I won't have it.'

'You shan't then,' said Lucia, relapsing into the vernacular of adults. 'Now all this house is spick and span, and Grosvenor tells me you've been paying all their wages, week by week.'

'Naturally,' said Georgie.

'It was very dear and thoughtful of you. You saw that my house was ready to welcome my return, and you must send me in all the bills and everything tomorrow and I'll pay them at once, and I thank you enormously for your care of it. And send me in the bill for the cenotaph too. I want to pay for it, I do indeed. It was a loving impulse of yours, Georgie, though, thank goodness, a hasty one. But I can't bear to think that you're out of pocket because I'm alive. Don't answer: I shan't listen. And now let's go straight to the piano and have one of our duets, the one we played last, that heavenly Mozartino.'

They went into the next room. There was the duet ready on the piano, which much looked as if Lucia had been at it already, and she slid on to the top music stool.

'We both come in on the third beat,' said she. 'Are you ready? Now! *Uno, due, TRE!*'

CHAPTER THIRTEEN

The wretched Major Benjy, who had not been out all day except for interviews with agents and miserable traverses between his house and the doorsteps of Mallards, dined alone that night (if you could call it dinner) on a pork pie and a bottle of Burgundy. A day's hard work had restored the lots of his abandoned sale to their proper places, and a little glue had restored its eye to the bald tiger. He felt worse than bald himself, he felt flayed, and God above alone knew what fresh skinnings were in store for him. All Tilling must have had its telephone bells (as well as the church bells) ringing from morning till night with messages of congratulation and suitable acknowledgements between the returned ladies and their friends, and he had never felt so much like a pariah before. Diva had just passed his windows (clearly visible in the lamplight, for he had not put up the curtains of his snuggery yet) and he had heard her knock on the door of Mallards. She must have gone to dine with the fatal Elizabeth, and what were they talking about now? Too well he knew, for he knew Elizabeth.

If in spirit he could have been present in the dining room, where only last night he had so sumptuously entertained Diva and Georgie and Mrs Bartlett, and had bidden them punish the port, he would not have felt much more cheerful.

'In my best spare room, Diva, would you believe it?' said Elizabeth, 'with all the drawers full of socks and shirts and false teeth, wasn't it so, Withers? and the cellar full of wine. What he has consumed of my things, goodness only knows. There was that *pâté* which Lucia gave me only the day before we were whisked out to sea – '

'But that was three months ago,' said Diva.

' – and he used my coal and my electric light as if they were his own, not to mention firing,' said Elizabeth, going on exactly where she had left off, 'and a whole row of beetroot.'

Diva was bursting to hear the story of the voyage. She knew that Georgie was dining with Lucia, and he would be telling everybody about it tomorrow, but if only Elizabeth would leave the beetroot alone and speak of the other she herself would be another focus of information instead of being obliged to listen to Georgie.

'Dear Elizabeth,' she said, 'what does a bit of beetroot matter compared to what you've been through? When an old friend like you has had such marvellous experiences as I'm sure you must have, nothing else counts. Of course I'm sorry about your beetroot: most annoying, but I do want to hear about your adventures.'

'You'll hear all about them soon,' said Elizabeth, 'for tomorrow I'm going to begin a full history of it all. Then, as soon as it's finished, I shall have a big tea party, and instead of bridge afterwards I shall read it to you. That's absolutely confidential, Diva. Don't say a word about it, or Lucia may steal my idea or do it first.'

'Not a word,' said Diva. 'But surely you can tell me some bits.'

'Yes, there is a certain amount which I shan't mention publicly,' Elizabeth said. 'Things about Lucia which I should never dream of stating openly.'

'Those are just the ones I should like to hear about most,' said Diva. 'Just a few little titbits.'

Elizabeth reflected a moment.

'I don't want to be hard on her,' she said, 'for after all we were together, and what would have happened if I had not been there, I can't think. A little off her head perhaps with panic: that is the most charitable explanation. As we swept by the town on our way out to sea she shrieked out – "*Au reservoir*: just wait till we come back." Diva, I am not easily shocked, but I must say I was appalled. Death stared us in the face and all she could do was to make jokes! There was I sitting quiet and calm, preparing myself to meet the solemn moment as a Christian should, with this screaming hyena for my companion. Then out we went to sea, in that blinding fog, tossing and pitching on the waves, till we went crash into the side of a ship which was invisible in the darkness.'

'How awful!' said Diva. 'I wonder you didn't upset.'

'Certainly it was miraculous,' said Elizabeth. 'We were battered about, the blows against the table were awful, and if I hadn't kept my head and clung on to the ship's side, we must have upset. They had heard our calls by then, and I sprang on to the rope ladder they put down without a moment's pause, so as to lighten the table for Lucia, and then she came up too.'

Elizabeth paused a moment.

'Diva, you will bear me witness that I always said, in spite of Amelia Faraglione, that Lucia didn't know a word of Italian, and it was proved I was right. It was an Italian boat, and our great Italian scholar was absolutely flummoxed, and the captain had to talk to us in English. There!'

'Go on,' said Diva breathlessly.

'The ship was a fishing trawler bound for the Gallagher Banks, and we were there for two months, and then we found another trawler on its way home to Tilling, and it was from that we landed this morning. But I shan't tell you of our life and adventures, for I'm reserving that for my reading to you.'

'No, never mind then,' said Diva. 'Tell me intimate things about Lucia.'

Elizabeth sighed.

'We mustn't judge anybody,' she said, 'and I won't: but oh, the nature that revealed itself! The Italians were a set of coarse, lascivious men of the lowest type, and Lucia positively revelled in their society. Every day she used to walk about the deck, often with bare feet, and skip and do her callisthenics, and learn a few words of Italian; she sat with this one or that, with her fingers actually entwined with his, while he pretended to teach her to tie a knot or a clove hitch or something that probably had an improper meaning as well. Such flirtation (at her age too), such promiscuousness, I have never seen. But I don't judge her, and I beg you won't.'

'But didn't you speak to her about it?' asked Diva.

'I used to try to screw myself up to it,' said Elizabeth, 'but her lightness positively repelled me. We shared a cabin about as big as a dog kennel, and oh, the sleepless nights when I used to be thrown from the shelf where I lay! Even then she wanted to instruct me, and show me how to wedge myself in. Always that dreadful superior attitude, that mania to teach everybody everything except Italian, which we have so often deplored. But that was nothing. It was her levity from the time when the flood poured into the kitchen at Grebe – '

'Do tell me about that,' cried Diva. 'That's almost the most interesting thing of all. Why had she taken you into the kitchen?'

Elizabeth laughed.

'Dear thing!' she said. 'What a lovely appetite you have for details! You might as well expect me to remember what I had for breakfast that morning. She and I had both gone into the kitchen; there we were, and we were looking at the Christmas tree. Such a tawdry tinselly tree! Rather like her. Then the flood poured in, and I saw that our only chance was to embark on the kitchen table. By the way, was it ever washed up?'

'Oh yes, without a scratch on it,' said Diva, thinking of the battering it was supposed to have undergone against the side of the trawler . . .

Elizabeth had evidently not reckoned on its having come ashore, and rose.

'I am surprised that it didn't go to bits,' she said. 'But let us go into the garden room. We must really talk about that wretched sponger next door. Is it true he's bought a motor car out of the money he hoped my death would bring him? And all that wine: bottles and bottles, so Withers told me. Oceans of champagne. How is he to pay for it all now with his miserable little income on which he used to pinch and scrape along before?'

'That's what nobody knows,' said Diva. 'An awful crash for him. So rash and hasty, as we all felt.'

They settled themselves comfortably by the fire, after Elizabeth had had one peep between the curtains.

'I'm not the least sorry for having been a little severe with him this morning,' she said. 'Any woman would have done the same.'

Withers entered with a note. Elizabeth glanced at the handwriting, and turned pale beneath the tan acquired on the cod banks.

'From him,' she said. 'No answer, Withers.'

'Shall I read it?' said Elizabeth, when Withers had left the room, 'or throw it, as it deserves, straight into the fire.'

'Oh, read it,' said Diva, longing to know what was in it. 'You must see what he has to say for himself.'

Elizabeth adjusted her pince-nez and read it in silence.

'Poor wretch,' she said. 'But very proper as far as it goes. Shall I read it you?'

'Do, do, do,' said Diva.

Elizabeth read:

'My Dear Miss Elizabeth (if you will still permit me to call you so) –'

'Very proper,' said Diva.

'Don't interrupt, dear, or I shan't read it,' said Elizabeth.

' – call you so. I want first of all to congratulate you with all my heart on your return after adventures and privations which I know you bore with Christian courage.

Secondly I want to tender you my most humble apologies for my atrocious conduct in your absence, which was unworthy of a soldier and Christian, and, in spite of all, a gentleman. Your forgiveness, should you be so gracious as to extend it to me, will much mitigate my present situation.

Most sincerely yours (if you will allow me to say so),

Benjamin Flint.'

'I call that very nice,' said Diva. 'He didn't find that easy to write!'

'And I don't find it very easy to forgive him,' retorted Elizabeth.

'Elizabeth, you must make an effort,' said Diva energetically. 'Tilling society will all fly to smithereens if we don't take care. You and Lucia have come back from the dead, so that's a very good opportunity for showing a forgiving spirit and beginning again. He really can't say more than he has said.'

'Nor could he possibly, if he's a soldier, a Christian and a gentleman, have said less,' observed Elizabeth.

'No, but he's done the right thing.'

Elizabeth rose and had one more peep out of the window.

'I forgive him,' she said. 'I shall ask him to tea tomorrow.'

Elizabeth carried up to bed with her quantities of food for thought and lay munching it till a very late hour. She had got rid of a good deal of spite against Lucia, which left her head the clearer, and she would be very busy tomorrow writing her account of the great adventure. But it was the thought of Major Benjy that most occupied her. Time had been when he had certainly come very near making honourable proposals to her which she always was more than ready to accept. They used to play golf together in those days before that firebrand Lucia descended on Tilling; he used to drop in casually, and she used to put flowers in his buttonhole for him. Tilling had expected their union, and Major Benjy had without doubt been on the brink. Now, she reflected, was the precise moment to extend to him a forgiveness so plenary that it would start a new chapter in the golden book of pardon. Though only this morning she had ejected his golf clubs and his socks and his false teeth with every demonstration of contempt, this appeal of his revived in her hopes that had hitherto found no fruition. There should be fatted calves for him as for a prodigal son, he should find in this house that he had violated a cordiality and a welcome for the future and an oblivion of the past that could not fail to undermine his celibate propensities. Discredited owing to his precipitate occupation of Mallards, humiliated by his degrading expulsion from it, and impoverished by the imprudent purchase of wines, motor car and steel-shafted drivers, he would surely take advantage of the wonderful opportunity which she presented to him. He might be timid at first, unable to believe the magnitude of his good fortune, but with a little tact, a proffering of saucers of milk, so to speak, as to a stray and friendless cat, with comfortable invitations to sweet Pussie to be fed and stroked, with stealthy butterings of his paws, and with, frankly, a sudden slam of the door when sweet Pussie had begun to make himself at home, it seemed that unless Pussie was a lunatic, he could not fail to wish to domesticate himself. 'I think I can manage it,' thought Elizabeth, 'and then poor Lulu will only be a widow, and I a married woman with a well-controlled husband. How will she like that?'

Such sweet thoughts as these gradually lulled her to sleep.

It was soon evident that the return of the lost, an event in itself of the first magnitude, was instantly to cause a revival of those rivalries which during the autumn had rendered life at Tilling so thrilling a business. Georgie, walking down to see Lucia three days after her return, found a bill poster placarding the High Street with notices of a lecture to be delivered at the Institute in two days' time by Mrs Lucas, admission free and no collection of any sort before, during or after. 'A modern odyssey' was the title of the discourse. He hurried on to Grebe, and found her busy correcting the typewritten manuscript which she had been dictating to her secretary all yesterday with scarcely a pause for meals.

'Why, I thought it was to be just an after-dinner reading,' he said, straight off, without any explanation of what he was talking about.

Lucia put a paperknife in the page she was at, and turned back to the first.

'My little room would not accommodate all the people who, I understand, are most eager to hear about what I went through,' she said. 'You see, Georgie, I think it is a duty laid upon those who have been privileged to pass unscathed through tremendous adventures to let others share, as far as is possible, their experiences. In fact that is how I propose to open my lecture. I was reading the first sentence. What do you think of it?'

'Splendid,' said Georgie. 'So well expressed.'

'Then I make some allusion to Nansen, and Stanley and Amundsen,' said Lucia, 'who have all written long books about their travels, and say that as I do not dream of comparing my adventure to theirs, a short verbal recital of some of the strange things that happened to me will suffice. I calculate that it will not take much more than two hours, or at most two and a half. I finished it about one o'clock this morning.'

'Well, you have been quick about it,' said Georgie. 'Why, you've only been back three days.'

Lucia pushed the pile of typewritten sheets aside.

'Georgie, it has been terrific work,' she said, 'but I had to rid myself of the incubus of these memories by writing them down. Aristotle, you know; the purging of the mind. Besides, I'm sure I'm right in hurrying up. It would be like Elizabeth to be intending to do something of the sort. I've hired the Institute anyhow – '

'Now that is interesting,' said Georgie. 'Practically every time that I've passed Mallards during these last two days Elizabeth has been writing in the window of the garden room. Frightfully busy:

hardly looking up at all. I don't know for certain that she is writing her odyssey – such a good title – but she is writing something, and surely it must be that. And two of those times Major Benjy was sitting with her on the piano stool and she was reading to him from a pile of blue foolscap. Of course I couldn't hear the words, but there were her lips going on like anything. So busy that she didn't see me, but I think he did.'

'No!' said Lucia, forgetting her lecture for the moment. 'Has she made it up with him then?'

'She must have. He dined there once, for I saw him going in, and he lunched there once, for I saw him coming out, and then there was tea, when she was reading to him, and I passed them just now in his car. All their four hands were on the wheel, and I think he was teaching her to drive, or perhaps learning himself.'

'And fancy his forgiving all the names she called him, and putting his teeth on the doorstep,' said Lucia. 'I believe there's more than meets the eye.'

'Oh, much more,' said he. 'You know she wanted to marry him and nearly got him, Diva says, just before we came here. She's having another go.'

'Clever of her,' said Lucia appreciatively. 'I didn't think she had so much ability. She's got him on the hop, you see, when he's ever so grateful for her forgiving him. But cunning, Georgie, rather low and cunning. And it's quite evident she's writing our adventures as hard as she can. It's a good thing I've wasted no time.'

'I should like to see her face when she comes back from her drive,' said Georgie. 'They were pasting the High Street with you, as I came. Friday afternoon, too: that's a good choice because it's early closing.'

'Yes, of course, that's why I chose it,' said Lucia. 'I don't think she can possibly be ready a whole day before me, and if she hires the Institute the day after me, nobody will go, because I shall have told them everything already. Then she can't have hired the Institute on the same day as I, because you can't have two lectures, especially on the same subject, going on in the same room simultaneously. Impossible.'

Grosvenor came in with the afternoon post.

'And one by hand, ma'am,' she said.

Lucia, of course, looked first at the one by hand. Nothing that came from outside Tilling could be as urgent as a local missive.

'Georgie!' she cried. 'Delicious complication! Elizabeth asks me – me – to attend her reading in the garden room called "Lost to Sight", at three o'clock on Friday afternoon. Major Benjamin Flint has kindly consented to take the chair. At exactly that hour the Padre will be taking the chair at the Institute for me. I know what I shall do. I shall send a special invitation to Elizabeth to sit on the platform at my lecture, and I shall send another note to her two hours later as if I had only just received hers, to say that as I am lecturing myself that afternoon at the Institute, I much regret that, etc. Then she can't say I haven't asked her.'

'And when they come back from their drive this afternoon, she and Major Benjy,' cried Georgie, 'they'll see the High Street placarded with your notices. I've never been so excited before except when you came home.'

The tension next day grew very pleasant. Elizabeth, hearing that Lucia had taken the Institute, did her best to deprive her of an audience, and wrote personal notes not only to her friends of the immediate circle, but to chemists and grocers and auctioneers and butchers to invite them to the garden room at Mallards at three o'clock on the day of battle in order to hear a *true* (underlined) account of her adventure. Lucia's reply to that was to make a personal canvass of all the shops, pay all her bills, and tell everyone that in the interval between the two sections of her lecture, tea would be provided gratis for the audience. She delayed this manoeuvre till Friday morning, so that there could scarcely be a counter-attack.

That same morning, the Padre, feeling that he must do his best to restore peace after the engagement that was now imminent, dashed off two notes to Lucia and Elizabeth, saying that a few friends (this was a lie because he had thought of it himself) had suggested to him how suitable it would be that he should hold a short service of thanksgiving for their escape from the perils of the sea and of cod-fisheries. He proposed therefore that this service should take place directly after the baptisms on Sunday afternoon. It would be quite short, a few prayers, the general thanksgiving, a hymn ('Fierce raged the tempest o'er the deep'), and a few words from himself. He hoped the two ladies would sit together in the front pew which had been occupied at the memorial service by the chief mourners. Both of them were charmed with the idea, for neither dared refuse for fear of putting herself in the wrong. So after about three forty-five on Sunday afternoon (and it was already two forty-five on Friday afternoon) there must be peace, for who could go on after that joint thanksgiving?

By three o'clock on Friday there was not a seat to be had at the Institute, and many people were standing. At the same hour every seat was to be had at the garden room, for nobody was sitting down in any of them. At half-past three Lucia was getting rather mixed about the latitude and longitude of the Gallagher Bank, and the map had fallen down. At half-past three Elizabeth and Major Benjy were alone in the garden room. It would be fatiguing for her, he said, to read again the lecture she had read him yesterday, and he wouldn't allow her to do it. Every word was already branded on his memory. So they seated themselves comfortably by the fire and Elizabeth began to talk of the loneliness of loneliness and of affinities. At half-past four Lucia's audience, having eaten their sumptuous tea, had ebbed away, leaving only Irene, Georgie, Mr and Mrs Wyse, and Mr and Mrs Padre to listen to the second half of the lecture. At half-past four in the garden room Elizabeth and Major Benjy were engaged to be married. There was no reason for (in fact every reason against) a long engagement, and the banns would be put up in church next Sunday morning.

'So they'll all know about it, *Benjino mio*,' said Elizabeth, 'when we have our little thanksgiving service on Sunday afternoon, and I shall ask all our friends, Lucia included, to a cosy lunch on Monday to celebrate our engagement. You must send me across some of your best bottles of wine, dear.'

'As if you didn't know that all my cellar was at your disposal,' said he.

Elizabeth jumped up and clapped her hands. 'Oh, I've got such a lovely idea for that lunch,' she said. 'Don't ask me about it, for I shan't tell you. A splendid surprise for everybody, especially Lulu.'

*   *   *

Elizabeth was slightly chagrined next day, when she offered to read her lecture on practically any afternoon to the inmates of the workhouse, to find that Lucia had already asked all those who were not bedridden or deaf to tea at Grebe that very day, and hear an abridged form of what she had read at the Institute: an hour was considered enough, since perhaps some of them would find the excitement and the strain of a longer intellectual effort too much for them. But this chagrin was altogether wiped from her mind when on Sunday morning at the end of the second lesson the Padre published banns of marriage. An irrepressible buzz of conversation like a sudden irruption of bluebottle flies filled the church, and Lucia, who was sitting behind the choir and assisting the altos, said 'I thought so' in an audible voice. Elizabeth was assisting the trebles on the Cantoris side, and had she not been a perfect lady, and the scene a sacred edifice, she might have been tempted to put out her tongue or make a face in the direction of the Decani altos. Then in the afternoon came the service of thanksgiving, and the two heroines were observed to give each other a stage kiss. Diva, who sat in the pew immediately behind them, was certain that actual contact was not established. They resumed their seats, slightly apart.

As was only to be expected, notes of congratulation and acceptance to the lunch on Monday poured in upon the young couple. All the intimate circle of Tilling was there, the sideboard groaned with Major Benjy's most expensive wines, and everyone felt that the hatchet which had done so much interesting chopping in the past was buried, for never had two folk been so cordial to each other as were Lucia and Elizabeth.

They took their places at the table. Though it was only lunch there were menu cards, and written on them as the first item of the banquet was 'Lobster *à la Riseholme*'.

Georgie saw it first, though his claim was passionately disputed by Diva, but everybody else, except Lucia, saw it in a second or two and the gay talk dropped dead. What could have happened? Had Lucia, one day on the Gallagher Banks, given their hostess the secret which she had so firmly withheld? Somehow it seemed scarcely credible. The eyes of the guests, pair by pair, grew absorbed in meditation, for all were beginning to recall a mystery that had baffled them. The presence of Elizabeth in Lucia's kitchen when the flood poured in had never been fathomed, but surely . . . A slight catalepsy seized the party, and all eyes were turned on Lucia who now for the first time looked at the menu. If she had given the recipe to Elizabeth, she would surely say something about it.

Lucia read the menu and slightly moistened her lips. She directed on Elizabeth a long penetrating gaze that mutely questioned her. Then the character of that look altered. There was no reproach in it, only comprehension and unfathomable contempt.

The ghastly silence continued as the lobster was handed round. It came to Lucia first. She tasted it and found that it was exactly right. She laid down her fork, and grubbed up the imperfectly buried hatchet.

'Are you sure you copied the recipe out quite correctly, *Elizabetha mia*?' she asked. 'You must pop into my kitchen some afternoon when you are going for your walk – never mind if I am in or not – and look at it again. And if my cook is out too, you will find the recipe in a book on the kitchen shelf. But you know that, don't you?'

'Thank you, dear,' said Elizabeth. 'Sweet of you.'

Then everybody began to talk in a great hurry.